THE TALISMAN

'Chilling horror story or fantastic journey though a strange world . . . this book works like . . . well, like magic' – *Mirror*

'A classic . . . a journey to rival the greatest adventure stories ever told . . . rare and dazzling' – *New York Daily News*

'Extraordinary . . . makes your hair stand on end' – *Washington Post*

'Gripping . . . immensely satisfying' – *Los Angeles Times*

'Well written . . . the world is strong; the characters are strong' – *Guardian*

Stephen King and Peter Straub are co-authors of *The Talisman, Black House* and *Other Worlds Than These: A Talisman novel.*

STEPHEN KING is the author of more than seventy books, all of them worldwide bestsellers. Among his bestselling fiction titles are *Fairy Tale, Never Flinch* and *The Dark Tower* series.

Many of King's titles are the basis for major motion pictures, TV series and streamed events, including *The Green Mile, IT* and *The Shawshank Redemption*, which is IMDb's top-rated movie of all time.

King is the recipient of *The Sunday Times* Award for Literary Excellence 2022, the 2020 Audio Publishers Association Lifetime Achievement Award, the 2018 PEN America Literary Service Award, the 2014 National Medal of Arts, and the 2003 National Book Foundation Medal for Distinguished Contribution to American Letters. He lives in Maine, with his wife, novelist Tabitha King.

PETER STRAUB authored numerous bestselling novels, including *Ghost Story, A Dark Matter, Floating Dragon* and *Koko.* He also published short fiction, poetry and a graphic novel. For the Library of America, he edited the volume *H.P. Lovecraft: Tales* and the anthology *American Fantastic Tales.*

A prolific Grand Master of Horror, he received numerous literary honours including the British Fantasy Award; the Bram Stoker Award; the World Fantasy Award, and the International Horror Guild Award. He was also the recipient of several lifetime achievement awards. He passed away in 2022.

By Stephen King and published by Hodder & Stoughton

NOVELS:

Carrie
'Salem's Lot
The Shining
The Stand
The Dead Zone
Firestarter
Cujo
Cycle of the Werewolf
Christine
Pet Sematary
IT
The Talisman (with Peter Straub)
The Eyes of the Dragon
Misery
The Tommyknockers
The Dark Half
Needful Things
Gerald's Game
Dolores Claiborne
Insomnia
Rose Madder
Desperation
Bag of Bones
The Girl Who Loved Tom Gordon
Dreamcatcher
Black House (with Peter Straub)
From a Buick 8
Cell
Lisey's Story
Duma Key
Under the Dome
11.22.63
Doctor Sleep
Mr Mercedes
Revival
Finders Keepers
End of Watch
Gwendy's Button Box
(with Richard Chizmar)
Sleeping Beauties (with Owen King)
The Outsider
Elevation
The Institute
Billy Summers
Gwendy's Final Task
(with Richard Chizmar)
Fairy Tale
Holly
Never Flinch
The Life of Chuck

The Dark Tower

The Dark Tower I: The Gunslinger
The Dark Tower II:
The Drawing of the Three
The Dark Tower III: The Waste Lands
The Dark Tower IV: Wizard and Glass
The Dark Tower V: Wolves of the Calla
The Dark Tower VI: Song of Susannah
The Dark Tower VII: The Dark Tower
The Wind through the Keyhole:
A Dark Tower Novel

As Richard Bachman

Thinner
The Running Man
The Bachman Books
The Regulators
Blaze

STORY COLLECTIONS:

Night Shift
Different Seasons
Skeleton Crew
Four Past Midnight
Nightmares and Dreamscapes
Hearts in Atlantis
Everything's Eventual
Just After Sunset
Stephen King Goes to the Movies
Full Dark, No Stars
The Bazaar of Bad Dreams
If It Bleeds
You Like It Darker

NON-FICTION:

Danse Macabre
On Writing (A Memoir of the Craft)

By Peter Straub and published by Hodder & Stoughton

Ghost Story
The Talisman (with Stephen King)
The Hellfire Club
Black House (with Stephen King)
A Dark Matter

STEPHEN KING

AND

PETER STRAUB

THE TALISMAN

HODDER &
STOUGHTON

This book is for
Ruth King
Elvena Straub

First published in Great Britain in 1985 by Penguin Books Limited

This Hodder & Stoughton paperback edition of *The Talisman* published in 2026

4

A CIP catalogue record for this title is available from the British Library

Paperback ISBN 978 1 399 76481 0
ebook ISBN 978 1 409 10387 5

Printed and bound in Great Britain by Clays Ltd, Elcograf S.p.A.

Hodder & Stoughton policy is to use papers that are natural, renewable and recyclable products and made from wood grown in sustainable forests. The logging and manufacturing processes are expected to conform to the environmental regulations of the country of origin.

Hodder & Stoughton Limited
Carmelite House
50 Victoria Embankment
London EC4Y 0DZ

The authorised representative in the EEA is Hachette Ireland, 8 Castlecourt Centre, Dublin 15, D15 XTP3, Ireland (email: info@hbgi.ie)

www.hodder.co.uk

Well, when Tom and me got to the edge of the hilltop, we looked away down into the village and could see three or four lights twinkling, where there was sick folks, may be; and stars over us was sparkling ever so fine; and down by the village was the river, a whole mile broad, and awful still and grand.

– Mark Twain, *Huckleberry Finn*

My new clothes was all greased up and clayey, and I was dog-tired.

– Mark Twain, *Huckleberry Finn*

Grateful acknowledgement is made to the following for permission to reprint copyrighted material:

Bourne Co. Music Publishers: portions of lyrics from 'Who's Afraid of the Big Bad Wolf?', by Frank E. Churchill and Ann Ronell. Copyright 1933 by Bourne Co. Copyright renewed.

Bourne Co. Music Publishers and Callicoon Music: portions of lyrics from 'When the Red, Red Robin Goes Bob-Bob-Bobbing Along', music and lyrics by Harry Woods. Copyright 1926 by Bourne Co. and Callicoon Music. Copyright renewed.

CBS Songs, A Division of CBS, Inc.: portions of lyrics from 'Ruben James', by Barry Etris and Alex Harvey. Copyright © Unart Music Corporation, 1969. Rights assigned to CBS Catalogue Partnership. All rights controlled and administered by CBS Unart Catalog, Inc. All rights reserved. International copyright secured. An excerpt from 'The Wizard of Oz', lyrics by E.Y. Harburg, music by Harold Arlen. Copyright © 1938, renewed 1966, Metro-Goldwyn Mayer, Inc. Copyright 1939, renewed 1967 by Leo Feist, Inc. Rights assigned to CBS Catalogue Partnership. All rights controlled and administered by CBS Feist Catalog, Inc. All rights reserved. International copyright secured.

Hudson Bay Music, Inc., and T.M. Music Ltd: portions of lyrics from 'Long Line Rider' (Bobby Darin). Copyright © Alley Music Corporation and Trio Music Company, Inc. All rights administered by Hudson Bay Music, Inc. All rights reserved.

Jondora Music: portions of lyrics from 'Run Through the Jungle', by John Fogarty. Copyright © Jondora Music, 1973, courtesy Fantasy, Inc., Berkeley, California.

Sanga Music, Inc., and Harmony Music Ltd: portions of lyrics from 'Gotta Travel On', by Paul Clayton, David Lazar, Larry Ehrlich, and Tom Six. Copyright © Sanga Music, Inc., 1958, 1960. All rights reserved.

CONTENTS

I

Jack Lights Out

CHAPTER ONE
THE ALHAMBRA INN AND GARDENS

1

On September 15th, 1981, a boy named Jack Sawyer stood where the water and land come together, hands in the pockets of his jeans, looking out at the steady Atlantic. He was twelve years old and tall for his age. The sea-breeze swept back his brown hair, probably too long, from a fine, clear brow. He stood there, filled with the confused and painful emotions he had lived with for the last three months – since the time when his mother had closed their house on Rodeo Drive in Los Angeles and, in a flurry of furniture, checks, and real-estate agents, rented an apartment on Central Park West. From that apartment they had fled to this quiet resort on New Hampshire's tiny seacoast. Order and regularity had disappeared from Jack's world. His life seemed as shifting, as uncontrolled, as the heaving water before him. His mother was moving him through the world, twitching him from place to place; but what moved his mother?

His mother was running, running.

Jack turned around, looking up the empty beach first to the left, then to the right. To the left was Arcadia Funworld, an amusement park that ran all racket and roar from Memorial

Day to Labor Day. It stood empty and still now, a heart between beats. The roller coaster was a scaffold against that featureless, overcast sky, the uprights and angled supports like strokes done in charcoal. Down there was his new friend, Speedy Parker, but the boy could not think about Speedy Parker now. To the right was the Alhambra Inn and Gardens, and that was where the boy's thoughts relentlessly took him. On the day of their arrival Jack had momentarily thought he'd seen a rainbow over its dormered and gambreled roof. A sign of sorts, a promise of better things. But there had been no rainbow. A weathervane spun right-left, left-right, caught in a crosswind. He had got out of their rented car, ignoring his mother's unspoken desire for him to do something about the luggage, and looked up. Above the spinning brass cock of the weathervane hung only a blank sky.

'Open the trunk and get the bags, sonny boy,' his mother had called to him. 'This broken-down old actress wants to check in and hunt down a drink.'

'An elementary martini,' Jack had said.

'"You're not so old," you were supposed to say.' She was pushing herself effortfully off the carseat.

'You're not so old.'

She gleamed at him – a glimpse of the old, go-to-hell Lily Cavanaugh (Sawyer), queen of two decades' worth of B movies. She straightened her back. 'It's going to be okay here, Jacky,' she had said. 'Everything's going to be okay here. This is a good place.'

A seagull drifted over the roof of the hotel, and for a second Jack had the disquieting sensation that the weathervane had taken flight.

'We'll get away from the phone calls for a while, right?'

'Sure,' Jack had said. She wanted to hide from Uncle

Morgan, she wanted no more wrangles with her dead husband's business partner, she wanted to crawl into bed with an elementary martini and hoist the covers over her head . . .

Mom, what's wrong with you?

There was too much death, the world was half-made of death. The gull cried out overhead.

'Andelay, kid, andelay,' his mother had said. 'Let's get into the Great Good Place.'

Then, Jack had thought: *At least there's always Uncle Tommy to help out in case things get really hairy.*

But Uncle Tommy was already dead; it was just that the news was still on the other end of a lot of telephone wires.

2

The Alhambra hung out over the water, a great Victorian pile on gigantic granite blocks which seemed to merge almost seamlessly with the low headland – a jutting collarbone of granite here on the few scant miles of New Hampshire seacoast. The formal gardens on its landward side were barely visible from Jack's beachfront angle – a dark green flip of hedge, that was all. The brass cock stood against the sky, quartering west by northwest. A plaque in the lobby announced that it was here, in 1838, that the Northern Methodist Conference had held the first of the great New England abolition rallies. Daniel Webster had spoken at fiery, inspired length. According to the plaque, Webster had said: 'From this day forward, know that slavery as an American institution has begun to sicken and must soon die in all our states and territorial lands.'

3

So they had arrived on that day last week which had ended the turmoil of their months in New York. In Arcadia Beach there were no lawyers employed by Morgan Sloat popping out of cars and waving papers which had to be signed, *had* to be filed, Mrs Sawyer. In Arcadia Beach the telephones did not ring out from noon until three in the morning (Uncle Morgan appeared to forget that residents of Central Park West were not on California time). In fact the telephones in Arcadia Beach rang not at all.

On the way into the little resort town, his mother driving with squinty-eyed concentration, Jack had seen only one person on the streets – a mad old man desultorily pushing an empty shopping cart along a sidewalk. Above them was that blank gray sky, an uncomfortable sky. In total contrast to New York, here there was only the steady sound of the wind, hooting up deserted streets that looked much too wide with no traffic to fill them. Here were empty shops with signs in the windows saying OPEN WEEKENDS ONLY or, even worse, SEE YOU IN JUNE! There were a hundred empty parking places on the street before the Alhambra, empty tables in the Arcadia Tea and Jam Shoppe next door.

And shabby-crazy old men pushed shopping carts along deserted streets.

'I spent the happiest three weeks of my life in this funny little place,' Lily told him, driving past the old man (who turned, Jack saw, to look after them with frightened suspicion – he was mouthing something but Jack could not tell what it was) and then swinging the car up the curved drive through the front gardens of the hotel.

For that was why they had bundled everything they

could not live without into suitcases and satchels and plastic shopping bags, turned the key in the lock on the apartment door (ignoring the shrill ringing of the telephone, which seemed to penetrate that same keyhole and pursue them down the hall); that was why they had filled the trunk and back seat of the rented car with all their overflowing boxes and bags and spent hours crawling north along the Henry Hudson Parkway, then many more hours pounding up I-95 – because Lily Cavanaugh Sawyer had once been happy here. In 1968, the year before Jack's birth, Lily had been nominated for an Academy Award for her role in a picture called *Blaze*. *Blaze* was a better movie than most of Lily's, and in it she had been able to demonstrate a much richer talent than her usual bad-girl roles had revealed. Nobody expected Lily to win, least of all Lily; but for Lily the customary cliché about the real honor being in the nomination was honest truth – she did feel honored, deeply and genuinely, and to celebrate this one moment of real professional recognition, Phil Sawyer had wisely taken her for three weeks to the Alhambra Inn and Gardens, on the other side of the continent, where they had watched the Oscars while drinking champagne in bed. (If Jack had been older, and had he had an occasion to care, he might have done the necessary subtraction and discovered that the Alhambra had been the place of his essential beginning.)

When the Supporting Actress nominations were read, according to family legend, Lily had growled to Phil, 'If I win this thing and I'm not there, I'll do the Monkey on your chest in my *stiletto heels*.'

But when Ruth Gordon had won, Lily had said, 'Sure, she deserves it, she's a great kid.' And had immediately poked her husband in the middle of the chest and said, 'You'd better get me another part like that, you big-shot agent you.'

There had been no more parts like that. Lily's last role, two years after Phil's death, had been that of a cynical ex-prostitute in a film called *Motorcycle Maniacs*.

It was that period Lily was commemorating now, Jack knew as he hauled the baggage out of the trunk and the back seat. A D'Agostino bag had torn right down through the big D'AG, and a jumble of rolled-up socks, loose photographs, chessmen and the board, comic books, had dribbled over all else in the trunk. Jack managed to get most of this stuff into other bags. Lily was moving slowly up the hotel steps, pulling herself along on the railing like an old lady. 'I'll find the bellhop,' she said without turning around.

Jack straightened up from the bulging bags and looked again at the sky where he was sure he had seen a rainbow. There was no rainbow, only that uncomfortable, shifting sky.

Then:

'Come to me,' someone said behind him in a small and perfectly audible voice.

'What?' he asked, turning around. The empty gardens and drive stretched out before him.

'Yes?' his mother said. She looked crickle-backed, leaning over the knob of the great wooden door.

'Mistake,' he said. There had been no voice, no rainbow. He forgot both and looked up at his mother, who was struggling with the vast door. 'Hold on, I'll help,' he called, and trotted up the steps, awkwardly carrying a big suitcase and a straining paper bag filled with sweaters.

4

Until he met Speedy Parker, Jack had moved through the days at the hotel as unconscious of the passage of time as a sleeping dog. His entire life seemed almost dreamlike to him during these days, full of shadows and inexplicable transitions. Even the terrible news about Uncle Tommy which had come down the telephone wires the night before had not entirely awakened him, as shocking as it had been. If Jack had been a mystic, he might have thought that other forces had taken him over and were manipulating his mother's life and his own. Jack Sawyer at twelve was a being who required things to do, and the noiseless passivity of these days, after the hubbub of Manhattan, had confused and undone him in some basic way.

Jack had found himself standing on the beach with no recollection of having gone there, no idea of what he was doing there at all. He supposed he was mourning Uncle Tommy, but it was as though his mind had gone to sleep, leaving his body to fend for itself. He could not concentrate long enough to grasp the plots of the sitcoms he and Lily watched at night, much less keep the nuances of fiction in his head.

'You're tired from all this moving around,' his mother said, dragging deeply on a cigarette and squinting at him through the smoke. 'All you have to do, Jack-O, is relax for a little while. This is a good place. Let's enjoy it as long as we can.'

Bob Newhart, before them in a slightly too-reddish color on the set, bemusedly regarded a shoe he held in his right hand.

'That's what I'm doing, Jacky.' She smiled at him. 'Relaxing and enjoying it.'

He peeked at his watch. Two hours had passed while they sat in front of the television, and he could not remember anything that had preceded this program.

Jack was getting up to go to bed when the phone rang. Good old Uncle Morgan Sloat had found them. Uncle Morgan's news was never very great, but this was apparently a blockbuster even by Uncle Morgan's standards. Jack stood in the middle of the room, watching as his mother's face grew pale, paler, palest. Her hand crept to her throat, where new lines had appeared over the last few months, and pressed lightly. She said barely a word until the end, when she whispered, 'Thank you, Morgan,' and hung up. She had turned to Jack then, looking older and sicker than ever.

'Got to be tough now, Jacky, all right?'

He hadn't felt tough.

She took his hand then and told him.

'Uncle Tommy was killed in a hit-and-run accident this afternoon, Jack.'

He gasped, feeling as if the wind had been torn out of him.

'He was crossing La Cienega Boulevard and a van hit him. There was a witness who said it was black, and that the words WILD CHILD were written on the side, but that was . . . was all.'

Lily began to cry. A moment later, almost surprised, Jack began to cry as well. All of that had happened three days ago, and to Jack it seemed forever.

5

On September 15th, 1981, a boy named Jack Sawyer stood looking out at the steady water as he stood on an unmarked beach before a hotel that looked like a castle in a Sir Walter Scott novel. He wanted to cry but was unable to release his tears. He was surrounded by death, death made up half the world, there were no rainbows. The WILD CHILD van had subtracted Uncle Tommy from the world. Uncle Tommy, dead in L.A., too far from the east coast, where even a kid like Jack knew he really belonged. A man who felt he had to put on a tie before going out to get a roast beef sandwich at Arby's had no business on the west coast at all.

His father was dead, Uncle Tommy was dead, his mother might be dying. He felt death here, too, at Arcadia Beach, where it spoke through telephones in Uncle Morgan's voice. It was nothing as cheap or obvious as the melancholy feel of a resort in the off-season, where one kept stumbling over the Ghosts of Summers Past; it seemed to be in the texture of things, a smell on the ocean breeze. He was scared . . . and he had been scared for a long time. Being here, where it was so quiet, had only helped him to realize it – had helped him to realize that maybe Death had driven all the way up I-95 from New York, squinting out through cigarette smoke and asking him to find some bop on the car radio.

He could remember – vaguely – his father telling him that he was born with an old head, but his head didn't feel old now. Right now, his head felt very young. *Scared*, he thought. *I'm pretty damn scared. This is where the world ends, right?*

Seagulls coursed the gray air overhead. The silence was as gray as the air – as deadly as the growing circles under her eyes.

6

When he had wandered into Funworld and met Lester Speedy Parker after he did not quite know how many days of numbly drifting through time, that passive feeling of being *on hold* had somehow left him. Lester Parker was a black man with crinkly gray hair and heavy lines cutting through his cheeks. He was utterly unremarkable now despite whatever he had accomplished in his earlier life as a travelling blues musician. Nor had he said anything particularly remarkable. Yet as soon as Jack had walked aimlessly into Funworld's game arcade and met Speedy's pale eyes he felt all the fuzziness leave him. He had become himself again. It was as if a magical current had passed directly from the old man into Jack. Speedy had smiled at him and said, 'Well, it looks like I got me some company. Little travellin man just walked in.'

It was true, he was not *on hold* anymore: just an instant before, he had seemed to be wrapped in wet wool and cotton candy, and now he was set free. A silvery nimbus seemed to play about the old man for an instant, a little aureole of light which disappeared as soon as Jack blinked. For the first time Jack saw that the man was holding the handle of a wide heavy push-broom.

'You okay, son?' The handyman put one hand in the small of his back, and stretched backward. 'The world just get worse, or did she get better?'

'Uh, better,' Jack said.

'Then you come to the right place, I'd say. What do they call you?'

Little travellin man, Speedy had said that first day, *ole Travellin Jack.* He had leaned his tall angular body against the Skee-Ball machine and wrapped his arms around the broomhandle as though it were a girl at a dance. *The man you see here is Lester Speedy Parker, formerly a travellin man hisself, son, hee hee – oh, yeah, Speedy knew the road, he knew all the roads, way back in the old days. Had me a band, Travellin Jack, played the blues. Git-tar blues. Made me a few records, too, but I won't shame you by asking if you ever heard em.* Every syllable had its own rhythmic lilt, every phrase its rimshot and backbeat; Speedy Parker carried a broom instead of a guitar, but he was still a musician. Within the first five seconds of talking to Speedy, Jack had known that his jazz-loving father would have relished this man's company.

He had tagged along behind Speedy for the better part of three or four days, watching him work and helping out when he could. Speedy let him bang in nails, sand down a picket or two that needed paint; these simple tasks done under Speedy's instructions were the only schooling he was getting, but they made him feel better. Jack now saw his first days in Arcadia Beach as a period of unrelieved wretchedness from which his new friend had rescued him. For Speedy Parker was a friend, that was certain – so certain, in fact, that in it was a quantity of mystery. In the few days since Jack had shaken off his daze (or since Speedy had shaken it off for him by dispelling it with one glance of his light-colored eyes), Speedy Parker had become closer to him than any other friend, with the possible exception of Richard Sloat, whom Jack had known approximately since the cradle. And now, counteracting his terror at losing Uncle Tommy and his fear that his mother was actually dying, he felt the tug of Speedy's warm wise presence from just down the street.

Again, and uncomfortably, Jack had his old sense of *being directed*, of being manipulated: as if a long invisible wire had pulled himself and his mother up to this abandoned place by the sea.

They had wanted him here, whoever *they* were.

Or was that just crazy? In his inner vision he saw a bent old man, clearly out of his mind, muttering to himself as he pushed an empty shopping cart down the sidewalk.

A gull screamed in the air, and Jack promised himself that he would *make* himself talk about some of his feelings with Speedy Parker. Even if Speedy thought he was nuts; even if he laughed at Jack. He would not laugh, Jack secretly knew. They were old friends because one of the things Jack understood about the old custodian was that he could say almost anything to him.

But he was not ready for all that yet. It was all too crazy, and he did not understand it yet himself. Almost reluctantly Jack turned his back on Funworld and trudged across the sand toward the hotel.

CHAPTER TWO
THE FUNNEL OPENS

1

It was a day later, but Jack Sawyer was no wiser. He *had*, however, had one of the greatest nightmares of all time last night. In it, some terrible creature had been coming for his mother – a dwarvish monstrosity with misplaced eyes and rotting, cheesy skin. '*Your mother's almost dead, Jack, can you say hallelujah?*' this monstrosity had croaked, and Jack knew – the way you knew things in dreams – that it was radioactive, and that if it touched him, he would die, too. He had awakened with his body drenched in sweat, on the edge of a bitter scream. It took the steady pounding of the surf to reacquaint him with where he was, and it was hours before he could go back to sleep.

He had meant to tell his mother about the dream this morning, but Lily had been sour and uncommunicative, hiding in a cloud of cigarette smoke. It was only as he started out of the hotel coffee shop on some trumped-up errand that she smiled at him a little.

'Think about what you want to eat tonight.'

'Yeah?'

'Yeah. Anything but fast food. I did not come all the way from L.A. to New Hampshire in order to poison myself with hotdogs.'

'Let's try one of those seafood places in Hampton Beach,' Jack said.

'Fine. Go on and play.'

Go on and play, Jack thought with a bitterness utterly unlike him. *Oh yeah, Mom, way to go. Too cool. Go on and play. With who? Mom, why are you here? Why are we here? How sick are you? How come you won't talk to me about Uncle Tommy? What's Uncle Morgan up to? What –*

Questions, questions. And not one of them worth a darned thing, because there was no one to answer them.

Unless Speedy –

But that was ridiculous; how could one old black man he'd just met solve any of his problems?

Still, the thought of Speedy Parker danced at the edge of his mind as Jack ambled across the boardwalk and down to the depressingly empty beach.

2

This is where the world ends, right? Jack thought again.

Seagulls coursed the gray air overhead. The calendar said it was still summer, but summer ended here at Arcadia Beach on Labor Day. The silence was as gray as the air.

He looked down at his sneakers and saw that there was some sort of tarry goo on them. *Beach crud*, he thought. *Some kind of pollution.* He had no idea where he had picked it up and he stepped back from the edge of the water, uneasy.

The gulls in the air, swooping and crying. One of them screamed overhead and he heard a flat cracking that was almost metallic. He turned in time to see it come in for a fluttering, awkward landing on a hump of rock. The gull turned its head in rapid, almost robotic movements, as if to verify it was alone, and then it hopped down to where the clam it had dropped lay on the smooth, hard-packed sand. The clam cracked open like an egg and Jack saw raw meat inside, still twitching . . . or perhaps that was his imagination.

Don't want to see this.

But before he could turn away, the gull's yellow, hooked beak was pulling at the meat, stretching it like a rubber band, and he felt his stomach knot into a slick fist. In his mind he could hear that stretched tissue screaming – nothing coherent, only stupid flesh crying out in pain.

He tried to look away from the seagull again and he couldn't. The gull's beak opened, giving him a brief glimpse of dirty pink gullet. The clam snapped back into its cracked shell and for a moment the gull was looking at him, its eyes a deadly black, confirming every horrible truth: fathers die, mothers die, uncles die even if they went to Yale and look as solid as bank walls in their three-piece Savile Row suits. Kids die too, maybe . . . and at the end all there may be is the stupid, unthinking scream of living tissue.

'Hey,' Jack said aloud, not aware he was doing anything but thinking inside his own head. 'Hey, give me a break.'

The gull sat over its catch, regarding him with its beady black eyes. Then it began to dig at the meat again. *Want some, Jack? It's still twitching! By God, it's so fresh it hardly knows it's dead!*

The strong yellow beak hooked into the meat again and pulled. *Stretttchhhhhh* –

It snapped. The gull's head went up toward the gray September sky and its throat worked. And again it seemed to be looking at him, the way the eyes in some pictures seemed always to look at you no matter where you went in the room. And the eyes . . . he knew those eyes.

Suddenly he wanted his mother – her dark blue eyes. He could not remember wanting her with such desperation since he had been very, very small. *La-la,* he heard her sing inside his head, and her voice was the wind's voice, here for now, somewhere else all too soon. *La-la, sleep now, Jacky, baby-bunting, daddy's gone a-hunting. And all that jazz.* Memories of being rocked, his mother smoking one Herbert Tareyton after another, maybe looking at a script – blue pages, she called them, he remembered that: blue pages. *La-la, Jacky, all is cool. I love you, Jacky. Shhh . . . sleep. La-la.*

The gull was looking at him.

With sudden horror that engorged his throat like hot salt water he saw *it really was looking at him.* Those black eyes (*whose?*) were *seeing* him. And he knew that look.

A raw strand of flesh still dangled from the gull's beak. As he looked, the gull sucked it in. Its beak opened in a weird but unmistakable grin.

He turned then and ran, head down, eyes shut against the hot salt tears, sneakers digging against the sand, and if there was a way to go up, go up and up, up to some gull's-eye view, one would have seen only him, only his tracks, in all that gray day; Jack Sawyer, twelve and alone, running back toward the inn, Speedy Parker forgotten, his voice nearly lost in tears and wind, crying the negative over and over again: *no* and *no* and *no.*

3

He paused at the top of the beach, out of breath. A hot stitch ran up his left side from the middle of his ribs to the deepest part of his armpit. He sat down on one of the benches the town put out for old people and pushed his hair out of his eyes.

Got to get control of yourself. If Sergeant Fury goes Section Eight, who's gonna lead the Howling Commandos?

He smiled and actually did feel a little better. From up here, fifty feet from the water, things looked a little better. Maybe it was the change in barometric pressure, or something. What had happened to Uncle Tommy was horrible, but he supposed he would get over it, learn to accept. That was what his mother said, anyway. Uncle Morgan had been unusually pesty just lately, but then, Uncle Morgan had *always* been sort of a pest.

As for his mother . . . well, that was the big one, wasn't it?

Actually, he thought, sitting on the bench and digging at the verge of the sand beyond the boardwalk with one toe, actually his mother might still be all right. She *could* be all right; it was certainly *possible*. After all, no one had come right out and *said* it was the big C, had they? No. If she had cancer, she wouldn't have brought him here, would she? More likely they'd be in Switzerland, with his mother taking cold mineral baths and scoffing goat-glands, or something. And she would do it, too.

So maybe –

A low, dry whispering sound intruded on his consciousness. He looked down and his eyes widened. The sand had begun to move by the instep of his left sneaker. The fine white grains were sliding around in a small circle perhaps a finger's length in diameter. The sand in the middle of this circle suddenly collapsed, so that now there was a dimple in the sand. It was maybe two inches deep. The sides of this dimple were also in motion: around and around, moving in rapid counterclockwise circuits.

Not real, he told himself immediately, but his heart began to speed up again. His breathing also began to come faster. *Not real, it's one of the Daydreams, that's all, or maybe it's a crab or something . . .*

But it wasn't a crab and it wasn't one of the Daydreams – this was not the other place, the one he dreamed about when things were boring or maybe a little scary, and it sure as hell wasn't any crab.

The sand spun faster, the sound arid and dry, making him think of static electricity, of an experiment they had done in science last year with a Leyden jar. But more than either of these, the minute sound was like a long lunatic gasp, the final breath of a dying man.

More sand collapsed inward and began to spin. Now it was not a dimple; it was a funnel in the sand, a kind of reverse dust-devil. The bright yellow of a gum wrapper was revealed, covered, revealed, covered, revealed again – each time it showed up again, Jack could read more of it as the funnel grew: JU, then JUI, then JUICY F. The funnel grew and the sand jerked away from the gum wrapper again. It was as quick and rude as an unfriendly hand jerking down the covers on a made bed. JUICY FRUIT, he read, and then the wrapper flapped upward.

The sand turned faster and faster, in a hissing fury. *Hhhhhhaaaaahhhhhhhh* was the sound the sand made. Jack stared at it, fascinated at first, and then horrified. The sand was opening like a large dark eye: it was the eye of the gull that had dropped the clam on the rock and then pulled the living meat out of it like a rubber band.

Hhhhhhaaaahhhhh, the sand-spout mocked in its dead,

dry voice. That was not a mind-voice. No matter how much Jack wished it were only in his head, that voice was real. *His false teeth flew, Jack, when the old* WILD CHILD *hit him, out they went, rattledybang! Yale or no Yale, when the old* WILD CHILD *van comes and knocks your false teeth out, Jacky, you got to go. And your mother –*

Then he was running again, blindly, not looking back, his hair blown off his forehead, his eyes wide and terrified.

4

Jack walked as quickly as he could through the dim lobby of the hotel. All the atmosphere of the place forbade running: it was as quiet as a library, and the gray light which fell through the tall mullioned windows softened and blurred the already faded carpets. Jack broke into a trot as he passed the desk, and the stooped ashen-skinned day-clerk chose that second to emerge through an arched wooden passage. The clerk said nothing, but his permanent scowl dragged the corners of his mouth another centimeter downward. It was like being caught running in church. Jack wiped his sleeve across his forehead, made himself walk the rest of the way to the elevators. He punched the button, feeling the desk clerk's frown burning between his shoulder-blades. The only time this week that Jack had seen the desk clerk smile had been when the man had recognized his mother. The smile had met only the minimum standards for graciousness.

'I suppose that's how old you have to be to remember Lily Cavanaugh,' she had said to Jack as soon as they were alone in their rooms. There had been a time, and not so long ago, when being identified, recognized from any one of the fifty movies she had made during the fifties and sixties

('Queen of the Bs', they called her; her own comment: 'Darling of the Drive-ins') – whether by a cabdriver, waiter, or the lady selling blouses at the Wilshire Boulevard Saks – perked her mood for hours. Now even that simple pleasure had gone dry for her.

Jack jigged before the unmoving elevator doors, hearing an impossible and familiar voice lifting to him from a whirling funnel of sand. For a second he saw Thomas Woodbine, solid familiar Uncle Tommy Woodbine, who was supposed to have been one of his guardians – a strong wall against trouble and confusion – crumpled and dead on La Cienega Boulevard, his teeth like popcorn twenty feet away in the gutter. He stabbed the button again.

Hurry *up!*

Then he saw something worse – his mother hauled into a waiting car by two impassive men. Suddenly Jack had to urinate. He flattened his palm against the button, and the bent gray man behind the desk uttered a phlegmy sound of disapproval. Jack pressed the edge of his other hand into that magic place just beneath his stomach which lessened the pressure on his bladder. Now he could hear the slow whir of the descending elevator. He closed his eyes, squeezing his legs together. His mother looked uncertain, lost and confused, and the men forced her into the car as easily as they would a weary collie dog. But that was not really happening, he knew; it was a memory – part of it must have been one of the Daydreams – and it had happened not to his mother but to him.

As the mahogany doors of the elevator slid away to reveal a shadowy interior from which his own face met him in a foxed and peeling mirror, that scene from his seventh year wrapped around him once again, and he saw one man's eyes turn to yellow, felt the other's hand alter into something clawlike, hard and inhuman . . . he jumped into the elevator as if he had been jabbed with a fork.

Not possible: the Daydreams were not possible, he had *not* seen a man's eyes turning from blue to yellow, and his mother was fine and dandy, there was nothing to be scared of, nobody was dying, and danger was what a seagull meant to a clam. He closed his eyes and the elevator toiled upward.

That thing in the sand had laughed at him.

Jack squeezed through the opening as soon as the doors began to part. He trotted past the closed mouths of the other elevators, turned right into the panelled corridor and ran past the sconces and paintings toward their rooms. Here running seemed less a sacrilege. They had 407 and 408, consisting of two bedrooms, a small kitchen, and a living room with a view of the long smooth beach and the vastness of the ocean. His mother had appropriated flowers from somewhere, arranged them in vases, and set her little array of framed photographs beside them. Jack at five, Jack at eleven, Jack as an infant in the arms of his father. His father, Philip Sawyer, at the wheel of the old DeSoto he and Morgan Sloat had driven to California in the unimaginable days when they had been so poor they had often slept in the car.

When Jack threw open 408, the door to the living room, he called out, 'Mom? Mom?'

The flowers met him, the photographs smiled; there was no answer. 'Mom!' The door swung shut behind him. Jack felt his stomach go cold. He rushed through the living room to the large bedroom on the right. *'Mom!'* Another vase of tall bright flowers. The empty bed looked starched and ironed, so stiff a quarter would bounce off the quilt.

On the bedside table stood an assortment of brown bottles containing vitamins and other pills. Jack backed out. His mother's window showed black waves rolling and rolling toward him.

Two men getting out of a nondescript car, themselves nondescript, reaching for her . . .

'Mom!' he shouted.

'I hear you, Jack,' came his mother's voice through the bathroom door. 'What on earth . . . ?'

'Oh,' he said, and felt all his muscles relax. 'Oh, sorry. I just didn't know where you were.'

'Taking a bath,' she said. 'Getting ready for dinner. Is that still allowed?'

Jack realized that he no longer had to go to the bathroom. He dropped into one of the overstuffed chairs and closed his eyes in relief. She was still okay –

Still okay for now, a dark voice whispered, and in his mind he saw that sand funnel open again, whirling.

5

Seven or eight miles up the coast road, just outside Hampton Township, they found a restaurant called The Lobster Chateau. Jack had given a very sketchy account of his day – already he was backing away from the terror he had experienced on the beach, letting it diminish in his memory. A waiter in a red jacket printed with the yellow image of a lobster across the back showed them to a table beside a long streaky window.

'Would Madam care for a drink?' The waiter had a stony-cold off-season New England face, and looking at it, suspecting the resentment of his Ralph Lauren sport coat and his mother's carelessly worn Halston afternoon dress behind those watery blue eyes, Jack felt a more familiar terror needle him – simple homesickness. *Mom, if you're not really sick, what the hell are we doing here? The place is empty! It's creepy! Jesus!*

'Bring me an elementary martini,' she said.

The waiter raised his eyebrows. 'Madam?'

'Ice in a glass,' she said. 'Olive on ice. Tanqueray gin over olive. Then – are you getting this?'

Mom, for God's sake, can't you see his eyes? You think you're being charming – he thinks you're making fun of him! Can't you see his eyes?

No. She couldn't. And that failure of empathy, when she had always been so sharp about how other people were feeling, was another stone against his heart. She was withdrawing . . . in all ways.

'Yes, madam.'

'Then,' she said, 'you take a bottle of vermouth – any brand – and hold it against the glass. Then you put the vermouth back on the shelf and bring the glass to me. 'Kay?'

'Yes, madam.' Watery-cold New England eyes, staring at his mother with no love at all. *We're alone here*, Jack thought, really realizing it for the first time. *Jeez*, are *we*. 'Young sir?'

'I'd like a Coke,' Jack said miserably.

The waiter left. Lily rummaged in her purse, came up with a package of Herbert Tarrytoons (so she had called them since he had been a baby, as in 'Bring me my Tarrytoons from over there on the shelf, Jacky,' and so he still thought them) and lit one. She coughed out smoke in three harsh bursts.

It was another stone against his heart. Two years ago,

his mother had given up smoking entirely. Jack had waited for her to backslide with that queer fatalism which is the flip side of childish credulity and innocence. His mother had always smoked; she would soon smoke again. But she had not . . . not until three months ago, in New York. Carltons. Walking around the living room in the apartment on Central Park West, puffing like a choo-choo, or squatting in front of the record cabinet, pawing through her old rock records or her dead husband's old jazz records.

'You smoking again, Mom?' he'd asked her.

'Yeah, I'm smoking cabbage leaves,' she'd said.

'I wish you wouldn't.'

'Why don't you turn on the TV?' she'd responded with uncharacteristic sharpness, turning toward him, her lips pressed tightly together. 'Maybe you can find Jimmy Swaggart or Reverend Ike. Get down there in the hallelujah corner with the amen sisters.'

'Sorry,' he'd muttered.

Well – it was only Carltons. Cabbage leaves. But here were the Herbert Tarrytoons – the blue-and-white old-fashioned pack, the mouthpieces that looked like filters but which weren't. He could remember, vaguely, his father telling somebody that he smoked Winstons and his wife smoked Black Lungers.

'See anything weird, Jack?' she asked him now, her overbright eyes fixed on him, the cigarette held in its old, slightly eccentric position between the second and third fingers of the right hand. Daring him to say something. Daring him to say, 'Mom, I notice you're smoking Herbert Tarrytoons again – does this mean you figure you don't have anything left to lose?'

'No,' he said. That miserable, bewildered homesickness

swept him again, and he felt like weeping. 'Except this place. *It's* a little weird.'

She looked around and grinned. Two other waiters, one fat, one thin, both in red jackets with golden lobsters on the back, stood by the swing doors to the kitchen, talking quietly. A velvet rope hung across the entrance to a huge dining room beyond the alcove where Jack and his mother sat. Chairs were overturned in ziggurat shapes on the tables in this dark cave. At the far end, a huge window-wall looked out on a gothic shorescape that made Jack think of *Death's Darling*, a movie his mother had been in. She had played a young woman with a lot of money who married a dark and handsome stranger against her parents' wishes. The dark and handsome stranger took her to a big house by the ocean and tried to drive her crazy. *Death's Darling* had been more or less typical of Lily Cavanaugh's career – she had starred in a lot of black-and-white films in which handsome but forgettable actors drove around in Ford convertibles with their hats on.

The sign hanging from the velvet rope barring the entrance to this dark cavern was ludicrously understated: THIS SECTION CLOSED.

'It *is* a little grim, isn't it?' she said.

'It's like the Twilight Zone,' he replied, and she barked her harsh, infectious, somehow lovely laugh.

'Yeah, Jacky, Jacky, Jacky,' she said, and leaned over to ruffle his too-long hair, smiling.

He pushed her hand away, also smiling (but oh, her fingers felt like bones, didn't they? *She's almost dead, Jack . . .*). 'Don't touch-a da moichendise.'

'Off my case.'

'Pretty hip for an old bag.'

'Oh boy, try to get movie money out of me this week.'

'Yeah.'

They smiled at each other, and Jack could not ever remember a need to cry so badly, or remember loving her so much. There was a kind of desperate toughness about her now . . . going back to the Black Lungers was part of that.

Their drinks came. She tipped her glass toward his. 'Us.'

'Okay.'

They drank. The waiter came with menus.

'Did I pull his string a little hard before, Jacky?'

'Maybe a little,' he said.

She thought about it, then shrugged it away. 'What are you having?'

'Sole, I guess.'

'Make it two.'

So he ordered for both of them, feeling clumsy and embarrassed but knowing it was what she wanted – and he could see in her eyes when the waiter left that he hadn't done too bad a job. A lot of that was Uncle Tommy's doing. After a trip to Hardee's Uncle Tommy had said: 'I think there's hope for you, Jack, if we can just cure this revolting obsession with processed yellow cheese.'

The food came. He wolfed his sole, which was hot and lemony and good. Lily only toyed with hers, ate a few green beans, and then pushed things around on her plate.

'School started up here two weeks ago,' Jack announced halfway through the meal. Seeing the big yellow buses with ARCADIA DISTRICT SCHOOLS written on the sides had made him feel guilty – under the circumstances he thought that was probably absurd, but there it was. He was playing hooky.

She looked at him, enquiring. She had ordered and finished a second drink; now the waiter brought a third.

Jack shrugged. 'Just thought I'd mention it.'

'Do you want to go?'

'Huh? No! Not here!'

'Good,' she said. 'Because I don't have your goddam vaccination papers. They won't let you in school without a pedigree, chum.'

'Don't call me chum,' Jack said, but Lily didn't crack a smile at the old joke.

Boy, why ain't you in school?

He blinked as if the voice had spoken aloud instead of only in his mind.

'Something?' she asked.

'No. Well . . . there's a guy at the amusement park. Funworld. Janitor, caretaker, something like that. An old black guy. He asked me why I wasn't in school.'

She leaned forward, no humor in her now, almost frighteningly grim. 'What did you tell him?'

Jack shrugged. 'I said I was getting over mono. You remember that time Richard had it? The doctor told Uncle Morgan Richard had to stay out of school for six weeks, but he could walk around outside and everything.' Jack smiled a little. 'I thought he was lucky.'

Lily relaxed a little. 'I don't like you talking to strangers, Jack.'

'Mom, he's just a—'

'I don't care *who* he is. I don't want you talking to strangers.'

Jack thought of the black man, his hair gray steel wool, his dark face deeply lined, his odd, light-colored eyes. He had been pushing a broom in the big arcade on the pier – the arcade was the only part of Arcadia Funworld that stayed open the year around, but it had been deserted then except for Jack and the black man and two old men far in the back. The two were playing Skee-Ball in apathetic silence.

But now, sitting here in this slightly creepy restaurant with his mother, it wasn't the black man who asked the question; it was himself.

Why aren't I in school?

It be just like she say, son. Got no vaccination, got no pedigree. You think she come down here with your birth certificate? That what you think? She on the run, son, and you on the run with her. You –

'Have you heard from Richard?' she broke in, and when she said it, it came to him – no, that was too gentle. It crashed into him. His hands twitched and his glass fell off the table. It shattered on the floor.

She's almost dead, Jack.

The voice from the swirling sand-funnel. The one he had heard in his mind.

It had been Uncle Morgan's voice. Not maybe, not almost, not sorta like. It had been a *real* voice. The voice of Richard's father.

6

Going home in the car, she asked him, 'What happened to you in there, Jack?'

'Nothing. My heart did this funny little Gene Krupa riff.' He ran off a quick one on the dashboard to demonstrate. 'Threw a PCV, just like on *General Hospital*.'

'Don't wise off to me, Jacky.' In the glow of the dashboard instruments she looked pale and haggard. A cigarette smouldered between the second and third fingers of her right hand. She was driving very slowly – never over forty – as she always drove when she'd had too much to drink. Her seat was pulled all the way forward, her skirt was hiked up so her knees floated, storklike, on either side of the steering column, and her chin seemed to hang over the wheel. For a moment she looked haglike, and Jack quickly looked away.

'I'm not,' he mumbled.

'What?'

'I'm not wising off,' he said. 'It was like a twitch, that's all. I'm sorry.'

'It's okay,' she said. 'I thought it was something about Richard Sloat.'

'No.' *His father talked to me out of a hole in the sand down on the beach, that's all. In my head he talked to me, like in a movie where you hear a voiceover. He told me you were almost dead.*

'Do you miss him, Jack?'

'Who, Richard?'

'No – Spiro Agnew. Of course Richard.'

'Sometimes.' Richard Sloat was now going to school in Illinois – one of those private schools where chapel was compulsory and no one had acne.

'You'll see him.' She ruffled his hair.

'Mom, are you all right?' The words burst out of him. He could feel his fingers biting into his thighs.

'Yes,' she said, lighting another cigarette (she slowed down to twenty to do it; an old pick-up swept by them, its horn blatting). 'Never better.'

'How much weight have you lost?'

'Jacky, you can never be too thin or too rich.' She

paused and then smiled at him. It was a tired, hurt smile that told him all the truth he needed to know.

'Mom—'

'No more,' she said. 'All's well. Take my word for it. See if you can find us some be-bop on the FM.'

'But—'

'Find us some bop, Jacky, and shut up.'

He found some jazz on a Boston station – an alto saxophone elucidating 'All the Things You Are'. But under it, a steady, senseless counterpoint, was the ocean. And later, he could see the great skeleton of the roller coaster against the sky. And the rambling wings of the Alhambra Inn. If this was home, they were home.

CHAPTER THREE
SPEEDY PARKER

1

The next day the sun was back – a hard bright sun that layered itself like paint over the flat beach and the slanting, red-tiled strip of roof Jack could see from his bedroom window. A long low wave far out in the water seemed to harden in the light and sent a spear of brightness straight toward his eyes. To Jack this sunlight felt different from the light in California. It seemed somehow thinner; colder; less nourishing. The wave out in the dark ocean melted away, then hoisted itself up again, and a hard dazzling streak of gold leaped across it. Jack turned away from his window. He had already showered and dressed, and his body's clock told him that it was time to start moving toward the schoolbus stop. Seven-fifteen. But of course he would not go to school today, nothing was normal anymore, and he and his mother would just drift like ghosts through another twelve hours of daytime. No schedule, no responsibilities, no homework . . . no order at all except for that given them by mealtimes.

Was today even a schoolday? Jack stopped short beside his bed, feeling a little flicker of panic that his world had become so formless . . . he didn't *think* this was a Saturday.

Jack counted back to the first absolutely identifiable day his memory could find, which was the previous Sunday. Counting forward made it Thursday. On Thursdays he had computer class with Mr Balgo and an early sports period. At least that was what he'd had when his life had been normal, a time that now seemed – though it had come to an end only months ago – irretrievably lost.

He wandered out of his bedroom into the living room. When he tugged at the drawstring for the curtains the hard bright light flooded into the room, bleaching the furniture. Then he punched the button on the television set and dropped himself onto the stiff couch. His mother would not be up for at least another fifteen minutes. Maybe longer, considering that she'd had three drinks with dinner the night before.

Jack glanced toward the door to his mother's room.

Twenty minutes later he rapped softly at her door. 'Mom?' A thick mumble answered him. Jack pushed the door open a crack and looked in. She was lifting her head off the pillow and peering back through half-closed eyes.

'Jacky. Morning. What time?'

'Around eight.'

'God. You starving?' She sat up and pressed the palms of her hands to her eyes.

'Kind of. I'm sort of sick of sitting in here. I just wondered if you were getting up soon.'

'Not if I can help it. You mind? Go down to the dining room, get some breakfast. Mess around on the beach, okay? You'll have a much better mother today if you give her another hour in bed.'

'Sure,' he said. 'Okay. See you later.'

Her head had already dropped back down on the pillow.

Jack switched off the television and let himself out of the room after making sure his key was in the pocket of his jeans.

The elevator smelled of camphor and ammonia – a maid had tipped a bottle off a cart. The doors opened, and the gray desk clerk frowned at him and ostentatiously turned away. *Being a movie star's brat doesn't make you anything special around here, sonny . . . and why aren't you in school?* Jack turned into the panelled entrance to the dining room – The Saddle of Lamb – and saw rows of empty tables in a shadowy vastness. Perhaps six had been set up. A waitress in a white blouse and red ruffled skirt looked at him, then looked away. Two exhausted-looking old people sat across a table from each other at the other end of the room. There were no other breakfasters. As Jack looked on, the old man leaned over the table and unselfconsciously cut his wife's fried egg into four inch-square sections.

'Table for one?' The woman in charge of The Saddle of Lamb during the day had materialized beside him, and was already plucking a menu off a stack beside the reservation book.

'Changed my mind, sorry.' Jack escaped.

The Alhambra's coffee shop, The Beachcomber Lounge, lay all the way across the lobby and down a long bleak corridor lined with empty display cases. His hunger died at the thought of sitting by himself at the counter and watching the bored cook slap down strips of bacon on the crusty grill. He would wait until his mother got up: or, better yet, he would go out and see if he could get a doughnut and a little carton of milk at one of the shops up the street on the way into town.

He pushed open the tall heavy front door of the hotel

and went out into the sunlight. For a moment the sudden brightness stung his eyes – the world was a flat glaring dazzle. Jack squinted, wishing he had remembered to bring his sunglasses downstairs. He went across the apron of red brick and down the four curving steps to the main pathway through the gardens at the front of the hotel.

What happened if she died?

What happened to him – where would he go, who would take care of him, if the worst thing in the world actually took place and she died, for good and all *died*, up in that hotel room?

He shook his head, trying to send the terrible thought away before a lurking panic could rush up out of the Alhambra's well-ordered gardens and blast him apart. He would not cry, he would not let that happen to him – and he would not let himself think about the Tarrytoons and the weight she had lost, the feeling that he sometimes had that she was too helpless and without direction. He was walking very quickly now, and he shoved his hands into his pockets as he jumped down off the curving path through the gardens onto the hotel's drive. *She on the run, son, and you on the run with her.* On the run, but from whom? And to where? Here – just to here, this deserted resort?

He reached the wide street that travelled up the shoreline toward the town, and now all of the empty landscape before him was a whirlpool that could suck him down into itself and spit him out into a black place where peace and safety had never existed. A gull sailed out over the empty road, wheeled around in a wide curve, and dipped back toward the beach. Jack watched it go, shrinking in the air to a smudge of white above the erratic line of the roller-coaster track.

Lester Speedy Parker, a black man with crinkly gray hair and heavy lines cutting down through his cheeks, was down there somewhere inside Funworld and it was Speedy he had to see. That was as clear to Jack as his sudden insight about his friend Richard's father.

A gull screeched, a wave bounced hard gold light toward him, and Jack saw Uncle Morgan and his new friend Speedy as figures almost allegorically opposed, as if they were statues of NIGHT and DAY, stuck up on plinths, MOON and SUN – the dark and the light. What Jack had understood as soon as he had known that his father would have liked Speedy Parker was that the ex-bluesman had no harm in him. Uncle Morgan, now . . . he was another kind of being altogether. Uncle Morgan lived for business, for deal-making and hustling; and he was so ambitious that he challenged every even faintly dubious call in a tennis match, so ambitious in fact that he cheated in the penny-ante card games his son had now and then coaxed him into joining. At least, Jack *thought* that Uncle Morgan had been cheating in a couple of their games . . . not a man who thought that defeat demanded graciousness.

NIGHT and DAY, MOON and SUN; DARK and LIGHT, and the black man was the light in these polarities. And when Jack's mind had pushed him this far, all that panic he had fought off in the hotel's tidy gardens swarmed toward him again. He lifted his feet and ran.

2

When the boy saw Speedy kneeling down outside the gray and peeling arcade building – wrapping electrician's tape around a thick cord, his steel-wool head bent almost to the pier and his skinny buttocks poking out the worn green seat of his workpants, the dusty soles of his boots toed down like a pair of upended surfboards – he realized that he had no idea of what he had been planning to say to the custodian, or even if he intended to say anything at all. Speedy gave the roll of black tape another twist around the cord, nodded, took a battered Palmer knife from the flat pocket of his workshirt and sliced the tape off the roll with a flat surgical neatness. Jack would have escaped from here too, if he could – he was intruding on the man's work, and anyhow, it was crazy to think that Speedy could really help him in any way. What kind of help could he give, an old janitor in an empty amusement park?

Then Speedy turned his head and registered the boy's presence with an expression of total and warming welcome – not so much a smile as a deepening of all those heavy lines in his face – and Jack knew that he was at least no intrusion.

'Travellin Jack,' Speedy said. 'I was beginnin to get afraid you decided to stay away from me. Just when we got to be friends, too. Good to see you again, son.'

'Yeah,' Jack said. 'Good to see you, too.'

Speedy popped the metal knife back into his shirt pocket and lifted his long bony body upright so easily, so athletically, that he seemed weightless. 'This whole place comin down around my ears,' he said. 'I just fix it a little bit at a time, enough so everything works more or less the way it should.' He stopped in mid-sentence, having had a good look at Jack's face. 'Old world's not so fine right now, seems like. Travellin Jack got bucked up to a load of worries. That the way it is?'

'Yeah, sort of,' Jack began – he still had no idea of

how to begin expressing the things that troubled him. They could not be put into ordinary sentences, for ordinary sentences made everything seem rational. One . . . two . . . three: Jack's world no longer marched in those straight lines. All he could not say weighed in his chest.

He looked miserably at the tall thin man before him. Speedy's hands were thrust deep into his pockets; his thick gray eyebrows pushed toward the deep vertical furrow between them. Speedy's eyes, so light they were almost no color at all, swung up from the blistered paint of the pier and met Jack's own – and suddenly Jack felt better again. He did not understand why, but Speedy seemed to be able to communicate emotion directly to him: as if they had not met just a week before, but years ago, and had shared far more than a few words in a deserted arcade.

'Well, that's enough work for now,' Speedy said, glancing up in the direction of the Alhambra. 'Do any more and I just spoil em. Don't suppose you ever saw my office, did you?'

Jack shook his head.

'Time for a little refreshment, boy. The *time* is *right*.'

He set off down the pier in his long-legged gait, and Jack trotted after him. As they jumped down the steps of the pier and began going across the scrubby grass and packed brown earth toward the buildings on the far side of the park, Speedy astonished Jack by starting to sing.

Travellin Jack, ole Travellin Jack,
Got a far long way to go,
Longer way to come back.

It was not exactly singing, Jack thought, but sort of halfway between singing and talking. If it were not for the words, he would have enjoyed listening to Speedy's rough, confident voice.

Long long way for that boy to go,
Longer way to come back.

Speedy cast an almost twinkling look at him over his shoulder.

'Why do you call me that?' Jack asked him. 'Why am I Travelling Jack? Because I'm from California?'

They had reached the pale blue ticket booth at the entrance to the roller-coaster enclosure, and Speedy thrust his hands back in the pockets of his baggy green workpants, spun on his heel, and propped his shoulders on the little blue enclosure. The efficiency and quickness of his movements had a quality almost theatrical – as if, Jack thought, he had known the boy was going to ask that particular question at that precise moment.

He say he come from California,
Don he know he gotta go right back . . .

sang Speedy, his ponderous sculptured face filled with emotion that seemed almost reluctant to Jack.

Say he come all that way,
Poor Travellin Jack gotta go right back . . .

'What?' Jack said. 'Go back? I think my mom even sold the house – or she rented it or something. I don't know what the hell you're trying to do, Speedy.'

He was relieved when Speedy did not answer him in

his chanting, rhythmic sing-song, but said in a normal voice: 'Bet you don't remember meetin me before, Jack. You don't, do you?'

'Meeting you before? Where was this?'

'California – at least, I *think* we met back there. Not so's you'd remember, Travellin Jack. It was a pretty busy couple of minutes. Would have been in . . . let me see . . . would have been about four – five years ago. Nineteen seventy-six.'

Jack looked up at him in pure befuddlement. Nineteen seventy-six? He would have been seven years old.

'Let's go find my little office,' Speedy said, and pushed himself off the ticket booth with that same weightless grace.

Jack followed after him, winding through the tall supports of the roller coaster – black shadows like the grids of tic-tac-toe diagrams overlaid a dusty wasteland sprinkled with beercans and candy wrappers. The tracks of the roller coaster hung above them like an unfinished skyscraper. Speedy moved, Jack saw, with a basketball player's rangy ease, his head up and his arms dangling. The angle of his body, his posture in the crisscrossed gloom beneath the struts, seemed very young – Speedy could have been in his twenties.

Then the custodian stepped out again into the harsh sunlight, and fifty extra years grayed his hair and seamed the back of his neck. Jack paused as he reached the final row of uprights, sensing as if Speedy Parker's illusory juvenescence were the key to them that the Daydreams were somehow very near, hovering all about him.

Nineteen seventy-six? California? Jack trailed off after Speedy, who was going toward a tiny red-painted wooden shack back up against the smooth-wire fence on the far side of the amusement park. He was sure that he had never met Speedy in California . . . but the almost visible presence of his fantasies had brought back to him another specific memory of those days, the visions and sensations of a late afternoon of his sixth year, Jacky playing with a black toy taxi behind the couch in his father's office . . . and his father and Uncle Morgan unexpectedly, magically talking about the Daydreams. *They have magic like we have physics, right? An agrarian monarchy, using magic instead of science. But can you begin to understand how much fucking clout we'd swing if we gave them electricity? If we got modern weapons to the right guys over there? Do you have any idea?*

Hold on there, Morgan, I have a lot of ideas that apparently have yet to occur to you . . .

Jack could almost hear his father's voice, and the peculiar and unsettling realm of the Daydreams seemed to stir in the shadowy wasteland beneath the roller coaster. He began again to trot after Speedy, who had opened the door of the little red shack and was leaning against it, smiling without smiling.

'You got something on your mind, Travellin Jack. Something that's buzzin in there like a bee. Get on inside the executive suite and tell me about it.'

If the smile had been broader, more obvious, Jack might have turned and run: the spectre of mockery still hung humiliatingly near. But Speedy's whole being seemed to express a welcoming concern – the message of all those deepened lines in his face – and Jack went past him through the door.

Speedy's 'office' was a small board rectangle – the same red as its exterior – without a desk or a telephone. Two upended orange crates leaned against one of the side walls, flanking an unplugged electrical heater that resembled the grille of a mid-fifties Pontiac. In the middle of the room a wooden round-back school chair kept company with an overstuffed chair of faded gray material.

The arms of the overstuffed chair seemed to have been clawed open by several generations of cats: dingy wisps of stuffing lay across the arms like hair; on the back of the school chair was a complex graffito of scratched-in initials. Junkyard furniture. In one of the corners stood two neat foot-high piles of paperback books, in another the square fake-alligator cover of a cheap record player. Speedy nodded at the heater and said, 'You come round here in January, February, boy, you see why I got that. Cold? Shoo.' But Jack was now looking at the pictures taped to the wall over the heater and orange crates.

All but one of the pictures were nudes cut from men's magazines. Women with breasts as large as their heads lolled back against uncomfortable trees and splayed columnar, hard-worked legs. To Jack, their faces looked both fascinating and rapacious – as if these women would take bites out of his skin after they kissed him. Some of the women were no younger than his mother; others seemed only a few years older than himself. Jack's eyes grazed over this needful flesh – all of it, young and unyoung, pink or chocolate-brown or honey-yellow, seemed to press toward his touch, and he was too conscious of Speedy Parker standing beside him, watching. Then he saw the landscape in the midst of the nude photographs, and for a second he probably forgot to breathe.

It too was a photograph; and it too seemed to reach out for him, as if it were three-dimensional. A long grassy plain of a particular, aching green unfurled toward a low, ground-down range of mountains. Above the plain and the mountains ranged a deeply transparent sky. Jack could very nearly smell the freshness of this landscape. He knew that place. He had never been there, not really, but he knew it. That was one of the places of the Daydreams.

'Kind of catch the eye, don't it?' Speedy said, and Jack remembered where he was. A Eurasian woman with her back to the camera tilted a heart-shaped rear and smiled at him over her shoulder. Yes, Jack thought. 'Real pretty face,' Speedy said. 'I put that one up myself. All these here girls met me when I moved in. Didn't have the heart to rip em off the wall. They sort of do remind me of way back when, times I was on the road.

Jack looked up at Speedy, startled, and the old man winked at him.

'Do you know that place, Speedy?' Jack asked. 'I mean, do you know where it is?'

'Maybe so, maybe not. It might be Africa – someplace in Kenya. Or that might be just my memory. Sit down, Travellin Jack. Take the com'fable chair.'

Jack twisted the chair so that he could still see the picture of the Daydream place. 'That's *Africa*?'

'Might be somewhere a lot closer. Might be somewhere a fellow could get to – get to anytime he liked, that is, if he wanted to see it bad enough.'

Jack suddenly realized that he was trembling, and had been for some time. He balled his hands into fists, and felt the trembling displace itself into his stomach.

He was not sure that he wanted ever to see the Daydream place, but he looked questioningly over at Speedy, who had perched himself on the school chair. 'It isn't anyplace in Africa, is it?'

'Well, I don't know. Could be. I got my own name for it, son. I just call it the Territories.'

Jack looked back up at the photograph – the long, dimpled plain, the low brown mountains. The Territories. That was right; that was its name.

They have magic like we have physics, right? An agrarian monarchy . . . modern weapons to the right guys over there . . . Uncle Morgan plotting. His father answering, putting on the brakes: *We have to be careful about the way we go in there, partner . . . remember, we owe them, by which I mean we really owe them . . .*

'The Territories,' he said to Speedy, tasting the name in his mouth as much as asking a question.

'Air like the best wine in a rich man's cellar. Soft rain. That's the place, son.'

'You've been there, Speedy?' Jack asked, fervently hoping for a straightforward answer.

But Speedy frustrated him, as Jack had almost known he would. The custodian smiled at him, and this time it was a real smile, not just a subliminal flare of warmth.

After a moment Speedy said, 'Hell, I never been outside these United States, Travellin Jack. Not even in the war. Never got any farther than Texas and Alabama.'

'How do you know about the . . . the Territories?' The name was just beginning to fit his mouth.

'Man like me, he hear all kinds of stories. Stories about two-headed parrots, men that fly with their own wings, men who turn into wolves, stories about queens. Sick queens.'

. . . magic like we have physics, right?

Angels and werewolves. 'I've heard stories about werewolves,' Jack said. 'They're even in cartoons. That doesn't mean anything, Speedy.'

'Probably it don't. But I heard that if a man pulls a radish out of the ground, another man half a mile away will be able to smell that radish – the air so sweet and clear.'

'But angels . . .'

'Men with wings.'

'And sick queens,' Jack said, meaning it as a joke – *man, this is some dumb place you made up, broom jockey*. But the instant he spoke the words, he felt sick himself. He had remembered the black eye of a gull fixing him with his own mortality as it yanked a clam from its shell: and he could hear hustlin, bustlin Uncle Morgan asking if Jack could put Queen Lily on the line.

Queen of the Bs. Queen Lily Cavanaugh.

'Yeah,' Speedy said softly. 'Troubles everywhere, son. Sick Queen . . . maybe dyin. *Dyin*, son. And a world or two waitin out there, just waitin to see if anyone can save her.'

Jack stared at him open-mouthed, feeling more or less as if the custodian had just kicked him in the stomach. Save her? Save his mother? The panic started to flood toward him once again – how could *he* save her? And did all this crazy talk mean that she really was dying, back there in that room?

'You got a job, Travellin Jack,' Speedy told him. 'A job that ain't gonna let you go, and that's the Lord's truth. I wish it was different.'

'I don't know what you're talking about,' Jack said. His breath seemed to be trapped in a hot little pocket situated at the base of his neck. He looked into another corner of the small red room and in the shadow saw a battered guitar propped against the wall. Beside it lay the neat tube of a thin rolled-up mattress. Speedy slept next to his guitar.

'I wonder,' Speedy said. 'There comes times, you know

what I mean, you know more than you think you know. One hell of a lot more.'

'But I don't—' Jack began, and then pulled himself up short. He had just remembered something. Now he was even more frightened – another chunk of the past had rushed out at him, demanding his attention. Instantly he was filmed with perspiration, and his skin felt very cold – as if he had been misted by a fine spray from a hose. This memory was what he had fought to repress yesterday morning, standing before the elevators, pretending that his bladder was not about to burst.

'Didn't I say it was time for a little refreshment?' Speedy asked, reaching down to push aside a loose floorboard.

Jack again saw two ordinary-looking men trying to push his mother into a car. Above them a huge tree dipped scalloped fronds over the automobile's roof.

Speedy gently extracted a pint bottle from the gap between the floorboards. The glass was dark green, and the fluid inside looked black. 'This gonna help you, son. Just a little taste all you need – send you some new places, help you get started findin that job I told you bout.'

'I can't stay, Speedy,' Jack blurted out, now in a desperate hurry to get back to the Alhambra. The old man visibly checked the surprise in his face, then slid the bottle back under the loose floorboard. Jack was already on his feet. 'I'm worried,' he said.

'Bout your mom?'

Jack nodded, moving backward toward the open door.

'Then you better settle your mind and go see she's all right. You can come back here anytime, Travellin Jack.'

'Okay,' the boy said, and then hesitated before running outside. 'I think . . . I remember when we met before.'

'Nah, nah, my brains got twisted,' Speedy said, shaking his head and waving his hands back and forth before him. 'You had it right. We never met before last week. Get on back to your mom and set your mind at ease.'

Jack sprinted out the door and ran through the dimensionless sunlight to the wide arch leading to the street. Above it he could see the letters DLROWNUF AIDACRA outlined against the sky: at night, colored bulbs would spell out the park's name in both directions. Dust puffed up beneath his Nikes. Jack pushed himself against his own muscles, making them move faster and harder, so that by the time he burst out through the arch, he felt almost as though he were flying.

Nineteen seventy-six. Jack had been puttering his way up Rodeo Drive on an afternoon in June? July? . . . some afternoon in the drought season, but before that time of the year when everybody started worrying about brushfires in the hills. Now he could not even remember where he had been going. A friend's house? It had not been an errand of any urgency. He had, Jack remembered, just reached the point where he no longer thought of his father in every unoccupied second – for many months after Philip Sawyer's death in a hunting accident, his shade, his loss had sped toward Jack at a bruising speed whenever the boy was least prepared to meet it. Jack was only seven, but he knew that a part of his childhood had been stolen from him – his six-year-old self now seemed impossibly naive and thoughtless – but he had learned to trust his mother's strength. Formless and savage threats no longer seemed to conceal themselves in dark corners, closets with half-open doors, shadowy streets, empty rooms.

The events of that aimless summer afternoon in 1976 had murdered this temporary peace. After it, Jack slept with his light on for six months; nightmares roiled his sleep.

The car pulled across the street just a few houses up from the Sawyers' white three-story Colonial. It had been a green car, and that was all that Jack had known about it except that it was not a Mercedes – Mercedes was the only kind of automobile he knew by sight. The man at the wheel had rolled down his window and smiled at Jack. The boy's first thought had been that he knew this man – the man had known Phil Sawyer, and wanted just to say hello to his son. Somehow that was conveyed by the man's smile, which was easy and unforced and familiar. Another man leaned forward in the passenger seat and peered toward Jack through blind-man's glasses – round and so dark they were nearly black. This second man was wearing a pure white suit. The driver let his smile speak for him a moment longer.

Then he said, 'Sonny, do you know how we get to the Beverly Hills Hotel?' So he was a stranger after all. Jack experienced an odd little flicker of disappointment.

He pointed straight up the street. The hotel was right up there, close enough so that his father had been able to walk to breakfast meetings in the Loggia.

'Straight ahead?' the driver asked, still smiling.

Jack nodded.

'You're a pretty smart little fellow,' the man told him, and the other man chuckled. 'Any idea of how far up it is?' Jack shook his head. 'Couple of blocks, maybe?'

'Yeah.' He had begun to get uncomfortable. The driver was still smiling, but now the smile looked bright and hard and empty. And the passenger's chuckle had been wheezy and damp, as if he were sucking on something wet.

'Five, maybe? Six? What do you say?'

'About five or six, I guess,' Jack said, stepping backward.

'Well, I sure do want to thank you, little fellow,' the driver said. 'You don't happen to like candy, do you?' He extended a closed fist through the window, turned it palm-up, and opened his fingers: a Tootsie Roll. 'It's yours. Take it.'

Jack tentatively stepped forward, hearing in his mind the words of a thousand warnings involving strange men and candy. But this man was still in his car; if he tried anything, Jack could be half a block away before the man got his door open. And to not take it somehow seemed a breach of civility. Jack took another step nearer. He looked at the man's eyes, which were blue and as bright and hard as his smile. Jack's instincts told him to lower his hand and walk away. He let his hand drift an inch or two nearer the Tootsie Roll. Then he made a little stabbing peck at it with his fingers.

The driver's hand clamped around Jack's, and the passenger in blind-man's glasses laughed out loud. Astonished, Jack stared into the eyes of the man gripping his hand and saw them start to change – *thought* he saw them start to change – from blue to yellow.

But later they were yellow.

The man in the other seat pushed his door open and trotted around the back of the car. He was wearing a small gold cross in the lapel of his silk suit coat. Jack pulled frantically away, but the driver smiled brightly, emptily and held him fast. 'NO!' Jack yelled. 'HELP!'

The man in dark glasses opened the rear door on Jack's side.

'HELP ME!' Jack screamed.

The man holding him began to squeeze him down into a shape that would fit into the open door. Jack bucked, still yelling, but the man effortlessly tightened his hold. Jack struck at his hands, then tried to push the hands off him. With horror, he realized that what he felt beneath his fingers was not skin. He twisted his head and saw that clamped to his side and protruding from the black sleeve was a hard, pinching thing like a claw or a jointed talon. Jack screamed again.

From up the street came a loud voice: 'Hey, stop messin with that boy! You! Leave that boy alone!'

Jack gasped with relief, and twisted as hard as he could in the man's arms. Running toward them from the end of the block was a tall thin black man, still shouting. The man holding him dropped Jack to the sidewalk and took off around the back of the car. The front door of one of the houses behind Jack slammed open – another witness.

'Move, *move*,' said the driver, already stepping on the accelerator. White Suit jumped back into the passenger seat, and the car spun its wheels and squealed diagonally across Rodeo Drive, barely missing a long white Clenet driven by a suntanned man in tennis whites. The Clenet's horn blared.

Jack picked himself up off the sidewalk. He felt dizzy. A bald man in a tan safari suit appeared beside him and said, 'Who were they? Did you get their names?'

Jack shook his head.

'How do you feel? We ought to call the police.'

'I want to sit down,' Jack said, and the man backed away a step.

'You want me to call the police?' he asked, and Jack shook his head.

'I can't believe this,' the man said. 'Do you live around here? I've seen you before, haven't I?'

'I'm Jack Sawyer. My house is just down there.'

'The white house,' the man said, nodding. 'You're Lily Cavanaugh's kid. I'll walk you home, if you like.'

'Where's the other man?' Jack asked him. 'The black man – the one who was shouting.'

He took an uneasy step away from the man in the safari suit. Apart from the two of them, the street was empty.

Lester Speedy Parker had been the man running toward him. Speedy had saved his life back then, Jack realized, and ran all the harder toward the hotel.

3

'You get any breakfast?' his mother asked him, spilling a cloud of smoke out of her mouth. She wore a scarf over her hair like a turban, and with her hair hidden that way, her face looked bony and vulnerable to Jack. A half-inch of cigarette smouldered between her second and third fingers, and when she saw him glance at it, she snubbed it out in the ashtray on her dressing table.

'Ah, no, not really,' he said, hovering in the door of her bedroom.

'Give me a clear yes or no,' she said, turning back to the mirror. 'The ambiguity is killing me.' Her mirror-wrist and mirror-hand, applying the makeup to Lily's face, looked stick-thin.

'No,' he said.

'Well, hang on for a second and when your mother has made herself beautiful she'll take you downstairs and buy you whatever your heart desires.'

'Okay,' he said. 'It just seemed so depressing, being there all alone.'

'I swear, what you have to be depressed about . . .' She leaned forward and inspected her face in the mirror. 'I don't suppose you'd mind waiting in the living room, Jacky? I'd rather do this alone. Tribal secrets.'

Jack wordlessly turned away and wandered back into the living room.

When the telephone rang, he jumped about a foot.

'Should I get that?' he called out.

'Thank you,' her cool voice came back.

Jack picked up the receiver and said hello.

'Hey kid, I finally got you,' said Uncle Morgan Sloat. 'What in the *world* is going on in your momma's head? Jesus, we could have a real situation here if somebody doesn't start paying attention to details. Is she there? Tell her she has to talk to me – I don't care what she says, she has to talk to me. Trust me, kiddo.'

Jack let the phone dangle in his hand. He wanted to hang up, to get in the car with his mother and drive to another hotel in another state. He did not hang up. He called out, 'Mom, Uncle Morgan's on the phone. He says you have to talk to him.'

She was silent for a moment, and he wished he could have seen her face. Finally she said, 'I'll take it in here, Jacky.'

Jack already knew what he was going to have to do. His mother gently shut her bedroom door; he heard her walking back to the dressing table. She picked up the telephone in her bedroom. 'Okay, Jacky,' she called through the door. 'Okay,' he called back. Then he put the telephone back to his ear and covered the mouthpiece with his hand so that no one would hear him breathing.

'Great stunt, Lily,' Uncle Morgan said. 'Terrific. If you were still in pictures, we could probably get a little mileage out of this. Kind of a "Why Has This Actress Disappeared?"

thing. But don't you think it's time you started acting like a rational person again?'

'How did you find me?' she asked.

'You think you're hard to find? Give me a break, Lily, I want you to get your ass back to New York. It's time you stopped running away.'

'Is that what I'm doing, Morgan?'

'You don't exactly have all the time in the world, Lily, and I don't have enough time to waste to chase you all over New England. Hey, hold on. Your kid never hung up his phone.'

'Of course he did.'

Jack's heart had stopped some seconds earlier.

'Get off the line, kid,' Morgan Sloat's voice said to him.

'Don't be ridiculous, Sloat,' his mother said.

'I'll tell you what's ridiculous, lady. You holing up in some seedy resort when you ought to be in the hospital, *that's* ridiculous. Jesus, don't you know we have about a million business decisions to make? I care about your son's education too, and it's a damn good thing I do. You seem to have given up on that.'

'I don't want to talk to you anymore,' Lily said.

'You don't want to, but you have to. I'll come up there and put you in a hospital by force if I have to. We gotta make *arrangements*, Lily. You own half of the company I'm trying to run – and Jack gets your half after you're gone. I want to make sure Jack's taken care of. And if you think that taking care of Jack is what you're doing up there in goddam New Hampshire, then you're a lot sicker than you know.'

'What do you want, Sloat?' Lily asked in a tired voice.

'You know what I want – I want everybody taken care of. I want what's fair. I'll take care of Jack, Lily. I'll give him fifty thousand dollars a year – you think about that, Lily. I'll see he goes to a good college. You can't even keep him in school.'

'Noble Sloat,' his mother said.

'Do you think that's an answer? Lily, you need help and I'm the only one offering.'

'What's your cut, Sloat?' his mother asked.

'You know damn well. I get what's fair. I get what's coming to me. Your interest in Sawyer and Sloat – I worked my ass off for that company, and it ought to be mine. We could get the paperwork done in a morning, Lily, and then concentrate on getting you taken care of.'

'Like Tommy Woodbine was taken care of,' she said. 'Sometimes I think you and Phil were *too* successful, Morgan. Sawyer and Sloat was more manageable before you got into real-estate investments and production deals. Remember when you had only a couple of deadbeat comics and a half-dozen hopeful actors and screenwriters as clients? I liked life better before the megabucks.'

'Manageable, who are you kidding?' Uncle Morgan yelled. 'You can't even manage yourself!' Then he made an effort to calm himself. 'And I'll forget you mentioned Tom Woodbine. That was beneath even you, Lily.'

'I'm going to hang up now, Sloat. Stay away from here. And stay away from Jack.'

'You are going into a hospital, Lily, and this running around is going to—'

His mother hung up in the middle of Uncle Morgan's sentence; Jack gently put down his own receiver. Then he took a couple of steps closer to the window, as if not to be seen anywhere near the living-room phone. Only silence came from the closed bedroom.

'Mom?' he said.

'Yes, Jacky?' He heard a slight wobble in her voice.

'You okay? Is everything all right?'

'Me? Sure.' Her footsteps came softly to the door, which cracked open. Their eyes met, his blue to her blue. Lily swung the door all the way open. Again their eyes met, for a moment of uncomfortable intensity. 'Of course everything's all right. Why shouldn't it be?' Their eyes disengaged. Knowledge of some kind had passed between them, but what? Jack wondered if she knew that he had listened to her conversation; then he thought that the knowledge they had just shared was – for the first time – the fact of her illness.

'Well,' he said, embarrassed now. His mother's disease, that great unspeakable subject, grew obscenely large between them. 'I don't know, exactly. Uncle Morgan seemed . . .' He shrugged.

Lily shivered, and Jack came to another great recognition. His mother was afraid – at least as afraid as he was.

She plugged a cigarette in her mouth and snapped open her lighter. Another stabbing look from her deep eyes. 'Don't pay any attention to that pest, Jack. I'm just irritated because it really doesn't seem that I'll ever be able to get away from him. Your Uncle Morgan likes to bully me.' She exhaled gray smoke. 'I'm afraid that I don't have much appetite for breakfast anymore. Why don't you take yourself downstairs and have a real breakfast this time?'

'Come with me,' he said.

'I'd like to be alone for a while, Jack. Try to understand that.'

Try to understand that.

Trust me.

These things that grown-ups said, meaning something else entirely.

'I'll be more companionable when you get back,' she said. 'That's a promise.'

And what she was really saying was *I want to scream, I can't take any more of this, get out, get out!*

'Should I bring you anything?'

She shook her head, smiling toughly at him, and he had to leave the room, though he no longer had any stomach for breakfast either. Jack wandered down the corridor to the elevators. Once again, there was only one place to go, but this time he knew it before he ever reached the gloomy lobby and the ashen, censorious desk clerk.

4

Speedy Parker was not in the small red-painted shack of an office; he was not out on the long pier, in the arcade where the two old boys were back playing Skee-Ball as if it were a war they both knew they would lose; he was not in the dusty vacancy beneath the roller coaster. Jack Sawyer turned aimlessly in the harsh sunlight, looking down the empty avenues and deserted public places of the park. Jack's fear tightened itself up a notch. Suppose something had happened to Speedy? It was impossible, but what if Uncle Morgan had found out about Speedy (found out what, though?) and had . . . Jack mentally saw the WILD CHILD van careering around a corner, grinding its gears and picking up speed.

He jerked himself into motion, hardly knowing which way he meant to go. In the bright panic of his mood, he saw Uncle Morgan running past a row of distorting mirrors, turned by them into a series of monstrous and deformed figures. Horns grew on his bald brow, a hump flowered between his fleshy shoulders, his wide fingers became shovels. Jack veered sharply off to the right, and found himself moving toward an oddly shaped, almost round building of white slat-like boards.

From within it he suddenly heard a rhythmic *tap tap tap*. The boy ran toward the sound – a wrench hitting a pipe, a hammer striking an anvil, a noise of work. In the midst of the slats he found a doorknob and pulled open a fragile slat-door.

Jack went forward into striped darkness, and the sound grew louder. The darkness changed form around him, altered its dimensions. He stretched out his hands and touched canvas. This slid aside; instantly, glowing yellow light fell about him. 'Travellin Jack,' said Speedy's voice.

Jack turned toward the voice and saw the custodian seated on the ground beside a partially dismantled merry-go-round. He held a wrench in his hand, and before him a white horse with a foamy mane lay impaled by a long silver stake from pommel to belly. Speedy gently put the wrench on the ground. 'Are you ready to talk now, son?' he asked.

CHAPTER FOUR
JACK GOES OVER

1

'Yes, I'm ready now,' Jack said in a perfectly calm voice, and then burst into tears.

'Say, Travellin Jack,' Speedy said, dropping his wrench and coming to him. 'Say, son, take her easy, take her easy now . . .'

But Jack couldn't take her easy. Suddenly it was too much, all of it, too much, and it was cry or just sink under a great wave of blackness – a wave which no bright streak of gold could illuminate. The tears hurt, but he sensed the terror would kill him if he did not cry it out.

'You do your weepin, Travellin Jack,' Speedy said, and put his arms around him. Jack put his hot, swollen face against Speedy's thin shirt, smelling the man's smell – something like Old Spice, something like cinnamon, something like books that no one has taken out of the library in a long time. Good smells, comforting smells. He groped his arms around Speedy; his palms felt the bones in Speedy's back, close to the surface, hardly covered by scant meat.

'You weep if it put you easy again,' Speedy said, rocking him. 'Sometimes it does. I know. Speedy knows how far you been, Travellin Jack, and how far you got to go, and how you tired. So you weep if it put you easy.'

Jack barely understood the words – only the sounds of them, soothing and calming.

'My mother's really sick,' he said at last against Speedy's chest. 'I think she came here to get away from my father's old partner. Mr Morgan Sloat.' He sniffed mightily, let go of Speedy, stepped back, and rubbed at his swollen eyes with the heels of his hands. He was surprised at his lack of embarrassment – always before, his tears had disgusted and shamed him . . . it was almost like peeing your pants. Was that because his mother had always been so tough? He supposed that was part of it, all right; Lily Cavanaugh had little use for tears.

'But that ain't the only reason she come here, was it?'

'No,' Jack said in a low voice. 'I think . . . she came here to die.' His voice rose impossibly on the last word, making a squeak like an unoiled hinge.

'Maybe,' Speedy said, looking at Jack steadily. 'And maybe you here to save her. Her . . . and a woman just like her.'

'Who?' Jack said through numb lips. He knew who. He didn't know her name, but he knew who.

'The Queen,' Speedy said. 'Her name is Laura DeLoessian, and she is the Queen of the Territories.'

2

'Help me,' Speedy grunted. 'Catch old Silver Lady right under the tail. You be takin liberties with the Lady, but I guess she ain't gonna mind if you're helpin me get her back where she belongs.'

'Is that what you call her? Silver Lady?'

'Yeah-bob,' Speedy said, grinning, showing perhaps a dozen teeth, top and bottom. 'All carousel horses is named, don't you know that? Catch on, Travellin Jack!'

Jack reached under the white horse's wooden tail and locked his fingers together. Grunting, Speedy wrapped his big brown hands around the Lady's forelegs. Together they carried the wooden horse over to the canted dish of the carousel, the pole pointing down, its far end sinister with layers of Quaker State oil.

'Little to the left . . .' Speedy gasped. 'Yeah . . . now peg her, Travellin Jack! Peg her down good!'

They seated the pole and then stood back, Jack panting, Speedy grinning and gasping wheezily. The black man armed sweat from his brow and then turned his grin on Jack.

'My, ain't we cool?'

'If you say so,' Jack answered, smiling.

'I say so! Oh yes!' Speedy reached into his back pocket and pulled out the dark green pint bottle. He unscrewed the cap, drank – and for a moment Jack felt a weird certainty: he could see through Speedy. Speedy had become transparent, as ghostly as one of the spirits on the *Topper* show, which they showed on one of the indy stations out in L.A. Speedy was disappearing. *Disappearing*, Jack thought, *or going someplace else?* But that was another nutty thought; it made no sense at all.

Then Speedy was as solid as ever. It had just been a trick his eyes had played, a momentary –

No. No it wasn't. For just a second he almost wasn't here!

– hallucination.

Speedy was looking shrewdly at him. He started to hold the bottle out to Jack, then shook his head a little. He recapped it instead, and then slid it into his back pocket again. He turned to study the Silver Lady, back in her place on the carousel, now needing only to have her post bolted securely into place. He was smiling. 'We just as cool as we can be, Travellin Jack.'

'Speedy—'

'All of em is named,' Speedy said, walking slowly around the canted dish of the carousel, his footfalls echoing in the high building. Overhead, in the shadowy crisscross of the beams, a few barnswallows cooed softly. Jack followed him. 'Silver Lady . . . Midnight . . . this here roan is Scout . . . this mare's Ella Speed.'

The black man threw back his head and sang, startling the barnswallows into flight:

'"*Ella Speed was havin her lovin fun . . . let me tell you what old Bill Martin done . . .*" Hoo! Look at em fly!' He laughed . . . but when he turned to Jack, he was serious again. 'You like to take a shot at savin your mother's life, Jack? Hers, and the life of that other woman I tole you about?'

'I . . .' . . . *don't know how*, he meant to say, but a voice inside – a voice which came from that same previously locked room from which the memory of the two men and the attempted kidnapping had come that morning – rose up powerfully: *You do know! You might need Speedy to get you started, but you do know, Jack. You do.*

He knew that voice so very well. It was his father's voice.

'I will if you tell me how,' he said, his voice rising and falling unevenly.

Speedy crossed to the room's far wall – a great circular shape made of narrow slatted boards, painted with a primitive but wildly energetic mural of dashing horses. To Jack, the wall looked like the pull-down lid of his father's rolltop desk (and that desk had been in Morgan Sloat's office the last time Jack and his mother had been there, he suddenly remembered – the thought brought a thin, milky anger with it).

Speedy pulled out a gigantic ring of keys, picked thoughtfully through them, found the one he wanted, and turned it in a padlock. He pulled the lock out of the hasp, clicked it shut, and dropped it into one of his breast pockets. Then he shoved the entire wall back on its track. Gorgeously bright sunlight poured in, making Jack narrow his eyes. Water ripples danced benignly across the ceiling. They were looking at the magnificent sea-view the riders of the Arcadia Funworld Carousel got each time Silver Lady and Midnight and Scout carried them past the east side of the round carousel building. A light sea-breeze pushed Jack's hair back from his forehead.

'Best to have sunlight if we're gonna talk about this,' Speedy said. 'Come over here, Travellin Jack, and I'll tell you what I can . . . which ain't all I know. God forbid you should ever have to get all of that.'

3

Speedy talked in his soft voice – it was as mellow and soothing to Jack as leather that has been well broken in. Jack listened, sometimes frowning, sometimes gaping.

'You know those things you call the Daydreams?'

Jack nodded.

'Those things ain't dreams, Travellin Jack. Not daydreams, not nightdreams, either. That place is a real place. Real enough, anyway. It's a lot different from here, but it's real.'

'Speedy, my mom says—'

'Never mind that right now. She don't know about the Territories . . . but, in a way, she *do* know about them. Because your Daddy, *he* knew. And this other man—'

'Morgan Sloat?'

'Yeah, I reckon. He knows too.' Then, cryptically, Speedy added, 'I know who he is over there, too. Don't I? Whooo!'

'The picture in your office . . . not Africa?'

'Not Africa.'

'Not a trick?'

'Not a trick.'

'And my father went to this place?' he asked, but his heart already knew the answer – it was an answer that clarified too many things not to be true. But, true or not, Jack wasn't sure how much of it he wanted to *believe*. Magic lands? Sick queens? It made him uneasy. It made him uneasy about his mind. Hadn't his mother told him over and over again when he was small that he shouldn't confuse his Daydreaming with what was really real? She had been very stern about that, and she had frightened Jack a little. Perhaps, he thought now, she had been frightened herself. Could she have lived with Jack's father for so long and not known *something*? Jack didn't think so. *Maybe*, he thought, *she didn't know very much . . . just enough to scare her.*

Going nuts. That's what she was talking about. People who couldn't tell the difference between real things and make-believe were going nuts.

But his father had known a different truth, hadn't he? Yes. He and Morgan Sloat.

They have magic like we have physics, right?

'Your father went often, yes. And this other man, Groat—'

'Sloat.'

'Yeah-bob! Him. He went, too. Only your dad, Jacky, he went to see and learn. The other fella, he just went to plunder him out a fortune.'

'Did Morgan Sloat kill my Uncle Tommy?' Jack asked.

'Don't know nuthin bout that. You just listen to me, Travellin Jack. Because time is short. If you really think this fellow Sloat is gonna turn up here –'

'He sounded awful mad,' Jack said. Just thinking about Uncle Morgan showing up in Arcadia Beach made him feel nervous.

'– then time is shorter than ever. Because maybe he wouldn't mind so bad if your mother died. And his Twinner is sure hopin that Queen Laura dies.'

'Twinner?'

'There's people in this world have got Twinners in the Territories,' Speedy said. 'Not many, because there's a lot less people over there – maybe only one for every hundred thousand over here. But Twinners can go back and forth the easiest.'

'This Queen . . . she's my mother's . . . her Twinner?'

'Yeah, seems like she is.'

'But my mother never—?'

'No. She never has. No reason.'

'My father had a . . . a Twinner?'

'Yes indeed he did. A fine man.'

Jack wet his lips – what a crazy conversation this was! Twinners and Territories! 'When my father died over here, did his Twinner die over there?'

'Yeah. Not zackly the same time, but almost.'

'Speedy?'

'What?'

'Have I got a Twinner? In the Territories?'

And Speedy looked at him so seriously that Jack felt a deep chill go up his back. 'Not you, son. There's only one of you. You special. And this fella Smoot –'

'Sloat,' Jack said, smiling a little.

'– yeah, whatever, he knows it. That be one of the reasons he be coming up here soon. And one of the reasons you got to get movin.'

'*Why?*' Jack burst out. 'What good can I do if it's cancer? If it's cancer and she's here instead of in some clinic, it's because there's no *way*, if she's here, see, it means—' The tears threatened again and he swallowed them back frantically. 'It means it must be all through her.'

All through her. Yes. That was another truth his heart knew: the truth of her accelerating weight-loss, the truth of the brown shadows under her eyes. *All through her*, but please God, hey, God, please, man, she's my *mother* –

'I mean,' he finished in a thick voice, 'what good is that Daydream place going to do?'

'I think we had enough jaw-chin for now,' Speedy said. 'Just believe this here, Travellin Jack: I'd never tell you you ought to go if you couldn't do her some good.'

'But—'

'Get quiet, Travellin Jack. Can't talk no more till I show you some of what I mean. Wouldn't do no good. Come on.'

Speedy put an arm around Jack's shoulders and led him around the carousel dish. They went out the door together and walked down one of the amusement park's deserted byways. On their left was the Demon Dodgem Cars building, now boarded and shuttered. On their right was a series of booths: Pitch Til U Win, Famous Pier Pizza & Dough-Boys, the Rimfire Shooting Gallery, also boarded up (faded wild animals pranced across the boards – lions and tigers and bears, o my).

They reached the wide main street, which was called Boardwalk Avenue in vague imitation of Atlantic City – Arcadia Funworld had a pier, but no real boardwalk. The arcade building was now a hundred yards down to their left and the arch marking the entrance to Arcadia Funworld about two hundred yards down to their right. Jack could hear the steady, grinding thunder of the breaking waves, the lonely cries of the gulls.

He looked at Speedy, meaning to ask him what now, what next, could he mean any of it or was it all a cruel joke . . . but he said none of those things. Speedy was holding out the green glass bottle.

'That—' Jack began.

'Takes you there,' Speedy said. 'Lot of people who visit over there don't need nothin like this, but you ain't been there in a while, have you, Jacky?'

'No.' When had he last closed his eyes in this world and opened them in the magic world of the Daydreams, that world with its rich, vital smells and its deep, transparent sky? Last year? No. Further back than that . . . California . . . after his father had died. He would have been about . . .

Jack's eyes widened. Nine years old? That long? Three *years*?

It was frightening to think how quietly, how unobtrusively, those dreams, sometimes sweet, sometimes darkly unsettling, had slipped away – as if a large part of his imagination had died painlessly and unannounced.

He took the bottle from Speedy quickly, almost dropping it. He felt a little panicky. Some of the Daydreams had been disturbing, yes, and his mother's carefully worded admonitions not to mix up reality and make-believe (*in other words don't go crazy, Jacky, ole kid old sock, okay?*) had been a little scary, yes, but he discovered now that he didn't want to lose that world after all.

He looked in Speedy's eyes and thought: *He knows it, too. Everything I just thought, he knows. Who are you, Speedy?*

'When you ain't been there for a while, you kinda forget how to get there on your own hook,' Speedy said. He nodded at the bottle. 'That's why I got me *some* magic juice. This stuff is *special*.' Speedy spoke this last in tones that were almost reverential.

'Is it from there? The Territories?'

'Nope. They got *some* magic right here, Travellin Jack. Not much, but a little. This here magic juice come from California.'

Jack looked at him doubtfully.

'Go on. Have you a little sip and see if you don't go travellin.' Speedy grinned. 'Drink enough of that, you can go just about anyplace you want. You're lookin at one who knows.'

'Jeez, Speedy, but—' He began to feel afraid. His mouth had gone dry, the sun seemed much too bright, and he could feel his pulsebeat speeding up in his temples. There was a coppery taste under his tongue and Jack thought: *That's how his 'magic juice' will taste – horrible.*

'If you get scared and want to come back, have another sip,' Speedy said.

'It'll come with me? The bottle? You promise?' The thought of getting stuck there, in that mystical other place, while his mother was sick and Sloat-beset back here, was awful.

'I promise.'

'Okay.' Jack brought the bottle to his lips . . . and then let it fall away a little. The smell was awful – sharp and rancid. 'I don't want to, Speedy,' he whispered.

Lester Parker looked at him, and his lips were smiling, but there was no smile in his eyes – they were stern. Uncompromising. Frightening. Jack thought of black eyes: eye of gull, eye of vortex. Terror swept through him.

He held the bottle out to Speedy. 'Can't you take it back?' he asked, and his voice came out in a strengthless whisper. 'Please?'

Speedy made no reply. He did not remind Jack that his mother was dying, or that Morgan Sloat was coming. He didn't call Jack a coward, although he had never in his life felt so much like a coward, not even the time he had backed away from the high board at Camp Accomac and some of the other kids had booed him. Speedy merely turned around and whistled at a cloud.

Now loneliness joined the terror, sweeping helplessly through him. Speedy had turned away from him; Speedy had shown him his back.

'Okay,' Jack said suddenly. 'Okay, if it's what you need me to do.'

He raised the bottle again, and before he could have any second or third thoughts, he drank.

The taste was worse than anything he had anticipated. He had had wine before, had even developed some taste for it (he especially liked the dry white wines his mother served with sole or snapper or swordfish), and this was something like wine . . . but at the same time it was a dreadful mockery of all the wines he had drunk before. The taste was high and sweet and rotten, not the taste of lively grapes but of dead grapes that had not lived well.

As his mouth flooded with that horrible sweet-purple taste, he could actually *see* those grapes – dull, dusty, obese and nasty, crawling up a dirty stucco wall in a thick, syrupy sunlight that was silent except for the stupid buzz of many flies.

He swallowed and thin fire printed a snail-trail down his throat.

He closed his eyes, grimacing, his gorge threatening to rise. He did not vomit, although he believed that if he had eaten any breakfast he would have done.

'Speedy—'

He opened his eyes, and further words died in his throat. He forgot about the need to sick up that horrible parody of wine. He forgot about his mother, and Uncle Morgan, and his father, and almost everything else.

Speedy was gone. The graceful arcs of the roller coaster against the sky were gone. Boardwalk Avenue was gone.

He was someplace else now. He was –

'In the Territories,' Jack whispered, his entire body crawling with a mad mixture of terror and exhilaration. He could feel the hair stirring on the nape of his neck, could feel a goofed-up grin pulling at the corners of his mouth. 'Speedy, I'm here, my God, I'm here in the Territories! I—'

But wonder overcame him. He clapped a hand over his mouth and slowly turned in a complete circle, looking at this place to which Speedy's 'magic juice' had brought him.

4

The ocean was still there, but now it was a darker, richer blue – the truest indigo Jack had ever seen. For a moment he stood transfixed, the sea-breeze blowing in his hair, looking at the horizon-line where that indigo ocean met a sky the color of faded denim.

That horizon-line showed a faint but unmistakable curve.

He shook his head, frowning, and turned the other way. Sea-grass, high and wild and tangled, ran down from the headland where the round carousel building had been only a minute ago. The arcade pier was also gone; where it had been, a wild tumble of granite blocks ran down to the ocean. The waves struck the lowest of these and ran into ancient cracks and channels with great hollow boomings. Foam as thick as whipped cream jumped into the clear air and was blown away by the wind.

Abruptly Jack seized his left cheek with his left thumb and forefinger. He pinched hard. His eyes watered, but nothing changed.

'It's real,' he whispered, and another wave boomed onto the headland, raising white curds of foam.

Jack suddenly realized that Boardwalk Avenue *was* still here . . . after a fashion. A rutted cart-track ran from the top of the headland – where Boardwalk Avenue had ended at the entrance to the arcade in what his mind persisted in thinking of as 'the real world' – down to where he was standing and then on to the north, just as Boardwalk Avenue ran north, becoming Arcadia Avenue after it passed under the arch at the border of Funworld. Sea-grass grew up along the center of this track, but it had a bent and matted look that made Jack think that the track was still used, at least once in a while.

He started north, still holding the green bottle in his right hand. It occurred to him that somewhere, in another world, Speedy was holding the cap that went on this bottle.

Did I disappear right in front of him? I suppose I must have. Jeez!

About forty paces along the track, he came upon a tangle of blackberry bushes. Clustered amid the thorns were the fattest, darkest, most lush-looking blackberries he had ever seen. Jack's stomach, apparently over the indignity of the 'magic juice', made a loud *goinging* sound.

Blackberries? In September?

Never mind. After all that had happened today (and it was not yet ten o'clock), sticking at blackberries in September seemed a little bit like refusing to take an aspirin after one has swallowed a doorknob.

Jack reached in, picked a handful of berries, and tossed them into his mouth. They were amazingly sweet, amazingly good. Smiling (his lips had taken on a definite bluish cast), thinking it quite possible that he had lost his mind, he picked another handful of berries . . . and then a third. He had never tasted anything so fine – although, he thought later, it was not just the berries themselves; part of it was the incredible clarity of the air.

He got a couple of scratches while picking a fourth helping – it was as if the bushes were telling him to lay off, enough was enough, already. He sucked at the deepest of the scratches, on the fleshy pad below the thumb, and then headed north along the twin ruts again, moving slowly, trying to look everywhere at once.

He paused a little way from the blackberry tangles to

look up at the sun, which seemed somehow smaller and yet more fiery. Did it have a faint orange cast, like in those old medieval pictures? Jack thought perhaps it did. And –

A cry, as rusty and unpleasant as an old nail being pulled slowly out of a board, suddenly arose on his right, scattering his thoughts. Jack turned toward it, his shoulders going up, his eyes widening.

It was a gull – and its size was mind-boggling, almost unbelievable (but there it was, as solid as stone, as real as houses). It was, in fact, the size of an eagle. Its smooth white bullet-head cocked to one side. Its fishhook of a beak opened and closed. It fluttered great wings, rippling the sea-grass around it.

And then, seemingly without fear, it began to hop toward Jack.

Faintly, Jack heard the clear, brazen note of many horns blown together in a simple flourish, and for no reason at all he thought of his mother.

He glanced to the north momentarily, in the direction he had been travelling, drawn by that sound – it filled him with a sense of unfocussed urgency. It was, he thought (when there was *time* to think), like being hungry for a specific *something* that you haven't had in a long time – ice cream, potato chips, maybe a taco. You don't know until you see it – and until you do, there is only a need without a name, making you restless, making you nervous.

He saw pennons and the peak of what might have been a great tent – a pavilion – against the sky.

That's where the Alhambra is, he thought, and then the gull shrieked at him. He turned toward it and was alarmed to see it was now less than six feet away. Its beak opened again, showing that dirty pink lining, making him think of yesterday, the gull that had dropped the clam on the rock and then fixed him with a horrid stare exactly like this one. The gull was grinning at him – he was sure of it. As it hopped closer, Jack could smell a low and noisome stink hanging about it – dead fish and rotted seaweed.

The gull hissed at him and flurried its wings again.

'Get out of here,' Jack said loudly. His heart was pumping quick blood and his mouth had gone dry, but he did not want to be scared off by a seagull, even a big one. 'Get out!'

The gull opened its beak again . . . and then, in a terrible, open-throated series of pulses, it spoke – or seemed to.

'Other's iyyyin Ack . . . other's iyyyyyyyyyyin—'

Mother's dying, Jack . . .

The gull took another clumsy hop toward him, scaly feet clutching at the grassy tangles, beak opening and closing, black eyes fixed on Jack's. Hardly aware of what he was doing. Jack raised the green bottle and drank.

Again that horrible taste made him wince his eyes shut – and when he opened them he was looking stupidly at a yellow sign which showed the black silhouettes of two running kids, a little boy and a little girl. SLOW CHILDREN, this sign read. A seagull – this one of perfectly normal size – flew up from it with a squawk, no doubt startled by Jack's sudden appearance.

He looked around, and was walloped by disorientation. His stomach, full of blackberries and Speedy's pustulant 'magic juice', rolled over, groaning. The muscles in his legs began to flutter unpleasantly, and all at once he sat down on the curb at the base of the sign with a bang that travelled up his spine and made his teeth click together.

He suddenly leaned over between his splayed knees and opened his mouth wide, sure he was just going to yark up the whole works. Instead he hiccuped twice, half-gagged, and then felt his stomach slowly relax.

It was the berries, he thought. *If it hadn't been for the berries, I would have puked for sure.*

He looked up and felt the unreality wash over him again. He had walked no more than sixty paces down the cart-track in the Territories world. He was sure of that. Say his stride was two feet – no, say two and a half feet, just to be on the safe side. That meant he had come a paltry hundred and fifty feet. But –

He looked behind him and saw the arch, with its big red letters: ARCADIA FUNWORLD. Although his vision was 20/20, the sign was now so far away he could barely read it. To his right was the rambling, many-winged Alhambra Inn, with the formal gardens before it and the ocean beyond it.

In the Territories world he had come a hundred and fifty feet.

Over here he had somehow come half a mile.

'Jesus Christ,' Jack Sawyer whispered, and covered his eyes with his hands.

5

'Jack! Jack, boy! Travellin Jack!'

Speedy's voice rose over the washing-machine roar of an old flathead-six engine. Jack looked up – his head felt impossibly heavy, his limbs leaden with weariness – and saw a very old International Harvester truck rolling slowly toward him. Homemade stake sides had been added to the back of the truck, and they rocked back and forth like loose teeth as the truck moved up the street toward him. The body was painted a hideous turquoise. Speedy was behind the wheel.

He pulled up at the curb, gunned the engine (*Whup! Whup! Whup-whup-whup!*), and then killed it (*Hahhhhhhhhh* . . .). He climbed down quickly.

'You all right, Jack?'

Jack held the bottle out for Speedy to take. 'Your magic juice really sucks, Speedy,' he said wanly.

Speedy looked hurt . . . then he smiled. 'Whoever tole you medicine supposed to taste good, Travellin Jack?'

'Nobody, I guess,' Jack said. He felt some of his strength coming back – slowly – as that thick feeling of disorientation ebbed.

'You believe now, Jack?'

Jack nodded.

'No,' Speedy said. 'That don't git it. Say it out loud.'

'The Territories,' Jack said. 'They're there. Real. I saw a bird—' He stopped and shuddered.

'What kind of a bird?' Speedy asked sharply.

'Seagull. Biggest damn seagull—' Jack shook his head. 'You wouldn't believe it.' He thought and then said, 'No, I guess *you* would. Nobody else, maybe, but *you* would.'

'Did it talk? Lots of birds over there do. Talk foolishness, mostly. And there's some that talks a kind of sense . . . but it's a evil kind of sense, and mostly it's lies.'

Jack was nodding. Just hearing Speedy talk of these things, as if it were utterly rational and utterly lucid to do so, made him feel better.

'I think it did talk. But it was like—' He thought hard. 'There was a kid at the school Richard and I went to in L.A. Brandon Lewis. He had a speech impediment, and when he talked you could hardly understand him. The bird was like that. But I knew what it said. It said my mother was dying.'

Speedy put an arm around Jack's shoulders and they sat quietly together on the curb for a time. The desk clerk from the Alhambra, looking pale and narrow and suspicious of every living thing in the universe, came out with a large stack of mail. Speedy and Jack watched him go down to the corner of Arcadia and Beach Drive and dump the inn's correspondence into the mailbox. He turned back, marked Jack and Speedy with his thin gaze, and then turned up the Alhambra's main walk. The top of his head could barely be descried over the tops of the thick box hedges.

The sound of the big front door opening and closing was clearly audible, and Jack was struck by a terrible sense of this place's autumn desolation. Wide, deserted streets. The long beach with its empty dunes of sugar-sand. The empty amusement park, with the roller-coaster cars standing on a siding under canvas tarps and all the booths padlocked. It came to him that his mother had brought him to a place very like the end of the world.

Speedy cocked his head back and sang in his true and mellow voice, '*Well I've laid around . . . and played around . . . this old town too long . . . summer's almost gone, yes, and winter's coming on . . . winter's coming on, and I feel like . . . I got to travel on—*'

He broke off and looked at Jack.

'You feel like you got to travel, ole Travellin Jack?'

Flagging terror stole through his bones.

'I guess so,' he said. 'If it will help. Help her. Can I help her, Speedy?'

'You can,' Speedy said gravely.

'But—'

'Oh, there's a whole string of buts,' Speedy said. 'Whole *trainload* of buts, Travellin Jack. I don't promise you no cake-walk. I don't promise you success. Don't promise that you'll come back alive, or if you do, that you'll come back with your mind still bolted together.

'You gonna have to do a lot of your ramblin in the Territories, because the Territories is a whole lot smaller. You notice that?'

'Yes.'

'Figured you would. Because you sure did get a whole mess down the road, didn't you?'

Now an earlier question recurred to Jack, and although it was off the subject, he had to know. 'Did I disappear, Speedy? Did you see me disappear?'

'You went,' Speedy said, and clapped his hands once, sharply, 'just like *that*.'

Jack felt a slow, unwilling grin stretch his mouth . . . and Speedy grinned back.

'I'd like to do it sometime in Mr Balgo's computer class,' Jack said, and Speedy cackled like a child. Jack joined him – and the laughter felt good, almost as good as those blackberries had tasted.

After a few moments Speedy sobered and said, 'There's a reason you got to be in the Territories, Jack. There's somethin you got to git. It's a mighty powerful somethin.'

'And it's over there?'

'Yeah-bob.'

'It can help my mother?'

'Her . . . and the other.'

'The Queen?'

Speedy nodded.

'What is it? Where is it? When do I—'

'Hold it! Stop!' Speedy held up a hand. His lips were smiling, but his eyes were grave, almost sorrowing. 'One thing at a time. And, Jack, I can't tell you what I don't know . . . or what I'm not allowed to tell.'

'Not allowed?' Jack asked bewildered. 'Who—'

'There you go again,' Speedy said. 'Now listen, Travellin Jack. You got to leave as soon as you can, before that man Bloat can show up an bottle you up—'

'Sloat.'

'Yeah, him. You got to get out before he comes.'

'But he'll bug my mother,' Jack said, wondering why he was saying it – because it was true, or because it was an excuse to avoid the trip that Speedy was setting before him, like a meal that might be poisoned. 'You don't know him! He—'

'I know him,' Speedy said quietly. 'I know him of old, Travellin Jack. And he knows me. He's got my marks on him. They're hidden – but they're on him. Your momma can take care of herself. At least, she's gonna have to, for a while. Because you got to go.'

'Where?'

'West,' Speedy said. 'From this ocean to the other.'

'*What?*' Jack cried, appalled by the thought of such distance. And then he thought of an ad he'd seen on TV not three nights ago – a man picking up goodies at a deli buffet some thirty-five thousand feet in the air, just as cool as a cucumber. Jack had flown from one coast to another with his mother a good two dozen times, and was always secretly delighted by the fact that when you flew from New York to L.A. you could have sixteen hours of daylight. It was like cheating time. And it was easy.

'Can I fly?' he asked Speedy.

'No!' Speedy almost yelled, his eyes widening in consternation. He gripped Jack's shoulder with one strong hand. 'Don't you let *nuthin* git you up in the sky! You dassn't! If you happened to flip over into the Territories while you was up there—'

He said no more; he didn't have to. Jack had a sudden, appalling picture of himself tumbling out of that clear, cloudless sky, a screaming boy-projectile in jeans with a red-and-white-striped rugby shirt, a sky-diver with no parachute.

'You *walk*,' Speedy said. 'And thumb what rides you think you can . . . but you got to be careful because there's strangers out there. Some are just crazy people, sissies that would like to touch you or thugs that would like to mug you. But some are real Strangers, Travellin Jack. They people with a foot in each world – they look that way and this like a goddamn Janus-head. I'm afraid they gonna know you comin before too long has passed. And they'll be on the watch.'

'Are they' – he groped – 'Twinners?'

'Some are. Some aren't. I can't say no more right now. But you get across if you can. Get across to the other ocean. You travel in the Territories when you can and you'll get across faster. You take the juice—'

'I hate it!'

'Never mind what you hate,' Speedy said sternly. 'You get across and you're gonna find a place – another Alhambra. You got to go in that place. It's a scary place, a bad place. But you got to go in.'

'How will I find it?'

'It will call you. You'll hear it loud and clear, son.'

'Why?' Jack asked. He wet his lips. 'Why do I have to go there, if it's so bad?'

'Because,' Speedy said, 'that's where the Talisman is. Somewhere in that other Alhambra.'

'I don't know what you're talking about!'

'You will,' Speedy said. He stood up, then took Jack's hand. Jack rose. The two of them stood face-to-face, old black man and young white boy.

'Listen,' Speedy said, and his voice took on a slow, chanting rhythm. 'Talisman be given unto your hand, Travellin Jack. Not too big, not too small, she look just like a crystal ball. Travellin Jack, ole Travellin Jack, you be goin to California to bring her back. But here's your burden, here's your cross: drop her, Jack, and all be lost.'

'I don't know what you're talking about,' Jack repeated with a scared kind of stubbornness. 'You have to—'

'No,' Speedy said, not unkindly. 'I got to finish with that carousel this morning, Jack, that's what I got to do. Got no time for any more jaw-chin. I got to get back and you got to get on. Can't tell you no more now. I guess I'll be seein you around. Here . . . or over there.'

'But I don't know what to *do*!' Jack said as Speedy swung up into the cab of the old truck.

'You know enough to get movin,' Speedy said. 'You'll go to the Talisman, Jack. She'll draw you to her.'

'I don't even know what a Talisman is!'

Speedy laughed and keyed the ignition. The truck started up with a big blue blast of exhaust. 'Look it up in the dictionary!' he shouted, and threw the truck into reverse.

He backed up, turned around, and then the truck was rattling back toward Arcadia Funworld. Jack stood by the curb, watching it go. He had never felt so alone in his life.

CHAPTER FIVE
JACK AND LILY

1

When Speedy's truck turned off the road and disappeared beneath the Funworld arch, Jack began to move toward the hotel. A Talisman. In another Alhambra. On the edge of another ocean. His heart seemed empty. Without Speedy beside him, the task was mountainous, so huge; vague, too – while Speedy had been talking, Jack had had the feeling of *almost* understanding that macaroni of hints and threats and instructions. Now it was close to just being macaroni. The Territories were real, though. He hugged that certainty as close as he could, and it both warmed and chilled him. They were a real place, and he was going there again. Even if he did not really understand everything yet – even if he was an ignorant pilgrim, he was going. Now all he had to do was to try to convince his mother. 'Talisman,' he said to himself, using the word as the thing, and crossed empty Boardwalk Avenue and jumped up the steps onto the path between the hedges. The darkness of the Alhambra's interior, once the great door had swung shut, startled him. The lobby was a long cave – you'd need a fire just to separate the shadows. The pale clerk flickered behind the long desk, stabbing at Jack with his white eyes. A message there: yes. Jack swallowed and turned away. The message made him stronger, it increased him, though its intention was only scornful.

He went toward the elevators with a straight back and an unhurried step. *Hang around with blackies, huh? Let them put their arms around you, huh?* The elevator whirred down like a great heavy bird, the doors parted, and Jack stepped inside. He turned to punch the button marked with a glowing 4. The clerk was still posed spectrally behind the desk, sending out his dumdum's message. *Niggerlover Niggerlover Niggerlover (like it that way, hey brat? Hot and black, that's for you, hey?).* The doors mercifully shut. Jack's stomach fell toward his shoes, the elevator lurched upward.

The hatred stayed down there in the lobby: the very air in the elevator felt better once it had risen above the first floor. Now all Jack had to do was to tell his mother that he had to go to California by himself.

Just don't let Uncle Morgan sign any papers for you . . .

As Jack stepped out of the elevator, he wondered for the first time in his life whether Richard Sloat understood what his father was really like.

2

Down past the empty sconces and paintings of little boats riding foamy, corrugated seas, the door marked 408 slanted inward, revealing a foot of the suite's pale carpet. Sunlight from the living-room windows made a long rectangle on the inner wall. 'Hey Mom,' Jack said, entering the suite. 'You didn't close the door, what's the big—' He was alone in the room. 'Idea?' he said to the furniture. 'Mom?' Disorder seemed to ooze from the tidy room – an overflowing ashtray, a half-full tumbler of water left on the coffee table.

This time, Jack promised himself, he would not panic.

He turned in a slow circle. Her bedroom door was open, the room itself as dark as the lobby because Lily had never pulled open the curtains.

'Hey, I know you're here,' he said, and then walked through her empty bedroom to knock at her bathroom door. No reply. Jack opened this door and saw a pink toothbrush beside the sink, a forlorn hairbrush on the dressing table. Bristles snarled with light hairs. *Laura DeLoessian*, announced a voice in Jack's mind, and he stepped backward out of the little bathroom – that name stung him.

'Oh, not again,' he said to himself. 'Where'd she *go*?'

Already he was seeing it.

He saw it as he went to his own bedroom, saw it as he opened his own door and surveyed his rumpled bed, his flattened knapsack and little stack of paperback books, his socks balled up on top of the dresser. He saw it when he looked into his own bathroom, where towels lay in oriental disarray over the floor, the sides of the tub, and the Formica counters.

Morgan Sloat thrusting through the door, grabbing his mother's arms and hauling her downstairs . . .

Jack hurried back into the living room and this time looked behind the couch.

. . . yanking her out a side door and pushing her into a car, his eyes beginning to turn yellow . . .

He picked up the telephone and punched 0. 'This is, ah, Jack Sawyer, and I'm in, ah, room four-oh-eight. Did my mother leave any message for me? She was supposed to be here and . . . and for some reason . . . ah . . .'

'I'll check,' said the girl, and Jack clutched the phone

for a burning moment before she returned. 'No message for four-oh-eight, sorry.'

'How about four-oh-seven?'

'That's the same slot,' the girl told him.

'Ah, did she have any visitors in the last half hour or so? Anybody come this morning? To see her, I mean.'

'That would be Reception,' the girl said. 'I wouldn't know. Do you want me to check for you?'

'Please,' Jack said.

'Oh, I'm happy to have something to do in this morgue,' she told him. 'Stay on the line.'

Another burning moment. When she came back to him, it was with 'No visitors. Maybe she left a note somewhere in your rooms.'

'Yes, I'll look,' Jack said miserably and hung up. Would the clerk tell the truth? Or would Morgan Sloat have held out a hand with a twenty-dollar bill folded like a stamp into his meaty palm? That too Jack could see.

He dropped himself on the couch, stifling an irrational desire to look under the cushions. Of course Uncle Morgan could not have come to the rooms and abducted her – he was still in California. But he could have sent other people to do it for him. Those people Speedy had mentioned, the Strangers with a foot in each world.

Then Jack could stay in the room no longer. He bounced off the couch and went back into the corridor, closing the door after him. When he had gone a few paces down the hall, he twirled around in mid-step, went back, and opened the door with his own key. He pushed the door an inch in, and then trotted back towards the elevators. It was always possible that she had gone out without her key – to the shop in the lobby, to the newsstand for a magazine or a paper.

Sure. He had not seen her pick up a newspaper since the beginning of summer. All the news she cared about came over an internal radio.

Out for a walk, then.

Yeah, out exercising and breathing deeply. Or jogging, maybe: maybe Lily Cavanaugh had suddenly gone in for the hundred-yard dash. She'd set up hurdles down on the beach and was in training for the next Olympics . . .

When the elevator deposited him in the lobby he glanced into the shop, where an elderly blond woman behind a counter peered at him over the tops of her glasses. Stuffed animals, a tiny pile of thin newspapers, a display rack of flavored Chap Stick. Leaning out of pockets in a wallstand were *People* and *Us* and *New Hampshire Magazine*.

'Sorry,' Jack said, and turned away.

He found himself staring at the bronze plaque beside a huge, dispirited fern . . . *has begun to sicken and must soon die*.

The woman in the shop cleared her throat. Jack thought that he must have been staring at those words of Daniel Webster's for entire minutes. 'Yes?' the woman said behind him.

'Sorry,' Jack repeated, and pulled himself into the center of the lobby. The hateful clerk lifted an eyebrow, then turned sideways to stare at a deserted staircase. Jack made himself approach the man.

'Mister,' he said when he stood before the desk. The clerk was pretending to try to remember the capital of North Carolina or the principal export of Peru. 'Mister.' The man scowled to himself: he was nearly there, he could not be disturbed.

All of this was an act, Jack knew, and he said, 'I wonder if you can help me.'

The man decided to look at him after all. 'Depends on what the help is, sonny.'

Jack consciously decided to ignore the hidden sneer. 'Did you see my mother go out a little while ago?'

'What's a little while?' Now the sneer was almost visible.

'Did you see her go out? That's all I'm asking.'

'Afraid she saw you and your sweetheart holding hands out there?'

'God, you're such a creep,' Jack startled himself by saying. 'No, I'm not afraid of that. I'm just wondering if she went out, and if you weren't such a creep, you'd tell me.' His face had grown hot, and he realized that his hands were bunched into fists.

'Well okay, she went out,' the clerk said, drifting away toward the bank of pigeonholes behind him. 'But you'd better watch your tongue, boy. You better apologize to me, fancy little Master Sawyer. I got eyes, too. I know things.'

'You run your mouth and I run my business,' Jack said, dredging the phrase up from one of his father's old records – perhaps it did not quite fit the situation, but it felt right in his mouth, and the clerk blinked satisfactorily.

'Maybe she's in the gardens, I don't know,' the man said gloomily but Jack was already on his way toward the door.

The Darling of the Drive-ins and Queen of the Bs was nowhere in the wide gardens before the hotel, Jack saw immediately – and he had known that she would not be in the gardens, for he would have seen her on his way into the hotel.

Besides, Lily Cavanaugh did not dawdle through gardens: that suited her as little as did setting up hurdles on the beach.

A few cars rolled down Boardwalk Avenue. A gull screeched far overhead, and Jack's heart tightened.

The boy pushed his fingers through his hair and looked up and down the bright street. Maybe she had been curious about Speedy – maybe she'd wanted to check out this unusual new pal of her son's and had wandered down to the amusement park. But Jack could not see her in Arcadia Funworld any more than he could see her lingering picturesquely in the gardens. He turned in the less familiar direction, toward the town line.

Separated from the Alhambra's grounds by a high thick hedge, the Arcadia Tea and Jam Shoppe stood first in a row of brightly colored shops. It and New England Drugs were the only shops in the terrace to remain open after Labor Day. Jack hesitated a moment on the cracked sidewalk. A tea shop, much less shoppe, was an unlikely situation for the Darling of the Drive-ins. But since it was the first place he might expect to find her, he moved across the sidewalk and peered in the window.

A woman with piled-up hair sat smoking before a cash register. A waitress in a pink rayon dress leaned against the far wall. Jack saw no customers. Then at one of the tables near the Alhambra end of the shop he saw an old woman lifting a cup. Apart from the help, she was alone. Jack watched the old woman delicately replace the cup in the saucer, then fish a cigarette from her bag, and realized with a sickening jolt that she was his mother. An instant later, the impression of age had disappeared.

But he could remember it – and it was as if he were seeing her through bifocals, seeing both Lily Cavanaugh

Sawyer and that fragile old woman in the same body.

Jack gently opened the door, but still he set off the tinkle of the bell that he had *known* was above it. The blond woman at the register nodded, smiling. The waitress straightened up and smoothed the lap of her dress. His mother stared at him with what looked like genuine surprise, and then gave him an open smile.

'Well, Wandering Jack, you're so tall that you looked just like your father when you came through that door,' she said. 'Sometimes I forget you're only twelve.'

3

'You called me "Wandering Jack",' he said, pulling a chair out and dropping himself into it.

Her face was very pale, and the smudges beneath her eyes looked almost like bruises.

'Didn't your father call you that? I just happened to think of it – you've been on the move all morning.'

'He called me Wandering Jack?'

'Something like that . . . sure he did. When you were tiny. *Travelling* Jack,' she said firmly. 'That was it. He used to call you Travelling Jack – you know, when we'd see you tearing down the lawn. It was funny, I guess. I left the door open, by the way. Didn't know if you remembered to take your key with you.'

'I saw,' he said, still tingling with the new information she had so casually given him.

'Want any breakfast? I just couldn't take the thought of eating another meal in that hotel.'

The waitress had appeared beside them. 'Young man?' she asked, lifting her order pad.

'How did you know I'd find you here?'

'Where else is there to go?' his mother reasonably asked, and told the waitress, 'Give him the three-star breakfast. He's growing about an inch a day.'

Jack leaned against the back of his chair. How could he begin this?

His mother glanced at him curiously, and he began – he had to begin, now. 'Mom, if I had to go away for a while, would you be all right?'

'What do you mean, all right? And what do you mean, go away for a while?'

'Would you be able – ah, would you have trouble from Uncle Morgan?'

'I can handle old Sloat,' she said, smiling tautly. 'I can handle him for a while, anyhow. What's this all about, Jacky? You're not going anywhere.'

'I have to,' he said. 'Honest.' Then he realized that he sounded like a child begging for a toy. Mercifully, the waitress arrived with toast in a rack and a stubby glass of tomato juice. He looked away for a moment, and when he looked back, his mother was spreading jam from one of the pots on the table over a triangular section of toast.

'I have to go,' he said. His mother handed him the toast; her face moved with a thought, but she said nothing.

'You might not see me for a while, Mom,' he said. 'I'm going to try to help you. That's why I have to go.'

'Help me?' she asked, and her cool incredulity, Jack reckoned, was about seventy-five per cent genuine.

'I want to try to save your life,' he said.

'Is that all?'

'I can do it.'

'You can save my life. That's very entertaining, Jacky-boy; it ought to make prime time someday. Ever think about going into network programming?' She had put down the red-smeared knife and was widening her eyes in mockery: but beneath the deliberate incomprehension he saw two things. A flare-up of her terror; a faint, almost unrecognized hope that he might after all be able to do something.

'Even if you say I can't try, I'm going to do it anyhow. So you might as well give me your permission.'

'Oh, that's a wonderful deal. Especially since I don't have any idea of what you're talking about.'

'I think you do, though – I think you do have some idea, Mom. Because Dad would have known exactly what I'm talking about.'

Her cheeks reddened; her mouth thinned into a line. 'That's so unfair it's despicable, Jacky. You can't use what Philip might have known as a weapon against me.'

'What he did know, not what he might have known.'

'You're talking total horseshit, sonny boy.'

The waitress, setting a plate of scrambled eggs, home fries, and sausages before Jack, audibly inhaled.

After the waitress had paraded off, his mother shrugged. 'I don't seem able to find the right *tone* with the help around here. But horseshit is still horseshit is still horseshit, to quote Gertrude Stein.'

'I'm going to save your life, Mom,' he repeated. 'And I have to go a long way away and bring something back to do it. And so that's what I'm going to do.'

'I wish I knew what you were talking about.'

Just an ordinary conversation, Jack told himself: as ordinary as asking permission to spend a couple of nights at a friend's house. He cut a sausage in half and popped one of the pieces in his mouth. She was watching him carefully.

Sausage chewed and swallowed, Jack inserted a forkful of egg into his mouth. Speedy's bottle lumped like a rock against his backside.

'I also wish you'd act as though you could hear the little remarks I send your way, as obtuse as they may be.'

Jack stolidly swallowed the eggs and inserted a salty wad of the crisp potatoes into his mouth.

Lily put her hands in her lap. The longer he said nothing, the more she would listen when he did talk. He pretended to concentrate on his breakfast, eggs sausage potatoes, sausage potatoes eggs, potatoes eggs sausage, until he sensed that she was near to shouting at him.

My father called me Travelling Jack, he thought to himself. *This is right; this is as right as I'll ever get.*

'Jack—'

'Mom,' he said, 'sometimes didn't Dad call you up from a long way away, and you knew he was supposed to be in town?'

She raised her eyebrows.

'And sometimes didn't you, ah, walk into a room because you thought he was there, maybe even *knew* he was there – but he wasn't.'

Let her chew on that.

'No,' she said.

Both of them let the denial fade away.

'Almost never.'

'Mom, it even happened to *me*,' Jack said.

'There was always an explanation, you know there was.'

'My father – this is what *you* know – was never too bad at explaining things. Especially the stuff that really couldn't be explained. He was very good at that. That's part of the reason he was such a good agent.'

Now she was silent again.

'Well, I know where he went,' Jack said. 'I've been there already. I was there this morning. And if I go there again, I can try to save your life.'

'*My life doesn't need you to save it, it doesn't need anyone to save it*,' his mother hissed. Jack looked down at his devastated plate and muttered something. 'What was that?' she drilled at him.

'I think it does, I said.' He met her eyes with his own.

'Suppose I ask you how you propose to go about saving my life, as you put it.'

'I can't answer. Because I don't really understand it yet. Mom, I'm not in school, anyhow . . . give me a chance. I might only be gone a week or so.'

She raised her eyebrows.

'It could be longer,' he admitted.

'I think you're nuts,' she said. But he saw that part of her wanted to believe him, and her next words proved it. 'If – *if* – I were mad enough to allow you to go off on this mysterious errand, I'd have to be sure that you wouldn't be in any danger.'

'Dad always came back,' Jack pointed out.

'I'd rather risk my life than yours,' she said, and this truth, too, lay hugely between them for a long moment.

'I'll call when I can. But don't get too worried if a couple of weeks go by without my calling. I'll come back, too, just like Dad always did.'

'This whole thing is nuts,' she said. 'Me included. How are you going to get to this place you have to go to? And where is it? Do you have enough money?'

'I have everything I need,' he said, hoping that she would not press him on the first two questions. The silence stretched out and out, and finally he said, 'I guess I'll mainly walk. I can't talk about it much, Mom.'

'Travelling Jack,' she said. 'I can almost believe . . .'

'Yes,' Jack said. '*Yes.*' He was nodding. *And maybe*, he thought, *you know some of what she knows, the real Queen, and that's why you are letting go this easily*. 'That's right. I can believe, too. That's what makes it right.'

'Well . . . since you say you'll go no matter what I say . . .'

'I will, too.'

'. . . then I guess it doesn't matter what I say.' She looked at him bravely. 'It does matter, though. I know. I want you to get back here as quick as you can, sonny boy. You're not going right away, are you?'

'I have to.' He inhaled deeply. 'Yes. I am going right away. As soon as I leave you.'

'I could almost believe in this rigamarole. You're Phil Sawyer's son, all right. You haven't found a girl somewhere in this place, have you . . . ?' She looked at him very sharply. 'No. No girl. Okay. Save my life. Off with you.' She shook her head, and he thought he saw an extra brightness in her eyes. 'If you're going to leave, get out of here, Jacky. Call me tomorrow.'

'If I can.' He stood up.

'If you can. Of course. Forgive me.' She looked down at nothing, and he saw that her eyes were unfocussed. Red dots burned in the middle of her cheeks.

Jack leaned over and kissed her, but she just waved him away. The waitress stared at the two of them as if they were performing a play. Despite what his mother had just said, Jack thought that he had brought the level of her disbelief down to something like fifty per cent; which meant that she no longer knew *what* to believe.

She focussed on him for a moment, and he saw that hectic brightness blazing in her eyes again. Anger: tears? 'Take care,' she said, and signalled the waitress.

'I love you,' Jack said.

'Never get off on a line like that.' Now she was almost smiling. 'Get travelling, Jack. Get going before I realize how crazy this is.'

'I'm gone,' he said, and turned away and marched out of the restaurant. His head felt tight, as if the bones of his skull had just grown too large for their covering of flesh. The empty yellow sunlight attacked his eyes. Jack heard the door of the Arcadia Tea and Jam Shoppe banging shut an instant after the little bell had sounded. He blinked; ran across Boardwalk Avenue without looking for cars. When he reached the pavement on the other side, he realized that he would have to go back to their suite for some clothes. His mother had still not emerged from the tea shop by the time Jack was pulling open the hotel's great front door.

The desk clerk stepped backward and sullenly stared. Jack felt some sort of emotion steaming off the man, but for a second could not remember why the clerk should react so strongly to the sight of him. The conversation with his mother – actually much shorter than he had imagined it would be – seemed to have lasted for days. On the other side of the vast gulf of time he'd spent in the Tea and Jam Shoppe, he had called the clerk a creep. Should he apologize? He no longer actually remembered what had caused him to flare up at the clerk . . .

His mother had agreed to his going – she had given him permission to take his journey, and as he walked through the crossfire of the deskman's glare he finally understood why. He had not mentioned the Talisman, not explicitly, but even if he had – if he had spoken of the most lunatic aspect of his mission – she would have accepted that too. And if he'd said that he was going to bring back a foot-long butterfly and roast it in the oven, she'd have agreed to eat roast butterfly. It would have been an ironic, but a real, agreement. In part this showed the depth of her fear, that she would grasp at such straws.

But she would grasp because at some level she knew that these were bricks, not straws. His mother had given him permission to go because somewhere inside her she too knew about the Territories.

Did she ever wake up in the night with that name, *Laura DeLoessian*, sounding in her mind?

Up in 407 and 408, he tossed clothes into his knapsack almost randomly: if his fingers found it in a drawer and it was not too large, in it went. Shirts, socks, a sweater, Jockey shorts. Jack tightly rolled up a pair of tan jeans and forced them in, too; then he realized that the pack had become uncomfortably heavy, and pulled out most of the shirts and socks. The sweater too came out. At the last minute he remembered his toothbrush. Then he slid the straps over his shoulders and felt the pull of the weight on his back – not too heavy. He could walk all day, carrying only these few pounds. Jack simply stood quiet in the suite's living room a moment, feeling – unexpectedly powerfully – the absence of any person or thing to whom he could say goodbye. His mother would not return to the suite until she could be sure he was gone: if she saw him now, she'd order him to stay. He could not say goodbye to these three rooms as he could to a house he had loved: hotel rooms accepted departures emotionlessly. In the end he went to the telephone pad printed with a drawing of the hotel on eggshell-thin paper, and with the Alhambra's blunt narrow pencil wrote the three lines that were most of what he had to say:

Thanks
I love you
and will be back

4

Jack moved down Boardwalk Avenue in the thin northern sun, wondering where he should . . . flip. That was the word for it. And should he see Speedy once more before he 'flipped' into the Territories? He almost *had* to talk to Speedy once more, because he knew so little about where he was going, whom he might meet, what he was looking for . . . *she look just like a crystal ball.* Was that all the instruction Speedy intended to give him about the Talisman? That, and the warning not to drop it? Jack felt almost sick with lack of preparation – as if he had to take a final exam in a course he'd never attended.

He also felt that he could flip right where he stood, he was that impatient to begin, to get started, to move. *He had to be in the Territories again*, he suddenly understood; in the welter of his emotions and longings, that thread brightly shone. He wanted to breathe that air; he hungered for it. The Territories, the long plains and ranges of low mountains, called him, the fields of tall grass and the streams that flashed through them. Jack's entire body yearned for that landscape. And he might have taken the bottle out of his pocket and forced a mouthful of the awful juice down his throat on the spot if he had not just then seen the bottle's former owner tucked up against a tree, butt on heels and hands laced across his knees. A brown grocery bag lay beside him, and atop the bag was an enormous sandwich of what looked like liver sausage and onion.

'You're movin now,' Speedy said, smiling up at him. 'You're on your way, I see. Say your goodbyes? Your momma know you won't be home for a while?'

Jack nodded, and Speedy held up the sandwich. 'You hungry? This one, it's too much for me.'

'I had something to eat,' the boy said. 'I'm glad I can say goodbye to you.'

'Ole Jack on fire, he rarin to go,' Speedy said, cocking his long head sideways. 'Boy gonna move.'

'Speedy?'

'But don't take off without a few little things I brought for you. I got em here in this bag, you wanna see?'

'Speedy?'

The man squinted up at Jack from the base of the tree.

'Did you know that my father used to call me Travelling Jack?'

'Oh, I probably heard that somewhere,' Speedy said, grinning at him. 'Come over here and see what I brought you. Plus, I have to tell you where to go first, don't I?'

Relieved, Jack walked across the sidewalk to Speedy's tree. The old man set his sandwich in his lap and fished the bag closer to him. 'Merry Christmas,' Speedy said, and brought forth a tall, battered old paperback book. It was, Jack saw, an old Rand McNally road atlas.

'Thanks,' Jack said, taking the book from Speedy's outstretched hand.

'Ain't no maps over there, so you stick as much as you can to the roads in ole Rand McNally. That way you'll get where you're goin.'

'Okay,' Jack said, and slipped out of the knapsack so that he could slide the big book down inside it.

'The next thing don't have to go in that fancy rig you carryin on your back,' Speedy said. He put the sandwich on the flat paper bag and stood up all in one long smooth motion. 'No, you can carry this right in your pocket.' He dipped his fingers into the left pocket of his workshirt. What emerged, clamped between his second and third fingers like one of Lily's Tarrytoons, was a white triangular object it took the boy a moment to recognize as a guitar-pick. 'You take this and keep it. You'll want to show it to a man. He'll help you.'

Jack turned the pick over in his fingers. He had never seen one like it – of ivory, with scrimshaw filigrees and patterns winding around it in slanted lines like some kind of unearthly writing. Beautiful in the abstract, it was almost too heavy to be a useful fingerpick.

'Who's the man?' Jack asked. He slipped the pick into one of his pants pockets.

'Big scar on his face – you'll see him pretty soon after you land in the Territories. He's a guard. Fact is, he's a Captain of the Outer Guards, and he'll take you to a place where you can see a lady you has to see. Well, a lady you ought to see. So you know the other reason you're puttin your neck on the line. My friend over there, he'll understand what you're doin and he'll figure out a way to get you to the lady.'

'This lady . . .' Jack began.

'Yep,' Speedy said. 'You got it.'

'She's the Queen.'

'You take a good look at her, Jack. You see what you see when you sees her. You see what she *is*, understand? Then you hit out for the west.' Speedy stood examining him gravely, almost as if he were just now doubting that he'd ever see Jack Sawyer again, and then the lines in his face twitched and he said, 'Steer clear of ole Bloat. Watch for his trail – his own and his Twinner's. Old Bloat can find out where you went if you're not careful, and if he finds out he's gonna be after you like a fox after a goose.' Speedy shoved his hands in his pockets and regarded Jack again, looking very much as though he wished he could think of more to say. 'Get the Talisman, son,' he concluded. 'Get it and bring it back safe. It gonna be your burden but you got to be bigger than your burden.'

Jack was concentrating so hard on what Speedy was telling him that he squinted into the man's seamed face. Scarred man, Captain of the Outer Guards. The Queen. Morgan Sloat, after him like a predator. In an evil place over on the other side of the country. A burden. 'Okay,' he said, wishing suddenly that he were back in the Tea and Jam Shoppe with his mother.

Speedy smiled jaggedly, warmly. 'Yeah-bob. Ole Travellin Jack is okey-doke.' The smile deepened. 'Bout time for you to sip at that special juice, wouldn't you say?'

'I guess it is,' Jack said. He tugged the dark bottle out of his hip pocket and unscrewed the cap. He looked back up at Speedy, whose pale eyes stabbed into his own.

'Speedy'll help you when he can.'

Jack nodded, blinked, and raised the neck of the bottle to his mouth. The sweetly rotten odor which leaped out of the bottle nearly made his throat close itself in an involuntary spasm. He tipped the bottle up and the taste of the odor invaded his mouth. His stomach clenched. He swallowed, and rough, burning liquid spilled down his throat.

Long seconds before Jack opened his eyes, he knew from the richness and clarity of the smells about him that he had flipped into the Territories. Horses, grass, a dizzying scent of raw meat; dust; the clear air itself.

INTERLUDE
SLOAT IN THIS WORLD (I)

'I know I work too hard,' Morgan Sloat told his son Richard that evening. They were speaking on the telephone, Richard standing at the communal telephone in the downstairs corridor of his dormitory, his father sitting at his desk on the top floor of one of Sawyer & Sloat's first and sweetest real-estate deals in Beverly Hills. 'But I tell you kid, there are a lot of times when you have to do something yourself to get it done right. Especially when my late partner's family is involved. It's just a short trip, I hope. Probably I'll get everything nailed down out there in goddam New Hampshire in less than a week. I'll give you another call when it's all over. Maybe we'll go railroading in California, just like the old days. There'll be justice yet. Trust your old man.'

The deal for the building had been particularly sweet because of Sloat's willingness to do things himself. After he and Sawyer had negotiated the purchase of a short-term lease, then (after a gunfire of lawsuits) a long-term lease, they had fixed their rental rates at so much per square foot, done the necessary alterations, and advertised for new tenants. The only holdover tenant was the Chinese restaurant on the ground floor, dribbling in rent at about a third of what the space was worth. Sloat had tried reasonable discussions with the Chinese, but when they saw that he was trying to talk them into paying more rent, they suddenly lost the ability to speak or understand English. Sloat's attempts at negotiation limped along for a few days, and then he happened to see one of the kitchen help carrying a bucket of grease out through the back door of the kitchen. Feeling better already, Sloat followed the man into a dark, narrow cul-de-sac and watched him tip the grease into a garbage can. He needed no more than that. A day later, a chain-link fence separated the cul-de-sac from the restaurant; yet another day later, a Health Department inspector served the Chinese with a complaint and a summons. Now the kitchen help had to take all their refuse, grease included, out through the dining area and down a chain-link dog run Sloat had constructed alongside the restaurant. Business fell off: the customers caught odd, unpleasant odors from the nearby garbage. The owners rediscovered the English language, and volunteered to double their monthly payment. Sloat responded with a grateful-sounding speech that said nothing. And that night, having primed himself with three large martinis, Sloat drove from his house to the restaurant and took a baseball bat from the trunk of his car and smashed in the long window which had once given a pleasant view of the street but now looked out at a corridor of fencing which ended in a huddle of metal bins.

He had done those things . . . but he hadn't exactly been Sloat when he did them.

The next morning the Chinese requested another meeting and this time offered to quadruple their payment. 'Now you're talking like men,' Sloat told the stony-faced

Chinese. 'And I'll tell you what! Just to prove we're all on the same team, we'll pay half the cost of replacing your window.'

Within nine months of Sawyer & Sloat's taking possession of the building, all the rents had increased significantly and the initial cost and profit projections had begun to look wildly pessimistic. By now this building was one of Sawyer & Sloat's more modest ventures, but Morgan Sloat was as proud of it as of the massive new structures they had put up downtown. Just walking past the place where he'd put up the fence as he came in to work in the morning reminded him – daily – of how much he had contributed to Sawyer & Sloat, how reasonable were his claims!

This sense of the justice of his ultimate desires kindled within him as he spoke to Richard – after all, it was for Richard that he wanted to take over Phil Sawyer's share of the company. Richard was, in a sense, his immortality. His son would be able to go to the best business schools and then pick up a law degree before he came into the company; and thus fully armed, Richard Sloat would carry all the complex and delicate machinery of Sawyer & Sloat into the next century. The boy's ridiculous ambition to become a chemist could not long survive his father's determination to murder it – Richard was smart enough to see that what his father did was a hell of a lot more interesting, not to mention vastly more remunerative, than working with a test tube over a Bunsen burner. That 'research chemist' stuff would fade away pretty quickly, once the boy had a glimpse of the real world. And if Richard was concerned about being fair to Jack Sawyer, he could be made to understand that fifty thousand a year and a guaranteed college education was not only fair but magnanimous. Princely. Who could say that Jack wanted any part of the business, anyhow, or that he would possess any talent for it?

Besides, accidents happened. Who could even say that Jack Sawyer would live to see twenty?

'Well, it's really a matter of getting all the papers, all the ownership stuff, finally straight,' Sloat told his son. 'Lily's been hiding out from me for too long. Her brain is strictly cottage cheese by now, take my word for it. She probably has less than a year to live. So if I don't hump myself off to see her now that I have her pinned down, she could stall long enough to put everything into probate – or into a trust fund, and I don't think your friend's momma would let me administer it. Hey, I don't want to bore you with my troubles. I just wanted to tell you that I won't be home for a few days, in case you call. Send me a letter or something. And remember about the train, okay? We gotta do that again.'

The boy promised to write, to work hard, to not worry about his father or Lily Cavanaugh or Jack.

And sometime when this obedient son was, say, in his senior year at Stanford or Yale, Sloat would introduce him to the Territories. Richard would be six or seven years younger than he had been himself when Phil Sawyer, cheerfully crack-brained on grass in their first little North Hollywood office, had first puzzled, then infuriated (because Sloat had been certain Phil was laughing at him), then intrigued his partner (for surely Phil was too stoned to have invented all this science-fiction crapola about another world). And when Richard saw the Territories, that would be it – if he had not already done it by himself, they'd change his mind for him. Even a small peek into the Territories shook your confidence in the omniscience of scientists.

Sloat ran the palm of his hand over the shiny top of

his head, then luxuriantly fingered his moustache. The sound of his son's voice had obscurely, irrelevantly comforted him: as long as there was Richard politely coming along behind him, all was well and all was well and all manner of things was well. It was night already in Springfield, Illinois, and in Nelson House, Thayer School, Richard Sloat was padding down a green corridor back to his desk, perhaps thinking of the good times they'd had, and would have again, aboard Morgan's toy train line in coastal California. He'd be asleep by the time his father's jet punished the resistant air far above and some hundred miles farther north; but Morgan Sloat would push aside the panel over his first-class window and peer down, hoping for moonlight and a parting of the clouds.

He wanted to go home immediately – home was only thirty minutes away from the office – so that he could change clothes and get something to eat, maybe snort a little coke, before he had to get to the airport. But instead he had to pound along the freeway to the Marina: an appointment with a client who had freaked out and was on the verge of being dumped from a picture, then a meeting with a crowd of spoilers who claimed that a Sawyer & Sloat project just up from Marina del Rey was polluting the beach – things that could not be postponed. Though Sloat promised himself that as soon as he had taken care of Lily Cavanaugh and her boy he was going to begin dropping clients from his list – he had much bigger fish to fry now. Now there were whole worlds to broker, and his piece of the action would be no mere ten per cent. Looking back on it, Sloat wasn't sure how he had tolerated Phil Sawyer for as long as he had. His partner had never played to win, not seriously; he had been encumbered by sentimental notions of loyalty and honor, corrupted by the stuff you told kids to get them halfway civilized before you finally tore the blindfold off their eyes. Mundane as it might be in light of the stakes he now played for, he could not forget that the Sawyers owed him, all right – indigestion flowered in his chest like a heart attack at the thought of how much, and before he reached his car in the still-sunny lot beside the building, he shoved his hand into his jacket pocket and fished out a crumpled package of Di-Gel.

Phil Sawyer had underestimated him, and that still rankled. Because Phil had thought of him as a sort of trained rattlesnake to be let out of his cage only under controlled circumstances, so had others. The lot attendant, a hillbilly in a broken cowboy hat, eyed him as he marched around his little car, looking for dents and dings. The Di-Gel melted most of the fiery ball in his chest. Sloat felt his collar growing clammy with sweat. The attendant knew better than to try to buddy up: Sloat had verbally peeled the man's hide weeks ago, after discovering a tiny wrinkle in the BMW's door. In the midst of his rant, he had seen violence begin to darken in the hillbilly's green eyes, and a sudden upsurge of joy had made him waddle in toward the man, still cutting off skin, almost hoping that the attendant would take a poke at him. Abruptly, the hillbilly had lost his momentum; feebly, indeed apologetically suggested that maybe that-there l'il *nuthin* of a ding came from somewhere else? Parking service at a restaurant, maybe? The way those bozos treat cars, y'know, and the light ain't so good that time of night, why . . .

'Shut your stinking mouth,' Sloat had said. 'That little nothing, as you call it, is going to cost me about twice what you make in a week. I should fire you right now, cowpoke, and the only reason I'm not going to is that there's about a two per cent chance you might be right; when I came out of Chasen's last night maybe I didn't look under the door handle, maybe I DID and maybe I DIDN'T, but if you ever talk to me again, if you ever say any more than "Hello, Mr Sloat" or "Goodbye, Mr Sloat", I'll get you fired so fast you'll think you were beheaded.' So the hillbilly watched him inspect his car, knowing that if Sloat found any imperfections in the car's finish he would bring down the axe, afraid even to come close enough to utter the ritual goodbye. Sometimes from the window that overlooked the parking lot Sloat had seen the attendant furiously wiping some flaw, bird dropping or splash of mud, off the BMW's hood. And that's management, buddy.

When he pulled out of the lot he checked the rear-view mirror and saw on the hillbilly's face an expression very like the last one Phil Sawyer had worn in the final seconds of his life, out in the middle of nowhere in Utah. He smiled all the way to the freeway on-ramp.

Philip Sawyer had underestimated Morgan Sloat from the time of their first meeting, when they were freshmen at Yale. It could have been, Sloat reflected, that he had been easy to underestimate – a pudgy eighteen-year-old from Akron, graceless, overweighted with anxieties and ambitions, out of Ohio for the first time in his life. Listening to his classmates talk easily about New York, about '21' and the Stork Club, about seeing Brubeck at Basin Street and Erroll Garner at the Vanguard, he'd sweated to hide his ignorance. 'I really like the downtown part,' he'd thrown in, as casually as he could. Palms wet, cramped by curled-in fingers. (Mornings, Sloat often found his palms tattooed with dented bruises left by his fingernails.) 'What downtown part, Morgan?' Tom

Woodbine had asked him. The others cackled. 'You know, Broadway and the Village. Around there.' More cackles, harsher. He had been unattractive and badly dressed; his wardrobe consisted of two suits, both charcoal-gray and both apparently made for a man with a scarecrow's shoulders. He had begun losing his hair in high school, and pink scalp showed through his short, flattened-down haircuts.

No, no beauty had Sloat been, and that had been part of it. The others made him feel like a clenched fist: those morning bruises were shadowy little photographs of his soul. The others, all interested in the theater like himself and Sawyer, possessed good profiles, flat stomachs, easy careless manners. Sprawled across the lounge chairs of their suite in Davenport while Sloat, in a haze of perspiration, stood that he might not wrinkle his suit pants and thereby get a few more days' wear out of them, they sometimes resembled a gathering of young gods – cashmere sweaters draped over their shoulders like the golden fleece. They were on their way to becoming actors, playwrights, songwriters. Sloat had seen himself as a director: entangling them all in a net of complications and designs which only he could unwind.

Sawyer and Tom Woodbine, both of whom seemed unimaginably rich to Sloat, were roommates. Woodbine had only a lukewarm interest in theater and hung around their undergraduate drama workshop because Phil did. Another gilded private-school boy, Thomas Woodbine differed from the others because of his absolute seriousness and straightforwardness. He intended to become a lawyer, and already seemed to have the probity and impartiality of a judge. (In fact, most of Woodbine's acquaintances imagined that he would wind up on the Supreme Court, much to the embarrassment of the boy himself.) Woodbine was without ambition in Sloat's terms, being interested far more in living rightly than in living well. Of course he had everything, and what he by some accident lacked other people were quick to give him: how could he, so spoiled by nature and friendships, be ambitious? Sloat almost unconsciously detested Woodbine, and could not bring himself to call him 'Tommy'.

Sloat directed two plays during his four years at Yale: *No Exit*, which the student paper called 'a furious confusion', and *Volpone*. This was described as 'churning, cynical, sinister, and almost unbelievably messy'. Sloat was held responsible for most of these qualities. Perhaps he was not a director after all – his vision too intense and crowded. His ambitions did not lessen, they merely shifted. If he was not eventually to be behind the camera, he could be behind the people in front of it. Phil Sawyer had also begun to think this way – Phil had never been certain where his love of theater might take him, and thought he might have a talent for representing actors and writers. 'Let's go to Los Angeles and start an agency,' Phil said to him in their senior year. 'It's nutty as hell and our parents will hate it, but maybe we'll make it work. So we starve for a couple of years.'

Phil Sawyer, Sloat had learned since their freshman year, was not rich after all. He just *looked* rich.

'And when we can afford him, we'll get Tommy to be our lawyer. He'll be out of law school by then.'

'Sure, okay,' Sloat had said, thinking that he could stop that one when the time came. 'What should we call ourselves?'

'Anything you like. Sloat and Sawyer? Or should we stick to the alphabet?'

'Sawyer and Sloat, sure, that's great, alphabetical order,' Sloat said, seething because he imagined that his partner had euchred him into forever suggesting that he was somehow secondary to Sawyer.

Both sets of parents did hate the idea, as Phil had predicted, but the partners in the infant talent agency drove to Los Angeles in the old DeSoto (Morgan's, another demonstration of how much Sawyer owed him), set up an office in a North Hollywood building with a happy population of rats and fleas, and started hanging around the clubs, passing out their spandy-new business cards. Nothing – nearly four months of total failure. They had a comic who got too drunk to be funny, a writer who couldn't write, a stripper who insisted on being paid in cash so that she could stiff her agents. And then late one afternoon, high on marijuana and whiskey, Phil Sawyer had gigglingly told Sloat about the Territories.

'You know what I can do, you ambitious so-and-so? Oh, can I travel, partner. All the way.'

Shortly after that, both of them travelling now, Phil Sawyer met a rising young actress at a studio party and within an hour had their first important client. And she had three friends similarly unhappy with their agents. And one of the friends had a boyfriend who had actually written a decent filmscript and needed an agent, and the boyfriend had a boyfriend . . . Before their third year was over, they had a new office, new apartments, a slice of the Hollywood pie. The Territories, in a fashion that Sloat accepted but never understood, had blessed them.

Sawyer dealt with the clients; Sloat with the money, the investments, the business side of the agency. Sawyer spent money – lunches, airplane tickets – Sloat saved it, which was all the justification he needed to skim a little of the cream off the top. And it was Sloat who kept pushing them into new areas, land development, real estate, production deals. By the time Tommy Woodbine arrived in Los Angeles, Sawyer & Sloat was a five-million-dollar business.

Sloat discovered that he still detested his old classmate; Tommy Woodbine had put on thirty pounds, and looked and acted, in his blue three-piece suits, more than ever like a judge. His cheeks were always slightly flushed (alcoholic? Sloat wondered), his manner still kindly and ponderous. The world had left its marks on him – clever little wrinkles at the corners of his eyes, the eyes themselves infinitely more guarded than those of the gilded boy at Yale. Sloat understood almost at once, and knew that Phil Sawyer would never see it unless he were told, that Tommy Woodbine lived with an enormous secret: whatever the gilded boy might have been, Tommy was now a homosexual. Probably he'd call himself gay. And that made everything easier – in the end, it even made it easier to get rid of Tommy.

Because queers are always getting killed, aren't they? And did anybody really want a two-hundred-and-ten-pound pansy responsible for bringing up a teenage boy? You could say that Sloat was just saving Phil Sawyer from the posthumous consequences of a serious lapse of judgment. If Sawyer had made Sloat the executor of his estate and the guardian of his son, there would have been no problems. As it was, the murderers from the Territories – the same two who had bungled the abduction of the boy – had blasted through a stoplight and nearly been arrested before they could return home.

Things all would have been so much simpler, Sloat reflected for perhaps the thousandth time, if Phil Sawyer had never married. If no Lily, no Jack; if no Jack, no problems. Phil may never even have looked at the reports about Lily

Cavanaugh's early life Sloat had compiled: they listed where and how often and with whom, and should have killed that romance as readily as the black van turned Tommy Woodbine into a lump on the road. If Sawyer read those meticulous reports, they left him amazingly unaffected. He wanted to marry Lily Cavanaugh, and he did. As his damned Twinner had married Queen Laura. More underestimation. And repaid in the same fashion, which seemed fitting.

Which meant, Sloat thought with some satisfaction, that after a few details were taken care of, everything would finally be settled. After so many years – when he came back from Arcadia Beach, he should have all of Sawyer & Sloat in his pocket. And in the Territories, all was placed just *so*: poised on the brink, ready to fall into Morgan's hands. As soon as the Queen died, her consort's former deputy would rule the country, introducing all the interesting little changes both he and Sloat desired. And then watch the money roll in, Sloat thought, turning off the freeway into Marina del Rey. Then watch *everything* roll in!

His client, Asher Dondorf, lived in the bottom half of a new condo in one of the Marina's narrow, alleylike streets just off the beach. Dondorf was an old character actor who had achieved a surprising level of prominence and visibility in the late seventies through a role on a television series; he'd played the landlord of the young couple – private detectives, and both cute as baby pandas – who were the series' stars. Dondorf got so much mail from his few appearances in the early episodes that the writers increased his part, making him an unofficial father to the young detectives, letting him solve a murder or two, putting him in danger, etc., etc. His salary doubled, tripled, quadrupled, and when the series was cancelled after six years, he went back into film work. Which was the problem. Dondorf thought he was a star, but the studios and producers still considered him a character actor – popular, but not a serious asset to any project. Dondorf wanted flowers in his dressing room, he wanted his own hairdresser and dialogue coach, he wanted more money, more respect, more love, more everything. Dondorf, in fact, was a putz.

When he pulled his car tight into the parking bay and eased himself out, being careful not to scratch the edge of his door on the brick, Sloat came to a realization: if he learned, or even suspected, sometime in the next few days, that Jack Sawyer had discovered the existence of the Territories, he would kill him. There was such a thing as an unacceptable risk.

Sloat smiled to himself, popping another Di-Gel into his mouth, and rapped on the condo's door. He knew it already: Asher Dondorf was going to kill himself. He'd do it in the living room in order to create as much mess as possible. A temperamental jerk like his soon-to-be-ex-client would think a really sloppy suicide was revenge on the bank that held his mortgage. When a pale, trembling Dondorf opened the door, the warmth of Sloat's greeting was quite genuine.

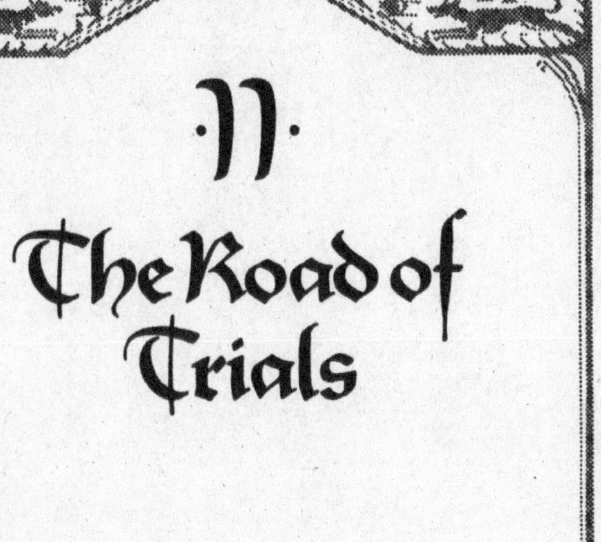

II
The Road of Trials

CHAPTER SIX
THE QUEEN'S PAVILION

1

The saw-toothed blades of grass directly before Jack's eyes seemed as tall and stiff as sabres. They would cut the wind, not bend to it. Jack groaned as he lifted his head. He did not possess such dignity. His stomach still felt threateningly liquid, his forehead and eyes burned. Jack pushed himself up on his knees and then forced himself to stand. A long horse-drawn cart rumbled toward him down the dusty track, and its driver, a bearded red-faced man roughly the same shape and size as the wooden barrels rattling behind him, was staring at him. Jack nodded and tried to take in as much as he could about the man while giving the appearance of a loafing boy who had perhaps run off for an illicit snooze. Upright, he no longer felt ill; he felt, in fact, better than at any time since leaving Los Angeles, not merely healthy but somehow harmonious, mysteriously in tune with his body. The warm, drifting air of the Territories patted his face with the gentlest, most fragrant of touches – its own delicate and flowery scent quite distinct beneath the stronger odor of raw meat it carried. Jack ran his hands over his face and peeked at the driver of the cart, his first sample of Territories Man.

If the driver addressed him, how should he answer? Did they even speak English here? His kind of English? For a moment Jack imagined himself trying to pass unnoticed in a world where people said 'Prithee' and 'Dost thou go cross-gartered, yonder varlet?' and decided that if that was how things went, he'd pretend to be a mute.

The driver finally took his eyes off Jack and clucked something decidedly not 1980s American English to his horses. But perhaps that was just the way you spoke to horses. *Slusha, slusha!* Jack edged backward into the sea-grass, wishing that he had managed to get on his feet a couple of seconds earlier. The man glanced at him again, and surprised Jack by nodding – a gesture neither friendly nor unfriendly, merely a communication between equals. *I'll be glad when this day's work is done, brother.* Jack returned the nod, tried to put his hands in his pockets, and for a moment must have looked half-witted with astonishment. The driver laughed, not unpleasantly.

Jack's clothes had changed – he wore coarse, voluminous woolen trousers instead of the corduroy jeans. Above the waist a close-fitting jacket of soft blue fabric covered him. Instead of buttons, the jacket – a jerkin? he speculated – had a row of cloth hooks and eyes. Like the trousers, it was clearly handmade. The Nikes, too, were gone, replaced by flat leather sandals. The knapsack had been transmogrified into a leather sack held by a thin strap over his shoulder. The cart-driver wore clothing almost exactly similar – his jerkin was of leather stained so deeply and continuously that it showed rings within rings, like an old tree's heart.

All rattle and dust, the cart pulled past Jack. The barrels radiated a yeasty musk of beer. Behind the barrels stood a triple pile of what Jack unthinkingly took to be truck tires.

He smelled the 'tires' and noticed that they were perfectly, flawlessly bald in the same moment – it was a creamy odor, full of secret depths and subtle pleasures, that instantly made him hungry. Cheese, but no cheese that he had ever tasted. Behind the wheels of cheese, near the back of the cart, an irregular mound of raw meat – long, peeled-looking sides of beef, big slablike steaks, a heap of ropy internal organs he could not identify – slithered beneath a glistening mat of flies. The powerful smell of the raw meat assailed Jack, killing the hunger evoked by the cheese. He moved into the middle of the track after the cart had passed him and watched it jounce toward the crest of a little rise. A second later he began to follow after, walking north.

He had gone only halfway up the rise when he once again saw the peak of the great tent, rigid in the midst of a rank of narrow fluttering flags. That, he assumed, was his destination. Another few steps past the blackberry bushes where he'd paused the last time (remembering how good they'd been, Jack popped two of the enormous berries in his mouth) and he could see the whole of the tent. It was actually a big rambling pavillion, long wings on each side, with gates and a courtyard. Like the Alhambra, this eccentric structure – a summer palace, Jack's instincts told him – stood just above the ocean. Little bands of people moved through and around the great pavillion, driven by forces as powerful and invisible as the effect on iron filings of a magnet. The little groups met, divided, poured on again.

Some of the men wore bright, rich-looking clothes, though many seemed to be dressed much as Jack was. A few women in long shining white gowns or robes marched through the courtyard, as purposeful as generals. Outside the gates stood a collection of smaller tents and impromptu-looking wooden huts; here too people moved, eating or buying or talking, though more easily and randomly. Somewhere down in that busy crowd he would have to find the man with a scar.

But first he looked behind him, down the length of the rutted track, to see what had happened to Funworld.

When he saw two small dark horses pulling plows, perhaps fifty yards off, he thought that the amusement park had become a farm, but then he noticed the crowd watching the plowing from the top of the field and understood that this was a contest. Next his eye was taken by the spectacle of a huge red-haired man, stripped to the waist, whirling about like a top. His outstretched hands held some long heavy object. The man abuptly stopped whirling and released the object, which flew a long way before it thudded and bounced on the grass and revealed itself to be a hammer. Funworld was a fair, not a farm – Jack now saw tables heaped with food, children on their fathers' shoulders.

In the midst of the fair, making sure that every strap and harness was sound, every oven stoked with wood, was there a Speedy Parker? Jack hoped so.

And was his mother still sitting by herself in the Tea and Jam Shoppe, wondering why she had let him go?

Jack turned back and watched the long cart rattle through the gates of the summer palace and swing off to the left, separating the people who moved there as a car making a turn off Fifth Avenue separates pedestrians on a cross-town street. A moment later he set off after it.

2

He had feared that all the people on the pavillion grounds would turn toward him staring, instantly sensing his difference from them. Jack carefully kept his eyes lowered whenever he could and imitated a boy on a complicated errand – he had been sent out to assemble a list of things; his face showed how he was concentrating to remember them. *A shovel, two picks, a ball of twine, a bottle of goose grease* . . . But gradually he became aware that none of the adults before the summer palace paid him any attention at all. They rushed or dawdled, inspected the merchandise – rugs, iron pots, bracelets – displayed in the little tents, drank from wooden mugs, plucked at another's sleeve to make a comment or start a conversation, argued with the guards at the gate, each wholly taken up by his own business. Jack's impersonation was so unnecessary as to be ridiculous. He straightened up and began to work his way, moving generally in an irregular half-circle, toward the gate.

He had seen almost immediately that he would not be able just to stroll through it – the two guards on either side stopped and questioned nearly everyone who tried to reach the interior of the summer palace. Men had to show their papers, or display badges or seals which gave them access. Jack had only Speedy Parker's fingerpick, and he didn't think that would get him past the guards' inspection. One man just now stepping up to the gate flashed a round silver badge and was waved through; the man following him was stopped. He argued; then the tone of his manner changed, and Jack saw that he was pleading. The guard shook his head and ordered the man off.

'*His* men don't have any trouble getting in,' someone to Jack's right said, instantly solving the problem of Territories language, and Jack turned his head to see if the man had spoken to him.

But the middle-aged man walking beside him was speaking to another man, also dressed in the plain, simple clothes of most of the men and women outside the palace grounds. 'They'd better not,' the second man answered. 'He's on his way – supposed to be here today sometime, I guess.'

Jack fell in behind these two and followed them toward the gate.

The guards stepped forward as the men neared, and as they both approached the same guard, the other gestured to the man nearest him. Jack hung back. He still had not seen anyone with a scar, nor had he seen any officers. The only soldiers in sight were the guards, both young and countrified – with their broad red faces above the elaborately pleated and ruffled uniforms, they looked like farmers in fancy dress. The two men Jack had been following must have passed the guards' tests, for after a few moments' conversation the uniformed men stepped back and admitted them. One of the guards looked sharply at Jack, and Jack turned his head and stepped back.

Unless he found the Captain with the scar, he would never get inside the palace grounds.

A group of men approached the guard who had stared at Jack, and immediately began to wrangle. They had an appointment, it was crucial they be let in, much money depended on it, regrettably they had no papers. The guard shook his head, scraping his chin across his uniform's white ruff. As Jack watched, still wondering how he could find the Captain, the leader of the little group waved his hands in the air, pounded his fist into a palm. He had become as red-faced as the guard. At length he began jabbing the guard with his forefinger. The guard's companion joined him – both guards looked bored and hostile.

A tall straight man in a uniform subtly different from the guards' – it might have been the way the uniform was worn, but it looked as though it might serve in battle as well as in an operetta – noiselessly materialized beside them. He did not wear a ruff, Jack noticed a second later, and his hat was peaked instead of three-cornered. He spoke to the guards, and then turned to the leader of the little group. There was no more shouting, no more finger-jabbing. The man spoke quietly. Jack saw the danger ebb out of the group. They shifted on their feet, their shoulders sank. They began to drift away. The officer watched them go, then turned back to the guards for a final word.

For a moment while the officer faced in Jack's direction, in effect shooing the group of men away with his presence, Jack saw a long pale lightning-bolt of a scar zigzagging from beneath his right eye to just above his jawline.

The officer nodded to the guards and stepped briskly away. Looking neither to the left nor to the right, he wove through the crowd, apparently headed for whatever lay to the side of the summer palace. Jack took off after him.

'Sir!' he yelled, but the officer marched on through the slow-moving crowd.

Jack ran around a group of men and women hauling a pig toward one of the little tents, shot through a gap between two other bands of people approaching the gate, and finally was close enough to the officer to reach out and touch his elbow. 'Captain?'

The officer wheeled around, freezing Jack where he stood. Up close, the scar seemed thick and separate, a living creature riding on the man's face. Even unscarred, Jack thought, this man's face would express a forceful impatience. 'What is it, boy?' the man asked.

'Captain, I'm supposed to talk to you – I have to see the Lady, but I don't think I can get into the palace. Oh, you're supposed to see this.' He dug into the roomy pocket of the unfamiliar pants and closed his fingers around a triangular object.

When he displayed it on his palm, he felt shock boom through him – what he held in his hand was not a finger-pick but a long tooth, a shark's tooth perhaps, inlaid with a winding, intricate pattern of gold.

When Jack looked up at the Captain's face, half-expecting a blow, he saw his shock echoed there. The impatience which had seemed so characteristic had utterly vanished. Uncertainty and even fear momentarily distorted the man's strong features. The Captain lifted his hand to Jack's, and the boy thought he meant to take the ornate tooth: he would have given it to him, but the man simply folded the boy's fingers over the object on his palm. 'Follow me,' he said.

They went around to the side of the great pavillion, and the Captain led Jack behind the shelter of a great sail-shaped flap of stiff pale canvas. In the glowing darkness behind the flap, the soldier's face looked as though someone had drawn on it with thick pink crayon. 'That sign,' he said calmly enough. 'Where did you get it?'

'From Speedy Parker. He said that I should find you and show it to you.'

The man shook his head. 'I don't know the name. I want you to give me the sign now. Now.' He firmly grasped Jack's wrist. 'Give it to me, and then tell me where you stole it.'

'I'm telling the truth,' Jack said. 'I got it from Lester Speedy Parker. He works at Funworld. But it wasn't a tooth when he gave it to me. It was a guitar-pick.'

'I don't think you understand what's going to happen to you, boy.'

'You *know* him,' Jack pleaded. 'He described you – he

told me you were a Captain of the Outer Guards. Speedy *told* me to find you.'

The Captain shook his head and gripped Jack's wrist more firmly. 'Describe this man. I'm going to find out if you're lying right now, boy, so I'd make this good if I were you.'

'Speedy's old,' Jack said. 'He used to be a musician.' He thought he saw recognition of some kind flash in the man's eyes. 'He's black – a black man. With white hair. Deep lines in his face. And he's pretty thin, but he's a lot stronger than he looks.'

'A black man. You mean, a *brown* man?'

'Well, black people aren't really black. Like white people aren't really white.'

'A brown man named Parker.' The Captain gently released Jack's wrist. 'He is called Parkus here. So you are from . . .' He nodded toward some distant invisible point on the horizon.

'That's right,' Jack said.

'And Parkus . . . Parker . . . sent you to see our Queen.'

'He said he wanted me to see the Lady. And that you could take me to her.'

'This will have to be fast,' the Captain said. 'I think I know how to do it, but we don't have any time to waste.' He had shifted his mental direction with a military smoothness. 'Now listen to me. We have a lot of bastards around here, so we're going to pretend that you are my son on t'other side of the sheets. You have disobeyed me in connection with some little job, and I am angry with you. I *think* no one will stop us if we make this performance convincing. At least I can get you inside – but it might be a little trickier once we are in. You think you can do it? Convince people that you're my son?'

'My mother's an actress,' Jack said, and felt that old pride in her.

'Well then, let's see what you've learned,' the Captain said, and surprised Jack by winking at him. 'I'll try not to cause you any pain.' Then he startled Jack again, and clamped a very strong hand over the boy's upper arm. 'Let's go,' he said, and marched out of the shelter of the flap, half-dragging Jack behind him.

'When I tell you to wash the flagstones behind the kitchen, wash flagstones is what you'll do,' the Captain said loudly, not looking at him. 'Understand that? You will *do your job*. And if you do not do your job, you must be punished.'

'But I washed some of the flagstones . . .' Jack wailed.

'I didn't tell you to wash *some* of the flagstones!' the Captain yelled, hauling Jack along behind him. The people around them parted to let the Captain through. Some of them grinned sympathetically at Jack.

'I was going to do it all, honest, I was going to go back in a minute . . .'

The soldier pulled him toward the gate without even glancing at the guards, and yanked him through. 'No, Dad!' Jack squalled. 'You're hurting me!'

'Not as much as I'm *going* to hurt you,' the Captain said, and pulled him across the wide courtyard Jack had seen from the cart-track.

At the other end of the court the soldier pulled him up wooden steps and into the great palace itself. 'Now your acting had better be good,' the man whispered, and immediately set off down a long corridor, squeezing Jack's arm hard enough to leave bruises.

'I promise I'll be good!' Jack shouted.

The man hauled him into another, narrower corridor.

The interior of the palace did not at all resemble the inside of a tent, Jack saw. It was a mazelike warren of passages and little rooms, and it smelled of smoke and grease.

'Promise!' the Captain bawled out.

'I promise! I do!'

Ahead of them as they emerged from yet another corridor, a group of elaborately clothed men either leaning against a wall or draped over couches turned their heads to look at this noisy duo. One of them, who had been amusing himself by giving orders to a pair of women carrying stacks of sheets folded flat across their arms, glanced suspiciously at Jack and the Captain.

'And I promise to beat the sin out of you,' the Captain said loudly.

A couple of the men laughed. They wore soft wide-brimmed hats trimmed with fur and their boots were of velvet. They had greedy, thoughtless faces. The man talking to the maids, the one who seemed to be in charge, was skeletally tall and thin. His tense, ambitious face tracked the boy and the soldier as they hurried by.

'Please don't!' Jack wailed. 'Please!'

'Each *please* is another strapping,' the soldier growled, and the men laughed again. The thin one permitted himself to display a smile as cold as a knife-blade before he turned back to the maids.

The Captain yanked the boy into an empty room filled with dusty wooden furniture. Then at last he released Jack's aching arm. 'Those were *his* men,' he whispered. 'What life will be like when—' He shook his head, and for a moment seemed to forget his haste. 'It says in *The Book of Good Farming* that the meek shall inherit the earth, but those fellows don't have a teaspoonful of meekness among them.

Taking's all they're good for. They want wealth, they want—' He glanced upward, unwilling or unable to say what else the men outside wanted. Then he looked back at the boy. 'We'll have to be quick about this, but there are still a few secrets his men haven't learned about the place.' He nodded sideways, indicating a faded wooden wall.

Jack followed him, and understood when the Captain pushed two of the flat brown nailheads left exposed at the end of a dusty board. A panel in the faded wall swung inward, exposing a narrow black passageway no taller than an upended coffin. 'You'll only get a glimpse of her, but I suppose that's all you need. It's all you can have, anyhow.'

The boy followed the silent instruction to slip into the passageway. 'Just go straight ahead until I tell you,' the Captain whispered. When he closed the panel behind them, Jack began to move slowly forward through perfect blackness.

The passage wound this way and that, occasionally illuminated by faint light spilling in through a crack in a concealed door or through a window set above the boy's head. Jack soon lost all sense of direction, and blindly followed the whispered directions of his companion. At one point he caught the delicious odor of roasting meat, at another the unmistakable stink of sewage.

'Stop,' the Captain finally said. 'Now I'll have to lift you up. Raise your arms.'

'Will I be able to see?'

'You'll know in a second,' the Captain said, and put a hand just beneath each of Jack's armpits and lifted him cleanly off the floor. 'There is a panel in front of you now,' he whispered. 'Slide it to the left.'

Jack blindly reached out before him and touched smooth wood. It slid easily aside, and enough light fell into the passage for him to see a kitten-sized spider scrambling toward the ceiling. He was looking down into a room the size of a hotel lobby, filled with women in white and furniture so ornate that it brought back to the boy all the museums he and his parents had visited. In the center of the room a woman lay sleeping or unconscious on an immense bed, only her head and shoulders visible above the sheets.

And then Jack nearly shouted with shock and terror, because the woman on the bed was his mother. That was his mother, and she was dying.

'You saw her,' the Captain whispered, and braced his arms more firmly.

Open-mouthed, Jack stared in at his mother. She was dying, he could not doubt that any longer: even her skin seemed bleached and unhealthy, and her hair too had lost several shades of color. The nurses around her bustled about, straightening the sheets or rearranging books on a table, but they assumed this busy and purposeful manner because they had no real idea of how to help their patient. The nurses knew that for such a patient there was no real help. If they could stave off death for another month, or even a week, they were at the fullest extent of their powers.

He looked back at the face turned upward like a waxen mask and finally saw that the woman on the bed was not his mother. Her chin was rounder, the shape of her nose slightly more classical. The dying woman was his mother's Twinner; she was Laura DeLoessian. If Speedy had wanted him to see more, he was not capable of it: that white moveless face told him nothing of the woman behind it.

'Okay,' he whispered, pushing the panel back into place, and the Captain lowered him to the floor.

In the darkness he asked, 'What's wrong with her?'

'Nobody can find that out,' came from above him. 'The Queen cannot see, she cannot speak, she cannot move . . .' There was silence for a moment, and then the Captain touched his hand and said, 'We must return.'

They quietly emerged from blackness into the dusty empty room. The Captain brushed ropy cobwebs from the front of his uniform. His head cocked to one side, he considered Jack for a long moment, worry very plain upon his face. 'Now you must answer a question of mine,' he said.

'Yes.'

'Were you sent here to save her? To save the Queen?'

Jack nodded. 'I think so – I think that's part of it. Tell me just one thing.' He hesitated. 'Why don't those creeps out there just take over? She sure couldn't stop them.'

The Captain smiled. There was no humor in that smile. 'Me,' he said. 'My men. *We'd* stop them. I know not what they may have gotten up to in the Outposts, where order is thin – but here we hold to the Queen.'

A muscle just below the eye on the unscarred cheekbone jumped like a fish. He was pressing his hands together, palm to palm. 'And your directions, your orders, whatever, are to . . . ah, to *go* west, is that correct?'

Jack could practically feel the man vibrating, controlling his growing agitation only from a lifetime's habit of self-discipline. 'That's right,' he said. 'I'm supposed to go west. Isn't that right? Shouldn't I go west? To the other Alhambra?'

'I can't say, I can't say,' the Captain blurted, taking a step backward. 'We have to get you out of here right now. I can't tell you what to do.' He could not even look at Jack now, the boy saw. 'But you can't stay here a minute longer

– let's, ah, let's see if we can get you out and away before Morgan gets here.'

'Morgan?' Jack said, almost thinking that he had not heard the name correctly. 'Morgan Sloat? Is he coming here?'

CHAPTER SEVEN
FARREN

1

The Captain appeared not to have heard Jack's question. He was looking away into the corner of this empty unused room as if there were something there to see. He was thinking long and hard and fast; Jack recognized that. And Uncle Tommy had taught him that interrupting an adult who was thinking hard was just as impolite as interrupting an adult who was speaking. But –

Steer clear of ole Bloat. Watch for his trail – his own and his Twinner's . . . he's gonna be after you like a fox after a goose.

Speedy had said that, and Jack had been concentrating so hard on the Talisman that he had almost missed it. Now the words came back and came home with a nasty double-thud that was like being hit in the back of the neck.

'What does he look like?' he asked the Captain urgently.

'Morgan?' the Captain asked, as if startled out of some interior dream.

'Is he fat? Is he fat and sorta going bald? Does he go like this when he's mad?' And employing the innate gift for mimicry he'd always had – a gift which had made his father roar with laughter even when he was tired and feeling down – Jack 'did' Morgan Sloat. Age fell into his face as he laddered his brow the way Uncle Morgan's brow laddered into lines when he was pissed off about something. At the same time, Jack sucked his cheeks in and pulled his head down to create a double chin. His lips flared out in a fishy pout and he began to waggle his eyebrows rapidly up and down. 'Does he go like that?'

'No,' the Captain said, but something flickered in his eyes, the way something had flickered there when Jack told him that Speedy Parker was old. 'Morgan's tall. He wears his hair long' – the Captain held a hand by his right shoulder to show Jack how long – 'and he has a limp. One foot's deformed. He wears a built-up boot, but—' He shrugged.

'You looked like you knew him when I did him! You—'

'Shhh! Not so God-pounding loud, boy!'

Jack lowered his voice. 'I think I know the guy,' he said – and for the first time he felt fear as an informed emotion . . . something he could grasp in a way he could not as yet grasp this world. *Uncle Morgan here? Jesus!*

'Morgan is just Morgan. No one to fool around with, boy. Come on, let's get out of here.'

His hand closed around Jack's upper arm again. Jack winced but resisted.

Parker becomes Parkus. And Morgan . . . it's just too big a coincidence.

'Not yet,' he said. Another question had occurred to him. 'Did she have a son?'

'The Queen?'

'Yes.'

'She had a son,' the Captain replied reluctantly. 'Yes. Boy, we can't stay here. We—'

'Tell me about him!'

'There is nothing to tell,' the Captain answered. 'The babe died an infant, not six weeks out of her womb. There was talk that one of Morgan's men – Osmond, perhaps – smothered the lad. But talk of that sort is always cheap. I have no love for Morgan of Orris but everyone knows that one child in every dozen dies a-crib. No one knows why; they die mysteriously, of no cause. There's a saying – *God pounds His nails*. Not even a royal child is excepted in the eyes of the Carpenter. He . . . Boy? are you all right?'

Jack felt the world go gray around him. He reeled, and when the Captain caught him, his hard hands felt as soft as feather pillows.

He had almost died as an infant.

His mother had told him the story – how she had found him still and apparently lifeless in his crib, his lips blue, his cheeks the color of funeral candles after they have been capped and thus put out. She had told him how she had run screaming into the living room with him in her arms. His father and Sloat were sitting on the floor, stoned on wine and grass, watching a wrestling match on TV. His father had snatched him from his mother's arms, pinching his nostrils savagely shut with his left hand (*You had bruises there for almost a month, Jacky*, his mother had told him with a jittery laugh) and then plunging his mouth over Jack's tiny mouth, while Morgan cried: *I don't think that's going to help him, Phil, I don't think that's going to help him!*

(*Uncle Morgan was funny, wasn't he, Mom?* Jack had said. *Yes, very funny, Jack-O*, his mother had replied, and she had smiled an oddly humorless smile, and lit another Herbert Tarrytoon from the butt of the one smouldering in the ashtray.)

'Boy!' the Captain whispered, and shook him so hard

that Jack's lolling head snapped on his neck. 'Boy! Dammit! If you faint on me . . .'

'I'm okay,' Jack said – his voice seemed to come from far away; it sounded like the voice of the Dodgers announcer when you were cruising by Chavez Ravine at night with the top down, echoing and distant, the play-by-play of baseball in a sweet dream. 'Okay, lay off me, what do you say? Give me a break.'

The Captain stopped shaking him but looked at him warily.

'Okay,' Jack said again, and abruptly he slapped his own cheek as hard as he could – *Ow!* But the world came swimming back into focus.

He had almost died in his crib. In that apartment they'd had back then, the one he barely remembered, the one his mother always called the Technicolor Dream Palace because of the spectacular view of the Hollywood Hills from the living room. He had almost died in his crib, and his father and Morgan Sloat had been drinking wine, and when you drank a lot of wine you had to pee a lot, and he remembered the Technicolor Dream Palace well enough to know that you got from the living room to the nearest bathroom by going through the room that had been his when he was a baby.

He saw it: Morgan Sloat getting up, grinning easily, saying something like *Just a sec while I make some room, Phil*; his father hardly looking around because Haystack Calhoun was getting ready to put the Spinner or the Sleeper on some hapless opponent; Morgan passing from the TV-brightness of the living room into the ashy dimness of the nursery, where little Jacky Sawyer lay sleeping in his Pooh pajamas with the feet, little Jacky Sawyer warm and secure in a dry diaper. He saw Uncle Morgan glancing furtively back at the bright square of the door to the living room, his balding brow turning to ladder-rungs, his lips pursing like the chilly mouth of a lake bass; he saw Uncle Morgan take a throw-pillow from a nearby chair, saw him put it gently and yet firmly over the sleeping baby's entire head, holding it there with one hand while he held the other hand flat on the baby's back. And when all movement had stopped, he saw Uncle Morgan put the pillow back on the chair where Lily sat to nurse, and go into the bathroom to urinate.

If his mother hadn't come in to check on him almost immediately . . .

Chilly sweat broke out all over his body.

Had it been that way? It could have been. His heart told him it *had* been. The coincidence was too utterly perfect, too seamlessly complete.

At the age of six weeks, the son of Laura DeLoessian, Queen of the Territories, had died in his crib.

At the age of six weeks, the son of Phil and Lily Sawyer had *almost* died in his crib . . . *and Morgan Sloat had been there.*

His mother always finished the story with a joke: how Phil Sawyer had almost racked up their Chrysler, roaring to the hospital after Jacky had already started breathing again.

Pretty funny, all right. Yeah.

2

'Now come *on*,' the Captain said.

'All right,' Jack said. He still felt weak, dazed. 'All right, let's g—'

'*Shhhh!*' The Captain looked around sharply at the sound of approaching voices. The wall to their right was not wood but heavy canvas. It stopped four inches short of the floor, and Jack saw booted feet passing by in the gap. Five pairs. Soldiers' boots.

One voice cut through the babble: '. . . didn't know he *had* a son.'

'Well,' a second answered, 'bastards sire bastards – a fact you should well know, Simon.'

There was a roar of brutal, empty laughter at this – the sort of laughter Jack heard from some of the bigger boys at school, the ones who busted joints behind the woodshop and called the younger boys mysterious but somehow terrifying names: *queerboy* and *humpa-jumpa* and *morphadite*. Each of these somehow slimy terms was followed by a coarse ribband of laughter exactly like this.

'Cork it! Cork it up!' – a third voice. 'If *he* hears you, you'll be walking Outpost Line before thirty suns have set!'

Mutters.

A muffled burst of laughter.

Another jibe, this one unintelligible. More laughter as they passed on.

Jack looked at the Captain, who was staring at the short canvas wall with his lips drawn back from his teeth all the way to the gumlines. No question who they were talking about. And if they were talking, there might be someone listening . . . the wrong somebody. Somebody who might be wondering just who this suddenly revealed bastard might really be. Even a kid like him knew that.

'You heard enough?' the Captain said. 'We've got to *move*.' He looked as if he would like to shake Jack . . . but did not quite dare.

Your directions, your orders, whatever, are to . . . ah, go *west, is that correct?*

He changed, Jack thought. *He changed twice.*

Once when Jack showed him the shark's tooth that had been a filigreed guitar-pick in the world where delivery trucks instead of horse-drawn carts ran the roads. And he had changed again when Jack confirmed that he was going west. He had gone from threat to a willingness to help to . . . what?

I can't say . . . I can't tell you what to do.

To something like religious awe . . . or religious terror.

He wants to get out of here because he's afraid we'll be caught, Jack thought. *But there's more, isn't there? He's afraid of me. Afraid of –*

'Come on,' the Captain said. 'Come *on*, for Jason's sake.'

'*Whose* sake?' Jack asked stupidly, but the Captain was already propelling him out. He pulled Jack hard left and half-led, half-dragged him down a corridor that was wood on one side and stiff, mouldy-smelling canvas on the other.

'This isn't the way we came,' Jack whispered.

'Don't want to go past those fellows we saw coming in,' the Captain whispered back. 'Morgan's men. Did you see the tall one? Almost skinny enough to look through?'

'Yes.' Jack remembered the thin smile, and the eyes which did not smile. The others had looked soft. The thin man had looked hard. He had looked crazy. And one thing more: he had looked dimly familiar.

'Osmond,' the Captain said, now pulling Jack to the right.

The smell of roasting meat had been growing gradually stronger, and now the air was redolent of it. Jack had never smelled meat he wanted so badly to taste in his whole life. He was scared, he was mentally and emotionally on the ropes, perhaps rocking on the edge of madness . . . but his mouth was watering crazily.

'Osmond is Morgan's right-hand man,' the Captain grunted. 'He sees too much, and I'd just as soon he didn't see *you* twice, boy.'

'What do you mean?'

'*Hssst!*' He clamped Jack's aching arm even tighter. They were approaching a wide cloth drape that hung in a doorway. To Jack it looked like a shower-curtain – except the cloth was burlap of a weave so coarse and wide that it was almost netlike, and the rings it hung from were bone rather than chrome. 'Now *cry*,' the Captain breathed warmly in Jack's ear.

He swept the curtain back and pulled Jack into a huge kitchen which fumed with rich aromas (the meat still predominating) and billows of steamy heat. Jack caught a confused glimpse of braziers, of a great stonework chimney, of women's faces under billowy white kerchiefs that reminded him of nuns' wimples. Some of them were lined up at a long iron trough which stood on trestles, their faces red and beaded with sweat as they washed pots and cooking utensils. Others stood at a counter which ran the width of the room, slicing and dicing and coring and paring. Another was carrying a wire rack filled with uncooked pies. They all stared at Jack and the Captain as they pushed through into the kitchen.

'Never again!' the Captain bellowed at Jack, shaking him as a terrier shakes a rat . . . and all the while he continued to move them both swiftly across the room, toward the double-hung doors at the far side. 'Never again, do you hear me? The next time you shirk your duty, I'll split your skin down the back and peel you like a baked potato!'

And under his breath, the Captain hissed, 'They'll all remember and they'll all talk, so *cry*, dammit!'

And now, as the Captain with the scarred face dragged him across the steaming kitchen by the scruff of his neck and one throbbing arm, Jack deliberately called up the dreadful image of his mother lying in a funeral parlor. He saw her in billowing folds of white organdy – she was lying in her coffin and wearing the wedding dress she had worn in *Drag Strip Rumble* (RKO, 1953). Her face came clearer and clearer in Jack's mind, a perfect wax effigy, and he saw she was wearing her tiny gold-cross earrings, the ones Jack had given her for Christmas two years ago. Then the face changed. The chin became rounder, the nose straighter and more patrician. The hair went a shade lighter and became somehow coarser. Now it was Laura DeLoessian he saw in that coffin – and the coffin itself was no longer a smoothly anonymous funeral parlor special, but something that looked as if it had been hacked with rude fury from an old log – a Viking's coffin, if there had ever been such a thing; it was easier to imagine this coffin being torched alight on a bier of oiled logs than it was to imagine it being lowered into the unprotesting earth. It was Laura DeLoessian, Queen of the Territories, but in this imagining which had become as clear as a vision, the Queen was wearing his mother's wedding dress from *Drag Strip Rumble* and the gold-cross earrings Uncle Tommy had helped him pick out in Sharp's of Beverly Hills. Suddenly his tears came in a hot and burning flood – not sham tears but real ones, not just for his mother but for both of these lost women, dying universes apart, bound by some unseen cord which might rot but would never break – at least, not until they were both dead.

Through the tears he saw a giant of a man in billowing whites rush across the room toward them. He wore a red bandanna instead of a puffy chef's hat on his head, but Jack thought its purpose was the same – to identify the wearer as the boss of the kitchen. He was also brandishing a wicked-looking three-tined wooden fork.

'*Ged-OUT!*' the chef screeched at them, and the voice emerging from that huge barrel chest was absurdly flutelike – it was the voice of a willowy gay giving a shoe-clerk a piece of his mind. But there was nothing absurd about the fork; it looked deadly.

The women scattered before his charge like birds. The bottom-most pie dropped out of the pie-woman's rack and she uttered a high, despairing cry as it broke apart on the boards. Strawberry juice splattered and ran, the red as fresh and bright as arterial blood.

'GED-DOUT MY KIDCHEN, YOU SLUGS! DIS IS NO SHORD-CUD! DIS IS NO RAZE-TRAG! DIS IS MY KIDCHEN AND IF YOU CAD'T REMEMBER DAT, I'LL BY GOD THE CARBENDER CARVE YOUR AZZES FOR YOU!'

He jabbed the fork at them, simultaneously half-turning his head and squinching his eyes mostly shut, as if in spite of his tough talk the thought of hot flowing blood was just too *gauche* to be borne. The Captain removed the hand that had been on the scruff of Jack's neck and reached out – almost casually, it seemed to Jack. A moment later the chef was on the floor, all six and a half feet of him. The meat-fork was lying in a puddle of strawberry sauce and chunks of white unbaked pastry. The chef rolled back and forth, clutching his broken right wrist and screaming in that high, flutelike voice. The news he screamed out to the room in general was certainly woeful enough: he was dead, the Captain had surely murdered him (pronounced mur-dirt in the chef's odd, almost Teutonic accent); he was at the very least crippled, the cruel and heartless Captain of the Outer Guards having destroyed his good right hand and thus his livelihood, and so ensuring a miserable beggar's life for him in the years to come; the Captain had inflicted terrible pain on him, a pain beyond belief, such as was not to be borne –

'*Shut up!*' the Captain roared, and the chef did. Immediately. He lay on the floor like a great baby, his right hand curled on his chest, his red bandanna drunkenly askew so that one ear (a small black pearl was set in the center of the lobe) showed, his fat cheeks quivering. The kitchen women gasped and twittered as the Captain bent over the dreaded chief ogre of the steaming cave where they spent their days and nights. Jack, still weeping, caught a glimpse of a black boy (*brown* boy, his mind amended) standing at one end of the largest brazier. The boy's mouth was open, his face as comically surprised as a face in a minstrel show, but he kept turning the crank in his hands, and the haunch suspended over the glowing coals kept revolving.

'Now listen and I'll give you some advice you won't find in *The Book of Good Farming*,' the Captain said. He bent over the chef until their noses almost touched (his paralyzing grip on Jack's arm – which was now going mercifully numb – never loosened the smallest bit). 'Don't you ever . . . don't you *ever* . . . come at a man with a knife . . . or a fork . . . or a spear . . . or with so much as a God-pounding *splinter* in your hand unless you intend to kill him with it. One expects temperament from chefs, but temperament does not extend to assaults upon the person of the Captain of the Outer Guards. Do you understand me?'

The chef moaned out a teary, defiant something-or-other. Jack couldn't make it all out – the man's accent seemed to be growing steadily thicker – but it had something to do with the Captain's mother and the dump-dogs beyond the pavillion.

'That may well be,' the Captain said. 'I never knew the lady. But it certainly doesn't answer my question.' He prodded the chef with one dusty, scuffed boot. It was a gentle enough prod, but the chef screeched as if the Captain had drawn his foot back and kicked him as hard as he could. The women twittered again.

'Do we or do we not have an understanding on the subject of chefs and weapons and Captains? Because if we don't, a little more instruction might be in order.'

'We do!' the chef gasped. 'We do! We do! We—'

'Good. Because I've had to give far too much instruction already today.' He shook Jack by the scruff of the neck. 'Haven't I, boy?' He shook him again, and Jack uttered a wail that was completely unfeigned. 'Well . . . I suppose that's all he can say. The boy's a simpleton. Like his mother.'

The Captain threw his dark, gleaming glance around the kitchen.

'Good day, ladies. Queen's blessings upon you.'

'And you, good sir,' the eldest among them managed, and dropped an awkward, ungraceful curtsey. The others followed suit.

The Captain dragged Jack across the kitchen. Jack's hip bumped the edge of the washing trough with excruciating force and he cried out again. Hot water flew. Smoking droplets hit the boards and ran, hissing between them. *Those women had their hands in that,* Jack thought. *How do they stand it?* Then the Captain, who was almost carrying him by now, shoved Jack through another burlap curtain and into the hallway beyond.

'Phew!' the Captain said in a low voice. 'I don't like this, not any of it, it all smells bad.'

Left, right, then right again. Jack began to sense that they were approaching the outer walls of the pavillion, and he had time to wonder how the place could seem so much bigger on the inside than it looked from the outside. Then the Captain was pushing him through a flap and they were in daylight again – mid-afternoon daylight so bright after the shifting dimness of the pavillion that Jack had to wince his eyes shut against a burst of pain.

The Captain never hesitated. Mud squelched and smooched underfoot. There was the smell of hay and horses and shit. Jack opened his eyes again and saw they were crossing what might have been a paddock or a corral or maybe just a barnyard. He saw an open canvas-sided hallway and heard chickens clucking somewhere beyond it. A scrawny man, naked except for a dirty kilt and thong sandals, was tossing hay into an open stall, using a pitchfork with wooden tines to do the job. Inside the stall, a horse not much bigger than a Shetland pony looked moodily out at them. They had already passed the stall when Jack's mind was finally able to accept what his eyes had seen: the horse had two heads.

'Hey!' he said. 'Can I look back in that stall? That—'

'No time.'

'But that horse had—'

'No time, I said.' He raised his voice and shouted: 'And if I ever catch you laying about again when there's work to be done, you'll get *twice* this!'

'You won't!' Jack screamed (in truth he felt as if this scene were getting a bit old). 'I swear you won't! I told you I'd be good!'

Just ahead of them, tall wooden gates loomed in a wall

made of wooden posts with the bark still on them – it was like a stockade wall in an old Western (his mother had made a few of those, too). Heavy brackets were screwed into the gates, but the bar the brackets were meant to hold was not in place. It leaned against the woodpile to the left, thick as a railroad crosstie. The gates stood open almost six inches. Some muddled sense of direction in Jack's head suggested that they had worked their way completely around the pavilion to its far side.

'Thank God,' the Captain said in a more normal voice. 'Now—'

'Captain,' a voice called from behind them. The voice was low but carrying, deceptively casual. The Captain stopped in his tracks. It had called just as Jack's scarred companion had been in the act of reaching for the left gate to push it open; it was as if the voice's owner had watched and waited for just that second.

'Perhaps you would be good enough to introduce me to your . . . ah . . . son.'

The Captain turned, turning Jack with him. Standing halfway across the paddock area, looking unsettlingly out of place there, was the skeletal courtier the Captain had been afraid of – Osmond. He looked at them from dark gray melancholy eyes. Jack saw something stirring in those eyes, something deep down. His fear was suddenly sharper, something with a point, jabbing into him. *He's crazy* – this was the intuition which leaped spontaneously into his mind. *Nuttier than a damned fruitcake.*

Osmond took two steps toward them. In his left hand he held the rawhide-wrapped half of a bullwhip. The handle narrowed only slightly into a dark, limber tendon coiled thrice around his shoulder – the whip's central stalk was as thick as a timber rattlesnake. Near its tip, this central stalk gave birth to perhaps a dozen smaller offshoots, each of woven rawhide, each tipped with a crudely made but bright metal spur.

Osmond tugged the whip's handle and the coils slithered from his shoulder with a dry hiss. He wiggled the handle, and the metal-tipped strands of rawhide writhed slowly in the straw-littered mud.

'Your son?' Osmond repeated, and took another step toward them. And Jack suddenly understood why this man had looked familiar before. The day he had almost been kidnapped – hadn't this man been White Suit?

Jack thought that perhaps he had been.

3

The Captain made a fist, brought it to his forehead, and bent forward. After only a moment's hesitation, Jack did the same.

'My son, Lewis,' the Captain said stiffly. He was still bent over, Jack saw, cutting his eyes to the left. So he remained bent over himself, his heart racing.

'Thank you, Captain. Thank you, Lewis. Queen's blessings upon you.' When he touched him with the haft of the bullwhip, Jack almost cried out. He stood straight again, biting the cry in.

Osmond was only two paces away now, regarding Jack with that mad, melancholy gaze. He wore a leather jacket and what might have been diamond studs. His shirt was extravagantly ruffled. A bracelet of links clanked ostentatiously upon his right wrist (from the way he handled the bullwhip, Jack guessed that his left was his working hand).

His hair was drawn back and tied with a wide ribbon that might have been white satin. There were two odors about him. The top was what his mother called 'all those men's perfumes', meaning after-shave, cologne, whatever. The smell about Osmond was thick and powdery. It made Jack think of those old black-and-white British films where some poor guy was on trial in the Old Bailey. The judges and lawyers in those films always wore wigs, and Jack thought the boxes those wigs came out of would smell like Osmond – dry and crumbly-sweet, like the world's oldest powdered doughnut. Beneath it, however, was a more vital, even less pleasant smell: it seemed to pulse out at him. It was the smell of sweat in layers and dirt in layers, the smell of a man who bathed seldom, if ever.

Yes. This was one of the creatures that had tried to steal him that day.

His stomach knotted and roiled.

'I did not know you had a son, Captain Farren,' Osmond said. Although he spoke to the Captain, his eyes remained on Jack. *Lewis*, he thought, *I'm Lewis, don't forget* –

'Would that I did not,' the Captain replied, looking at Jack with anger and contempt. 'I honor him by bringing him to the great pavillion and then he slinks away like a dog. I caught him playing at d—'

'Yes, yes,' Osmond said, smiling remotely. *He doesn't believe a word*, Jack thought wildly, and felt his mind take another clumsy step toward panic. *Not one single word!* 'Boys are bad. All boys are bad. It's axiomatic.'

He tapped Jack lightly on the wrist with the haft of the bullwhip. Jack, his nerves screwed up to an unbearable pitch, screamed . . . and immediately flushed with hot shame.

Osmond giggled. 'Bad, oh yes, it's axiomatic, all boys

are bad. *I* was bad; and I'll wager *you* were bad, Captain Farren. Eh? Eh? Were you bad?'

'Yes, Osmond,' the Captain said.

'Very bad?' Osmond asked. Incredibly, he had begun to prance in the mud. Yet there was nothing swishy about this: Osmond was willowy and almost delicate, but Jack got no feeling of true homosexuality from the man; if there was that innuendo in his words, then Jack sensed intuitively that it was hollow. No, what came through most clearly here was a sense of malignity . . . and madness. '*Very* bad? Most *awfully* bad?'

'Yes, Osmond,' Captain Farren said woodenly. His scar glowed in the afternoon light, more red than pink now.

Osmond ceased his impromptu little dance as abruptly as he had begun it. He looked coldly at the Captain.

'*No one* knew you had a son, Captain.'

'He's a bastard,' the Captain said. 'And simple. Lazy as well, it now turns out.' He pivoted suddenly and struck Jack on the side of the face. There was not much force behind the blow, but Captain Farren's hand was as hard as a brick. Jack howled and fell into the mud, clutching his ear.

'*Very* bad, most *awfully* bad,' Osmond said, but now his face was a dreadful blank, thin and secretive. 'Get up, you bad boy. Bad boys who disobey their fathers must be punished. And bad boys must be questioned.' He flicked the whip to one side. It made a dry pop. Jack's tottery mind made another strange connection – reaching, he supposed later, for home in every way it knew how. The sound of Osmond's whip was like the pop of the Daisy air rifle he'd had when he was eight. He and Richard Sloat had both had rifles like that.

Osmond reached out and grasped Jack's muddy arm

with one white, spiderlike hand. He drew Jack toward him, into those smells – old sweet powder and old rancid filth. His weird gray eyes peered solemnly into Jack's blue ones. Jack felt his bladder grow heavy, and he struggled to keep from wetting his pants.

'Who are you?' Osmond asked.

4

The words hung in the air over the three of them.

Jack was aware of the Captain looking at him with a stern expression that could not quite hide his despair. He could hear hens clucking; a dog barking; somewhere the rumble of a large approaching cart.

Tell me the truth; I will know a lie, those eyes said. *You look like a certain bad boy I first met in California – are you that boy?*

And for a moment, everything trembled on his lips:

Jack, I'm Jack Sawyer, yeah, I'm the kid from California, the Queen of this world was my mother, only I died, and I know your boss, I know Morgan – Uncle Morgan – and I'll tell you anything you want to know if only you'll stop looking at me with those freaked-out eyes of yours, sure, because I'm only a kid, and that's what kids do, they tell, they tell everything –

Then he heard his mother's voice, tough, on the edge of a jeer:

You gonna spill your guts to this guy, Jack-O? THIS guy? He smells like a distress sale at the men's cologne counter and he looks like a medieval version of Charles Manson . . . but you suit yourself. You can fool him if you want – no sweat – but you suit yourself.

'Who are you?' Osmond asked again, drawing even closer, and on his face Jack now saw total confidence – he was used to getting the answers he wanted from people . . . and not just from twelve-year-old kids, either.

Jack took a deep, trembling breath (*When you want max volume – when you want to get it all the way up to the back row of the balcony – you gotta bring it from your diaphragm, Jacky. It just kind of gets passed through the old vox-box on the way up*) and screamed:

'*I WAS GOING TO GO RIGHT BACK! HONEST TO GOD!*'

Osmond, who had been leaning even farther forward in anticipation of a broken and strengthless whisper, recoiled as if Jack had suddenly reached out and slapped him. He stepped on the trailing rawhide tails of his whip with one booted foot and came close to tripping over them.

'You damned God-pounding little—'

'*I WAS GOING TO! PLEASE DON'T WHIP ME OSMOND I WAS GOING TO GO BACK! I NEVER WANTED TO COME HERE I NEVER I NEVER I NEVER—*'

Captain Farren lunged forward and struck him in the back. Jack sprawled full-length in the mud, still screaming.

'He's simple-minded, as I told you,' he heard the Captain saying. 'I apologize, Osmond. You can be sure he'll be beaten within an inch of his life. He—'

'*What's he doing here in the first place?*' Osmond shrieked. His voice was now as high and shrewish as any fishwife's. 'What's your snot-nosed puling brat-bastard doing here at all? Don't offer to show me his pass! I know he has no pass! You sneaked him in to feed at the Queen's table . . . to steal the Queen's silver, for all I know . . . he's *bad* . . . one look's enough to tell anyone that he's very, intolerably, most indubitably *bad*!'

The whip came down again, not the mild cough of a Daisy air rifle this time but the loud clean report of a .22, and Jack had time to think *I know where that's going*, and then a large fiery hand clawed into his back. The pain seemed to sink into his flesh, not diminishing but actually intensifying. It was hot and maddening. He screamed and writhed in the mud.

'*Bad!* Most awfully *bad*! Indubitably *bad*!'

Each 'bad' was punctuated by another crack of Osmond's whip, another fiery handprint, another scream from Jack. His back was burning. He had no idea how long it might have gone on – Osmond seemed to be working himself into a hotter frenzy with each blow – but then a new voice shouted: 'Osmond! Osmond! There you are! Thank God!'

A commotion of running footsteps.

Osmond's voice, furious and slightly out of breath: 'Well? Well? What is it?'

A hand grasped Jack's elbow and helped him to his feet. When he staggered, the arm attached to the hand slipped around his waist and supported him. It was difficult to believe that the Captain who had been so hard and sure during their bewildering tour of the pavillion could now be so gentle.

Jack staggered again. The world kept wanting to swim out of focus. Trickles of warm blood ran down his back. He looked at Osmond with swift-awakening hatred, and it was good to feel that hatred. It was a welcome antidote to the fear and the confusion.

You did that – you hurt me, you cut me. And listen to me, Jiggs, if I get a chance to pay you back –

'Are you all right?' the Captain whispered.

'Yes.'

'*What?*' Osmond screamed at the two men who had interrupted Jack's whipping.

The first was one of the dandies Jack and the Captain had passed going to the secret room. The other looked a bit like the carter Jack had seen almost immediately upon his return to the Territories. This fellow looked badly frightened, and hurt as well – blood was welling from a gash on the left side of his head and had covered most of the left side of his face. His left arm was scraped and his jerkin was torn. '*What are you saying, you jackass?*'

'My wagon overturned coming around the bend on the far side of All-Hands' Village,' the carter said. He spoke with the slow, dazed patience of one in deep shock. 'My son's kilt, my Lord. Crushed to death under the barrels. He was just sixteen last May-Farm Day. His mother—'

'*What?*' Osmond screamed again. 'Barrels? *Ale?* Not the Kingsland? *You don't mean to tell me you've overturned a full wagonload of Kingsland Ale, you stupid goat's penis? You don't mean to tell me that, do yoooooouuuuuuu?*'

Osmond's voice rose on the last word like the voice of a man making savage mockery of an operatic diva. It wavered and warbled. At the same time he began to dance again . . . but in rage this time. The combination was so weird that Jack had to raise both hands to stifle an involuntary giggle. The movement caused his shirt to scrape across his welted back, and that sobered him even before the Captain muttered a warning word.

Patiently, as if Osmond had missed the only important fact (and so it must have seemed to him), the carter began again: 'He was just sixteen last May-Farm Day. His mother didn't want him to come with me. I can't think what—'

Osmond raised his whip and brought it whickering

down with blinding and unexpected speed. At one moment the handle was grasped loosely in his left hand, the whip with its rawhide tails trailing in the mud; at the next there was a whipcrack not like the sound of a .22 but more like that of a toy rifle. The carter staggered back, shrieking, his hands clapped to his face. Fresh blood ran loosely through his dirty fingers. He fell over, screaming, '*My Lord! My Lord! My Lord!*' in a muffled, gargling voice.

Jack moaned: 'Let's get out of here. Quick!'

'Wait,' the Captain said. The grim set of his face seemed to have loosened the smallest bit. There might have been hope in his eyes.

Osmond whirled to the dandy, who took a step back, his thick red mouth working.

'Was it the Kingsland?' Osmond panted.

'Osmond, you shouldn't tax yourself so—'

Osmond flicked his left wrist upward; the whip's steel-tipped rawhide tails clattered against the dandy's boots. The dandy took another step backward.

'Don't tell me what I should or shouldn't do,' he said. 'Only answer my questions. I'm vexed, Stephen, I'm most intolerably, indubitably vexed. Was it the Kingsland?'

'Yes,' Stephen said. 'I regret to say it, but—'

'On the Outpost Road?'

'Osmond—'

'On the Outpost Road, you dripping penis?'

'Yes,' Stephen gulped.

'Of course,' Osmond said, and his thin face was split by a hideous white grin. 'Where is All-Hands' Village, if not on the Outpost Road? Can a village fly? Huh? Can a village somehow fly from one road to another, Stephen? Can it? Can it?'

'No, Osmond, of course not.'

'No. And so there are barrels all over the Outpost Road, is that correct? Is it correct for me to assume that there are barrels and an overturned ale-wagon blocking the Outpost Road while the best ale in the Territories soaks into the ground for the earthworms to carouse on? Is that correct?'

'Yes . . . yes. But—'

'*Morgan is coming by the Outpost Road!*' Osmond screamed. '*Morgan is coming and you know how he drives his horses!* If his diligence comes around a bend and upon that mess, his driver may not have time to stop! *He could be overturned! He could be killed!*'

'Dear-God,' Stephen said, all as one word. His pallid face went two shades whiter.

Osmond nodded slowly. 'I think, if Morgan's diligence were to overturn, we would all do better to pray for his death than for his recovery.'

'But – but—'

Osmond turned from him and almost ran back to where the Captain of the Outer Guards stood with his 'son'. Behind Osmond, the hapless carter still writhed in the mud, bubbling *My Lords*.

Osmond's eyes touched Jack and then swept over him as if he weren't there. 'Captain Farren,' he said. 'Have you followed the events of the last five minutes?'

'Yes, Osmond.'

'Have you followed them closely? Have you *gleaned* them? Have you gleaned them most closely?'

'Yes. I think so.'

'Do you think so? What an excellent Captain you are, Captain! We will talk more, I think, about how such an excellent Captain could produce such a frog's testicle of a son.'

His eyes touched Jack's face briefly, coldly.

'But there's no time for that now, is there? No. I suggest that you summon a dozen of your brawniest men and that you double-time them – no, *triple*-time them – out to the Outpost Road. You'll be able to follow your nose, to the site of the accident, won't you?'

'Yes, Osmond.'

Osmond glanced quickly at the sky. 'Morgan is expected at six of the clock – perhaps a little sooner. It is now – two. I would say two. Would you say two, Captain?'

'Yes, Osmond.'

'And what would you say, you little turd? Thirteen? Twenty-three? Eighty-one of the clock?'

Jack gaped. Osmond grimaced contemptuously, and Jack felt the clear tide of his hate rise again.

You hurt me, and if I get the chance—!

Osmond looked back at the Captain. 'Until five of the clock, I suggest that you be at pains to save whatever barrels may still be whole. After five, I suggest you simply clear the road as rapidly as you can. Do you understand?'

'Yes, Osmond.'

'Then get out there.'

Captain Farren brought a fist to his forehead and bowed. Gaping stupidly, still hating Osmond so fiercely that his brains seemed to pulse, Jack did the same. Osmond had whirled away from them before the salute was even fairly begun. He was striding back toward the carter, popping his whip, making it cough out those Daisy air rifle sounds.

The carter heard Osmond's approach and began to scream.

'Come on,' the Captain said, pulling Jack's arm for the last time. 'You don't want to see this.'

'No,' Jack managed. 'God, no.'

But as Captain Farren pushed the right-hand gate open and they finally left the pavillion, Jack heard it – and he heard it in his dreams that night: one whistling carbine-crack after another, each followed by a scream from the doomed carter. And Osmond was making a sound. The man was panting, out of breath, and so it was hard to tell exactly what that sound was, without turning around to look at his face – something Jack did not want to do.

He was pretty sure he knew, though.

He thought Osmond was laughing.

5

They were in the public area of the pavillion grounds now. The strollers glanced at Captain Farren from the corners of their eyes . . . and gave him a wide berth. The Captain strode swiftly, his face tight and dark with thought. Jack had to trot in order to catch up.

'We were lucky,' the Captain said suddenly. 'Damned lucky. I think he meant to kill you.'

Jack gaped at him, his mouth dry and hot.

'He's mad, you know. Mad as the man who chased the cake.'

Jack had no idea what that might mean, but he agreed that Osmond was mad.

'What—'

'Wait,' the Captain said. They had come back around to the small tent where the Captain had taken Jack after seeing the shark's tooth. 'Stand right here and wait for me. Speak to no one.'

The Captain entered the tent. Jack stood watching and waiting. A juggler passed him, glancing at Jack but never losing his rhythm as he tossed half a dozen balls in a complex and airy pattern. A straggle of dirty children followed him as the children followed the Piper out of Hamelin. A young woman with a dirty baby at one huge breast told him she could teach him something to do with his little man besides let piss out of it, if he had a coin or two. Jack looked uncomfortably away, his face hot.

The girl cawed laughter. '*Oooooo, this pretty young man's SHY! Come over here, pretty! Come—*'

'Get out, slut, or you'll finish the day in the under-kitchens.'

It was the Captain. He had come out of the tent with another man. This second fellow was old and fat, but he shared one characteristic with Farren – he looked like a real soldier rather than one from Gilbert and Sullivan. He was trying to fasten the front of his uniform over his bulging gut while holding a curly, French horn-like instrument at the same time.

The girl with the dirty baby scurried away with never another look at Jack. The Captain took the fat man's horn so he could finish buttoning and passed another word with him. The fat man nodded, finished with his shirt, took his horn back, and then strode off, blowing it. It was not like the sound Jack had heard on his first flip into the Territories; that had been many horns, and their sound had been somehow showy: the sound of heralds. This was like a factory whistle, announcing work to be done.

The Captain returned to Jack.

'Come with me,' he said.

'Where?'

'Outpost Road,' Captain Farren said, and then he cast a wondering half-fearful eye down on Jack Sawyer. 'What my father's father called Western Road. It goes west through smaller and smaller villages until it reaches the Outposts. Beyond the Outposts it goes into nowhere . . . or hell. If you're going west, you'll need God with you, boy. But I've heard it said He Himself never ventures beyond the Outposts. Come on.'

Questions crowded Jack's mind – a million of them – but the Captain set a killer pace and he didn't have the spare breath to ask them. They breasted the rise south of the great pavillion and passed the spot where he had first flipped back out of the Territories. The rustic fun-fair was now close – Jack could hear a barker cajoling patrons to try their luck on Wonder the Devil-Donkey; to stay on two minutes was to win a prize, the barker cried. His voice came on the sea-breeze with perfect clarity, as did the mouthwatering smell of hot food – roast corn as well as meat this time. Jack's stomach rumbled. Now safely away from Osmond the Great and Terrible, he was ravenous.

Before they quite reached the fair, they turned right on a road much wider than the one which led toward the great pavillion. *Outpost Road*, Jack thought, and then, with a little chill of fear and anticipation in his belly, he corrected himself: *No . . . Western Road. The way to the Talisman.*

Then he was hurrying after Captain Farren again.

6

Osmond had been right; they could have followed their noses, if necessary. They were still a mile outside the village with that odd name when the first sour tang of spilled ale came to them on the breeze.

Eastward-bearing traffic on the road was heavy. Most of it was wagons drawn by lathered teams of horses (none with two heads, however). The wagons were, Jack supposed, the Diamond Reos and Peterbilts of this world. Some were piled high with bags and bales and sacks, some with raw meat, some with clacking cages of chickens. On the outskirts of All-Hands' Village, an open wagon filled with women swept by them at an alarming pace. The women were laughing and shrieking. One got to her feet, raised her skirt all the way to her hairy crotch, and did a tipsy bump and grind. She would have tumbled over the side of the wagon and into the ditch – probably breaking her neck – if one of her colleagues hadn't grabbed her by the back of the skirt and pulled her rudely back down.

Jack blushed again: he saw the girl's large white breast, its nipple in the dirty baby's working mouth. *Oooooo, this pretty young man's SHY!*

'God!' Farren muttered, walking faster than ever. 'They were all drunk! Drunk on spilled Kingsland! Whores and driver both! He's apt to wreck them on the road or drive them right off the seacliffs – no great loss. Diseased sluts!'

'At least,' Jack panted, 'the road must be fairly clear, if all this traffic can get through. Mustn't it?

They were in All-Hands' Village now. The wide Western Road had been oiled here to lay the dust. Wagons came and went, groups of people crossed the street, and everyone seemed to be talking too loudly. Jack saw two men arguing outside what might have been a restaurant. Abruptly, one of them threw a punch. A moment later, both men were rolling on the ground. *Those whores aren't the only ones drunk on*

Kingsland, Jack thought. *I think everyone in this town's had a share.*

'All of the big wagons that passed us came from here,' Captain Farren said. 'Some of the smaller ones may be getting through, but Morgan's diligence isn't small, boy.'

'Morgan—'

'Never mind Morgan now.'

The smell of the ale grew steadily sharper as they passed through the center of the village and out the other side. Jack's legs ached as he struggled to keep up with the Captain. He guessed they had now come perhaps three miles. *How far is that in my world?* he thought, and that thought made him think of Speedy's magic juice. He groped frantically in his jerkin, convinced it was no longer there – but it was, held securely within whatever Territories undergarment had replaced his Jockey shorts.

Once they were on the western side of the village, the wagon-traffic decreased, but the pedestrian traffic headed east increased dramatically. Most of the pedestrians were weaving, staggering, laughing. They all reeked of ale. In some cases, their clothes were dripping, as if they had lain full-length in it and drunk of it like dogs. Jack supposed they had. He saw a laughing man leading a laughing boy of perhaps eight by the hand. The man bore a nightmarish resemblance to the hateful desk clerk at the Alhambra, and Jack understood with perfect clarity that this man was that man's Twinner. Both he and the boy he led by the hand were drunk, and as Jack turned to look after them, the little boy began to vomit. His father – or so Jack supposed him to be – jerked him hard by the arm as the boy attempted to flounder his way into the brushy ditch, where he could be sick in relative privacy. The kid reeled back to his father like a cur-dog on a short leash, spraying puke on an elderly man who had collapsed by the side of the road and was snoring there.

Captain Farren's face grew blacker and blacker. 'God pound them all,' he said.

Even those furthest into their cups gave the scarred Captain a wide and prudent berth. While in the guard-post outside the pavillion, he had belted a short, businesslike leather scabbard around his waist. Jack assumed (not unreasonably) that it contained a short, businesslike sword. When any of the sots came too close, the Captain touched the sword and the sot detoured quickly away.

Ten minutes later – as Jack was becoming sure he could no longer keep up – they arrived at the site of the accident. The driver had been coming out of the turn on the inside when the wagon had tilted and gone over. As a result, the kegs had sprayed all the way across the road. Many of them were smashed, and the road was a quagmire for twenty feet. One horse lay dead beneath the wagon, only its hindquarters visible. Another lay in the ditch, a shattered chunk of barrel-stave protruding from its ear. Jack didn't think that could have happened by accident. He supposed the horse had been badly hurt and someone had put it out of its misery by the closest means at hand. The other horses were nowhere to be seen.

Between the horse under the wagon and the one in the ditch lay the carter's son, spreadeagled on the road. Half of his face stared up at the bright blue Territories sky with an expression of stupid amazement. Where the other half had been was now only red pulp and splinters of white bone like flecks of plaster.

Jack saw that his pockets had been turned out.

Wandering around the scene of the accident were

perhaps a dozen people. They walked slowly, often bending over to scoop ale two-handed from a hoofprint or to dip a handkerchief or a torn-off piece of singlet into another puddle. Most of them were staggering. Voices were raised in laughter and in quarrelsome shouts. After a good deal of pestering, Jack's mother had allowed him to go with Richard to see a midnight double feature of *Night of the Living Dead* and *Dawn of the Dead* at one of Westwood's dozen or so movie theaters. The shuffling, drunken people here reminded him of the zombies in those two films.

Captain Farren drew his sword. It was as short and businesslike as Jack had imagined, the very antithesis of a sword in a romance. It was little more than a long butcher's knife, pitted and nicked and scarred, the handle wrapped in old leather that had been sweated dark. The blade itself was dark . . . except for the cutting edge. That looked bright and keen and *very* sharp.

'Make away, then!' Farren bawled. 'Make away from the Queen's ale, God-pounders! Make away and keep your guts where they belong!'

Growls of displeasure met this, but they moved away from Captain Farren – all except one hulk of a man with tufts of hair growing at wildly random points from his otherwise bald skull. Jack guessed his weight at close to three hundred pounds, his height at just shy of seven feet.

'D'you like the idea of taking on all of us, sojer?' this hulk asked, and waved one grimy hand at the knot of villagers who had stepped away from the swamp of ale and the litter of barrels at Farren's order.

'Sure,' Captain Farren said, and grinned at the big man. 'I like it fine, just as long as you're first, you great drunken clot of shit.' Farren's grin widened, and the big man faltered away from its dangerous power. 'Come for me, if you like. Carving you will be the first good thing that's happened to me all day.'

Muttering, the drunken giant slouched away.

'Now, all of you!' Farren shouted. 'Make away! There's a dozen of my men just setting out from the Queen's pavilion! They'll not be happy with this duty and I don't blame them and I can't be responsible for them! I think you've just got time to get back to the village and hide in your cellars before they arrive there! It would be prudent to do so! Make away!'

They were already streaming back toward the village of All-Hands', the big man who had challenged the Captain in their van. Farren grunted and then turned back to the scene of the accident. He removed his jacket and covered the face of the carter's son with it.

'I wonder which of them robbed the lad's pockets as he lay dead or dying in the roadstead,' Farren said meditatively. 'If I knew, I'd have them hung on a cross by nightfall.'

Jack made no answer.

The Captain stood looking down at the dead boy for a long time, one hand rubbing at the smooth, ridged flesh of the scar on his face. When he looked up at Jack, it was as if he had just come to.

'You've got to leave now, boy. Right away. Before Osmond decides he'd like to investigate my idiot son further.'

'How bad is it going to be with you?' Jack asked.

The Captain smiled a little. 'If you're gone, I'll have no trouble. I can say that I sent you back to your mother, or that I was overcome with rage and hit you with a chunk of wood and killed you. Osmond would believe either. He's distracted. They all are. They're waiting for her to die. It will be soon. Unless . . .'

He didn't finish.

'Go,' Farren said. 'Don't tarry. And when you hear Morgan's diligence coming, get off the road and get deep into the woods. *Deep*. Or he'll smell you like a cat smells a rat. He knows instantly if something is out of order. *His* order. He's a devil.'

'Will I hear it coming? His diligence?' Jack asked timidly. He looked at the road beyond the litter of barrels. It rose steadily upward, toward the edge of a piney forest. It would be dark in there, he thought . . . and Morgan would be coming the other way. Fear and loneliness combined in the sharpest, most disheartening wave of unhappiness he had ever known. *Speedy, I can't do this! Don't you know that? I'm just a kid!*

'Morgan's diligence is drawn by six pairs of horses and a thirteenth to lead,' Farren said. 'At the full gallop, that damned hearse sounds like thunder rolling along the earth. You'll hear it, all right. Plenty of time to burrow down. Just make sure you do.'

Jack whispered something.

'What?' Farren asked sharply.

'I said I don't want to go,' Jack said, only a little louder. Tears were close and he knew that once they began to fall he was going to lose it, just blow his cool entirely and ask Captain Farren to get him out of it, protect him, *something* –

'I think it's too late for your wants to enter into the question,' Captain Farren said. 'I don't know your tale, boy, and I don't want to. I don't even want to know your name.'

Jack stood looking at him, shoulders slumped, eyes burning, his lips trembling.

'Get your shoulders up!' Farren shouted at him with

sudden fury. 'Who are you going to save? Where are you going? Not ten feet, looking like that! You're too young to be a man, but you can at least *pretend*, can't you? You look like a kicked dog!'

Stung, Jack straightened his shoulders and blinked his tears back. His eyes fell on the remains of the carter's son and he thought: *At least I'm not like that, not yet. He's right. Being sorry for myself is a luxury I can't afford.* It was true. All the same, he could not help hating the scarred Captain a little for reaching inside him and pushing the right buttons so easily.

'Better,' Farren said dryly. 'Not much, but a little.'

'Thanks,' Jack said sarcastically.

'You can't cry off, boy. Osmond's behind you. Morgan will soon be behind you as well. And perhaps . . . perhaps there are problems wherever you came from, too. But take this. If Parkus sent you to me, he'd want me to give you this. So take it, and then go.'

He was holding out a coin. Jack hesitated, then took it. It was the size of a Kennedy half-dollar, but much heavier – as heavy as gold, he guessed, although its color was dull silver. What he was looking at was the face of Laura DeLoessian in profile – he was struck again, briefly but forcibly, by her resemblance to his mother. No, not just resemblance – in spite of such physical dissimilarities as the thinner nose and rounder chin, she *was* his mother. Jack knew it. He turned the coin over and saw an animal with the head and wings of an eagle and the body of a lion. It seemed to be looking at Jack. It made him a little nervous, and he put the coin inside his jerkin, where it joined the bottle of Speedy's magic juice.

'What's it for?' he asked Farren.

'You'll know when the time comes,' the Captain replied. 'Or perhaps you won't. Either way, I've done my duty by you. Tell Parkus so, when you see him.'

Jack felt wild unreality wash over him again.

'Go, son,' Farren said. His voice was lower, but not necessarily more gentle. 'Do your job . . . or as much of it as you can.'

In the end, it was that feeling of unreality – the pervasive sense that he was no more than a figment of someone else's hallucination – that got him moving. Left foot, right foot, hay foot, straw foot. He kicked aside a splinter of ale-soaked wood. Stepped over the shattered remnants of a wheel. Detoured around the end of the wagon, not impressed by the blood drying there or the buzzing flies. What was blood or buzzing flies in a dream?

He reached the end of the muddy, wood- and barrel-littered stretch of road, and looked back . . . but Captain Farren had turned the other way, perhaps to look for his men, perhaps so he would not have to look at Jack. Either way, Jack reckoned, it came to the same thing. A back was a back. Nothing to look at.

He reached inside his jerkin, tentatively touched the coin Farren had given him, and then gripped it firmly. It seemed to make him feel a little better. Holding it as a child might hold a quarter given him to buy a treat at the candy store, Jack went on.

7

It might have been as little as two hours later when Jack heard the sound Captain Farren had described as 'thunder rolling along the earth' – or it might have been as long as four. Once the sun passed below the western rim of the forest (and it did that not long after Jack had entered it), it became difficult to judge the time.

On a number of occasions vehicles came out of the west, presumably bound for the Queen's pavillion. Hearing each one come (and vehicles could be heard a long way away here; the clarity with which sound carried made Jack think of what Speedy had said about one man pulling a radish out of the ground and another smelling it half a mile away) made him think of Morgan, and each time he hurried first down into the ditch and then up the other side, and so into the woods. He didn't *like* being in these dark woods – not even a little way in, where he could still peer around the trunk of a tree and see the road; it was no rest-cure for the nerves, but he liked the idea of Uncle Morgan (for so he still believed Osmond's superior to be, in spite of what Captain Farren had said) catching him out on the road even less.

So each time he heard a wagon or carriage approaching he got out of sight, and each time the vehicle passed he went back to the road. Once, while he was crossing the damp and weedy right-hand ditch, something ran – or slithered – over his foot, and Jack cried out.

The traffic was a pain in the tail, and it wasn't exactly helping him to make better time, but there was also something comforting about the irregular passage of wagons – they served notice that he wasn't alone, at least.

He wanted to get the hell out of the Territories altogether.

Speedy's magic juice was the worst medicine he'd ever had in his life, but he would gladly have taken a belly-choking swig of it if someone – Speedy himself, for example – had just happened to appear in front of him and assure him that, when he opened his eyes again, the first thing he would see would be a set of McDonald's golden arches – what his mother called The Great Tits of America. A sense of oppressive danger was growing in him – a feeling that the forest was indeed dangerous, that there were things in it aware of his passage, that perhaps the forest *itself* was aware of his passage. The trees had gotten closer to the road, hadn't they? Yes. Before, they had stopped at the ditches. Now they infested those as well. Before, the forest had seemed composed solely of pines and spruces. Now other sorts of trees had crept in, some with black boles that twisted together like gnarls of rotted strings, some that looked like weird hybrids of firs and ferns – these latter had nasty-looking gray roots that gripped at the ground like pasty fingers. *Our boy?* these nasty things seemed to whisper inside of Jack's head. *O U R boy?*

All in your mind, Jack-O. You're just freaking out a little.

Thing was, he didn't really believe that.

The trees *were* changing. That sense of thick oppression in the air – that sense of being *watched* – was all too real. And he had begun to think that his mind's obsessive return to monstrous thoughts was almost something he was picking up from the forest . . . as if the trees themselves were sending to him on some horrible shortwave.

But Speedy's bottle of magic juice was only half-full. Somehow that had to last him all the way across the United States. It wouldn't last until he was out of New England if he sipped a little every time he got the willies.

His mind also kept returning to the amazing distance he had travelled in his world when he had flipped back from the Territories. A hundred and fifty feet over here had equalled half a mile over there. At that rate – unless the ratio of distance travelled were somehow variable, and Jack recognized that it might be – he could walk ten miles over here and be damn near out of New Hampshire over there. It was like wearing seven-league boots.

Still, the trees . . . those gray, pasty roots . . .

When it starts to get really dark – when the sky goes from blue to purple – I'm flipping back. That's it; that's all she wrote. I'm not walking through these woods after dark. And if I run out of magic juice in Indiana or something, ole Speedy can just send me another bottle by UPS, or something.

Still thinking these thoughts – and thinking how much better it made him feel to have a plan (even if the plan only encompassed the next two hours or so) – Jack suddenly realized he could hear another vehicle and a great many horses.

Cocking his head, he stopped in the middle of the road. His eyes widened, and two pictures suddenly unspooled behind his eyes with shutterlike speed: the big car the two men had been in – the car that had not been a Mercedes – and then the WILD CHILD van, speeding down the street and away from Uncle Tommy's corpse, blood dripping from the broken plastic fangs of its grille. He saw the hands on the van's steering wheel . . . but they weren't hands. They were weird, articulated hooves.

At the full gallop, that damned hearse sounds like thunder rolling along the earth.

Now, hearing it – the sound still distant but perfectly clear in the pure air – Jack wondered how he could have even thought those other approaching wagons might be Morgan's diligence. He would certainly never make such a mistake again. The sound he heard now was perfectly ominous, thick with a potential for evil – the sound of a hearse, yes, a hearse driven by a devil.

He stood frozen in the road, almost hypnotized, as a rabbit is hypnotized by headlights. The sound grew steadily louder – the thunder of the wheels and hooves, the creak of leather rigging. Now he could hear the driver's voice: '*Hee-yah! Heee-yahhh! HEEEEE-YAHHHH!*'

He stood in the road, stood there, his head drumming with horror. *Can't move, oh dear God oh dear Christ I can't move Mom Mom Muhhhhhmeeeee—!*

He stood in the road and the eye of his imagination saw a huge black thing like a stagecoach tearing up the road, pulled by black animals that looked more like pumas than horses; he saw black curtains flapping in and out of the coach's windows; he saw the driver standing on the teeter-board, his hair blown back, his eyes as wild and crazed as those of a psycho with a switchblade.

He saw it coming toward him, never slowing.

He saw it run him down.

That broke the paralysis. He ran to the right, skidding down the side of the road, catching his foot under one of those gnarled roots, falling, rolling. His back, relatively quiet for the last couple of hours, flared with fresh pain, and Jack drew his lips back with a grimace.

He got to his feet and scurried into the woods, hunched over.

He slipped first behind one of the black trees, but the touch of the gnarly trunk – it was a bit like the banyans he had seen while on vacation in Hawaii year before last – was oily and unpleasant. Jack moved to the left and behind the trunk of a pine.

The thunder of the coach and its outriders grew steadily louder. At every second Jack expected the company to flash by toward All-Hands' Village. Jack's fingers squeezed and relaxed on the pine's gummy bark. He bit at his lips.

Directly ahead was a narrow but perfectly clear sightline back to the road, a tunnel with sides of leaf and fern and pine needles. And just when Jack had begun to think that Morgan's party would never arrive, a dozen or more mounted soldiers passed heading east, riding at a gallop. The one in the lead carried a banner, but Jack could not make out its device . . . nor was he sure he wanted to. Then the diligence flashed across Jack's narrow sightline.

The moment of its passage was brief – no more than a second, perhaps less than that – but Jack's recall of it was total. The diligence was a gigantic vehicle, surely a dozen feet high. The trunks and bundles lashed with stout cord to the top added another three feet. Each horse in the team which pulled it wore a black plume on its head – these plumes were blown back almost flat in a speed-generated wind. Jack thought later that Morgan must need a new team for every run, because these looked close to the end of their endurance. Foam and blood sprayed back from their working mouths in curds; their eyes rolled crazily, showing arcs of white.

As in his imagining – or his vision – black crepe curtains flew and fluttered through glassless windows. Suddenly a white face appeared in one of those black oblongs, a white face framed in strange, twisted carving-work. The sudden appearance of that face was as shocking as the face of a ghost in the ruined window of a haunted house. It was not the face of Morgan Sloat . . . but it *was*.

And the owner of that face knew that Jack – or some other danger, just as hated and just as *personal* – was out there. Jack saw this in the widening of the eyes and the sudden vicious downtwist of the mouth.

Captain Farren had said *He'll smell you like a rat*, and now Jack thought dismally: *I've been smelled, all right. He knows I'm here, and what happens now? He'll stop the whole bunch of them, I bet, and send the soldiers into the woods after me.*

Another band of soldiers – these protecting Morgan's diligence from the rear – swept by. Jack waited, his hands frozen to the bark of the pine, sure that Morgan would call a halt. But no halt came; soon the heavy thunder of the diligence and its outriders began to fade.

His eyes. That's what's the same. Those dark eyes in that white face. And –

Our boy? Y E S S S S!

Something slithered over his foot . . . and up his ankle. Jack screamed and floundered backward, thinking it must be a snake. But when he looked down he saw that one of those gray roots had slipped up his foot . . . and now it ringed his calf.

That's impossible, he thought stupidly. *Roots don't* move –

He pulled back sharply, yanking his leg out of the rough gray manacle the root had formed. There was thin pain in his calf, like the pain of a rope-burn. He raised his eyes and felt sick fear slip into his heart. He thought he knew now why Morgan had sensed him and gone on anyway; Morgan knew that walking in this forest was like walking into a jungle stream infested with piranhas. Why hadn't Captain Farren warned him? All Jack could think was that the scarred Captain must not have known; must never have been this far west.

The grayish roots of those fir-fern hybrids were all moving now – rising, falling, scuttling along the mulchy ground toward him. *Ents and Entwives*, Jack thought crazily. *B A D Ents and Entwives.* One particularly thick root, its last six inches dark with earth and damp, rose and wavered in front of him like a cobra piped up from a fakir's basket. *O U R boy! Y E S S!*

It darted toward him and Jack backed away from it, aware that the roots had now formed a living screen between him and the safety of the road. He backed into a tree . . . and then lurched away from it, screaming, as its bark began to ripple and twitch against his back – it was like feeling a muscle which has begun to spasm wildly. Jack looked around and saw one of those black trees with the gnarly trunks. Now the trunk was moving, writhing. Those twisted knots of bark formed something like a dreadful runnelled face, one eye widely, blackly open, the other drawn down in a hideous wink. The tree split open lower down with a grinding, rending sound, and whitish-yellow sap began to drool out. *O U R S! Oh, yesssss!*

Roots like fingers slipped between Jack's upper arm and ribcage, as if to tickle.

He tore away, holding on to the last of his rationality with a huge act of will, groping in his jerkin for Speedy's bottle. He was aware – faintly – of a series of gigantic ripping sounds. He supposed the trees were tearing themselves right out of the ground. Tolkien had never been like this.

He got the bottle by the neck and pulled it out. He scrabbled at the cap, and then one of those gray roots slid easily around his neck. A moment later it pulled as bitterly tight as a hangman's noose.

Jack's breath stopped. The bottle tumbled from his fingers as he grappled with the thing that was choking him. He managed to work his fingers under the root. It was not cold and stiff but warm and limber and fleshlike. He struggled with it, aware of the choked gargling sound coming from him and the slick of spittle on his chin.

With a final convulsive effort he tore the root free. It tried to circle his wrist then, and Jack whipped his arm away from it with a cry. He looked down and saw the bottle twisting and bumping away, one of those gray roots coiled about its neck.

Jack leaped for it. Roots grabbed his legs, circled them. He fell heavily to the earth, stretching, reaching, the tips of his fingers digging at the thick black forest soil for an extra inch –

He touched the bottle's slick green side . . . and seized it. He pulled as hard as he could, dimly aware that the roots were all over his legs now, crisscrossing like bonds, holding him firmly. He spun the cap off the bottle. Another root floated down, cobweblight, and tried to snatch the bottle away from him. Jack pushed it away and raised the bottle to his lips. That smell of sickish fruit suddenly seemed everywhere, a living membrane.

Speedy, please let it work!

As more roots slid over his back and around his waist, turning him helplessly this way and that, Jack drank, cheap wine splattering both of his cheeks. He swallowed, groaning, praying, and it was no good, *it wasn't working*, his eyes were still closed but he could feel the roots entangling his arms and legs, could feel

8

the water soaking into his jeans and his shirt, could smell

Water?

mud and damp, could hear

Jeans? Shirt?

the steady croak of frogs and

Jack opened his eyes and saw the orange light of the setting sun reflected from a wide river. Unbroken forest grew on the east side of this river; on the western side, the side that he was on, a long field, now partially obscured with evening ground-mist, rolled down to the water's edge. The ground here was wet and squelchy. Jack was lying at the edge of the water, in the boggiest area of all. Thick weeds still grew here – the hard frosts that would kill them were still a month or more away – and Jack had gotten entangled in them, the way a man awakening from a nightmare may entangle himself in the bedclothes.

He scrambled and stumbled to his feet, wet and slimed with the fragrant mud, the straps of his pack pulling under his arms. He pushed the weedy fragments from his arms and face with horror. He started away from the water, then looked back and saw Speedy's bottle lying in the mud, the cap beside it. Some of the 'magic juice' had either run out or been spilled in his struggle with the malignant Territories trees. Now the bottle was no more than a third full.

He stood there a moment, his caked sneakers planted in the oozy muck, looking out at the river. This was his world; this was the good old United States of America. He didn't see the golden arches he had hoped for, or a skyscraper, or an earth satellite blinking overhead in the darkening sky, but he knew where he was as well as he knew his own name. The question was, had he ever been in that other world at all?

He looked around at the unfamiliar river, the likewise unfamiliar countryside, and listened to the distant mellow mooing of cows. He thought: *You're somewhere different. This sure isn't Arcadia Beach anymore, Jack-O.*

No, it wasn't Arcadia Beach, but he didn't know the area surrounding Arcadia Beach well enough to say for sure that he was more than four or five miles away – just enough inland, say, to no longer be able to smell the Atlantic. He had come back as if waking from a nightmare – was it not possible that was all it had been, the whole thing, from the carter with his load of fly-crawling meat to the living trees? A sort of waking nightmare in which sleepwalking had played a part? It made sense. His mother was dying, and he now thought he had known that for quite a while – the signs had been there, and his subconscious had drawn the correct conclusion even while his conscious mind denied it. That would have contributed the correct atmosphere for an act of self-hypnosis, and that crazy wino Speedy Parker had gotten him in gear. Sure. It all hung together.

Uncle Morgan would have loved it.

Jack shivered and swallowed hard. The swallow hurt. Not the way a sore throat hurts, but the way an abused muscle hurts.

He raised his left hand, the one not holding the bottle, and rubbed his palm gently against his throat. For a moment he looked absurdly like a woman checking for dewlaps or wrinkles. He found a welted abrasion just above his adam's apple. It hadn't bled much, but it was almost too painful to touch. The root that had closed about his throat had done that.

'True,' Jack whispered, looking out at the orange water, listening to the *twank* of the bullfrogs and the mooing, distant cows. 'All true.'

9

Jack began walking up the slope of the field, setting the river – and the east – at his back. After he had gone half a mile, the steady rub and shift of the pack against his throbbing back (the strokes Osmond had laid on were still there too, the shifting pack reminded him) triggered a memory. He had refused Speedy's enormous sandwich, but hadn't Speedy slipped the remains into his pack anyway, while Jack was examining the guitar-pick?

His stomach pounced on the idea.

Jack unshipped the pack then and there, standing in a curdle of ground-mist beneath the evening star. He unbuckled one of the flaps, and there was the sandwich, not just a piece or a half, but the whole thing, wrapped up in a sheet of newspaper. Jack's eyes filled with a warmth of tears and he wished that Speedy were here so he could hug him.

Ten minutes ago you were calling him a crazy old wino.

His face flamed at that, but his shame didn't stop him from gobbling the sandwich in half a dozen big bites. He rebuckled his pack and reshouldered it. He went on, feeling better – with that whistling hole in his gut stopped up for the time being, Jack felt himself again.

Not long after, lights twinkled up out of the growing darkness. A farmhouse. A dog began to bark – the heavy bark of a really big fellow – and Jack froze for a moment.

Inside, he thought. *Or chained up. I hope.*

He bore to the right, and after a while the dog stopped barking. Keeping the lights of the farmhouse as a guide, Jack soon came out on a narrow blacktop road. He stood looking from right to left, having no idea which way to go.

Well, folks, here's Jack Sawyer, halfway between hoot and

holler, wet through to the skin and sneakers packed with mud. Way to go, Jack!

The loneliness and homesickness rose in him again. Jack fought them off. He put a drop of spit on his left index finger, then spanked the drop sharply. The larger of the two halves flew off to the right – or so it seemed to Jack – and so he turned that way and began to walk. Forty minutes later, drooping with weariness (and hungry again, which was somehow worse), he saw a gravel-pit with a shed of some sort standing beyond a chained-off access road.

Jack ducked under the chain and went to the shed. The door was padlocked shut, but he saw that the earth had eroded under one side of the small outbuilding. It was the work of a minute to remove his pack, wriggle under the shed's side, and then pull the pack in after him. The lock on the door actually made him feel safer.

He looked around and saw that he was in with some very old tools – this place hadn't been used in a long time, apparently, and that suited Jack just fine. He stripped to the skin, not liking the feel of his clammy, muddy clothes. He felt the coin Captain Farren had given him in one of his pants pockets, resting there like a giant amid his little bit of more ordinary change. Jack took it out and saw that Farren's coin, with the Queen's head on one side and the winged lion on the other – had become a 1921 silver dollar. He looked fixedly at the profile of Lady Liberty on the cart-wheel for some time, and then slipped it back into the pocket of his jeans.

He rooted out fresh clothes, thinking he would put the dirty ones in his pack in the morning – they would be dry then – and perhaps clean them along the way, maybe in a Laundromat, maybe just in a handy stream.

While searching for socks, his hand encountered something slim and hard. Jack pulled it out and saw it was his toothbrush. At once, images of home and safety and rationality – all the things a toothbrush could represent – rose up and overwhelmed him. There was no way that he could beat these emotions down or turn them aside this time. A toothbrush was a thing meant to be seen in a well-lighted bathroom, a thing to be used with cotton pajamas on the body and warm slippers on the feet. It was nothing to come upon in the bottom of your knapsack in a cold, dark toolshed on the edge of a gravel-pit in a deserted rural town whose name you did not even know.

Loneliness raged through him; his realization of his outcast status was now complete. Jack began to cry. He did not weep hysterically or shriek as people do when they mask rage with tears; he cried in the steady sobs of one who has discovered just how alone he is, and is apt to remain for a long time yet. He cried because all safety and reason seemed to have departed from the world. Loneliness was here, a reality; but in this situation, insanity was also too much of a possibility.

Jack fell asleep before the sobs had entirely run their course. He slept curled around his pack, naked except for clean underpants and socks. The tears had cut clean courses down his dirty cheeks, and he held his toothbrush loosely in one hand.

CHAPTER EIGHT

THE OATLEY TUNNEL

1

Six days later, Jack had climbed nearly all the way out of his despair. By the end of his first days on the road, he seemed to himself to have grown from childhood right through adolescence into adulthood – into competence. It was true that he had not returned to the Territories since he had awakened on the western bank of the river, but he could rationalize that, and the slower travelling it involved, by telling himself that he was saving Speedy's juice for when he really needed it.

And anyhow, hadn't Speedy told him to travel mainly on the roads in this world? Just following orders, pal.

When the sun was up and the cars whirled him thirty, forty miles west and his stomach was full, the Territories seemed unbelievably distant and dreamlike: they were like a movie he was beginning to forget, a temporary fantasy. Sometimes, when Jack leaned back into the passenger seat of some schoolteacher's car and answered the usual questions about the Story, he actually did forget. The Territories left him, and he was again – or nearly so – the boy he had been at the start of the summer.

Especially on the big state highways, when a ride dropped

him off near the exit ramp, he usually saw the next car pulling off to the side ten or fifteen minutes after he stuck his thumb into the air. Now he was somewhere near Batavia, way over in the western part of New York State, walking backward down the breakdown lane of I-90, his thumb out again, working his way toward Buffalo – after Buffalo, he would start to swing south. It was a matter, Jack thought, of working out the best way to accomplish something and then just doing it. Rand McNally and the Story had gotten him this far; all he needed was enough luck to find a driver going all the way to Chicago or Denver (or Los Angeles, if we're going to daydream about luck, Jacky-baby), and he could be on his way home again before the middle of October.

He was suntanned, he had fifteen dollars in his pocket from his last job – dishwasher at the Golden Spoon Diner in Auburn – and his muscles felt stretched and toughened. Though sometimes he wanted to cry, he had not given in to his tears since that first miserable night. He was in control, that was the difference. Now that he knew how to proceed, had worked it out so painstakingly, he was on top of what was happening to him; he thought he could see the end of his journey already, though it was so far ahead of him. If he travelled mainly in this world, as Speedy had told him, he could move as quickly as he had to and get back to New Hampshire with the Talisman in plenty of time. It was going to work, and he was going to have many fewer problems than he had expected.

That, at least, was what Jack Sawyer was imagining as a dusty blue Ford Fairlane swerved off to the shoulder of the road and waited for him to run up to it, squinting into the lowering sun. *Thirty or forty miles*, he thought to himself.

He pictured the page from Rand McNally he had studied that morning, and decided: *Oatley*. It sounded dull, small, and safe – he was on his way, and nothing could hurt him now.

2

Jack bent down and looked in the window before opening the Fairlane's door. Fat sample books and printed fliers lay messily over the back seat; two oversize briefcases occupied the passenger seat. The slightly paunchy black-haired man who now seemed almost to be mimicking Jack's posture, bending over the wheel and peering through the open window at the boy, was a salesman. The jacket to his blue suit hung from the hook behind him; his tie was at half-mast, his sleeves were rolled. A salesman in his mid-thirties, tooling comfortably through his territory. He would love to talk, like all salesmen. The man smiled at him and picked up first one of the outsize briefcases, hoisting it over the top of the seat and onto the litter of papers behind, then the other. 'Let's create a little room,' he said.

Jack knew that the first thing the man would ask him was why he was not at school.

He opened the door, said, 'Hey, thanks,' and climbed in.

'Going far?' the salesman asked, checking the rear-view mirror as he slid the gear-lever down into Drive and swung back out onto the road.

'Oatley,' Jack said. 'I think it's about thirty miles.'

'You just flunked geography,' the salesman said. 'Oatley's more like forty-five miles.' He turned his head to look at Jack, and surprised the boy by winking at him. 'No offense,' he said, 'but I hate to see young kids hitching. That's why

I always pick em up when I see em. At least I know they're safe with me. No touchie-feelie, know what I mean? Too many crazies out there, kid. You read the papers? I mean, I'm talking carnivores. You could turn yourself into an endangered species.'

'I guess you're right,' Jack said. 'But I try to be pretty careful.'

'You live somewhere back there, I take it?'

The man was still looking straight at him, snatching little birdlike peeks ahead down the road, and Jack frantically searched his memory for the name of a town back down the road. 'Palmyra. I'm from Palmyra.'

The salesman nodded, said, 'Nice enough old place,' and turned back to the highway. Jack relaxed back into the comfortable plush of the seat. Then the man finally said, 'I guess you're not actually playing hooky, are you?' and it was time yet again for the Story.

He had told it so often, varying the names of the towns involved as he worked westward, that it had a slick, monologue-like feel in his mouth. 'No, sir. It's just that I have to go over to Oatley to live with my Aunt Helen for a little while. Helen Vaughan? That's my mom's sister. She's a schoolteacher. My dad died last winter, see, and things have been pretty tough – then two weeks ago my mom's cough got a lot worse and she could hardly get up the stairs and the doctor said she had to stay in bed for as long as she could and she asked her sister if I could come stay with her for a while. Her being a teacher and all, I guess I'll be in the Oatley school for sure. Aunt Helen wouldn't let any kid play hooky, you bet.'

'You mean your mother told you to hitchhike all the way from Palmyra to *Oatley*?' the man asked.

'Oh no, not at all – she'd never do that. No, she gave me bus money but I decided to save it. There won't be much money from home for a long time, I guess, and Aunt Helen doesn't really have any money. My mom would hate it if she knew I was thumbing it. But it seemed like a waste of money to me. I mean, five bucks is five bucks, and why give it to a bus driver?'

The man looked sideways at him. 'How long do you think you'll be in Oatley?'

'Hard to say. I sure hope my mom gets well pretty soon.'

'Well, don't hitch back, okay?'

'We don't have a car anymore,' Jack said, adding to the Story. He was beginning to enjoy himself. 'Can you believe this? They came out in the middle of the night and repossessed it. Dirty cowards. They knew everybody would be asleep. They just came out in the middle of the night and stole the car right out of the garage. Mister, I would have fought for that car – and not so I could get a ride to my aunt's house. When my mom goes to the doctor, she has to walk all the way down the hill and then go about another five blocks just to get to the bus stop. They shouldn't be able to do that, should they? Just come in and steal your own car? As soon as we could, we were going to start making the payments again. I mean, wouldn't you call that stealing?'

'If it happened to me, I suppose I would,' the man said. 'Well, I hope your mother gets better in a hurry.'

'You and me both,' Jack said with perfect honesty.

And that held them until the signs for the Oatley exit began to appear. The salesman pulled back into the breakdown lane just after the exit ramp, smiled again at Jack and said, 'Good luck, kid.'

Jack nodded and opened the door.

'I hope you don't have to spend much time in Oatley, anyhow.'

Jack looked at him questioningly.

'Well, you know the place, don't you?'

'A little. Not really.'

'Ah, it's a real pit. Sort of place where they eat what they run over on the road. Gorillaville. You eat the beer, then you drink the glass. Like that.'

'Thanks for the warning,' Jack said and got out of the car. The salesman waved and dropped the Fairlane into Drive. In moments it was only a dark shape speeding toward the low orange sun.

3

For a mile or so the road took him through flat dull countryside – far off, Jack saw small two-story frame houses perched on the edges of fields. The fields were brown and bare, and the houses were not farmhouses. Widely separated, the houses overlooking the desolate fields existed in a gray moveless quiet broken only by the whine of traffic moving along I-90. No cows lowed, no horses whinnied – there were no animals, and no farm equipment. Outside one of the little houses squatted half a dozen junked and rusting cars. These were the houses of men who disliked their own species so thoroughly that even Oatley was too crowded for them. The empty fields gave them the moats they needed around their peeling frame castles.

At length he came to a crossroads. It looked like a crossroads in a cartoon, two narrow empty roads bisecting each other in an absolute nowhere, then stretching on toward another kind of nowhere. Jack had begun to feel insecure about his sense of direction, and he adjusted the pack on his back and moved up toward the tall rusted iron pipe supporting the black rectangles, themselves rusting, of the street names. Should he have turned left instead of right off the exit ramp? The sign pointing down the road running parallel to the highway read DOGTOWN ROAD. Dogtown? Jack looked down this road and saw only endless flatness, fields full of weeds and the black streak of asphalt rolling on. His own particular streak of asphalt was called MILL ROAD, according to the sign. About a mile ahead it slipped into a tunnel nearly overgrown by leaning trees and an oddly pubic mat of ivy. A white sign hung in the thickness of ivy, seemingly supported by it. The words were too small to be read. Jack put his right hand in his pocket and clutched the coin Captain Farren had given him.

His stomach talked to him. He was going to need dinner soon, so he had to move off this spot and find a town where he could earn his meals. Mill Road it was – at least he could go far enough to see what was on the other side of the tunnel. Jack pushed himself toward it, and the dark opening in the bank of trees enlarged with every step.

Cool and damp and smelling of brick dust and overturned earth, the tunnel seemed to take the boy in and then tighten down around him. For a moment Jack feared that he was being led underground – no circle of light ahead showed the tunnel's end – but then realized that the asphalt floor was level. TURN ON LIGHTS, the sign outside the tunnel had read. Jack bumped into a brick wall and felt grainy powder crumble onto his hands. 'Lights,' he said to himself, wishing he had one to turn on. The tunnel must, he realized, bend somewhere along its length. He had cautiously, slowly, carefully, walked straight into the wall, like a blind man with his hands extended. Jack groped his way along the wall. When the coyote in the Roadrunner cartoons did something like this, he usually wound up splashed across the front of a truck.

Something rattled busily along the floor of the tunnel, and Jack froze.

A rat, he thought. Maybe a rabbit out taking a shortcut between fields. But it had sounded bigger than that.

He heard it again, farther away in the dark, and took another blind step forward. Ahead of him, just once, he heard an intake of breath. And stopped, wondering: *Was that an animal?* Jack held his fingertips against the damp brick wall, waiting for the exhalation. It had not sounded like an animal – certainly no rat or rabbit inhaled so deeply. He crept a few inches forward, almost unwilling to admit to himself that whatever was up there had frightened him.

Jack froze again, hearing a quiet little sound like a raspy chuckle come out of the blackness before him. In the next second a familiar but unidentifiable smell, coarse, strong, and musky, drifted toward him out of the tunnel.

Jack looked back over his shoulder. The entrance was now only half-visible, half-obscured by the curve of the wall, a long way off and looking about the size of a rabbit-hole.

'What's in here?' he called out. 'Hey! Anything in here with me? Anybody?'

He thought he heard something whisper deeper into the tunnel.

He was not in the Territories, he reminded himself – at the worst he might have startled some imbecilic dog who had come into the cool dark for a nap. In that case, he'd be saving its life by waking it up before a car came along. 'Hey, dog!' he yelled. '*Dog!*'

And was rewarded instantly by the sound of paws trotting through the tunnel. But were they . . . going out or coming in? He could not tell, listening to the soft *pad pad pad*, whether the animal was leaving or approaching. Then it occurred to him that maybe the noise was coming toward him from behind, and he twisted his neck and looked back and saw that he had moved far enough along so that he could not see that entrance, either.

'Where are you, dog?' he said.

Something scratched the ground only a foot or two behind him, and Jack jumped forward and struck his shoulder, hard, against the curve of the wall.

He sensed a shape – doglike, perhaps – in the darkness. Jack stepped forward – and was stopped short by a sense of dislocation so great that he imagined himself back in the Territories. The tunnel was filled with that musky, acrid zoo-odor, and whatever was coming toward him was not a dog.

A gust of cold air smelling of grease and alcohol pushed toward him. He sensed that shape getting nearer.

Only for an instant he had a glimpse of a face hanging in the dark, glowing as if with its own sick and fading interior light, a long, bitter face that should have been almost youthful but was not. Sweat, grease, a stink of alcohol on the breath that came from it. Jack flattened himself against the wall, raising his fists, even as the face faded back into the dark.

In the midst of his terror he thought he heard footfalls softly, quickly covering the ground toward the tunnel's entrance, and turned his face from the square foot of darkness which had spoken to him to look back. Darkness, silence. The tunnel was empty now. Jack squeezed his hands under his armpits and gently fell back against the brick, taking the blow on his knapsack. A moment later he began to edge forward again.

As soon as Jack was out of the tunnel, he turned around to face it. No sounds emerged, no weird creatures slunk toward him. He took three steps forward, peered in. And then his heart nearly stopped, because coming toward him were two huge orange eyes. They halved the distance between themselves and Jack in seconds. He could not move – his feet were past the ankles in asphalt. Finally he managed to extend his hands, palm-out, in the instinctive gesture of warding-off. The eyes continued toward him, and a horn blasted. Seconds before the car burst out of the tunnel, revealing a red-faced man waving a fist, Jack threw himself out of the way.

'SHIIITHEEAAA . . .' came from the contorted mouth.

Still dazed, Jack turned and watched the car speed downhill toward a village that had to be Oatley.

4

Situated in a long depression in the land, Oatley spread itself out meagerly from two principal streets. One, the continuation of Mill Road, dipped past an immense and shabby building set in the midst of a vast parking lot – a factory, Jack thought – to become a strip of used-car lots (sagging pennants), fast-food franchises (The Great Tits of America), a bowling alley with a huge neon sign (BOWL-A-RAMA!), grocery stores, gas stations. Past all this, Mill Road became

Oatley's five or six blocks of downtown, a strip of old two-story brick buildings before which cars were parked nose-in. The other street was obviously the location of Oatley's most important houses – large frame buildings with porches and long slanting lawns. Where these streets intersected stood a traffic light winking its red eye in the late afternoon. Another light perhaps eight blocks down changed to green before a high dingy many-windowed building that looked like a mental hospital, and so was probably the high school. Fanning out from the two streets was a jumble of little houses interspersed with anonymous buildings fenced in behind tall wire mesh.

Many of the windows in the factory were broken, and some of the windows in the strip of downtown had been boarded over. Heaps of garbage and fluttering papers littered the fenced-in concrete yards. Even the important houses seemed neglected, with their sagging porches and bleached-out paint jobs. These people would own the used-car lots filled with unsaleable automobiles.

For a moment Jack considered turning his back on Oatley and making the hike to Dogtown, wherever that was. But that would mean walking through the Mill Road tunnel again. From down in the middle of the shopping district a car horn blatted, and the sound unfurled toward Jack full of an inexpressible loneliness and nostalgia.

He could not relax until he was all the way to the gates of the factory, the Mill Road tunnel far up behind him. Nearly a third of the windows along the dirty-brick facade had been broken in, and many of the others showed blank brown squares of cardboard. Even out on the road, Jack could smell machine oil, grease, smouldering fanbelts, and clashing gears. He put his hands in his pockets and walked downhill as quickly as he could.

5

Seen close up, the town was even more depressed than it had looked from the hill. The salesmen at the car lots leaned against the windows in their offices, too bored to come outside. Their pennants hung tattered and joyless, the once-optimistic signs propped along the cracked sidewalk fronting the rows of cars – ONE OWNER! FANTASTIC BUY! CAR OF THE WEEK! – had yellowed. The ink had feathered and run on some of the signs, as if they had been left out in the rain. Very few people moved along the streets. As Jack went toward the center of town, he saw an old man with sunken cheeks and gray skin trying to wrestle an empty shopping cart up onto a curb. When he approached, the old man screeched something hostile and frightened and bared gums as black as a badger's. He thought Jack was going to steal his cart! 'Sorry,' Jack said, his heart pounding again. The old man was trying to hug the whole cumbersome body of the cart, protecting it, all the while showing those blackened gums to his enemy. 'Sorry,' Jack repeated. 'I was just going to . . .'

'Fusshhingfeef! FusshhingFEEEFF!' the old man screeched, and tears crawled into the wrinkles on his cheeks.

Jack hurried off.

Twenty years before, during the sixties, Oatley must have prospered. The relative brightness of the strip of Mill Road leading out of town was the product of that era when stocks went go-go and gas was still cheap and nobody had heard the term 'discretionary income' because they had plenty of it. People had sunk their money into franchise operations and little shops and for a time had, if not actually flourished, held their heads above the waves. This short series of blocks still had that superficial hopefulness – but only a few bored teenagers sat in the franchise restaurants, nursing medium Cokes, and in the plate-glass windows of too many of the little shops placards as faded as those in the used-car lots announced EVERYTHING MUST GO! CLOSING SALE. Jack saw no signs advertising for help, and kept on walking.

Downtown Oatley showed the reality beneath the happy clown's colors left behind by the sixties. As Jack trudged along these blocks of baked-looking brick buildings, his pack grew heavier, his feet more tender. He would have walked to Dogtown after all, if it were not for his feet and the necessity of going through the Mill Road tunnel again. Of course there was no snarling man-wolf lurking in the dark there – he'd worked that out by now. No one could have spoken to him in the tunnel. The Territories had shaken him. First the sight of the Queen, then that dead boy beneath the cart with half his face gone. Then Morgan; the trees. But that was *there*, where such things could be – were, perhaps, even normal. *Here*, normality did not admit such gaudiness.

He was before a long, dirty window above which the flaking slogan FURNITURE DEPOSITORY was barely legible on the brickwork. He put his hands to his eyes and stared in. A couch and a chair, each covered by a white sheet, sat fifteen feet apart on a wide wooden floor. Jack moved farther down the block, wondering if he was going to have to beg for food.

Four men sat in a car before a boarded-up shop a little way down the block. It took Jack a moment to see that the car, an ancient black DeSoto that looked as though Broderick Crawford should come bustling out of it, had no tires. Taped to the windshield was a yellow five-by-eight card which read FAIR WEATHER CLUB. The men inside, two in front and two in back, were playing cards. Jack stepped up to the front passenger window.

'Excuse me,' he said, and the cardplayer closest to him rolled a fishy gray eye toward him. 'Do you know where—'

'Get lost,' the man said. His voice sounded squashed and phlegmy, unfamiliar with speech. The face half-turned to Jack was deeply pitted with acne scars and oddly flattened out, as if someone had stepped on it when the man was an infant.

'I just wondered if you knew somewhere I could get a couple days' work.'

'Try Texas,' said the man in the driver's seat, and the pair in the back seat cracked up, spitting beer out over their hands of cards.

'I told you, kid, get lost,' said the flatfaced gray-eyed man closest to Jack. 'Or I'll personally pound the shit out of you.'

It was just the truth, Jack understood – if he stayed there a moment longer, this man's rage would boil over and he would get out of the car and beat him senseless. Then the man would get back in the car and open another beer. Cans of Rolling Rock covered the floor, the opened ones tipped every which way, the fresh ones linked by white plastic nooses. Jack stepped backward, and the fish-eye rolled away from him. 'Guess I'll try Texas after all,' he said. He listened for the sound of the DeSoto's door creaking open as he walked away, but all he heard being opened was another Rolling Rock.

Crack! Hiss!

He kept moving.

He got to the end of the block and found himself looking across the town's other main street at a dying lawn filled with yellow weeds from which peeked fiberglass statues of Disneylike fawns. A shapeless old woman gripping a flyswatter stared at him from a porch swing.

Jack turned away from her suspicious gaze and saw before him the last of the lifeless brick buildings on Mill Road. Three concrete steps led up to a propped-open screen door. A long, dark window contained a glowing BUDWEISER sign and, a foot to the right of that, the painted legend UPDIKE'S OATLEY TAP. And several inches beneath that, hand-written on a yellow five-by-eight card like the one on the DeSoto, were the miraculous words HELP WANTED. Jack pulled the knapsack off his back, bunched it under one arm, and went up the steps. For no more than an instant, moving from the tired sunlight into the darkness of the bar, he was reminded of stepping past the thick fringe of ivy into the Mill Road tunnel.

CHAPTER NINE
JACK IN THE PITCHER PLANT

1

Not quite sixty hours later a Jack Sawyer who was in a very different frame of mind from that of the Jack Sawyer who had ventured into the Oatley tunnel on Wednesday was in the chilly storeroom of the Oatley Tap, hiding his pack behind the kegs of Busch which sat in the room's far corner like aluminum bowling pins in a giant's alley. In less than two hours, when the Tap finally shut down for the night, Jack meant to run away. That he should even think of it in such a fashion – not *leaving*, not *moving on*, but *running away* – showed how desperate he now believed his situation to be.

I was six, six, John B. Sawyer was six, Jacky was six. Six.

This thought, apparently nonsensical, had fallen into his mind this evening and had begun to repeat there. He supposed it went a long way toward showing just how scared he was now, how certain he was that things were beginning to close in on him. He had no idea what the thought meant; it just circled and circled, like a wooden horse bolted to a carousel.

Six. I was six. Jacky Sawyer was six.

Over and over, round and round she goes.

The storeroom shared a wall in common with the taproom itself, and tonight that wall was actually vibrating with noise; it throbbed like a drumhead. Until twenty minutes before, it had been Friday night, and both Oatley Textiles and Weaving and Dogtown Custom Rubber paid on Friday. Now the Oatley Tap was full to the overflow point . . . and past. A big poster to the left of the bar read OCCUPANCY BY MORE THAN 220 PERSONS IS IN VIOLATION OF GENESEE COUNTY FIRE CODE 331. Apparently fire code 331 was suspended on the weekends, because Jack guessed there were more than three hundred people out there now, boogying away to a country-western band which called itself The Genny Valley Boys. It was a terrible band, but they had a pedal-steel guitar. 'There's guys around here that'd fuck a pedal-steel, Jack,' Smokey had said.

'*Jack!*' Lori yelled over the wall of sound.

Lori was Smokey's woman. Jack still didn't know what her last name was. He could barely hear her over the juke, which was playing at full volume while the band was on break. All five of them were standing at the far end of the bar, Jack knew, tanking up on half-price Black Russians. She stuck her head through the storeroom door. Tired blond hair, held back with childish white plastic barrettes, glittered in the overhead fluorescent.

'Jack if you don't run that keg out real quick, I guess he'll give your arm a try.'

'Okay,' Jack said. 'Tell him I'll be right there.'

He felt gooseflesh on his arms, and it didn't come entirely from the storeroom's damp chill. Smokey Updike was no one to fool with – Smokey who wore a succession of paper fry-cook's hats on his narrow head, Smokey with his large plastic mail-order dentures, grisly and somehow funereal in their perfect evenness, Smokey with his violent brown eyes, the scleras an ancient, dirty yellow. Smokey Updike who in some way still unknown to Jack – and who was all the more frightening for that – had somehow managed to take him prisoner.

The juke-box fell temporarily silent, but the steady roar of the crowd actually seemed to go up a notch to make up for it. Some Lake Ontario cowboy raised his voice in a big, drunken '*Yeeeee-H A W!*' A woman screamed. A glass broke. Then the juke-box took off again, sounding a little like a Saturn rocket achieving escape velocity.

Sort of place where they eat what they run over on the road.

Raw.

Jack bent over one of the aluminum kegs and dragged it out about three feet, his mouth screwed down in a painful wince, sweat standing out on his forehead in spite of the air-conditioned chill, his back protesting. The keg gritted and squealed on the unadorned cement. He stopped, breathing hard, his ears ringing.

He wheeled the hand-truck over to the keg of Busch, stood it up, then went around to the keg again. He managed to rock it up on its rim and walk it forward, toward where the hand-truck stood. As he was setting it down he lost control of it – the big barkeg weighed only a few pounds less than Jack did himself. It landed hard on the foot of the hand-truck, which had been padded with a remnant of carpet so as to soften just such landings. Jack tried to both steer it and get his hands out of the way in time. He was slow. The keg mashed his fingers against the back of the hand-truck. There was an agonizing thud, and he somehow managed to get his throbbing, pulsing fingers out of there. Jack stuck all the fingers of his left hand in his mouth and sucked on them, tears standing in his eyes.

Worse than jamming his fingers, he could hear the slow sigh of gases escaping through the breather-cap on top of the keg. If Smokey hooked up the keg and it came out foamy . . . or, worse yet, if he popped the cap and the beer went a gusher in his face . . .

Best not to think of those things.

Last night, Thursday night, when he'd tried to 'run Smokey out a keg', the keg had gone right over on its side. The breather-cap had shot clear across the room. Beer foamed white-gold across the storeroom floor and ran down the drain. Jack had stood there, sick and frozen, oblivious to Smokey's shouts. It wasn't Busch, it was Kingsland. Not beer but ale – the Queen's Own.

That was when Smokey hit him for the first time – a quick looping blow that drove Jack into one of the storeroom's splintery walls.

'There goes your pay for today,' Smokey had said, 'And you never want to do that again, Jack.'

What chilled Jack most about that phrase *you never want to do that again* was what it assumed: that there would be lots of opportunities for him to do that again; as if Smokey Updike expected him to be here a long, long time.

'Jack, hurry it up!'

'*Coming.*' Jack puffed. He pulled the hand-truck across the room to the door, felt behind himself for the knob, turned it, and pushed the door open. He hit something large and soft and yielding.

'Christ, watch it!'

'Whoops, sorry,' Jack said.

'I'll whoops you, asshole,' the voice replied.

Jack waited until he heard heavy steps moving on down the hall outside the storeroom and then tried the door again.

The hall was narrow and painted a bilious green. It stank of shit and piss and TidyBowl. Holes had been punched through both plaster and lath here and there; graffiti lurched and staggered everywhere, written by bored drunks waiting to use either POINTERS or SETTERS. The largest of them all had been slashed across the green paint with a black Magic Marker, and it seemed to scream out all of Oatley's dull and objectless fury. SEND ALL AMERICAN NIGGERS AND JEWS TO IRAN, it read.

The noise from the taproom was loud in the storeroom; out here it was a great wave of sound which never seemed to break. Jack took one glance back into the storeroom over the top of the keg tilted on the hand-truck, trying to make sure his pack wasn't visible.

He had to get out. *Had* to. The dead phone that had finally spoken, seeming to encase him in a capsule of dark ice . . . that had been bad. Randolph Scott was worse. The guy wasn't *really* Randolph Scott; he only looked the way Scott had looked in his fifties films. Smokey Updike was perhaps worse still . . . although Jack was no longer sure of that. Not since he had seen (or thought he had seen) the eyes of the man who looked like Randolph Scott change color.

But that Oatley itself was worst of all . . . he was sure of that.

Oatley, New York, deep in the heart of Genny County, seemed now to be a horrible trap that had been laid for him . . . a kind of municipal pitcher plant. One of nature's real marvels, the pitcher plant. Easy to get in. Almost impossible to get out.

2

A tall man with a great swinging gut porched in front of him stood waiting to use the men's room. He was rolling a plastic toothpick from one side of his mouth to the other and glaring at Jack. Jack supposed that it was the big man's gut that he had hit with the door.

'Asshole,' the fat man repeated, and then the men's room door jerked open. A man strode out. For a heart-stopping moment his eyes and Jack's eyes met. It was the man who looked like Randolph Scott. But this was no movie-star; this was just an Oatley millhand drinking up his week's pay. Later on he would leave in a half-paid-for doorsucker Mustang or maybe on a three-quarters-paid-for motorcycle – a big old Harley with a BUY AMERICAN sticker plastered on the nacelle, probably.

His eyes turned yellow.

No, your imagination, Jack, just your imagination. He's just –

– just a millhand who was giving him the eye because he was new. He had probably gone to high school here in town, played football, knocked up a Catholic cheerleader and married her, and the cheerleader had gotten fat on chocolates and Stouffer's frozen dinners; just another Oatley oaf, just –

But his eyes turned yellow.

Stop it! They did not!

Yet there was something about him that made Jack think of what had happened when he was coming into town . . . what had happened in the dark.

The fat man who had called Jack an asshole shrank back from the rangy man in the Levi's and the clean white

T-shirt. Randolph Scott started toward Jack. His big, veined hands swung at his sides.

His eyes sparkled an icy blue . . . and then began to change, to moil and lighten.

'Kid,' he said, and Jack fled with clumsy haste, butting the swinging door open with his fanny, not caring who he hit.

Noise pounced on him. Kenny Rogers was bellowing an enthusiastic redneck paean to someone named Reuben James. '*You allus turned your other CHEEK,*' Kenny testified to this room of shuffling, sullen-faced drunks, '*and said there's a better world waitin for the MEEK!*' Jack saw no one here who looked particularly meek. The Genny Valley Boys were trooping back onto the bandstand and picking up their instruments. All of them but the pedal-steel player looked drunk and confused . . . perhaps not really sure of where they were. The pedal-steel player only looked bored.

To Jack's left, a woman was talking earnestly on the Tap's pay phone – a phone Jack would never touch again if he had his way about it, not for a thousand dollars. As she talked, her drunken companion probed and felt inside her half-open cowboy shirt. On the big dancefloor, perhaps seventy couples groped and shuffled, oblivious of the current song's bright up-tempo, simply squeezing and grinding, hands gripping buttocks, lips spit-sealed together, sweat running down cheeks and making large circles under the armpits.

'Well thank *Gawd,*' Lori said, and flipped up the hinged partition at the side of the bar for him. Smokey was halfway down the bar, filling up Gloria's tray with gin-and-tonics, vodka sours, and what seemed to be beer's only competition for the Oatley Town Drink: Black Russians.

Jack saw Randolph Scott come out through the

swinging door. He glanced toward Jack, his blue eyes catching Jack's again at once. He nodded slightly, as if to say: *We'll talk. Yessirree. Maybe we'll talk about what might or might not be in the Oatley tunnel. Or about bullwhips. Or sick mothers. Maybe we'll talk about how you're gonna be in Genny County for a long, long time . . . maybe until you're an old man crying over a shopping cart. What do you think, Jacky?*

Jack shuddered.

Randolph Scott smiled, as if he had seen the shudder . . . or felt it. Then he moved off into the crowd and the thick air.

A moment later Smokey's thin, powerful fingers bit into Jack's shoulder – hunting for the most painful place and, as always, finding it. They were educated, nerve-seeking fingers.

'Jack, you just got to move faster,' Smokey said. His voice sounded almost sympathetic, but his fingers dug and moved and probed. His breath smelled of the pink Canada Mints he sucked almost constantly. His mail-order false teeth clicked and clacked. Sometimes there was an obscene slurping as they slipped a little and he sucked them back into place. 'You got to move faster or I'm going to have to light a fire under your ass. You understand what I'm saying?'

'Y-yeah,' Jack said. Trying not to moan.

'All right. That's good, then.' For an excruciating second Smokey's fingers dug even deeper, grinding with a bitter enthusiasm at the neat little nest of nerves there. Jack *did* moan. That was good enough for Smokey. He let up.

'Help me hook this keg up, Jack. And let's make it fast. Friday night, people got to drink.'

'Saturday morning,' Jack said stupidly.

'Then too. Come on.'

Jack somehow managed to help Smokey lift the keg into the square compartment under the bar. Smokey's thin, ropey muscles bulged and writhed under his Oatley Tap T-shirt. The paper fry-cook's hat on his narrow weasel's head stayed in place, its leading edge almost touching his left eyebrow, in apparent defiance of gravity. Jack watched, holding his breath, as Smokey flicked off the red plastic breather-cap on the keg. The keg breathed more gustily than it should have done . . . but it didn't foam. Jack let his breath out in a silent gust.

Smokey spun the empty toward him. 'Get that back in the storeroom. And then swamp out the bathroom. Remember what I told you this afternoon.'

Jack remembered. At three o'clock a whistle like an air-raid siren had gone off, almost making him jump out of his skin. Lori had laughed, had said: *Check out Jack, Smokey – I think he just went wee-wee in his Tuffskins*. Smokey had given her a narrow, unsmiling look and motioned Jack over. Told Jack that was the payday whistle at the Oatley T & W. Told Jack that a whistle very much like it was going off at Dogtown Rubber, a company that made beach-toys, inflatable rubber dolls, and condoms with names like Ribs of Delight. Soon, he said, the Oatley Tap would begin filling up.

'And you and me and Lori and Gloria are going to move just as fast as lightning,' Smokey said, 'because when the eagle screams on Friday, we got to make up for what this place don't make every Sunday, Monday, Tuesday, Wednesday, and Thursday. When I tell you to run me out a keg, you want to have it out to me before I finish yelling. And you're in the men's room every half an hour with your mop. On Friday nights, a guy blows his groceries every fifteen minutes or so.'

'I got the women's,' Lori said, coming over. Her hair was thin, wavy gold, her complexion as white as a comic-book vampire's. She either had a cold or a bad coke habit; she kept sniffing. Jack guessed it was a cold. He doubted if anyone in Oatley could afford a bad coke habit. 'Women ain't as bad as men, though. Almost, but not quite.'

'Shut up, Lori.'

'Up yours,' she said, and Smokey's hand flickered out like lightning. There was a crack and suddenly the imprint of Smokey's palm was printed red on one of Lori's pallid cheeks like a child's Tattoodle. She began to snivel . . . but Jack was sickened and bewildered to see an expression in her eyes that was almost happy. It was the look of a woman who believed such treatment was a sign of caring.

'You just keep hustling and we'll have no problem,' Smokey said. 'Remember to move fast when I yell for you to run me out a keg. And remember to get in the men's can with your mop every half an hour and clean up the puke.'

And then he had told Smokey again that he wanted to leave and Smokey had reiterated his false promise about Sunday afternoon . . . but what good did it do to think of that?

There were louder screams now, and harsh caws of laughter. The crunch of a breaking chair and a wavering yell of pain. A fistfight – the third of the night – had broken out on the dancefloor. Smokey uttered a curse and shoved past Jack. 'Get rid of that keg,' he said.

Jack got the empty onto the dolly and trundled it back toward the swinging door, looking around uneasily for Randolph Scott as he went. He saw the man standing in the crowd that was watching the fight, and relaxed a little.

In the storeroom he put the empty keg with the others by the loading-bay – Updike's Oatley Tap had already gone through six kegs tonight. That done, he checked his pack again. For one panicky moment he thought it was gone, and his heart began to hammer in his chest – the magic juice was in there, and so was the Territories coin that had become a silver dollar in this world. He moved to the right, sweat now standing out on his forehead, and felt between two more kegs. There it was – he could trace the curve of Speedy's bottle through the green nylon of the pack. His heartbeat began to slow down, but he felt shaky and rubber-legged – the way you feel after a narrow escape.

The men's toilet was a horror. Earlier in the evening Jack might have vomited in sympathy, but now he actually seemed to be getting used to the stench . . . and that was somehow the worst thing of all. He drew hot water, dumped in Comet, and began to run his soapy mop back and forth through the unspeakable mess on the floor. His mind began to go back over the last couple of days, worrying at them the way an animal in a trap will worry at the limb that has been caught.

3

The Oatley Tap had been dark, and dingy, and apparently dead empty when Jack first walked into it. The plugs on the juke, the pinball machine, and the Space Invaders game were all pulled. The only light in the place came from the Busch display over the bar – a digital clock caught between the peaks of two mountains, looking like the weirdest UFO ever imagined.

Smiling a little, Jack walked toward the bar. He was

almost there when a flat voice said from behind him, 'This is a bar. No minors. What are you, stupid? Get out.'

Jack almost jumped out of his skin. He had been touching the money in his pocket, thinking it would go just as it had at the Golden Spoon: he would sit on a stool, order something, and then ask for the job. It was of course illegal to hire a kid like him – at least without a work permit signed by his parents or a guardian – and that meant they could get him for under the minimum wage. Way under. So the negotiations would start, usually beginning with Story #2 – Jack and the evil Stepfather.

He whirled around and saw a man sitting alone in one of the booths, looking at him with chilly, contemptuous alertness. The man was thin, but ropes of muscle moved under his white undershirt and along the sides of his neck. He wore baggy white cook's pants. A paper cap was cocked forward over his left eyebrow. His head was narrow, weasel-like. His hair was cut short, graying at the edges. Between his big hands were a stack of invoices and a Texas Instruments calculator.

'I saw your Help Wanted sign,' Jack said, but now without much hope. This man was not going to hire him, and Jack was not sure he would want to work for him anyway. This guy looked mean.

'You did, huh?' the man in the booth said. 'You must have learned to read on one of the days you weren't playing hooky.' There was a package of Phillies Cheroots on the table. He shook one out.

'Well, I didn't know it was a bar,' Jack said, taking a step back toward the door. The sunlight seemed to come through the dirty glass and then just fall dead on the floor, as if the Oatley Tap were located in a slightly different dimension. 'I guess I thought it was . . . you know, a bar and grill. Something like that. I'll just be going.'

'Come here.' The man's brown eyes were looking at him steadily now.

'No, hey, that's all right,' Jack said nervously. 'I'll just—'

'Come here. Sit down.' The man popped a wooden match alight with his thumbnail and lit the cigar. A fly which had been preening on his paper hat buzzed away into the darkness. His eyes remained on Jack. 'I ain't gonna bite you.'

Jack came slowly over to the booth, and after a moment he slipped in on the other side and folded his hands in front of him neatly. Some sixty hours later, swamping out the men's toilet at twelve-thirty in the morning with his sweaty hair hanging in his eyes, Jack thought – no, he *knew* – that it was his own stupid confidence that had allowed the trap to spring shut (and it had shut the moment he sat down opposite Smokey Updike, although he had not known it then). The Venus flytrap is able to close on its hapless, insectile victims; the pitcher plant, with its delicious smell and its deadly, glassy-smooth sides, only waits for some flying asshole of a bug to buzz on down and inside . . . where it finally drowns in the rainwater the pitcher collects. In Oatley the pitcher was full of beer instead of rainwater – that was the only difference.

If he had run –

But he hadn't run. And maybe, Jack thought, doing his best to meet that cold brown stare, there would be a job here after all. Minette Banberry, the woman who owned and operated the Golden Spoon in Auburn, had been pleasant enough to Jack, had even given him a little hug and a peck of a kiss as well as three thick sandwiches when he left, but he had not been fooled. Pleasantness and even a remote sort of kindness did not preclude a cold interest in profits, or even something very close to outright greed.

The minimum wage in New York was three dollars and forty cents an hour – that information had been posted in the Golden Spoon's kitchen by law, on a bright pink piece of paper almost the size of a movie poster. But the short-order cook was a Haitian who spoke little English and was almost surely in the country illegally, Jack thought. The guy cooked like a whiz, though, never allowing the spuds or the fried clams to spend a moment too long in the Fryolaters. The girl who helped Mrs Banberry with the waitressing was pretty but vacant and on a work-release program for the retarded in Rome. In such cases, the minimum wage did not apply, and the lisping, retarded girl told Jack with unfeigned awe that she was getting a dollar and twenty-five cents *each hour*, and *all for her.*

Jack himself was getting a dollar-fifty. He had bargained for that, and he knew that if Mrs Banberry hadn't been strapped – her old dishwasher had quit just that morning, had gone on his coffee-break and just never come back – she would not have bargained at all; would have simply told him take the buck and a quarter, kid, or see what's down the road. It's a free country.

Now, he thought, with the unknowing cynicism that was also a part of his new self-confidence, here was another Mrs Banberry. Male instead of female, rope-skinny instead of fat and grandmotherly, sour instead of smiling, but almost surely a Mrs Banberry for a' that and a' that.

'Looking for a job, huh?' The man in the white pants and the paper hat put his cigar down in an old tin ashtray with the words CAMELS embossed on the bottom. The fly stopped washing its legs and took off.

'Yes, sir, but like you say, this is a bar and all—'

The unease stirred in him again. Those brown eyes and yellowed scleras troubled him – they were the eyes of some old hunting cat that had seen plenty of errant mice like him before.

'Yeah, it's my place,' the man said. 'Smokey Updike.' He held his hand out. Surprised, Jack shook it. It squeezed Jack's hand once, hard, almost to the point of pain. Then it relaxed . . . but Smokey didn't let go. 'Well?' he said.

'Huh?' Jack said, aware he sounded stupid and a little afraid – he *felt* stupid and a little afraid. And he wanted Updike to let go of his hand.

'Didn't your folks ever teach you to innerduce yourself?'

This was so unexpected that Jack came close to gabbling out his real name instead of the one he had used at the Golden Spoon, the name he also used if the people who picked him up asked for his handle. That name – what he was coming to think of as his 'road-name' – was Lewis Farren.

'Jack Saw – ah – Sawtelle,' he said.

Updike held his hand yet a moment longer, those brown eyes never moving. Then he let it go. 'Jack Saw-ah-Sawtelle,' he said. 'Must be the longest fucking name in the phonebook, huh, kid?'

Jack flushed but said nothing.

'You ain't very big,' Updike said. 'You think you could manage to rock a ninety-pound keg of beer up on its side and walk it onto a hand-dolly?'

'I think so,' Jack said, not knowing if he could or not.

It didn't look as if it would be much of a problem, anyway – in a place as dead as this, the guy probably only had to change kegs when the one hooked up to the taps went flat.

As if reading his mind, Updike said, 'Yeah, nobody here now. But we get pretty busy by four, five o'clock. And on weekends the place really fills up. That's when you'd earn your keep, Jack.'

'Well, I don't know,' Jack said. 'How much would the job pay?'

'Dollar an hour,' Updike said. 'Wish I could pay you more, but—' He shrugged and tapped the stack of bills. He even smiled a little, as if to say *You see how it is, kid, everything in Oatley is running down like a cheap pocket-watch someone forgot to wind – ever since about 1971 it's been running down.* But his eyes did not smile. His eyes were watching Jack's face with still, catlike concentration.

'Gee, that's not very much,' Jack said. He spoke slowly but he was thinking as fast as he could.

The Oatley Tap was a tomb – there wasn't even a single bombed-out old alky at the bar nursing a beer and watching *General Hospital* on the tube. In Oatley you apparently drank in your car and called it a club. A dollar-fifty an hour was a hard wage when you were busting your buns; in a place like this, a buck an hour might be an easy one.

'Nope,' Updike agreed, going back to his calculator, 'it ain't.' His voice said Jack could take it or leave it; there would be no negotiations.

'Might be all right,' Jack said.

'Well, that's good,' Updike said. 'We ought to get one other thing straight, though. Who you running from and who's looking for you?' The brown eyes were on him again, and they drilled hard. 'If you got someone on your back-trail, I don't want him fucking up my life.'

This did not shake Jack's confidence much. He wasn't the world's brightest kid, maybe, but bright enough to know he wouldn't last long on the road without a second cover story for prospective employers. This was Story #2 – The Wicked Stepfather.

'I'm from a little town in Vermont,' he said. 'Fenderville. My mom and dad got divorced two years ago. My dad tried to get custody of me, but the judge gave me to my mom. That's what they do most of the time.'

'Fucking-A they do.' He had gone back to his bills and was bent so far over the pocket calculator that his nose was almost touching the keys. But Jack thought he was listening all the same.

'Well, my dad went out to Chicago and he got a job in a plant out there,' Jack said. 'He writes to me just about every week, I guess, but he quit coming back last year, when Aubrey beat him up. Aubrey's—'

'Your stepfather,' Updike said, and for just a moment Jack's eyes narrowed and his original distrust came back. There was no sympathy in Updike's voice. Instead, Updike seemed almost to be laughing at him, as if he knew the whole tale was nothing but a great big swatch of whole cloth.

'Yeah,' he said. 'My mom married him a year and a half ago. He beats on me a lot.'

'Sad, Jack. Very sad.' Now Updike did look up, his eyes sardonic and unbelieving. 'So now you're off to Shytown, where you and Dads will live happily ever after.'

'Well, I hope so,' Jack said, and he had a sudden inspiration. 'All I know is that my *real* dad never hung me up by the neck in my closet.' He pulled down the neck of his

T-shirt, baring the mark there. It was fading now; during his stint at the Golden Spoon it had still been a vivid, ugly red-purple – like a brand. But at the Golden Spoon he'd never had occasion to uncover it. It was, of course, the mark left by the root that had nearly choked the life from him in that other world.

He was gratified to see Smokey Updike's eyes widen in surprise and what might almost have been shock. He leaned forward, scattering some of his pink and yellow pages. 'Holy *Jesus*, kid,' he said. 'Your stepfather did that?'

'That's when I decided I had to split.'

'Is he going to show up here, looking for his car or his motorcycle or his wallet or his fucking dope-stash?'

Jack shook his head.

Smokey looked at Jack for a moment longer, and then pushed the OFF button on the calculator. 'Come on back to the storeroom with me, kid,' he said.

'Why?'

'I want to see if you can really rock one of those kegs up on its side. If you can run me out a keg when I need one, you can have the job.'

4

Jack demonstrated to Smokey Updike's satisfaction that he could get one of the big aluminum kegs up on its rim and walk it forward just enough to get it on the foot of the dolly. He even made it look fairly easy – dropping a keg and getting punched in the nose was still a day away.

'Well, that ain't too bad,' Updike said. 'You ain't big enough for the job and you'll probably give yourself a fucking rupture, but that's your nevermind.'

He told Jack he could start at noon and work through until one in the morning ('For as long as you can hack it, anyway'). Jack would be paid, Updike said, at closing time each night. Cash on the nail.

They went back out front and there was Lori, dressed in dark blue basketball shorts so brief that the edges of her rayon panties showed, and a sleeveless blouse that had almost surely come from Mammoth Mart in Batavia. Her thin blond hair was held back with plastic barrettes and she was smoking a Pall Mall, its end wet and heavily marked with lipstick. A large silver crucifix dangled between her breasts.

'This is Jack,' Smokey said. 'You can take the Help Wanted sign out of the window.'

'Run, kid,' Lori said. 'There's still time.'

'Shut the fuck up.'

'Make me.'

Updike slapped her butt, not in a loving way but hard enough to send her against the padded edge of the bar. Jack blinked and thought of the sound Osmond's whip had made.

'Big man,' Lori said. Her eyes brimmed with tears . . . and yet they also looked contented, as if this was just the way things were supposed to be.

Jack's earlier unease was now clearer, sharper . . . now it was almost fright.

'Don't let us get on your case, kid,' Lori said, headed past him to the sign in the window. 'You'll be okay.'

'Name's Jack, not *kid*,' Smokey said. He had gone back to the booth where he had 'interviewed' Jack and began gathering up his bills. 'A kid's a fucking baby goat. Didn't they teach you that in school? Make the kid a couple of burgers. He's got to go to work at four.'

She got the HELP WANTED sign out of the window and put it behind the juke-box with the air of one who has done this a good many times before. Passing Jack, she winked at him.

The telephone rang.

All three of them looked toward it, startled by its abrupt shrilling. To Jack it looked for a moment like a black slug stuck to the wall. It was an odd moment, almost timeless. He had time to notice how pale Lori was – the only color in her cheeks came from the reddish pocks of her fading adolescent acne. He had time to study the cruel, rather secretive planes of Smokey Updike's face and to see the way the veins stood out on the man's long hands. Time to see the yellowed sign over the phone reading PLEASE LIMIT YOUR CALLS TO THREE MINUTES.

The phone rang and rang in the silence.

Jack thought, suddenly terrified: *It's for me. Long distance . . . long, LONG distance.*

'Answer that, Lori,' Updike said, 'what are you, simple?'

Lori went to the phone.

'Oatley Tap,' she said in a trembling, faint voice. She listened. 'Hello? Hello? . . . Oh, fuck off.'

She hung up with a bang.

'No one there. Kids. Sometimes they want to know if we got Prince Albert in a can. How do you like your burgers, kid?'

'Jack!' Updike roared.

'Jack, okay, okay, *Jack*. How do you like your burgers, Jack?'

Jack told her and they came medium, just right, hot with brown mustard and Bermuda onions. He gobbled them and drank a glass of milk. His unease abated with his hunger.

Kids, as she had said. Still, his eyes drifted back to the phone every once in a while, and he wondered.

5

Four o'clock came, and as if the Tap's total emptiness had been only a clever piece of stage setting to lure him in – like the pitcher plant with its innocent look and its tasty smell – the door opened and nearly a dozen men in work-clothes came sauntering in. Lori plugged in the juke, the pinball machine, the Space Invaders game. Several of the men bellowed greetings at Smokey, who grinned his narrow grin, exposing the big set of mail-order dentures. Most ordered beer. Two or three ordered Black Russians. One of them – a member of the Fair Weather Club, Jack was almost sure – dropped quarters into the juke-box, summoning up the voices of Mickey Gilley, Eddie Rabbit, Waylon Jennings, others. Smokey told him to get the mop-bucket and squeegee out of the storeroom and swab down the dancefloor in front of the bandstand, which waited, deserted, for Friday night and The Genny Valley Boys. He told Jack when it was dry he wanted him to put the Pledge right to it. 'You'll know it's done when you can see your own face grinnin up at you,' Smokey said.

6

So his time of service at Updike's Oatley Tap began.

We get pretty busy by four, five o'clock.

Well, he couldn't very well say that Smokey had lied to him. Up until the very moment Jack pushed away his plate and began making his wage, the Tap had been deserted.

But by six o'clock there were maybe fifty people in the Tap, and the brawny waitress – Gloria – came on duty to yells and hooraws from some of the patrons. Gloria joined Lori, serving a few carafes of wine, a lot of Black Russians, and oceans of beer.

Besides the kegs of Busch, Jack lugged out case after case of bottled beer – Budweiser, of course, but also such local favorites as Genesee, Utica Club, and Rolling Rock. His hands began to blister, his back to ache.

Between trips to the storeroom for cases of bottled beer and trips to the storeroom to 'run me out a keg, Jack' (a phrase for which he was already coming to feel an elemental dread), he went back to the dancefloor, the mop-bucket, and the big bottle of Pledge. Once an empty beer-bottle flew past his head, missing him by inches. He ducked, heart racing, as it shattered against the wall. Smokey ran the drunken perpetrator out, his dentures bared in a great false alligator grin. Looking out the window, Jack saw the drunk hit a parking-meter hard enough to pop the red VIOLATION flag up.

'Come on, Jack,' Smokey called impatiently from the bar, 'it missed you, didn't it? Clean that mess up!'

Smokey sent him into the men's can half an hour later. A middle-aged man with a Joe Pyne haircut was standing woozily at one of the two ice-choked urinals, one hand braced against the wall, the other brandishing a huge uncircumcised penis. A puddle of puke steamed between his spraddled work-boots.

'Clean her up, kid,' the man said, weaving his way back toward the door and clapping Jack on the back almost hard enough to knock him over. 'Man's gotta make room any way he can, right?'

Jack was able to wait until the door closed, and then he could control his gorge no longer.

He managed to make it into the Tap's only stall, where he was faced with the unflushed and sickeningly fragrant spoor of the last customer. Jack vomited up whatever remained of his dinner, took a couple of hitching breaths, and then vomited again. He groped for the flush with a shaking hand and pushed it. Waylon and Willie thudded dully through the walls, singing about Luckenbach, Texas.

Suddenly his mother's face was before him, more beautiful than it had ever been on any movie screen, her eyes large and dark and sorrowing. He saw her alone in their rooms at the Alhambra, a cigarette smouldering forgotten in an ashtray beside her. She was crying. Crying for him. His heart seemed to hurt so badly that he thought he would die from love for her and want of her – for a life where there were no things in tunnels, no women who somehow wanted to be slapped and made to cry, no men who vomited between their own feet while taking a piss. He wanted to be with her and hated Speedy Parker with a black completeness for ever having set his feet on this awful road west.

In that moment whatever might have remained of his self-confidence was demolished – it was demolished utterly and forever. Conscious thought was overmastered by a deep, elemental, wailing, childish cry: *I want my mother please God I want my MOTHER –*

He trembled his way out of the stall on watery legs, thinking *Okay that's it everybody out of the pool fuck you Speedy this kid's going home. Or whatever you want to call it.* In that moment he didn't care if his mother might be dying. In that moment of inarticulate pain he became totally Jack's Jack, as unconsciously self-serving as an animal on which any carnivore may prey: deer, rabbit, squirrel, chipmunk. In that moment he would have been perfectly willing to let her die of the cancer metastasizing wildly outward from her lungs if only she would hold him and then kiss him goodnight and tell him not to play his goddam transistor in bed or read with a flashlight under the covers for half the night.

He put his hand against the wall and little by little managed to get hold of himself. This taking-hold was no conscious thing but a simple tightening of the mind, something that was very much Phil Sawyer and Lily Cavanaugh. He'd made a mistake, a big mistake, yeah, but he wasn't going back. The Territories were real and so the Talisman might also be real; he was not going to murder his mother with faintheartedness.

Jack filled his mop-bucket with hot water from the spigot in the storeroom and cleaned up the mess.

When he came out again, it was half past ten and the crowd in the Tap had begun to thin out – Oatley was a working town, and its working drinkers went home early on weeknights.

Lori said, 'You look as pale as pastry, Jack. You okay?'

'Do you think I could have a gingerale?' he asked.

She brought him one and Jack drank it while he finished waxing the dancefloor. At quarter to twelve Smokey ordered him back to the storeroom to 'run out a keg'. Jack managed the keg – barely. At quarter to one Smokey started bawling for people to finish up. Lori unplugged the juke – Dick Curless died with a long, unwinding groan – to a few half-hearted cries of protest. Gloria unplugged the games, donned her sweater (it was as pink as the Canada Mints Smokey ate regularly, as pink as the false gums of his dentures), and left.

Smokey began to turn out the lights and to urge the last four or five drinkers out the door.

'Okay, Jack,' he said when they were gone. 'You did good. There's room for improvement, but you got a start, anyway. You can doss down in the storeroom.'

Instead of asking for his pay (which Smokey did not offer anyway), Jack stumbled off toward the storeroom, so tired that he looked like a slightly smaller version of the drunks so lately ushered out.

In the storeroom he saw Lori squatting down in one corner – the squat caused her basketball shorts to ride up to a point that was nearly alarming – and for a moment Jack thought with dull alarm that she was going through his knapsack. Then he saw that she had spread a couple of blankets on a layer of burlap apple-sacks. Lori had also put down a small satin pillow which said NEW YORK WORLD'S FAIR on one side.

'Thought I'd make you a little nest, kid,' she said.

'Thanks,' he said. It was a simple, almost offhand act of kindness, but Jack found himself having to struggle from bursting into tears. He managed a smile instead. 'Thanks a lot, Lori.'

'No problem. You'll be all right here, Jack. Smokey ain't so bad. Once you get to know him, he ain't half bad.' She said this with an unconscious wistfulness, as if wishing it were so.

'Probably not,' Jack said, and then he added impulsively, 'but I'm moving on tomorrow. Oatley's just not for me, I guess.'

She said: 'Maybe you'll go, Jack . . . and maybe you'll decide to stay awhile. Why don't you sleep on it?' There was something forced and unnatural about this little speech – it had none of the genuineness of her grin when she'd said *Thought I'd make you a little nest.* Jack noticed it, but was too tired to do more than that.

'Well, we'll see,' he said.

'Sure we will,' Lori agreed, going to the door. She blew a kiss toward him from the palm of one dirty hand. 'Good night, Jack.'

'Good night.'

He started to pull off his shirt . . . and then left it on, deciding he would just take off his sneakers. The storeroom was cold and chilly. He sat down on the apple-sacks, pulled the knots, pushed off first one and then the other. He was about to lie back on Lori's New York World's Fair souvenir – and he might well have been sound asleep before his head ever touched it – when the telephone began to ring out in the bar, shrilling into the silence, *drilling* into it, making him think of wavering, pasty-gray roots and bullwhips and two-headed ponies.

Ring, ring, ring, into silence, into the dead silence.

Ring, ring, ring, long after the kids who call up to ask about Prince Albert in a can have gone to bed. Ring, ring, ring, *Hello, Jacky it's Morgan and I felt you in my woods, you smart little shit. I SMELLED you in my woods, and how did you ever get the idea that you were safe in your world? My woods are there, too. Last chance, Jacky. Get home or we send out the troops. You won't have a chance. You won't –*

Jack got up and ran across the storeroom floor in his stocking feet. A light sweat that felt freezing cold seemed to cover his entire body.

He opened the door a crack.

Ring, ring, ring, ring.

Then, finally: 'Hello, Oatley Tap. And this better be good.'

Smokey's voice. A pause. 'Hello?' Another pause. 'Fuck *off*!' Smokey hung up with a bang, and Jack heard him re-cross the floor and then start up the stairs to the small overhead apartment he and Lori shared.

7

Jack looked unbelievingly from the green slip of paper in his left hand to the small pile of bills – all ones – and change by his right. It was eleven o'clock the next morning. Thursday morning, and he had asked for his pay.

'What *is* this?' he asked, still unable to believe it.

'You can read,' Smokey said, 'and you can count. You don't move as fast as I'd like, Jack – at least not yet – but you're bright enough.'

Now he sat with the green slip in one hand and the money by the other. Dull anger began to pulse in the middle of his forehead like a vein. GUEST CHECK, the green slip was headed. It was the exact same form Mrs Banberry had used in the Golden Spoon. It read:

1 hmbrg	$1.35
1 hmbrg	$1.35
1 lrg mk	.55
1 gin-ale	.55
Tx	.30

At the bottom the figure $4.10 was written in large numbers and circled. Jack had made nine dollars for his four-to-one stint. Smokey had charged off nearly half of it; what he had left by his right hand was four dollars and ninety cents.

He looked up, furious – first at Lori, who looked away as if vaguely embarrassed, and then at Smokey, who simply looked back.

'This is a cheat,' he said thinly.

'Jack, that's not true. Look at the menu prices—'

'That's not what I mean and you know it!'

Lori flinched a little, as if expecting Smokey to clout him one . . . but Smokey only looked at Jack with a kind of terrible patience.

'I didn't charge you for your bed, did I?'

'Bed!' Jack shouted, feeling the hot blood boil up into his cheeks. 'Some *bed*! Cut-open burlap bags on a concrete floor! Some *bed*! I'd like to see you try to charge me for it, you dirty *cheat*!'

Lori made a scared sound and shot a look at Smokey . . . but Smokey only sat across from Jack in the booth, the thick blue smoke of a Cheroot curling up between them. A fresh paper fry-cook's hat was cocked forward on Smokey's narrow head.

'We talked about you dossing down back there,' Smokey said. 'You asked if it came with the job. I said it did. No mention was made of your meals. If it had been brought up, maybe something could have been done. Maybe not. Point is, you never brought it up, so now you got to deal with that.'

Jack sat shaking, tears of anger standing in his eyes. He tried to talk and nothing came out but a small strangled groan. He was literally too furious to speak.

'Of course, if you wanted to discuss an employees' discount on your meals now—'

'Go to *hell*!' Jack managed finally, snatching up the four singles and the little screw of change. 'Teach the next kid who comes in here how to look out for number one! I'm *going*!'

He crossed the floor toward the door, and in spite of his anger he knew – did not just think but flat-out *knew* – that he wasn't going to make the sidewalk.

'Jack.'

He touched the doorknob, thought of grasping it and turning it – but that voice was undeniable and full of a certain threat. He dropped his hand and turned around, his anger leaving him. He suddenly felt shrunken and old. Lori had gone behind the bar, where she was sweeping and humming. She had apparently decided that Smokey wasn't going to work Jack over with his fists, and since nothing else really mattered, everything was all right.

'You don't want to leave me in the lurch with my weekend crowd coming up.'

'I want to get out of here. You cheated me.'

'No sir,' Smokey said, 'I explained that. If anyone blotted your copybook, Jack, it was you. Now we could discuss your meals – fifty per cent off the food, maybe, and even free sodas. I never went that far before with the younger help I hire from time to time, but this weekend's going to be especially hairy, what with all the migrant labor in the county for the apple-picking. And I *like* you, Jack. That's why I didn't clout you one when you raised your voice to me, although maybe I should have. But I need you over the weekend.'

Jack felt his rage return briefly, and then die away again.

'What if I go anyhow?' he asked. 'I'm five dollars to the good, anyway, and being out of this shitty little town might be just as good as a bonus.'

Looking at Jack, still smiling his narrow smile, Smokey

said, 'You remember going into the men's last night to clean after some guy who whoopsed his cookies?'

Jack nodded.

'You remember what he looked like?'

'Crewcut. Khakis. So what?'

'That's Digger Atwell. His real name's Carlton, but he spent ten years taking care of the town cemeteries, so everyone got calling him Digger. That was – oh, twenty or thirty years ago. He went on the town cops back around the time Nixon got elected President. Now he's Chief of Police.'

Smokey picked up his Cheroot, puffed at it, and looked at Jack.

'Digger and me go back,' Smokey said. 'And if you was to just walk out of here now, Jack, I couldn't guarantee that you wouldn't have some trouble with Digger. Might end up getting sent home. Might end up picking the apples on the town's land – Oatley Township's got . . . oh, I guess forty acres of good trees. Might end up getting beat up. Or . . . I've heard that Old Digger's got a taste for kids on the road. Boys, mostly.'

Jack thought of that clublike penis. He felt both sick and cold.

'In here, you're under my wing, so to speak,' Smokey said.

'Once you hit the street, who can say? Digger's apt to be cruising anyplace. You might get over the town line with no sweat. On the other hand, you might just see him pulling up beside you in that big Plymouth he drives. Digger ain't totally bright, but he does have a nose, sometimes. Or . . . someone might give him a call.'

Behind the bar, Lori was doing dishes. She dried her

hands, turned on the radio, and began to sing along with an old Steppenwolf song.

'Tell you what,' Smokey said. 'Hang in there, Jack. Work the weekend. Then I'll pack you into my pick-up and drive you over the town line myself. How would that be? You'll go out of here Sunday noon with damn near thirty bucks in your poke that you didn't have coming in. You'll go out thinking that Oatley's not such a bad place after all. So what do you say?'

Jack looked into those brown eyes, noted the yellow scleras and the small flecks of red; he noted Smokey's big, sincere smile lined with false teeth; he even saw with a weird and terrifying sense of *déjà vu* that the fly was back on the paper fry-cook's hat, preening and washing its hair-thin forelegs.

He suspected Smokey *knew* that *he* knew that everything Updike had said was a lie, and didn't even care. After working into the early hours of Saturday morning and then Sunday morning, Jack would sleep until maybe two Sunday afternoon. Smokey would tell him he couldn't give him that ride because Jack had woken up too late; now he, Smokey, was too busy watching the Colts and the Patriots. And Jack would not only be too tired to walk, he would be too afraid that Smokey might lose interest in the Colts and Patriots just long enough to call his good friend Digger Atwell and say, 'He's walking down Mill Road right now, Digger old boy, why don't you pick him up? Then get over here for the second half. Free beer, but don't you go puking in my urinal until I get the kid back here.'

That was one scenario. There were others that he could think of, each a little different, each really the same at bottom.

Smokey Updike's smile widened a little.

CHAPTER TEN
ELROY

1

When I was six . . .

The Tap, which had begun to wind down by this time on his previous two nights, was roaring along as if the patrons expected to greet the dawn. He saw two tables had vanished – victims of the fistfight that had broken out just before his last expedition into the john. Now people were dancing where the tables had been.

'About time,' Smokey said as Jack staggered the length of the bar on the inside and put the case down by the refrigerator compartments. 'You get those in there and go back for the fucking Bud. You should have brought that first, anyway.'

'Lori didn't say—'

Hot, incredible pain exploded in his foot as Smokey drove one heavy shoe down on Jack's sneaker. Jack uttered a muffled scream and felt tears sting his eyes.

'Shut up,' Smokey said. 'Lori don't know shit from Shinola. and you are smart enough to know it. Get back in there and run me out a case of Bud.'

He went back to the storeroom, limping on the foot Smokey had stomped, wondering if the bones in some of his toes might be broken. It seemed all too possible. His head roared with smoke and noise and the jagged ripsaw rhythm of The Genny Valley Boys, two of them now noticeably weaving on the bandstand. One thought stood out clearly: it might not be possible to wait until closing. He really might not be able to last that long. If Oatley was a prison and the Oatley Tap was his cell, then surely exhaustion was as much his warder as Smokey Updike – maybe even more so.

In spite of his worries about what the Territories might be like at this place, the magic juice seemed more and more to promise him his only sure way out. He could drink some and flip over . . . and if he could manage to walk a mile west over there, two at the most, he could drink a bit more and flip back into the U.S.A. well over the town line of this horrible little place, perhaps as far west as Bushville or even Pembroke.

When I was six, when Jack-O was six, when –

He got the Bud and stumble-staggered out through the door again . . . and the tall, rangy cowboy with the big hands, the one who looked like Randolph Scott, was standing there, looking at him.

'Hello, Jack,' he said, and Jack saw with rising terror that the irises of the man's eyes were as yellow as chicken-claws. 'Didn't somebody tell you to get gone? You don't listen very good, do you?'

Jack stood with the case of Bud dragging at the end of his arms, staring into those yellow eyes, and suddenly a horrid idea hammered into his mind: that *this* had been the lurker in the tunnel – this man-thing with its dead yellow eyes.

'Leave me alone,' he said – the words came out in a wintery little whisper.

He crowded closer. 'You were supposed to get *gone.*'

Jack tried to back up . . . but now he was against the wall, and as the cowboy who looked like Randolph Scott leaned toward him, Jack could smell dead meat on its breath.

2

Between the time Jack started work on Thursday at noon and four o'clock, when the Tap's usual after-work crowd started to come in, the pay phone with the PLEASE LIMIT YOUR CALLS TO THREE MINUTES sign over it rang twice.

The first time it rang, Jack felt no fear at all – and it turned out to be only a solicitor for the United Fund.

Two hours later, as Jack was banging up the last of the previous night's bottles, the telephone began to shrill again. This time his head snapped up like an animal which scents fire in a dry forest . . . except it wasn't fire he sensed, but ice. He turned toward the telephone, which was only four feet from where he was working, hearing the tendons in his neck creak. He thought he must see the pay phone caked with ice, ice that was sweating through the phone's black plastic case, extruding from the holes in the earpiece and the mouthpiece in lines of blue ice as thin as pencil-leads, hanging from the rotary dial and the coin return in icicle beards.

But it was just the phone, and all the coldness and death was on the inside.

He stared at it, hypnotized.

'Jack!' Smokey yelled. 'Answer the goddam phone! What the fuck am I paying you for?'

* * *

Jack looked toward Smokey, as desperate as a cornered animal . . . but Smokey was staring back with that thin-lipped, out-of-patience expression that he got on his face just before he popped Lori one. He started toward the phone, barely aware that his feet were moving; he stepped deeper and deeper into the capsule of coldness, feeling the gooseflesh run up his arms, feeling the moisture crackle in his nose.

He reached out and grasped the phone. His hand went numb.

He put it to his ear. His ear went numb.

'Oatley Tap,' he said into that deadly blackness, and his mouth went numb.

The voice that came out of the phone was the cracked, rasping croak of something long dead, some creature which could never be seen by the living: the sight of it would drive a living person insane, or strike him dead with frost-etchings on his lips and staring eyes blinded by cataracts of ice. '*Jack,*' this scabrous, rattling voice whispered up out of the earpiece, and his face went numb, the way it did when you needed to spend a heavy day in the dentist's chair and the guy needled you up with a little too much Novocain. '*You get your ass back home, Jack.*'

From far away, a distance of light-years, it seemed, he could hear his voice repeating: 'Oatley Tap, is anyone there? Hello? . . . Hello? . . .'

Cold, so cold.

His throat was numb. He drew breath and his lungs seemed to freeze. Soon the chambers of his heart would ice up and he would simply drop dead.

That chilly voice whispered, '*Bad things can happen to a boy alone on the road, Jack. Ask anybody.*'

He hung the phone up with a quick, clumsy reaching

gesture. He pulled his hand back and then stood looking at the phone.

'Was it that asshole, Jack?' Lori asked, and her voice was distant . . . but a little closer than his own voice had seemed a few moments ago. The world was coming back. On the handset of the pay phone he could see the shape of his hand, outlined in a glittering rime of frost. As he looked, the frost began to melt and run down the black plastic.

3

That was the night – Thursday night – that Jack first saw Genny County's answer to Randolph Scott. The crowd was a little smaller than it had been Wednesday night – very much a day-before-payday crowd – but there were still enough men present to fill the bar and spill over into the tables and booths.

They were town men from a rural area where the plows were now probably rusting forgotten in back sheds, men who perhaps wanted to be farmers but had forgotten how. There were a lot of John Deere caps in evidence, but to Jack very few of these men looked as if they would be at home riding a tractor. These were men in gray chinos and brown chinos and green chinos; men with their names stitched on blue shirts in gold thread; men in squaretoed Dingo Boots and men in great big clumping Survivors. These men carried their keys on their belts. These men had wrinkles but no laugh-lines; their mouths were dour. These men wore cowboy hats and when Jack looked at the bar from in back of the stools, there were as many as eight who looked like Charlie Daniels in the chewing-tobacco ads. But these men didn't chew; these men smoked cigarettes, and a lot of them.

Jack was cleaning the bubble front of the juke-box when Digger Atwell came in. The juke was turned off; the Yankees were on the cable, and the men at the bar were watching intently. The night before, Atwell had been in the Oatley male's version of sports clothes (chinos, khaki shirt with a lot of pens in one of the two big pockets, steel-toed workboots). Tonight he was wearing a blue cop's uniform. A large gun with wood grips hung in a holster on his creaking leather belt.

He glanced at Jack, who thought of Smokey saying *I've heard that ole Digger's got a taste for kids on the road. Boys, mostly*, and flinched back as if guilty of something. Digger Atwell grinned a wide, slow grin. 'Decided to stick around for a while, boy?'

'Yes, sir,' Jack muttered, and squirted more Windex onto the juke's bubble front, although it was already as clean as it was going to get. He was only waiting for Atwell to go away. After a while, Atwell did. Jack turned to watch the beefy cop cross to the bar . . . and that was when the man at the far left end of the bar turned around and looked at him.

Randolph Scott, Jack thought at once, *that's just who he looks like.*

But in spite of the rangy and uncompromising lines of his face, the real Randolph Scott had had an undeniable look of heroism; if his good looks had been harsh, they had also been part of a face that could smile. This man looked both bored and somehow crazy.

And with real fright, Jack realized the man was looking at him, at *Jack*. Nor had he simply turned around during the commercial to see who might be in the bar; he had turned around to look at Jack. Jack knew this was so.

The phone. The ringing phone.

With a tremendous effort, Jack pulled his gaze away. He looked back into the bubble front of the juke and saw his own frightened face hovering, ghostlike, over the records inside.

The telephone began to shriek on the wall.

The man at the left end of the bar looked at it . . . and then looked back at Jack, who stood frozen by the jukebox with his bottle of Windex in one hand and a rag in the other, his hair stiffening, his skin freezing.

'If it's that asshole again, I'm gonna get me a whistle to start blowing down the phone when he calls, Smokey,' Lori was saying as she walked toward it. 'I swear to God I am.'

She might have been an actress in a play, and all the customers extras paid the standard SAG rate of thirty-five dollars a day. The only two real people in the world were him and this dreadful cowboy with the big hands and the eyes Jack could not . . . quite . . . see.

Suddenly, shockingly, the cowboy mouthed these words: *Get your ass home.* And winked.

The phone stopped ringing even as Lori stretched out her hand to it.

Randolph Scott turned around, drained his glass, and yelled, 'Bring me another tapper, okay?'

'I'll be damned,' Lori said. 'That phone's got the ghosts.'

4

Later on, in the storeroom, Jack asked Lori who the guy was who looked like Randolph Scott.

'Who looks like *who*?' she asked.

'An old cowboy actor. He was sitting down at the end of the bar.'

She shrugged. 'They all look the same to me, Jack. Just a bunch of swinging dicks out for a good time. On Thursday nights they usually pay for it with the little woman's Beano money.'

'He calls beers "tappers".'

Her eyes lit. 'Oh yeah! Him. He looks mean.' She said this last with actual appreciation . . . as if admiring the straightness of his nose or the whiteness of his smile.

'Who is he?'

'I don't know his name,' Lori said. 'He's only been around the last week or two. I guess the mill must be hiring again. It—'

'For Christ's sake, Jack, did I tell you to run me out a keg or not?'

Jack had been in the process of walking one of the big kegs of Busch onto the foot of the hand-dolly. Because his weight and the keg's weight were so close, it was an act requiring a good deal of careful balancing. When Smokey shouted from the doorway, Lori screamed and Jack jumped. He lost control of the keg and it went over on its side, the cap shooting out like a champagne cork, beer following in a white-gold jet. Smokey was still shouting at him but Jack could only stare at the beer, frozen . . . until Smokey popped him one.

When he got back out to the taproom perhaps twenty minutes later, holding a Kleenex against his swelling nose, Randolph Scott had been gone.

5

I'm six.

John Benjamin Sawyer is six.

Six –

Jack shook his head, trying to clear this steady, repeating thought out as the rangy millhand who was not a millhand leaned closer and closer. His eyes . . . yellow and somehow scaly. He – *it* – blinked, a rapid, milky, swimming blink, and Jack realized it had nictitating membranes over its eyeballs.

'You were supposed to get *gone*,' it whispered again, and reached toward Jack with hands that were beginning to twist and plate and harden.

The door banged open, letting in a raucous flood of the Oak Ridge Boys.

'Jack, if you don't quit lollygagging, I'm going to have to make you sorry,' Smokey said from behind Randolph Scott. Scott stepped backward. No melting, hardening hooves here; his hands were just hands again – big and powerful, their backs crisscrossed with prominent ridged veins. There was another milky, swirling sort of blink that didn't involve the eyelids at all . . . and then the man's eyes were not yellow but a simple faded blue. He gave Jack a final glance and then headed toward the men's room.

Smokey came toward Jack now, his paper cap tipped forward, his narrow weasel's head slightly inclined, his lips parted to show his alligator teeth.

'Don't make me speak to you again,' Smokey said. 'This is your last warning, and don't you think I don't mean it.'

As it had against Osmond, Jack's fury suddenly rose up – that sort of fury, closely linked as it is to a sense of hopeless injustice, is perhaps never as strong as it is at twelve

– college students sometimes think they feel it, but it is usually little more than an intellectual echo.

This time it boiled over.

'I'm not your dog, so don't you treat me like I am,' Jack said, and took a step toward Smokey Updike on legs that were still rubbery with fear.

Surprised – possibly even flabbergasted – by Jack's totally unexpected anger, Smokey backed up a step.

'Jack, I'm warning you—'

'No, man. I'm warning *you*,' Jack heard himself say. 'I'm not Lori. I don't want to be hit. And if you hit me, I'm going to hit you back, or something.'

Smokey Updike's discomposure was only momentary. He had most assuredly not seen everything – not living in Oatley, he hadn't – but he *thought* he had, and even for a minor leaguer, sometimes assurance can be enough.

He reached out to grab Jack's collar.

'Don't you smart off to me, Jack,' he said, drawing Jack close. 'As long as you're in Oatley, my dog is just what you are. As long as you're in Oatley I'll pet you when I want and I'll beat you when I want.'

He administered a single neck-snapping shake. Jack bit his tongue and cried out. Hectic spots of anger now glowed in Smokey's pale cheeks like cheap rouge.

'You may not think that is so right now, but Jack, it is. As long as you're in Oatley you're my dog, and you'll be in Oatley until I decide to let you go. And we might as well start getting that learned right now.'

He pulled his fist back. For a moment the three naked sixty-watt bulbs which hung in this narrow hallway sparkled crazily on the diamond chips of the horseshoe-shaped pinky ring he wore. Then the fist pistoned forward and slammed into the side of Jack's face. He was driven backward into the graffiti-covered wall, the side of his face first flaring and then going numb. The taste of his own blood washed into his mouth.

Smokey looked at him – the close, judgemental stare of a man who might be thinking about buying a heifer or a lottery number. He must not have seen the expression he wanted to see in Jack's eye, because he grabbed the dazed boy again, presumably the better to center him for a second shot.

At that moment a woman shrieked, from the Tap, *'No, Glen! No!'* There was a tangle of bellowing male voices, most of them alarmed. Another woman screamed – a high, drilling sound. Then a gunshot.

'Shit on *toast*!' Smokey cried, enunciating each word as carefully as an actor on a Broadway stage. He threw Jack back against the wall, whirled, and slammed out through the swinging door. The gun went off again and there was a scream of pain.

Jack was sure of only one thing – the time had come to get out. Not at the end of tonight's shift, or tomorrow's, or on Sunday morning. Right *now*.

The uproar seemed to be quieting down. There were no sirens, so maybe nobody had gotten shot . . . but, Jack remembered, cold, the millhand who looked like Randolph Scott was still down in the men's can.

Jack went into the chilly, beer-smelling storeroom, knelt by the kegs, and felt around for his pack. Again there was that suffocating certainty, as his fingers encountered nothing but thin air and the dirty concrete floor, that one of them – Smokey or Lori – had seen him hide the pack and had taken it. All the better to keep you in Oatley, my dear. Then relief, almost as suffocating as the fear, when his fingers touched the nylon.

Jack donned the pack and looked longingly toward the loading door at the back of the storeroom. He would much rather use that door – he didn't want to go down to the fire-door at the end of the hall. That was too close to the men's bathroom. But if he opened the loading door, a red light would go on at the bar. Even if Smokey was still sorting out the ruckus on the floor, Lori would see that light and tell him.

So . . .

He went to the door which gave on the back corridor. He eased it open a crack and applied one eye. The corridor was empty. All right, that was cool. Randolph Scott had tapped a kidney and gone back to where the action was while Jack was getting his backpack. Great.

Yeah, except maybe he's still in there. You want to meet him in the hall, Jacky? Want to watch his eyes turn yellow again? Wait until you're sure.

But he couldn't do that. Because Smokey would see he wasn't out in the Tap, helping Lori and Gloria swab tables, or behind the bar, unloading the dishwasher. He would come back here to finish teaching Jack what his place was in the great scheme of things. So –

So what? Get going!

Maybe he's in there waiting for you, Jacky . . . maybe he's going to jump out just like a big bad Jack-in-the-Box . . .

The lady or the tiger? Smokey or the millhand? Jack hesitated a moment longer in an agony of indecision. That the man with the yellow eyes was still in the bathroom was a possibility; that Smokey would be back was a certainty.

Jack opened the door and stepped out into the narrow

hallway. The pack on his back seemed to gain weight – an eloquent accusation of his planned escape to anyone who might see it. He started down the hallway, moving grotesquely on tiptoe in spite of the thundering music and the roar of the crowd, his heart hammering in his chest.

I was six, Jacky was six.

So what? Why did that keep coming back?

Six.

The corridor seemed longer. It was like walking on a treadmill. The fire-door at the far end seemed to draw closer only by agonizing degrees. Sweat now coated his brow and his upper lip. His gaze flicked steadily toward the door to the right, with the black outline of a dog on it. Beneath this outline was the word POINTERS. And at the end of the corridor, a door of fading, peeling red. The sign on the door said EMERGENCY USE ONLY! ALARM WILL SOUND! In fact, the alarm bell had been broken for two years. Lori had told him so when Jack had hesitated about using the door to take out the trash.

Finally almost there. Directly opposite POINTERS.

He's in there, I know he is . . . and if he jumps out I'll scream . . . I . . . I'll . . .

Jack put out a trembling right hand and touched the crash-bar of the emergency door. It felt blessedly cool to his touch. For one moment he really believed he would simply fly out of the pitcher plant and into the night . . . free.

Then the door *behind* him suddenly banged open, the door to SETTERS, and a hand grabbed his backpack. Jack uttered the high-pitched, despairing shriek of a trapped animal and lunged at the emergency door, heedless of the pack and the magic juice inside it. If the straps had broken he would have simply gone fleeing through the trashy, weedy vacant lot behind the Tap, and never mind anything else.

But the straps were tough nylon and didn't break. The door opened a little way, revealing a brief dark wedge of the night, and then thumped shut again. Jack was pulled into the women's room. He was whirled around and then thrown backward. If he had hit the wall dead on, the bottle of magic juice would undoubtedly have shattered in the pack, drenching his few clothes and good old Rand McNally with the odor of rotting grapes. Instead, he hit the room's one wash-basin with the small of his back. The pain was giant, excruciating.

The millhand was walking toward him slowly, hitching up his jeans with hands that had begun to twist and thicken.

'You were supposed to be gone, kid,' he said, his voice roughening, becoming at every moment more like the snarl of an animal.

Jack began to edge to his left, his eyes never leaving the man's face. His eyes now seemed almost transparent, not just yellow but lighted from within . . . the eyes of a hideous Halloween jack-o'-lantern.

'But you can trust old Elroy,' the cowboy-thing said, and now it grinned to reveal a mouthful of great curving teeth, some of them jaggedly broken off, some black with rot. Jack screamed. 'Oh, you can trust Elroy,' it said, its words now hardly discernible from a doglike growl. 'He ain't gonna hurt you *too* bad.

'You'll be all right,' it growled, moving toward Jack, 'you'll be all right, oh yeah, you'll . . .' It continued to talk, but Jack could no longer tell what it was saying. Now it was only snarling.

Jack's foot hit the tall wastecan by the door. As the

cowboy-thing reached for him with its hooflike hands, Jack grabbed the can and threw it. The can bounced off the Elroy-thing's chest. Jack tore open the bathroom door and lunged to the left, toward the emergency door. He slammed into the crash-bar, aware that Elroy was right behind him. He lurched into the dark behind the Oatley Tap.

There was a colony of overloaded garbage cans to the right of the door. Jack blindly swept three of them behind him, heard them clash and rattle – and then a howl of fury as Elroy stumbled into them.

He whirled in time to see the thing go down. There was even a moment to realize – *Oh dear Jesus a tail it's got something like a tail* – that the thing was now almost entirely an animal. Golden light fell from its eyes in weird rays, like bright light falling through twin keyholes.

Jack backed away from it, pulling the pack from his back, trying to undo the catches with fingers which felt like blocks of wood, his mind a roaring confusion –

– *Jacky was six God help me Speedy Jacky was SIX God please* –

– of thoughts and incoherent pleas. The thing snarled and flailed at the garbage cans. Jack saw one hoof-hand go up and then come whistling down, splitting the side of one corrugated metal can in a jagged slash a yard long. It got up again, stumbled, almost fell, and then began to lurch toward Jack, its snarling, rippling face now almost at chest level. And somehow, through its barking growls, he was able to make out what it was saying. 'Now I'm not just gonna ream you, little chicken. Now I'm gonna kill you . . . *after*.'

Hearing it with his *ears*? Or in his *head*?

It didn't matter. The space between this world and that had shrunk from a universe to a mere membrane.

The Elroy-thing snarled and came toward him, now unsteady and awkward on its rear feet, its clothes bulging in all the wrong places, its tongue swinging from its fanged mouth. Here was the vacant lot behind Smokey Updike's Oatley Tap, yes, here it was at last, choked with weeds and blown trash – a rusty bedspring here, the grille of a 1957 Ford over there, and a ghastly sickle moon like a bent bone in the sky overhead, turning every shard of broken glass into a dead staring eye, and this hadn't begun in New Hampshire, had it? No. It hadn't begun when his mother got sick, or with the appearance of Lester Parker. It had begun when –

Jacky was six. When we all lived in California and no one lived anywhere else and Jack was –

He fumbled at the straps of his pack.

It came again, seeming almost to dance, for a moment reminding him of some animated Disney cartoon-figure in the chancy moonlight. Crazily, Jack began to laugh. The thing snarled and leaped at him. The swipe of those heavy hoof-claws again missed him by barest inches as he danced back through the weeds and litter. The Elroy-thing came down on the bedspring and somehow became entangled in it. Howling, snapping white gobbets of foam into the air, it pulled and twisted and lunged, one foot buried deep in the rusty coils.

Jack groped inside his pack for the bottle. He dug past socks and dirty undershorts and a wadded, fragrant pair of jeans. He seized the neck of the bottle and yanked it out.

The Elroy-thing split the air with a howl of rage, finally pulling free of the bedspring.

Jack hit the cindery, weedy, scruffy ground and rolled over, the last two fingers of his left hand hooked around one pack-strap, his right hand holding the bottle. He worked at the cap with the thumb and forefinger of his left hand, the pack dangling and swinging. The cap spun off.

Can it follow me? he wondered incoherently, tipping the bottle to his lips. *When I go, do I punch some kind of hole through the middle of things? Can it follow me through and finish me on the other side?*

Jack's mouth filled with that rotten dead-grape taste. He gagged, his throat closing, seeming to actually reverse direction. Now that awful taste filled his sinuses and nasal passages as well and he uttered a deep, shaking groan. He could hear the Elroy-thing screaming now, but the scream seemed far away, as if it were on one end of the Oatley tunnel and he, Jack, were falling rapidly toward the other end. And this time there *was* a sense of falling and he thought: *Oh my God what if I just flipped my stupid self over a cliff or off a mountain over there?*

He held on to the pack and the bottle, his eyes screwed desperately shut, waiting for whatever might happen next – Elroy-thing or no Elroy-thing, Territories or oblivion – and the thought which had haunted him all night came swinging back like a dancing carousel horse – Silver Lady, maybe Ella Speed. He caught it and rode it down in a cloud of the magic juice's awful smell, holding it, waiting for whatever would happen next, feeling his clothes change on his body.

Six oh yes when we were all six and nobody was anything else and it was California who blows that sax daddy is it Dexter Gordon or is it is it what does Mom mean when she says we're living on a fault-line and where where oh where do you go Daddy you and Uncle Morgan oh Daddy sometimes he looks at you like like oh like there is a fault-line in his head and an earthquake going on behind his eyes and you're dying in it oh Daddy!

Falling, twisting, turning in the middle of limbo, in

the middle of a smell like a purple cloud, Jack Sawyer, John Benjamin Sawyer, Jacky, Jacky

– *was six when it started to happen, and who blew that sax, Daddy? Who blew it when I was six, when Jacky was six, when Jacky –*

CHAPTER ELEVEN

THE DEATH OF JERRY BLEDSOE

1

was six . . . when it really started, Daddy, when the engines that eventually pulled him to Oatley and beyond began to chug away. There had been loud saxophone music. *Six. Jacky was six.* At first his attention had been entirely on the toy his father had given him, a scale model of a London taxi – the toy car was heavy as a brick, and on the smooth wooden floors of the new office a good push sent it rumbling straight across the room. Late afternoon, first grade all the way on the other side of August, a neat new car that rolled like a tank on the strip of bare wood behind the couch, a contented, relaxed feeling in the air-conditioned office . . . no more work to do, no more phone calls that couldn't wait until the next day. Jack pushed the heavy toy taxi down the strip of bare wood, barely able to hear the rumbling of the solid rubber tires under the soloing of a saxophone. The black car struck one of the legs of the couch, spun sideways, and stopped. Jack crawled down the length of the couch after it. His father had his feet up on his desk, and Uncle Morgan had parked himself in one of the chairs on the other side of the couch. Each man nursed a drink; soon they would put down their glasses, switch off the turntable and the amplifier, and go downstairs to their cars.

when we were all six and nobody was anything else and it was California

'Who's playing that sax?' he heard Uncle Morgan ask, and, half in a reverie, heard that familiar voice in a new way: something whispery and hidden in Morgan Sloat's voice coiled into Jacky's ear. He touched the top of the toy taxi and his fingers were as cold as if it were of ice, not English steel.

'That's Dexter Gordon, is who that is,' his father answered. His voice was as lazy and friendly as it always was, and Jack slipped his hand around the heavy taxi.

'Good record.'

'*Daddy Plays the Horn.* It is a nice old record, isn't it?'

'I'll have to look for it.' And then Jack thought he knew what that strangeness in Uncle Morgan's voice was all about – Uncle Morgan didn't really like jazz at all, he just pretended to in front of Jack's father. Jack had known this fact about Morgan Sloat for most of his childhood, and he thought it was silly that his father couldn't see it too. Uncle Morgan was never going to look for a record called *Daddy Plays the Horn*, he was just flattering Phil Sawyer – and maybe the reason Phil Sawyer didn't see it was that like everyone else he never paid quite enough attention to Morgan Sloat. Uncle Morgan, smart and ambitious ('smart as a wolverine, sneaky as a courthouse lawyer,' Lily said), good old Uncle Morgan deflected observation – your eye just sort of naturally slid off him. When he was a kid, Jacky would have bet, his teachers would have had trouble even remembering his name.

'Imagine what this guy would be like over there,' Uncle

Morgan said, for once fully claiming Jack's attention. That falsity still played through his voice, but it was not Sloat's hypocrisy that jerked up Jacky's head and tightened his fingers on his heavy toy – the words *over there* had sailed straight into his brain and now were gonging like chimes. Because *over there* was the country of Jack's Daydreams. He had known that immediately. His father and Uncle Morgan had forgotten that he was behind the couch, and they were going to talk about the Daydreams.

His father knew about the Daydream-country. Jack could never have mentioned the Daydreams to either his father or his mother, but his father knew about the Daydreams because he had to – simple as that. And the next step, felt along Jack's emotions more than consciously expressed, was that his dad helped keep the Daydreams safe.

But for some reason, equally difficult to translate from emotion into language, the conjunction of Morgan Sloat and the Daydreams made the boy uneasy.

'Hey?' Uncle Morgan said. 'This guy would really turn em around, wouldn't he? They'd probably make him Duke of the Blasted Lands, or something.'

'Well, probably not that,' Phil Sawyer said. 'Not if they liked him as much as we do.'

But Uncle Morgan doesn't like him, Dad, Jacky thought, suddenly clear that this was important. *He doesn't like him at all, not really, he thinks that music is too* loud, *he thinks it takes something from him . . .*

'Oh, you know a lot more about it than I do,' Uncle Morgan said in a voice that sounded easy and relaxed.

'Well, I've been there more often. But you're doing a good job of catching up.' Jacky heard that his father was smiling.

'Oh, I've learned a few things, Phil. But really, you know – I'll never get over being grateful to you for showing all that to me.' The two syllables of *grateful* filled with smoke and the sound of breaking glass.

But all of these little warnings could not do more than dent Jack's intense, almost blissful satisfaction. They were talking about the Daydreams. It was magical, that such a thing was possible. What they said was beyond him, their terms and vocabulary were too adult, but six-year-old Jack experienced again the wonder and joy of the Daydreams, and was at least old enough to understand the direction of their conversation. The Daydreams were real, and Jacky somehow shared them with his father. That was half his joy.

2

'Let me just get some things straight,' Uncle Morgan said, and Jacky saw the word *straight* as a pair of lines knotting around each other like snakes. 'They have magic like we have physics, right? We're talking about an agrarian monarchy, using magic instead of science.'

'Sure,' Phil Sawyer said.

'And presumably they've gone on like that for centuries. Their lives have never changed very much.'

'Except for political upheavals, that's right.'

Then Uncle Morgan's voice tightened, and the excitement he tried to conceal cracked little whips within his consonants. 'Well, forget about the political stuff. Suppose we think about us for a change. You'll say – and I'd agree with you, Phil – that we've done pretty well out of the Territories already, and that we'd have to be careful about how we introduce changes there. I have no problems at all with that position. I feel the same way myself.'

Jacky could feel his father's silence.

'Okay,' Sloat continued. 'Let's go with the concept that, within a situation basically advantageous to ourselves, we can spread the benefits around to anybody on our side. We don't sacrifice the advantage, but we're not greedy about the bounty it brings. We owe these people, Phil. Look what they've done for us. I think we could put ourselves into a really synergistic situation over there. Our energy can feed their energy and come up with stuff we've never even thought of, Phil. And we end up looking generous, which we are – but which also doesn't hurt us.' He would be frowning forward, the palms of his hands pressed together. 'Of course I don't have a total window on this situation, you know that, but I think the synergy alone is worth the price of admission, to tell you the truth. But Phil – can you imagine how much fucking clout we'd swing if we gave them electricity? If we got modern weapons to the right guys over there? Do you have any idea? I think it'd be awesome. *Awesome*.' The damp, squashy sound of his clapping hands. 'I don't want to catch you unprepared or anything, but I thought it might be time for us to think along those lines – to think, Territories-wise, about increasing our involvement.'

Phil Sawyer still said nothing. Uncle Morgan slapped his hands together again. Finally Phil Sawyer said, in a noncommittal voice, 'You want to think about increasing our involvement.'

'I think it's the way to go. And I can give you chapter and verse, Phil, but I shouldn't have to. You can probably remember as well as I can what it was like before we started going there together. Hey, maybe we could have made it all on our own, and maybe we would have, but as for me, I'm grateful not to be representing a couple of broken-down strippers and Little Timmy Tiptoe anymore.'

'Hold on,' Jack's father said.

'Airplanes,' Uncle Morgan said. 'Think airplanes.'

'Hold on, hold on there, Morgan, I have a lot of ideas that apparently have yet to occur to you.'

'I'm always ready for new ideas,' Morgan said, and his voice was smoky again.

'Okay. I think we have to be careful about what we do over there, partner. I think anything major – any real changes we bring about – just might turn around and bite our asses back here. Everything has consequences, and some of those consequences might be on the uncomfortable side.'

'Like what?' Uncle Morgan asked.

'Like war.'

'That's nuts, Phil. We've never seen anything . . . unless you mean Bledsoe . . .'

'I do mean Bledsoe. Was that a coincidence?'

Bledsoe? Jack wondered. He had heard the name before; but it was vague.

'Well, that's a long way from war, to put it mildly, and I don't concede the connection anyhow.'

'All right. Do you remember hearing about how a Stranger assassinated the old King over there – a long time ago? You ever hear about that?'

'Yeah, I suppose,' Uncle Morgan said, and Jack heard again the falseness in his voice.

His father's chair squeaked – he was taking his feet off his desk, leaning forward. 'The assassination touched off a minor war over there. The followers of the old King had to put down a rebellion led by a couple of disgruntled nobles. These guys saw their chance to take over and run things – seize lands, impound property, throw their enemies in jail, make themselves rich.'

'Hey, be fair,' Morgan broke in. 'I heard about this stuff, too. They also wanted to bring some kind of political order to a crazy inefficient system – sometimes you have to be tough, starting out. I can see that.'

'And it's not for us to make judgments about their politics, I agree. But here's my point. That little war over there lasted about three weeks. When it was over, maybe a hundred people had been killed. Fewer, probably. Did anyone ever tell you when that war began? What year it was? What day?'

'No,' Uncle Morgan muttered in a sulky voice.

'It was the first of September, 1939. Over here, it was the day Germany invaded Poland.' His father stopped talking, and Jacky, clutching his black toy taxi behind the couch, yawned silently but hugely.

'That's screwball,' Uncle Morgan finally said. '*Their* war started *our?* Do you really believe that?'

'I do believe that,' Jack's father said. 'I believe a three-week squabble over there in some way sparked off a war here that lasted six years and killed millions of people. Yes.'

'Well . . .' Uncle Morgan said, and Jack could see him beginning to huff and blow.

'There's more. I've talked to lots of people over there about this, and the feeling I get is that the stranger who assassinated the King was a *real* Stranger, if you see what I mean. Those who saw him got the feeling that he was uncomfortable with Territories clothes. He acted like he was unsure of local customs – he didn't understand the money right away.'

'Ah.'

'Yes. If they hadn't torn him to pieces right after he stuck a knife into the King, we could be sure about this, but I'm sure anyhow that he was—'

'Like us.'

'Like us. That's right. A visitor. Morgan, I don't think we can mess around too much over there. Because we simply don't know what the effects will be. To tell you the truth, I think we're affected all the time by things that go on in the Territories. And should I tell you another crazy thing?'

'Why not?' Sloat answered.

'That's not the only other world out there.'

3

'Bullshit,' Sloat said.

'I mean it. I've had the feeling, once or twice when I was there, that I was near to somewhere *else* – the Territories' Territories.'

Yes, Jack thought, *that's right, it has to be, the Daydreams' Daydreams, someplace even more beautiful, and on the other side of that is the Daydreams' Daydreams' Daydreams, and on the other side of that is another place, another world nicer still . . . He realized for the first time that he had become very sleepy.*

The Daydreams' Daydreams

And then he was almost immediately asleep, the heavy little taxi in his lap, his whole body simultaneously weighty with sleep, anchored to the strip of wooden floor, and so blissfully light.

The conversation must have continued – there must have been much that Jacky missed. He rose and fell, heavy and light, through the second whole side of *Daddy Plays the*

Horn, and during that time Morgan Sloat must at first have argued – gently, but with what squeezings of his fists, what contortions of his forehead! – for his plan; then he must have allowed himself to seem persuadable, then finally persuaded by his partner's doubts. At the end of this conversation, which returned to the twelve-year-old Jacky Sawyer in the dangerous borderland between Oatley, New York, and a nameless Territories village, Morgan Sloat had allowed himself to seem not only *persuaded* but positively grateful for the lessons. When Jack woke up, the first thing he heard was his father asking, 'Hey, did Jack disappear or something?' and the second thing was Uncle Morgan saying, 'Hell, I guess you're right, Phil. You have a way of seeing right to the heart of things, you're great the way you do that.'

'Where the hell is Jack?' his father said, and Jack stirred behind the couch, really waking up now. The black taxi thudded to the floor.

'Aha,' Uncle Morgan said. 'Little pitchers and big ears, *peut-être*?'

'You behind there, kiddo?' his father said. Noises of chairs pushing back across the wooden floor, of men standing up.

He said, '*Oooh*,' and slowly lifted the taxi back into his lap. His legs felt stiff and uncomfortable – when he stood, they would tingle.

His father laughed. Footsteps came toward him. Morgan Sloat's red, puffy face appeared over the top of the couch. Jack yawned and pushed his knees into the back of the couch. His father's face appeared beside Sloat's. His father was smiling. For a moment, both of those grown-up adult male heads seemed to be floating over the top of the couch. 'Let's move on home, sleepyhead,' his father said. When the boy looked into Uncle Morgan's face, he saw calculation sink into his skin, slide underneath his jolly-fat-man's cheeks like a snake beneath a rock. He looked like Richard Sloat's daddy again, like good old Uncle Morgan who always gave spectacular Christmas and birthday presents, like good old sweaty Uncle Morgan, so easy not to notice. But what had he looked like before? *like a human earthquake, like a man crumbling apart over the fault-line behind his eyes, like something all wound up and waiting to explode . . .*

'How about a little ice cream on the way home, Jack?' Uncle Morgan said to him. 'That sound good to you?'

'Uh,' Jack said.

'Yeah, we can stop off at that place in the lobby,' his father said.

'Yummy-yummy-yum,' Uncle Morgan said. 'Now we're really talking about synergy,' and smiled at Jack once more.

This happened when he was six, and in the midst of his weightless tumble through limbo, it happened again – the horrible purple taste of Speedy's juice backed up into his mouth, into the passages behind his nose, and all of that languid afternoon of six years before replayed itself out in his mind. He saw it just as if the magic juice brought total recall, and so speedily that he lived through that afternoon in the same few seconds which told him that this time the magic juice really was going to make him vomit.

Uncle Morgan's eyes smoking, and inside Jack, a question smoking too, demanding and demanding to finally come out . . .

Who played
What changes what changes
Who plays those changes, daddy?
Who

killed Jerry Bledsoe? The magic juice forced itself into the boy's mouth, stinging threads of it nauseatingly trickled into his nose, and just as Jack felt loose earth beneath his hands he gave up and vomited rather than drown. *What* killed Jerry Bledsoe? Foul purple stuff shot from Jack's mouth, choking him, and he blindly pushed himself backward – his feet and legs snagged in tall stiff weeds. Jack pushed himself up on his hands and knees and waited, patient as a mule, his mouth drooping open, for the second attack. His stomach clenched, and he did not have time to groan before more of the stinking juice burned up through his chest and throat and spattered out of his mouth. Ropey pink strings of saliva hung from his lips, and Jack feebly brushed them away. He wiped his hand on his pants. Jerry Bledsoe, yes. *Jerry* – who'd always had his name spelled out on his shirt, like a gas-station attendant. Jerry, who had died when – The boy shook his head and wiped his hands across his mouth again. He spat into a nest of sawtoothed wild grass sprouting like a giant's corsage out of the gray-brown earth. Some dim animal instinct he did not understand made him push loose earth over the pinkish pool of vomit. Another reflex made him brush the palms of his hands against his trousers. Finally he looked up.

He was kneeling, in the last of the evening light, on the edge of a dirt lane. No horrible Elroy-thing pursued him – he had known that immediately. Dogs penned in a wooden, cagelike enclosure barked and snarled at him, thrusting their snouts through the cracks of their jail. On the other side of the fenced-in dogs was a rambling wooden structure, and from here too doggy noises rose up into the immense sky. These were unmistakably similar to the noises Jack had just been hearing from the other side of a wall in the Oatley Tap: the sounds of drunken men bellowing at each other. A bar – here it would be an inn or a public house, Jack imagined. Now that he was no longer sickened by Speedy's juice, he could smell the pervasive, yeasty odors of malt and hops. He could not let the men from the inn discover him.

For a moment he imagined himself running from all those dogs yipping and growling through the cracks in their enclosure, and then he stood up. The sky seemed to tilt over his head, to darken. And back home, in *his* world, what was happening? A nice little disaster in the middle of Oatley? Maybe a nice little flood, a sweet little fire? Jack slipped quietly backward away from the inn, then began to move sideways through the tall grass. Perhaps sixty yards away, thick candles burned in the windows of the only other building he could see. From somewhere not far off to his right drifted the odor of pigs. When Jack had gone half the distance between the inn and the house, the dogs ceased growling and snapping, and he slowly began walking forward toward the Western Road. The night was dark and moonless.

Jerry Bledsoe.

4

There were other houses, though Jack did not see them until he was nearly before them. Except for the noisy drinkers behind him at the inn, here in the country Territories people went to bed when the sun did. No candles burned in these small square windows. Themselves squarish and dark, the houses on either side of the Western Road sat in a puzzling isolation – something was wrong, as in a visual game from a child's magazine, but Jack could not identify it. Nothing hung upside down, nothing burned, nothing seemed extravagantly out of place. Most of the houses had thick fuzzy roofs which resembled haystacks with crewcuts, but Jack assumed that these were thatch – he had heard of it, but never seen it before. *Morgan*, he thought with a sudden thrill of panic, *Morgan of Orris*, and saw the two of them, the man with long hair and a built-up boot and his father's sweaty workaholic partner, for a moment jumbled up together – Morgan Sloat with pirate's hair and a hitch in his walk. But Morgan – this world's Morgan – was not what was Wrong with This Picture.

Jack was just now passing a short squat one-story building like an inflated rabbit hutch, crazily half-timbered with wide black wooden X's. A fuzzy crewcut thatch capped this building too. If he were walking out of Oatley – or even running out of Oatley to be closer to the truth – what would he expect to see in the single dark window of this hutch for giant rabbits? He knew: the dancing glimmer of a television screen. But of course Territories houses did not have television sets inside them, and the absence of that colorful glimmer was not what had puzzled him. It was something else, something so much an aspect of any grouping of houses along a road that its absence left a hole in the landscape. You noticed the hole even if you could not quite identify what was absent.

Television, television sets . . . Jack continued past the half-timbered little building and saw ahead of him, its front door set only inches back from the verge of the road, another gnomishly small dwelling. This one seemed to have a sod, not thatched, roof, and Jack smiled to himself – this tiny village had reminded him of Hobbiton. Would a Hobbit cable-stringer pull up here and say to the lady of the . . . shack? doghouse? . . . anyhow, would he say, 'Ma'am, we're installing cable in your area, and for a small monthly fee – hitch you up right now – you get fifteen new channels, you get *Midnight Blue*, you get the all-sports and all-weather channels, you get . . .'?

And that, he suddenly realized, was it. In front of these houses were no poles. No wiring! No TV antennas complicated the sky, no tall wooden poles marched the length of the Western Road, because in the Territories there was no electricity. Which was why he had not permitted himself to identify the absent element. Jerry Bledsoe had been, at least part of the time, Sawyer & Sloat's electrician and handyman.

5

When his father and Morgan Sloat used that name, *Bledsoe*, he thought he had never heard it before – though, having remembered it, he must have heard the handyman's last name once or twice. But Jerry Bledsoe was almost always just *Jerry*, as it said above the pocket on his workshirt. 'Can't Jerry do something about the air conditioning?' 'Get Jerry to oil the hinges on that door, will you? The squeaks are driving me batshit.' And Jerry would appear, his work-clothes clean and pressed, his thinning rust-red hair combed flat, his glasses round and earnest, and quietly fix whatever was wrong. There was a Mrs Jerry, who kept the creases sharp and clean in the tan workpants, and several small Jerrys, whom Sawyer & Sloat invariably remembered at Christmas. Jack had been small enough to associate the name *Jerry* with Tom Cat's eternal adversary, and so imagined that the handyman and Mrs Jerry and the little Jerrys lived in a giant mouse-hole, accessible by a curved arch cut into a baseboard.

But who had killed Jerry Bledsoe? His father and Morgan Sloat, always so sweet to the Bledsoe children at Christmastime?

Jack stepped forward into the darkness of the Western Road, wishing that he had forgotten completely about Sawyer & Sloat's handyman, that he had fallen asleep as soon as he had crawled behind the couch. Sleep was what he wanted now – wanted it far more than the uncomfortable thoughts which that six-years-dead conversation had aroused in him. Jack promised himself that as soon as he was sure he was at least a couple of miles past the last house, he would find someplace to sleep. A field would do, even a ditch. His legs did not want to move anymore; all his muscles, even his bones, seemed twice their weight.

It had been just after one of those times when Jack had wandered into some enclosed place after his father and found that Phil Sawyer had somehow contrived a disappearance. Later, his father would manage to vanish from his bedroom, from the dining room, from the conference room at Sawyer & Sloat. On this occasion he executed his mystifying trick in the garage beside the house on Rodeo Drive.

Jack, sitting unobserved on the little knob of raised land which was the closest thing to a hill offered by this section of Beverly Hills, saw his father leave their house by the front door, cross the lawn while digging in his pockets for money or keys, and let himself into the garage by the side door. The white door on the right side should have swung up seconds later; but it remained stubbornly closed. Then Jack realized that his father's car was where it had been all this Saturday morning, parked at the curb directly in front of the house. Lily's car was gone – she'd plugged a cigarette into her mouth and announced that she was taking herself off to a screening of *Dirt Track*, the latest film by the director of *Death's Darling*, and nobody by God had better try to stop her – and so the garage was empty. For minutes.

Jack waited for something to happen. Neither the side door nor the big front doors opened. Eventually Jack slid down off the grassy elevation, went to the garage, and let himself in. That wide familiar space was entirely empty. Dark oil stains patterned the gray cement floor. Tools hung from silvery hooks set into the walls. Jack grunted in astonishment, called out, 'Dad?' and looked at everything again, just to make sure. This time he saw a cricket hop toward the shadowy protection of a wall, and for a second *almost* could have believed that magic was real and some malign wizard had happened along and . . . the cricket reached the wall and slipped into an invisible crack. No, his father had not been turned into a cricket. Of course he had not. 'Hey,' the boy said – to himself it seemed. He walked backward to the side door and left the garage. Sunlight fell on the lush, springy lawns of Rodeo Drive. He would have called someone, but whom? The police? *My daddy walked into the garage and I couldn't find him in there and now I'm scared . . .*

Two hours later Phil Sawyer came walking up from the Beverly Wilshire end of the street. He carried his jacket over his shoulder, had pulled down the knot of his tie – to Jack, he looked like a man returning from a journey around the world.

Jack jumped down from his anxious elevation and tore toward his father. 'You sure cover the ground,' his father said, smiling, and Jack flattened himself against his legs. 'I thought you were taking a nap, Travelling Jack.'

They heard the telephone ringing as they came up the walk, and some instinct – perhaps the instinct to keep his father close – made Jacky pray that it had already rung a dozen times, that whoever was calling would hang up before they reached the front door. His father ruffled the hair on his crown, put his big warm hand on the back of his neck, then pulled open the door and made it to the phone in five long strides. 'Yes, Morgan,' Jacky heard his father say. 'Oh? Bad news? You'd better tell me, yes.' After a long moment of silence in which the boy could hear the tinny, rasping sound of Morgan Sloat's voice stealing through the telephone wires: 'Oh, Jerry. My God. Poor Jerry. I'll be right over.' Then his father looked straight at him, not smiling, not winking, not doing anything but taking him in. 'I'll come over, Morgan. I'll have to bring Jack, but he can wait in the car.' Jack felt his muscles relax, and was so relieved that he did not ask why he had to wait in the car, as he would have at any other time.

Phil drove up Rodeo Drive to the Beverly Hills Hotel, turned left onto Sunset, and pointed the car toward the office building. He said nothing.

His father zipped through the oncoming traffic and swung the car into the parking lot beside the office building. Already in the lot were two police cars, a fire truck, Uncle Morgan's pocket-size white Mercedes convertible, the rusted old Plymouth two-door that had been the handyman's car. Just inside the entrance Uncle Morgan was talking to a policeman, who shook his head slowly, slowly, in evident sympathy. Morgan Sloat's right arm squeezed the shoulders of a slim young woman in a dress too large for her who had twisted her face into his chest. Mrs Jerry, Jack knew, seeing that most of her face was obscured by a white handkerchief she had pressed to her eyes. A behatted, raincoated fireman pushed a mess of twisted metal and plastic, ashes and broken glass into a disorderly heap far past them down the hall. Phil said, 'Just sit here for a minute or two, okay, Jacky?' and sprinted toward the entrance. A young Chinese woman sat talking to a policeman on a concrete abutment at the end of the parking lot. Before her lay a crumpled object it took Jack a moment to recognize as a bike. When Jack inhaled, he smelled bitter smoke.

Twenty minutes later, both his father and Uncle Morgan left the building. Still gripping Mrs Jerry, Uncle Morgan waved goodbye to the Sawyers. He led the woman around to the passenger door of his tiny car. Jack's father twirled his own car out of the lot and back into the traffic on Sunset.

'Is Jerry hurt?' Jack asked.

'Some kind of freak accident,' his father said. 'Electricity – the whole building could've gone up in smoke.'

'Is Jerry hurt?' Jack repeated.

'Poor son of a bitch got hurt so bad he's dead,' said his father.

Jack and Richard Sloat needed two months to really put the story together out of the conversations they overheard. Jack's mother and Richard's housekeeper supplied other details – the housekeeper, the goriest.

Jerry Bledsoe had come in on a Saturday to try to iron out some of the kinks in the building's security system. If he tampered with the delicate system on a weekday, he was sure to confuse or irritate the tenants with the klaxon alarm whenever he accidentally set it off. The security system was wired into the building's main electrical board, set behind two large removable walnut panels on the ground floor. Jerry had set down his tools and lifted off the panels, having already seen that the lot was empty and nobody would jump out of his skin when the alarm went off. Then he went downstairs to the telephone in his basement cubicle and told the local precinct house to ignore any signals from the Sawyer & Sloat address until his next telephone call. When he went back upstairs to tackle the mare's nest of wires coming into the board from all the contact points, a twenty-three-year-old woman named Lorette Chang was just riding her bicycle into the building's lot – she was distributing a leaflet advertising a restaurant which was due to open down the street in fifteen days.

Miss Chang later told the police that she looked through the glass front door and saw a workman enter the hall from the basement. Just before the workman picked up his screwdriver and touched the wiring panel, she felt the parking lot wobble beneath her feet. It was, she assumed, a mini-earthquake: a lifelong resident of Los Angeles, Lorette Chang was untroubled by any seismic event that did not actually knock anything down. She saw Jerry Bledsoe set his feet (so he felt it, too, though no one else did), shake his head, then gently insert the tip of the screwdriver into a hive of wires.

And then the entry and downstairs corridor of the Sawyer & Sloat building turned into a holocaust.

The entire wiring panel turned instantly to a solid rectangular body of flame; bluish-yellow arcs of what looked like lightning shot out and encased the workman. Electronic horns bawled and bawled: KA-WHAAAAM! KA-WHAAAM! A ball of fire six feet high fell right out of the wall, slammed the already dead Jerry Bledsoe aside, and rolled down the corridor toward the lobby. The transparent front door blew into flying glass and smoking, twisted pieces of frame. Lorette Chang dropped her bike and sprinted toward the pay telephone across the street. As she told the fire department the building's address and noticed that her bicycle had been twisted nearly in half by whatever force had burst through the door, Jerry Bledsoe's roasted corpse still swayed upright back and forth before the devastated panel. Thousands of volts poured through his body, twitching it with regular surges, snapping it back and forth in a steady pulse. All the handyman's body hair and most of his clothes had fried off, and his skin had become a cooked blotchy gray. His eyeglasses, a solidifying lump of brown plastic, covered his nose like a poultice.

Jerry Bledsoe. *Who plays those changes, daddy?* Jack made his feet move until he had gone half an hour without seeing another of the little thatched cottages. Unfamiliar stars in unfamiliar patterns lay all over the sky above him – messages in a language he could not read.

CHAPTER TWELVE
JACK GOES TO THE MARKET

1

He slept that night in a sweetly fragrant Territories haystack, first burrowing his way in and then turning around so the fresh air could reach him along the tunnel he had made. He listened apprehensively for small scuttering sounds – he had heard or read somewhere that fieldmice were great haystack fans. If they were in this one, then a great big mouse named Jack Sawyer had scared them into silence. He relaxed little by little, his left hand tracing the shape of Speedy's bottle – he had plugged the top with a piece of springy moss from a small stream where he had stopped to drink. He supposed it was entirely possible that some of the moss would fall into the bottle, or already had. What a pity, it would spoil the piquant flavor and the delicate bouquet.

As he lay in here, warm at last, heavily sleepy, the feeling he was most aware of was relief . . . as if there had been a dozen ten-pound weights strapped to his back and some kind soul had undone the buckles and allowed them to fall to the ground. He was in the Territories again, the place which such charming folks as Morgan of Orris,

Osmond the Bullwhipper, and Elroy the Amazing Goat-man all called home, the Territories, where anything could happen.

But the Territories could be good, too. He remembered that from his earliest childhood, when everyone had lived in California and no one had lived anyplace else. The Territories could be good, and it seemed he felt the goodness around him now, as calmly, inarguably sweet as the smell of the haystack, as clear as the smell of the Territories air.

Does a fly or a ladybug feel relief if an unexpected gust of wind comes along and tilts the pitcher plant just enough to allow the drowning insect to fly out? Jack didn't know . . . but he knew that he was out of Oatley, away from Fair Weather Clubs and old men who wept over their stolen shopping carts, away from the smell of beer and the smell of puke . . . most important of all, he was away from Smokey Updike and the Oatley Tap.

He thought he might travel in the Territories for a while, after all.

And so thinking, fell asleep.

2

He had walked two, perhaps three miles along the Western Road the following morning, enjoying the sunshine and the good, earthy smell of fields almost ready for the harvests of summer's end, when a cart pulled over and a whiskery farmer in what looked like a toga with rough breeches under it pulled up and shouted:

'Are you for market-town, boy?'

Jack gaped at him, half in a panic, realizing that the man was not speaking English – never mind 'prithee' or 'Dost thou go cross-gartered, varlet,' it wasn't English *at all.*

There was a woman in a voluminous dress sitting beside the whiskery farmer; she held a boy of perhaps three on her lap. She smiled pleasantly enough at Jack and rolled her eyes at her husband. 'He's a simpleton, Henry.'

They're not speaking English . . . but whatever it is they're speaking, I understand it. I'm actually thinking in that language . . . and that's not all – I'm seeing in it, or with it, or whatever it is I mean.

Jack realized he had been doing it the last time he had been in the Territories, too – only then he had been too confused to realize it; things had moved too fast, and *everything* had seemed strange.

The farmer leaned forward. He smiled, showing teeth which were absolutely horrid. 'Are you a simpleton, laddie?' he asked, not unkindly.

'No,' he said, smiling back as best he could, aware that he had not said *no* but some Territories word which meant *no* – when he had flipped, he had changed his speech and his way of thinking (his way of *imaging*, anyway – he did not have that word in his vocabulary, but understood what he meant just the same), just as he had changed his clothes. 'I'm not simple. It's just that my mother told me to be careful of people I might meet along the road.'

Now the farmer's wife smiled. 'Your mother was right,' she said. 'Are you for the market?'

'Yes,' Jack said. 'That is, I'm headed up the road – west.'

'Climb up in the back, then,' Henry the farmer said. 'Daylight's wasting. I want to sell what I have if I can and be home again before sunset. Corn's poor but it's the last of the season. Lucky to have corn in ninemonth at all. Someone may buy it.'

'Thank you,' Jack said, climbing into the back of the

low wagon. Here, dozens of corn were bound with rough hanks of rope and stacked like cordwood. If the corn was poor, then Jack could not imagine what would constitute good corn over here – they were the biggest ears he had ever seen in his life. There were also small stacks of squashes and gourds and things that looked like pumpkins – but they were reddish instead of orange. Jack didn't know what they were, but he suspected they would taste wonderful. His stomach rumbled busily. Since going on the road, he had discovered what hunger was – not as a passing acquaintance, something you felt dimly after school and which could be assuaged with a few cookies and a glass of milk souped up with Nestlé's Quik, but as an intimate friend, one that sometimes moved away to a distance but who rarely left entirely.

He was sitting with his back to the front of the wagon, his sandal-clad feet dangling down, almost touching the hard-packed dirt of the Western Road. There was a lot of traffic this morning, most of it bound for the market, Jack assumed. Every now and then Henry bawled a greeting to someone he knew.

Jack was still wondering how those apple-colored pumpkins might taste – and just where his next meal was going to come from, anyway – when small hands twined in his hair and gave it a brisk tug – brisk enough to make his eyes water.

He turned and saw the three-year-old standing there in his bare feet, a big grin on his face and a few strands of Jack's hair in each of his hands.

'Jason!' his mother cried – but it was, in its way, an indulgent cry (*Did you see the way he pulled that hair? My, isn't he strong!*) – 'Jason, that's not *nice*!'

Jason grinned, unabashed. It was a big, dopey, sunshiney

grin, as sweet in its way as the smell of the haystack in which Jack had spent the night. He couldn't help returning it . . . and while there had been no politics or calculation in his returning grin, he saw he had made a friend of Henry's wife.

'Sit,' Jason said, swaying back and forth with the unconscious movement of a veteran sailor. He was still grinning at Jack.

'Huh?'

'Yap.'

'I'm not getting you, Jason.'

'Sit-yap.'

'I'm not—'

And then Jason, who was husky for a three-year-old, plopped into Jack's lap, still grinning.

Sit-yap, oh yeah, I get it, Jack thought, feeling the dull ache from his testicles spreading up into the pit of his stomach.

'Jason, *bad*!' his mother called back in that same indulgent, but-isn't-he-cute voice . . . and Jason, who knew who ruled the roost, grinned his dopey, sweetly charming grin.

Jack realized that Jason was wet. Very, extremely, indubitably wet.

Welcome back to the Territories, Jack-O.

And sitting there with the child in his arms and warm wetness slowly soaking through his clothes, Jack began to laugh, his face turned up to the blue, blue sky.

3

A few minutes later Henry's wife worked her way to where Jack was sitting with the child on his lap and took Jason back.

'Oooh, wet, bad baby,' she said in her indulgent voice. *Doesn't my Jason wet big!* Jack thought, and laughed again. That made Jason laugh, and Mrs Henry laughed with them.

As she changed Jason, she asked Jack a number of questions – ones he had heard often enough in his own world. But here he would have to be careful. He was a stranger, and there might be hidden trapdoors. He heard his father telling Morgan, . . . *a* real *Stranger, if you see what I mean.*

Jack sensed that the woman's husband was listening closely. He answered her questions with a careful variation of the Story – not the one he told when he was applying for a job but the one he told when someone who had picked him up thumbing got curious.

He said he had come from the village of All-Hands' – Jason's mother had a vague recollection of hearing of the place, but that was all. Had he really come so far? she wanted to know. Jack told her that he had. And where was he going? He told her (and the silently listening Henry) that he was bound for the village of California. That one she had not heard of, even vaguely, in such stories as the occasional peddler told. Jack was not exactly very surprised . . . but he was grateful that neither of them exclaimed, 'California? Whoever heard of a village named California? Who are you trying to shuck and jive, boy?' In the Territories there had to be lots of places – whole areas as well as villages – of which people who lived in their own little areas had never heard. No power poles. No electricity. No movies. No cable TV to tell them how wonderful things were in Malibu or Sarasota. No Territories version of Ma Bell, advertising that a three-minute call to the Outposts after five p.m. cost only $5.83, plus tax, rates may be higher on God-Pounders' Eve and some other holidays. *They live in a mystery*, he thought.

When you live in a mystery, you don't question a village simply because you never heard of it. California doesn't sound any wilder than a place named All-Hands'.

Nor did they question. He told them that his father had died the year before, and that his mother was quite ill (he thought of adding that the Queen's repossession men had come in the middle of the night and taken away their donkey, grinned, and decided that maybe he ought to leave that part out). His mother had given him what money she could (except the word that came out in that strange language wasn't really *money* – it was something like *sticks*) and had sent him off to the village of California, to stay with his Aunt Helen.

'These are hard times,' Mrs Henry said, holding Jason, now changed, more closely to her.

'All-Hands' is near the summer palace, isn't it, boy?' It was the first time Henry had spoken since inviting Jack aboard.

'Yes,' Jack said. 'That is, fairly near. I mean—'

'You never said what your father died of.'

Now he had turned his head. His gaze was narrow and assessing, the former kindness gone; it had been blown out of his eyes like candle-flames in a wind. Yes, there were trapdoors here.

'Was he ill?' Mrs Henry asked. 'So much illness these days – pox, plague – hard times . . .'

For a wild moment Jack thought of saying, *No, he wasn't ill, Mrs Henry. He took a lot of volts, my dad. You see he went off one Saturday to do some work, and he left Mrs Jerry and all the little Jerrys – including me – back at home. This was when we all lived in a hole in the baseboard and nobody lived anywhere else, you see. And do you know what? He stuck his screwdriver into a bunch of wires and Mrs Feeny, she works over at Richard Sloat's house, she heard Uncle Morgan talking on the phone and he said the electricity came out, all of the electricity, and it cooked him, it cooked him so bad that his glasses melted all over his nose, only you don't know about glasses because you don't have them here. No glasses . . . no electricity . . . no* Midnight Blue *. . . no airplanes. Don't end up like Mrs Jerry, Mrs Henry. Don't –*

'Never mind was he ill,' the whiskered farmer said. 'Was he *political*?'

Jack looked at him. His mouth was working but no sounds came out. He didn't know what to say. There were too many trapdoors.

Henry nodded, as if he had answered. 'Jump down, laddie. Market's just over the next rise. I reckon you can ankle it from here, can't you?'

'Yes,' Jack said. 'I reckon I can.'

Mrs Henry looked confused . . . but she was now holding Jason away from Jack, as if he might have some contagious disease.

The farmer, still looking back over his shoulder, smiled a bit ruefully. 'I'm sorry. You seem a nice enough lad, but we're simple people here – whatever's going on back yonder by the sea is something for great lords to settle. Either the Queen will die or she won't . . . and of course, someday she must. God pounds all His nails sooner or later. And what happens to little people when they meddle into the affairs of the great is that they get hurt.'

'My father—'

'I don't want to know about your father!' Henry said sharply. His wife scrambled away from Jack, still holding Jason to her bosom. 'Good man or bad, I don't know and I don't *want* to know – all I know is that he's a dead man,

I don't think you lied about that, and that his son has been sleeping rough and has all the smell of being on the dodge. The son doesn't talk as if he comes from any of these parts. So climb down. I've a son of my own, as you see.'

Jack got down, sorry for the fear in the young woman's face – fear he had put there. The farmer was right – little people had no business meddling in the affairs of the great. Not if they were smart.

CHAPTER THIRTEEN
THE MEN IN THE SKY

1

It was a shock to discover that the money he had worked so hard to get literally *had* turned into sticks – they looked like toy snakes made by an inept craftsman. The shock lasted only for a moment, however, and he laughed ruefully at himself. The sticks *were* money, of course. When he came over here, *everything* changed. Silver dollar to gryphon-coin, shirt to jerkin, English to Territories speech, and good old American money to – well, to jointed sticks. He had flipped over with about twenty-two dollars in all, and he guessed that he had exactly the same amount in Territories money, although he had counted fourteen joints on one of the money-sticks and better than twenty on the other.

The problem wasn't so much money as cost – he had very little idea of what was cheap and what was dear, and as he walked through the market, Jack felt like a contestant on *The New Price is Right* – only, if he flubbed it here, there wouldn't be any consolation prize and a clap on the back from Bob Barker; if he flubbed it here, they might . . . well, he didn't know for sure *what* they might do. Run him out for sure. Hurt him, rough him up? Maybe. Kill him? Probably not, but it was impossible to be absolutely certain. They were little people. They were not political. And he was a stranger.

Jack walked slowly from one end of the loud and busy market-day throng to the other, wrestling with the problem. It now centered mostly in his stomach – he was dreadfully hungry. Once he saw Henry, dickering with a man who had goats to sell. Mrs Henry stood near him, but a bit behind, giving the men room to trade. Her back was to Jack, but she had the baby hoisted in her arms – *Jason, one of the little Henrys*, Jack thought – and Jason saw him. The baby waved one chubby hand at Jack and Jack turned away quickly, putting as much crowd as he could between himself and the Henrys.

Everywhere was the smell of roasting meat, it seemed. He saw vendors slowly turning joints of beef over charcoal fires both small and ambitious; he saw 'prentices laying thick slices of what looked like pork on slabs of homemade bread and taking them to the buyers. They looked like runners at an auction. Most of the buyers were farmers like Henry, and it appeared that they also called for food the way people entered a bid at an auction – they simply raised one of their hands imperiously, the fingers splayed out. Jack watched several of these transactions closely, and in every case the medium of exchange was the jointed sticks . . . but how many knuckles would be enough? he wondered. Not that it mattered. He had to eat, whether the transaction marked him as a stranger or not.

He passed a mime-show, barely giving it a glance although the large audience that had gathered – women and children, most of them – roared with appreciative laughter and applauded. He moved toward a stall with canvas sides where a big man with tattoos on his slabbed biceps stood on one side of a trench of smouldering charcoal in the earth. An iron spit about seven feet long ran over the charcoal. A sweating, dirty boy stood at each end. Five large roasts were impaled along the length of the pit, and the boys were turning them in unison.

'Fine meats!' the big man was droning. 'Fine meats! *Fiiine* meats! Buy my fine meats! Fine meats here! Fine meats right here!' In an aside to the boy closest to him: 'Put your back into it, God pound you.' Then back to his droning, huckstering cry.

A farmer passing with his adolescent daughter raised his hand, and then pointed at the joint of meat second from the left. The boys stopped turning the spit long enough for their boss to hack a slab from the roast and put it on a chunk of bread. One of them ran with it to the farmer, who produced one of the jointed sticks. Watching closely, Jack saw him break off two knuckles of wood and hand them to the boy. As the boy ran back to the stall the customer pocketed his money-stick with the absent but careful gesture of any man repocketing his change, took a gigantic bite of his open-faced sandwich, and handed the rest to his daughter, whose first chomp was almost as enthusiastic as her father's.

Jack's stomach boinged and goinged. He had seen what he had to see . . . he hoped.

'Fine meats! Fine meats! Fine—' The big man broke off and looked down at Jack, his beetling brows drawing together over eyes that were small but not entirely stupid. 'I hear the song your stomach is singing, friend. If you have money, I'll take your trade and bless you to God in my prayers tonight. If you haven't, then get your stupid sheep's face out of here and go to the devil.'

Both boys laughed, although they were obviously tired – they laughed as if they had no control over the sounds they were making.

But the maddening smell of the slowly cooking meat would not let him leave. He held out the shorter of his jointed sticks and pointed to the roast which was second from the left. He didn't speak. It seemed safer not to. The vendor grunted, produced his crude knife from his wide belt again, and cut a slice – it was a smaller slice than the one he had cut the farmer, Jack observed, but his stomach had no business with such matters; it was rumbling crazily in anticipation.

The vendor slapped the meat on bread and brought it over himself instead of handing it to either of the boys. He took Jack's money-stick. Instead of two knuckles, he broke off three.

His mother's voice, sourly amused, spoke up in his mind: *Congratulations, Jack-O . . . you've just been screwed.*

The vendor was looking at him, grinning around a mouthful of wretched, blackish teeth, daring him to say anything, to protest in any way. *You just ought to be grateful I only took three knuckles instead of all fourteen of them. I could have, you know. You might as well have a sign hung around your neck, boy: I AM A STRANGER, AND ON MY OWN. So tell me, Sheep's-Face: do you want to make an issue of it?*

What he wanted didn't matter – he obviously *couldn't* make an issue of it. But he felt that thin, impotent anger again.

'Go on,' the vendor said, tiring of him. He flapped a big hand in Jack's face. His fingers were scarred, and there was blood under his nails. 'You got your food. Now get out of here.'

Jack thought, *I could show you a flashlight and you'd run*

like all the devils of hell were after you. Show you an airplane and you'd probably go crazy. You're maybe not as tough as you think, chum.

He smiled, and perhaps there was something in his smile that the meat-vendor didn't like, because he drew away from Jack, his face momentarily uneasy. Then his brows beetled together again.

'Get out, I said!' he roared. 'Get out, God pound you!' And this time Jack went.

2

The meat was delicious. Jack gobbled it and the bread it sat on, and then unselfconsciously licked the juice from his palms as he strolled along. The meat *did* taste like pork . . . and yet it didn't. It was somehow richer, tangier than pork. Whatever it was, it filled the hole in the middle of him with authority. Jack thought he could take it to school in bag lunches for a thousand years.

Now that he had managed to shut his belly up – for a little while, anyway – he was able to look about himself with more interest . . . and although he didn't know it, he had finally begun to blend into the crowd. Now he was only one more rube from the country come to the market-town, walking slowly between the stalls, trying to gawk in every direction at once. Hucksters recognized him, but only as one more potential mark among many. They yelled and beckoned at him, and as he passed by they yelled and beckoned at whoever happened to be behind him – man, woman, or child. Jack gaped frankly at the wares scattered all around him, wares both wonderful and strange, and amidst all the others staring at them he ceased to be a stranger himself – perhaps because he had given up his effort to seem blasé in a place where *no one acted blasé*. They laughed, they argued, they haggled . . . but no one seemed bored.

The market-town reminded him of the Queen's pavillion without the air of strained tension and too-hectic gaiety – there was the same absurdly rich mingle of smells (dominated by roasting meat and animal ordure), the same brightly dressed crowds (although even the most brightly dressed people Jack saw couldn't hold a candle to some of the dandies he had seen inside the pavillion), the same unsettling but somehow exhilarating juxtaposition of the perfectly normal, cheek by jowl with the extravagantly strange.

He stopped at a stall where a man was selling carpets with the Queen's portrait woven into them. Jack suddenly thought of Hank Scoffler's mom and smiled. Hank was one of the kids Jack and Richard Sloat had hung around with in L.A. Mrs Scoffler had a thing for the most garish decorations Jack had ever seen. And God, wouldn't she have loved these rugs, with the image of Laura DeLoessian, her hair done up in a high, regal coronet of braids, woven into them! Better than her velvet paintings of Alaskan stags or the ceramic diorama of the Last Supper behind the bar in the Scoffler living room . . .

Then the face woven into the rugs seemed to change even as he looked at it. The face of the Queen was gone and it was his mother's face he saw, repeated over and over and over, her eyes too dark, her skin much too white.

Homesickness surprised Jack again. It rushed through his mind in a wave and he called out for her in his heart – *Mom! Hey, Mom! Jesus, what am I doing here? Mom!!* – wondering with a lover's longing intensity what she was doing now, right this minute. Sitting at the window, smoking, looking out at the ocean, a book open beside her? Watching TV? At a movie? Sleeping? Dying?

Dead? an evil voice added before he could stop it. *Dead, Jack? Already dead?*

Stop it.

He felt the burning sting of tears.

'Why so sad, my little lad?'

He looked up, startled, and saw the rug salesman looking at him. He was as big as the meat-vendor, and his arms were also tattooed, but his smile was open and sunny. There was no meanness in it. That was a big difference.

'It's nothing,' Jack said.

'If it's nothing makes you look like that, you ought to be thinking of *something*, my son, my son.'

'I looked that bad, did I?' Jack asked, smiling a little. He had also grown unselfconscious about his speech – at least for the moment – and perhaps that was why the rug salesman heard nothing odd or off-rhythm in it.

'Laddie, you looked as if you only had one friend left on this side o' the moon and you just saw the Wild White Wolf come out o' the north an' gobble him down with a silver spoon.'

Jack smiled a little. The rug salesman turned away and took something from a smaller display to the right of the largest rug – it was oval and had a short handle. As he turned it over the sun flashed across it – it was a mirror. To Jack it looked small and cheap, the sort of thing you might get for knocking over all three wooden milk-bottles in a carnival game.

'Here, laddie,' the rug salesman said. 'Take a look and see if I'm not right.'

Jack looked into the mirror and gaped, for a moment so stunned he thought his heart must have forgotten to beat. It was him, but he looked like something from Pleasure Island in the Disney version of *Pinocchio*, where too much pool-shooting and cigar-smoking had turned boys into donkeys. His eyes, normally as blue and round as an Anglo-Saxon heritage could make them, had gone brown and almond-shaped. His hair, coarsely matted and falling across the middle of his forehead, had a definite manelike look. He raised one hand to brush it away, and touched only bare skin – in the mirror, his fingers seemed to fade right through the hair. He heard the vendor laugh, pleased. Most amazing of all, long jackass-ears dangled down to below his jawline. As he stared, one of them twitched.

He thought suddenly: *I HAD* one of these!

And on the heels of that: *In the* Daydreams *I had one of these. Back in the regular world it was . . . was . . .*

He could have been no more than four. In the regular world (he had stopped thinking of it as the *real* world without even noticing) it had been a great big glass marble with a rosy center. One day while he was playing with it, it had rolled down the cement path in front of their house and before he could catch it, it had fallen down a sewer grate. It had been gone – forever, he had thought then, sitting on the curb with his face propped on his dirty hands and weeping. But it wasn't; here was that old toy rediscovered, just as wonderful now as it had been when he was three or four. He grinned, delighted. The image changed and Jack the Jackass became Jack the Cat, his face wise and secret with amusement. His eyes went from donkey-brown to tomcat-green. Now pert little gray-furred ears cocked alertly where the droopy donkey-ears had dangled.

'Better,' the vendor said. 'Better, my son. I like to see a happy boy. A happy boy is a healthy boy, and a healthy boy finds his way in the world. *Book of Good Farming* says that, and if it doesn't, it should. I may just scratch it in my copy, if I ever scratch up enough scratch from my pumpkin-patch to buy a copy someday. Want the glass?'

'Yes!' Jack cried. 'Yeah, great!' He groped for his sticks. Frugality was forgotten. 'How much?'

The vendor frowned and looked around swiftly to see if they were being watched. 'Put it away, my son. Tuck it down deep, that's the way. You show your scratch, you're apt to lose the batch. Dips abound on market-ground.'

'What?'

'Never mind. No charge. Take it. Half of em get broken in the back of my wagon when I drag em back to my store come ten-month. Mothers bring their little 'uns over and they try it but they don't buy it.'

'Well, at least you don't deny it,' Jack said.

The vendor looked at him with some surprise and then they both burst out laughing.

'A happy boy with a snappy mouth,' the vendor said. 'Come see me when you're older and bolder, my son. We'll take your mouth and head south and treble what we peddle.'

Jack giggled. This guy was better than a rap record by the Sugarhill Gang.

'Thanks,' he said (a large, improbable grin had appeared on the chops of the cat in the mirror). 'Thanks very much!'

'Thank me to God,' the vendor said . . . then, as an afterthought: 'And watch your wad!'

Jack moved on, tucking the mirror-toy carefully into his jerkin, next to Speedy's bottle.

And every few minutes he checked to make sure his sticks were still there.

He guessed he knew what dips were, after all.

3

Two stalls down from the booth of the rhyming rug-vendor, a depraved-looking man with a patch askew over one eye and the smell of strong drink about him was trying to sell a farmer a large rooster. He was telling the farmer that if he bought this rooster and put it in with his hens, the farmer would have nothing but double-yolkers for the next twelve-month.

Jack, however, had neither eyes for the rooster nor ears for the salesman's pitch. He joined a crowd of children who were staring at the one-eyed man's star attraction. This was a parrot in a large wicker cage. It was almost as tall as the youngest children in the group, and it was as smoothly, darkly green as a Heineken beer-bottle. Its eyes were a brilliant gold . . . its four eyes. Like the pony he had seen in the pavillion stables, the parrot had two heads. It gripped its perch with its big yellow feet and looked placidly in two directions at once, its two tufted crowns almost touching.

The parrot was talking to itself, to the amusement of the children – but even in his amazement Jack noted that, while they were paying close attention to the parrot, they seemed neither stunned nor even very wondering. They weren't like kids seeing their first movie, sitting stupefied in their seats and all eyes; they were more like kids getting their regular Saturday-morning cartoon-fix. This was a wonder, yes, but not a wholly new one. And to whom do wonders pall more rapidly than the very young?

'*Bawwwrk!* How high is up?' East-Head enquired.

'As low as low,' West-Head responded, and the children giggled.

'*Graaak!* What's the great truth of noblemen?' East-Head now asked.

'That a king will be a king all his life, but once a knight's enough for any man!' West-Head replied pertly. Jack smiled and several of the older children laughed, but the younger ones only looked puzzled.

'And what's in Mrs Spratt's cupboard?' East-Head now posed.

'A sight no man shall see!' West-Head rejoined, and although Jack was mystified, the children went into gales of laughter.

The parrot solemnly shifted its talons on its perch and made droppings into the straw below it.

'And what frightened Alan Destry to death in the night?'

'He saw his wife – *growwwwk!* – getting out of the bath!'

The farmer was now walking away and the one-eyed salesman still had charge of the rooster. He rounded furiously on the children. 'Get out of here! Get out of here before I kick your asses square!'

The children scattered. Jack went with them, sparing a last bemused look over his shoulder at the wonderful parrot.

4

At another stall he gave up two knuckles of wood for an apple and a dipper of milk – the sweetest, richest milk he had ever tasted. Jack thought that if they had milk like that back at home, Nestlé's and Hershey's would go bankrupt in a week.

He was just finishing the milk when he saw the Henry family moving slowly in his direction. He handed the dipper back to the woman in the stall, who poured the lees thriftily back into a large wooden cask beside her. Jack hurried on, wiping a milk moustache from his upper lip and hoping uneasily that no one who had drunk from the dipper before him had had leprosy or herpes or anything like that. But he somehow didn't think such awful things even existed over here.

He walked up the market-town's main thoroughfare, past the mimers, past two fat women selling pots and pans (*Territories Tupperware*, Jack thought, and grinned), past that wonderful two-headed parrot (its one-eyed owner was now drinking quite openly from a clay bottle, reeling wildly from one end of his booth to the other, holding the dazed-looking rooster by the neck and yelling truculently at passersby – Jack saw the man's scrawny right arm was caked with yellowish-white guano, and grimaced), past an open area where farmers were gathered. He paused there for a moment, curious. Many of the farmers were smoking clay pipes, and Jack saw several clay bottles, much the same as the one the bird-salesman had been brandishing, go from hand to hand. In a long, grassy field, men were hitching stones behind large shaggy horses with lowered heads and mild, stupid eyes.

Jack passed the rug-stall. The vendor saw him and raised a hand. Jack raised one in turn and thought of calling *Use it, my man, but don't abuse it!* He decided he better not. He was suddenly aware that he felt blue. That feeling of strangeness, of being an outsider, had fallen over him again.

He reached the crossroads. The way going north and south was little more than a country lane. The Western Road was much wider.

Old Travelling Jack, he thought, and tried to smile. He straightened his shoulders and heard Speedy's bottle clink lightly against the mirror. *Here goes old Travelling Jack along the Territories version of Interstate 90.* Feets don't fail me now!

He set off again, and soon that great dreaming land swallowed him.

5

About four hours later, in the middle of the afternoon, Jack sat down in the tall grass by the side of the road and watched as a number of men – from this distance they looked little bigger than bugs – climbed a tall, rickety-looking tower. He had chosen this place to rest and eat his apple because it was here that the Western Road seemed to make its closest approach to that tower. It was still at least three miles away (and perhaps much more than that – the almost supernatural clarity of the air made distances extremely hard to judge), but it had been in Jack's view for an hour or more.

Jack ate his apple, rested his tired feet, and wondered what that tower could be, standing out there all by itself in a field of rolling grass. And, of course, he wondered why those men should be climbing it. The wind had blown quite steadily ever since he had left the market-town, and the tower was down-wind of Jack, but whenever it died away for a minute, Jack could hear them calling to each other . . . and laughing. There was a lot of laughing going on.

Some five miles west of the market, Jack had walked through a village – if your definition of a village stretched to cover five tiny houses and one store that had obviously been closed for a long time. Those had been the last human habitations he had seen between then and now. Just before glimpsing the tower, he had been wondering if he had already come to the Outposts without even knowing it. He remembered well enough what Captain Farren had said: *Beyond the Outposts the Western Road goes into nowhere . . . or into hell. I've heard it said that God Himself never ventures beyond the Outposts . . .*

Jack shivered a little.

But he didn't really believe he had come so far. Certainly there was none of the steadily deepening unease he had been feeling before he floundered into the living trees in his effort to get away from Morgan's diligence . . . the living trees which now seemed like a hideous prologue to all the time he had spent in Oatley.

Indeed, the good emotions he had felt from the time he woke up warm and rested inside the haystack until the time Henry the farmer had invited him to jump down from his wagon had now resurfaced: that feeling that the Territories, in spite of whatever evil they might harbor, were fundamentally good, and that he could be a part of this place anytime he wanted . . . that he was really no Stranger at all.

He had come to realize that he *was* part of the Territories for long periods of time. A strange thought had come to him as he swung easily along the Western Road, a thought which came half in English and half in whatever the Territories language was: *When I'm having a dream, the only time I really KNOW it's a dream is when I'm starting to wake up. If I'm dreaming and just wake up all at once – if the alarm clock goes off, or something – then I'm the most surprised guy alive. At first it's the waking that seems like a dream. And I'm no stranger over here when the dream gets deep – is that what I mean? No, but it's getting close. I bet my dad dreamed deep a lot. And I'll bet Uncle Morgan almost never does.*

He had decided he would take a swig out of Speedy's bottle and flip back the first time he saw anything that might be dangerous . . . even if he saw anything scary. Otherwise he would walk all day over here before returning to New York. In fact, he might have been tempted to spend the night in the Territories, if he'd had anything to eat beyond the one apple. But he didn't, and along the wide, deserted dirt track of the Western Road there was not a 7-Eleven or a Stop-'n-Go in sight.

The old trees which had surrounded the crossroads and the market-town had given way to open grassland on either side once Jack got past that final small settlement. He began to feel that he was walking along an endless causeway which crossed the middle of a limitless ocean. He travelled the Western Road alone that day under a sky that was bright and sunny but cool (*late September now, of course it's cool*, he thought, except the word which came to mind was not *September* but a Territories word which really did translate better as *ninemonth*). No pedestrians passed him, no wagons either loaded or empty. The wind blew pretty steadily, sighing through the ocean of grasses with a low sound that was both autumnal and lonely. Great ripples ran across the grasses before that wind.

If asked 'How do you feel, Jack?', the boy would have responded: 'Pretty good, thanks. Cheerful.' *Cheerful* is the word which would have come into his mind as he hiked through those empty grasslands: *rapture* was a word he associated most easily with the pop hit of the same name by the rock group Blondie. And he would have been astounded if told he had wept several times as he stood watching those great ripples chase each other toward the horizon, drinking in a sight that only a very few American children of his time had ever seen – huge empty tracts of land under a blue sky of dizzying width and breadth and, yes, even depth. It was a sky unmarked by either jet contrails across its dome or smutty bands of smog at any of its lower edges.

Jack was having an experience of remarkable sensory impact, seeing and hearing and smelling things which were brand-new to him, while other sensory input to which he had grown utterly accustomed was missing for the first time. In many ways he was a remarkably sophisticated child – brought up in a Los Angeles family where his father had been an agent and his mother a movie actress, it would have been odder if he had been naive – but he was still just a child, sophisticated or not, and that was undeniably his gain . . . at least in a situation such as this. That lonely day's journey across the grasslands would surely have produced sensory overload, perhaps even a pervasive sense of madness and hallucination, in an adult. An adult would have been scrabbling for Speedy's bottle – probably with fingers too shaky to grasp it very successfully – an hour west of the market-town, maybe less.

In Jack's case, the wallop passed almost completely through his conscious mind and into his subconscious. So when he blissed out entirely and began to weep, he was really unaware of the tears (except as a momentary doubling of vision which he attributed to sweat) and thought only: *Jeez, I feel good . . . it should feel spooky out here with no one around, but it doesn't.*

That was how Jack came to think of his rapture as no more than a good, cheerful feeling as he walked alone up the Western Road with his shadow gradually growing longer behind him. It did not occur to him that part of his emotional radiance might stem from the fact that hardly less than twelve hours before he had been a prisoner of Updike's Oatley Tap (the blood-blisters from the last keg to land on his fingers were still fresh); that hardly less than twelve hours ago he had escaped – barely! – some sort of murdering beast that he had begun to think of as a were-goat; that for the first time in his life he was on a wide, open road that was utterly deserted except for him; there was not a Coca-Cola sign anywhere in view, or a Budweiser billboard showing the World-Famous Clydesdales; no ubiquitous wires ran beside the road on either side or criss-crossed above it, as had been the case *on every road Jack Sawyer had ever travelled in his entire life*; there was not so much as even the distant rolling sound of an airplane, let alone the rolling thunder of the 747s on their final approaches to LAX, or the F-111s that were always blasting off from the Portsmouth Naval Air Station and then cracking the air over the Alhambra like Osmond's whip as they headed out over the Atlantic; there was only the sound of his feet on the road and the clean ebb and flow of his own respiration.

Jeez, I feel good, Jack thought, wiping absently at his eyes, and defined it all as 'cheerful'.

6

Now there was this tower to look at and wonder about.

Boy, you'd never get me up on that thing, Jack thought. He had gnawed the apple right down to the core, and without thinking about what he was doing or even taking his eyes off the tower, he dug a hole in the tough, springy earth with his fingers and buried the apple-core in it.

The tower seemed made of barn-boards, and Jack guessed it had to be at least five hundred feet high. It appeared to be a big hollow square, the boards rising on all sides in X after X. There was a platform on top, and Jack, squinting, could see a number of men strolling around up there.

Wind pushed by him in a gentle gust as he sat at the side of the road, his knees against his chest and his arms wrapped around them. Another of those grassy ripples ran away in the direction of the tower. Jack imagined the way that rickety thing must be swaying and felt his stomach turn over.

NEVER get me up there, he thought, not for a million bucks.

And then the thing he had been afraid might happen since the moment he had observed that there were men on the tower now *did* happen: one of them fell.

Jack came to his feet. His face wore the dismayed, slack-jawed expression of anyone who has ever been present at a circus performance where some dangerous trick has gone wrong – the tumbler who falls badly and lies in a huddled heap, the aerialist who misses her grip and bounces off the net with a thud, the human pyramid that unexpectedly collapses, spilling bodies into a heap.

Oh shit, oh cripes, oh –

Jack's eyes suddenly widened. For a moment his jaw sagged even farther – until it was almost lying on his breastbone, in fact – and then it came up and his mouth spread in a dazed, unbelieving grin. The man hadn't fallen from the tower, nor had he been blown off it. There were tonguelike protrusions on two sides of the platform – they looked like diving boards – and the man had simply walked out to the end of one of these and jumped off. Halfway down something began to unfurl – a parachute, Jack thought, but it would never have time to open.

Only it hadn't been a parachute.

It was wings.

The man's fall slowed and then stopped completely while he was still some fifty feet above the high fieldgrass. Then it reversed itself. The man was now flying upward and outward, the wings going up so high they almost touched – like the crowns on the heads of that Henny Youngman parrot – and then driving downward again with immense power, like the arms of a swimmer in a finishing sprint.

Oh wow, Jack thought, driven back to the dumbest cliché he knew by his total, utter amazement. This topped everything; this was an utter pisser. *Oh wow, look at that, oh wow.*

Now a second man leaped from the diving board at the top of the tower; now a third; now a fourth. In less than five minutes there must have been fifty men in the air, flying complicated but discernible patterns: out from the tower, describe a figure-eight, back over the tower and out to the other side, another figure-eight, back to the tower, alight on the platform, do it all again.

They spun and danced and crisscrossed in the air. Jack began to laugh with delight. It was a little like watching the water ballets in those corny old Esther Williams movies. Those swimmers – Esther Williams herself most of all, of course – always made it look easy, as if you yourself could dip and swirl like that, or as if you and a few of your friends could easily come off the opposite sides of the diving board in timed choreography, making a kind of human fountain.

But there was a difference. The men flying out there did not give that sense of effortlessness; they seemed to be expending prodigious amounts of energy to stay in the air, and Jack felt with sudden certainty that it hurt, the way some of the calisthenics in phys ed – leg-lifts, or halfway sit-ups, for instance – hurt. *No pain, no gain!* Coach would roar if someone had the nerve to complain.

And now something else occurred to him – the time his mother had taken him with her to see her friend Myrna, who was a *real* ballet dancer, practicing in the loft of a dance studio on lower Wilshire Boulevard. Myrna was part of a ballet troupe and Jack had seen her and the other dancers perform – his mother often made him go with her and it was mostly boring stuff, like church or *Sunrise Semester* on TV. But he had never seen Myrna in practice . . . never that close up. He had been impressed and a little frightened by the contrast between seeing ballet on stage, where everyone seemed to either glide or mince effortlessly on the tips of their *pointes*, and seeing it from less than five feet away, with harsh daylight pouring in the floor-to-ceiling windows and no music – only the choreographer rhythmically clapping his hands and yelling harsh criticisms. No praise; only criticisms. Their faces ran with sweat. Their leotards were wet with sweat. The room, as large and airy as it was, stank of sweat. Sleek muscles trembled and fluttered on the nervous edge of exhaustion. Corded tendons stood out like insulated cables. Throbbing veins popped out on foreheads and necks. Except for the choreographer's clapping and angry, hectoring shouts, the only sounds were the *thrupthud* of ballet dancers on *pointe* moving across the floor and harsh, agonized panting for breath. Jack had suddenly realized that these dancers were not just earning a living; they were killing themselves. Most of all he remembered their expressions – all that exhausted concentration, all that pain . . . but transcending the pain, or at least creeping around its edges, he had seen joy. Joy was unmistakably what that look was, and it had scared Jack because it had seemed inexplicable. What kind of person could get off by subjecting himself or herself to such steady, throbbing, excruciating pain?

And pain that he was seeing here, he thought. Were they actual winged men, like the bird-people in the old *Flash Gordon* serials, or were the wings more in the Icarus and Daedalus line, something that you strapped on? Jack found that it didn't really matter . . . at least, not to him.

Joy.

They live in a mystery, these people live in a mystery.

It's joy that holds them up.

That was what mattered. It was joy that held them up, no matter if the wings grew out of their backs or were somehow held on with buckles and clamps. Because what he saw, even from this distance, was the same sort of effort he had seen in the loft on lower Wilshire that day. All that profligate investment of energy to effect a splendid, momentary reversal of natural law. That such a reversal should demand so much and last such a short time was terrible; that people would go for it anyway was both terrible and wonderful.

And it's all just a game, he thought, and suddenly felt sure of it. A game, or maybe not even that – maybe it was only *practice* for a game, the way that all the sweat and trembling exhaustion in the Wilshire loft that day had just been practice. Practice for a show that only a few people would probably care to attend and which would probably close quickly.

Joy, he thought again, standing now, his face turned up to look at the flying men in the distance, the wind spilling his hair across his forehead. His time of innocence was fast approaching its end (and, if pressed, even Jack would have reluctantly agreed that he felt such an end approaching – a boy couldn't go on the road for long, couldn't go through many experiences such as the one he had gone through in Oatley, and expect to remain an innocent), but in those moments as he stood looking into the sky, innocence seemed to surround him; like the young fisherman during his brief moment of epiphany in the Elizabeth Bishop poem, everything was rainbow, rainbow, rainbow.

Joy – damn, but that's a cheerful little word.

Feeling better than he had since all of this began – and only God knew just how long ago *that* had been – Jack set off along the Western Road again, his step light, his face wreathed in that same silly, splendid grin. Every now and then he looked back over his shoulder, and he was able to see the fliers for a very long time. The Territories air was so clear it almost seemed to magnify. And even after he could no longer see them, that feeling of joy remained, like a rainbow inside his head.

7

When the sun began to go down, Jack realized he was putting off his return to the other world – to the *American*

Territories – and not just because of how terrible the magic juice tasted, either. He was putting it off because he didn't want to leave here.

A streamlet had flowed out of the grasslands (where small groves of trees had again begun to appear – billowy trees with oddly flat tops, like eucalyptus trees) and had hooked a right so that it flowed along beside the road. Farther off, to the right and ahead, was a huge body of water. It was *so* huge, in fact, that until the last hour or so Jack had thought it was a patch of sky that somehow had a slightly bluer color than the rest. But it wasn't sky; it was a lake. *A great lake*, he thought, smiling at the pun. He guessed that in the other world that would be Lake Ontario.

He felt good. He was headed in the right direction – maybe a little too far north, but he had no doubt that the Western Road would bend away from that direction soon enough. That feeling of almost manic joy – what he had defined as cheerfulness – had mellowed to a lovely sort of calm serenity, a feeling that seemed as clear as the Territories air. Only one thing marred his good feeling, and that was the memory

(*six, is six, Jack was six*)

of Jerry Bledsoe. Why had his mind given him such a hard time about coughing that memory up?

No – not the memory . . . the two memories. First me and Richard hearing Mrs Feeny telling her sister that the electricity came out and cooked him, that it melted his glasses all over his nose, that she heard Mr Sloat talking on the phone and he said so . . . and then being behind the couch, not really meaning to snoop or eavesdrop, and hearing my dad say 'Everything has consequences, and some of those consequences might be on the uncomfortable side.' And something surely made Jerry Bledsoe uncomfortable, didn't it? When your glasses end up melted all over your nose, I'd say you'd been through something mildly uncomfortable, yes . . .

Jack stopped. Stopped dead.

What are you trying to say?

You know what I'm trying to say, Jack. Your father was gone that day – he and Morgan both. They were over here. Where, over here? I think they were at the same spot over here where their building is in California, over in the American Territories. And they did something, or one of them did. Maybe something big, maybe no more than tossing a rock . . . or burying an applecore in the dirt. And it somehow . . . it echoed over there. It echoed over there and it killed Jerry Bledsoe.

Jack shivered. Oh yes, he supposed he knew why it had taken his mind so long to cough up the memory – the toy taxi, the murmur of the men's voices, Dexter Gordon blowing his horn. It hadn't wanted to cough it up. Because

(*who plays those changes daddy*)

it suggested that just by being over here he could be doing something terrible in the other world. Starting World War III? No, probably not. He hadn't assassinated any kings lately, young or old. But how much had it taken to set up the echo which had fried Jerry Bledsoe? Had Uncle Morgan shot Jerry's Twinner (if Jerry had had one)? Tried to sell some Territories bigwig on the concept of electricity? Or had it been just some little thing . . . something no more earth-shattering than buying a chunk of meat in a rural market-town? Who played those changes? *What* played those changes?

A nice flood, a sweet fire.

Suddenly Jack's mouth was as dry as salt.

He crossed to the little stream by the side of the road,

dropped to his knees, and put a hand down to scoop up water. His hand froze suddenly. The smooth-running stream had taken on the colors of the coming sunset . . . but these colors suddenly suffused with red, so that it seemed to be a stream of blood rather than water running beside the road. Then it went black. A moment later it had become transparent and Jack saw –

A little mewling sound escaped him as he saw Morgan's diligence roaring along the Western Road, pulled by its foaming baker's dozen of black-plumed horses. Jack saw with almost swooning terror that the driver sitting up high in the peak-seat, his booted feet on the splashboard and a ceaselessly cracking whip in one hand, was Elroy. But it was not a hand at all that held that whip. It was some sort of hoof. Elroy was driving that nightmare coach, Elroy grinning with a mouth that was filled with dead fangs, Elroy who just couldn't wait to find Jack Sawyer again and split open Jack Sawyer's belly and pull out Jack Sawyer's intestines.

Jack knelt before the stream, eyes bulging, mouth quivering with dismay and horror. He had seen one final thing in this vision, not a large thing, no, but by implication it was the most frightful thing of all: the eyes of the horses seemed to glow. They seemed to glow because they were full of light – full of the sunset.

The diligence was travelling west along this same road . . . and it was after him.

Crawling, not sure he could stand even if he had to, Jack retreated from the stream and lurched clumsily out into the road. He fell flat in the dust, Speedy's bottle and the mirror the rug salesman had given him digging into his guts. He turned his head sideways so that his right cheek and ear were pressed tightly against the surface of the Western Road.

He could feel the steady rumble in the hard, dry earth. It was distant . . . but coming closer.

Elroy up on top . . . and Morgan inside. Morgan Sloat? Morgan of Orris? Didn't matter. Both were one.

He broke the hypnotic effect of that rumbling in the earth with an effort and got up again. He took Speedy's bottle – the same over here in the Territories as in the U.S.A. – out of his jerkin and pulled as much of the moss-plug out of the neck as he could, never minding the shower of particles into the little bit of liquid remaining – no more than a couple of inches now. He looked nervously to his left, as if expecting to see the black diligence appear at the horizon, the sunset-filled eyes of the horses glowing like weird lanterns. Of course he saw nothing. Horizons were closer over here in the Territories, as he had already noticed, and sounds travelled farther. Morgan's diligence had to be ten miles to the east, maybe as much as twenty.

Still right on top of me, Jack thought, and raised the bottle to his lips. A bare second before he drank from it, his mind shouted, *Hey, wait a minute! Wait a minute, dummy, you want to get killed?* He would look cute, wouldn't he, standing in the middle of the Western Road and then flipping back into the other world in the middle of some road over there, maybe getting run down by a highballing semi or a UPS truck.

Jack shambled over to the side of the road . . . and then walked ten or twenty paces into the thigh-high grass for good measure. He took one final deep breath, inhaling the sweet smell of this place, groping for that feeling of serenity . . . that feeling of rainbow.

Got to try and remember how that felt, he thought. I may need it . . . and I may not get back here for a long time.

He looked out at the grasslands, darkening now as night stole over them from the east. The wind gusted, chilly now but still fragrant, tossing his hair – it was getting shaggy now – as it tossed the grass.

You ready, Jack-O?

Jack closed his eyes and steeled himself against the awful taste and the vomiting that was apt to follow.

'Banzai,' he whispered, and drank.

CHAPTER FOURTEEN
BUDDY PARKINS

1

He vomited up a thin purple drool, his face only inches from the grass covering the long slope down to a four-lane highway; shook his head and rocked backward onto his knees, so that only his back was exposed to the heavy gray sky. The world, this world, stank. Jack pushed himself backward, away from the threads of puke settling over the blades of grass, and the stench altered but did not diminish. Gasoline, other nameless poisons floated in the air; and the air itself stank of exhaustion, fatigue – even the noises roaring up from the highway punished this dying air. The back end of a roadsign reared like a gigantic television screen over his head. Jack wobbled to his feet. Far down the other side of the highway glinted an endless body of water only slightly less gray than the sky. A sort of malignant luminescence darted across the surface. From here, too, rose an odor of metal filings and tired breath. Lake Ontario: and the snug little city down there might be Olcott or Kendall. He'd gone miles out of his way – lost a hundred miles or more and just about four and a half days. Jack stepped under the sign, hoping it was no worse than that. He looked up at the black letters. Wiped his mouth. ANGOLA. Angola? Where was that?

He peered down at the smokey little city through the already nearly tolerable air.

And Rand McNally, that invaluable companion, told him that the acres of water way down there were Lake Erie – instead of losing days of travel time, he had gained them.

But before the boy could decide that he'd be smarter after all if he jumped back into the Territories as soon as he thought it might be safe – which is to say, as soon as Morgan's diligence had roared long past the place he had been – before he could do that, before he could even begin to think about doing that, he had to go down into the smokey little city of Angola and see if this time Jack Sawyer, Jack-O, had played any of those changes, Daddy. He began to make his way down the slope, a twelve-year-old boy in jeans and a plaid shirt, tall for his age, already beginning to look uncared-for, with suddenly too much worry in his face.

Halfway down the long slope, he realized that he was thinking in English again.

2

Many days later, and a long way west: the man, Buddy Parkins by name, who, just out of Cambridge, Ohio, on U.S. 40, had picked up a tall boy calling himself Lewis Farren, would have recognized that look of worry – this kid Lewis looked like worry was about to sink into his face for good. *Lighten up, son, for your own sake if no one else's*, Buddy wanted to tell the boy. But the boy had troubles enough for ten, according to his story. Mother sick, father dead, sent off to some schoolteacher aunt in Buckeye Lake . . . Lewis Farren had plenty to trouble him. He looked as though he had not seen as much as five dollars all together since the previous Christmas. Still . . . Buddy thought that somewhere along the line this Farren kid was jiving him.

For one thing, he smelled like farm, not town. Buddy Parkins and his brothers ran three hundred acres not far from Amanda, about thirty miles southeast of Columbus, and Buddy knew that he could not be wrong about this. This boy smelled like Cambridge, and Cambridge was country. Buddy had grown up with the smell of farmland and barnyard, of manure and growing corn and pea vineries, and the unwashed clothes of this boy beside him had absorbed all these familiar odors.

And there were the clothes themselves. Mrs Farren must have been awful sick, Buddy thought, if she sent her boy off down the road in ripped jeans so stiff with dirt the wrinkles seemed bronzed. And the shoes! Lewis Farren's sneakers were about to fall off his feet, the laces all spliced together and the fabric split or worn through in a couple of places on each shoe.

'So they got yore daddy's car, did they, Lewis?' Buddy asked.

'Just like I said, that's right – the lousy cowards came out after midnight and just stole it right out of the garage. I don't think they should be allowed to do that. Not from people who work hard and really are going to start making their payments as soon as they can. I mean, do you? You don't, do you?'

The boy's honest, sunburned face was turned toward him as if this were the most serious question since the Nixon Pardon or maybe the Bay of Pigs, and all Buddy's instincts were to agree – he would be inclined to agree with any generally good-hearted opinion uttered by a boy so redolent of farm work. 'I guess there's two sides to everything when you come down to it,' Buddy Parkins said, not very happily. The boy blinked, and then turned away to face forward again. Again Buddy felt his anxiety, the cloud of worry that seemed to hang over the boy, and was almost sorry he had not given Lewis Farren the agreement he seemed to need.

'I suppose yore aunt's in the grade school over there in Buckeye Lake,' Buddy said, at least in part hoping to lighten the boy's misery. Point to the future, not the past.

'Yes, sir, that's right. She teaches in the grade school. Helen Vaughan.' His expression did not change.

But Buddy had heard it again – he didn't consider himself any Henry Higgins, the professor guy in that musical, but he knew for certain sure that young Lewis Farren didn't talk like anyone who had been raised in Ohio. The kid's voice was all wrong, too pushed-together and full of the wrong ups and downs. It wasn't an Ohio voice at all. It especially was not a rural Ohioan's voice. It was an *accent*.

Or was it possible that some boy from Cambridge, Ohio, could learn to talk like that? Whatever his crazy reason might be? Buddy supposed it was.

On the other hand, the newspaper this Lewis Farren had never once unclamped from beneath his left elbow seemed to validate Buddy Parkins's deepest and worst suspicion, that his fragrant young companion was a runaway and his every word a lie. The name of the paper, visible to Buddy with only the slightest tilt of his head, was *The Angola Herald*. There was that Angola in Africa that a lot of Englishmen had rushed off to as mercenaries, and there was Angola, New York – right up there on Lake Erie. He'd seen pictures of it on the news not long ago, but could not quite remember why.

'I'd like to ask you a question, Lewis,' he said, and cleared his throat.

'Yes?' the boy said.

'How come a boy from a nice little burg on U.S. Forty is carrying around a paper from Angola, New York? Which is one hell of a long way away. I'm just curious, son.'

The boy looked down at the paper flattened under his arm and hugged it even closer to him, as if he were afraid it might squirm away. 'Oh,' he said. 'I found it.'

'Oh, hell,' Buddy said.

'Yes, sir. It was on a bench at the bus station back home.'

'You went to the bus station this morning?'

'Right before I decided to save the money and hitch. Mr Parkins, if you can get me to the turnoff at Zanesville, I'll only have a short ride left. Could probably get to my aunt's house before dinner.'

'Could be,' Buddy said, and drove in an uncomfortable silence for several miles. Finally he could bear it no longer, and he said, very quietly and while looking straight ahead, 'Son, are you running away from home?'

Lewis Farren astonished him by smiling – not grinning and not faking it, but actually smiling. He thought the whole notion of running away from home was funny. It tickled him. The boy glanced at him a fraction of a second after Buddy had looked sideways, and their eyes met.

For a second, for two seconds, three . . . for however long that moment lasted, Buddy Parkins saw that this unwashed boy sitting beside him was beautiful. He would have thought himself incapable of using that word to describe any male human being above the age of nine months, but underneath the road-grime this Lewis Farren was beautiful. His sense of humor had momentarily murdered his worries, and what shone out of him at Buddy – who was fifty-two years old and had three teenage sons – was a kind of straightforward goodness that had only been dented by a host of unusual experiences. This Lewis Farren, twelve years old by his own account, had somehow gone farther and seen more than Buddy Parkins, and what he had seen and done had made him beautiful.

'No, I'm not a runaway, Mr Parkins,' the boy said.

Then he blinked, and his eyes went inward again and lost their brightness, their light, and the boy slumped back against his seat. He pulled up a knee, rested it on the dashboard, and snugged the newspaper up under his bicep.

'No, I guess not,' Buddy Parkins said, snapping his eyes back to the highway. He felt relieved, though he was not quite sure why. 'I guess yore not a runaway, Lewis. Yore something, though.'

The boy did not respond.

'Been workin on a farm, haven't you?'

Lewis looked up at him, surprised. 'I did, yeah. The past three days. Two dollars an hour.'

And yore mommy didn't even take the time out from bein sick to wash yore clothes before she sent you to her sister, is that right? Buddy thought. But what he said was 'Lewis, I'd like you to think about coming home with me. I'm not saying yore on the run or anything, but if yore from anywhere around Cambridge I'll eat this beat-up old car, tires and all, and I got three boys myself and the youngest one, Billy, he's only about three years older'n you, and we know how to feed *boys* around my house. You can stay about as long as you like, depending on how many questions you want to answer. 'Cuz I'll be asking em, at least after the first time we break bread together.'

He rubbed one palm over his gray crewcut and glanced across the seat. Lewis Farren was looking more like a boy and less like a revelation. 'You'll be welcome, son.'

Smiling, the boy said, 'That's really nice of you, Mr Parkins, but I can't. I have to go see my, ah, aunt in . . .'

'Buckeye Lake,' Buddy supplied.

The boy swallowed and looked forward again.

'I'll give you help, if you want help,' Buddy repeated.

Lewis patted his forearm, sunburned and thick. 'This ride is a big help, honest.'

Ten nearly silent minutes later he was watching the boy's forlorn figure trudge down the exit ramp outside Zanesville. Emmie would probably have brained him if he'd come home with a strange dirty boy to feed, but once she'd seen him and talked to him, Emmie would have brought out the good glasses and the plates her mother had given her. Buddy Parkins didn't believe that there was any woman named Helen Vaughan in Buckeye Lake, and he wasn't so sure this mysterious Lewis Farren even had a mother – the boy seemed such an orphan, off on a vast errand. Buddy watched until the boy was taken by the curve of the off-ramp, and he was staring out at space and the enormous yellow-and-purple sign of a shopping mall.

For a second he thought of jumping out of the car and running after the kid, trying to get him back . . . and then he had a moment of recall of a crowded, smokey scene on the six-o'clock news. Angola, New York. Some disaster too small to be reported more than once, that was what had happened in Angola; one of those little tragedies the world shovels under a mountain of newsprint. All Buddy could catch, in this short, probably flawed moment of memory, was a picture of girders strewn like giant straws over battered cars, jutting up out of a fuming hole in the ground – a hole that might lead down into hell. Buddy Parkins looked once more at the empty place on the road where the boy had been, and then stamped on his clutch and dropped the old car into Low.

3

Buddy Parkins's memory was more accurate than he imagined. If he could have seen the first page of the month-old *Angola Herald* 'Lewis Farren', that enigmatic boy, had been holding so protectively yet fearfully beneath his arm, these are the words he would have read:

FREAK EARTHQUAKE KILLS 5
by Herald staff reporter Joseph Gargan

Work on the Rainbird Towers, intended to be Angola's tallest and most luxurious condominium development and still six months from completion, was tragically halted yesterday as an unprecedented earth tremor collapsed the structure of the building, burying many construction workers beneath the rubble. Five bodies have been retrieved from the ruins of the proposed condominium, and two other workers have not yet been found but these are presumed dead. All seven workers were welders and fitters in the employ of Speiser Construction, and all were on the girders of the building's top two floors at the time of the incident.

Yesterday's tremor was the first earthquake in Angola's recorded history. Armin Van Pelt of New York University's Geology Department, contacted today by

> telephone, described the fatal quake as a 'seismic bubble'. Representatives of the State Safety Commission are continuing their examinations of the site, as is a team of . . .

The dead men were Robert Heidel, twenty-three; Thomas Thielke, thirty-four; Jerome Wild, forty-eight; Michael Hagen, twenty-nine; and Bruce Davey, thirty-nine. The two men still missing were Arnold Schulkamp, fifty-four, and Theodore Rasmussen, forty-three. Jack no longer had to look at the newspaper's front page to remember their names. The first earthquake in the history of Angola, New York, had occurred on the day he had flipped away from the Western Road and landed on the town's border. Part of Jack Sawyer wished that he could have gone home with big kindly Buddy Parkins, eaten dinner around the table in the kitchen with the Parkins family – boiled beef and deep-dish apple pie – and then snuggled into the Parkinses' guest bed and pulled the homemade quilt up over his head. And not moved, except toward the table, for four or five days. But part of the trouble was that he saw that knotty-pine kitchen table heaped with crumbly cheese, and on the other side of the table a mouse-hole was cut into a giant baseboard; and from holes in the jeans of the three Parkins boys protruded thin long tails. Who plays these Jerry Bledsoe changes, Daddy? *Heidel, Thielke, Wild, Hagen, Davey; Schulkamp and Rasmussen.* Those Jerry changes? He knew who played them.

4

The huge yellow-and-purple sign reading BUCKEYE MALL floated ahead of Jack as he came around the final curve of the off-ramp, drifted past his shoulder and reappeared on his other side, at which point he could finally see that it was erected on a tripod of tall yellow poles in the shopping-center parking lot. The mall itself was a futuristic assemblage of ochre-colored buildings that seemed to be windowless – a second later, Jack realized that the mall was covered, and what he was seeing was only the illusion of separate buildings. He put his hand in his pocket and fingered the tight roll of twenty-three single dollar bills which was his earthly fortune.

In the cool sunlight of an early autumn afternoon, Jack sprinted across the street toward the mall's parking lot.

If it had not been for his conversation with Buddy Parkins, Jack would very likely have stayed on U.S. 40 and tried to cover another fifty miles – he wanted to get to Illinois, where Richard Sloat was, in the next two or three days. The thought of seeing his friend Richard again had kept him going during the weary days of nonstop work on Elbert Palamountain's farm: the image of spectacled, serious-faced Richard Sloat in his room at Thayer School, in Springfield, Illinois, had fueled him as much as Mrs Palamountain's generous meals. Jack still wanted to see Richard, and as soon as he could: but Buddy Parkins's inviting him home had somehow unstrung him. He could not just climb into another car and begin all over again on the Story. (In any case, Jack reminded himself, the Story seemed to be losing its potency.) The shopping mall gave him a perfect chance to drop out for an hour or two, especially if there was a movie theater somewhere in there – right now, Jack could have watched the dullest, soppiest *Love Story* of a movie.

And before the movie, were he lucky enough to find a theater, he would be able to take care of two things he had been putting off for at least a week. Jack had seen Buddy Parkins looking at his disintegrating Nikes. Not only were the running shoes falling apart, the soles, once spongy and elastic, had mysteriously become hard as asphalt. On days when he had to walk great distances – or when he had to work standing up all day – his feet stung as if they'd been burned.

The second task, calling his mother, was so loaded with guilt and other fearful emotions that Jack could not quite allow it to become conscious. He did not know if he could keep from weeping, once he'd heard his mother's voice. What if she sounded weak – what if she sounded really sick? Could he really keep going west if Lily hoarsely begged him to come back to New Hampshire? So he could not admit to himself that he was probably going to call his mother. His mind gave him the suddenly very clear image of a bank of pay telephones beneath their hairdryer plastic bubbles, and almost immediately bucked away from it – as if Elroy or some other Territories creature could reach out of the receiver and clamp a hand around his throat.

Just then three girls a year or two older than Jack bounced out of the back of a Subaru Brat which had swung recklessly into a parking spot near the mall's main entrance. For a second they had the look of models contorted into awkwardly elegant poses of delight and astonishment. When they had adjusted into more conventional postures the girls glanced incuriously at Jack and began to flip their hair expertly back into place. They were leggy in their tight jeans, these confident little princesses of the tenth grade, and when they laughed they put their hands over their mouths in a fashion which suggested that laughter itself was laughable. Jack slowed his walk into a kind of sleepwalker's stroll. One of the princesses glanced at him and muttered something to the brownhaired girl beside her.

I'm different now, Jack thought: *I'm not like them anymore.* The recognition pierced him with loneliness.

A thickset blond boy in a blue sleeveless down vest climbed out of the driver's seat and gathered the girls around him by the simple expedient of pretending to ignore them. The boy, who must have been a senior and at the very least in the varsity backfield, glanced once at Jack and then looked appraisingly at the facade of the mall. 'Timmy?' said the tall brownhaired girl. 'Yeah, yeah,' the boy said. 'I was just wondering what smells like shit out here.' He rewarded the girls with a superior little smile. The brownhaired girl looked smirkingly toward Jack, then swung herself across the asphalt with her friends. The three girls followed Timmy's arrogant body through the glass doors into the mall.

Jack waited until the figures of Timmy and his court, visible through the glass, had shrunk to the size of puppies far down the long mall before he stepped on the plate which opened the doors.

Cold pre-digested air embraced him.

Water trickled down over a fountain two stories high set in a wide pool surrounded by benches. Open-fronted shops on both levels faced the fountain. Bland Muzak drifted down from the ochre ceiling, as did the peculiar bronzy light; the smell of popcorn, which had struck Jack the moment the glass doors had whooshed shut behind him, emanated from an antique popcorn wagon, painted fire-engine red and stationed outside a Waldenbooks to the left of the fountain on the ground level. Jack had seen immediately that there was no movie theater in the Buckeye Mall. Timmy and his leggy princesses were floating up the escalator at the mall's other end, making, Jack thought, for a fast-food restaurant called The Captain's Table right at the top of the escalator. Jack put his hand in his pants pocket again and touched his roll of bills. Speedy's guitar-pick and Captain Farren's coin nested at the bottom of the pocket, along with a handful of dimes and quarters.

On Jack's level, sandwiched between a Mr Chips cookie shop and a liquor store advertising NEW LOW PRICES for Hiram Walker bourbon and Inglenook Chablis, a Fayva shoe store drew him toward its long table of running shoes. The clerk at the cash register leaned forward and watched Jack pick over the shoes, clearly suspicious that he might try to steal something. Jack recognized none of the brands on the table. There were no Nikes or Pumas here – they were called Speedster or Bullseye or Zooms, and the laces of each pair were tied together. These were sneakers, not true running shoes. They were good enough, Jack supposed.

He bought the cheapest pair the store had in his size, blue canvas with red zigzag stripes down the sides. No brand name was visible anywhere on the shoes. They seemed indistinguishable from most of the other shoes on the table. At the register he counted out six limp one-dollar bills and told the clerk that he did not need a bag.

Jack sat on one of the benches before the tall fountain and toed off the battered Nikes without bothering to unlace them. When he slipped on the new sneakers, his feet fairly sighed with gratitude. Jack left the bench and dropped his old shoes in a tall black wastebasket with DON'T BE A LITTERBUG stencilled on it in white. Beneath that, in smaller letters, the wastebasket read *The earth is our only home.*

Jack began to move aimlessly through the long lower

arcade of the mall, searching for the telephones. At the popcorn wagon he parted with fifty cents and was handed a quart-size tub of fresh popcorn glistening with grease. The middle-aged man in a bowler hat, a walrus moustache, and sleeve garters who sold him the popcorn told him that the pay phones were around a corner next to 31 Flavors, upstairs. The man gestured vaguely toward the nearest escalator.

Scooping the popcorn into his mouth, Jack rode up behind a woman in her twenties and an older woman with hips so wide they nearly covered the entire width of the escalator, both of them in pants suits.

If Jack were to flip inside the Buckeye Mall – or even a mile or two from it – would the walls shake and the ceiling crumble down, dropping bricks and beams and Muzak speakers and light fixtures down on everybody unlucky enough to be inside? And would the tenth-grade princesses, and even arrogant Timmy, and most of the others, too, wind up with skull fractures and severed limbs and mangled chests and . . . for a second just before he reached the top of the escalator Jack saw giant chunks of plaster and metal girders showering down, heard the terrible cracking of the mezzanine floor, the screams, too – inaudible, they were still printed in the air.

Angola. The Rainbird Towers.

Jack felt his palms begin to itch and sweat, and he wiped them on his jeans.

THIRTY-ONE FLAVORS, gleamed out a chilly incandescent white light to his left, and when he turned that way he saw a curving hallway on its other side. Shiny brown tiles on the walls and floor; as soon as the curve of the hallway took him out of sight of anyone on the mezzanine level, Jack saw three telephones, which were indeed under transparent plastic bubbles. Across the hall from the telephones were doors to MEN and LADIES.

Beneath the middle bubble, Jack dialled 0, followed by the area code and the number for the Alhambra Inn and Gardens. 'Billing?' asked the operator, and Jack said, 'This is a collect call for Mrs Sawyer in four-oh-seven and four-oh-eight. From Jack.'

The hotel operator answered, and Jack's chest tightened. She transferred the call to the suite. The telephone rang once, twice, three times.

Then his mother said, 'Jesus, kid, I'm glad to hear from you! This absentee-mother business is hard on an old girl like me. I kind of miss you when you're not moping around and telling me how to act with waiters.'

'You're just too classy for most waiters, that's all,' Jack said, and thought that he might begin to cry with relief.

'Are you all right, Jack? Tell me the truth.'

'I'm fine, sure,' he said. 'Yeah, I'm fine. I just had to make sure that you . . . you know.'

The phone whispered electronically, a skirl of static that sounded like sand blowing across a beach.

'I'm okay,' Lily said. 'I'm great. I'm not any worse, anyhow, if that's what you're worried about. I suppose I'd like to know where you are.'

Jack paused, and the static whispered and hissed for a moment. 'I'm in Ohio now. Pretty soon I'm going to be able to see Richard.'

'When are you coming home, Jack-O?'

'I can't say. I wish I could.'

'You can't say. I swear, kid, if your father hadn't called you that silly name – and if you'd asked me about this ten minutes earlier or ten minutes later . . .'

A rising tide of static took her voice, and Jack remembered how she'd looked in the tea shop, haggard and feeble, an old woman. When the static receded he asked, 'Are you having any trouble with Uncle Morgan? Is he bothering you?'

'I sent your Uncle away from here with a flea in his ear,' she said.

'He was there? He did come? Is he still bothering you?'

'I got rid of the Stoat about two days after you left, baby. Don't waste time worrying about him.'

'Did he say where he was going?' Jack asked her, but as soon as the words were out of his mouth the telephone uttered a tortured electronic squeal that seemed to bore right into his head. Jack grimaced and jerked the receiver away from his ear. The awful whining noise of static was so loud that anyone stepping into the corridor would have heard it. 'MOM!' Jack shouted, putting the phone as close to his head as he dared. The squeal of static increased, as if a radio between stations had been turned up to full volume.

The line abruptly fell silent. Jack clamped the receiver to his ear and heard only the flat black silence of dead air. 'Hey,' he said, and jiggled the hook. The flat silence in the phone seemed to press up against his ear.

Just as abruptly, and as if his jiggling the hook had caused it, the dial tone – an oasis of sanity, of regularity, now – resumed. Jack jammed his right hand in his pocket, looking for another coin.

He was holding the receiver, awkwardly, in his left hand as he dug in his pocket; he froze when he heard the dial tone suddenly slot off into outer space.

Morgan Sloat's voice spoke to him as clearly as if good

old Uncle Morgan were standing at the next telephone. 'Get your ass back home, Jack.' Sloat's voice carved the air like a scalpel. 'You just get your ass back home before we have to take you back ourselves.'

'Wait,' Jack said, as if he were begging for time: in fact, he was too terrified to know quite what he was saying.

'Can't wait any longer, little pal. You're a murderer now. That's right, isn't it? You're a murderer. So we're not able to give you any more chances. You just get your can back to that resort in New Hampshire. Now. Or maybe you'll go home in a bag.'

Jack heard the click of the receiver. He dropped it. The telephone Jack had used shuddered forward, then sagged off the wall. For a second it drooped on a network of wires; then crashed heavily to the floor.

The door to the men's room banged open behind Jack, and a voice yelled, 'Holy SHIT!'

Jack turned to see a thin crewcut boy of about twenty staring at the telephones. He was wearing a white apron and a bow tie: a clerk at one of the shops.

'I didn't do it,' Jack said. 'It just happened.'

'Holy shit.' The crewcut clerk goggled at Jack for a split-second, jerked as if to run, and then ran his hands over the crown of his head.

Jack backed away down the hall. When he was halfway down the escalator he finally heard the clerk yelling, 'Mr Olafson! The phone, Mr Olafson!' Jack fled.

Outside, the air was bright, surprisingly humid. Dazed, Jack wandered across the sidewalk. A half-mile away across the parking lot, a black-and-white police car swung in toward the mall. Jack turned sideways and began to walk down the pavement. Some way ahead, a family of six struggled to get a lawn chair in through the next entrance to the mall. Jack slowed down and watched the husband and wife tilt the long chair diagonally, hindered by the attempts of the smaller children to either sit on the chair or to assist them. At last, nearly in the posture of the flagraisers in the famous photograph of Iwo Jima, the family staggered through the doors. The police car lazily circled through the big parking lot.

Just past the door where the disorderly family had succeeded in planting their chair, an old black man sat on a wooden crate, cradling a guitar in his lap. As Jack slowly drew nearer, he saw the metal cup beside the man's feet. The man's face was hidden behind big dirty sunglasses and beneath the brim of a stained felt hat. The sleeves of his denim jacket were as wrinkled as an elephant's hide.

Jack swerved out to the edge of the pavement to give the man all the room he seemed to warrant, and noticed that around the man's neck hung a sign handwritten in big shaky capital letters on discolored white cardboard. A few steps later he could read the letters.

BLIND SINCE BIRTH
WILL PLAY ANY SONG
GOD BLESS YOU

He had nearly walked past the man holding the beat-up old guitar when he heard him utter, his voice a cracked and juicy whisper, 'Yeah-bob.'

CHAPTER FIFTEEN
SNOWBALL SINGS

1

Jack swung back toward the black man, his heart hammering in his chest.

Speedy?

The black man groped for his cup, held it up, shook it. A few coins rattled in the bottom.

It *is* Speedy. Behind those dark glasses, it *is* Speedy.

Jack was sure of it. But a moment later he was just as sure that it *wasn't* Speedy. Speedy wasn't built square in the shoulders and broad across the chest; Speedy's shoulders were rounded, a little slumped over, and his chest consequently had a slightly caved-in look. Mississippi John Hurt, not Ray Charles.

But I could tell one way or the other for sure if he'd take off those shades.

He opened his mouth to speak Speedy's name aloud, and suddenly the old man began to play, his wrinkled fingers, as dully dark as old walnut that had been faithfully oiled but never polished, moving with limber speed and grace on both strings and frets. He played well, finger-picking the melody. And after a moment, Jack recognized the tune. It had been on one of his father's older records. A Vanguard album called *Mississippi John Hurt Today*. And although the blind man didn't sing, Jack knew the words:

O kindly friends, tell me, ain't it hard?
To see ole Lewis in a new graveyard,
The angels laid him away . . .

The blond football player and his three princesses came out of the mall's main doors. Each of the princesses had an ice cream cone. Mr All-America had a chili-dog in each hand. They sauntered toward where Jack stood. Jack, whose whole attention was taken up by the old black man, had not even noticed them. He had been transfixed by the idea that it was Speedy, and Speedy had somehow read his mind. How else could it be that this man had begun to play a Mississippi John Hurt composition just as Jack happened to think Speedy looked like that very man? And a song containing his own road-name, as well?

The blond football player transferred both chili-dogs to his left hand and slapped Jack on the back with his right as hard as he could. Jack's teeth snapped on his own tongue like a bear-trap. The pain was sudden and excruciating.

'You just shake her easy, urine-breath,' he said. The princesses giggled and shrieked.

Jack stumbled forward and kicked over the blind man's cup. Coins spilled and rolled. The gentle lilt of the blues tune came to a jangling halt.

Mr All-America and the Three Little Princesses were already moving on. Jack stared after them and felt the now-familiar impotent hate. This was how it felt to be on your own, just young enough to be at everyone's mercy and to be anyone's meat – anyone from a psychotic like Osmond to a humorless old Lutheran like Elbert Palamountain, whose idea of a pretty fair work-day was to slog and squelch through gluey fields for twelve hours during a steady cold downpour of October rain, and to sit bolt-upright in the cab of his International Harvester truck during lunch hour, eating onion sandwiches and reading from the Book of Job.

Jack had no urge to 'get' them, although he had a strange idea that if he wanted to, he could – that he was gaining some sort of power, almost like an electrical charge. It sometimes seemed to him that other people knew that, too – that it was in their faces when they looked at him. But he didn't *want* to get them; he only wanted to be left alone. He –

The blind man was feeling around himself for the spilled money, his pudgy hands moving gently over the pavement, almost seeming to read it. He happened on a dime, set his cup back again, and dropped the dime in. *Plink!*

Faintly, Jack heard one of the princesses: 'Why do they let him stay there, he's so *gross*, you know?'

Even more faintly still: 'Yeah, *rilly*!'

Jack got down on his knees and began to help, picking up coins and putting them into the blind man's cup. Down here, close to the old man, he could smell sour sweat, mildew, and some sweet bland smell like corn. Smartly dressed mall shoppers gave them a wide berth.

'Thankya, thankya,' the blind man croaked monotonously. Jack could smell dead chili on his breath. 'Thankya, blessya, God blessya, thankya.'

He *is* Speedy.

He's *not* Speedy.

What finally forced him to speak – and this was not really so odd – was remembering just how little of the magic juice he had left. Barely two swallows now. He did not know if, after what had happened in Angola, he could ever bring himself to travel in the Territories again, but he was still determined to save his mother's life, and that meant he might have to.

And, whatever the Talisman was, he might have to flip into the other world to get it.

'Speedy?'

'Blessya, thankya, God blessya, didn't I hear one go over there?' He pointed.

'*Speedy!* It's Jack!'

'Ain't nothin speedy round here, boy. No *sir.*' His hands began to whisper-walk along the concrete in the direction he had just pointed. One of them found a nickel and he dropped it into the cup. His other happened to touch the shoe of a smartly dressed young woman who was passing by. Her pretty, empty face wrinkled in almost painful disgust as she drew away from him.

Jack picked the last coin out of the gutter. It was a silver dollar – a big old cartwheel with Lady Liberty on one side.

Tears began to spill out of his eyes. They ran down his dirty face and he wiped them away with an arm that shook. He was crying for Thielke, Wild, Hagen, Davey, and Heidel. For his mother. For Laura DeLoessian. For the carter's son lying dead in the road with his pockets turned out. But most of all for himself. He was tired of being on the road. Maybe when you rode it in a Cadillac it was a road of dreams, but when you had to hitch it, riding on your thumb and a story that was just about worn out, when you were at everybody's mercy and anyone's meat, it was nothing but a road of trials. Jack felt that he had been tried enough . . . but there was no way to cry it off. If he cried it off, the cancer would take his mother, and Uncle Morgan might well take *him.*

'I don't think I can do it, Speedy,' he wept. 'I don't think so, man.'

Now the blind man groped for Jack instead of the spilled coins. Those gentle, reading fingers found his arm and closed around it. Jack could feel the hard pad of callus in the tip of each finger. He drew Jack to him, into those odors of sweat and heat and old chili. Jack pressed his face against Speedy's chest.

'Hoo, boy. I don't know no Speedy, but it sounds like you puttin an awful lot on him. You—'

'I miss my mom, Speedy,' Jack wept, 'and Sloat's after me. It was him on the phone inside the mall, *him.* And that's not the worst thing. The worst thing was in Angola . . . the Rainbird Towers . . . earthquake . . . five men . . . *me, I did it, Speedy, I killed those men when I flipped into this world, I killed them just like my dad and Morgan Sloat killed Jerry Bledsoe that time!*'

Now it was out, the worst of it. He had sicked up the stone of guilt that had been in his throat, threatening to choke him, and a storm of weeping seized him – but this time it was relief rather than fear. It was said. It had been confessed. He was a murderer.

'Hooo-*eeee*!' the black man cried. He sounded perversely delighted. He held Jack with one thin, strong arm, rocked him. 'You tryin to carry you one heavy load, boy. You sure am. Maybe you ought to put some of it down.'

'I killed em,' Jack whispered. 'Thielke, Wild, Hagen, Davey . . .'

'Well, if yo friend Speedy was here,' the black man said, '*whoever* he might be, or *wherever* he might be in this wide old world, he might tell you that you cain't carry the world on yo shoulders, son. You cain't do that. No one can. Try to carry the world on yo shoulders, why, first it's gonna break yo *back*, and then it's gonna break yo *sperrit*.'

'I killed—'

'Put a gun to their heads and shot somebodies, didya?'

'No . . . the earthquake . . . I flipped . . .'

'Don't know nothin bout *dat*,' the black man said. Jack had pulled away from him a bit and was staring up into the black man's seamed face with wondering curiosity, but the black man had turned his head toward the parking lot. If he *was* blind, then he had picked out the smoother, slightly more powerful beat of the police car's engine from the others as it approached, because he was looking right at it. 'All I know is you seem to have this idear of "moider" a little broad. Prolly if some fella dropped dead of a heart-attack goin around us as we sit here, you'd think you killed him. "Oh look, I done moidered that fella on account of where I was sittin, oh woe, oh *doom*, oh *glooooom*, oh *this* . . . oh *that*!"' As he spoke *this* and *that*, the blind man punctuated it with a quick change from G to C and back to G again. He laughed, pleased with himself.

'Speedy—'

'Nothin speedy round here,' the black man reiterated, and then showed yellow teeth in a crooked grin. 'Cept maybe how speedy some folks are to put the blame on themselves for things others might have got started. Maybe you runnin, boy, and maybe you being *chased*.'

G-chord.

'Maybe you be just a little off-*base*.'

C-chord, with a nifty little run in the middle that made Jack grin in spite of himself.

'Might be somebody else gettin on yo *case*.'

Back down to G again, and the blind man laid his guitar aside (while, in the police car, the two cops were flipping to see which of them would actually have to touch Old Snowball if he wouldn't get into the back of the cruiser peaceably).

'Maybe dooom an maybe glooooom an maybe *this* an maybe *that* . . .' He laughed again, as if Jack's fears were the funniest thing he'd ever heard.

'But I don't know what could happen if I—'

'No one ever knows what could happen if they do anything, do dey?' the black man who might or might not be Speedy Parker broke in. 'No. Dey do *not*. If you thought about it, you'd stay in yo house all day, ascairt to come out! I don't know yo problems, boy. Don't want to know em. Could be crazy, talkin bout earthquakes and all. But bein as how you helped me pick up my money and didn't steal none – I counted every *plinkety-plink*, so I know – I'll give you some advice. Some things you cain't help. Sometimes people get killed because somebody does something . . . but if somebody *didn't* do that somethin, a whole lot of more people would have got killed. Do you see where I'm pushin, son?'

The dirty sunglasses inclined down toward him.

Jack felt a deep, shuddery relief. He saw, all right. The blind man was talking about hard choices. He was suggesting that maybe there was a difference between hard choices and criminal behavior. And that maybe the criminal wasn't here.

The criminal might have been the guy who had told him five minutes ago to get his ass home.

'Could even be,' the blind man remarked, hitting a dark D-minor chord on his box, 'that all things soive the

Lord, just like my momma tole me and your momma might have tole you, if she was a Christian lady. Could be we think we doin one thing but are really doin another. Good Book says all things, even those that seem evil, soive the Lord. What you think, boy?'

'I don't know,' Jack said honestly. He was all mixed up. He only had to close his eyes and he could see the telephone tearing off the wall, hanging from its wires like a weird puppet.

'Well, it *smells* like you lettin it drive you to drink.'

'What?' Jack asked, astonished. Then he thought, *I thought that Speedy looked like Mississippi John Hurt, and this guy started playing a John Hurt blues . . . and now he's talking about the magic juice. He's being careful, but I swear that's what he's talking about – it's got to be!*

'You're a mind-reader,' Jack said in a low voice. 'Aren't you? Did you learn it in the Territories, Speedy?'

'Don't know nothin bout readin minds,' the blind man said, 'but my lamps have been out forty-two year come November, and in forty-two year your nose and ears take up some of the slack. I can smell cheap wine on you, son. Smell it *all over you*. It's almost like you washed yo hair widdit!'

Jack felt an odd, dreamy guilt – it was the way he always felt when accused of doing something wrong when he was in fact innocent – mostly innocent, anyway. He had done no more than touch the almost-empty bottle since flipping back into this world. Just touching it filled him with dread – he had come to feel about it the way a fourteenth-century European peasant might have felt about a splinter of the One True Cross or the fingerbone of a saint. It was magic, all right. *Powerful* magic. And sometimes it got people killed.

'I haven't been drinking it, honest,' he finally managed. 'What I started with is almost gone. It . . . I . . . man, I don't even *like* it!' His stomach had begun to clench nervously; just thinking about the magic juice was making him feel nauseated. 'But I need to get some more. Just in case.'

'More Poiple Jesus? Boy your age?' The blind man laughed and made a shooing gesture with one hand. 'Hell, you don't need *dat*. No boy needs *dat* poison to travel with.'

'But—'

'Here. I'll sing you a song to cheer you up. Sounds like you could use it.'

He began to sing, and his singing voice was nothing at all like his speaking voice. It was deep and powerful and thrilling, without the Nigger Jim 'My-Huck-dat-sure-is-*gay*!' cadences of his talk. It was, Jack thought, awed, almost the trained, cultured voice of an opera singer, now amusing itself with a little piece of popular fluff. Jack felt goosebumps rise on his arms and back at that rich, full voice. Along the sidewalk which ran along the dull, ochre flank of the mall, heads turned.

'When the red, red robin goes bob-bob-bobbin along, ALONG, there'll be no more sobbin when he starts throbbin his old . . . sweet SONG—'

Jack was struck by a sweet and terrible familiarity, a sense that he had heard this before, or something very like it, and as the blind man bridged, grinning his crooked, yellowing smile, Jack realized where the feeling was coming from. He knew what had made all those heads turn, as they would have turned if a unicorn had gone galloping across the mall's parking lot. There was a beautiful, alien clarity in the man's voice. It was the clarity of, say, air so pure that you could smell a radish when a man pulled one out of the ground half a mile away. It was a good old Tin Pan Alley song . . . but the voice was pure Territories.

'Get up . . . get up, you sleepyhead . . . get out . . . get out, get outta bed . . . live, love, laugh and be ha—'

Both guitar and voice came to a sudden halt. Jack, who had been concentrating fiercely on the blind man's face (trying subconsciously to peer right through those dark glasses, perhaps, and see if Speedy Parker's eyes were behind them), now widened his focus and saw two cops standing beside the blind man.

'You know, I don't *hear* nothin,' the blind guitarist said, almost coyly, 'but I b'lieve I *smell* somethin blue.'

'Goddammit, Snowball, you know you're not supposed to work the mall!' one of the cops cried. 'What did Judge Hallas tell you the last time he had you in chambers? Downtown between Center Street and Mural Street. Noplace else. Damn, boy, how senile have you got? Your pecker rotted off yet from that whatall your woman gave you before she took off? Christ, I just don't—'

His partner put a hand on his arm and nodded toward Jack in a little-pitchers-have-big-ears gesture.

'Go tell your mother she wants you, kid,' the first cop said curtly.

Jack started walking down the sidewalk. He couldn't stay. Even if there was something he could do, he couldn't stay. He was lucky the cops' attention had been taken up by the man they called Snowball. If they had given him a second glance, Jack had no doubt he would have been asked to produce his bona fides. New sneakers or not, the rest of him looked used and battered. It doesn't take cops long to get good at spotting road-kids, and Jack was a boy on the road if there ever had been one.

He imagined being tossed into the Zanesville pokey while the Zanesville cops, fine upstanding boys in blue who listened to Paul Harvey every day and supported President Reagan, tried to find out whose little boy *he* was.

No, he didn't want the Zanesville cops giving him more than the one passing glance.

A motor, throbbing smoothly, coming up behind him.

Jack hunched his pack a little higher on his back and looked down at his new sneakers as if they interested him tremendously. From the corners of his eyes he saw the police cruiser slide slowly by.

The blind man was in the back seat, the neck of his guitar poking up beside him.

As the cruiser swung into one of the outbound lanes, the blind man abruptly turned his head and looked out the back window, looked directly at Jack . . .

. . . and although Jack could not see through the dirty dark glasses, he knew perfectly well that Lester 'Speedy' Parker had winked at him.

2

Jack managed to keep further thought at bay until he reached the turnpike ramps again. He stood looking at the signs, which seemed the only clear-cut things left in a world

(worlds?)

where all else was a maddening gray swirl. He felt a dark depression swirling all around him, sinking into him, trying to destroy his resolve. He recognized that homesickness played a part in this depression, but this feeling made his former homesickness seem boyish and callow indeed. He felt utterly adrift, without a single firm thing to hold on to.

Standing by the signs, watching the traffic on the turnpike, Jack realized he felt damn near suicidal. For quite a while he had been able to keep himself going with the thought that he would see Richard Sloat soon (and, although he had hardly admitted the thought to himself, the idea that Richard might head west with him had done more than cross Jack's mind – after all, it would not be the first time that a Sawyer and a Sloat had made strange journeys together, would it?), but the hard work at the Palamountain farm and the peculiar happenings at the Buckeye Mall had given even that the false glitter of fool's gold.

Go home, Jacky, you're beaten, a voice whispered. *If you keep on, you're going to end up getting the living shit kicked out of you . . . and next time it may be fifty people that die. Or five hundred.*

I-70 East.

I-70 West.

Abruptly he fished in his pocket for the coin – the coin that was a silver dollar in this world. Let whatever gods there were decide this, once and for all. He was too beaten to do it for himself. His back still smarted where Mr All-America had whacked him. Come up tails, and he would go down the eastbound ramp and head home. Come up heads, he would go on . . . and there would be no more looking back.

He stood in the dust of the soft shoulder and flicked the coin into the chilly October air. It rose, turning over and over, kicking up glints of sun. Jack craned his head to follow its course.

A family passing in an old station-wagon stopped squabbling long enough to look at him curiously. The man driving the wagon, a balding C.P.A. who sometimes awoke in the middle of the night fancying that he could feel shooting pains in his chest and down his left arm, had a sudden and absurd series of thoughts: Adventure. Danger. A quest of some noble purpose. Dreams of fear and glory. He shook his head, as if to clear it, and glanced at the boy in the wagon's rear-view mirror just as the kid leaned over to look at something. *Christ*, the balding C.P.A. thought. *Get it out of your head, Larry, you sound like a fucking boys' adventure book.*

Larry shot into traffic, quickly getting the wagon up to seventy, forgetting about the kid in the dirty jeans by the side of the road. If he could get home by three, he'd be in good time to watch the middleweight title fight on ESPN.

The coin came down. Jack bent over it. It was heads . . . but that was not all.

The lady on the coin wasn't Lady Liberty. It was Laura DeLoessian, Queen of the Territories. But God, what a difference here from the pale, still, sleeping face he had glimpsed for a moment in the pavillion, surrounded by anxious nurses in their billowing white wimples! This face was alert and aware, eager and beautiful. It was not a classic beauty; the line of the jaw was not clear enough for that, and the cheekbone which showed in profile was a little soft. Her beauty was in the regal set of her head combined with the clear sense that she was kind as well as capable.

And oh it was so like the face of his mother.

Jack's eyes blurred with tears and he blinked them hard, not wanting the tears to fall. He had cried enough for one day. He had his answer, and it was not for crying over.

When he opened his eyes again, Laura DeLoessian was gone; the woman on the coin was Lady Liberty again.

He had his answer all the same.

Jack bent over, picked the coin out of the dust, put it in his pocket, and headed down the westbound ramp of Interstate 70.

3

A day later; white overcast in the air that tasted of chilly rain on its way; the Ohio-Indiana border not much more than a lick and a promise from here.

'Here' was in a scrub of woods beyond the Lewisburg rest area on I-70. Jack was standing concealed – he hoped – among the trees, patiently waiting for the large bald man with the large bald voice to get back into his Chevy Nova and drive away. Jack hoped he would go soon, before it started to rain. He was cold enough without getting wet, and all morning his sinuses had been plugged, his voice foggy. He thought he must finally be getting a cold.

The large bald man with the large bald voice had given his name as Emory W. Light. He had picked Jack up around eleven o'clock, north of Dayton, and Jack had felt a tired sinking sensation in the pit of his belly almost at once. He had gotten rides with Emory W. Light before. In Vermont Light had called himself Tom Ferguson, and said he was a shoe-shop foreman; in Pennsylvania the alias had been Bob Darrent ('Almost like that fellow who sang "Splish-Splash", ah-ha-hah-hah'), and the job had changed to District High School Superintendent; this time Light said he was President of The First Mercantile Bank of Paradise Falls, in the town of Paradise Falls, Ohio. Ferguson had been lean and dark, Darrent as portly and pink as a freshly tubbed baby, and this Emory W. Light was large and owlish, with eyes like boiled eggs behind his rimless glasses.

Yet all of these differences were only superficial, Jack had found. They all listened to the Story with the same breathless interest. They all asked him if he had had any girl-friends back home. Sooner or later he would find a hand (a large bald hand) lying on his thigh, and when he looked at Ferguson/Darrent/Light, he would see an expression of half-mad hope in the eyes (mixed with half-mad guilt) and a stipple of sweat on the upper lip (in the case of Darrent, the sweat had gleamed through a dark moustache like tiny white eyes peering through scant under-brush).

Ferguson had asked him if he would like to make ten dollars.

Darrent had upped that to twenty.

Light, in a large bald voice that nonetheless cracked and quivered through several registers, asked him if he couldn't use fifty dollars – he always kept a fifty in the heel of his left shoe, he said, and he'd just love to give it to Master Lewis Farren. There was a place they could go near Randolph. An empty barn.

Jack did not make any correlation between the steadily increasing monetary offers from Light in his various incarnations and any changes his adventures might be working on him – he was not introspective by nature and had little interest in self-analysis.

He had learned quickly enough how to deal with fellows like Emory W. Light. His first experience with Light, when Light had been calling himself Tom Ferguson, had taught him that discretion was by far the better part of valor. When Ferguson put his hand on Jack's thigh, Jack had responded automatically out of a California sensibility in which gays had been merely part of the scenery: 'No thanks, mister. I'm strictly A.C.'

He had been groped before, certainly – in movie theaters, mostly, but there had been the men's-shop clerk in North Hollywood who had cheerfully offered to blow him in a changing booth (and when Jack told him no thanks, the clerk said, 'Fine, now try on the blue blazer, okay?').

These were annoyances a good-looking twelve-year-old boy in Los Angeles simply learned to put up with, the way a pretty woman learns to put up with being groped occasionally on the subway. You eventually find a way to cope without letting it spoil your whole day. The deliberate passes, such as the one this Ferguson was making, were less of a problem than the sudden gropes from ambush. They could simply be shunted aside.

At least in California they could. Eastern gays – especially out here in the sticks – apparently had a different way of dealing with rejection.

Ferguson had come to a screeching, sliding halt, leaving forty yards of rubber behind his Pontiac and throwing a cloud of shoulder-dust into the air.

'Who you calling *D.C.*?' he screamed. 'Who you calling *queer*? I'm not *queer*! Jesus! Give a kid a fucking ride and he calls you a fucking *queer*!'

Jack was looking at him, dazed. Unprepared for the sudden stop, he had thumped his head a damned good one on the padded dash. Ferguson, who had only a moment before been looking at him with melting brown eyes, now looked ready to kill him.

'*Get out!*' Ferguson yelled. '*You're the queer, not me! You're the queer! Get out, you little queerboy! Get out! I've got a wife! I've got kids! I've probably got bastards scattered all over New*

England! I'm not queer! You're the queer, not me, SO GET OUT OF MY CAR!'

More terrified than he had been since his encounter with Osmond, Jack had done just that. Ferguson tore out, spraying him with gravel, still raving. Jack staggered over to a rock wall, sat down, and began to giggle. The giggles became shrieks of laughter, and he decided right then and there that he would have to develop A POLICY, at least until he got out of the boondocks. 'Any serious problem demands A POLICY,' his father had said once. Morgan had agreed vigorously, but Jack decided he shouldn't let that hold him back.

His POLICY had worked well enough with Bob Darrent, and he had no reason to believe it wouldn't also work with Emory Light . . . but in the meantime he was cold and his nose was running. He wished Light would head em up and move em out. Standing in the trees, Jack could see him down there, walking back and forth with his hands in his pockets, his large bald head gleaming mellowly under the white-out sky. On the turnpike, big semis droned by, filling the air with the stink of burned diesel fuel. The woods here were trashed-out, the way the woods bordering any interstate rest area always were. Empty Dorito bags. Squashed Big Mac boxes. Crimped Pepsi and Budweiser cans with pop-tops that rattled inside if you kicked them. Smashed bottles of Wild Irish Rose and Five O'Clock gin. A pair of shredded nylon panties over there, with a mouldering sanitary napkin still glued to the crotch. A rubber poked over a broken branch. Plenty of nifty stuff, all right, hey-hey. And lots of graffiti jotted on the walls of the men's room, almost all of it the sort a fellow like Emory W. Light could really relate to: I LIKE TO SUK BIG FAT COX. BE HERE AT 4 FOR

THE BEST BLOJOB YOU EVER HAD. REEM OUT MY BUTT. And here was a gay poet with large aspirations: LET THE HOLE HUMAN RACE/JERK OFF ON MY SMILING FACE.

I'm homesick for the Territories, Jack thought, and there was no surprise at all in the realization. Here he stood behind two brick outhouses off I-70 somewhere in western Ohio, shivering in a ragged sweater he had bought in a thrift store for a buck and a half, waiting for that large bald man down there to get back on his horse and ride.

Jack's POLICY was simplicity itself: don't antagonize a man with large bald hands and a large bald voice.

Jack sighed with relief. Now it was starting to work. An expression that was half-anger, half-disgust, had settled over Emory W. Light's large bald face. He went back to his car, got in, backed up so fast he almost hit the pick-up truck passing behind him (there was a brief blare of horns and the passenger in the truck shot Emory W. Light the finger), and then left.

Now it was only a matter of standing on the ramp where the rest-area traffic rejoined the turnpike traffic with his thumb out . . . and, he hoped, catching a ride before it started to rain.

Jack spared another look around. *Ugly, wretched.* These words came quite naturally to mind as he looked around at the littery desolation here on the rest area's pimply backside. It occurred to Jack that there was a feeling of death here – not just at this rest area or on the interstate roads but pressed deep into all the country he had travelled. Jack thought that sometimes he could even see it, a desperate shade of hot dark brown, like the exhaust from the short-stack of a fast-moving Jimmy-Pete.

The new homesickness came back – the wanting to

go to the Territories and see that dark blue sky, the slight curve at the edge of the horizon . . .

But it plays those Jerry Bledsoe changes.

Don't know nothin bout dat . . . All I know is you seem to have this idear of 'moider' a little broad . . .

Walking down to the rest area – now he really did have to urinate – Jack sneezed three times, quickly. He swallowed and winced at the hot prickle in his throat. Getting sick, oh yeah. Great. Not even into Indiana yet, fifty degrees, rain in the forecast, no ride, and now I'm –

The thought broke off cleanly. He stared at the parking lot, his mouth falling wide open. For one awful moment he thought he was going to wet his pants as everything below his breastbone seemed to cramp and squeeze.

Sitting in one of the twenty or so slant parking spaces, its deep green surface now dulled with road-dirt, was Uncle Morgan's BMW. No chance of a mistake; no chance at all. California vanity plates MLS, standing for Morgan Luther Sloat. It looked as if it had been driven fast and hard.

But if he flew to New Hampshire, how can his car be here? Jack's mind yammered. *It's a coincidence, Jack, just a –*

Then he saw the man standing with his back to him at the pay telephone and knew it was no coincidence. He was wearing a bulky Army-style anorak, fur-lined, a garment more suited to five below than to fifty degrees. Back-to or not, there was no mistaking those broad shoulders and that big, loose, hulking frame.

The man at the phone started to turn around, crooking the phone between his ear and shoulder.

Jack drew back against the brick side of the men's toilet.

Did he see me?

No, he answered himself. *No, I don't think so. But –*

But Captain Farren had said that Morgan – that other Morgan – would smell him like a cat smells a rat, and so he had. From his hiding place in that dangerous forest, Jack had seen the hideous white face in the window of the diligence change.

This Morgan would smell him, too. If given the time.

Footfalls around the corner, approaching.

Face numb and twisted with fear, Jack fumbled off his pack and then dropped it, knowing he was too late, too slow, that Morgan would come around the corner and seize him by the neck, smiling. *Hi, Jacky! Allee-allee-in-free! Game's over now, isn't it, you little prick?*

A tall man in a houndstooth-check jacket passed the corner of the rest-room, gave Jack a disinterested glance, and went to the drinking fountain.

Going back. He was going back. There was no guilt, at least not now; only that terrible trapped fear mingling with feelings of relief and pleasure. Jack fumbled his pack open. Here was Speedy's bottle, with less than an inch of the purple liquid now left

(*no boy needs* dat *poison to travel with but I do Speedy I do!*)

sloshing around in the bottom. No matter. He was going back. His heart leaped at the thought. A big Saturday-night grin dawned on his face, denying both the gray day and the fear in his heart. *Going back, oh yeah, dig it.*

More footsteps approaching, and this was Uncle Morgan, no doubt about that heavy yet somehow mincing step. But the fear was gone. Uncle Morgan had smelled something, but when he turned the corner he would see nothing but empty Dorito bags and crimped beercans.

Jack pulled in breath – pulled in the greasy stink of diesel fumes and car exhausts and cold autumn air. Tipped the bottle up to his lips. Took one of the two swallows left. And even with his eyes shut he squinted as –

CHAPTER SIXTEEN

WOLF

1

– the strong sunlight struck his closed lids.

Through the gagging-sweet odor of the magic juice he could smell something else . . . the warm smell of animals. He could hear them, too, moving all about him.

Frightened, Jack opened his eyes but at first could see nothing – the difference in the light was so sudden and abrupt that it was as if someone had suddenly turned on a cluster of two-hundred-watt bulbs in a black room.

A warm, hide-covered flank brushed by him, not in a threatening way (or so Jack hoped), but most definitely in an I'm-in-a-hurry-to-be-gone-thank-you-very-much way. Jack, who had been getting up, thumped back to the ground again.

'*Hey! Hey! Get away from im! Right here and right now!*' A loud, healthy whack followed by a disgruntled animal sound somewhere between a moo and a baa. '*God's nails! Got no sense! Get away from im fore I bite your God-pounding eyes out!*'

Now his eyes had adjusted enough to the brightness of this almost flawless Territories autumn day to make out a young giant standing in the middle of a herd of milling animals, whacking their sides and slightly humped backs with what appeared to be great gusto and very little real force. Jack sat up, automatically finding Speedy's bottle with its one precious swallow left and putting it away. He never took his eyes from the young man who stood with his back to him.

Tall he was – six-five at least, Jack guessed – and with shoulders so broad that his across still looked slightly out of proportion to his high. Long, greasy black hair shagged down his back to the shoulderblades. Muscles bulged and rippled as he moved amid the animals, which looked like pygmy cows. He was driving them away from Jack and toward the Western Road.

He was a striking figure, even when seen from behind, but what amazed Jack was his dress. Everyone he had seen in the Territories (including himself) had been wearing tunics, jerkins, or rough breeches.

This fellow appeared to be wearing Oshkosh bib overalls.

Then he turned around and Jack felt a horrible shocked dismay well up in his throat. He shot to his feet.

It was the Elroy-thing.

The herdsman was the Elroy-thing.

2

Except it wasn't.

Jack perhaps would not have lingered to see that, and everything that happened thereafter – the movie theater, the shed, and the hell of the Sunlight Home – would not have happened (or would, at the very least, have happened in some completely different way), but in the extremity of his terror he froze completely after getting up. He was no more able to run than a deer is when it is frozen in a hunter's jacklight.

As the figure in the bib overalls approached, he thought: *Elroy wasn't that tall or that broad. And his eyes were yellow –* The eyes of this creature were a bright, impossible shade of orange. Looking into them was like looking into the eyes of a Halloween pumpkin. And while Elroy's grin had promised madness and murder, the smile on this fellow's face was large and cheerful and harmless.

His feet were bare, huge, and spatulate, the toes clumped into groups of three and two, barely visible through curls of wiry hair. Not hooflike, as Elroy's had been, Jack realized, half-crazed with surprise, fear, a dawning amusement, but padlike-pawlike.

As he closed the distance between himself and Jack,

(*his? its?*)

eyes flared an even brighter orange, going for a moment to the Day-Glo shade favored by hunters and flagmen on road-repair jobs. The color faded to a muddy hazel. As it did, Jack saw that his smile was puzzled as well as friendly, and understood two things at once: first, that there was no harm in this fellow, not an ounce of it, and second, that he was slow. Not feeble, perhaps, but slow.

'Wolf!' the big, hairy boy-beast cried, grinning. His tongue was long and pointed, and Jack thought with a shudder that a wolf was exactly what he looked like. Not a goat but a wolf. He hoped he was right about there not being any harm in him. *But if I made a mistake about that, at least I won't have to worry about making any more mistakes . . . ever again.* 'Wolf! Wolf!' He stuck out one hand, and Jack saw that, like his feet, his hands were covered with hair, although this hair was finer and more luxuriant – actually quite handsome. It grew especially thick in the palms, where it was the soft white of a blaze on a horse's forehead.

My God, I think he wants to shake hands with me!

Gingerly, thinking of Uncle Tommy, who had told him he must never refuse a handshake, not even with his worst enemy ('Fight him to the death afterward if you must, but shake his hand first,' Uncle Tommy had said), Jack put his own hand out, wondering if it was about to be crushed . . . or perhaps eaten.

'Wolf! Wolf! Shakin hands right here and now!' the boy-thing in the Oshkosh biballs cried, delighted. 'Right here and now! Good old Wolf! God-pound it! Right here and now! *Wolf!*'

In spite of this enthusiasm, Wolf's grip was gentle enough, cushioned by the crisp, furry growth of hair on his hand. *Bib overalls and a big handshake from a guy who looks like an overgrown Siberian husky and smells a little bit like a hayloft after a heavy rain,* Jack thought. *What next? An offer to come to his church this Sunday?*

'Good old Wolf, you bet! Good old Wolf right here and now!' Wolf wrapped his arms around his huge chest and laughed, delighted with himself. Then he grabbed Jack's hand again.

This time his hand was pumped vigorously up and down. Something seemed required of him at this point, Jack reflected. Otherwise, this pleasant if rather simple young man might go on shaking his hand until sundown.

'Good old Wolf,' he said. It seemed to be a phrase of which his new acquaintance was particularly fond.

Wolf laughed like a child and dropped Jack's hand.

This was something of a relief. The hand had been neither crushed nor eaten, but it did feel a bit seasick. Wolf had a faster pump than a slot-machine player on a hot streak.

'Stranger, ain'tcha?' Wolf asked. He stuffed his hairy hands into the slit sides of his biballs and began playing pocket-pool with a complete lack of self-consciousness.

'Yes,' Jack said, thinking of what that word meant over here. It had a very specific meaning over here. 'Yes, I guess that's just what I am. A stranger.'

'God-pounding right! I can smell it on you! Right here and now, oh yeah, oh boy! Got it! Doesn't smell bad, you know, but it sure is *funny*. Wolf! That's me. Wolf! Wolf! Wolf!' He threw back his head and laughed. The sound ended being something that was disconcertingly like a howl.

'Jack,' Jack said. 'Jack Saw—'

His hand was seized again and pumped with abandon.

'Sawyer,' he finished, when he was released again. He smiled, feeling very much as though someone had hit him with a great big goofystick. Five minutes ago he had been standing scrunched against the cold brick side of a shithouse on I-70. Now he was standing here talking to a young fellow who seemed to be more animal than man.

And damned if his cold wasn't completely gone.

3

'Wolf meet Jack! Jack meet Wolf! Here and now! Okay! Good! Oh, Jason! Cows in the road! Ain't they stupid! Wolf! Wolf!'

Yelling, Wolf loped down the hill to the road, where about half of his herd was standing, looking around with expressions of bland surprise, as if to ask where the grass had gone. They really did look like some strange cross between cows and sheep, Jack saw, and wondered what you would call such a crossbreed. The only word to come immediately to mind was *creeps* – or perhaps, he thought, the singular would be more proper in this case, as in *Here's Wolf taking care of his flock of creep. Oh yeah. Right here and now.*

The goofystick came down on Jack's head again. He sat down and began to giggle, his hands crisscrossed over his mouth to stifle the sounds.

Even the biggest creep stood no more than four feet high. Their fur was woolly, but of a muddy shade that was similar to Wolf's eyes – at least, when Wolf's eyes weren't blazing like Halloween jack-o'-lanterns. Their heads were topped with short, squiggly horns that looked good for absolutely nothing. Wolf herded them back out of the road. They went obediently, with no sign of fear. *If a cow or a sheep on my side of the jump got a whiff of that guy,* Jack thought, *it'd kill itself trying to get out of his way.*

But Jack liked Wolf – liked him on sight, just as he had feared and disliked Elroy on sight. And that contrast was particularly apt, because the comparison between the two was undeniable. Except that Elroy had been goatish while Wolf was . . . well, wolfish.

Jack walked slowly toward where Wolf had set his herd to graze. He remembered tiptoeing down the stinking back hall of the Oatley Tap toward the fire-door, sensing Elroy somewhere near, smelling him, perhaps, as a cow on the other side would undoubtedly smell Wolf. He remembered the way Elroy's hands had begun to twist and thicken, the way his neck had swelled, the way his teeth had become a mouthful of blackening fangs.

'Wolf?'

Wolf turned and looked at him, smiling. His eyes flared a bright orange and looked for a moment both savage and intelligent. Then the glow faded and they were only that muddy, perpetually puzzled hazel again.

'Are you . . . sort of a werewolf?'

'Sure am,' Wolf said, smiling. 'You pounded that nail, Jack. Wolf!'

Jack sat down on a rock, looking at Wolf thoughtfully. He believed it would be impossible for him to be further surprised than he had already been, but Wolf managed the trick quite nicely.

'How's your father, Jack?' he asked, in that casual, by-the-way tone reserved for enquiring after the relatives of others. 'How's Phil doing these days? Wolf!'

4

Jack made a queerly apt cross-association: he felt as if all the wind had been knocked out of his mind. For a moment it just sat there in his head, not a thought in it, like a radio station broadcasting nothing but a carrier wave. Then he saw Wolf's change. The expression of happiness and childish curiosity was replaced by one of sorrow. Jack saw that Wolf's nostrils were flaring rapidly.

'He's dead, isn't he? Wolf! I'm sorry, Jack. God pound me! I'm stupid! *Stupid!*' Wolf crashed a hand into his fore-head and this time he really *did* howl. It was a sound that chilled Jack's blood. The herd of creep looked around uneasily.

'That's all right,' Jack said. He heard his voice more in his ears than in his head, as if someone else had spoken.

'But . . . how did you know?'

'Your smell changed,' Wolf said simply. 'I knew he was dead because it was in your smell. Poor Phil! What a good guy! Tell you that right here and now, Jack! Your father was a good guy! Wolf!'

'Yes,' Jack said, 'he was. But how did you know him? And how did you know he was my father?'

Wolf looked at Jack as though he had asked a question so simple it barely needed answering. 'I remember his smell, of course. Wolfs remember all smells. You smell just like him.'

Whack! The goofystick came down on his head again. Jack felt an urge to just roll back and forth on the tough, springy turf, holding his gut and howling. People had told him he had his father's eyes and his father's mouth, even his father's knack for quick-sketching, but never before had he been told that he smelled like his father. Yet he supposed the idea had a certain crazy logic, at that.

'How did you know him?' Jack asked again.

Wolf looked at a loss. 'He came with the other one,' he said at last. 'The one from Orris. I was just little. The other one was bad. The other one stole some of us. Your father didn't know,' he added hastily, as if Jack had shown anger. 'Wolf! No! He was good, your father. Phil. The other one . . .'

Wolf shook his head slowly. On his face was an expression even more simple than his pleasure. It was the memory of some childhood nightmare.

'Bad,' Wolf said. 'He made himself a place in this world, my father says. Mostly he was in his Twinner, but he was from your world. We knew he was bad, we could tell, but who listens to Wolfs? No one. Your father knew he was bad, but he couldn't smell him as good as we could. He knew he was bad, but not *how* bad.'

And Wolf threw his head back and howled again, a long, chilly ululation of sorrow that resounded against the deep blue sky.

INTERLUDE

SLOAT IN THIS WORLD (II)

From the pocket of his bulky parka (he had bought it convinced that from the Rockies east, America was a frigid wasteland after October 1st or so – now he was sweating rivers), Morgan Sloat took a small steel box. Below the latch were ten small buttons and an oblong of cloudy yellow glass a quarter of an inch high and two inches long. He pushed several of the buttons carefully with the fingernail of his left-hand pinky, and a series of numbers appeared briefly in the readout window. Sloat had bought this gadget, billed as the world's smallest safe, in Zurich. According to the man who had sold it to him, not even a week in a crematory oven would breach its carbon-steel integrity.

Now it clicked open.

Sloat folded back two tiny wings of ebony jeweler's velvet, revealing something he had had for well over twenty years – since long before the odious little brat who was causing all this trouble had been born. It was a tarnished tin key, and once it had gone into the back of a mechanical toy soldier. Sloat had seen the toy soldier in the window of a junkshop in the odd little town of Point Venuti, California – a town in which he had a great interest. Acting under a compulsion much too strong to deny (and he hadn't even wanted to deny it, not really; he had always made a virtue of compulsion, had Morgan Sloat), he had gone in and paid five dollars for the dusty, dented soldier . . . and it wasn't the soldier he had wanted, anyway. It was the key that had caught his eye and then whispered to him. He had removed the key from the soldier's back and pocketed it as soon as he was outside the junkshop door. The soldier itself he threw in a litter-basket outside the Dangerous Planet Bookstore.

Now, as Sloat stood beside his car in the Lewisburg rest area, he held the key up and looked at it. Like Jack's croaker, the tin key became something else in the Territories. Once, when coming back, he had dropped that key in the lobby of the old office building. And there must have been some Territories magic left in it, because that idiot Jerry Bledsoe had gotten himself fried not an hour later. Had Jerry picked it up? Stepped on it, perhaps? Sloat didn't know and didn't care. Nor had he cared a tinker's damn about Jerry – and considering the handyman had had an insurance policy specifying double indemnity for accidental death (the building's super, with whom Sloat sometimes shared a hash-pipe, had passed this little tidbit on to him), Sloat imagined that Nita Bledsoe had done nip-ups – but he had been nearly frantic about the loss of his key. It was Phil Sawyer who had found it, giving it back to him with no comment other than 'Here, Morg. Your lucky charm, isn't it? Must have a hole in your pocket. I found it in the lobby after they took poor old Jerry away.'

Yes, in the lobby. In the lobby where everything smelled like the motor of a Waring Blendor that had been running continuously on Hi Speed for about nine hours. In the lobby where everything had been blackened and twisted and fused.

Except for this humble tin key.

Which, in the other world, was a queer kind of lightning-rod – and which Sloat now hung around his neck on a fine silver chain.

'Coming for you, Jacky,' said Sloat in a voice that was almost tender. 'Time to bring this entire ridiculous business to a crashing halt.'

CHAPTER SEVENTEEN
WOLF AND THE HERD

1

Wolf talked of many things, getting up occasionally to shoo his cattle out of the road and once to move them to a stream about half a mile to the west. When Jack asked him where he lived, Wolf only waved his arm vaguely northward. He lived, he said, with his family. When Jack asked for clarification a few minutes later, Wolf looked surprised and said he had no mate and no children – that he would not come into what he called the 'big rut-moon' for another year or two. That he looked forward to the 'big rut-moon' was quite obvious from the innocently lewd grin that overspread his face.

'But you said you lived with your family.'

'Oh, family! Them! Wolf!' Wolf laughed. 'Sure. *Them!* We all live together. Have to keep the cattle, you know. *Her* cattle.'

'The Queen's?'

'Yes. May she never, never die.' And Wolf made an absurdly touching salute, bending briefly forward with his right hand touching his forehead.

Further questioning straightened the matter out somewhat in Jack's mind . . . at least, he thought it did. Wolf was a bachelor (although that word barely fit, somehow). The family of which he spoke was a hugely extended one – literally, the Wolf family. They were a nomadic but fiercely loyal race that moved back and forth in the great empty areas east of the Outposts but west of 'The Settlements', by which Wolf seemed to mean the towns and villages of the east.

Wolfs (never Wolves – when Jack once used the proper plural, Wolf had laughed until tears spurted from the corners of his eyes) were solid, dependable workers, for the most part. Their strength was legendary, their courage unquestioned. Some of them had gone east into The Settlements, where they served the Queen as guards, soldiers, even as personal bodyguards. Their lives, Wolf explained to Jack, had only two great touchstones: the Lady and the family. Most of the Wolfs, he said, served the Lady as he did – watching the herds.

The cow-sheep were the Territories' primary source of meat, cloth, tallow, and lamp-oil (Wolf did not tell Jack this, but Jack inferred it from what he said). All the cattle belonged to the Queen, and the Wolf family had been watching over them since time out of mind. It was their job. In this Jack found an oddly persuasive correlative to the relationship that had existed between the buffalo and the Indians of the American Plains . . . at least until the white man had come into those territories and upset the balance.

'Behold, and the lion shall lie down with the lamb, and the Wolf with the creep,' Jack murmured, and smiled. He was lying on his back with his hands laced behind his head. The most marvellous feeling of peace and ease had stolen over him.

'What, Jack?'

'Nothing,' he said. 'Wolf, do you really change into an animal when the moon gets full?'

''Course I do!' Wolf said. He looked astounded, as if Jack had asked him something like *Wolf, do you really pull up your pants after you finish taking a crap?* 'Strangers don't, do they? Phil told me *that.*'

'The, ah, herd,' Jack said. 'When you change, do they—'

'Oh, we don't go *near* the herd when we change,' Wolf said seriously. 'Good Jason, no! We'd eat them, don't you know that? And a Wolf who eats of his herd must be put to death. *The Book of Good Farming* says so. Wolf! Wolf! We have places to go when the moon is full. So does the herd. They're stupid, but they know they have to go away at the time of the big moon. Wolf! They better know, God pound them!'

'But you *do* eat meat, don't you?' Jack asked.

'Full of questions, just like your father,' Wolf said. 'Wolf! I don't mind. Yeah, we eat meat. Of course we do. We're Wolfs, aren't we?'

'But if you don't eat from the herds, what do you eat?'

'We eat well,' Wolf said, and would say no more on that subject.

Like everything else in the Territories, Wolf was a mystery – a mystery that was both gorgeous and frightening. The fact that he had known both Jack's father and Morgan Sloat – had, at least, met their Twinners on more than one occasion – contributed to Wolf's particular aura of mystery, but did not define it completely. Everything Wolf told him led Jack to a dozen more questions, most of which Wolf couldn't – or wouldn't – answer.

The matter of Philip Sawtelle's and Orris's visits was

a case in point. They had first appeared when Wolf was in the 'little moon' and living with his mother and two 'litter-sisters'. They were apparently just passing through, as Jack himself was now doing, only they had been heading east instead of west ('Tell you the truth, you're just about the only human I've ever seen this far west who was still *going* west,' Wolf said).

They had been jolly enough company, both of them. It was only later that there had been trouble . . . trouble with Orris. That had been after the partner of Jack's father had 'made himself a place in this world', Wolf told Jack again and again – only now he seemed to mean Sloat, in the physical guise of Orris. Wolf said that Morgan had stolen one of his litter-sisters ('My mother bit her hands and toes for a month after she knew for certain that he took her,' Wolf told Jack matter-of-factly) and had taken other Wolfs from time to time. Wolf dropped his voice and, with an expression of fear and superstitious awe on his face, told Jack that the 'limping man' had taken some of these Wolfs into the other world, the Place of the Strangers, and had taught them to eat of the herd.

'That's very bad for guys like you, isn't it?' Jack asked.

'They're damned,' Wolf replied simply.

Jack had thought at first that Wolf was speaking of kidnapping – the verb Wolf had used in connection with his litter-sister, after all, was the Territories version of *take*. He began to see now that kidnapping wasn't what was going on at all – unless Wolf, with unconscious poetry, had been trying to say that Morgan had kidnapped the minds of some of the Wolf family. Jack now thought that Wolf was really talking about werewolves who had thrown over their ancient allegiance to the Crown and the herd and had given it to Morgan instead . . . Morgan Sloat and Morgan of Orris.

Which led naturally enough to thoughts of Elroy.

A Wolf who eats of his herd must be put to death.

To thoughts of the men in the green car who had stopped to ask him directions, and offered him a Tootsie Roll, and who had then tried to pull him into their car. The eyes. *The eyes had changed.*

They're damned.

He made himself a place in this world.

Until now he had felt both safe and delighted: delighted to be back in the Territories where there was a nip in the air but nothing like the dull, cold gray bite of western Ohio, safe with big, friendly Wolf beside him, way out in the country, miles from anything or anyone.

Made himself a place in this world.

He asked Wolf about his father – Philip Sawtelle in this world – but Wolf only shook his head. He had been a God-pounding good guy, and a Twinner – thus obviously a Stranger – but that was all Wolf seemed to know. Twinners, he said, was something that had something to do with litters of *people*, and about such business he could not presume to say. Nor could he describe Philip Sawtelle – he didn't remember. He only remembered the smell. All *he* knew, he told Jack, was that, while both of the Strangers had *seemed* nice, only Phil Sawyer had really *been* nice. Once he had brought presents for Wolf and his litter-sisters and litter-brothers. One of the presents, unchanged from the world of the Strangers, had been a set of bib overalls for Wolf.

'I wore em all the time,' Wolf said. 'My mother wanted to throw em away after I'd wore em for five years or so.

Said they were worn out! Said I was too big for them! Wolf! Said they were only patches holding more patches together. I wouldn't give em up, though. Finally, she bought some cloth from a drummer headed out toward the Outposts. I don't know how much she paid, and Wolf! I'll tell you the truth, Jack, I'm afraid to ask. She dyed it blue and made me six pairs. The ones your father brought me, I sleep on them now. Wolf! Wolf! It's my God-pounding pillow, I guess.' Wolf smiled so openly – and yet so wistfully – that Jack was moved to take his hand. It was something he never could have done in his old life, no matter what the circumstances, but that now seemed like his loss. He was glad to take Wolf's warm, strong hand.

'I'm glad you liked my dad, Wolf,' he said.

'I did! I did! Wolf! Wolf!'

And then all hell broke loose.

2

Wolf stopped talking and looked around, startled.

'Wolf? What's wr—'

'Shhhh!'

Then Jack heard it. Wolf's more sensitive ears had picked the sound up first, but it swelled quickly; before long, a deaf man would have heard it, Jack thought. The cattle looked around and then began to move away from the source of the sound in a rough, uneasy clot. It was like a radio sound-effect where someone is supposed to be ripping a bedsheet down the middle, very slowly. Only the volume kept going up and up and up until Jack thought he was going to go crazy.

Wolf leaped to his feet, looking stunned and confused

and frightened. That ripping sound, a low, ragged purr, continued to grow. The bleating of the cattle became louder. Some were backing into the stream, and as Jack looked that way he saw one go down with a splash and a clumsy flailing of legs. It had been pushed over by its milling, retreating comrades. It let out a shrill, *baaa*-ing cry. Another cow-sheep stumbled over it and was likewise trampled into the water by the slow retreat. The far side of the stream was low and wet, green with reeds, muddy-marshy. The cow-sheep who first reached this muck quickly became mired in it.

'*Oh you God-pounding good-for-nothing cattle!*' Wolf bellowed, and charged down the hill toward the stream, where the first animal to fall over now looked as if it were in its death-throes.

'Wolf!' Jack shouted, but Wolf couldn't hear him. Jack could barely hear himself over that ragged ripping sound. He looked a little to the right, on this side of the stream, and gaped with amazement. Something was happening to the air. A patch of it about three feet off the ground was rippling and blistering, seeming to twist and pull at itself. Jack could see the Western Road through this patch of air, but the road seemed blurry and shimmery, as if seen through the heated, rippling air over an incinerator.

Something's pulling the air open like a wound – something's coming through – from our side? Oh Jason, is that what I do when I come through? But even in his own panic and confusion he knew it was not.

Jack had a good idea who *would* come through like this, like a rape in progress.

Jack began to run down the hill.

3

The ripping sound went on and on and on. Wolf was down on his knees in the stream, trying to help the second downed animal to its feet. The first floated limply downstream, its body tattered and mangled.

'Get up! God pound you, get up! Wolf!'

Wolf shoved and slapped as best he could at the cow-sheep who milled and backed into him, then got both arms around the drowning animal's midriff and pulled upward. *'WOLF! HERE AND NOW!'* he screamed. The sleeves of his shirt split wide open along the biceps, reminding Jack of David Banner having one of the gamma-ray-inspired tantrums that turned him into The Incredible Hulk. Water sprayed everywhere and Wolf lurched to his feet, eyes blazing orange, blue overalls now soaked black. Water streamed from the nostrils of the animal, which Wolf held clutched against his chest as if it were an overgrown puppy. Its eyes were turned up to sticky whites.

'Wolf!' Jack screamed. 'It's Morgan! It's—'

'The herd!' Wolf screamed back. *'Wolf! Wolf! My God-pounding herd! Jack! Don't try—'*

The rest was drowned out by a grinding clap of thunder that shook the earth. For a moment the thunder even covered that maddening, monotonous ripping sound. Almost as confused as Wolf's cattle, Jack looked up and saw a clear blue sky, innocent of clouds save for a few puffy white ones that were miles away.

The thunder ignited outright panic in Wolf's herd. They tried to bolt, but in their exquisite stupidity, many of them tried to do it by backing up. They crashed and splashed and were rolled underwater. Jack heard the bitter snap of a breaking bone, followed by the *baaaa*-ing scream of an animal in pain. Wolf bellowed in rage, dropped the cow-sheep he had been trying to save, and floundered toward the muddy far bank of the stream.

Before he could get there, half a dozen cattle struck him and bore him down. Water splashed and flew in thin, bright sprays. Now, Jack saw, Wolf was the one in danger of being simultaneously trampled and drowned by the stupid, fleeing animals.

Jack pushed into the stream, which was now dark with roiling mud. The current tried continually to push him off-balance. A bleating cow-sheep, its eyes rolling madly, splashed past him, almost knocking him down. Water sprayed into his face and Jack tried to wipe it out of his eyes.

Now that sound seemed to fill the whole world: *RRRRRIIIPPPP* –

Wolf. Never mind Morgan, at least not for the moment. Wolf was in trouble.

His shaggy, drenched head was momentarily visible above the water, and then three of the animals ran right over him and Jack could only see one waving, fur-covered hand. He pushed forward again, trying to weave through the cattle, some still up, others floundering and drowning underfoot.

'*Jack!*' A voice bellowed over that ripping noise. It was a voice Jack knew. Uncle Morgan's voice.

'*Jack!*'

There was another clap of thunder, this one a huge oaken thud that rolled through the sky like an artillery shell.

Panting, his soaked hair hanging in his eyes, Jack looked over his shoulder . . . and directly into the rest area on I-70 near Lewisburg, Ohio. He was seeing it as if through ripply, badly made glass . . . but he was *seeing* it. The edge of the brick toilet was on the left side of that blistered, tortured patch of air. The snout of what looked like a Chevrolet pick-up truck was on the right, floating three feet above the field where he and Wolf had been sitting peacefully and talking not five minutes ago. And in the center, looking like an extra in a film about Admiral Byrd's assault on the South Pole, was Morgan Sloat, his thick red face twisted with murderous rage. Rage, and something else. Triumph? Yes. Jack thought that was what it was.

He stood at midstream in water that was crotch-deep, cattle passing on either side of him, *baa*-ing and bleating, staring at that window which had been torn in the very fabric of reality, his eyes wide, his mouth wider.

He's found me, oh dear God, he's found me.

'There you are, you little shithead!' Morgan bellowed at him. His voice carried, but it had a muffled, dead quality as it came from the reality of that world into the reality of this one. It was like listening to a man shout inside a telephone booth. '*Now we'll see, won't we? Won't we?*'

Morgan started forward, his face swimming and rippling as if made of limp plastic, and Jack had time to see there was something clutched in his hand, something hung around his neck, something small and silvery.

Jack stood, paralyzed, as Sloat bulled his way through the hole between the two universes. As he came he did his own werewolf number, changing from Morgan Sloat, investor, land speculator, and sometime Hollywood agent, into Morgan of Orris, pretender to the throne of a dying Queen. His flushed, hanging jowls thinned. The color faded out of them. His hair renewed itself, growing forward, first tinting the rondure of his skull, as if some invisible being were coloring

Uncle Morgan's head, then covering it. The hair of Sloat's Twinner was long, black, flapping, somehow dead-looking. It had been tied at the nape of his neck, Jack saw, but most of it had come loose.

The parka wavered, disappeared for a moment, then came back as a cloak and hood.

Morgan Sloat's suede boots became dark leather knee-boots, their tops turned down, what might have been the hilt of a knife poking out of one.

And the small silvery thing in his hand had turned to a small rod tipped with crawling blue fire.

It's a lightning-rod. Oh Jesus, it's a –

'Jack!'

The cry was low, gargling, full of water.

Jack whirled clumsily around in the stream, barely avoiding another cow-sheep, this one floating on its side, dead in the water. He saw Wolf's head going down again, both hands waving. Jack fought his way toward those hands, still dodging the cattle as best he could. One of them bunted his hip hard and Jack went over, inhaling water. He got up again quick, coughing and choking, one hand feeling inside his jerkin for the bottle, afraid it might have washed away. It was still there.

'Boy! Turn around and look at me, boy!'

No time just now, Morgan. Sorry, but I've got to see if I can avoid getting drowned by Wolf's herd before I see if I can avoid getting fried by your doomstick there. I –

Blue fire arched over Jack's shoulder, sizzling – it was like a deadly electric rainbow. It struck one of the cow-sheep caught in the reedy muck on the other side of the stream and the unfortunate beast simply exploded, as if it had swallowed dynamite. Blood flew in a needle-spray of droplets. Gobbets of flesh began to rain down around Jack.

'Turn and look at me, boy!'

He could feel the *force* of that command, gripping his face with invisible hands, trying to turn it.

Wolf struggled up again, his hair plastered against his face, his dazed eyes peering through a curtain of it like the eyes of an English sheepdog. He was coughing and staggering, seemingly no longer aware of where he was.

'Wolf!' Jack screamed, but thunder exploded across the blue sky again, drowning him out.

Wolf bent over and retched up a great muddy sheet of water. A moment later another of the terrified cow-sheep struck him and bore him under again.

That's it, Jack thought despairingly. *That's it, he's gone, must be, let him go, get out of here –*

But he struggled on toward Wolf, pushing a dying, weakly convulsing cow-sheep out of his way to get there.

'Jason!' Morgan of Orris screamed, and Jack realized that Morgan was not cursing in the Territories argot; he was calling his, Jack's, name. Only here he was not Jack. Here he was Jason.

But the Queen's son died an infant, died, he –

The wet, sizzling zap of electricity again, seeming almost to part his hair. Again it struck the other bank, this time vaporizing one of Wolf's cattle. No, Jack saw, at least not utterly. The animal's legs were still there, mired in the mud like shakepoles. As he watched, they began to sag tiredly outward in four different directions.

'TURN AND LOOK AT ME, GOD POUND YOU!'

The water, why doesn't he throw it at the water, fry me, Wolf, all these animals at the same time?

Then his fifth-grade science came back to him. Once electricity went to water, it could go anywhere . . . including back to the generator of the current.

Wolf's dazed face, floating underwater, drove these thoughts from Jack's flying mind. Wolf was still alive, but partially pinned under a cow-sheep, which, although apparently unhurt, had frozen in panic. Wolf's hands waved with pathetic, flagging energy. As Jack closed the last of the distance, one of those hands dropped and simply floated, limp as a water-lily.

Without slowing, Jack lowered his left shoulder and hit the cow-sheep like Jack Armstrong in a boy's sports story.

If it had been a full-sized cow instead of a Territories compact model, Jack would probably not have budged it, not with the stream's fairly stiff current working against him. But it was smaller than a cow, and Jack was pumped up. It bawled when Jack hit it, floundered backward, sat briefly on its haunches, and then lunged for the far bank. Jack grabbed Wolf's hands and pulled with all of his might.

Wolf came up as reluctantly as a waterlogged tree-trunk, his eyes now glazed and half-closed, water streaming from his ears and nose and mouth. His lips were blue.

Twin forks of lightning blazed to the right and left of where Jack stood holding Wolf, the two of them looking like a pair of drunks trying to waltz in a swimming pool. On the far bank, another cow-sheep flew in all directions, its severed head still bawling. Hot rips of fire zigzagged through the marshy area, lighting the reeds on the tussocks and then finding the drier grass of the field where the land began to rise again.

'Wolf!' Jack screamed. *'Wolf, for Christ's sake!'*

'Auh,' Wolf moaned, and vomited warm muddy water over Jack's shoulder. '*Auhhhhhhhhhh . . .*'

Now Jack saw Morgan standing on the other bank, a tall, Puritanical figure in his black cloak. His hood framed his pallid, vampirelike face with a kind of cheerless romance. Jack had time to think that the Territories had worked their magic even here, on behalf of his dreadful uncle. Over here, Morgan was not an overweight, hypertensive actuarial toad with piracy in his heart and murder in his mind; over here, his face had narrowed and found a frigid masculine beauty. He pointed the silver rod like a toy magic wand, and blue fire tore the air open.

'*Now you and your dumb friend!*' Morgan screamed. His thin lips split in a triumphant grin, revealing sunken yellow teeth that spoiled Jack's blurred impression of beauty once and forever.

Wolf screamed and jerked in Jack's aching arms. He was staring at Morgan, his eyes orange and bulging with hate and fear.

'*You, devil!*' Wolf screamed. '*You, devil! My sister! My litter-sister! Wolf! Wolf! You, devil!*'

Jack pulled the bottle out of his jerkin. There was a single swallow left anyway. He couldn't hold Wolf up with his one arm; he was losing him, and Wolf seemed unable to support himself. Didn't matter. Couldn't take him back through into the other world anyway . . . or could he?

'*You, devil!*' Wolf screamed, weeping, his wet face sliding down Jack's arm. The back of his bib overalls floated and belled in the water.

Smell of burning grass and burning animals.

Thunder, exploding.

This time the river of fire in the air rushed by Jack so close that the hairs in his nostrils singed and curled.

'OH YES, BOTH OF YOU, BOTH OF YOU!' Morgan howled. *'I'LL TEACH YOU TO GET IN MY WAY, YOU LITTLE BASTARD! I'LL BURN BOTH OF YOU! I'LL POUND YOU DOWN!'*

'Wolf, hold on!' Jack yelled. He gave up his effort to hold Wolf up; instead, he snatched Wolf's hand in his own and held it as tightly as he could. 'Hold on to me, do you hear?'

'Wolf!'

He tipped the bottle up, and the awful cold taste of rotted grapes filled his mouth for the last time. The bottle was empty. As he swallowed, he heard it shatter as one of Morgan's bolts of lightning struck it. But the sound of the breaking glass was faint . . . the tingle of electricity . . . even Morgan's screams of rage.

He felt as if he were falling over backward into a hole. A grave, maybe. Then Wolf's hand squeezed down on Jack's so hard that Jack groaned. That feeling of vertigo, of having done a complete dipsy-doodle, began to fade . . . and then the sunlight faded, too, and became the sad purplish gray of an October twilight in the heartland of America. Cold rain struck Jack in the face, and he was faintly aware that the water he was standing in seemed much colder than it had only seconds ago. Somewhere not far away he could hear the familiar snoring drone of the big rigs on the interstate . . . except that now they seemed to be coming from directly overhead.

Impossible, he thought, but was it? The bounds of that word seemed to be stretching with plastic ease. For one dizzy moment he had an image of flying Territories trucks driven by flying Territories men with big canvas wings strapped to their backs.

Back, he thought. Back again, same time, same turnpike.

He sneezed.

Same cold, too.

But two things were not the same now.

No rest area here. They were standing thigh-deep in the icy water of a stream beneath a turnpike overpass.

Wolf was with him. That was the other change.

And Wolf was screaming.

CHAPTER EIGHTEEN
WOLF GOES TO THE MOVIES

1

Overhead, another truck pounded across the overpass, big diesel engine bellowing. The overpass shook. Wolf wailed and clutched at Jack, almost knocking them both into the water.

'Quit it!' Jack shouted. 'Let go of me, Wolf! It's just a truck! Let *go!*'

He slapped at Wolf, not wanting to do it – Wolf's terror was pathetic. But, pathetic or not, Wolf had the best part of a foot and maybe a hundred and fifty pounds on Jack, and if he overbore him, they would both go into this freezing water and it would be pneumonia for sure.

'Wolf! Don't like it! Wolf! Don't like it! Wolf! Wolf!'

But his hold slackened. A moment later his arms dropped to his sides. When another truck snored by overhead, Wolf cringed but managed to keep from grabbing Jack again. But he looked at Jack with a mute, trembling appeal that said *Get me out of this, please get me out of this, I'd rather be dead than in this world.*

Nothing I'd like better, Wolf, but Morgan's over there. Even if he weren't, I don't have the magic juice anymore.

He looked down at his left hand and saw he was holding the jagged neck of Speedy's bottle, like a man getting ready to do some serious barroom brawling. Just dumb luck Wolf hadn't gotten a bad cut when he grabbed Jack in his terror.

Jack tossed it away. *Splash.*

Two trucks this time – the noise was doubled. Wolf howled in terror and plastered his hands over his ears. Jack could see that most of the hair had disappeared from Wolf's hands in the flip – most, but not all. And, he saw, the first two fingers of each of Wolf's hands were exactly the same length.

'Come on, Wolf,' Jack said when the racket of the trucks had faded a little. 'Let's get out of here. We look like a couple of guys waiting to get baptized on a *PTL Club* special.'

He took Wolf's hand, and then winced at the panicky way Wolf's grip closed down. Wolf saw his expression and loosened up . . . a little.

'Don't leave me, Jack,' Wolf said. 'Please, please don't leave me.'

'No, Wolf, I won't,' Jack said. He thought: *How do you get into these things, you asshole? Here you are, standing under a turnpike overpass somewhere in Ohio with your pet werewolf. How do you do it? Do you practice? And, oh, by the way, what's happening with the moon, Jack-O? Do you remember?*

He didn't, and with clouds blanketing the sky and a cold rain falling, there was no way to tell.

What did that make the odds? Thirty to one in his favor? Twenty-eight to two?

Whatever the odds were, they weren't good enough. Not the way things were going.

'No, I won't leave you,' he repeated, and then led Wolf toward the far bank of the stream. In the shallows, the decayed remains of some child's dolly floated belly-up, her glassy blue eyes staring into the growing dark. The muscles of Jack's arm ached from the strain of pulling Wolf through into this world, and the joint in his shoulder throbbed like a rotted tooth.

As they came out of the water onto the weedy, trashy bank, Jack began to sneeze again.

2

This time, Jack's total progress in the Territories had been half a mile west – the distance Wolf had moved his herd so they could drink in the stream where Wolf himself had later almost been drowned. Over here, he found himself ten miles farther west, as best he could figure. They struggled up the bank – Wolf actually ended up pulling Jack most of the way – and in the last of the daylight Jack could see an exit-ramp splitting off to the right some fifty yards up the road. A reflectorized sign read: ARCANUM LAST EXIT IN OHIO STATE LINE 15 MILES.

'We've got to hitch,' Jack said.

'Hitch?' Wolf said doubtfully.

'Let's have a look at you.'

He thought Wolf would do, at least in the dark. He was still wearing the bib overalls, which now had an actual OSHKOSH label on them. His homespun shirt had become a machine-produced blue chambray that looked like an Army-Navy Surplus special. His formerly bare feet were clad in a huge pair of dripping penny loafers and white socks.

Oddest of all, a pair of round steel-rimmed spectacles

of the sort John Lennon used to wear sat in the middle of Wolf's big face.

'Wolf, did you have trouble seeing? Over in the Territories?'

'I didn't know I did,' Wolf said. 'I guess so. Wolf! I sure see better over here, with these glass eyes. Wolf, right here and now!' He looked out at the roaring turnpike traffic, and for just a moment Jack saw what he must be seeing: great steel beasts with huge yellow-white eyes, snarling through the night at unimaginable speeds, rubber wheels blistering the road. 'I see better than I want to,' Wolf finished forlornly.

3

Two days later a pair of tired, footsore boys limped past the MUNICIPAL TOWN LIMITS sign on one side of Highway 32 and the 10–4 Diner on the other side, and thus into the city of Muncie, Indiana. Jack was running a fever of a hundred and two degrees and coughing pretty steadily. Wolf's face was swollen and discolored. He looked like a pug that has come out on the short end in a grudge match. The day before, he had tried to get them some late apples from a tree growing in the shade of an abandoned barn beside the road. He had actually been in the tree and dropping shrivelled autumn apples into the front of his overalls when the wall-wasps, which had built their nest somewhere in the eaves of the old barn, had found him. Wolf had come back down the tree as fast as he could, with a brown cloud around his head. He was howling. And still, with one eye completely closed and his nose beginning to resemble a large purple turnip, he had insisted that Jack have the best of the apples. None of them was very good – small and sour and wormy

– and Jack didn't feel much like eating anyway, but after what Wolf had gone through to get them, he hadn't had the heart to refuse.

A big old Camaro, jacked in the back so that the nose pointed at the road, blasted by them. '*Heyyyyy, assholes!*' someone yelled, and there was a burst of loud, beer-fueled laughter. Wolf howled and clutched at Jack. Jack had thought that Wolf would eventually get over his terror of cars, but now he was really beginning to wonder.

'It's all right, Wolf,' he said wearily, peeling Wolf's arms off for the twentieth or thirtieth time that day. 'They're gone.'

'So *loud*!' Wolf moaned. 'Wolf! Wolf! Wolf! So *loud*, Jack, my *ears*, my *ears*!'

'Glasspack muffler,' Jack said, thinking wearily: *You'd love the California freeways, Wolf. We'll check those out if we're still travelling together, okay? Then we'll try a few stock-car races and motorcycle scrambles. You'll be nuts about them.* 'Some guys like the sound, you know. They—' But he went into another coughing fit that doubled him over. For a moment the world swam away in gray shades. It came back very, very slowly.

'*Like* it,' Wolf muttered. 'Jason! How could anyone *like* it, Jack? And the *smells* . . .'

Jack knew that, for Wolf, the smells were the worst. They hadn't been over here four hours before Wolf began to call it the Country of Bad Smells. That first night Wolf had retched half a dozen times, at first throwing up muddy water from a stream which existed in another universe onto the Ohio ground, then simply dry-heaving. It was the smells, he explained miserably. He didn't know how Jack could stand them, how anyone could stand them.

Jack knew – coming back from the Territories, you were bowled over by odors you barely noticed when you were living with them. Diesel fuel, car exhausts, industrial wastes, garbage, bad water, ripe chemicals. Then you got used to them again. Got used to them or just went numb. Only that wasn't happening to Wolf. He hated the cars, he hated the smells, he hated this world. Jack didn't think he was ever going to get used to it. If he didn't get Wolf back into the Territories fairly soon, Jack thought he might go crazy. *He'll probably drive me crazy while he's at it,* Jack thought. *Not that I've got far to go anymore.*

A clattering farm-truck loaded with chickens ground by them, followed by an impatient line of cars, some of them honking. Wolf almost jumped into Jack's arms. Weakened by the fever, Jack reeled into the brushy, trash-littered ditch and sat down so hard his teeth clicked together.

'I'm sorry, Jack,' Wolf said miserably. 'God pound me!'

'Not your fault,' Jack said. 'Fall out. Time to take five.'

Wolf sat down beside Jack, remaining silent, looking at Jack anxiously. He knew how hard he was making it for Jack; he knew that Jack was in a fever to move faster, partly to outdistance Morgan, but mostly for some other reason. He knew that Jack moaned about his mother in his sleep, and sometimes cried. But the only time he had cried when awake was after Wolf went a little crazy on the Arcanum turnpike ramp. That was when he realized what Jack meant by 'hitching'. When Wolf told Jack he didn't think he could hitch rides – at least not for a while and maybe not ever – Jack had sat down on the top strand of guardrail cable and had wept into his hands. And then he had stopped, which was good . . . but when he took his face out of his hands, he had looked at Wolf in a way that made Wolf feel sure that Jack would leave him in this horrible Country of Bad Smells . . . and without Jack, Wolf would soon go quite mad.

4

They had walked up to the Arcanum exit in the breakdown lane, Wolf cringing and pawing at Jack each time a car or truck passed in the deepening dusk. Jack had heard a mocking voice drift back on the slipstream: 'Where's your car, faggots?' He shook it off like a dog shaking water out of his eyes, and had simply kept going, taking Wolf's hand and pulling him after when Wolf showed signs of lagging or drifting toward the woods. The important thing was to get off the turnpike proper, where hitchhiking was forbidden, and onto the westbound Arcanum entrance ramp. Some states had legalized hitching from the ramps (or so a road-bum with whom Jack had shared a barn one night had told him), and even in states where thumbing was technically a crime, the cops would usually wink if you were on a ramp.

So first, get to the ramp. Hope no state patrol happened along while you were getting there. What a state trooper might make of Wolf Jack didn't want to think about. He would probably think he had caught an eighties incarnation of Charles Manson in Lennon glasses.

They made the ramp and crossed over to the westbound lane. Ten minutes later a battered old Chrysler had pulled up. The driver, a burly man with a bull neck and a cap which read CASE FARM EQUIPMENT tipped back on his head, leaned over and opened the door.

'Hop in, boys! Dirty night, ain't it?'

'Thanks, mister, it sure is,' Jack said cheerfully. His mind was in overdrive, trying to figure out how he could work Wolf into the Story, and he barely noticed Wolf's expression.

The man noticed it, however.

His face hardened.

'You smell anything bad, son?'

Jack was snapped back to reality by the man's tone, which was as hard as his face. All cordiality had departed it, and he looked as if he might have just wandered into the Oatley Tap to eat a few beers and drink a few glasses.

Jack whipped around and looked at Wolf.

Wolf's nostrils were flaring like the nostrils of a bear which smells a blown skunk. His lips were not just pulled back from his teeth; they were *wrinkled* back from them, the flesh below his nose stacked in little ridges.

'What is he, retarded?' the man in the CASE FARM EQUIPMENT hat asked Jack in a low voice.

'No, ah, he just—'

Wolf began to growl.

That was it.

'Oh, Christ,' the man said in the tones of one who simply cannot believe this is happening. He stepped on the gas and roared down the exit ramp, the passenger door flopping shut. His taillights dot-dashed briefly in the rainy dark at the foot of the ramp, sending reflections in smeary red arrows up the pavement toward where they stood.

'Boy, that's *great*,' Jack said, and turned to Wolf, who shrank back from his anger. 'That's just *great*! If he'd had a CB radio, he'd be on Channel Nineteen right now, yelling for a cop, telling anyone and everyone that there are a couple of loonies trying to hitch a ride out of Arcanum! Jason! Or Jesus! Or Whoever, I don't care! You want to see some fucking nails get pounded, Wolf? You do that a few more times and you'll *feel* them get pounded! Us! *We'll* get pounded!'

Exhausted, bewildered, frustrated, almost used up, Jack advanced on the cringing Wolf, who could have torn his head from his shoulders with one hard, swinging blow if he had wanted to, and Wolf backed up before him.

'Don't shout, Jack,' he moaned. 'The smells . . . to be in there . . . shut up in there with those *smells* . . .'

'I didn't smell *anything*!' Jack shouted. His voice broke, his sore throat hurt more than ever, but he couldn't seem to stop; it was shout or go mad. His wet hair had fallen in his eyes. He shook it away and then slapped Wolf on the shoulder. There was a smart crack and his hand began to hurt at once. It was as if he had slapped a stone. Wolf howled abjectly, and this made Jack angrier. The fact that he was lying made him angrier still. He had been in the Territories less than six hours this time, but that man's car had smelled like a wild animal's den. Harsh aromas of old coffee and fresh beer (there had been an open can of Stroh's between his legs), an air-freshener hanging from the rear-view mirror that smelled like dry sweet powder on the cheek of a corpse. And there had been something else, something darker, something wetter . . .

'Not *anything*!' he shouted, his voice breaking hoarsely. He slapped Wolf's other shoulder. Wolf howled again and turned around, hunching like a child who is being beaten by an angry father. Jack began to slap at his back, his smarting hands spatting up little sprays of water from Wolf's overalls. Each time Jack's hand descended, Wolf howled. 'So you better get *used* to it *(Slap!)* because the *next* car to come along might be a *cop* *(Slap!)* or it might be Mr Morgan Bloat in his puke-green BMW *(Slap!)* and if all you can be is a big *baby*, we're going to be in one big fucking *world* of *hurt*! *(Slap!)* Do you understand that?'

Wolf said nothing. He stood hunched in the rain, his back to Jack, quivering. Crying. Jack felt a lump rise in his own throat, felt his eyes grow hot and stinging. All of this only increased his fury. Some terrible part of him wanted most of all to hurt himself, and knew that hurting Wolf was a wonderful way to do it.

'Turn around!'

Wolf did. Tears ran from his muddy brown eyes behind the round spectacles. Snot ran from his nose.

'Do you understand me?'

'Yes,' Wolf moaned. 'Yes, I understand, but I couldn't ride with him, Jack.'

'Why not?' Jack looked at him angrily, fisted hands on his hips. Oh, his head was aching.

'Because he was dying,' Wolf said in a low voice.

Jack stared at him, all his anger draining away.

'Jack, didn't you know?' Wolf asked softly. 'Wolf! You couldn't *smell* it?'

'No,' Jack said in a small, whistling, out-of-breath voice. Because he had smelled *something*, hadn't he? Something he had never smelled before. Something like a mixture of . . .

It came to him, and suddenly his strength was gone. He sat down heavily on the guardrail cable and looked at Wolf.

Shit and rotting grapes. That was what that smell had been like. That wasn't it a hundred per cent, but it was too hideously close.

Shit and rotting grapes.

'It's the worst smell,' Wolf said. 'It's when people forget how to be healthy. We call it – *Wolf!* – the Black Disease. I don't even think he knew he had it. And . . . these Strangers can't smell it, can they, Jack?'

'No,' he whispered. If he were to be suddenly teleported back to New Hampshire, to his mother's room in the Alhambra, would he smell that stink on *her*?

Yes. He would smell it on his mother, drifting out of her pores, the smell of shit and rotting grapes, the Black Disease.

'We call it cancer,' Jack whispered. *We call it cancer and my mother has it.*

'I just don't know if I can hitch,' Wolf said. 'I'll try again if you want, Jack, but the smells . . . inside . . . they're bad enough in the outside air, *Wolf!* but inside . . .'

That was when Jack put his face in his hands and wept, partly out of desperation, mostly out of simple exhaustion. And, yes, the expression Wolf believed he had seen on Jack's face really had been there; for an instant the temptation to leave Wolf was more than a temptation, it was a maddening imperative. The odds against his ever making it to California and finding the Talisman – whatever it might be – had been long before; now they were so long they dwindled to a point on the horizon. Wolf would do more than slow him down; Wolf would sooner or later get both of them thrown in jail. Probably sooner. And how could he ever explain Wolf to Rational Richard Sloat?

What Wolf saw on Jack's face in that moment was a look of cold speculation that unhinged his knees. He fell on them and held his clasped hands up to Jack like a suitor in a bad Victorian melodrama.

'Don't go away an' leave me, Jack,' he wept. 'Don't leave old Wolf, don't leave me here, *you* brought me here, please, please don't leave me alone . . .'

Beyond this, conscious words were lost; Wolf was perhaps trying to talk but all he really seemed able to do was sob. Jack felt a great weariness fall over him. It fitted well, like a jacket that one has worn often. *Don't leave me here,* you *brought me here . . .*

There it was. Wolf was his responsibility, wasn't he? Yes. Oh yes indeed. He had taken Wolf by the hand and dragged him out of the Territories and into Ohio and he had the throbbing shoulder to prove it. He had had no choice, of course; Wolf had been drowning, and even if he hadn't drowned, Morgan would have crisped him with whatever that lightning-rod thing had been. So he could have turned on Wolf again, could have said: *Which would you prefer, Wolf old buddy? To be here and scared, or there and dead?*

He could, yes, and Wolf would have no answer because Wolf wasn't too swift in the brains department. But Uncle Tommy had been fond of quoting a Chinese proverb that went: *The man whose life you save is your responsibility for the rest of your life.*

Never mind the ducking, never mind the fancy footwork; Wolf was his responsibility.

'Don't leave me, Jack,' Wolf wept. 'Wolf-Wolf! Please don't leave good old Wolf, I'll help you, I'll stand guard at night, I can do lots, only don't don't—'

'Quit bawling and get up,' Jack said quietly. 'I won't leave you. But we've got to get out of here in case that guy does send a cop back to check on us. Let's move it.'

5

'Did you figure out what to do next, Jack?' Wolf asked timidly. They had been sitting in the brushy ditch just over the Muncie town line for more than half an hour, and when Jack turned toward Wolf, Wolf was relieved to see he was smiling. It was a weary smile, and Wolf didn't like the dark, tired circles under Jack's eyes (he liked Jack's smell even less – it was a sick smell), but it was a smile.

'I think I see what we should do next right over there,' Jack said. 'I was thinking about it just a few days ago, when I got my new sneakers.'

He bowed his feet. He and Wolf regarded the sneakers in depressed silence. They were scuffed, battered, and dirty. The left sole was bidding a fond adieu to the left upper. Jack had owned them for . . . he wrinkled his forehead and thought. The fever made it hard to think. Three days. Only three days since he had picked them out of the bargain bin of the Fayva store. Now they looked old. Old.

'Anyway . . .' Jack sighed. Then he brightened. 'See that building over there, Wolf?'

The building, an explosion of uninteresting angles in gray brick, stood like an island in the middle of a giant parking lot. Wolf knew what the asphalt in that parking lot would smell like: dead, decomposing animals. That smell would almost suffocate him, and Jack would barely notice it.

'For your information, the sign there says Town Line Sixplex,' Jack said. 'It sounds like a coffee pot, but actually it's a movie with six shows. There ought to be one we like.' *And in the afternoon, there won't be many people there and that's good because you have this distressing habit of going Section Eight, Wolf.* 'Come on.' He got unsteadily to his feet.

'What's a movie, Jack?' Wolf asked. He had been a dreadful problem to Jack, he knew – such a dreadful problem that he now hesitated to protest about anything, or even express unease. But a frightening intuition had come to him: that *going to a movie* and *hitching a ride* might be the same thing. Jack called the roaring carts and carriages 'cars', and 'Chevys', and 'Jartrans', and 'station-wagons' (these latter, Wolf thought, must be like the coaches in the Territories which carried passengers from one coach-station to the next). Might the bellowing, stinking carriages also be called 'movies'? It sounded very possible.

'Well,' Jack said, 'it's easier to show you than to tell you. I think you'll like it. Come on.'

Jack stumbled coming out of the ditch and went briefly to his knees. 'Jack, are you okay?' Wolf asked anxiously.

Jack nodded. They started across the parking lot, which smelled just as bad as Wolf had known it would.

6

Jack had come a good part of the thirty-five miles between Arcanum, Ohio, and Muncie, Indiana, on Wolf's broad back. Wolf was frightened of cars, terrified of trucks, nauseated by the smells of almost everything, apt to howl and run at sudden loud noises. But he was also almost tireless. *As far as that goes, you can strike the 'almost'*, Jack thought now. *So far as I know, he is tireless.*

Jack had moved them away from the Arcanum ramp as fast as he could, forcing his wet, aching legs into a rusty trot. His head had been throbbing like a slick, flexing fist inside his skull, waves of heat and cold rushing through him. Wolf moved easily to his left, his stride so long that he was keeping up with Jack easily by doing no more than a moderately fast walk. Jack knew that he had maybe gotten paranoid about the cops, but the man in the CASE FARM EQUIPMENT hat had looked really scared. And pissed.

They hadn't gone even a quarter of a mile when a deep, burning stitch settled into his side and he asked Wolf if he could give him a piggyback for a while.

'Huh?' Wolf asked.

'You know,' Jack said, and pantomimed.

A big grin had overspread Wolf's face. Here at last was something he understood; here was something he could *do*.

'You want a *horsey*back!' he cried, delighted.

'Yeah, I guess . . .'

'Oh, yeah! Wolf! Here and now! Used to give em to my litter-brothers! Jump up, Jack!' Wolf bent down, holding his curved hands ready, stirrups for Jack's thighs.

'Now when I get too heavy, just put me d—'

Before he could finish, Wolf had swept him up and was running lightly down the road with him into the dark – really running. The cold, rainy air flipped Jack's hair back from his hot brow.

'Wolf, you'll wear yourself out!' Jack shouted.

'Not me! Wolf! Wolf! Runnin here and now!' For the first time since they had come over, Wolf sounded actually happy. He ran for the next two hours, until they were well west of Arcanum and travelling along a dark, unmarked stretch of two-lane blacktop. Jack saw a deserted barn standing slumped in a shaggy, untended field, and they slept there that night.

Wolf wanted nothing to do with downtown areas where the traffic was a roaring flood and the stinks rose up to heaven in a noxious cloud, and Jack didn't want anything to do with them, either. Wolf stuck out too much. But he had forced one stop, at a roadside store just across the Indiana line, near Harrisville. While Wolf waited nervously out by the road, hunkering down, digging at the dirt, getting up, walking around in a stiff little circle, then hunkering again, Jack bought a newspaper and checked the weather page carefully. The next full moon was on October 31st – Halloween, that was fitting enough. Jack turned back to the front page so he could see what day it was today . . . yesterday, that had been now. It had been October 26th.

7

Jack pulled open one of the glass doors and stepped inside the lobby of the Town Line Sixplex. He looked around sharply at Wolf, but Wolf looked – for the moment, at least – pretty much okay. Wolf was, in fact, cautiously optimistic . . . at least for the moment. He didn't like being inside a building, but at least it wasn't a car. There was a good smell in here – light and sort of tasty. Or would have been, except for a bitter, almost rancid undersmell. Wolf looked left and saw a glass box full of white stuff. That was the source of the good light smell.

'Jack,' he whispered.

'Huh?'

'I want some of that white stuff, please. But none of the pee.'

'Pee? What are you talking about?'

Wolf searched for a more formal word and found it. 'Urine.' He pointed at a thing with a light going off and on inside it. BUTTERY FLAVORING, it read. 'That's some kind of urine, isn't it? It's got to be, the way it smells.'

Jack smiled tiredly. 'A popcorn without the fake butter, right,' he said. 'Now pipe down, okay?'

'Sure, Jack,' Wolf said humbly. 'Right here and now.'

The ticket-girl had been chewing a big wad of grape-flavored bubble gum. Now she stopped. She looked at Jack, then at Jack's big, hulking companion. The gum sat on her tongue inside her half-open mouth like a large purple tumor. She rolled her eyes at the guy behind the counter.

'Two, please,' Jack said. He took out his roll of bills, dirty, tageared ones with an orphan five hiding in the middle.

'Which show?' Her eyes moved back and forth, back and forth, Jack to Wolf and Wolf to Jack. She looked like a woman watching a hot table-tennis match.

'What's just starting?' Jack asked her.

'Well . . .' She glanced down at the paper Scotch-taped beside her. 'There's *The Flying Dragon* in Cinema Four. It's a kung-fu movie with Chuck Norris.' Back and forth went her eyes, back and forth, back and forth. 'Then, in Cinema Six, there's a double feature. Two Ralph Bakshi cartoons. *Wizards* and *The Lord of the Rings*.'

Jack felt relieved. Wolf was nothing but a big, overgrown kid, and kids loved cartoons. This could work out after all. Wolf would maybe find at least one thing in the Country of Bad Smells that would amuse him, and Jack could sleep for three hours.

'That one,' he said. 'The cartoons.'

'That'll be four dollars,' she said. 'Bargain Matinee prices end at two.' She pushed a button and two tickets poked out of a slot with a mechanical ratcheting noise. Wolf flinched backward with a small cry.

The girl looked at him, eyebrows raised.

'You jumpy, mister?'

'No, I'm Wolf,' Wolf said. He smiled, showing a great many teeth. Jack would have sworn that Wolf showed more teeth now when he smiled than he had a day or two ago. The girl looked at all those teeth. She wet her lips.

'He's okay. He just—' Jack shrugged. 'He doesn't get off the farm much. You know.' He gave her the orphan five. She handled it as if she wished she had a pair of tongs to do it with.

'Come on, Wolf.'

As they turned away to the candy-stand, Jack stuffing the one into the pocket of his grimy jeans, the ticket-girl mouthed to the counterman: *Look at his nose!*

Jack looked at Wolf and saw Wolf's nose flaring rhythmically.

'Stop that,' he muttered.

'Stop what, Jack?'

'Doing that thing with your nose.'

'Oh. I'll try, Jack, but—'

'Shh.'

'Help you, son?' the counterman asked.

'Yes, please. A Junior Mints, a Reese's Pieces, and an extra-large popcorn without the grease.'

The counterman got the stuff and pushed it across to them. Wolf got the tub of popcorn in both hands and immediately began to snaffle it up in great jaw-cracking chomps.

The counterman looked at this silently.

'Doesn't get off the farm much,' Jack repeated. Part of him was already wondering if these two had seen enough of sufficient oddness to get them thinking that a call to the police might be in order. He thought – not for the first time – that there was a real irony in all this. In New York or L.A., probably no one would have given Wolf a second look . . . or if a second look, certainly not a third. Apparently the weirdness-toleration level was a lot lower out in the middle of the country. But, of course, Wolf would have flipped out of his gourd long since if they had been in New York or L.A.

'I'll bet he don't,' the counterman said. 'That'll be two-eighty.'

Jack paid it with an inward wince, realizing he had just laid out a quarter of his cash for their afternoon at the movies.

Wolf was grinning at the counterman through a mouthful of popcorn. Jack recognized it as Wolf's A #1 Friendly Smile, but he somehow doubted that the counterman was seeing it that way. There were all those teeth in that smile . . . hundreds of them, it seemed.

And Wolf was flaring his nostrils again.

Screw it, let them call the cops, if that's what they want to do, he thought with a weariness that was more adult than child. *It can't slow us down much more than we're slowed down already. He can't ride in the new cars because he can't stand the smell of the catalytic convertors and he can't ride in old cars because they smell like exhaust and sweat and oil and beer and he probably can't ride in any cars because he's so goddam claustrophobic. Tell the truth, Jack-O, even if it's only to yourself. You're going along telling yourself he's going to get over it pretty soon, but it's probably not going to happen. So what are we going to do? Walk across Indiana, I guess. Correction, Wolf is going to walk across Indiana. Me, I'm going to cross Indiana riding horseyback. But first I'm going to take Wolf into this damn movie theater and sleep either until both pictures are over or until the cops arrive. And that is the end of my tale, sir.*

'Well, enjoy the show,' the counterman said.

'You bet,' Jack replied. He started away and then realized Wolf wasn't with him. Wolf was staring at something over the counterman's head with vacant, almost superstitious wonder. Jack looked up and saw a mobile advertising the re-issue of Steven Spielberg's *Close Encounters* floating around on drafts of convection.

'Come on, Wolf,' he said.

8

Wolf knew it wasn't going to work as soon as they went through the door.

The room was small, dim, and dank. The smells in here were terrible. A poet, smelling what Wolf was smelling at that moment, might have called it the stink of sour dreams. Wolf was no poet. He only knew that the smell of the popcorn-urine predominated, and that he felt suddenly like throwing up.

Then the lights began to dim even further, turning the room into a cave.

'Jack,' he moaned, clutching at Jack's arm. 'Jack, we oughtta get out of here, okay?'

'You'll like it, Wolf,' Jack muttered, aware of Wolf's distress but not of its depth. Wolf was, after all, always distressed to some degree. In this world, the word *distress* defined him. 'Try it.'

'Okay,' Wolf said, and Jack heard the agreement but not the thin waver that meant Wolf was holding on to the last thread of his control with both hands. They sat down with Wolf on the aisle, his knees accordioned up uncomfortably, the tub of popcorn (which he no longer wanted) clutched to his chest.

In front of them a match flared briefly yellow. Jack smelled the dry tang of pot, so familiar in the movies that it could be dismissed as soon as identified. Wolf smelled a forest-fire.

'Jack—!'

'Shhh, picture's starting.'

And I'm dozing off.

Jack would never know of Wolf's heroism in the next

few minutes; Wolf did not really know of it himself. He only knew that he had to try and stick this nightmare out for Jack's sake. *It must be all right*, he thought, *look, Wolf, Jack's going right to sleep, right to sleep right here and now. And you know Jack wouldn't take you to a Hurt-Place, so just stick it out . . . just wait . . . Wolf! . . . it'll be all right . . .*

But Wolf was a cyclic creature, and his cycle was approaching its monthly climax. His instincts had become exquisitely refined, almost undeniable. His rational mind told him that he would be all right in here, that Jack wouldn't have brought him otherwise. But that was like a man with an itchy nose telling himself not to sneeze in church because it was impolite.

He sat there smelling forest-fire in a dark, stinking cave, twitching each time a shadow passed down the aisle, waiting numbly for something to fall on him from the shadows overhead. And then a magic window opened at the front of the cave and he sat there in the acrid stink of his own terror-sweat, eyes wide, face a mask of horror, as cars crashed and overturned, as buildings burned, as one man chased another.

'Previews,' Jack mumbled. 'Told you you'd like it . . .'

There were Voices. One said *nosmoking*. One said *don'tlitter*. One said *groupratesavailable*. One said *BargainMatineepricesevery weekdayuntilfourp.m.*

'Wolf, we got screwed,' Jack mumbled. He started to say something else, but it turned into a snore.

A final voice said *andnowourfeaturepresentation* and that was when Wolf lost control. Bakshi's *The Lord of the Rings* was in Dolby sound, and the projectionist had orders to really crank it in the afternoons, because that's when the heads drifted in, and the heads really liked loud Dolby.

There was a screeching, discordant crash of brass. The magic window opened again and now Wolf could *see* the fire – shifting oranges and reds.

He howled and leaped to his feet, pulling with him a Jack who was more asleep than awake.

'Jack!' he screamed. '*Get out! Got to get out! Wolf! See the fire! Wolf! Wolf!'*

'Down in front!' someone shouted.

'Shut up, hoser!' someone else yelled.

The door at the back of Cinema 6 opened. 'What's going on in here?'

'Wolf, shut up!' Jack hissed. 'For God's sake—'

'OWWWWWWW-OOOOOOOOOOOOOOOO OOOO!' Wolf howled.

A woman got a good look at Wolf as the white light from the lobby fell on him. She screamed and began dragging her little boy out by one arm. Literally *dragging* him; the kid had fallen to his knees and was skidding up the popcorn-littered carpet of the center aisle. One of his sneakers had come off.

'OWWWWWWWWW-OOOOOOOOOOOOOO OOOHHHHHHHOOOOOOOHHHHOOOOOO!'

The pothead three rows down had turned around and was looking at them with bleary interest. He held a smouldering joint in one hand; a spare was cocked behind his ear. 'Far . . . *out*,' he pronounced. 'Fucking werewolves of London strike again, right?'

'Okay,' Jack said. 'Okay, we'll get out. No problem. Just . . . just don't do that anymore, okay? Okay?'

He started leading Wolf out. The weariness had fallen over him again.

The light of the lobby hit his eyes sharply, needling

them. The woman who had dragged the little boy out of the theater was backed into a corner with her arms around the kid. When she saw Jack lead the still-howling Wolf through the double doors of Cinema 6, she swept the kid up and made a break for it.

The counterman, the ticket-girl, the projectionist, and a tall man in a sportcoat that looked as if it belonged on the back of a racetrack tout were clustered together in a tight little group. Jack supposed the guy in the checkered sportcoat and white shoes was the manager.

The doors of the other cinemas in the hive had opened partway. Faces peered out of the darkness to see what all the hooraw was. To Jack, they all looked like badgers peering out of their holes.

'Get out!' the man in the checkered sportcoat said. 'Get out, I've called the police already, they'll be here in five minutes.'

Bullshit you did, Jack thought, feeling a ray of hope. You didn't have time. And if we blow right away, maybe – just maybe – you won't bother.

'We're going,' he said. 'Look, I'm sorry. It's just that . . . my big brother's an epileptic and he just had a seizure. We . . . we forgot his medicine.'

At the word *epileptic*, the ticket-girl and the counterman recoiled. It was as if Jack had said *leper*.

'Come on, Wolf.'

He saw the manager's eyes drop, saw his lip curl with distaste. Jack followed the glance and saw the wide dark stain on the front of Wolf's Oshkosh biballs. He had wet himself.

Wolf also saw. Much in Jack's world was foreign to him, but he apparently knew well enough what that look of contempt meant. He burst into loud, braying, heartbroken sobs.

'Jack, I'm sorry, Wolf is so SORRY!'

'Get him out of here,' the manager said contemptuously, and turned away.

Jack put an arm around Wolf and got him started toward the door. 'Come on, Wolf,' he said. He spoke quietly, and with an honest tenderness. He had never felt quite so keenly for Wolf as he did now. 'Come on, it was my fault, not yours. Let's go.'

'Sorry.' Wolf wept brokenly. 'I'm no good, God pound me, just no good.'

'You're plenty good,' Jack said. 'Come on.'

He pushed open the door and they went out into the thin, late-October warmth.

The woman with the child was easily twenty yards away, but when she saw Jack and Wolf, she retreated backward toward her car, holding her kid in front of her like a cornered gangster with a hostage.

'Don't let him come near me!' she screamed. 'Don't let that monster come near my baby! Do you hear? *Don't let him come near me!'*

Jack thought he should say something to calm her down, but he couldn't think what it might be. He was too tired.

He and Wolf started away, heading across the parking lot at an angle. Halfway back to the road, Jack staggered. The world went briefly gray.

He was vaguely aware of Wolf sweeping him up in his arms and carrying him that way, like a baby. Vaguely aware that Wolf was crying.

'Jack, I'm so sorry, please don't hate Wolf, I can be a good old Wolf, you wait, you'll see . . .'

'I don't hate you,' Jack said. 'I know you're . . . you're a good old—

But before he could finish, he had fallen asleep. When he woke up it was evening and Muncie was behind him. Wolf had gotten off the main roads and on to a web of farm roads and dirt tracks. Totally unconfused by the lack of signs and the multitude of choices, he had continued west with all the unerring instinct of a migrating bird.

They slept that night in an empty house north of Cammack, and Jack thought in the morning that his fever had gone down a little.

It was midmorning – midmorning of October 28th – when Jack realized that the hair was back on Wolf's palms.

CHAPTER NINETEEN
JACK IN THE BOX

1

They camped that night in the ruins of a burned-out house with a wide field on one side and a copse of woods on another. There was a farmhouse on the far side of the field, but Jack thought that he and Wolf would be safe enough if they were quiet and stayed in most of the time. After the sun went down, Wolf went off into the woods. He was moving slowly, his face close to the ground. Before Jack lost sight of him, he thought that Wolf looked like a nearsighted man hunting for his dropped spectacles. Jack became quite nervous (visions of Wolf caught in a steel-jawed trap had begun to come to him, Wolf caught and grimly not howling as he gnawed at his own leg . . .) before Wolf returned, walking almost upright this time, and carrying plants in both hands, the roots dangling out of his fists.

'What have you got there, Wolf?' Jack asked.

'Medicine,' Wolf said morosely. 'But it's not very good, Jack. *Wolf! Nothing's* much good in your world!'

'Medicine? What do you mean?'

But Wolf would say no more. He produced two wooden matches from the bib pocket of his overalls and started a smokeless fire and asked Jack if he could find a can. Jack found a beercan in the ditch. Wolf smelled it and wrinkled his nose.

'More bad smells. Need water, Jack. Clean water. I'll go, if you're too tired.'

'Wolf, I want to know what you're up to.'

'I'll go,' Wolf said. 'There's a farm right across that field. *Wolf!* There'll be water there. You rest.'

Jack had a vision of some farmer's wife looking out the kitchen window as she did the supper dishes and seeing Wolf skulking around in the dooryard with a beercan in one hairy paw and a bunch of roots and herbs in the other.

'*I'll* go,' he said.

The farm was not five hundred feet away from where they had camped; the warm yellow lights were clearly visible across the field. Jack went, filled the beercan at a shed faucet without incident, and started back. Halfway across the field he realized he could see his shadow, and looked up at the sky.

The moon, now almost full, rode the eastern horizon.

Troubled, Jack went back to Wolf and gave him the can of water. Wolf sniffed, winced again, but said nothing. He put the can over the fire and began to sift crumbled bits of the things he had picked in through the pop-top hole. Five minutes or so later, a terrible smell – a reek, not to put too fine a point on it – began to rise on the steam. Jack winced. He had no doubt at all that Wolf would want him to drink that stuff, and Jack also had no doubt it would kill him. Slowly and horribly, probably.

He closed his eyes and began snoring loudly and theatrically. If Wolf thought he was sleeping, he wouldn't wake him up. No one woke up sick people, did they? And Jack *was* sick; his fever had come back at dark, raging through him, punishing him with chills even while he oozed sweat from every pore.

Looking through his lashes, he saw Wolf set the can aside to cool. Wolf sat back and looked skyward, his hairy hands locked around his knees, his face dreamy and somehow beautiful.

He's looking at the moon, Jack thought, and felt a thread of fear.

We don't go near the herd when we change. Good Jason, no! We'd eat them!

Wolf, tell me something: am I the herd now?

Jack shivered.

Five minutes later – Jack almost *had* gone to sleep by then – Wolf leaned over the can, sniffed, nodded, picked it up, and came over to where Jack was leaning against a fallen, fire-blackened beam with an extra shirt behind his neck to pad the angle. Jack closed his eyes tightly and resumed snoring.

'Come on, Jack,' Wolf said jovially. 'I know you're awake. You can't fool Wolf.'

Jack opened his eyes and looked at Wolf with bleary resentment. 'How did you know?'

'People have a sleep-smell and a wake-smell,' Wolf said. 'Even Strangers must know that, don't they?'

'I guess we don't,' Jack said.

'Anyway, you have to drink this. It's medicine. Drink it up, Jack, right here and now.'

'I don't want it,' Jack said. The smell coming from the can was swampy and rancid.

'Jack,' Wolf said, 'you've got a sick-smell, too.'

Jack looked at him, saying nothing.

'Yes,' Wolf said. 'And it keeps getting worse. It's not

really bad, not yet, but – *Wolf!* – it's going to *get* bad if you don't take some medicine.'

'Wolf, I'll bet you're great at sniffing out herbs and things back in the Territories, but this is the Country of Bad Smells, remember? You've probably got ragweed in there, and poison oak, and bitter vetch, and—'

'They're good things,' Wolf said. 'Just not very strong, God pound them.' Wolf looked wistful. 'Not everything smells bad here, Jack. There are good smells, too. But the good smells are like the medicine plants. Weak. I think they were stronger, once.'

Wolf was looking dreamily up at the moon again, and Jack felt a recurrence of his earlier unease.

'I'll bet this was a good place once,' Wolf said. 'Clean and full of power . . .'

'Wolf?' Jack asked in a low voice. 'Wolf, the hair's come back on your palms.'

Wolf started and looked at Jack. For a moment – it might have been his feverish imagination, and even if not, it was only for a moment – Wolf looked at Jack with a flat, greedy hunger. Then he seemed to shake himself, as if out of a bad dream.

'Yes,' he said. 'But I don't want to talk about that, and I don't want you to talk about that. It doesn't matter, not yet. *Wolf!* Just drink your medicine, Jack, that's all *you* have to do.'

Wolf was obviously not going to take no for an answer; if Jack didn't drink the medicine, then Wolf might feel duty-bound to simply pull open his jaws and pour it down his throat.

'Remember, if this kills me, you'll be alone,' Jack said grimly, taking the can. It was still warm.

A look of terrible distress spread over Wolf's face. He pushed the round glasses up on his nose. 'Don't want to hurt you, Jack – Wolf never wants to hurt Jack.' The expression was so large and so full of misery that it would have been ludicrous had it not been so obviously genuine.

Jack gave in and drank the contents of the can. There was no way he could stand against that expression of hurt dismay. The taste was as awful as he had imagined it would be . . . *and for a moment didn't the world waver? Didn't it waver as if he were about to flip back into the Territories?*

'Wolf!' he yelled. *'Wolf, grab my hand!'*

Wolf did, looking both concerned and excited. 'Jack? Jacky? What is it?'

The taste of the medicine began to leave his mouth. At the same time, a warm glow – the sort of glow he got from a small sip of brandy on the few occasions his mother had allowed him to have one – began to spread in his stomach. And the world grew solid around him again. That brief wavering might also have been imagination . . . but Jack didn't think so.

We almost went. For a moment there it was very close. Maybe I can do it without the magic juice . . . maybe I can!

'Jack? What is it?'

'I feel better,' he said, and managed a smile. 'I feel better, that's all.' He discovered that he did, too.

'You smell better, too,' Wolf said cheerfully. '*Wolf! Wolf!*'

2

He continued to improve the next day, but he was weak. Wolf carried him 'horseyback' and they made slow progress west. Around dusk they started looking for a place to lie up for the night. Jack spotted a woodshed in a dirty little gully. It was surrounded by trash and bald tires. Wolf agreed without saying much. He had been quiet and morose all day long.

Jack fell asleep almost at once and woke up around eleven needing to urinate. He looked beside him and saw that Wolf's place was empty. Jack thought he had probably gone in search of more herbs in order to administer the equivalent of a booster shot. Jack wrinkled his nose, but if Wolf wanted him to drink more of the stuff, he would. It surely had made him feel one hell of a lot better.

He went around to the side of the shed, a straight slim boy wearing Jockey shorts, unlaced sneakers, and an open shirt. He peed for what seemed a very long time indeed, looking up at the sky as he did so. It was one of those misleading nights which sometimes come to the midwest in October and early November, not so long before winter comes down with a cruel, iron snap. It was almost tropically warm, and the mild breeze was like a caress.

Overhead floated the moon, white and round and lovely. It cast a clear and yet eerily misleading glow over everything, seeming to simultaneously enhance and obscure. Jack stared at it, aware that he was almost hypnotized, not really caring.

We don't go near *the herd when we change. Good Jason, no!*

Am I the herd now, Wolf?

There was a face on the moon. Jack saw with no surprise that it was Wolf's face . . . except it was not wide and open and a little surprised, a face of goodness and simplicity. This face was narrow, ah yes, and dark; it was dark with hair, but the hair didn't matter. It was dark with intent.

We don't go near *them, we'd eat them, eat them, we'd eat them, Jack, when we change we'd –*

The face in the moon, a chiaroscuro carved in bone, was the face of a snarling beast, its head cocked in that final moment before the lunge, the mouth open and filled with teeth.

We'd eat we'd kill we'd kill, kill, KILL KILL

A finger touched Jack's shoulder and ran slowly down to his waist.

Jack had only been standing there with his penis in his hand, the foreskin pinched lightly between thumb and forefinger, looking at the moon. Now a fresh, hard jet of urine spurted out of him.

'I scared you,' Wolf said from behind him. 'I'm sorry, Jack. God pound me.'

But for a moment Jack didn't think Wolf was sorry.

For a moment it sounded as if Wolf were grinning.

And Jack was suddenly sure he was going to be eaten up.

House of bricks? he thought incoherently. *I don't even have a house of straw that I can run to.*

Now the fear came, dry terror in his veins hotter than any fever.

Who's afraid of the big bad Wolf the big bad Wolf the big bad –

'Jack?'

I am, I am, oh God I am afraid of the big Bad Wolf –

He turned around slowly.

Wolf's face, which had been lightly scruffed with stubble when the two of them crossed to the shed and lay down, was now heavily bearded from a point so high on his cheekbones that the hair almost seemed to begin at his temples. His eyes glared a bright red-orange.

'Wolf, are you all right?' Jack asked in a husky, breathy whisper. It was as loud as he could talk.

'Yes,' Wolf said. 'I've been running with the moon. It's beautiful. I ran . . . and ran . . . and ran. But I'm all right, Jack.' Wolf smiled to show how all right he was, and revealed a mouthful of giant, rending teeth. Jack recoiled in numb horror. It was like looking into the mouth of that *Alien* thing in the movies.

Wolf saw his expression, and dismay crossed his roughened, thickening features. But under the dismay – and not far under, either – was something else. Something that capered and grinned and showed its teeth. Something that would chase prey until blood flew from the prey's nose in its terror, until it moaned and begged. Something that would laugh as it tore the screaming prey open.

It would laugh even if *he* were the prey.

Especially if he were the prey.

'Jack, I'm sorry,' he said. 'The time . . . it's coming. We'll have to do something. We'll . . . tomorrow. We'll have to . . . have to . . .' He looked up and that hypnotized expression spread over his face as he looked into the sky.

He raised his head and howled.

And Jack thought he heard – very faintly – the Wolf in the moon howl back.

Horror stole through him, quietly and completely. Jack slept no more that night.

3

The next day Wolf was better. A little better, anyway, but he was almost sick with tension. As he was trying to tell Jack what to do – as well as he could, anyway – a jet plane passed high overhead. Wolf jumped to his feet, rushed out, and howled at it, shaking his fists at the sky. His hairy feet were bare again. They had swelled and split the cheap penny loafers wide open.

He tried to tell Jack what to do, but he had little to go on except old tales and rumors. He knew what the change was in his own world, but he sensed it might be much worse – more powerful and more dangerous – in the land of the Strangers. And he felt that now. He felt that power sweeping through him, and tonight when the moon rose he felt sure it would sweep him away.

Over and over again he reiterated that he didn't want to hurt Jack, that he would rather kill himself than hurt Jack.

4

Daleville was the closest small town. Jack got there shortly after the courthouse clock struck noon, and went into the True Value hardware store. One hand was stuffed into his pants pocket, touching his depleted roll of bills.

'Help you, son?'

'Yes sir,' Jack said. 'I want to buy a padlock.'

'Well, step over here and let's us have a look. We've got Yales, and Mosslers, and Lok-Tites, and you name it. What kind of padlock you want?'

'A big one,' Jack said, looking at the clerk with his shadowed, somehow disquieting eyes. His face was gaunt but still persuasive in its odd beauty.

'A big one,' the clerk mused. 'And what would you be wanting it for, might I ask?'

'My dog,' Jack said steadily. A Story. Always they wanted a Story. He had gotten this one ready on the way in from the shed where they had spent the last two nights. 'I need it for my dog. I have to lock him up. He bites.'

5

The padlock he picked out cost ten dollars, leaving Jack with about ten dollars to his name. It hurt him to spend that much, and he almost went for a cheaper item . . . and then he had a memory of how Wolf had looked the night before, howling at the moon with orange fire spilling from his eyes.

He paid the ten dollars.

He stuck out his thumb at every passing car as he hurried back to the shed, but of course none of them stopped. Perhaps he looked too wild-eyed, too frantic. He certainly *felt* wild-eyed and frantic. The newspaper the hardware store clerk had let him look at promised sunset at six o'clock p.m. on the dot. Moonrise was not listed, but Jack guessed seven, at the latest. It was already one p.m., and he had no idea where he was going to put Wolf for the night.

You have to lock me up, Jack, Wolf had said. *Have to lock me up good. Because if I get out, I'll hurt anything I can run down and catch hold of. Even you, Jack. Even you. So you have to lock me up and keep me locked up, no matter what I do or what I say. Three days, Jack, until the moon starts to get thin again. Three days . . . even four, if you're not completely sure.*

Yes, but where? It had to be someplace away from people, so no one would hear Wolf if – *when*, he amended reluctantly – he began to howl. And it had to be someplace a lot stronger than the shed they had been staying in. If Jack used his fine new ten-dollar padlock on the door of that place, Wolf would bust right out through the back.

Where?

He didn't know, but he knew he had only six hours to find a place . . . maybe less.

Jack began to hurry along even faster.

6

They had passed several empty houses to come this far, had even spent the night in one, and Jack watched all the way back from Daleville for the signs of lack of occupancy: for blank uncovered windows and FOR SALE signs, for grass grown as high as the second porch step and the sense of lifelessness common to empty houses. It was not that he hoped he could lock Wolf into some farmer's bedroom for the three days of his Change. Wolf would be able to knock down the door of the shed. But one farmhouse had a root cellar; that would have worked.

A stout oaken door set into a grassy mound like a door in a fairy tale, and behind it a room without walls or ceiling – an underground room, a cave no creature could dig its way out of in less than a month. The cellar would have held Wolf, and the earthen floor and walls would have kept him from injuring himself.

But the empty farmhouse, and the root cellar, must have been at least thirty or forty miles behind them. They would never make it back there in the time remaining before moonrise. And would Wolf still be willing to run forty miles, especially for the purpose of putting himself in a foodless solitary confinement, so close to the time of his Change?

Suppose, in fact, that too much time had passed. Suppose that Wolf had come too close to the edge and would refuse any sort of imprisonment? What if that capering, greedy underside of his character had climbed up out of the pit and was beginning to look around this odd new world, wondering where the food was hiding? The big padlock threatening to rip the seams out of Jack's pocket would be useless.

He could turn around, Jack realized. He could walk back to Daleville and keep on going. In a day or two he'd be nearly to Lapel or Cicero, and maybe he could work an afternoon at a feed store or get in some hours as a farm-hand, make a few dollars or scrounge a meal or two, and then push all the way to the Illinois border in the next few days. Illinois would be easy, Jack thought – he didn't know how he was going to do this, exactly, but he was pretty sure he could get to Springfield and the Thayer School only a day or two after he made it into Illinois.

And, Jack puzzled as he hesitated a quarter-mile down the road from the shed, how could he explain Wolf to Richard Sloat? His old buddy Richard, in his round glasses and ties and laced cordovans? Richard Sloat was thoroughly rational and, though very intelligent, hard-headed. If you couldn't see it, it probably didn't exist. Richard had never been interested in fairy tales as a child; he had remained unexcited by Disney films about fairy godmothers who turned pumpkins into coaches, about wicked queens who owned speaking mirrors. Such conceits were too absurd to snare Richard's six-year-old (or eight-year-old, or ten-year-old) fancy – unlike, say, a photograph of an electron microscope. Richard's enthusiasm had embraced Rubik's Cube, which he could solve in less than ninety seconds, but Jack did not think it would go so far as to accept a six-foot-five, sixteen-year-old werewolf.

For a moment Jack twisted helplessly on the road – for a moment he almost thought that he would be able to leave Wolf behind and get on with his journey toward Richard and then the Talisman.

What if I'm the herd? he asked himself silently. And what he thought of was Wolf scrambling down the bank after his poor terrified animals, throwing himself into the water to rescue them.

7

The shed was empty. As soon as Jack saw the door leaning open he knew that Wolf had taken himself off somewhere, but he scrambled down the side of the gully and picked his way through the trash almost in disbelief. Wolf could not have gone farther than a dozen feet by himself, yet he had done so. 'I'm back,' Jack called. 'Hey, Wolf? I got the lock.' He knew he was talking to himself, and a glance into the shed confirmed this. His pack lay on a little wooden bench; a stack of pulpy magazines dated 1973 stood beside it. In one corner of the windowless wooden shed odd lengths of deadwood had been carelessly heaped, as if someone had once half-heartedly made a stab at squirrelling away firewood. Otherwise the shed was bare. Jack turned around from the gaping door and looked helplessly up the banks of the gully.

Old tires scattered here and there among the weeds, a bundle of faded and rotting political pamphlets still bearing the name LUGAR, one dented blue-and-white Connecticut license plate, beer-bottles with labels so faded they were white . . . no Wolf. Jack raised his hands to cup his mouth. 'Hey, Wolf! I'm back!' He expected no reply, and got none. Wolf was gone.

'Shit,' Jack said, and put his hands on his hips. Conflicting emotions, exasperation and relief and anxiety, surged through him. Wolf had left in order to save Jack's life – that had to be the meaning of his disappearance. As soon as Jack had set off for Daleville, his partner had skipped out.

He had run away on those tireless legs and by now was miles away, waiting for the moon to come up. By now, Wolf could be anywhere.

This realization was part of Jack's anxiety. Wolf could have taken himself into the woods visible at the end of the long field bordered by the gully, and in the woods gorged himself on rabbits and fieldmice and whatever else might live there, moles and badgers and the whole cast of *The Wind in the Willows*. Which would have been dandy. But Wolf just might sniff out the livestock, wherever it was, and put himself in real danger. He might also, Jack realized, sniff out the farmer and his family. Or, even worse, Wolf might have worked his way close to one of the towns north of them. Jack couldn't be sure, but he thought that a transformed Wolf would probably be capable of slaughtering at least half a dozen people before somebody finally killed him.

'Damn, damn, damn,' Jack said, and began to climb up the far side of the gully. He had no real hopes of seeing Wolf – he would probably never see Wolf again, he realized. In some smalltown paper, a few days down the road, he'd find a horrified description of the carnage caused by an enormous wolf which had apparently wandered into Main Street looking for food. And there would be more names. More names like Thielke, Heidel, Hagen . . .

At first he looked toward the road, hoping even now to see Wolf's giant form skulking away to the east – he wouldn't want to meet Jack returning from Daleville. The long road was as deserted as the shed.

Of course.

The sun, as good a clock as the one he wore on his wrist, had slipped well below its meridian.

Jack turned despairingly toward the long field and the

edge of the woods behind it. Nothing moved but the tips of the stubble, which bent before a chill wandering breeze.

HUNT CONTINUES FOR KILLER WOLF, a headline would read, a few days down the road.

Then a large brown boulder at the edge of the woods did move, and Jack realized that the boulder was Wolf. He had hunkered down on his heels and was staring at Jack.

'Oh, you inconvenient son of a bitch,' Jack said, and in the midst of his relief knew that a part of him had been secretly delighted by Wolf's departure. He stepped toward him.

Wolf did not move, but his posture somehow intensified, became more electric and aware. Jack's next step required more courage than the first.

Twenty yards farther, he saw that Wolf had continued to change. His hair had become even thicker, more luxuriant, as if it had been washed and blow-dried; and now Wolf's beard really did seem to begin just beneath his eyes. His entire body, hunkered down as it was, seemed to have become wider and more powerful. His eyes, filled with liquid fire, blazed Halloween orange.

Jack made himself go nearer. He nearly stopped when he thought he saw that Wolf now had paws instead of hands, but a moment later realized that his hands and fingers were completely covered by a thatch of coarse dark hair. Wolf continued to gaze at him with his blazing eyes. Jack again halved the distance between them, then paused. For the first time since he had come upon Wolf tending his flock beside a Territories stream, he could not read his expression. Maybe Wolf had become too alien for that already, or maybe all the hair simply concealed too much of his face. What he was sure of was that some strong emotion had gripped Wolf.

A dozen feet away he stopped for good and forced himself to look into the werewolf's eyes.

'Soon now, Jacky,' Wolf said, and his mouth dropped open in a fearsome parody of a smile.

'I thought you ran away,' Jack said.

'Sat here to see you coming. Wolf!'

Jack did not know what to make of this declaration. Obscurely, it reminded him of Little Red Riding Hood. Wolf's teeth did look particularly crowded, sharp, and strong. 'I got the lock,' he said. He pulled it out of his pocket and held it up. 'You have any ideas while I was gone, Wolf?'

Wolf's whole face – eyes, teeth, everything – blazed out at Jack.

'You're the herd now, Jacky,' Wolf said. And lifted his head and released a long unfurling howl.

8

A less frightened Jack Sawyer might have said, 'Can that stuff, willya?' or 'We'll have every dog in the county around here if you keep that up,' but both of these statements died in his throat. He was too scared to utter a word. Wolf gave him his A #1 smile again, his mouth looking like a television commercial for Ginsu knives, and rose effortlessly to his feet. The John Lennon glasses seemed to be receding back into the bristly top of his beard and the thick hair falling over his temples. He looked at least seven feet tall to Jack, and as burly as the beer barrels in the back room of the Oatley Tap.

'You have good smells in this world, Jacky,' Wolf said.

And Jack finally recognized his mood. Wolf was exultant.

He was like a man who against steep odds had just won a particularly difficult contest. At the bottom of this triumphant emotion percolated that joyful and feral quality Jack had seen once before.

'Good smells! Wolf! Wolf!'

Jack took a delicate step backward, wondering if he was upwind of Wolf. 'You never said anything good about it before,' he said, not quite coherently.

'Before is before and now is now,' Wolf said. 'Good things. Many good things – all around. Wolf will find them, you bet.'

That made it worse, for now Jack could see – could nearly feel – a flat, confident greed, a wholly amoral hunger shining in the reddish eyes. I'll eat anything I catch and kill, it said. Catch and kill.

'I hope none of those good things are people, Wolf,' Jack said quietly.

Wolf lifted his chin and uttered a bubbling series of noises half-howl, half-laughter.

'Wolfs need to eat,' he said, and his voice, too, was joyous. 'Oh, Jacky, how Wolfs do need to eat. EAT! Wolf!'

'I'm going to have to put you in that shed,' Jack said. 'Remember, Wolf? I got the lock? We'll just have to hope it'll hold you. Let's start over there now, Wolf. You're scaring the shit out of me.'

This time the bubbling laughter ballooned out of Wolf's chest. 'Scared! Wolf knows! Wolf knows, Jacky! You have the fear-smell.'

'I'm not surprised,' Jack said. 'Let's get over to that shed now, okay?'

'Oh, I'm not going in the shed,' Wolf said, and a long pointed tongue curled out from between his jaws. 'No, not me, Jacky. Not Wolf. Wolf can't go in the shed.' The jaws widened, and the crowded teeth shone. 'Wolf remembered, Jacky. Wolf! Right here and now! Wolf remembered!'

Jack stepped backward.

'More fear-smell. Even on your shoes. Shoes, Jacky! Wolf!'

Shoes that smelled of fear were evidently deeply comic.

'You have to go in the shed, that's what you should remember.'

'Wrong! Wolf! *You* go in the shed, Jacky! Jacky goes in shed! I remembered! Wolf!'

The werewolf's eyes slid from blazing reddish-orange to a mellow, satisfied shade of purple. 'From *The Book of Good Farming*, Jacky. The story of the Wolf Who Would Not Injure His Herd. Remember it, Jacky? The herd goes in the barn. Remember? The lock goes on the door. When the Wolf knows his Change is coming on him, the herd goes in the barn and the lock goes on the door. He Would Not Injure His Herd.' The jaws split and widened again, and the long dark tongue curled up at the tip in a perfect image of delight. 'Not! Not! Not Injure His Herd! Wolf! Right here and now!'

'You want me to stay locked up in the shed for three days?' Jack said.

'I have to eat, Jacky,' Wolf said simply, and the boy saw something dark, quick, and sinister slide toward him from Wolf's changing eyes. 'When the moon takes me with her, I have to eat. Good smells here, Jacky. Plenty of food for Wolf. When the moon lets me go, Jacky comes out of the shed.'

'What happens if I don't want to be locked up for three days?'

'Then Wolf will kill Jacky. And then Wolf will be damned.'

'This is all in *The Book of Good Farming*, is it?'

Wolf nodded his head. 'I remembered. I remembered in time, Jacky. When I was waiting for you.'

Jack was still trying to adjust himself to Wolf's idea. He would have to go three days without food. Wolf would be free to wander. He would be in prison, and Wolf would have the world. Yet it was probably the only way he would survive Wolf's transformation. Given the choice of a three-day fast or death, he'd choose an empty stomach. And then it suddenly seemed to Jack that this reversal was really no reversal at all – he would still be free, locked in the shed, and Wolf out in the world would still be imprisoned. His cage would just be larger than Jack's. 'Then God bless *The Book of Good Farming*, because I would never have thought of it myself.'

Wolf gleamed at him again, and then looked up at the sky with a blank, yearning expression. 'Not long now, Jacky. You're the herd. I have to put you inside.'

'Okay,' Jack said. 'I guess you do have to.'

And this too struck Wolf as uproariously funny. As he laughed his howling laugh, he threw an arm around Jack's waist and picked him up and carried him all the way across the field. 'Wolf will take care of you, Jacky,' he said when he had nearly howled himself inside-out. He set the boy gently on the ground at the top of the gully.

'Wolf,' Jack said.

Wolf widened his jaws and began rubbing his crotch.

'You can't kill any people, Wolf,' Jack said. 'Remember that – if you remembered that story, then you can remember not to kill any people. Because if you do, they'll hunt you down for sure. If you kill any people, if you kill even one person, then a lot of people will come to kill you. And they'd get you, Wolf. I promise you. They'd nail your hide to a board.'

'No people, Jacky. Animals smell better than people. No people. Wolf!'

They walked down the slope into the gully. Jack removed the lock from his pocket and several times clipped it through the metal ring that would hold it, showing Wolf how to use the key. 'Then you slide the key under the door, okay?' he asked. 'When you've changed back, I'll push it back to you.' Jack glanced down at the bottom of the door – there was a two-inch gap between it and the ground.

'Sure, Jacky. You'll push it back to me.'

'Well, what do we do now?' Jack asked. 'Should I go in the shed right now?'

'Sit there,' Wolf said, pointing to a spot on the floor of the shed a foot from the door.

Jack looked at him curiously, then stepped inside the shed and sat down. Wolf hunkered back down just outside the shed's open door, and without even looking at Jack, held out his hand toward the boy. Jack took Wolf's hand. It was like holding a hairy creature about the size of a rabbit. Wolf squeezed so hard that Jack nearly cried out – but even if he had, he didn't think that Wolf would have heard him. Wolf was staring upward again, his face dreamy and peaceful and rapt. After a second or two Jack was able to shift his hand into a more comfortable position inside Wolf's grasp.

'Are we going to stay like this a long time?' he asked.

Wolf took nearly a minute to answer. 'Until,' he said, and squeezed Jack's hand again.

9

They sat like that, on either side of the doorframe, for hours, wordlessly, and finally the light began to fade. Wolf had been almost imperceptibly trembling for the previous twenty minutes, and when the air grew darker the tremor in his hand intensified. It was, Jack thought, the way a thoroughbred horse might tremble in its stall at the beginning of a race, waiting for the sound of a gun and the gate to be thrown open.

'She's beginning to take me with her,' Wolf said softly. 'Soon we'll be running, Jack. I wish you could, too.'

He turned his head to look at Jack, and the boy saw that while Wolf meant what he had just said, there was a significant part of him that was silently saying: *I could run after you as well as beside you, little friend.*

'We have to close the door now, I guess,' Jack said. He tried to pull his hand from Wolf's grasp, but could not free himself until Wolf almost disdainfully released him.

'Lock Jacky in, lock Wolf out.' Wolf's eyes flared for a moment, becoming red molten Elroy-eyes.

'Remember, you're keeping the herd safe,' Jack said. He stepped backward into the middle of the shed.

'The herd goes in the barn, and the lock goes on the door. He Would Not Injure His Herd.' Wolf's eyes ceased to drip fire, shaded toward orange.

'Put the lock on the door.'

'God pound it, that's what I'm doing now,' Wolf said. 'I'm putting the God-pounding lock on the God-pounding door, see?' He banged the door shut, immediately sealing Jack up in darkness. 'Hear that, Jacky? That's the God-pounding lock.' Jack heard the lock click against the metal loop, then heard its ratchets catch as Wolf slid it home.

'Now the key,' Jack said.

'God-pounding key, right here and now,' Wolf said, and a key rattled into a slot, rattled out. A second later the key bounced off the dusty ground beneath the door high enough to skitter onto the shed's floorboards.

'Thanks,' Jack breathed. He bent down and brushed his fingers along the boards until he touched the key. For a moment he clamped it so hard into his palm that he almost drove it through his skin – the bruise, shaped like the state of Florida, would endure nearly five days, when in the excitement of being arrested he would fail to notice that it had left him. Then Jack carefully slid the key into his pocket. Outside, Wolf was panting in hot regular agitated-sounding spurts.

'Are you angry with me, Wolf!' he whispered through the door.

A fist thumped the door, hard. 'Not! Not angry! Wolf!'

'All right,' Jack said. 'No people, Wolf. Remember that. Or they'll hunt you down and kill you.'

'No peopOOOWWW-OOOOOOOOHHH-OOOO!' The word turned into a long, liquid howl. Wolf's body bumped against the door, and his long black-furred feet slid into the opening beneath it. Jack knew that Wolf had flattened himself out against the shed door. 'Not angry, Jack,' Wolf whispered, as if his howl had embarrassed him. 'Wolf isn't angry. Wolf is *wanting*, Jacky. It's so soon now, so God-pounding *soon*.'

'I know,' Jack said, now suddenly feeling as if he had to cry – he wished he could have hugged Wolf. More painfully, he wished that they had stayed the extra days at the farmhouse, and that he were now standing outside a root cellar where Wolf was safely jailed.

The odd, disturbing thought came to him again that Wolf *was* safely jailed.

Wolf's feet slid back under the door, and Jack thought he had a glimpse of them becoming more concentrated, slimmer, narrower.

Wolf grunted, panted, grunted again. He had moved well back from the door. He uttered a noise very like 'Aaah'.

'Wolf?' Jack said.

An earsplitting howl lifted up from above Jack: Wolf had moved to the top of the gully.

'Be careful,' Jack said, knowing that Wolf would not hear him, and fearing that he would not understand him even if he were close enough to hear.

A series of howls followed soon after – the sound of a creature set free, or the despairing sound of one who wakes to find himself still confined, Jack could not tell which. Mournful and feral and oddly beautiful, the cries of poor Wolf flew up into the moonlit air like scarves flung into the night. Jack did not know he was trembling until he wrapped his arms around himself and felt his arms vibrating against his chest, which seemed to vibrate, too.

The howls diminished, retreating. Wolf was running with the moon.

10

For three days and three nights, Wolf was engaged in a nearly ceaseless search for food. He slept from each dawn until just past noon, in a hollow he had discovered beneath the fallen trunk of an oak. Certainly Wolf did not feel himself imprisoned, despite Jack's forebodings. The woods on the other side of the field were extensive, and full of a wolf's natural diet. Mice, rabbits, cats, dogs, squirrels – all these he found easily. He could have contained himself in the woods and eaten more than enough to carry him through to his next Change.

But Wolf was riding with the moon, and he could no more confine himself to the woods than he could have halted his transformation in the first place. He roamed, led by the moon, through barnyards and pastures, past isolated suburban houses and down unfinished roads where bulldozers and giant asymmetrical rollers sat like sleeping dinosaurs on the banks. Half of his intelligence was in his sense of smell, and it is not exaggerating to suggest that Wolf's nose, always acute, had now attained a condition of genius. He could not only smell a coop full of chickens five miles away and distinguish their odors from those of the cows and pigs and horses on the same farm – that was elementary – he could smell when the chickens moved. He could smell that one of the sleeping pigs had an injured foot, and one of the cows in the barn an ulcerated udder.

And this world – for was it not this world's moon which led him? – no longer stank of chemicals and death. An older, more primitive order of being met him on his travels. He inhaled whatever remained of the earth's original sweetness and power, whatever was left of qualities we might once have shared with the Territories. Even when he approached some human dwelling, even while he snapped the backbone of the family mutt and tore the dog into gristly rags he swallowed whole, Wolf was aware of pure cool streams moving far beneath the ground, of bright snow on a mountain somewhere a long way west. This seemed a perfect place for a transmogrified Wolf, and if he had killed any human being he would have been damned.

He killed no people.

He saw none, and perhaps that is why. During the three days of his Change, Wolf did kill and devour representatives of most other forms of life to be found in eastern Indiana, including one skunk and an entire family of bobcats living in limestone caves on a hillside two valleys away. On his first night in the woods he caught a low-flying bat in his jaws, bit off its head, and swallowed the rest while it was still jerking. Whole squadrons of domestic cats went down his throat, platoons of dogs. With a wild, concentrated glee he one night slaughtered every pig in a pen the size of a city block.

But twice Wolf found that he was mysteriously forbidden from killing his prey, and this too made him feel at home in the world through which he prowled. It was a question of place, not of any abstract moral concern – and on the surface, the places were merely ordinary. One was a clearing in the woods into which he had chased a rabbit, the other the scruffy back yard of a farmhouse where a whimpering dog lay chained to a stake. The instant he set a paw down in these places, his hackles rose and an electric tingling traversed the entire distance of his spine. These were sacred places, and in a sacred place a Wolf could not kill. That was all. Like all hallowed sites, they had been set apart a long time ago, so long ago that the word *ancient* could have been used to describe them – *ancient* is probably as close as we can come to representing the vast well of time Wolf sensed about him in the farmer's back yard and the little clearing, a dense envelope of years packed together in a small, highly charged location. Wolf simply backed off the sacred ground and took himself elsewhere. Like the wingmen Jack had seen, Wolf lived in a mystery and so was comfortable with all such things.

And he did not forget his obligations to Jack Sawyer.

11

In the locked shed, Jack found himself thrown upon the properties of his own mind and character more starkly than at any other time in his life.

The only furniture in the shed was the little wooden bench, the only distraction the nearly decade-old magazines. And these he could not actually read. Since there were no windows, except in very early morning when light came streaming under the door he had trouble just working out the pictures on the pages. The words were streams of gray worms, indecipherable. He could not imagine how he would get through the next three days. Jack went toward the bench, struck it painfully with his knee, and sat down to think.

One of the first things he realized was that shed-time was different from time on the outside. Beyond the shed, seconds marched quickly past, melted into minutes which melted into hours. Whole days ticked along like metronomes, whole weeks. In shed-time, the seconds obstinately refused to move – they stretched into grotesque monster-seconds, Plasticman-seconds. Outside, an hour might go by while four or five seconds swelled and bloated inside the shed.

The second thing Jack realized was that thinking about the slowness of time made it worse. Once you started concentrating on the passing of seconds, they more or less refused to move at all. So he tried to pace off the dimensions of his cell, just to take his mind off the eternity of seconds it took to make up three days. Putting one foot in front of another and counting his steps, he worked out that the shed was approximately seven feet by nine feet. At least there would be enough room for him to stretch out at night.

If he walked all the way around the inside of the shed, he'd walk about thirty-two feet.

If he walked around the inside of the shed a hundred and sixty-five times, he'd cover a mile.

He might not be able to eat, but he sure could walk. Jack took off his watch and put it in his pocket, promising himself that he would look at it only when he absolutely had to.

He was about one-fourth of the way through his first mile when he remembered that there was no water in the shed. No food and no water. He supposed that it took longer than three or four days to die of thirst. As long as Wolf came back for him, he'd be all right – well, maybe not all right, but at least alive. And if Wolf didn't come back? He would have to break the door down.

In that case, he thought, he'd better try it now, while he still had some strength.

Jack went to the door and pushed it with both hands. He pushed it harder, and the hinges squeaked. Experimentally, Jack threw his shoulder at the edge of the door, opposite the hinges. He hurt his shoulder, but he didn't think he had done anything to the door. He banged his shoulder against the door more forcefully. The hinges squealed but did not move a millimeter. Wolf could have torn the door off with one hand, but Jack did not think that he could move it if he turned his shoulders into hamburger by running into it. He would just have to wait for Wolf.

By the middle of the night, Jack had walked seven or eight miles – he'd lost count of the number of times he had reached one hundred and sixty-five, but it was something like seven or eight. He was parched, and his stomach was rumbling. The shed stank of urine, for Jack had been forced to pee against the far wall, where a crack in the boards meant that at least some of it went outside. His body was tired, but he did not think he could sleep. According to clock-time, Jack had been in the shed barely five hours; in shed-time it was more like twenty-four. He was afraid to lie down.

His mind would not let him go – that was how it felt. He had tried making lists of all the books he'd read in the past year, of every teacher he'd had, of every player on the Los Angeles Dodgers . . . but disturbing, disorderly images kept breaking in. He kept seeing Morgan Sloat tearing a hole in the air. Wolf's face floated underwater, and his hands drifted down like heavy weeds. Jerry Bledsoe twitched and rocked before the electrical panel, his glasses smeared over his nose. A man's eyes turned yellow, and his hand became a claw-hoof. Uncle Tommy's false teeth coruscated in the Sunset Strip gutter. Morgan Sloat came toward him, his bald scalp suddenly rippling with black hair – but then Uncle Morgan was coming toward his mother, not himself.

'Songs by Fats Waller,' he said, sending himself around another circuit in the dark. '"Your Feets Too Big". "Ain't Misbehavin". "Jitterbug Waltz". "Keepin Out of Mischief Now".'

The Elroy-thing reached out toward his mother, whispering lewdly, and clamped a hand down over her hip.

'Countries in Central America. Nicaragua. Honduras. Guatemala. Costa Rica . . .'

Even when he was so tired he finally had to lie down and curl into a ball on the floor, using his knapsack as a pillow, Elroy and Morgan Sloat rampaged through his mind.

Osmond flicked his bullwhip across Lily Cavanaugh's back, and his eyes danced. Wolf reared up, massive, absolutely inhuman, and caught a rifle bullet directly in the heart.

The first light woke him, and he smelled blood. His whole body begged for water, then for food. Jack groaned. Three more nights of this would be impossible to survive. The low angle of the sunlight allowed him dimly to see the walls and roof of the shed. It all looked larger than he had felt it to be last night. He had to pee again, though he could scarcely believe that his body could afford to give up any moisture. Finally he realized that the shed seemed larger because he was lying on the floor.

Then he smelled blood again, and looked sideways, toward the door. The skinned hindquarters of a rabbit had been thrust through the gap. They lay sprawled on the rough boards, leaking blood, glistening. Smudges of dirt and a long ragged scrape showed that they had been forced into the shed. Wolf was trying to feed him.

'Oh, Jeez,' Jack groaned. The rabbit's stripped legs were disconcertingly human. Jack's stomach folded into itself. But instead of vomiting, he laughed, startled by an absurd comparison. Wolf was like the family pet who each morning presents his owners with a dead bird, an eviscerated mouse.

With two fingers Jack delicately picked up the horrible offering and deposited it under the bench. He still felt like laughing, but his eyes were wet. Wolf had survived the first night of his transformation, and so had Jack.

The next morning brought an absolutely anonymous, almost ovoid knuckle of meat around a startlingly white bone splintered at both ends.

12

On the morning of the fourth day Jack heard someone sliding down into the gully. A startled bird squawked, then noisily lifted itself off the roof of the shed. Heavy footsteps advanced toward the door. Jack raised himself onto his elbows and blinked into the darkness.

A large body thudded against the door and stayed there. A pair of split and stained penny loafers was visible through the gap.

'Wolf?' Jack asked softly. 'That's you, isn't it?'

'Give me the key, Jack.'

Jack slipped his hand into his pocket, brought out the key, and pushed it directly between the penny loafers. A large brown hand dropped into view and picked up the key.

'Bring any water?' Jack asked. Despite what he had been able to extract from Wolf's gruesome presents, he had come close to serious dehydration – his lips were puffy and cracked, and his tongue felt swollen, baked. The key slid into the lock, and Jack heard it click open.

Then the lock came away from the door.

'A little,' Wolf said. 'Close your eyes, Jacky. You have night-eyes now.'

Jack clasped his hands over his eyes as the door opened, but the light which boomed and thundered into the shed still managed to trickle through his fingers and stab his eyes. He hissed with the pain. 'Better soon,' Wolf said, very close to him. Wolf's arms circled and lifted him. 'Eyes closed,' Wolf warned, and stepped backward out of the shed.

Even as Jack said, 'Water,' and felt the rusty lip of an old cup meet his own lips, he knew why Wolf had not lingered in the shed. The air outside seemed unbelievably fresh and sweet – it might have been imported directly from the Territories. He sucked in a double tablespoon of water that tasted like the best meal on earth and wound down through him like a sparkling little river, reviving everything it touched. He felt as though he were being irrigated.

Wolf removed the cup from his lips long before Jack considered he was through with it. 'If I give you more you'll just sick it up,' Wolf said. 'Open your eyes, Jack – but only a little bit.'

Jack followed directions. A million particles of light stormed into his eyes. He cried out.

Wolf sat down, cradling Jack in his arms. 'Sip,' he said, and put the cup once more to Jack's lips. 'Eyes open, little more.'

Now the sunlight hurt much less. Jack peered out through the screen of his eyelashes at a flaring dazzle while another miraculous trickle of water slipped down his throat.

'Ah,' Jack said. 'What makes water so delicious?'

'The western wind,' Wolf promptly replied.

Jack opened his eyes wider. The swarm and dazzle resolved into the weathered brown of the shed and the mixed green and lighter brown of the gully. His head rested against Wolf's shoulder. The bulge of Wolf's stomach pressed into his backbone.

'Are you okay, Wolf?' he asked. 'Did you get enough to eat?'

'Wolfs always get enough to eat,' Wolf said simply. He patted the boy's thigh.

'Thanks for bringing me those pieces of meat.'

'I promised. You were the herd. Remember?'

'Oh, yes, I remember,' Jack said. 'Can I have some more of that water?' He slid off Wolf's huge lap and sat on the ground, where he could face him.

Wolf handed him the cup. The John Lennon glasses were back; Wolf's beard was now little more than a scurf covering his cheeks; his black hair, though still long and greasy, fell well short of his shoulders. Wolf's face was friendly and peaceful, almost tired-looking. Over the bib overalls he wore a gray sweatshirt, about two sizes two small, with INDIANA UNIVERSITY ATHLETIC DEPARTMENT stencilled on the front.

He looked more like an ordinary human being than at any other time since he and Jack had met. He did not look as if he could have made it through the simplest college course, but he could have been a great high-school football player.

Jack sipped again – Wolf's hand hovered above the rusty tin cup, ready to snatch it away if Jack gulped. 'You're really okay?'

'Right here and now,' Wolf said. He rubbed his other hand over his belly, so distended that it stretched the fabric at the bottom of the sweatshirt as taut as a hand would a rubber glove. 'Just tired. Little sleep, Jack. Right here and now.'

'Where'd you get the sweatshirt?'

'It was hanging on a line,' Wolf said. 'Cold here, Jacky.'

'You didn't hurt any people, did you?'

'No people. Wolf! Drink that water slow, now.' His eyes disconcertingly shaded into happy Halloween orange for a second, and Jack saw that Wolf could never really be said to resemble an ordinary human being. Then Wolf opened his wide mouth and yawned. 'Little sleep.' He hitched himself into a more comfortable position on the slope and put down his head. He was almost immediately asleep.

·III·

A Collision of Worlds

CHAPTER TWENTY
TAKEN BY THE LAW

1

By two o'clock that afternoon they were a hundred miles west, and Jack Sawyer felt as if he too had been running with the moon – it had gone that easily. In spite of his extreme hunger, Jack sipped slowly at the water in the rusty can and waited for Wolf to awaken. Finally Wolf stirred, said, 'Ready now, Jack,' hitched the boy up onto his back, and trotted into Daleville.

While Wolf sat outside on the curb and tried to look inconspicuous, Jack entered the Daleville Burger King. He made himself go first to the men's room and strip to the waist. Even in the bathroom, the maddening smell of grilling meat caused the saliva to spill into his mouth. He washed his hands, arms, chest, face. Then he stuck his head under the tap and washed his hair with liquid soap. Crumpled paper towels fell, one after the other, to the floor.

At last he was ready to go to the counter. The uniformed girl there stared at him while he gave his order – his wet hair, he thought. While she waited for the order to come through, the girl stepped back and leaned against the service hatch, still unabashedly looking at him.

He was biting into the first Whopper as he turned

away toward the glass doors. Juice ran down his chin. He was so hungry he could scarcely bother to chew. Three enormous bites took most of the big sandwich. He had just worked his mouth far enough around the remainder to take a fourth when he saw through the doors that Wolf had attracted a crowd of children. The meat congealed in his mouth, and his stomach slammed shut.

Jack hurried outside, still trying to swallow his mouthful of ground chuck, limp bread, pickles, lettuce, tomatoes, and sauce. The kids stood in the street on three sides of Wolf, staring at him every bit as frankly as the waitress had stared at Jack. Wolf had hunched down on the curb as far as he was able, bowing his back and pulling in his neck like a turtle. His ears seemed flattened against his head. The wad of food stuck in Jack's throat like a golf-ball, and when he swallowed convulsively, it dropped down another notch.

Wolf glanced at him out of the side of his eye, and visibly relaxed. A tall blue-jeaned man in his twenties opened the door of a battered red pick-up five or six feet away down the curb, leaned against the cab, and watched, smiling. 'Have a burger, Wolf,' Jack said as carelessly as he could. He handed Wolf the box, which Wolf sniffed. Then Wolf lifted his head and took a huge bite out of the box. He began methodically to chew. The children, astounded and fascinated, stepped nearer. A few of them were giggling. 'What is he?' asked a little girl with blond pigtails tied with fuzzy pink gift-wrapping yarn. 'Is he a monster?' A crewcut boy of seven or eight shoved himself in front of the girl and said, 'He's the Hulk, isn't he? He's really the Hulk. Hey? Hey? Huh? Right?'

Wolf had managed to extract what was left of his

Whopper from its cardboard container. He pushed the whole thing into his mouth with his palm. Shreds of lettuce fell between his upraised knees, mayonnaise and meat juices smeared over his chin, his cheek. Everything else became a brownish pulp smacked to death between Wolf's enormous teeth. When he swallowed he started to lick the inside of the box.

Jack gently took the container out of his hands. 'No, he's just my cousin. He's not a monster, and he's not the Hulk. Why don't you kids get away and leave us alone, huh? Go on. Leave us alone.'

They continued to stare. Wolf was now licking his fingers.

'If you keep on gawping at him like that, you might make him mad. I don't know what he'd do if he got mad.'

The boy with the crewcut had seen David Banner's transformation often enough to have an idea of what anger might do to this monstrous Burger King carnivore. He stepped back. Most of the others moved back with him.

'Go on, please,' Jack said, but the children had frozen again.

Wolf rose up mountainously, his fists clenched. 'GOD POUND YOU, DON'T LOOK AT ME!' he bellowed. 'DON'T MAKE ME FEEL FUNNY! EVERYBODY MAKES ME FEEL FUNNY!'

The children scattered. Breathing hard, red-faced, Wolf stood and watched them disappear up Daleville's Main Street and around the corner. When they were gone, he wrapped his arms around his chest and looked dartingly at Jack. He was miserable with embarrassment. 'Wolf shouldn't have yelled,' he said. 'They were just little ones.'

'Big fat scare'll do them a lot of good,' a voice said,

and Jack saw that the young man from the red pick-up was still leaning against his cab, smiling at them. 'Never saw anything like that before myself. Cousins, are you?'

Jack nodded suspiciously.

'Hey, I didn't mean to get personal or anything.' He stepped forward, an easy, dark-haired young man in a sleeveless down vest and a plaid shirt. 'I especially don't want to make anybody feel funny now, ya know.' He paused, lifted his hands, palm-out. 'Really. I was just thinking that you guys look like you've been on the road awhile.'

Jack glanced at Wolf, who was still hugging himself in embarrassment but also glowering through his round glasses at this figure.

'I've been there myself,' the man said. 'Hey, dig it – the year I got out of good old DHS – Daleville High, you know – I hitched all the way to northern California and all the way back. Anyhow, if you're sort of going west, I can give you a lift.'

'Can't, Jacky.' Wolf spoke in a thunderous stage whisper.

'How far west?' Jack asked. 'We're trying to make it to Springfield. I have a friend in Springfield.'

'Hey, no probleema, seenyor.' He raised his hands again. 'I'm going just this side of Cayuga, right next to the Illinois border. You let me scarf a burger, we gone. Straight shot. An hour and a half, maybe less – you'll be about halfway to Springfield.'

'*Can't*,' Wolf rasped again.

'There's one problem, okay? I got some stuff on the front seat. One of you guys'll have to ride behind. It's gonna be windy back there.'

'You don't know how great that is,' Jack said, speaking nothing more than the truth. 'We'll see you when you come back out.' Wolf began to dance in agitation. 'Honest. We'll be out here, mister. And thanks.'

He turned to whisper to Wolf as soon as the man went through the doors.

And so when the young man – Bill 'Buck' Thompson, for that was his name – returned to his pick-up carrying the containers for two more Whoppers, he found a sedate-looking Wolf kneeling in the open back, his arms resting on the side panel, mouth open, nose already lifting. Jack was in the passenger seat, crowded by a stack of bulky plastic bags which had been taped, then stapled shut, and then sprayed extensively with room freshener, to judge by the smell. Through the translucent sides of the bags were visible long frondlike cuttings, medium green. Clusters of buds grew on these amputated fronds.

'I reckoned you still looked a little hungry,' he said, and tossed another Whopper to Wolf. Then he let himself in on the driver's side, across the pile of plastic bags from Jack. 'Thought he might catch it in his teeth, no reflection on your cousin. Here, take this one, he already pulverized his.'

And a hundred miles west they went, Wolf delirious with joy to have the wind whipping past his head, half-hypnotized by the speed and variety of the odors which his nose caught in flight. Eyes blazing and glowing, registering every nuance of the wind, Wolf twitched from side to side behind the cab, shoving his nose into the speeding air.

Buck Thompson spoke of himself as a farmer. He talked nonstop during the seventy-five minutes he kept his foot near the floor, and never once asked Jack any questions. And when he swung off onto a narrow dirt road just outside the

Cayuga town line and stopped the car beside a cornfield that seemed to run for miles, he dug in his shirt pocket and brought out a faintly irregular cigarette rolled in almost tissuelike white paper. 'I've heard of red-eye,' he said. 'But your cousin's ridiculous.' He dropped the cigarette into Jack's hand. 'Have him take some of this when he gets excited, willya? Doctor's orders.'

Jack absently stuffed the joint into his shirt pocket and climbed out of the cab. 'Thanks, Buck,' he called up to the driver.

'Man, I thought I'd seen something when I saw him eat,' Buck said. 'How do you get him to go places? Yell *mush! mush!* at him?'

Once Wolf realized that the ride was over, he bounded off the back of the truck.

The red pick-up rolled off, leaving a long plume of dust behind it.

'Let's do that again!' Wolf sang out. 'Jacky! Let's do that again!'

'Boy, I wish we could,' Jack said. 'Come on, let's walk for a while. Someone will probably come along.'

He was thinking that his luck had turned, that in no time at all he and Wolf would be over the border into Illinois – and he'd always been certain that things would go smoothly once he got to Springfield and Thayer School and Richard. But Jack's mind was still partially in shed-time, where what is unreal bloats and distorts whatever is real, and when the bad things started to happen again, they happened so quickly that he was unable to control them. It was a long time before Jack saw Illinois, and during that time he found himself back in the shed.

2

The bewilderingly rapid series of events which led to the Sunlight Home began ten minutes after the two boys had walked past the stark little roadsign telling them that they were now in Cayuga, pop. 23,568. Cayuga itself was nowhere visible. To their right the endless cornfield rolled across the land; to their left a bare field allowed them to see how the road bent, then arrowed straight toward the flat horizon. Just after Jack had realized that they would probably have to walk all the way into town to get their next ride, a car appeared on this road, travelling fast toward them.

'Ride in back?' Wolf yelled, joyfully raising his arms up over his head. 'Wolf ride in back! Right here and now!'

'It's going the wrong way,' Jack said. 'Just be calm and let it pass us, Wolf. Get your arms down or he'll think you're signalling him.'

Reluctantly Wolf lowered his arms. The car had come nearly to the bend in the road which would take it directly past Jack and Wolf. 'No ride in the back now?' Wolf asked, pouting almost childishly.

Jack shook his head. He was staring at an oval medallion painted on the car's dusty white doorpanel. County Parks Commission, this might have said, or State Wildlife Board. It might have been anything from the vehicle of the state agricultural agent to the property of the Cayuga Maintenance Department. But when it turned into the bend, Jack saw it was a police car.

'That's a cop, Wolf. A policeman. Just keep walking and stay nice and loose. We don't want him to stop.'

'What's a coppiceman?' Wolf's voice had dropped into a dark brown range; he had seen that the speeding car was now coming straight toward him. 'Does a coppiceman kill Wolfs?'

'No,' Jack said, 'they absolutely never kill Wolfs,' but it did no good. Wolf captured Jack's hand in his own, which trembled.

'Let go of me, please, Wolf,' Jack pleaded. 'He'll think it's funny.'

Wolf's hand dropped away.

As the police car advanced toward them, Jack glanced at the figure behind the wheel, and then turned around and walked back a few paces so that he could watch Wolf. What he had seen was not encouraging. The policeman driving the car had a wide doughy domineering face with livid slabs of fat where he'd once had cheekbones. And Wolf's terror was plain on his face. Eyes, nostrils flared; he was showing his teeth.

'You really liked riding in the back of that truck, didn't you?' Jack asked him.

Some of the terror disappeared, and Wolf nearly managed a smile. The police car roared past – Jack was conscious of the driver turning his head to inspect them. 'All right,' Jack said. 'He's on his way. We're okay, Wolf.'

He had turned around again when he heard the sound of the police car suddenly begin to grow louder again.

'Coppiceman's coming back!'

'Probably just going back to Cayuga,' Jack said. 'Turn around and just act like me. Don't stare at him.'

Wolf and Jack trudged along, pretending to ignore the car, which seemed to hang behind them deliberately. Wolf uttered a sound that was half-moan, half-howl.

The police car swung out into the road, passed them, flashed its brake lights, and then cut in diagonally before them. The officer pushed open his door and got his feet planted on the ground. Then he hoisted himself out of the seat. He was roughly Jack's height, and all his weight was in his face and his stomach – his legs were twig-skinny, his arms and shoulders those of a normally developed man. His gut, trussed in the brown uniform like a fifteen-pound turkey, bulged out on both sides of the wide brown belt.

'I can't wait for it,' he said, and cocked an arm and leaned on the open door. 'What's your story, anyhow? Give.'

Wolf padded up behind Jack and hunched his shoulders, his hands shoved deep into the pockets of his overalls.

'We're going to Springfield, officer,' Jack said. 'We've been hitching – I guess maybe we shouldn't.'

'You guess maybe you shouldn't. Hol-eee shit. What's this guy tryinna disappear behind you, a Wookiee?'

'He's my cousin.' Jack thought frantically for a moment – the Story had to be bent far enough to accommodate Wolf. 'I'm supposed to be taking him home. He lives in Springfield with his Aunt Helen, I mean my Aunt Helen, the one who's a school-teacher. In Springfield.'

'What'd he do, escape from somewhere?'

'No, no, nothing like that. It was just that—'

The cop looked at him neutrally, his face sizzling. 'Names.'

Now the boy met a dilemma: Wolf was certain to call him Jack, no matter what name he gave the cop. 'I'm Jack Parker,' he said. 'And he's—'

'Hold it. I want the feeb to tell me himself. Come on, you. You remember your name, basket case?'

Wolf squirmed behind Jack, digging his chin into the top of his overalls. He muttered something.

'I couldn't hear you, sonny.'

'Wolf,' he whispered.

'Wolf. Prob'ly I should have guessed. What's your first name, or did they just give you a number?'

Wolf had squeezed his eyes shut, and was twisting his legs together.

'Come on, Phil,' Jack said, thinking that it was one of the few names Wolf might remember.

But he had just finished saying it when Wolf pulled up his head and straightened his back and yelled, 'JACK! JACK! JACK WOLF!'

'We call him Jack sometimes,' the boy put in, knowing it was already too late. 'It's because he likes me so much, sometimes I'm the only one who can do anything with him. I might even stay there in Springfield a few days after I get him home, just to make sure he settles down okay.'

'I sure am sick of the sound of your voice, Jack boy. Why don't you and good old Phil-Jack get in the back seat here and we'll go into town and straighten everything out?' When Jack did not move, the policeman put a hand on the butt of the enormous pistol which hung from his straining belt. 'Get in the car. Him first. I want to find out why you're a hundred miles from home on a school day. In the car. Right now.'

'Ah, officer,' Jack began, and behind him Wolf rasped, 'No. Can't.'

'My cousin has this problem,' Jack said. 'He's claustrophobic. Small spaces, especially the insides of cars, drive him crazy. We can only get rides in pick-ups, so he can be in the back.'

'*Get in the car,*' the policeman said. He stepped forward and opened the back door.

'CAN'T!' Wolf wailed. 'Wolf CAN'T! Stinks, Jacky, it

stinks in there.' His nose and lip had wrinkled into corrugations.

'You get him in the car or I will,' the cop said to Jack.

'Wolf, it won't be for long,' Jack said, reaching for Wolf's hand. Reluctantly, Wolf allowed him to take it. Jack pulled him toward the back seat of the police car, Wolf literally dragging his feet across the surface of the road.

For a couple of seconds it looked as though it would work. Wolf got close enough to the police car to touch the doorframe. Then his entire body shook. He clamped both hands onto the top of the doorframe. It looked as though he were going to try to rip the top of the car in half, as a circus strongman tears a telephone book in two.

'Please,' Jack said quietly. 'We have to.'

But Wolf was terrified, and too disgusted by whatever he had smelled. He shook his head violently. Slobber ran from his mouth and dripped onto the top of the car.

The policeman stepped around Jack and released something from a catch on his belt. Jack had time only to see that it was not his pistol before the cop expertly whapped his blackjack into the base of Wolf's skull. Wolf's upper body dropped onto the top of the car, and then all of Wolf slid gracefully down onto the dusty road.

'You get on his other side,' the cop said, fastening the sap to his belt. 'We're gonna finally get this big bag of shit into the vehicle.'

Two or three minutes later, after they had twice dropped Wolf's heavy unconscious body back onto the road, they were speeding toward Cayuga. 'I already know what's gonna happen to you and your feeb cousin, if he is your cousin, which I doubt.' The cop looked up at Jack in his rear-view mirror, and his eyes were raisins dipped in fresh tar.

All the blood in Jack's body seemed to swing down, down in his veins, and his heart jumped in his chest. He had remembered the cigarette in his shirt pocket. He clapped his hand over it, then jerked his hand away before the cop could say anything.

'I gotta put his shoes back on,' Jack said. 'They sort of fell off.'

'Forget it,' the cop said, but did not object further when Jack bent over. Out of sight of the mirror, he first shoved one of the split-seamed loafers back up on Wolf's bare heel, then quickly snatched the joint out of his pocket and popped it in his mouth. He bit into it, and dry crumbly particles with an oddly herbal taste spilled over his tongue. Jack began to grind them between his teeth. Something scratched down into his throat, and he convulsively jerked upright, put his hand in front of his mouth, and tried to cough with his lips together. When his throat was clear, he hurriedly swallowed all of the dampened, now rather sludgy marijuana. Jack ran his tongue over his teeth, collecting all the flecks and traces.

'You got a few surprises ahead of you,' the policeman said. 'You're gonna get a little sunlight in your soul.'

'Sunlight in my soul?' Jack asked, thinking that the cop had seen him stuff the joint into his mouth.

'A few blisters on your hands, too,' the cop said, and glared happily at Jack's guilty image in the rear-view mirror.

The Cayuga Municipal Building was a shadowy maze of unlighted hallways and narrow staircases that seemed to wind unexpectedly upward alongside equally narrow rooms. Water sang and rumbled in the pipes. 'Let me explain something to you kids,' the policeman said, ushering them toward the last staircase to their right. 'You're not under arrest. Got that? You are being detained for questioning. I don't want to hear any bullshit about one phone call. You're in limbo until you tell us who you are and what you're up to,' the cop went on. 'You hear me? Limbo. Nowhere. We're gonna see Judge Fairchild, he's the magistrate, and if you don't tell us the truth, you're gonna pay some big fuckin consequences. Upstairs. Move it!'

At the top of the stairs the policeman pushed a door open. A middle-aged woman in wire glasses and a black dress looked up from a typewriter placed sideways against the far wall. 'Two more runaways,' the policeman said. 'Tell him we're here.'

She nodded, picked up her telephone, and spoke a few words. 'You may go in,' the secretary said to them, her eyes wandering from Wolf to Jack and back again.

The cop pushed them across the anteroom and opened the door to a room twice as large, lined with books on one long wall, framed photographs and diplomas and certificates on another. Blinds had been lowered across the long windows opposite. A tall skinny man in a dark suit, a wrinkled white shirt, and a narrow tie of no discernible pattern stood up behind a chipped wooden desk that must have been six feet long. The man's face was a relief map of wrinkles, and his hair was so black it must have been dyed. Stale cigarette smoke hung visibly in the air. 'Well, what have we got here, Franky?' His voice was startlingly deep, almost theatrical.

'Kids I picked up on French Lick Road, over by Thompson's place.'

Judge Fairchild's wrinkles contorted into a smile as he looked at Jack. 'You have any identification papers on you, son?'

'No sir,' Jack said.

'Have you told Officer Williams here the truth about everything? He doesn't think you have, or you wouldn't be here.'

'Yes sir,' Jack said.

'Then tell me your story.' He walked around his desk, disturbing the flat layers of smoke just over his head, and half-sat, half-leaned on the front corner nearest Jack. Squinting, he lit a cigarette – Jack saw the Judge's recessed pale eyes peering at him through the smoke and knew there was no charity in them.

It was the pitcher plant again.

Jack drew in a large breath. 'My name is Jack Parker. He's my cousin, and he's called Jack too. Jack Wolf. But his real name is Philip. He was staying with us in Daleville because his dad's dead and his mother got sick. I was just taking him back to Springfield.'

'Simple-minded, is he?'

'A little slow,' Jack said, and glanced up at Wolf. His friend seemed barely conscious.

'What's your mother's name?' the Judge asked Wolf. Wolf did not respond in any way. His eyes were clamped shut and his hands stuffed into his pockets.

'She's named Helen,' Jack said. 'Helen Vaughan.'

The Judge eased himself off the desk and walked slowly over to Jack. 'Have you been drinking, son? You're a little unsteady.'

'No.'

Judge Fairchild came to within a foot of Jack and bent down. 'Let me smell your breath.'

Jack opened his mouth and exhaled.

'Nope. No booze.' The Judge straightened up again.

'But that's the only thing you were telling the truth about, isn't it? You're trying to string me along, boy.'

'I'm sorry we were hitching,' Jack said, aware that he had to speak with great caution now. Not only might what he said determine whether he and Wolf were to be let free, but he was having a little trouble forming the words themselves – everything seemed to be happening with great slowness. As in the shed, the seconds had wandered off the metronome. 'In fact, we hardly ever hitch because Wolf – Jack, that is – hates being in cars. We'll never do it again. We haven't done anything wrong, sir, and that really is the truth.'

'You don't understand, sonny,' the Judge said, and his far-off eyes gleamed again. *He's enjoying this*, Jack understood. Judge Fairchild moved slowly back behind his desk. 'Hitching rides isn't the issue. You two boys are out on the roads by yourself, coming from nowhere, going nowhere – real targets for trouble.' His voice was like dark honey. 'Now we have here in this county what we think is a most unusual facility – state-approved and state-funded, by the way – which might have been set up expressly for the benefit of boys like yourselves. It's called the Sunlight Gardener Scripture Home for Wayward Boys. Mr Gardener's work with young fellows in trouble has been nothing short of miraculous. We've sent him some tough cases, and in no time at all he has those boys on their knees, begging Jesus for forgiveness. Now I'd say that was pretty special, wouldn't you?'

Jack swallowed. His mouth felt drier than it had been in the shed. 'Ah, sir, it's really urgent that we get to Springfield. Everybody's going to wonder—'

'I very much doubt that,' said the Judge, smiling with all his wrinkles. 'But I'll tell you what. As soon as you two wags are on your way to the Sunlight Home, I'll telephone Springfield and try to get the number of this Helen . . . Wolf, is it? Or is it Helen Vaughan?'

'Vaughan,' Jack said, and a red-hot blush covered his face like a fever.

'Yes,' the Judge said.

Wolf shook his head, blinking, and then put a hand on Jack's shoulder.

'Coming around are you, son?' the Judge said. 'Could you tell me your age?'

Wolf blinked again, and looked at Jack.

'Sixteen,' Jack said.

'And you?'

'Twelve.'

'Oh. I would have taken you for several years older. All the more reason for seeing you get help now before you get in real deep trouble, wouldn't you say, Franky?'

'Amen,' the policeman said.

'You boys come back here in a month,' said the Judge. 'Then we'll see if your memory is any better. Why are your eyes so bloodshot?'

'They feel kind of funny,' Jack said, and the policeman barked. He had laughed, Jack realized a second later.

'Take them away, Franky,' the Judge said. He was already picking up the telephone. 'You're going to be different boys thirty days from now. Depend on it.'

While they walked down the steps of the red-brick Municipal Building, Jack asked Franky Williams why the Judge had asked for their ages. The cop paused on the bottom step and half-turned to glare up at Jack out of his blazing face. 'Old Sunlight generally takes em in at twelve and turns em loose at nineteen.' He grinned. 'You tellin me you never heard him on the radio? He's about the most famous thing we got around here. I'm pretty sure they heard of old Sunlight Gardener even way over in Daleville.' His teeth were small discolored pegs, irregularly spaced.

3

Twenty minutes later they were in farmland again.

Wolf had climbed into the back seat of the police car with surprisingly little fuss. Franky Williams had pulled his sap from his belt and said, 'You want this again, you fuckin freak? Who knows, it might make you smart.' Wolf had trembled, Wolf's nose had wrinkled up, but he had followed Jack into the car. He had immediately clapped his hand over his nose and begun breathing through his mouth. 'We'll get away from this place, Wolf,' Jack had whispered into his ear. 'A couple of days, that's all, and we'll see how to do it.' 'No chatter' came from the front seat.

Jack was strangely relaxed. He was certain that they would find a way to escape. He leaned back against the plastic seat, Wolf's hand wrapped around his, and watched the fields go by.

'There she is,' Franky Williams called from the front seat. 'Your future home.'

Jack saw a meeting of tall brick walls planted surrealistically amidst the fields. Too tall to see over, the walls around the Sunlight Home were topped with three strands of barbed wire and shards of broken glass set in cement. The car was now driving past exhausted fields bordered with fences in which strands of barbed and smooth wire alternated.

'Got sixty acres out here,' Williams said. 'And all of it

is either walled or fenced – you better believe it. Boys did it themselves.'

A wide iron gate interrupted the expanse of wall where the drive turned into the Home's property. As soon as the police car turned into the drive, the gates swung open, triggered by some electronic signal. 'TV camera,' the policeman explained. 'They're a-waitin for you two fresh fish.'

Jack leaned forward and put his face to the window. Boys in denim jackets worked in the long fields to either side, hoeing and raking, pushing wheelbarrows.

'You two shitheads just earned me twenty bucks,' Williams said. 'Plus another twenty for Judge Fairchild. Ain't that great?'

CHAPTER TWENTY-ONE
THE SUNLIGHT HOME

1

The Home looked like something made from a child's blocks, Jack thought – it had grown randomly as more space was needed. Then he saw that the numerous windows were barred, and the sprawling building immediately seemed penal, rather than childish.

Most of the boys in the fields had put down their tools to watch the progress of the police car.

Franky Williams pulled up into the wide, rounded end of the drive. As soon as he had cut off his engine, a tall figure stepped through the front door and stood regarding them from the top of the steps, his hands knitted together before him. Beneath a full head of longish wavy white hair, the man's face seemed unrealistically youthful – as if these chipped, vitally masculine features had been created or at least assisted by plastic surgery. It was the face of a man who could sell anything, anywhere, to anybody. His clothes were as white as his hair: white suit, white shoes, white shirt, and a trailing white silk scarf around his neck. As Jack and Wolf got out of the back seat, the man in white pulled a pair of dark green sunglasses from his suitpocket, put them on, and appeared to examine the two boys for a moment before smiling – long creases split his cheeks. Then he removed the sunglasses and put them back in his pocket.

'Well,' he said. 'Well, well, well. Where would we all be without you, Officer Williams?'

'Afternoon, Reverend Gardener,' the policeman said.

'Is it the usual sort of thing, or were these two bold fellows actually engaged in criminal activity?'

'Vagrants,' said the cop. Hands on hips, he squinted up at Gardener as if all that whiteness hurt his eyes. 'Refused to give Fairchild their right names. This one, the big one,' he said, pointing a thumb at Wolf, 'he wouldn't talk at all. I had to nail him in the head just to get him in the car.'

Gardener shook his head tragically. 'Why don't you bring them up here so they can introduce themselves, and then we'll take care of the various formalities. Is there any reason why the two of them should look so, ah, shall we say, "befuddled"?'

'Just that I cracked that big one behind the ears.'

'Ummmmm.' Gardener stepped backward, steepling his fingers before his chest.

As Williams prodded the boys up the steps to the long porch, Gardener cocked his head and regarded his new arrivals. Jack and Wolf reached the top of the steps and moved tentatively onto the surface of the porch. Franky Williams wiped his forehead and huffed himself up beside them. Gardener was smiling mistily, but his eyes switched back and forth between the boys. The second after something hard, cold, and familiar jumped out of his eyes at Jack, the Reverend again twitched the sunglasses out of his pocket and put them on. The smile remained misty and delicate, but even wrapped as he was in a sense of false security, Jack felt frozen by that glance – because he had seen it before.

Reverend Gardener pulled the sunglasses below the bridge of his nose and peered playfully over the tops of the frames. 'Names? Names? Might we have some names from you two gentlemen?'

'I'm Jack,' the boy said, and then stopped – he did not want to say one more word until he had to. Reality seemed to fold and buckle about Jack for a moment: he felt that he had been jerked back into the Territories, but that now the Territories were evil and threatening, and that foul smoke, jumping flames, the screams of tortured bodies filled the air.

A powerful hand closed over his elbow and held him upright. Instead of the foulness and smoke, Jack smelled some heavy sweet cologne, applied too liberally. A pair of melancholy gray eyes were looking directly into his.

'And have you been a bad boy, Jack? Have you been a very bad boy?'

'No, we were just hitching, and—'

'I think you're a trifle stoned,' said the Reverend Gardener. 'We'll have to see that you get some special attention, won't we?' The hand released his elbow; Gardener stepped neatly away, and pushed the sunglasses up over his eyes again. 'You do possess a last name, I imagine.'

'Parker,' Jack said.

'Yesss.' Gardener whipped the glasses off his head, executed a dancing little half-turn, and was scrutinizing Wolf. He had given no indication whether he believed Jack or not.

'My,' he said. 'You're a healthy specimen, aren't you? Positively strapping. We'll certainly be able to find a use for a big strong boy like you around here, praise the Lord. And might I ask you to emulate Mr Jack Parker here, and give me your name?'

Jack looked uneasily at Wolf. His head was bowed, and he was breathing heavily. A glistening line of slobber went from the corner of his mouth to his chin. A black smudge, half-dirt, half-grease, covered the front of the stolen Athletic Department sweatshirt. Wolf shook his head, but the gesture seemed to have no content – he might have been shaking away a fly.

'Name, son? Name? Name? Are you called Bill? Paul? Art? Sammy? No – something exceedingly foursquare, I'm sure. George, perhaps?'

'Wolf,' said Wolf.

'Ah, that *is* nice.' Gardener beamed at both of them. 'Mr Parker and Mr Wolf. Perhaps you'll escort them inside, Officer Williams? And aren't we happy that Mr Bast is in residence already? For the presence of Mr Hector Bast – one of our stewards, by the way – means that we shall probably be able to outfit Mr Wolf.' He peered at the two boys over the frames of his sunglasses. 'One of our beliefs here at the Scripture Home is that the soldiers of the Lord march best when they march in uniform. And Heck Bast is nearly as large as your friend Wolf, young Jack Parker. So from the points of view of both clothing and discipline you shall be very well served indeed. A comfort, yes?'

'Jack,' Wolf said in a low voice.

'Yes.'

'My head hurts, Jack. Hurts bad.'

'Your little head pains you, Mr Wolf?' Reverend Sunlight Gardener half-danced toward Wolf and gently patted his arm. Wolf snatched his arm away, his face working into an exaggerated reflex of disgust. The cologne, Jack knew – that heavy cloying odor would have been like ammonia in Wolf's sensitive nostrils.

'Never mind, son,' said Gardener, seemingly unaffected by Wolf's withdrawal from him. 'Mr Bast or Mr Singer, our other steward, will see to that inside. Frank, I thought I told you to get them into the Home.'

Officer Williams reacted as if he had been jabbed in the back with a pin. His face grew more feverish, and he jerked his peculiar body across the porch to the front door.

Sunlight Gardener twinkled at Jack again, and the boy saw that all his dandified animation was only a kind of sterile self-amusement: the man in white was cold and crazy within. A heavy gold chain rattled out of Gardener's sleeve and came to rest against the base of his thumb. Jack heard the whistle of a whip cutting through the air, and this time he recognized Gardener's dark gray eyes.

Gardener was Osmond's Twinner.

'Inside, young fellows,' Gardener said, half-bowing and indicating the open door.

2

'By the way, Mr Parker,' Gardener said, once they had gone in, 'is it possible that we've met before? There must be some reason you look so familiar to me, mustn't there?'

'I don't know,' Jack said, looking carefully around the odd interior of the Scripture Home.

Long couches covered with a dark blue fabric sat against the wall on the forest-green carpet; two massive leather-topped desks had been placed against the opposite wall. At one of the desks a pimply teenager glanced at them dully, then returned to the video screen before him, where a TV preacher was inveighing against rock and roll. The teenage boy seated at the adjoining desk straightened up and fixed

Jack with an aggressive stare. He was slim and black-haired and his narrow face looked clever and bad-tempered. To the pocket of his white turtleneck sweater was pinned a rectangular nameplate of the sort worn by soldiers: SINGER.

'But I do think we have met each other somewhere, don't you, my lad? I assure you, we must have – I don't forget, I am literally incapable of forgetting, the face of a boy I have encountered. Have you ever been in trouble before this, Jack?'

Jack said, 'I never saw you before.'

Across the room, a massive boy had lifted himself off one of the blue couches and was now standing at attention. He too wore a white turtleneck sweater and a military nameplate. His hands wandered nervously from his sides to his belt, into the pockets of his blue jeans, back to his sides. He was at least six-three and seemed to weigh nearly three hundred pounds. Acne burned across his cheeks and forehead. This, clearly, was Bast.

'Well, perhaps it will come to me later,' Sunlight Gardener said. 'Heck, come up here and help our new arrivals at the desk, will you?'

Bast lumbered forward, scowling. He made a point of coming up very close to Wolf before he sidestepped past him, scowling more fiercely all the while – if Wolf had opened his eyes, which he did not, he would have seen no more than the ravaged moonscape of Bast's forehead and the mean small eyes, like a bear's eyes, bulging up at him from beneath crusty brows. Bast switched his gaze to Jack, muttered, 'C'mon,' and flapped a hand toward the desk.

'Registration, then take them up to the laundry for clothes,' Gardener said in a flat voice. He smiled with chrome-like brilliance at Jack. 'Jack Parker,' he said softly. 'I wonder who you really are, Jack Parker. Bast, make sure everything is out of his pockets.'

Bast grinned.

Sunlight Gardener drifted across the room toward an obviously impatient Franky Williams and languidly withdrew a long leather wallet from his jacket's inside pocket. Jack saw him begin to count money out into the policeman's hands.

'Pay attention, snotface,' said the boy behind the desk, and Jack snapped around to face him. The boy was playing with a pencil, the smirk on his face an utterly inadequate disguise for what seemed to Jack's keyed-up perceptions his characteristic anger – a rage that bubbled far down within him, eternally stoked. 'Can he write?'

'Jeez, I don't think so,' Jack said.

'Then you'll have to sign in for him.' Singer shoved two legal-sized sheets of paper at him. 'Print on the top line, write on the bottom one. Where the X's are.' He fell back into his chair, raising the pencil to his lips, and slumped eloquently into its corner. Jack supposed that was a trick learned from the very Reverend Sunlight Gardener.

JACK PARKER, he printed, and scrawled something like that at the bottom of the sheet. PHILIP JACK WOLF. Another scrawl, even less like his real handwriting.

'Now you're wards of the State of Indiana, and that's what you'll be for the next thirty days, unless you decide to stay longer.' Singer twitched the papers back toward himself. 'You'll be—'

'Decide?' Jack asked. 'What do you mean, decide?'

A trifle of red grew smooth beneath Singer's cheeks. He jerked his head to one side and seemed to smile. 'I guess you don't know that over sixty per cent of our kids are here voluntarily. It's possible, yeah. You could decide to stay here.'

Jack tried to keep his face expressionless.

Singer's mouth twitched violently, as if a fishhook had snagged it. 'This is a pretty good place, and if I ever hear you ranking it I'll pound the shit out of you – it's the best place you've ever been in, I'm sure. I'll tell you another thing: you got no choice. You have to respect the Sunlight Home. You understand?'

Jack nodded his head.

'How about him? Does he?'

Jack looked up at Wolf, who was blinking slowly and breathing through his mouth.

'I think so.'

'All right. The two of you will be bunkmates. The day starts at five in the morning, when we have chapel. Fieldwork until seven, then breakfast in the dining hall. Back to the field until noon, when we get lunch plus Bible readings – everybody gets a crack at this, so you better start thinking about what you'll read. None of that sexy stuff from the Song of Songs, either, unless you want to find out what discipline means. More work after lunch.'

He looked sharply up at Jack. 'Hey, don't think that you work for nothing at the Sunlight Home. Part of our arrangement with the state is that everybody gets a fair hourly wage, which is set against the cost of keeping you here – clothes and food, electricity, heating, stuff like that. You are credited fifty cents an hour. That means that you earn five dollars a day for the hours you put in – thirty dollars a week. Sundays are spent in the Sunlight Chapel, except for the hour when we actually put on the *Sunlight Gardener Gospel Hour*.'

The red smoothed itself out under the surface of his skin again, and Jack nodded in recognition, being more or less obliged to.

'If you turn out right and if you can talk like a human being, which most people can't, then you might get a shot at OS – Outside Staff. We've got two squads of OS, one that works the streets, selling hymn sheets and flowers and Reverend Gardener's pamphlets, and the other one on duty at the airport. Anyhow, we got thirty days to turn you two scumbags around and make you see how dirty and filthy and diseased your crummy lives were before you came here, and this is where we start, right now exactly.'

Singer stood up, his face the color of a blazing autumn leaf, and delicately set the tips of his fingers atop his desk. 'Empty your pockets. Right now.'

'Right here and now,' Wolf mumbled, as if by rote.

'TURN EM OUT!' Singer shouted. 'I WANT TO SEE IT ALL!'

Bast stepped up beside Wolf. Reverend Gardener, having seen Franky Williams to his car, drifted expressively into Jack's vicinity.

'Personal possessions tend to tie our boys too much to the past, we've found,' Gardener purred to Jack. 'Destructive. We find this a very helpful tool.'

'EMPTY YOUR POCKETS!' Singer bawled, now nearly in a straightforward rage.

Jack pulled from his pockets the random detritus of his time on the road. A red handkerchief Elbert Palamountain's wife had given him when she'd seen him wipe his nose on his sleeve, two matchbooks, the few dollars and scattered change that was all of his money – a total of six dollars and forty-two cents – the key to room 407 of the Alhambra Inn and Gardens. He closed his fingers over the three objects he intended to keep. 'I guess you want my pack, too,' he said.

'Sure, you sorry little fart,' Singer ranted, 'of course we want your foul backpack, but first we want whatever you're trying to hide. Get it out – right now.'

Reluctantly Jack took Speedy's guitar-pick, the croaker marble, and the big wheel of the silver dollar from his pocket and put them into the nest of the handkerchief. 'They're just good-luck stuff.'

Singer snatched up the pick. 'Hey, what's this? I mean, what is it?'

'Fingerpick.'

'Yeah, sure.' Singer turned it over in his fingers, sniffed it. If he had bitten it, Jack would have slugged him in the face. 'Fingerpick. You tellin me the truth?'

'A friend of mine gave it to me,' Jack said, and suddenly felt as lonely and adrift as he ever had during these weeks of travelling. He thought of Snowball outside the shopping mall, who had looked at him with Speedy's eyes, who in some fashion Jack did not understand had actually been Speedy Parker. Whose name he had just adopted for his own.

'Bet he stole it,' Singer said to no one in particular, and dropped the pick back into the handkerchief beside the coin and the marble. 'Now the knapsack.' When Jack had unshouldered the backpack, handed it over, Singer pawed through it for some minutes in growing distaste and frustration. The distaste was caused by the condition of the few clothes Jack had left, the frustration by the reluctance of the pack to yield up any drugs.

Speedy, where are you now?

'He's not holding,' Singer complained. 'You think we should do a skin search?'

Gardener shook his head. 'Let us see what we can learn from Mr Wolf.'

Bast shouldered up even closer. Singer said, 'Well?'

'He doesn't have anything in his pockets,' Jack said.

'I want those pockets EMPTY! EMPTY!' Singer yelled. 'ON THE TABLE!'

Wolf tucked his chin into his chest and clamped his eyes shut.

'You don't have anything in your pockets, do you?' Jack asked.

Wolf nodded once, very slowly.

'He's holding! The dummy's holding!' Singer crowed. 'Come on, you big dumb idiot, get the stuff out on the table.' He clapped his hands sharply together twice. 'Oh wow, Williams never searched him! Fairchild never did! This is incredible – they're going to look like such morons.'

Bast shoved his face up to Wolf's and snarled, 'If you don't empty your pockets onto that table in a hurry, I'm going to tear your face off.'

Jack softly said, 'Do it, Wolf.'

Wolf groaned. Then he removed his balled right hand from its overall pocket. He leaned over the desk, brought his hand forward, and opened his fingers. Three wooden matches and two small water-polished stones, grained and striated and colorful, fell out onto the leather. When his left hand opened, two more pretty little stones rolled alongside the others.

'Pills!' Singer snatched at them.

'Don't be an idiot, Sonny,' Gardener said.

* * *

'You made me look like a jerk,' Singer said in low but vehement tones to Jack as soon as they were on the staircase to the upper floors. These stairs were covered with a shabby rose-patterned carpet. Only the principal downstairs rooms of the Sunlight Scripture Home had been decorated, dressed up – the rest of it looked rundown and ill cared for. 'You're gonna be sorry, I promise you that – in this place, *nobody* makes Sonny Singer into a jackass. I practically run this place, you two idiots. Christ!' He pushed his burning narrow face into Jack's. 'That was a great stunt back there, the dummy and his fuckin stones. It'll be a long time before you get over that one.'

'I didn't know he had anything in his pockets,' Jack said.

A step ahead of Jack and Wolf, Singer abruptly stopped moving. His eyes narrowed; his entire face seemed to contract. Jack understood what was going to happen a second before Singer's hand slapped stingingly over the side of his face.

'Jack?' Wolf whispered.

'I'm okay,' he said.

'When you hurt me, I'll hurt you back twice as bad,' Singer said to Jack. 'When you hurt me in front of Reverend Gardener, I'll hurt you four times as bad, you got that?'

'Yeah,' Jack said. 'I think I got it. Aren't we supposed to get some clothes?'

Singer whirled around and marched upward, and for a second Jack stood still and watched the other boy's thin intense back go up the stairs. *You, too,* he said to himself. *You and Osmond. Someday.* Then he followed, and Wolf trudged after.

In a long room stacked with boxes Singer fidgeted at the door while a tall boy with a passionless bland face and the demeanor of a sleepwalker researched the shelves for their clothes.

'Shoes, too. You get him into regulation shoes or you're gonna be holding a shovel all day,' Singer said from the doorway, conspicuously not looking at the clerk. Weary disgust – it would have been another of Sunlight Gardener's lessons.

The boy finally located a size thirteen pair of the heavy square black lace-ups in a corner of the storeroom, and Jack got them on Wolf's feet. Then Singer took them up another flight to the dormitory floor. Here there was no attempt to disguise the real nature of the Sunlight Home. A narrow corridor ran the entire length of the top of the house – it might have been fifty feet long. Rows of narrow doors with inset eye-level windows marched down either side of the long corridor. To Jack, the so-called dormitory looked like a prison.

Singer took them a short way up the narrow hall and paused before one of the doors. 'On their first day, nobody works. You start the full schedule tomorrow. So get in here for now and look at your Bibles or something until five. I'll come back and let you out in time for the confession period. And change into the Sunlight clothes, hey?'

'You mean you're going to lock us in there for the next three hours?' Jack asked.

'You want me to hold your hand?' Singer exploded, his face reddening again. 'Look. If you were a voluntary, I could let you walk around, get a look at the place. But since you're a ward of the state on a referral from a local police department, you're one step up from being a convicted criminal. Maybe in thirty days you'll be voluntaries, if you're lucky. In the meantime, get in your room and start acting like a human being made in God's image instead of like an animal.' He impatiently fitted a key into the lock, swung the door open, and stood beside it. 'Get in there. I got work to do.'

'What happens to all our stuff?'

Singer theatrically sighed. 'You little creep, do you think we'd be interested in stealing anything you could have?'

Jack kept himself from responding.

Singer sighed again. 'Okay. We keep it all for you, in a folder with your name on it. In Reverend Gardener's office downstairs – that's where we keep your money, too, right up until the time you get released. Okay? Get in there now before I report you for disobedience. I mean it.'

Wolf and Jack went into the little room. When Singer slammed the door, the overhead light automatically went on, revealing a windowless cubicle with a metal bunkbed, a small corner sink, and a metal chair. Nothing more. On the white Sheetrock walls yellowing tape marks showed where pictures had been put up by the room's previous inhabitants. The lock clicked shut. Jack and Wolf turned to see Singer's driven face in the small rectangular window. 'Be good, now,' he said, grinning, and disappeared.

'No, Jacky,' Wolf said. The ceiling was no more than an inch from the top of his head. 'Wolf can't stay here.'

'You'd better sit down,' Jack said. 'You want the top or the bottom bunk?'

'Huh?'

'Take the bottom one and sit down. We're in trouble here.'

'Wolf knows, Jacky. Wolf knows. This is a bad bad place. Can't stay.'

'Why is it a bad place? How do you know it, I mean?'

Wolf sat heavily on the lower bunk, dropped his new clothes on the floor, and idly picked up the book and two pamphlets set out there. The book was a Bible bound in some artificial fabric that looked like blue skin; the pamphlets, Jack saw by looking at those on his own bunk, were entitled *The High Road to Everlasting Grace* and *God Loves You!* 'Wolf knows. You know, too, Jacky.' Wolf looked up at him, almost scowling. Then he glanced back down at the books in his hands, began turning them over, almost shuffling them. They were, Jack supposed, the first books Wolf had ever seen.

'The white man,' Wolf said, almost too softly for Jack to hear.

'White man?'

Wolf held up one of the pamphlets, its back cover showing. The whole rear cover was a black-and-white photograph of Sunlight Gardener, his beautiful hair lifting in a breeze, his arms outstretched – a man of everlasting grace, beloved of God.

'Him,' Wolf said. 'He kills, Jacky. With whips. This is one of *his* places. No Wolf should ever be in one of *his* places. No Jack Sawyer, either. Never. We have to get away from here, Jacky.'

'We'll get out,' Jack said. 'I promise you. Not today, not tomorrow – we have to work it out. But soon.'

Wolf's feet protruded far past the edge of his bunk. 'Soon.'

3

Soon, he had promised, and Wolf had required the promise. Wolf was terrified. Jack could not tell if Wolf had ever seen Osmond in the Territories, but he had certainly heard of him. Osmond's reputation in the Territories, at least among members of the Wolf family, appeared to be even worse than Morgan's. But though both Wolf and Jack had recognized Osmond in Sunlight Gardener, Gardener had not recognized them – which brought up two possibilities. Either Gardener was just having fun with them, pretending ignorance; or he was a Twinner like Jack's mother, profoundly connected to a Territories figure but unaware of the connection at any but the deepest level.

And if that was true, as Jack thought it was, then he and Wolf could wait for the really right moment to escape. They had time to watch, time to learn.

Jack put on the scratchy new clothes. The square black shoes seemed to weigh several pounds apiece, and to be suited to either foot. With difficulty, he persuaded Wolf to put on the Sunlight Home uniform. Then the two of them lay down. Jack heard Wolf begin to snore, and after a while, he drifted off himself. In his dreams his mother was somewhere in the dark, calling for him to help her, help her.

CHAPTER TWENTY-TWO
THE SERMON

1

At five that afternoon, an electric bell went off in the hallway, a long, toneless blare of sound. Wolf leaped from his bunk, thudding the metal frame of the upper with the side of his head hard enough to wake up Jack, who had been dozing, with a jolt.

The bell stopped shrieking after fifteen seconds or so; Wolf went right on.

He staggered over into the corner of the room, his hands wrapped around his head.

'*Bad place, Jack!*' he screamed. '*Bad place right here and now! Gotta get outta here! Gotta get outta here RIGHT HERE AND NOW!*'

Pounding on the wall.

'Shut the dummy up!'

From the other side, a shrieking, whinnying, horsey laugh. 'You gittin some sunlight in yo souls now, boys! And from de way dat big fella soun, it sho feel *fine*!' The giggling, whinnying laugh, too much like a horrified scream, came again.

'*Bad, Jack! Wolf! Jason! Bad! Bad, bad—*'

Doors were opening all up and down the hall. Jack

could hear the rumble of many feet dressed in blocky Sunlight Home shoes.

He got down from the top bunk, forcing himself to move. He felt cross-grained to reality – not awake, not really asleep, either. Moving across the mean little room to Wolf was like moving through Karo syrup instead of air.

He felt so tired now . . . so very tired.

'Wolf,' he said. 'Wolf, stop it.'

'Can't, Jacky!' Wolf sobbed. His arms were still wrapped around his head, as if to keep it from exploding.

'You got to, Wolf. We have to go out in the hall now.'

'Can't, Jacky,' Wolf sobbed, 'it's a bad place, bad smells . . .'

From the hallway, someone – Jack thought it was Heck Bast – yelled, 'Out for confession!'

'Out for confession!' someone else yelled, and they all took up the chant: *Out for confession! Out for confession!* It was like some weird football cheer.

'If we're going to get out of here with our skins on, we've got to stay cool.'

'Can't, Jacky, can't stay cool, bad . . .'

Their door was going to open in a minute and Bast or Sonny Singer would be there . . . maybe both. They were not 'out for confession', whatever that was, and while newcomers to the Sunlight Home might be allowed a few screw-ups during their orientation period, Jack thought their chances for escape would be better if they blended in as completely as they could as soon as they could. With Wolf, that wasn't going to be easy. *Christ, I'm sorry I got you into this, big guy,* Jack thought. *But the situation is what the situation is. And if we can't ride it, it's gonna ride us down. So if I'm hard with you, it's for your own good.* He added miserably to himself, *I hope.*

'Wolf,' he whispered, 'do you want Singer to start beating on me again?'

'No, Jack, no . . .'

'Then you better come out in the hall with me,' Jack said. 'You have to remember that what you do is going to have a lot to do with how Singer and that guy Bast treat me. Singer slapped me around because of your stones—'

'Someone might slap *him* around,' Wolf said. His voice was low and mild, but his eyes suddenly narrowed, flared orange. For a moment Jack saw the gleam of white teeth between Wolf's lips – not as if Wolf had grinned, but as if his teeth had grown.

'Don't even think of that,' Jack said grimly. 'It'll only make things worse.'

Wolf's arms fell away from his head. 'Jack, I don't know . . .'

'Will you try?' Jack asked. He threw another urgent glance at the door.

'I'll try,' Wolf whispered shakily. Tears shone in his eyes.

2

The upstairs corridor should have been bright with late-afternoon light, but it wasn't. It was as if some sort of filtering device had been fitted over the windows at the ends of the corridor so that the boys could see out – out to where the *real* sunlight was – but that the light itself wasn't allowed to enter. It seemed to drop dead on the narrow inner sills of those high Victorian windows.

There were forty boys standing in front of twenty doors, ten on each side. Jack and Wolf were by far the last to appear, but their lateness was not noticed. Singer, Bast, and two other boys had found someone to rag and could not be bothered with taking attendance.

Their victim was a narrow-chested, bespectacled kid of maybe fifteen. He was standing at a sorry approximation of attention with his chinos puddled around his black shoes. He wore no underpants.

'Have you stopped it yet?' Singer asked.

'I—'

'*Shut up!*' One of the other boys with Singer and Bast yelled this last. The four of them wore blue jeans instead of chinos, and clean white turtleneck sweaters. Jack learned soon enough that the fellow who had just shouted was Warwick. The fat fourth was Casey.

'When we want you to talk, we'll ask you!' Warwick shouted now. 'You still whipping your weasel, Morton?'

Morton trembled and said nothing.

'ANSWER HIM!' Casey shrieked. He was a tubby boy who looked a little bit like a malevolent Tweedledum.

'No,' Morton whispered.

'*WHAT? SPEAK UP!*' Singer yelled.

'No!' Morton moaned.

'If you can stop for a whole week, you'll get your underpants back,' Singer said with the air of one conferring a great favor on an undeserving subject. 'Now pull up your pants, you little creep.'

Morton, sniffling, bent over and pulled up his trousers.

The boys went down to confession and supper.

3

Confession was held in a large bare-walled room across the way from the dining hall. The maddening smells of baked beans and hotdogs drifted across, and Jack could see Wolf's nostrils flaring rhythmically. For the first time that day the dull expression left his eyes and he began to look interested.

Jack was more wary of 'confession' than he had let on to Wolf. Lying in his upper bunk with his hands behind his head, he had seen a black something in the upper corner of the room. He had thought for a moment or two that it was some sort of a dead beetle, or the husk of its shell – he thought if he got closer he would perhaps see the spider's web the thing was caught in. It had been a bug, all right, but not the organic kind. It was a small, old-fashioned-looking microphone gadget, screwed into the wall with an eyebolt. A cord snaked from the back of it and through a ragged hole in the plaster. There had been no real effort to conceal it. Just part of the service, boys. Sunlight Gardener Listens Better.

After seeing the bug, after the ugly little scene with Morton in the hall, he had expected confession to be an angry, perhaps scary, adversary situation. Someone, possibly Sunlight Gardener himself, more probably Sonny Singer or Hector Bast, would try to get him to admit that he had used drugs on the road, that he had broken into places in the middle of the night and robbed while on the road, that he had spit on every sidewalk he could find while on the road, and played with himself after a hard day on the road. If he hadn't done any of those things, they would keep after him until he admitted them, anyway. They would try to break him. Jack thought he could hold up under such treatment, but he wasn't sure Wolf could.

But what was most disturbing about confession was the eagerness with which the boys in the Home greeted it.

The inner cadre – the boys in the white turtlenecks

– sat down near the front of the room. Jack looked around and saw the others looking toward the open door with a sort of witless anticipation. He thought it must be supper they were anticipating – it smelled very damn good, all right, especially after all those weeks of pick-up hamburgers interspersed with large helpings of nothing at all. Then Sunlight Gardener walked briskly in and Jack saw the expressions of anticipation change to looks of gratification. Apparently it hadn't been dinner they had been looking forward to, after all. Morton, who had been cowering in the upper hallway with his pants puddled around his ankles only fifteen minutes ago, looked almost exalted.

The boys got to their feet. Wolf sat, nostrils flaring, looking puzzled and frightened, until Jack grabbed a fistful of shirt and pulled him up.

'Do what they do, Wolf,' he muttered.

'Sit down, boys,' Gardener said, smiling. 'Sit down, please.'

They sat. Gardener was wearing faded blue jeans overtopped with an open-throated shirt of blinding white silk. He looked at them, smiling benignly. The boys looked back worshipfully, for the most part. Jack saw one boy – wavy brown hair that came to a deep widow's peak on his brow, receding chin, delicate little hands as pale as Uncle Tommy's Delftware – turn aside and cup his mouth to hide a sneer, and he, Jack, felt some encouragement. Apparently not everyone's head *had* been blown by whatever was going on here . . . but a lot of heads *had* been. Wide-open they had been blown, from the way things looked. The fellow with the great buck teeth was looking at Sunlight Gardener adoringly.

'Let us pray. Heck, will you lead us?'

Heck did. He prayed fast and mechanically. It was like listening to a Dial-a-Prayer recorded by a dyslexic. After asking God to favor them in the days and weeks ahead, to forgive them their trespasses and to help them become better people, Heck Bast rapped out, 'For Jessussakeamen,' and sat down.

'Thank you, Heck,' Gardener said. He had taken an armless chair, had turned it around backward, and was sitting on it like a range-ridin cowpoke in a John Ford Western. He was at his most charming tonight; the sterile, self-referring craziness Jack had seen that morning was almost gone. 'Let us have a dozen confessions, please. No more than that. Will you lead us, Andy?'

Warwick, an expression of ludicrous piety on his face, took Heck's place.

'Thank you, Reverend Gardener,' he said, and then looked at the boys. 'Confession,' he said. 'Who will start?'

There was a rustling stir . . . and then hands began to go up. Two . . . six . . . nine of them.

'Roy Owdersfelt,' Warwick said.

Roy Owdersfelt, a tall boy with a pimple the size of a tumor on the end of his nose, stood up, twisting his rawboned hands in front of him. 'I stole ten bucks from my momma's purse last year!' he announced in a high, screamy voice. One scabbed, grimy hand wandered up to his face, settled on the pimple, and gave it a fearful tweak. 'I took it down to The Wizard of Odds and I turned it into quarters and I played all these different games like Pac-Man and Laser Strike until it was gone! That was money she had put away against the gas bill, and that's how come for a while they turned off our heat!' He blinked around at them. 'And my brother got sick and had to go in the hospital up in Indianapolis with pneumonia! Because I stole that money!

'That's my confession.'

Roy Owdersfelt sat down.

Sunlight Gardener said, 'Can Roy be forgiven?'

In unison the boys replied, '*Roy can be forgiven.*'

'Can anyone here forgive him, boys?'

'No one here.'

'Who can forgive him?'

'God through the power of His only begotten Son, Jesus.'

'Will you pray to Jesus to intercede for you?' Gardener asked Roy Owdersfelt.

'Sure am gonna!' Roy Owdersfelt cried in an unsteady voice, and tweaked the pimple again. Jack saw that Roy Owdersfelt was weeping.

'And the next time your momma comes here are you going to tell your momma that you know you sinned against her and your little brother and against the face of God and you're just as sorry a boy as ever there was?'

'You bet!'

Sunlight Gardener nodded to Andy Warwick.

'Confession,' Warwick said.

Before confession was over at six o'clock, almost everyone except Jack and Wolf had his hand up, hoping to relate some sin to those gathered. Several confessed petty theft. Others told of stealing liquor and drinking until they threw up. There were, of course, many tales of drugs.

Warwick called on them, but it was Sunlight Gardener they looked to for approval as they told . . . and told . . . and told.

He's got them liking *their sins*, Jack thought, troubled.

They love him, they want his approval, and I guess they only get it if they confess. Some of these sad sacks probably even make their crimes up.

The smells from the dining hall had been getting stronger. Wolf's stomach rumbled furiously and constantly next to Jack. Once, during one boy's tearful confession of having hooked a *Penthouse* magazine so he could look at those filthy pictures of what he called 'sexed-out women', Wolf's stomach rumbled so loudly that Jack elbowed him.

Following the last confession of the evening, Sunlight Gardener offered a short, melodious prayer. Then he stood in the doorway, informal and yet resplendent in his jeans and white silk shirt, as the boys filed out. As Jack and Wolf passed, he closed one of his hands around Jack's wrist.

'I've met you before.' *Confess*, Sunlight Gardener's eyes demanded.

And Jack felt an urge to do just that.

Oh yes, we know each other, yes. You whipped my back bloody.

'No,' he said.

'Oh yes,' Gardener said. 'Oh yes. I've met you before. In California? In Maine? Oklahoma? Where?'

Confess.

'I don't know you,' Jack said.

Gardener giggled. Inside his own head, Jack suddenly knew, Sunlight Gardener was jigging and dancing and snapping a bullwhip. 'So Peter said when he was asked to identify Jesus Christ,' he said. 'But Peter lied. So do you, I think. Was it in Texas, Jack? El Paso? Was it in Jerusalern in another life? On Golgotha, the place of the skull?'

'I tell you—'

'Yes, yes, I know, we've only just met.' Another giggle.

Wolf, Jack saw, had shied as far away from Sunlight Gardener as the doorway would allow. It was the smell. The gagging, cloying smell of the man's cologne. And under it, the smell of craziness.

'I never forget a face, Jack. I never forget a face or a place. I'll remember where we met.'

His eyes flicked from Jack to Wolf – Wolf whined a little and pulled back – and then back to Jack again.

'Enjoy your dinner, Jack,' he said. 'Enjoy your dinner, Wolf. Your real life at the Sunlight Home begins tomorrow.'

Halfway to the stairs, he turned and looked back.

'I never forget a place or a face, Jack. I'll remember.'

Coldly, Jack thought, God, I hope not. Not until I'm about two thousand miles away from this fucking pris—

Something slammed into him hard. Jack flew out into the hall, pin-wheeling his arms madly for balance. He hit his head on the bare concrete floor and saw a tangled shower of stars.

When he was able to sit up, he saw Singer and Bast standing together, grinning. Behind them was Casey, his gut pouching out his white turtleneck. Wolf was looking at Singer and Bast, and something in his tensed-down posture alarmed Jack.

'No, Wolf!' he said sharply.

Wolf slumped.

'No, go ahead, dummy,' Heck Bast said, laughing a little. 'Don't listen to him. Go on and try me, if you want. I always like a little warm-up before dinner.'

Singer glanced at Wolf and said, 'Leave the dummy alone, Heck. He's just the body.' He nodded at Jack. 'There's the *head*. There's the *head* we got to change.' He looked down at Jack, hands on his knees, like an adult bending to pass a pleasant word or two with a very small child. 'And we will change it, Mr Jack Parker. You can believe it.'

Deliberately, Jack said, 'Piss off, you bullying asshole.'

Singer recoiled as if slapped, a flush rising out of his collar, up his neck, and into his face. With a growl, Heck Bast stepped forward.

Singer grabbed Bast's arm. Still looking at Jack, he said, 'Not now. Later.'

Jack got to his feet. 'You want to watch out for me,' he said quietly to them both, and although Hector Bast only glowered, Sonny Singer looked almost scared. For a moment he seemed to see something in Jack Sawyer's face that was both strong and forbidding – something that had not been there almost two months ago, when a much younger boy had set the small seafront town of Arcadia Beach to his back and had begun walking west.

4

Jack thought that Uncle Tommy might have described dinner – not unkindly – as consisting of American Grange Hall Cuisine. The boys sat at long tables and were served by four of their number, who had changed into clean mess-whites following the confession period.

Following another prayer, chow was duly brought on. Big glass bowls full of home-baked beans were passed up and down the four tables, steaming platters of cheap red hotdogs, tureens of canned pineapple chunks, lots of milk in plain cartons marked DONATED COMMODITIES and INDIANA STATE DAIRY COMMISSION.

Wolf ate with grim concentration, his head down, a piece of bread always in one hand to serve as a combination pusher and mopper. As Jack watched, he gobbled five hotdogs and three helpings of the bullet-hard beans. Thinking of the small room with its closed window, Jack wondered if he were going to need a gas-mask tonight. He supposed so – not that he was likely to be issued one. He watched dismally as Wolf slopped a fourth helping of beans onto his plate.

Following dinner, all the boys rose, formed lines, and cleared the tables. As Jack took his dishes, a Wolf-decimated loaf of bread, and two milk-pitchers out into the kitchen, he kept his eyes wide open. The stark labels on the milk cartons had given him an idea.

This place wasn't a prison, and it wasn't a workhouse. It was probably classed as a boarding school or something, and the law would demand that some sort of state inspectors must keep an eye on it. The kitchen would be a place where the State of Indiana's eye would fall most often. Bars on the windows upstairs, okay. Bars on the kitchen windows? Jack didn't think so. They would raise too many questions.

The kitchen might make a good jumping-off point for an escape attempt, so Jack studied it carefully.

It looked a lot like the cafeteria kitchen at his school in California. The floor and walls were tiled, the big sinks and counters stainless steel. The cupboards were nearly the size of vegetable bins. An old conveyor-belt dishwasher stood against one wall. Three boys were already operating this hoary antique under the supervision of a man in cook's whites. The man was narrow, pallid, and possessed of a ratlike little face. An unfiltered cigarette was pasted to his upper lip, and that identified him in Jack's mind as a possible ally. He doubted if Sunlight Gardener would let any of his own people smoke cigarettes.

On the wall, he saw a framed certificate which announced that this public kitchen had been rated acceptable under standards set by the State of Indiana and the U.S. Government.

And no, there were no bars on the frosted-glass windows.

The ratlike man looked over at Jack, peeled his cigarette off his lower lip, and tossed it into one of the sinks.

'New fish, you and your buddy, huh?' he asked. 'Well, you'll be old fish soon enough. The fish get old real quick here in the Sunlight Home, don't they, Sonny?'

He grinned insolently at Sonny Singer. It was quite obvious that Singer did not know how to cope with such a smile; he looked confused and unsure, just a kid again.

'You know you're not supposed to talk to the boys, Rudolph,' he said.

'You can just cram it up your ass anytime you can't roll it down the alley or kick it in the air, buddy-roo,' Rudolph said, flicking his eyes lazily over Singer. 'You know that, don't you?'

Singer looked at him, lips first trembling, then writhing, then pushing together hard.

He suddenly turned around. 'Night-chapel!' he shouted furiously. 'Night-chapel, come on, let's go, get those tables cleared and let's get up the hall, we're late! Night-chapel!'

5

The boys trooped down a narrow staircase lit by naked bulbs enclosed in wire mesh. The walls were dank plaster, and Jack didn't like the way Wolf's eyeballs were rolling.

After that, the cellar chapel was a surprise. Most of the downstairs area – which was considerable – had been converted into a spare, modern chapel. The air down here was good – not too warm, not too cold. And fresh. Jack could hear the whispering of convection units somewhere near. There were five pews split by a central aisle, leading up to a dais with a lectern and a simple wooden cross hung on a purple velvet backdrop.

Somewhere, an organ was playing.

The boys filed quietly into the pews. The microphone on the lectern had a large, professional-looking baffle on the end of it. Jack had been in plenty of studio sound-rooms with his mother, often sitting patiently by and reading a book or doing his homework assignments while she did TV overdubs or looped unclear dialogue, and he knew that sort of baffle was meant to keep the speaker from 'popping' the mike. He thought it a strange thing to see in the chapel of a religious boarding home for wayward boys. Two video cameras stood at either side of the lectern, one to catch Sunlight Gardener's right profile, the other to catch his left. Neither was turned on this evening. There were heavy purple draperies on the walls. On the right, they were unbroken. Set into the left wall, however, was a glass rectangle. Jack could see Casey crouched over an extremely professional-looking soundboard, reel-to-reel tape recorder close to his right hand. As Jack watched, Casey grabbed a pair of cans from the board and slipped them over his ears.

Jack looked up and saw hardwood beams rising in a series of six modest arches. Between them was drilled white composition board . . . sound-proofing. The place looked like a chapel, but it was a very efficient combination-TV-and-radio studio. Jack suddenly thought of Jimmy Swaggart, Rex Humbard, Jack Van Impe.

Folks, just lay yo hand on yo television set, and you gone be HEALED!!!

He suddenly felt like screaming with laughter.

A small door to the left of the podium opened, and Sunlight Gardener stepped out. He was dressed in white from head to toe, and Jack saw expressions varying from exaltation to outright adoration on the faces of many of the boys, but Jack again had to restrain himself from a wild laughing-spree. The vision in white approaching the lectern reminded him of a series of commercials he had seen as a very young child.

He thought Sunlight Gardener looked like the Man from Glad.

Wolf turned toward him and whispered hoarsely, 'What's the matter, Jack? You smell like something's really funny.'

Jack snorted so hard into the hand cupped over his mouth that he blew colorless snot all over his fingers.

Sunlight Gardener, his face glowing with ruddy good health, turned the pages of the great Bible on the lectern, apparently lost in deepest meditation. Jack saw the glowering, scorched-earth landscape of Heck Bast's face, the narrow, suspicious face of Sonny Singer. He sobered up in a hurry.

In the glass booth, Casey was sitting up, watching Gardener alertly. And as Gardener raised his handsome face from his Bible and fastened his cloudy, dreaming, and utterly insane eyes upon his congregation, Casey flipped a switch. The reels of the big tape recorder began to turn.

6

'Fret not thyself because of evildoers,'

said Sunlight Gardener. His voice was low, musical, thoughtful.

'Neither be thou envious against
the workers of iniquity.
For they shall soon be cut down like the grass,
and wither as the green herb.
Trust in the Lord, and do good;
so shalt thou dwell in the Territories –'

(Jack Sawyer felt his heart take a nasty, leaping turn in his chest)

'– and verily thou shalt be fed.
Delight thyself also in the Lord;
and he shall give thee the desires of thine heart.
Commit thy way unto the Lord;
trust also in him;
and he shall bring it to pass . . .
Cease from anger, and forsake wrath:
fret not thyself in any wise to do evil.
For evildoers shall be cut off:
but those that wait upon the Lord,
they shall inherit his Territory.'

Sunlight Gardener closed the Book.

'May God,' he said, 'add His blessing to the reading of His Holy Word.'

He looked down at his hands for a long, long time.

In Casey's glass booth, the wheels of the tape recorder turned. Then he looked up again, and in his mind Jack suddenly heard this man scream: *Not the Kingsland? You don't mean to tell me you've overturned a full wagonload of Kingsland Ale, you stupid goat's penis? You don't mean to tell me that, do yoooooou-uuuuuu?*

Sunlight Gardener studied his young male congregation closely and earnestly. Their faces looked back at him – round faces, lean faces, bruised faces, faces flaring with acne, faces that were sly, and faces that were open and youthful and lovely.

'What does it *mean*, boys? Do you understand Psalm Thirty-seven? Do you understand this lovely, lovely song?'

No, their faces said – sly and open, clear and sweet, pitted and poxed. *Not too much, only got as far as the fifth grade, been on the road, been on the bum, been in trouble . . . tell me . . . tell me . . .*

Suddenly, shockingly, Gardener shrieked into the mike, 'It means *DON'T SWEAT IT!*'

Wolf recoiled, moaning a little.

'Now you know what that means, don't you? You boys have heard that one, haven't you?'

'*Yeah!*' someone shouted from behind Jack.

'*OH-YEAH!*' Sunlight Gardener echoed, beaming. 'DON'T SWEAT IT! *NEGATIVE PERSPIRATION!* They are good words, aren't they, boys? Those are some kind of *poooood* words, *OH-YEAH!*'

'*Yeah! . . . YEAH!*'

'This Psalm says you don't have to WORRY about the evildoers! *NO SWEAT! OH-YEAH!* It says you don't have to WORRY about the workers of sin and iniquity! *NEGATIVE PERSPIRATION!* This Psalm here says that if you WALK the Lord and TALK the Lord, *EVERYTHING'S GONNA BE SO COOL!* Do you understand that, boys? Do you have an understanding ear for that?'

'Yeah!'

'*Hallelujah!*' Heck Bast cried, grinning divinely.

'*Amen!*' a boy with a great lazy eye behind his magnifying spectacles returned.

Sunlight Gardener took the mike with practiced ease, and Jack was again reminded of a Las Vegas lounge performer. Gardener began to walk back and forth with nervous, mincing rapidity. He sometimes did a jigging little half-step in his clean white leather shoes; now he was Dizzy Gillespie, now Jerry Lee Lewis, now Stan Kenton, now Gene Vincent; he was in a fever of jive Godhead testimony.

'Naw, you don't have to fear! Ah, naw! You don't have to fear that kid who wants to show you dirty-book pictures! You don't have to fear that boy who says just one toke on just one joint won't hurt you and you'll be a sissy if you don't take it! Ah, naw! 'CAUSE WHEN YOU GOT THE LORD YOU GONNA WALK WITH THE LORD, AM I RIGHT?'

'YEAH!!!'

'OH-YEAH! AND WHEN YOU GOT THE LORD YOU GONNA TALK WITH THE LORD, AM I RIGHT?'

'YEAH!'

'I CAN'T HEAR YOU, AM I RIGHT?'

'YEAH!!!' They screamed it out, many of them rocking back and forth in a frenzy now.

'IF I'M RIGHT SAY HALLELUJAH!'

'HALLELUJAH!'

'IF I'M RIGHT SAY OH-YEAH!'

'OH-YEAH!'

They rocked back and forth; Jack and Wolf were rocked with them, helplessly. Jack saw that some of the boys were actually weeping.

'Now tell me this,' Gardener said, looking toward them warmly and confidentially. 'Is there any place for the evildoer here in the Sunlight Home? Huh? What do you think?'

'No *sir*!' cried out the thin boy with the buck teeth.

'That's right,' Sunlight Gardener said, approaching the podium again. He gave the mike a quick, professional flick to clear the cord out from under his feet and then he slipped it back into the clamp again. 'That's the ticket. No room here for tattletale liars and workers of iniquity, say hallelujah.'

'Hallelujah,' the boys replied.

'Amen,' Sunlight Gardener agreed. 'The Lord says – in the Book of Isaiah he says it – that if you lean on the Lord, you're gonna mount up – oh-yeah! – with wings as eagles, and your strength shall be the strength of ten and I say to you, boys, *THAT THE SUNLIGHT HOME IS A NEST FOR EAGLES, CAN YOU SAY OH-YEAH!'*

'OH-YEAH!'

There was another caesura. Sunlight Gardener gripped the sides of the podium, head down as if in prayer, gorgeous white hair hanging in disciplined waves. When he spoke again, his voice was low and brooding. He did not look up. The boys listened breathlessly.

'But we have enemies,' Sunlight Gardener said at last. This was little more than a whisper, but the mike picked it up and transmitted it perfectly.

The boys sighed – a rustle of wind through autumn leaves.

Heck Bast was looking around truculently, eyes rolling, pimples glowing such a deep red that he looked like a boy in the grip of a tropical illness. *Show me an enemy*, Heck Bast's face said. *Yeah, you go on, show me an enemy and just see what happens to him!*

Gardener looked up. Now his mad eyes appeared filled with tears.

'Yes, we have enemies,' he repeated. 'Twice now the State of Indiana has tried to shut me down. Do you know what? The radical humanists can barely stand to think of me down here at the Sunlight Home, teaching my boys to love Jesus and their country. It makes em mad, and do you want to know something, boys? Do you want to know a deep old dark secret?'

They leaned forward, eyes on Sunlight Gardener.

'We don't just make em mad,' Gardener said in a hoarse conspirator's whisper. 'We make em *scaaaaaared*.'

'Hallelujah!'

'Oh-yeah!'

'Amen!'

In a flash, Sunlight Gardener grabbed the mike again, and he was off! Up and down! back and forth! sometimes he jigged a two-step neat as a minstrel in a 1910 cakewalk! He bopped the word to them, pumping one arm first at the boys, then up toward heaven, where God had presumably dragged up His armchair to listen.

'We scare em, oh-yeah! Scare em so bad they got to have another cocktail, or another joint, or another sniff of cocaine! We scare em, because even smart old God-denying, Jesus-hating radical humanists like them can smell righteousness and the love of God, and when they smell that they can smell the brimstone coming out of their own pores, and they don't like that smell, oh no!

'So they send down an extra inspector or two to plant garbage under the kitchen counters, or to let loose some cock-a-roaches in the flour! They start a lot of vile rumors about how my boys are beaten. *Are you beaten*?'

'*NO!*' they roared indignantly, and Jack was dumbfounded to see Morton roaring the negative out as enthusiastically as all the rest, even though a bruise was already beginning to form on Morton's cheek.

'Why, they sent down a bunch of smart news reporters from some smart radical humanist news show!' Sunlight Gardener cried in a kind of disgusted wonder. 'They came down here and they said, "Okay, who are we supposed to do the hatchet-job on? We've done a hundred and fifty already, we're experts at smearing the righteous, don't worry about us, just give us a few joints and a few cocktails and point us in the right direction."

'But we fooled em, didn't we, boys?'

Rumbling, almost vicious assent.

'They didn't find no one chained to a beam in the barn, did they? Didn't find no boys in strait-jackets, like they heard down in town from some of those hellbound School Board jackals, did they? Didn't find no boys getting their fingernails pulled, or all their hair shaved off, or nothing like that! Most they could find was some boys who said they got spanked, and they DID get spanked, oh-yeah, they was spanked and I'd testify on that matter myself before the Throne of Almighty God, with a lie-detector strapped to each arm, because the Book says if you SPARE that rod, you gonna SPOIL that child, and if you believe that, boys, you gimme hallelujah!'

'HALLELUJAH!'

'Even the Indiana Board of Education, much as they'd

like to get rid of me and leave a clear field for the devil, even *they* had to admit that when it comes to spanking, God's law and the State of Indiana's law runs just about the same: that if you SPARE that rod, you gonna SPOIL that child!

'They found HAPPY boys! They found HEALTHY boys! They found boys who were willing to WALK the Lord and TALK the Lord, oh can you say hallelujah?'

They could.

'Can you say oh-yeah?'

They could do that, too.

Sunlight Gardener came back to the podium.

'The Lord protects those that love Him, and the Lord is not gonna see a bunch of dope-smoking, communist-loving radical humanists take away this resting place for tired, confused boys.

'There were a few boys who told tattletale lies to those so-called news-people,' Gardener said. 'I heard the lies repeated on that TV news show, and although the boys slinging that mud were too cowardly to show their own faces on the screen, I knew – oh-yeah! – I knew those voices. When you've fed a boy, when you've held his head tenderly against your breast when he cries for his momma in the night, why, I guess then you know his voice.

'Those boys are gone now. God may forgive them – I hope He does, oh-yeah – but Sunlight Gardener is just a man.'

He hung his head to show what a shameful admission this was. But when he raised it again, his eyes were still hot, sparkling with fury.

'Sunlight Gardener cannot forgive them. So Sunlight Gardener set them out on the road again. They have been sent out into the Territories, but there they shall not be fed; there even the trees may eat them up, like beasts which walk in the night.'

Terrified silence in the room. Behind the glass panel, even Casey looked pallid and strange.

'The Book says that God sent Cain out to the East of Eden, into the land of Nod. Being cast out onto the road is like that, my boys. You have a safe haven here.'

He surveyed them.

'But if you weaken . . . if you lie . . . then woe unto you! Hell awaits the backslider just as it awaits the boy or man who dives into it on purpose.

'Remember, boys.

'Remember.

'Let us pray.'

CHAPTER TWENTY-THREE
FERD JANKLOW

1

It took Jack less than a week to decide that a detour into the Territories was the only way they could possibly escape the Sunlight Home. He was willing to try that, but he found he would do almost anything, run any risk, if only he could avoid flipping from the Sunlight Home itself.

There was no concrete reason for this, only the voice of his undermind whispering that what was bad here would be worse over there. This was, perhaps, a bad place in all worlds . . . like a bad spot in an apple which goes all the way to the core. Anyway, the Sunlight Home was bad enough; he had no urge to see what its Territories counterpart looked like unless he had to.

But there might be a way.

Wolf and Jack and the other boys not lucky enough to be on the Outside Staff – and that was most of them – spent their days in what the long-timers called Far Field. It was about a mile and half down the road, at the edge of Gardener's property, and there the boys spent their days picking rocks. There was no other fieldwork to be done at this time of year. The last of the crops had been harvested in mid-October, but as Sunlight Gardener had pointed out each morning in Chapel Devotions, rocks were always in season.

Sitting in the back of one of the Home's two dilapidated farmtrucks each morning, Jack surveyed Far Field while Wolf sat beside him, head down, like a boy with a hangover. It had been a rainy fall in the midwest, and Far Field was a gluey, sticky, muddy mess. Day before yesterday one of the boys had cursed it under his breath and called it a 'real boot-sucker'.

Suppose we just take off? Jack thought for the fortieth time. *Suppose I just yell 'Go for it!' at Wolf and we start busting our buns? Where? North end, where those trees are, and the rock wall. That's where his land ends.*

There might be a fence.

We'll climb over it. For that matter, Wolf can throw me over it, if he has to.

Might be barbed wire.

Wiggle under it. Or –

Or Wolf could tear it apart with his bare hands. Jack didn't like to think of it, but he knew Wolf had the strength . . . and if he asked, Wolf would do it. It would rip up the big guy's hands, but he was getting ripped up in worse ways right now.

And then what?

Flip, of course. That was what. If they could just get off the land that belonged to the Sunlight Home, that undervoice whispered, they would have a fighting chance all the way clear.

And Singer and Bast (whom Jack had come to think of as the Thuggsy Twins) would not be able to use one of the trucks to run them down; the first truck to turn wheels into Far Field before the deep frosts of December would mire itself rocker-panel deep.

It'd be a footrace, pure and simple. Got to try it. Better than trying it back there, at the Home. And –

And it wasn't just Wolf's growing distress that was driving him; he was now nearly frantic about Lily, who was back in New Hampshire dying by inches while Jack said hallelujah under duress.

Go for it. Magic juice or no magic juice. Got to try.

But before Jack was quite ready, Ferd Janklow tried.

Great minds run in the same channel, can you say amen.

2

When it happened, it happened fast. At one moment Jack was listening to Ferd Janklow's usual line of cynical, amusing bullshit. At the next, Ferd was pelting north across the murky field toward the stone wall. Until Ferd went for it, the day had seemed as drearily ordinary as any other at the Sunlight Home. It was cold and overcast; there was a smell of rain, possibly even snow, in the air. Jack looked up to ease his aching back, and also to see if Sonny Singer was around. Sonny enjoyed harassing Jack. Most of the harassment was of the nuisance variety. Jack had his feet stepped on, he was pushed on the stairs, his plate had been knocked out of his hands for three meals running – until he had learned to simultaneously cradle it on the inner side of his body and hold it in a death-grip.

Jack wasn't completely sure why Sonny hadn't organized a mass stomping. Jack thought maybe it was because Sunlight Gardener was interested in the new boy. He didn't *want* to think that, it scared him to think that, but it made sense. Sonny Singer was holding off because Sunlight Gardener had told him to, and that was another reason to get out of here in a hurry.

He looked to his right. Wolf was about twenty yards away, grubbing rocks with his hair in his face. Closer by was a gantry-thin boy with buck teeth – Donald Keegan, his name was. Donny grinned at him worshipfully, baring those amazing buck teeth. Spit dribbled from the end of his lolling tongue. Jack looked away quickly.

Ferd Janklow was on his left – the boy with the narrow Delftware hands and the deep widow's peak. In the week since Jack and Wolf had been incarcerated in the Sunlight Home, he and Ferd had become good friends.

Ferd was grinning cynically.

'Donny's in love with you,' he said.

'Blow it out,' Jack said uncomfortably, feeling a flush rise in his cheeks.

'I bet *Donny'd* blow it out if you let him,' Ferd said. 'Wouldn't you, Donny?'

Donny Keegan laughed his big, rusty yuck-yuck, not having the slightest idea of what they were talking about.

'I wish you'd quit it,' Jack said. He felt more uncomfortable than ever.

Donny's in love with you.

The bloody hell of it was, he thought that maybe poor, retarded Donny Keegan really *was* in love with him . . . and Donny was maybe not the only one. Oddly, Jack found himself thinking of the nice man who had offered to take him home and who had then settled for dropping him off at the mall exit near Zanesville. *He* saw it first, Jack thought. *Whatever's new about me, that man saw it first.*

Ferd said, 'You've gotten very popular around here, Jack. Why, I think even old Heck Bast would blow it out for you, if you asked him.'

'Man, that's sick,' Jack said, flushing. 'I mean—'

Abruptly, Ferd dropped the rock he had been working at and stood up. He looked swiftly around, saw none of the white turtlenecks were looking at him, and then turned back to Jack. 'And now, my darling,' he said, 'it's been a *very* dull party, and I really must be going.'

Ferd made kissing noises at Jack, and then a grin of amazing radiance lit and broadened Ferd's narrow, pale face. A moment later he was in full flight, running for the rock wall at the end of Far Field, running in big gangling storklike strides.

He did indeed catch the guards napping – at least to a degree. Pedersen was talking about girls with Warwick and a horse-faced boy named Peabody, an Outside Staffer who had been rotated back to the Home for a while. Heck Bast had been granted the supreme pleasure of accompanying Sunlight Gardener to Muncie on some errand. Ferd got a good head-start before a startled cry went up:

'Hey! Hey, someone's takin off!'

Jack gaped after Ferd, who was already six rows over and humping like hell. In spite of seeing his own plan co-opted, Jack felt a moment of triumphant excitement, and in his heart he wished him nothing but well. *Go! Go, you sarcastic son of a bitch! Go, for Jason's sake!*

'It's Ferd Janklow,' Donny Keegan gurgled, and then laughed his big, whooping laugh.

3

The boys gathered for confession in the common room that night as they always did, but confession was cancelled. Andy Warwick strode in, announced the cancellation with abrupt baldness, and told them they could have an hour of 'fellowship' before dinner. Then he strode out.

Jack thought Warwick had looked, under his patina of goose-stepping authority, frightened.

And Ferd Janklow was not here.

Jack looked around the room and thought with glum humor that if this was 'fellowship one with the other', he would hate to see what would happen if Warwick had told them to have 'a quiet hour'. They sat around the big long room, thirty-nine boys between age nine and age seventeen, looking at their hands, picking at scabs, morosely biting their nails. They all shared a common look – junkies robbed of their fix. They wanted to hear confessions; even more, they wanted to *make* confessions.

No one mentioned Ferd Janklow. It was as though Ferd, with his grimaces at Sunlight Gardener's sermons and his pale Delftware hands, had never existed.

Jack found himself barely able to restrain an impulse to stand and scream at them. Instead, he began to think as hard as he ever had in his life.

He's not here because they killed him. They're all mad. You think madness isn't catching? Just look what happened at that nutty place down in South America – when the man in the reflector sunglasses told them to drink the purple grape drink, they said yassuh, boss, and drank it.

Jack looked around at the dreary, indrawn, tired, blank faces – and thought how they would light, how they would kindle, if Sunlight Gardener strode in here – if he strode in here right here and now.

They'd do it, too, if Sunlight Gardener asked them to. They'd drink it, and then they'd hold me and Wolf, and they'd pour it down our throats as well. Ferd was right – they see something on my face, or in it, something that came into me in the Territories, and maybe they do love me a little . . . I guess that's what pulled

Heck Bast's bell-rope, anyway. That slob isn't used to loving anything or anyone. So, yeah, maybe they do love me a little . . . but they love him a lot more. They'd do it. They're mad.

Ferd could have told him that, and, sitting there in the common room, Jack supposed that Ferd *had* told him.

He told Jack he had been committed to the Sunlight Home by his parents, born-again Christians who fell down on their knees in the living room whenever anyone on *The 700 Club* began to say a prayer. Neither of them had understood Ferd, who was cut from an entirely different bolt of cloth. They thought Ferd must be a child of the devil – a communistic, radical humanist changeling. When he ran away for the fourth time and was bagged by none other than Franky Williams, his parents came to the Sunlight Home – where Ferd had of course been stashed – and fell in love with Sunlight Gardener on sight. Here was the answer to all the problems their bright, troublesome, rebellious son had caused them. Sunlight Gardener would educate their son toward the Lord. Sunlight Gardener would show him the error of his ways. Sunlight Gardener would take him off their hands and get him off the streets of Anderson.

'They saw that story about the Sunlight Home on *Sunday Report*,' Ferd told Jack. 'They sent me a postcard saying God would punish liars and false prophets in a lake of fire. I wrote them back – Rudolph in the kitchen smuggled the letter out for me. Dolph's a pretty good guy.' He paused. 'You know what the Ferd Janklow definition of a good guy is, Jack?'

'No.'

'One who stays bought,' Ferd said, and laughed a cynical, hurt laugh. 'Two bucks buys Dolph's mailman services. So I wrote them a letter and I said that if God punished liars the way they said, then I hoped Sunlight Gardener could find a set of asbestos longjohns in the other world, because he was lying about what goes on here faster than a horse can trot. Everything they had on *Sunday Report* – the rumors about the strait-jackets and about the Box – it was all true. Oh, they couldn't prove it. The guy's a nut, Jack, but he's a *smart* nut. If you ever make a mistake about that, he'll put a real hurt on you and on Phil the Fearless Wolf-Boy for good measure.'

Jack said, 'Those *Sunday Report* guys are usually pretty good at catching people with their hands in the pork barrel. At least, that's what my mom says.'

'Oh, he was scared. He got real shrill and shrieky. Ever see Humphrey Bogart in *The Caine Mutiny*? He was like that for a week before they showed up. When they finally got here he was all sweetness and reason, but the week before was a living hell. Mr Ice Cream was shitting in his pants. That was the week he kicked Benny Woodruff down the stairs from the third floor because he caught him with a Superman comic. Benny was out cold for three hours, and he couldn't quite get it straight who he was or where he was until that night.'

Ferd paused.

'He knew they were coming. Same as he always knows when the state inspectors are going to pull a surprise inspection. He hid the strait-jackets in the attic and made believe the Box was a hay-drying shed.'

Ferd's cynical, hurt laugh again.

'Know what my folks did, Jack? They sent Sunny Gardener a Xerox of my letter to them. "For my own good," my pop says in his next letter to me. And guess what? It's Ferd's turn in the Box, courtesy of my own folks!'

The hurt laugh again.

'Tell you one other thing. He wasn't kidding at night-chapel. The kids that talked to the *Sunday Report* people all disappeared – the ones he could get hold of, anyway.'

The way Ferd himself has disappeared now, Jack thought, watching Wolf brood across the room. He shivered. His hands felt very, very cold.

Your friend Phil the Fearless Wolf-Boy.

Was Wolf starting to look hairier again? So soon? Surely not. But that was coming, of course – it was as relentless as the tides.

And by the way, Jack, while we're just sitting around here worrying about the dangers of just sitting around here, how's your mother? How's Darling Lil, Queen of the Bs? Losing weight? Having pain? Is she finally starting to feel it eat into her with its sharp, ratty little teeth as you sit here growing roots in this weird prison? Is Morgan maybe getting ready to wind up the lightning and give the cancer a hand?

He had been shocked at the idea of strait-jackets, and although he had seen the Box – a big ugly iron thing which sat in the Home's back yard like a weird abandoned refrigerator – he couldn't believe that Gardener actually put boys in it. Ferd had slowly convinced him, talking in a low voice as they harvested rocks in Far Field.

'He's got a great setup here,' Ferd had said. 'It's a license to coin money. His religious shows play all over the midwest on the radio and over most of the country on cable TV and the indy stations. We're his captive audience. We sound great on the radio and we look great on the tube – when Roy Owdersfelt isn't milking that fucking pimple on the end of his nose, that is. He's got Casey, his pet radio and TV producer – Casey videotapes every morning-chapel and audiotapes every night-chapel. He cuts all the sound and picture together and hypes everything until Gardener looks like Billy Graham and us guys sound like the crowd in Yankee Stadium during the seventh game of the World Series. That isn't all Casey does, either. He's the house genius. You see the bug in your room? Casey set up the bugs. Everything feeds into his control room, and the only way into that control room is through Gardener's private office. The bugs are voice-actuated, so he doesn't waste any tape. Anything juicy he saves for Sunlight Gardener. I've heard Casey put a blue box on Gardener's phone so he can make long-distance phone calls free, and I know damned well he's spliced a line into the pay-TV cable that goes by out front. You like the idea of Mr Ice Cream settling back and watching a big double feature on Cinemax after a hard day of selling Jesus to the masses? I like it. This guy is as American as spinner hubcaps, Jack, and here in Indiana they love him almost as much as they love high-school basketball.'

Ferd hawked back snot, grimaced, twisted his head, and spat into the dirt.

'You're kidding,' Jack said.

'Ferd Janklow never kids about the Marching Morons of the Sunlight Home,' Ferd said solemnly. 'He's rich, he doesn't have to declare any of it to the Internal Revenue, he's got the local school board buffaloed – I mean, they're scared to death of him; there's this one woman who practically *skitters* every time she's out here, looks like she'd like to give him the sign against the evil eye, or something – and like I said, he always seems to know when someone from the State Education Board is going to pay us a surprise visit. We clean this place from top to bottom, Bast the Bastard takes the canvas overcoats up to the attic, and the Box gets filled with hay from the barn. And when they come, we're always in class. How many classes you been in since you landed here in Indiana's version of the *Love Boat*, Jack?'

'None,' Jack said.

'None!' Ferd agreed, delighted. He laughed his cynical, hurt laugh again – that laugh said, *Guess what I found out when I turned eight or so? I found out that I was getting a royal fucking from life, and that things weren't going to change in a hurry. Or maybe they were never going to change. And although it bums me out, it also has its funny side. You know what I mean, jellybean?*

4

Such was the run of Jack's thoughts when hard fingers suddenly grasped the back of his neck at the pressure-points below the ears and lifted him out of his chair. He was turned around into a cloud of foul breath and treated – if that was the word – to the sterile moonscape of Heck Bast's face.

'Me and the Reverend was still in Muncie when they brought your queer troublemaker friend into the hospital,' he said. His fingers pulsed and squeezed, pulsed and squeezed. The pain was excruciating. Jack moaned and Heck grinned. The grin allowed bad breath to escape his mouth in even greater quantities. 'Reverend got the news on his beeper. Janklow looked like a taco that spent about forty-five minutes in a microwave oven. It's gonna be a while before they put *that* boy back together again.'

He's not talking to me, Jack thought. *He's talking to the whole room. We're supposed to get the message that Ferd's still alive.*

'You're a stinking liar,' he said. 'Ferd's—'

Heck Bast hit him. Jack went sprawling on the floor.

Boys scattered away from him. From somewhere, Donny Keegan heehawed.

There was a roar of rage. Jack looked up, dazed, and shook his head in an effort to clear it. Heck turned and saw Wolf standing protectively over Jack, his upper lip pulled back, the overhead lights sending weird orange glints off his round glasses.

'So the dumbhead finally wants to dance,' Heck said, beginning to grin. 'Hey, all right! I *love* to dance. Come on, snotface. Come on over here and let's dance.'

Still growling, saliva now coating his lower lip, Wolf began to move forward. Heck moved to meet him. Chairs scraped across linoleum as people moved back hurriedly to give them room.

'What's going on h—'

From the door. Sonny Singer. No need to finish his question; he saw what was going on here. Smiling, he pulled the door shut and leaned against it, watching, arms crossed over his narrow chest, his dark narrow face now alight.

Jack switched his gaze back to Wolf and Heck.

'Wolf, be careful!' he shouted.

'I'll be careful, Jack,' Wolf said, his voice little more than a growl. 'I'll—'

'Let's *dance*, asshole,' Heck Bast grunted, and threw a whistling, country-boy roundhouse. It hit Wolf high on the right cheekbone, driving him backward three or four steps. Donny Keegan laughed his high, whinnying laugh, which Jack now knew was as often a signal of dismay as of glee.

The roundhouse was a good, heavy blow. Under other circumstances, the fight would probably have ended right there. Unfortunately for Hector Bast, it was also the only blow he landed.

He advanced confidently, big fists up at chest height, and drove the roundhouse again. This time Wolf's arm moved upward and outward to meet it. Wolf caught Heck's fist.

Heck's hand was big. Wolf's hand was bigger.

Wolf's fist swallowed Heck's.

Wolf's fist clenched.

From within it came a sound like small dry sticks first cracking, then breaking.

Heck's confident smile first curdled, then froze solid. A moment later he began to shriek.

'Shouldn't have hurt the herd, you bastard,' Wolf whispered. 'Oh your Bible this and oh your Bible that – *Wolf!* – and all you have to do is hear six verses of *The Book of Good Farming* to know you never . . .'

Crackle!

'. . . never . . .'

Crunch!

'*NEVER* hurt the herd.'

Heck Bast fell to his knees, howling and weeping. Wolf still held Heck's fist in his own, and Heck's arm angled up. Heck looked like a Fascist giving a *Heil Hitler* salute on his knees. Wolf's arm was as rigid as stone, but his face showed no real effort; it was, except for the blazing eyes, almost serene.

Blood began to drip out of Wolf's fist.

'Wolf, stop! That's enough!'

Jack looked around swiftly and saw that Sonny was gone, the door standing open. Almost all of the boys were on their feet now. They had drawn away from Wolf as far as the room's walls would allow, their faces awed and fearful. And still the tableau held in the center of the room: Heck Bast on his knees, arm up and out, his fist swallowed in Wolf's, blood pouring onto the floor from Wolf's fist.

People crowded back into the doorway. Casey, Warwick, Sonny Singer, three more big guys. And Sunlight Gardener, with a small black case, like a glasses-case, in one hand.

'*That's enough, I said!*' Jack took one look at the newcomers and raced toward Wolf. '*Right here and now! Right here and now!*'

'All right,' Wolf said quietly. He let go of Heck's hand, and Jack saw a horrible crushed thing that looked like a mangled pinwheel. Heck's fingers stuck off at jagged angles. Heck mewled and held his destroyed hand against his chest.

'All right, Jack.'

The six of them grabbed Wolf. Wolf made a half-turn, slipped one arm free, pushed, and suddenly Warwick went rattling against the wall. Someone screamed.

'Hold him!' Gardener yelled. 'Hold him! Hold him, for Jesus' sake!' He was opening the flat black case.

'*No, Wolf!*' Jack shouted. '*Quit it!*'

For a moment Wolf went on struggling, and then he slumped back, allowing them to push him to the wall. To Jack they looked like Lilliputians clinging to Gulliver. Sonny looked afraid of Wolf at last.

'Hold him,' Gardener repeated, taking a glittering hypodermic out of the flat case. That mincing, almost coy smile had come onto his face. 'Hold him, praise Jesus!'

'You don't need that,' Jack said.

'Jack?' Wolf looked suddenly frightened. 'Jack? *Jack?*'

Gardener, headed for Wolf, pushed Jack as he went by. There was good whipcord muscle in that push. Jack went reeling into Morton, who squealed and shrank away as if Jack were contaminated. Belatedly, Wolf began to struggle again – but they were six, and that was too many. Perhaps, when the Change was on him, it wouldn't have been.

'*Jack!*' he howled. '*Jack! Jack!*'

'Hold him, praise God,' Gardener whispered, his lips skinned back brutally from his teeth, and plunged the hypodermic into Wolf's arm.

Wolf went rigid, threw his head back, and howled.

Kill you, you bastard, Jack thought incoherently. *Kill you, kill you, kill you.*

Wolf struggled and thrashed. Gardener stood back, watching coldly. Wolf got a knee up into Casey's expansive gut. Casey *whoofed* air out, staggered backward, then came back. A minute or two later, Wolf began first to flag . . . then to sag.

Jack got to his feet, weeping with rage. He tried to plunge toward the knot of white turtlenecks holding his friend – as he watched he saw Casey swing a fist into Wolf's drooping face, and saw blood begin to pour from Wolf's nose.

Hands held him back. He struggled, then looked around and saw the frightened faces of the boys he picked rocks with in Far Field.

'I want him in the Box,' Gardener said as Wolf's knees finally buckled. He looked slowly around at Jack: 'Unless . . . perhaps you'd like to tell me where we've met before, Mr Parker?'

Jack stood looking down at his feet, saying nothing. His eyes stung and burned with hot, hateful tears.

'The Box, then,' Gardener said. 'You may feel different when he starts to vocalize, Mr Parker.'

Gardener strode out.

5

Wolf was still screaming in the Box when Jack and the other boys were marched down to morning-chapel. Sunlight

Gardener's eyes seemed to dwell ironically on Jack's pale, strained face. *Perhaps now, Mr Parker?*

Wolf, it's my mother, my mother –

Wolf was still screaming when Jack and the other boys scheduled for field-work were split into two groups and marched out to the trucks. As he passed near the box. Jack had to suppress an urge to jam his hands over his ears. Those growls, those gibbering sobs.

All at once Sonny Singer was at his shoulder.

'Reverend Gardener's in his office waiting to take your confession right this minute, snotface,' he said. 'Told me to tell you he'll let the dummy out of the Box the minute you tell him what he wants to know.' Sonny's voice was silky, his face dangerous.

Wolf, screaming and howling to be let out, pounding the home-riveted iron sides of the Box with a fury of blows.

Ah, Wolf, she's my MOTHER –

'I can't tell him what he wants to know,' Jack said. He turned suddenly toward Sonny, turning the force of whatever had come into him in the Territories upon Sonny. Sonny took two giant steps backward, his face dismayed and sickly scared. He tripped over his own feet and stumbled into the side of one of the idling trucks. If it hadn't been there, he would have fallen down.

'All right,' Sonny said . . . the words came out in a breathy rush that was close to a whine. 'All right, all right, forget it.' His thin face grew arrogant again. 'Reverend Gardener told me if you said no that I should tell you that your friend's screaming for you. Do you get it?'

'I know who he's screaming for.'

'Get in the truck!' Pedersen said, grimly, barely looking at them as he passed by . . . but when he passed Sonny,

Pedersen grimaced as though he had smelled something rotten.

Jack could hear Wolf screaming even after the trucks got rolling, though the mufflers on both were little more than scallops of iron lace and the engines blatted stridently. Nor did Wolf's screams fade. He had made some sort of connection with Wolf's mind now, and he could hear Wolf screaming even after the work parties had reached Far Field. The understanding that these screams were only in his mind did nothing at all to improve matters.

Around lunchtime, Wolf fell silent, and Jack knew, suddenly and with no doubt at all, that Gardener had ordered him taken out of the Box before his screams and howls attracted the wrong sort of attention. After what had happened to Ferd, he wouldn't want any attention at all focussed on the Sunlight Home.

When the work parties returned that late afternoon, the door of the Box was standing open and the Box was empty. Upstairs in the room they shared, Wolf was lying on the lower bunk. He smiled wanly as Jack came in.

'How's your head, Jack? Bruise looks a little better. Wolf!'

'Wolf, are you all right?'

'Screamed, didn't I? Couldn't help it.'

'Wolf, I'm sorry,' Jack said. Wolf looked strange – too white, somehow diminished.

He's dying, Jack thought. No, his mind corrected; Wolf had been dying ever since they had flipped into this world to escape Morgan. But now he was dying faster. Too white . . . diminished . . . but . . .

Jack felt a creeping chill.

Wolf's bare legs and arms weren't really bare; they were

downed with a fine pelt of hair. It hadn't been there two nights ago, he was sure of that.

He felt an urge to rush over to the window and stare out, searching for the moon, trying to make sure he hadn't somehow misplaced about seventeen days.

'It's not the time of the Change, Jacky,' Wolf said. His voice was dry, somehow husked-out. The voice of an invalid. 'But I started to change in that dark smelly place they put me in. Wolf! I did. Because I was so mad and scared. Because I was yelling and screaming. Yelling and screaming can make the Change all by themselves, if a Wolf does it long enough.' Wolf brushed at the hair on his legs. 'It'll go away.'

'Gardener set a price for letting you out,' Jack said, 'but I couldn't pay it. I wanted to, but . . . Wolf . . . my mother . . .'

His voice blurred and wavered toward tears.

'Shhh, Jacky. Wolf knows. Right here and now.' Wolf smiled his terrible wan smile again, and took Jack's hand.

CHAPTER TWENTY-FOUR
JACK NAMES THE PLANETS

1

Another week in the Sunlight Home, praise God. The moon put on weight.

On Monday, a smiling Sunlight Gardener asked the boys to bow their heads and give thanks to God for the conversion of their brother Ferdinand Janklow. Ferd had made a soul-decision for Christ while recuperating in Parkland Hospital, Sunlight said, his smile radiant. Ferd had made a collect call to his parents and told them he wanted to be a soul-winner for the Lord, and they prayed for guidance right there over the long-distance line, and his parents had come to pick him up that very day. *Dead and buried under some frosty Indiana field . . . or over in the Territories, perhaps, where the Indiana State Patrol could never go.*

Tuesday was too coldly rainy for field-work. Most of the boys had been allowed to stay in their rooms and sleep or read, but for Jack and Wolf, the period of harassment had begun. Wolf was lugging load after load of garbage from the barn and the sheds out to the side of the road in the driving rain. Jack had been set to work cleaning toilets. He supposed that Warwick and Casey, who had assigned him this duty, thought they were giving him a really nasty job to do. It was obvious that they'd never seen the men's room of the world-famous Oatley Tap.

Just another week at the Sunlight Home, can you say oh-yeah.

Hector Bast returned on Wednesday, his right arm in a cast up to the elbow, his big, doughy face so pallid that the pimples on it stood out like garish dots of rouge.

'Doctor says I may never get the use of it back,' Heck Bast said. 'You and your numbnuts buddy have got a lot to answer for, Parker.'

'You aiming to have the same thing happen to your other hand?' Jack asked him . . . but he was afraid. It was not just a desire for revenge he saw in Heck's eyes; it was a desire to commit murder.

'I'm not afraid of him,' Heck said. 'Sonny says they took most of the mean out of him in the Box. Sonny says he'll do anything to keep from going back in. As for you—'

Heck's left fist flashed out. He was even clumsier with his left hand than with his right, but Jack, stunned by the big boy's pallid rage, never saw it coming. His lips spread into a weird smile under Heck's fist and broke open. He reeled back against the wall.

A door opened and Billy Adams looked out.

'*Shut that door or I'll see you get a helping!*' Heck screamed, and Adams, not anxious for a dose of assault and battery, complied in a hurry.

Heck started toward Jack. Jack pushed groggily away from the wall and raised his fists. Heck stopped.

'You'd like that, wouldn't you,' Heck said. 'Fighting with a guy that's only got one good hand.' Color rushed up into his face.

Footsteps rattled on the third floor, heading toward the stairs. Heck looked at Jack. 'That's Sonny. Go on. Get out of here. We're gonna get you, my friend. You and the dummy both. Reverend Gardener says we can, unless you tell him whatever it is he wants to know.'

Heck grinned.

'Do me a favor, snotface. Don't tell him.'

2

They had taken *something* out of Wolf in the Box, all right, Jack thought. Six hours had passed since his hallway confrontation with Heck Bast. The bell for confession would ring soon, but for now Wolf was sleeping heavily in the bunk below him. Outside, rain continued to rattle off the sides of the Sunlight Home.

It wasn't meanness, and Jack knew it wasn't just the Box that had taken it. Not even just the Sunlight Home. It was this whole world. Wolf was, simply, pining for home. He had lost most of his vitality. He smiled rarely and laughed not at all. When Warwick yelled at him at lunch for eating with his fingers, Wolf cringed.

It has to be soon, Jacky. Because I'm dying. Wolf's dying.

Heck Bast said he wasn't afraid of Wolf, and indeed there seemed nothing left to be afraid of; it seemed that crushing Heck's hand had been the last strong act of which Wolf was capable.

The confession bell rang.

That night, after confession and dinner and chapel, Jack and Wolf came back to their room to find both of their beds dripping wet and reeking of urine. Jack went to the door, yanked it open, and saw Sonny, Warwick, and a big lunk named Van Zandt standing in the hall, grinning.

'Guess we got the wrong room, snotface,' Sonny said. 'Thought it had to be the toilet, on account of the turds we always see floating around in there.'

Van Zandt almost ruptured himself laughing at this sally.

Jack stared at them for a long moment, and Van Zandt stopped laughing.

'Who you looking at, turd? You want your fucking nose broke off?'

Jack closed the door, looked around, and saw Wolf asleep in his wet bunk with all his clothes on. Wolf's beard was coming back, but still his face looked pale, the skin stretched and shiny. It was an invalid's face.

Leave him alone, then, Jack thought wearily. *If he's that tired, let him sleep in it.*

No. You will not leave him alone to sleep in that fouled bed. You will not!

Tiredly, Jack went to Wolf, shook him half-awake, got him off the wet, stinking mattress, and out of his biballs. They slept curled up together on the floor.

At four in the morning, the door opened and Sonny and Heck marched in. They yanked Jack up and half-carried him down to Sunlight Gardener's basement office.

Gardener was sitting with his feet up on the corner of his desk. He was fully dressed in spite of the hour. Behind him was a picture of Jesus walking on the Sea of Galilee while his disciples gawped in wonder. To his right was a glass window looking into the darkened studio where Casey worked his idiot-savant wonders. There was a heavy keychain attached to one of Gardener's beltloops. The keys, a heavy bunch of them, lay in the palm of his hand. He played with them while he spoke.

'You haven't given us a single confession since you got here, Jack,' Sunlight Gardener said, his tone one of mild reproof. 'Confession is good for the soul. Without confession we cannot be saved. Oh, I don't mean the idolatrous, heathenish confession of the Catholics. I mean confession before your brothers and your Saviour.'

'I'll keep it between me and my Saviour, if it's all the same to you,' Jack said evenly, and in spite of his fear and disorientation, he could not help relishing the expression of fury which overspread Gardener's face.

'It's *not* all the same to me!' Gardener screamed. Pain exploded in Jack's kidneys. He fell to his knees.

'Watch what you say to Reverend Gardener, snotface,' Sonny said. 'Some of us around here stand up for him.'

'God bless you for your trust and your love, Sonny,' Gardener said gravely, and turned his attention to Jack again. 'Get up, son.'

Jack managed to get up, holding on to the edge of Sunlight Gardener's expensive blondewood desk.

'What's your real name?'

'Jack Parker.'

He saw Gardener nod imperceptibly, and tried to turn, but it was a moment too late. Fresh pain exploded in his kidneys. He screamed and went down again, knocking the fading bruise on his forehead against the edge of Gardener's desk.

'Where are you from, you lying, impudent, devil's spawn of a boy?'

'Pennsylvania.'

Pain exploded in the meaty upper part of his left thigh.

He rolled into a fetal position on the white Karastan carpet, huddling with his knees against his chest.

'Get him up.'

Sonny and Heck got him up.

Gardener reached into the pocket of his white jacket and took out a Zippo lighter. He flicked the wheel, produced a big yellow flame, and brought the flame slowly toward Jack's face. Nine inches. He could smell the sweet, pungent reek of lighter fluid. Six inches. Now he could feel heat. Three inches. Another inch – maybe just half that – and discomfort would turn to pain. Sunlight Gardener's eyes were hazy-happy. His lips trembled on the edge of a smile.

'Yeah!' Heck's breath was hot, and it smelled like mouldy pepperoni. 'Yeah, do it!'

'Where do I know you from?'

'I never met you before!' Jack gasped.

The flame moved closer. Jack's eyes began to water, and he could feel his skin beginning to sear. He tried to pull his head back. Sonny Singer pushed it forward.

'Where have I met you?' Gardener rasped. The lighter's flame danced deep in his black pupils, each deep spark a twinner of the other. 'Last chance!'

Tell him, for God's sake tell him!

'If we ever met I don't remember it,' Jack gasped. 'Maybe California—'

The Zippo clicked closed. Jack sobbed with relief.

'Take him back,' Gardener said.

They yanked Jack toward the door.

'It won't do you any good, you know,' Sunlight Gardener said. He had turned around and appeared to be meditating on the picture of Christ walking on water. 'I'll get it out of you. If not tonight, then tomorrow night. If not tomorrow night, then the night after. Why not make it easy on yourself, Jack?'

Jack said nothing. A moment later he felt his arm twisted up to his shoulderblades. He moaned.

'*Tell him!*' Sonny whispered.

And part of Jack wanted to, not because he was hurt but because –

– *because confession was good for the soul.*

He remembered the muddy courtyard, he remembered this same man in a different envelope of skin asking who he was, he remembered thinking: *I'll tell you anything you want to know if only you'll stop looking at me with those freaked-out eyes of yours, sure, because I'm only a kid, and that's what kids do, they tell, they tell everything* –

Then he remembered his mother's voice, that tough voice, asking him if he was going to spill his guts to this guy.

'I can't tell you what I don't know,' he said.

Gardener's lips parted in a small, dry smile. 'Take him back to his room,' he said.

3

Just another week in the Sunlight Home, can you say amen, brothers and sisters. Just another long, long week.

Jack lingered in the kitchen after the others had taken in their breakfast dishes and left. He knew perfectly well that he was risking another beating, more harassment . . . but by this time, that seemed a minor consideration. Only three hours before, Sunlight Gardener had come within an ace of burning his lips off. He had seen it in the man's crazy eyes, had felt it in the man's crazy heart. After something like that, the risk of a beating seemed a very minor consideration indeed.

Rudolph's cook's whites were as gray as the lowering November sky outside. When Jack spoke his name in a near-whisper, Rudolph turned a bloodshot, cynical gaze on him. Cheap whiskey was strong on his breath.

'You better get outta here, new fish. They're keepin an eye on you pretty good.'

Tell me something I don't know.

Jack glanced nervously toward the antique dishwasher, which thumped and hissed and gasped its steamy dragon's breath at the boys loading it. They seemed not to be looking at Jack and Rudolph, but Jack knew that *seemed* was really the operant word. Tales would be carried. Oh yes. At the Sunlight Home they took away your dough, and carried tales became a kind of replacement currency.

'I need to get out of here,' Jack said. 'Me and my big friend. How much would you take to look the other way while we went out that back door?'

'More than you could pay me even if you could get your hands on what they took from you when they ho'd you in here, buddy-roo,' Rudolph said. His words were hard but he looked at Jack with a bleary sort of kindness.

Yes, of course – it was all gone, everything. The guitar-pick, the silver dollar, the big croaker marble, his six dollars . . . all gone. Sealed in an envelope and held somewhere, probably in Gardener's office downstairs. But –

'Look, I'd give you an IOU.'

Rudolph grinned. 'Comin from someone in this den of thieves and dope-addicts, that's almost funny,' he said. 'Piss on your fuckin IOU, old hoss.'

Jack turned all the new force that was in him upon Rudolph. There was a way to hide that force, that new beauty – to a degree, at least – but now he let it all come out, and saw Rudolph step back from it, his face momentarily confused and amazed.

'My IOU would be good and I think you know it,' Jack said quietly. 'Give me an address and I'll mail you the cash. How much? Ferd Janklow said that for two bucks you'd mail a letter for someone. Would ten be enough to look the other way just long enough for us to take a walk?'

'Not ten, not twenty, not a hundred,' Rudolph said quietly. He now looked at the boy with a sadness that scared Jack badly. It was that look as much as anything else – maybe more – that told him just how badly he and Wolf were caught. 'Yeah, I've done it before. Sometimes for five bucks. Sometimes, believe it or not, for free. I would have done it free for Ferdie Janklow. He was a good kid. These *fuckers*—' Rudolph raised one water-and detergent-reddened fist and shook it toward the green-tiled wall. He saw Morton, the accused pud-puller, looking at him, and Rudolph glared horribly at him. Morton looked away in a hurry.

'Then why *not*?' Jack asked desperately.

'Because I'm scared, hoss,' Rudolph said.

'What do you mean? The night I came here, when Sonny started to give you some trouble—'

'Singer!' Rudolph flapped one hand contemptuously. 'I ain't scared of Singer, and I ain't scared of Bast, no matter how big he is. It's *him* I'm afraid of.'

'Gardener?'

'He's a devil from hell,' Rudolph said. He hesitated and then added, 'I'll tell you something I never told nobody else. One week he was late givin me my pay envelope and

I went downstairs to his office. Most times I don't, I don't like to go down there, but this time I had to . . . well, I had to see a man. I needed my money in a hurry, you know what I mean? And I seen him go down the hall and into his office, so I knew he was there. I went down and knocked on the door, and it swung open when I did, because it hadn't completely latched. And you know what, kid? *He wasn't there.*'

Rudolph's voice had lowered steadily as he told this story, until Jack could barely hear the cook over the thump and wheeze of the dishwasher. At the same time, his eyes had widened like the eyes of a child reliving a scary dream.

'I thought maybe he was in that recordin-studio thing they got, but he wasn't. And he hadn't gone into the chapel because there's no direct connectin door. There's a door to the outside from his office, but it was locked and bolted *on the inside*. So where did he go, buddy-roo? *Where did he go?*'

Jack, who knew, could only look at Rudolph numbly.

'I think he's a devil from hell and he took some weird elevator down to report to fuckin HQ,' Rudolph said. 'I'd like to help you but I can't. There ain't enough money in Fort Knox for me to cross the Sunlight Man. Now you get out of here. Maybe they ain't noticed you're missin.'

But they had, of course. As he came out through the swinging doors, Warwick stepped up behind him and clubbed Jack in the middle of the back with hands interlaced to form one gigantic fist. As he went stumbling forward through the deserted cafeteria, Casey appeared from nowhere like an evil jack-in-the-box and stuck out a foot. Jack couldn't stop. He tripped over Casey's foot, his own feet went out from under him, and he sprawled in a tangle of chairs. He got up, fighting back tears of rage and shame.

'You don't want to be so slow taking in your dishes, snotface,' Casey said. 'You could get hurt.'

Warwick grinned. 'Yeah. Now get on upstairs. The trucks are waiting to leave.'

4

At four the next morning he was awakened and taken down to Sunlight Gardener's office again.

Gardener looked up from his Bible as if surprised to see him.

'Ready to confess, Jack Parker?'

'I have nothing—'

The lighter again. The flame, dancing a bare inch from the tip of his nose.

'Confess. Where have we met?' The flame danced a little closer yet. 'I mean to have it out of you, Jack. Where? *Where?*'

'*Saturn!*' Jack screamed. It was all he could think of. '*Uranus! Mercury! Somewhere in the asteroid belt! Io! Ganymede! Dei—*'

Pain, thick and leaden and excruciating, exploded in his lower belly as Hector Bast reached between his legs with his good hand and squeezed Jack's testes.

'There,' Heck Bast said, smiling cheerfully. 'Didn't you just have that coming, you hellbound mocker.'

Jack collapsed slowly to the floor, sobbing.

Sunlight Gardener leaned slowly down, his face patient – almost beatific. 'Next time, it will be your friend down here,' Sunlight Gardener said gently. 'And with him I will not hesitate. Think about it, Jack. Until tomorrow night.'

But tomorrow night, Jack decided, he and Wolf would not be here. If only the Territories were left, then the Territories it would be . . .

. . . if he could get them back there.

CHAPTER TWENTY-FIVE

JACK AND WOLF GO TO HELL

1

They had to flip from downstairs. He concentrated on that rather than on the question of whether or not they would be able to flip at all. It would be simpler to go from the room, but the miserable little cubicle he and Wolf shared was on the third floor, forty feet above the ground. Jack didn't know how exactly the Territories geography and topography corresponded to the geography and topography of Indiana, but he wasn't going to take a chance that could get their necks broken.

He explained to Wolf what they would do.

'You understand?'

'Yes,' Wolf said listlessly.

'Give it back to me, anyway, pal.'

'After breakfast, I go into the bathroom across from the common room. I go into the first stall. If no one notices I'm gone, you'll come in. And we'll go back to the Territories. Is that right, Jacky?'

'That's it,' Jack said. He put a hand on Wolf's shoulder and squeezed it. Wolf smiled wanly. Jack hesitated and said, 'I'm sorry I got you into this. It's all my fault.'

'No, Jack,' Wolf said kindly. 'We'll try this. Maybe . . .' A small, wistful hope seemed to glimmer briefly in Wolf's eyes.

'Yes,' Jack said. 'Maybe.'

2

Jack was too scared and excited to want breakfast, but he thought he might attract attention by not eating. So he shovelled in eggs and potatoes that tasted like sawdust, and even managed one fatty piece of bacon.

The weather had finally cleared. There had been frost the night before, and the rocks in Far Field would be like chunks of slag embedded in hardened plastic.

Plates taken out to the kitchen.

Boys allowed to go back to the common room while Sonny Singer, Hector Bast, and Andy Warwick got their day-rosters.

They sat around, looking blank. Pedersen had a fresh copy of the magazine the Gardener organization published, *The Sunlight of Jesus*. He turned the pages idly, glancing up every once in a while to look at the boys.

Wolf looked a question at Jack. Jack nodded. Wolf got up and lumbered from the room. Pedersen glanced up, saw Wolf cross the hall and go into the long, narrow bathroom across the way, and then went back to his magazine.

Jack counted to sixty, then forced himself to count to sixty again. They were the two longest minutes of his life. He was dreadfully afraid that Sonny and Heck would come back into the common room and order all the boys out to the trucks, and he wanted to get into the bathroom before that happened. But Pedersen wasn't stupid. If Jack followed Wolf too closely, Pedersen might suspect something.

At last Jack got up and walked across the room toward the door. It seemed impossibly far away, and his heavy feet seemed to bring him no closer; it was like an optical illusion.

Pedersen looked up. 'Where you going, snotface?'

'Bathroom,' Jack said. His tongue was dry. He had heard of people's *mouths* getting dry when they were afraid, but their *tongues*?

'They'll be upstairs in a minute,' Pedersen said, nodding toward the end of the hall, where the stairs led down to the chapel, the studio, and Gardener's office. 'You better hold it and water Far Field.'

'I got to take a crap,' Jack said desperately.

Sure. And maybe you and your big stupid friend like to pull each other's dorks a little before you start the day. Just to sort of perk yourselves up. Go sit down.

'Well, go on, then,' Pedersen said crossly. 'Don't just stand there and whine about it.'

He looked back at his magazine. Jack crossed the hall and stepped into the bathroom.

3

Wolf had picked the wrong stall – he was halfway down the line, his big, clunky workshoes unmistakable under the door. Jack pushed in. It was cramped with the two of them, and he was very aware of Wolf's strong, clearly animal odor.

'Okay,' Jack said. 'Let's try it.'

'Jack, I'm scared.'

Jack laughed shakily. 'I'm scared, too.'

'How do we—'

'I don't know. Give me your hands.' That seemed like a good start.

Wolf put his hairy hands – paws, almost – in Jack's hands, and Jack felt an eerie strength flow from them into him. Wolf's strength wasn't gone after all, then. It had simply gone underground, as a spring will sometimes go underground in a savagely hot season.

Jack closed his eyes.

'*Want* to get back,' he said. '*Want* to get back, Wolf. *Help* me!'

'I do,' Wolf breathed. 'I will if I can! Wolf!'

'Here and now.'

'Right here and now!'

Jack squeezed Wolf's paw-hands tighter. He could smell Lysol. Somewhere he could hear a car passing. A phone rang. He thought, *I am drinking the magic juice. In my mind I'm drinking it, right here and now I'm drinking it, I can smell it, so purple and so thick and new, I can taste it, I can feel my throat closing on it –*

As the taste filled his throat, the world swayed under them, around them. Wolf cried out, 'Jacky, it's working!'

It startled him out of his fierce concentration and for a moment he became aware that it was only a trick, like trying to get to sleep by counting sheep, and the world steadied again. The smell of the Lysol flooded back. Faintly he heard someone answer the phone querulously: 'Yes, hello, who is it?'

Never mind, it's not a trick, not a trick at all – it's magic. It's magic and I did it before when I was little and I can do it again, Speedy said so that blind singer Snowball said so, too, THE MAGIC JUICE IS IN MY MIND –

He bore down with all his force, all his effort of will . . . and the ease with which they flipped was stupefying, as if a punch aimed at something which looked like granite hit a cleverly painted papier-mâché shell instead, so that the blow you thought would break all your knuckles instead encountered no resistance at all.

4

To Jack, with his eyes screwed tightly shut, it felt as if the floor had first crumbled under his feet . . . and then disappeared completely.

Oh shit we're going to fall anyway, he thought dismally.

But it wasn't really a fall, only a minor sideslip. A moment later he and Wolf were standing firmly, not on hard bathroom tile but on dirt.

A reek of sulphur mingled with what smelled like raw sewage flooded in. It was a deathly smell, and Jack thought it meant the end of all hope.

'Jason! What's that *smell*?' Wolf groaned. 'Oh Jason that *smell*, can't stay here, Jacky, can't stay—'

Jack's eyes snapped open. At the same moment Wolf let go of Jack's hands and blundered forward, his own eyes still tightly shut. Jack saw that Wolf's ill-fitting chinos and checked shirt had been replaced by the Oshkosh biballs in which Jack had originally seen the big herdsman. The John Lennon glasses were gone. And –

– and Wolf was blundering toward the edge of a precipice less than four feet away.

'*Wolf!*' He lunged at Wolf and wrapped his arms around Wolf's waist. *'Wolf, no!'*

'Jacky, can't stay,' Wolf moaned. 'It's a Pit, one of the

Pits, Morgan made these places, oh I heard that Morgan made them, I can smell it—'

'Wolf, there's a cliff, you'll fall!'

Wolf's eyes opened. His jaw dropped as he saw the smokey chasm which spread at their feet. In its deepest, cloudy depths, red fire winked like infected eyes.

'A Pit,' Wolf moaned. 'Oh Jacky, it's a Pit. Furnaces of the Black Heart down there. Black Heart at the middle of the world. Can't stay, Jacky, it's the worst bad there is.'

Jack's first cold thought as he and Wolf stood at the edge of the Pit, looking down into hell, or the Black Heart at the middle of the world, was that Territories geography and Indiana geography *weren't* the same. There was no corresponding place in the Sunlight Home to this cliff, this hideous Pit.

Four feet to the right, Jack thought with sudden, sickening horror. *That's all it would have taken – just four feet to the right. And if Wolf had done what I told him –*

If Wolf had done just what Jack had told him, they would have flipped from that first stall. And if they had done that, they would have come into the Territories just over this cliff's edge.

The strength ran out of his legs. He groped at Wolf again, this time for support.

Wolf held him absently, his eyes wide and glowing a steady orange. His face was a grue of dismay and fear. 'It's a Pit, Jacky.'

It looked like the huge open-pit molybdenum mine he had visited with his mother when they had vacationed in Colorado three winters ago – they had gone to Vail to ski but one day it had been too bitterly cold for that and so they had taken a bus tour to the Continental Minerals molybdenum mine outside the little town of Sidewinder. 'It looks like Gehenna to me, Jack-O,' she had said, and her face as she looked out the frost-bordered bus window had been dreamy and sad. 'I wish they'd shut those places down, every one of them. They're pulling fire and destruction out of the earth. It's Gehenna, all right.'

Thick, choking vines of smoke rose from the depths of the Pit. Its sides were veined with thick lodes of some poisonous green metal. It was perhaps half a mile across. A road leading downward spiraled its inner circumference. Jack could see figures toiling both upward and downward upon this road.

It was a prison of some kind, just as the Sunlight Home was a prison, and these were the prisoners and their keepers. The prisoners were naked, harnessed in pairs to carts like rickshaws – carts filled with huge chunks of that green, greasy-looking ore. Their faces were drawn in rough woodcuts of pain. Their faces were blackened with soot. Their faces ran with thick red sores.

The guards toiled beside them, and Jack saw with numb dismay that they were not human; in no sense at all could they be called human. They were twisted and humped, their hands were claws, their ears pointed like Mr Spock's. *Why, they're gargoyles!* he thought. *All those nightmare monsters on those cathedrals in France – Mom had a book and I thought we were going to have to see every one in the whole country but she stopped when I had a bad dream and wet the bed – did they come from here? Did somebody see them here? Somebody from the Middle Ages who flipped over, saw this place, and thought he'd had a vision of hell?*

But this was no vision.

The gargoyles had whips, and over the rumble of the

wheels and the sounds of rock cracking steadily under some steady, baking heat, Jack heard their pop and whistle. As he and Wolf watched, one team of men paused near the very top of the spiral road, their heads down, tendons on their necks standing out in harsh relief, their legs trembling with exhaustion.

The monstrosity who was guarding them – a twisted creature with a breechclout twisted around its legs and a patchy line of stiff hair growing from the scant flesh over the knobs of its spine – brought its whip down first on one and then on the other, howling at them in a high, screeching language that seemed to drive silver nails of pain into Jack's head. Jack saw the same silver beads of metal that had decorated Osmond's whip, and before he could blink, the arm of one prisoner had been torn open and the nape of the other's neck lay in ruined flaps.

The men wailed and leaned forward even farther, their blood the deepest color in the yellowish murk. The thing screeched and gibbered and its grayish, plated right arm flexed as it whirled the whip over the slaves' heads. With a final staggering jerk, they yanked the cart up and onto the level. One of them fell forward onto his knees, exhausted, and the forward motion of the cart knocked him sprawling. One of the wheels rolled over his back. Jack heard the sound of the downed prisoner's spine as it broke. It sounded like a track referee's starter-gun.

The gargoyle shrieked with rage as the cart tottered and then fell over, dumping its load onto the split, cracked, arid ground at the top of the Pit. He reached the fallen prisoner in two lunging steps and raised his whip. As he did, the dying man turned his head and looked into Jack Sawyer's eyes.

It was Ferd Janklow.

Wolf saw, too.

They groped for each other.

And flipped back.

5

They were in a tight, closed place – a bathroom stall, in fact – and Jack could barely breathe because Wolf's arms were wrapped around him in a crushing embrace. And one of his feet was sopping wet. He had somehow managed to flip back with one foot in a toilet-bowl. Oh, great. *Things like this never happen to Conan the Barbarian*, Jack thought dismally.

'Jack *no*, Jack *no*, the Pit, it was the Pit, *no*, Jack—'

'Quit it! Quit it, Wolf! We're back!'

'No, no n—'

Wolf broke off. He opened his eyes slowly.

'Back?'

'You bet, right here and now, so let go of me, you're breaking my ribs, and besides, my foot's stuck in the damn—'

The door between the bathroom and the hall burst open with a bang. It struck the inner tile with enough force to shatter the frosted-glass panel.

The stall door was torn open. Andy Warwick took one look and spoke three furious, contemptuous words:

'You fucking queers.'

He grabbed the dazed Wolf by the front of his checked shirt and pulled him out. Wolf's pants caught on the steel hood over the toilet-paper dispenser and pulled the whole works off the wall. It went flying. The toilet-paper roll broke free and went unspooling across the floor. Warwick sent Wolf crashing into the sinks, which were just the right height to catch him in the privates. Wolf fell to the floor, holding himself.

Warwick turned to Jack, and Sonny Singer appeared at the stall door. He reached in and grabbed Jack by the front of his shirt.

'All right, you fag—' Sonny began, and that was as far as he got. Ever since he and Wolf had been dragooned into this place, Sonny Singer had been in Jack's face. Sonny Singer with his sly dark face that wanted to look just like Sunlight Gardener's face (and as soon as it could). Sonny Singer who had coined the charming endearment *snotface*. Sonny Singer whose idea it had undoubtedly been to piss in their beds.

Jack pistoned his right fist out, not swinging wildly in the Heck Bast style but driving strong and smooth from the elbow. His fist connected with Sonny's nose. There was an audible crunch. Jack felt a moment of satisfaction so perfect it was sublime.

'There,' Jack cried. He pulled his foot out of the john. A great grin suffused his face, and he shot a thought at Wolf just as hard as he could:

We ain't doing that bad, Wolf – you broke one bastard's hand, and I broke one bastard's nose.

Sonny stumbled backward, screaming, blood spouting through his fingers.

Jack came out of the stall, his fists held up in front of him in a pretty fair imitation of John L. Sullivan. 'I told you to watch out for me, Sonny. Now I'm gonna teach you to say hallelujah.'

'Heck!' Sonny screamed. 'Andy! Casey! Somebody!'

'Sonny, you sound scared,' Jack said. 'I don't know why—'

And then something – something that felt like a full hod of bricks – fell on the back of his neck, driving him forward into one of the mirrors over the sinks. If it had been glass, it would have broken and cut Jack badly. But all the mirrors here were polished steel. There were to be no suicides in the Sunlight Home.

Jack was able to get one arm up and cushion the blow a little, but he still felt woozy as he turned around and saw Heck Bast grinning at him. Heck Bast had hit him with the cast on his right hand.

As he looked at Heck, an enormous, sickening realization suddenly dawned on Jack. *It was you!*

'That hurt like hell,' Heck said, holding his plastered right hand in his left, 'but it was worth it, snotface.' He started forward.

It was you! It was you standing over Ferd in that other world, whipping him to death. It was you, you were the gargoyle, it was your Twinner!

A rage so hot it was like shame swept through Jack. As Heck came in range, Jack leaned back against the sink, grasped its edge tightly in both hands, and shot both of his feet out. They caught Heck Bast squarely in the chest and sent him reeling back into the open stall. The shoe that had come back to Indiana planted in a toilet-bowl left a clear wet print on Heck's white turtleneck sweater. Heck sat down in the toilet with a splash, looking stunned. His cast clunked on porcelain.

Others were bursting in now. Wolf was trying to get up. His hair hung in his face. Sonny was advancing on him, one hand still clapped over his squirting nose, obviously meaning to kick Wolf back down.

'Yeah, you go ahead and touch him, Sonny,' Jack said softly, and Sonny cringed away.

Jack caught one of Wolf's arms and helped him up. He saw as if in a dream that Wolf had come back hairier than ever. *It's putting him under too much stress, all of this. It's bringing on his Change and Christ this is never going to end, never . . . never . . .*

He and Wolf backed away from the others – Warwick, Casey, Pedersen, Peabody, Singer – and toward the rear of the bathroom. Heck was coming out of the stall Jack had kicked him into, and Jack saw something else. They had flipped from the fourth stall down the line. Heck Bast was coming out of the fifth. They had moved just far enough in that other world to come back into a different stall.

'They was buggering each other in there!' Sonny cried, his words muffled and nasal. 'The retard and the pretty boy! Warwick and me caught em with their dicks out!'

Jack's buttocks touched cold tile. Nowhere else to run. He let go of Wolf, who slumped, dazed and pitiful, and put up his fists.

'Come on,' he said. 'Who's first?'

'You gonna take us all on?' Pedersen asked.

'If I have to, I will,' Jack said. 'What are you going to do, put me in traction for Jesus? Come on!'

A flicker of unease on Pedersen's face; a cramp of outright fear on Casey's. They stopped . . . they actually stopped. Jack felt a moment of wild, stupid hope. The boys stared at him with the unease of men looking at a mad dog which can be brought down . . . but which may bite someone badly first.

'Stand aside, boys,' a powerful, mellow voice said, and they moved aside willingly, relief lighting their faces. It was Reverend Gardener. Reverend Gardener would know how to handle this.

He came toward the cornered boys, dressed this morning in charcoal slacks and a white satin shirt with full, almost Byronic, sleeves. In his hand he held that black hypodermic case.

He looked at Jack and sighed. 'Do you know what the Bible says about homosexuality, Jack?'

Jack bared his teeth at him.

Gardener nodded sadly, as if this were no more than he had expected.

'Well, all boys are bad,' he said. 'It's axiomatic.'

He opened the case. The hypo glittered.

'I think that you and your friend have been doing something even worse than sodomy, however,' Gardener went on in his mellow, regretful voice. 'Going to places better left to your elders and betters, perhaps.'

Sonny Singer and Hector Bast exchanged a startled, uneasy look.

'I think that some of this evil . . . this perversity . . . has been my own fault.' He took the hypo out, glanced at it, and then took out a vial. He handed the case to Warwick and filled the hypo. 'I have never believed in forcing my boys to confess, but without confession there can be no decision for Christ, and with no decision for Christ, evil continues to grow. So, although I regret it deeply, I believe that the time to ask has ended and the time to demand in God's name has come. Pedersen. Peabody. Warwick. Casey. Hold them!'

The boys surged forward on his command like trained dogs. Jack got in one blow at Peabody, and then his hands were grabbed and pinned.

'*Led me hid imb!*' Sonny cried in his new, muffled voice. He elbowed through the crowd of goggling boys, his eyes glittering with hate. '*I wand to hid imb!*'

'Not now,' Gardener said. 'Later, perhaps. We'll pray on it, won't we, Sonny?'

'Yeah.' The glitter in Sonny's eyes had become positively feverish. 'I'mb going to bray on id all day.'

Like a man who is finally waking up after a very long sleep, Wolf grunted and looked around. He saw Jack being held, saw the hypodermic needle, and peeled Pedersen's arm off Jack as if it had been the arm of a child. A surprisingly strong roar came from his throat.

'No! Let him GO!'

Gardener danced in toward Wolf's blind side with a fluid grace that reminded Jack of Osmond turning on the carter in that muddy stable-yard. The needle flashed and plunged. Wolf wheeled, bellowing as if he had been stung . . . which, in a way, was just what had happened to him. He swept a hand at the hypo, but Gardener avoided the sweep neatly.

The boys, who had been looking on in their dazed Sunlight Home way, now began to stampede for the door, looking alarmed. They wanted no part of big, simple Wolf in such a rage.

'Let him GO! Let . . . him . . . let him . . .'

'Wolf!'

'Jack . . . Jacky . . .'

Wolf looked at him with puzzled eyes that shifted like strange kaleidoscopes from hazel to orange to a muddy red. He held his hairy hands out to Jack, and then Hector Bast stepped up behind him and clubbed him to the floor.

'Wolf! Wolf!' Jack stared at him with wet, furious eyes. *'If you killed him, you son of a bitch—'*

'Shhh, Mr Jack Parker,' Gardener whispered in his ear, and Jack felt the needle sting his upper arm. 'Just be quiet now. We're going to get a little sunlight in your soul. And maybe then we'll see how you like pulling a loaded wagon up the spiral road. Can you say hallelujah?'

That one word followed him down into dark oblivion. *Hallelujah . . . hallelujah . . . hallelujah . . .*

CHAPTER TWENTY-SIX
WOLF IN THE BOX

1

Jack was awake for quite a long time before they knew he was awake, but he became aware of who he was and what had happened and what his situation was now only by degrees – he was, in a way, like a soldier who has survived a fierce and prolonged artillery barrage. His arm throbbed where Gardener had punched the hypodermic into it. His head ached so badly that his very eyeballs seemed to pulse. He was ragingly thirsty.

He advanced a step up the ladder of awareness when he tried to touch the hurt place on his upper right arm with his left hand. He couldn't do it. And the reason he couldn't do it was that his arms were somehow wrapped around himself. He could smell old, mouldy canvas – it was the smell of a Boy Scout tent found in an attic after many dark years. It was only then (although he had been looking at it stupidly through his mostly lidded eyes for the last ten minutes) that he understood what he was wearing. It was a strait-jacket.

Ferd would have figured that out quicker, Jack-O, he thought, and thinking of Ferd had a focussing effect on his mind in spite of the crushing headache. He stirred a little and the bolts of pain in his head and the throb in his arm made him moan. He couldn't help it.

Heck Bast: 'He's waking up.'

Sunlight Gardener: 'No, he's not. I gave him a shot big enough to paralyze a bull alligator. He'll be out until nine tonight at the earliest. He's just dreaming a little. Heck, I want you to go up and hear the boys' confessions tonight. Tell them there will be no night-chapel; I've got a plane to meet, and that's just the start of what's probably going to be a very long night. Sonny, you stay and help me do the book-work.'

Heck: 'It sure *sounded* like he was waking up.'

Sunlight: 'Go on, Heck. And have Bobby Peabody check on Wolf.'

Sonny (snickering): 'He doesn't like it in there much, does he?'

Ah, Wolf, they put you back in the Box, Jack mourned. *I'm sorry . . . my fault . . . all of this is my fault . . .*

'The hellbound rarely care much for the machinery of salvation,' Jack heard Sunlight Gardener say. 'When the devils inside them start to die, they go out screaming. Go on now, Heck.'

'Yes sir, Reverend Gardener.'

Jack heard but did not see Heck as he lumbered out. He did not as yet dare to look up.

2

Stuffed into the crudely made, home-welded and home-bolted Box like a victim of premature burial in an iron coffin, Wolf had howled the day away, battering his fists bloody against the sides of the Box, kicking with his feet at the double-bolted, Dutch-oven-type door at the coffin's foot until the jolts of pain travelling up his legs made his crotch ache. He wasn't going to get out battering with his fists or kicking with his feet, he knew that, just as he knew they weren't going to let him out just because he screamed to be let out. But he couldn't help it. Wolfs hated being shut up above all things.

His screams carried through the Sunlight Home's immediate grounds and even into the near fields. The boys who heard them glanced at each other nervously and said nothing.

'I seen him in the bathroom this morning, and he turned mean,' Roy Owdersfelt confided to Morton in a low, nervous voice.

'Was they queerin off, like Sonny said?' Morton asked.

Another Wolf-howl rose from the squat iron Box, and both boys glanced toward it.

'And how!' Roy said eagerly. 'I didn't exactly see it because I'm short, but Buster Oates was right up front and he said that big retarded boy had him a whanger the size of a Akron fire-plug. That's what he said.'

'Jesus!' Morton said respectfully, thinking perhaps of his own sub-standard whanger.

Wolf howled all day, but as the sun began to go down, he stopped. The boys found the new silence ominous. They looked at one another often, and even more often, and with more unease, toward that rectangle of iron standing in the center of a bald patch in the Home's back yard. The Box was six feet long and three feet high – except for the crude square cut in the west side and covered with heavy-gauge steel mesh, an iron coffin was exactly what it looked like. What was going on in there? they wondered. And even during confession, during which time the boys were usually held rapt, every other consideration forgotten, eyes turned toward the common room's one window, even though that window looked on the side of the house directly opposite the Box.

What's going on in there?

Hector Bast knew that their minds were not on confession and it exasperated him, but he was unable to bring them around because he did not know what precisely was wrong. A feeling of chilly expectation had gripped the boys in the Home. Their faces were paler than ever; their eyes glittered like the eyes of dope-fiends.

What's going on in there?

What was going on was simple enough.

Wolf was going with the moon.

He felt it happen as the patch of sun coming in through the ventilation square began to rise higher and higher, as the quality of the light became reddish. It was too early to go with the moon; she was not fully pregnant yet and it would hurt him. Yet it would happen, as it always happened to Wolfs eventually, in season or out of it, when they were pressed too long and too hard. Wolf had held himself in check for a long time because it was what Jacky wanted. He had performed great heroisms for Jack in this world. Jack would dimly suspect some of them, yet never come close to apprehending their incredible depth and breadth.

But now he was dying, and he was going with the moon, and because the latter made the former seem more than bearable – almost holy, and surely ordained – Wolf went in relief, and in gladness. It was wonderful not to have to struggle anymore.

His mouth, suddenly deep with teeth.

3

After Heck left, there were office sounds: the soft scrape of chairs being moved, a jingle of the keys on Sunlight Gardener's belt, a file-cabinet door running open and then closed.

'Abelson. Two hundred and forty dollars and thirty-six cents.'

Sounds of keys being punched. Peter Abelson was one of the boys on OS. Like all of the OS boys, he was bright, personable, and had no physical defects. Jack had seen him only a few times, but he thought Abelson looked like Dondi, that homeless waif with the big eyes in the comic strips.

'Clark. Sixty-two dollars and seventeen cents.'

Keys being punched. The machine rumbled as Sonny hit the TOTAL key.

'That's a real fall-off,' Sonny remarked.

'I'll talk to him, never fear. Now please don't chatter at me, Sonny. Mr Sloat arrives in Muncie at ten-fifteen and it's a long drive. I don't want to be late.'

'Sorry, Reverend Gardener.'

Gardener made some reply Jack didn't even hear. At the name *Sloat*, a great shock had walloped him – and yet part of him was unsurprised. Part of him had known this might be in the cards. Gardener had been suspicious from the first. He had not wanted to bother his boss with trivialities, Jack figured. Or maybe he had not wanted to admit he couldn't get the truth out of Jack without help. But at last he had called – where? East? West? Jack would have given a great lot just then to know. Had Morgan been in Los Angeles, or New Hampshire?

Hello, Mr Sloat. I hope I'm not disturbing you, but the local police have brought me a boy – two boys, actually, but it's only the intelligent one I'm concerned with. I seem to know him. Or perhaps it's my . . . ah, my other self who knows him. He gives his name as Jack Parker, but . . . what? Describe him? All right . . .

And the balloon had gone up.

Please don't chatter at me, Sonny. Mr Sloat arrives in Muncie at ten-fifteen . . .

Time had almost run out.

I told you to get your ass home, Jack . . . too late now.

All boys are bad. It's axiomatic.

Jack raised his head a tiny bit and looked across the room. Gardener and Sonny Singer sat together on the far side of the desk in Gardener's basement office. Sonny was punching the keys of an adding machine as Gardener gave him set after set of figures, each figure following the name of an Outside Staffer, each name neatly set in alphabetical order. In front of Sunlight Gardener was a ledger, a long steel file-box, and an untidy stack of envelopes. As Gardener held one of these envelopes up to read the amount scribbled on the front, Jack was able to see the back. There was a drawing of two happy children, each carrying a Bible, skipping down the road toward a church, hand-in-hand. Written below them was I'LL BE A SUNBEAM FOR JESUS.

'Temkin. A hundred and six dollars even.' The envelope went into the steel file-box with the others that had been recorded.

'I think he's been skimming again,' Sonny said.

'God sees the truth but waits,' Gardener said mildly. 'Victor's all right. Now shut up and let's get this done before six.'

Sonny punched the keys.

The picture of Jesus walking on the water had been swung outward, revealing a safe behind it. The safe was open.

Jack saw that there were other things of interest on Sunlight Gardener's desk: two envelopes, one marked JACK PARKER and the other PHILIP JACK WOLFE. And his good old pack.

The third thing was Sunlight Gardener's bunch of keys.

From the keys, Jack's eyes moved to the locked door on the left-hand side of the room – Gardener's private exit to the outside, he knew. If only there was a way –

'Yellin. Sixty-two dollars and nineteen cents.'

Gardener sighed, put the last envelope into the long steel tray, and closed his ledger. 'Apparently Heck was right. I believe our dear friend Mr Jack Parker has awakened.' He got up, came around the desk, and walked toward Jack. His mad, hazy eyes glittered. He reached into his pocket and came out with the lighter. Jack felt a panic rise inside him at the sight of it. 'Only your name isn't really Parker at all, is it, my dear boy? Your real name is Sawyer, isn't it? Oh yes. Sawyer. And someone with a great interest in you is going to arrive very, very soon. And we'll have all sorts of interesting things to tell him, won't we?'

Sunlight Gardener tittered and flicked back the Zippo's hood, revealing the blackened wheel, the smoke-darkened wick.

'Confession is so good for the soul,' he whispered, and struck a light.

4

Thud.

'What was that?' Rudolph asked, looking up from his bank of double-ovens. Supper – fifteen large turkey pies – was coming along nicely.

'What was what?' George Irwinson asked.

At the sink, where he was peeling potatoes, Donny Keegan uttered his loud yuck-yuck of a laugh.

'I didn't hear anything,' Irwinson said.

Donny laughed again.

Rudolph looked at him, irritated. 'You gonna peel those goddam potatoes down to nothing, you idiot?'

'Hyuck-hyuck-hyuck!'

Thud!

'There, you heard it that time, didn't you?'

Irwinson only shook his head.

Rudolph was suddenly afraid. Those sounds were coming from the Box – which, of course, he was supposed to believe was a hay-drying shed. Some fat chance. That big boy was in the Box – the one they were saying had been caught in sodomy that morning with his friend, the one who had tried to bribe their way out only the day before. They said the big boy had shown a mean streak before Bast whopped him one . . . and some of them were also saying that the big boy hadn't just broken Bast's hand; they were saying he had *squeezed* it to a pulp. That was a lie, of course, had to be, but –

THUD!

This time Irwinson looked around. And suddenly Rudolph decided he needed to go to the bathroom. And that maybe he would go all the way up to the third floor to do his business. And not come out for two, maybe three hours. He felt the approach of black work – very black work.

THUD-THUD!

Fuck the turkey pies.

Rudolph took off his apron, tossed it on the counter

over the salt cod he had been freshening for tomorrow night's supper, and started out of the room.

'Where you going?' Irwinson asked. His voice was suddenly too high. It trembled. Donny Keegan went right on furiously peeling potatoes the size of Nerf footballs down to potatoes the size of Spalding golfballs, his dank hair hanging in his face.

THUD! THUD! THUD-THUD-THUD!

Rudolph didn't answer Irwinson's question, and by the time he hit the second-floor stairs, he was nearly running. It was hard times in Indiana, work was scarce, and Sunlight Gardener paid cash.

All the same, Rudolph had begun to wonder if the time to look for a new job had not come, could you say get me outta here.

5

THUD!

The bolt at the top of the Box's Dutch-oven-type door snapped in two. For a moment there was a dark gap between the Box and the door.

Silence for a time. Then:

THUD!

The bottom bolt creaked, bent.

THUD!

It snapped.

The door of the Box creaked open on its big, clumsy, homemade hinges. Two huge, heavily pelted feet poked out, soles up. Long claws dug into the dust.

Wolf started to work his way out.

6

Back and forth the flame went in front of Jack's eyes; back and forth, back and forth. Sunlight Gardener looked like a cross between a stage hypnotist and some old-time actor playing the lead in the biography of a Great Scientist on *The Late Late Show*. Paul Muni, maybe. It was funny – if he hadn't been so terrified, Jack would have laughed. And maybe he would laugh, anyway.

'Now I have a few questions for you, and you are going to answer them,' Gardener said. 'Mr Morgan could get the answers out of you himself – oh, easily, indubitably! – but I prefer not to put him to the trouble. So . . . how long have you been able to Migrate?'

'I don't know what you mean.'

'How long have you been able to Migrate to the Territories?'

'I don't know what you're talking about.'

The flame came closer.

'Where's the nigger?'

'Who?'

'The nigger, the nigger!' Gardener shrieked. 'Parker, Parkus, whatever he calls himself? Where is he?'

'I don't know who you're talking about.'

'Sonny! Andy!' Gardener screamed. 'Unlace his left hand. Hold it out to me.'

Warwick bent over Jack's shoulder and did something. A moment later they were peeling Jack's hand away from the small of his back. It tingled with pins and needles, waking up. Jack tried to struggle, but it was useless. They held his hand out.

'Now spread his fingers open.'

Sonny pulled Jack's ring finger and his pinky in one direction; Warwick pulled his pointer and middle finger in the other. A moment later, Gardener had applied the Zippo's flame to the webbing at the base of the V they had created. The pain was exquisite, bolting up his left arm and from there seeming to fill his whole body. A sweet, charring smell drifted up. Himself. Burning. Himself.

After an eternity, Gardener pulled the Zippo back and snapped it shut. Fine beads of sweat covered his forehead. He was panting.

'Devils scream before they come out,' he said. 'Oh yes indeed they do. Don't they, boys?'

'Yes, praise God,' Warwick said.

'You pounded that nail,' Sonny said.

'Oh yes, I know it. Yes indeed I do. I know the secrets of both boys and devils.' Gardener tittered, then leaned forward until his face was an inch from Jack's. The cloying scent of cologne filled Jack's nose. Terrible as it was, he thought it was quite a lot better than his own burning flesh. 'Now, Jack. How long have you been Migrating? Where is the nigger? How much does your mother know? Who have you told? What has the nigger told you? We'll start with those.'

'I don't know what you're talking about.'

Gardener bared his teeth in a grin.

'Boys,' he said, 'we're going to get sunlight in this boy's soul yet. Lace up his left arm again and unlace his right.'

Sunlight Gardener opened his lighter again and waited for them to do it, his thumb resting lightly on the striker wheel.

7

George Irwinson and Donny Keegan were still in the kitchen.

'Someone's out there,' George said nervously.

Donny said nothing. He had finished peeling the potatoes and now stood by the ovens for their warmth. He didn't know what to do next. Confession was being held just down the hall, he knew, and that's where he wanted to be – confession was safe, and here in the kitchen he felt very, very nervous – but Rudolph hadn't dismissed them. Best to stay right here.

'I heard someone,' George said.

Donny laughed: '*Hyuck! Hyuck! Hyuck!*'

'Jesus, that laugh of yours barfs me out,' George said. 'I got a new Captain America funnybook under my mattress. If you take a look out there, I'll let you read it.'

Donny shook his head and honked his donkey-laugh again.

George looked toward the door. Sounds. Scratching. That's what it sounded like. Scratching at the door. Like a dog that wanted to be let in. A lost, homeless pup. Except what sort of lost, homeless pup scratched near the top of a door that was nearly seven feet tall?

George went to the window and looked out. He could see almost nothing in the gloom. The Box was just a darker shadow amid shadows.

George moved toward the door.

8

Jack shrieked so loud and so hard he thought that surely his throat would rupture. Now Casey had also joined them,

Casey with his big swinging gut, and that was a good thing for them, because now it took three of them – Casey, Warwick, and Sonny Singer – to grapple with Jack's arm and keep his hand applied to the flame.

When Gardener drew it away this time, there was a black, bubbling, blistered patch the size of a quarter on the side of Jack's hand.

Gardener got up, took the envelope marked JACK PARKER from his desk, and brought it back. He brought out the guitar-pick.

'What's this?'

'A guitar-pick,' Jack managed. His hands were burning agony.

'What is it in the Territories?'

'I don't know what you mean.'

'What's this?'

'A marble. What are you, blind?'

'Is it a toy in the Territories?'

'I don't—'

'Is it a mirror?'

'—know—'

'Is it a top that disappears when you spin it fast?'

'—what you're—'

'*YOU DO! YOU DO TOO, YOU FAGGOT HELLBOUND WHELP!*'

'—talking about.'

Gardener drove a hand across Jack's face.

He brought out the silver dollar. His eyes gleamed.

'What's this?'

'It's a lucky piece from my Aunt Helen.'

'What is it in the Territories?'

'Box of Rice Krispies.'

Gardener held up the lighter. 'Your last chance, boy.'

'It turns into a vibraphone and plays "Crazy Rhythm".'

'Hold out his right hand again,' Gardener said.

Jack struggled, but at last they got his hand out.

9

In the oven, the turkey pies had begun to burn.

George Irwinson had been standing by the door for almost five minutes, trying to get up nerve enough to open it. That scratching noise had not been repeated.

'Well, I'll show you there's nothing to be afraid of, chicken-guts,' George said heartily. 'When you're strong in the Lord, there's never any need to be afraid!'

With this grand statement, he threw open the door. A huge, shaggy, shadowy thing stood on the threshold, its eyes blazing red from deep sockets. George's eyes tracked one paw as it rose in the windy autumn dark and whickered down. Six-inch claws gleamed in the kitchen's light. They tore George Irwinson's head from his neck and his head flew across the room, spraying blood, to strike the shoes of the laughing Donny Keegan, the madly laughing Donny Keegan.

Wolf leaped into the kitchen, dropping down to all fours. He passed Donny Keegan with hardly a look and ran into the hall.

10

Wolf! Wolf! Right here and now!

It was Wolf's voice in his mind, all right, but it was deeper, richer, more commanding than Jack had ever heard it. It cut through the haze of pain in his mind like a fine Swedish knife.

He thought, *Wolf is riding with the moon.* The thought brought a mixture of triumph and sorrow.

Sunlight Gardener was looking upward, his eyes narrowed. In that moment he looked very much like a beast himself – a beast who has scented danger downwind.

'Reverend?' Sonny asked. Sonny was panting slightly, and the pupils of his eyes were very large. *He's been enjoying himself,* Jack thought. *If I start to talk, Sonny's going to be disappointed.*

'I heard something,' Gardener said. 'Casey. Go and listen to the kitchen and the common room.'

'Right.' Casey took off.

Gardener looked back at Jack. 'I'm going to have to leave for Muncie soon,' he said, 'and when I meet Mr Morgan, I want to be able to give him some information immediately. So you had better talk to me, Jack. Spare yourself further pain.'

Jack looked at him, hoping the jackhammer beat of his heart didn't show either in his face or as a faster, more noticeable pulse in his neck. If Wolf was out of the Box –

Gardener held up the pick Speedy had given him in one hand, the coin Captain Farren had given him in the other. 'What are they?'

'When I flip, they turn into tortoise testicles,' Jack said, and laughed wildly, hysterically.

Gardener's face darkened with angry blood.

'Lace up his arms again,' he said to Sonny and Andy. 'Lace up his arms and then pull down this hellhound bastard's pants. Let's see what happens when we heat up *his* testicles.'

11

Heck Bast was deathly bored with confession. He had heard them all before, these paltry mail-order sins. *I hooked money from my mother's purse, I used to blow joints in the schoolyard, we usta put glue in a paper bag and sniff it, I did this, I did that.* Little kids' stuff. No excitement. Nothing to take his mind off the steady drone of pain in his hand. Heck wanted to be downstairs, working on that kid Sawyer. And then they could get started on the big retard who had somehow surprised him and destroyed his good right hand. Yes, getting to work on the big retard would be a real pleasure. Preferably with a set of bolt-cutters.

A boy named Vernon Skarda was currently droning away.

'. . . so me and him, we seen the keys was in her, know what I mean? So he goes, "Let's jump in the whore and drive her around the block," he goes. But I knew it was wrong, and I said it was, so he goes, "You ain't nothin but a chickenshit." So I go, "I ain't no chickenshit." Like that. So he goes, "Prove it, prove it." "I ain't doin no joy-ride," I go, so he goes . . .'

Oh dear Christ, Heck thought. His hand was really starting to yell at him, and his pain-pills were up in his room. On the far side of the room, he saw Peabody stretch his jaws in a bone-cracking yawn.

'So we went around the block, and then he goes to me, he goes—'

The door suddenly slammed inward so hard it tore off its hinges. It hit the wall, bounced, struck a boy named Tom Cassidy, drove him to the floor, and pinned him there. Something leaped into the common room – at first Heck

Bast thought it was the biggest motherfucking dog he had ever seen. Boys screamed and bolted up from their chairs . . . and then froze, eyes wide and unbelieving, as the gray-black beast that was Wolf stood upright, shreds of chinos and checked shirt still clinging to him.

Vernon Skarda stared, eyes bulging, jaw hanging.

Wolf bellowed, eyes glaring around as the boys fell back from him. Pedersen made for the door. Wolf, towering so high his head almost brushed the ceiling, moved with liquid speed. He swung an arm as thick as a barn-beam. Claws tore a channel through Pedersen's back. For a moment his spine was clearly visible – it looked like a bloody extension cord. Gore splashed the walls. Pedersen took one great, shambling step out into the hall and then collapsed.

Wolf turned back . . . and his blazing eyes fastened on Heck Bast. Heck got up suddenly on nerveless legs, staring at this shaggy, red-eyed horror. He knew who it was . . . or, at least, who it had been.

Heck would have given anything in the world just then to be bored again.

12

Jack was sitting in the chair again, his burned and throbbing hands once more pressed against the small of his back – Sonny had laced the straitjacket cruelly tight and then unbuttoned Jack's chinos and pushed them down.

'Now,' Gardener said, holding his Zippo up where Jack could see it. 'You listen to me, Jack, and listen well. I'm going to begin asking you questions again. And if you don't answer them well and truly, then buggery is one temptation you will never have to worry about being led into again.'

Sonny Singer giggled wildly at this. That muddy, half-dead look of lust was back in his eyes again. He stared at Jack's face with a kind of sickly greed.

'Reverend Gardener! Reverend Gardener!' It was Casey, and Casey sounded distressed. Jack opened his eyes again. 'Some kind of hooraw going on upstairs!'

'I don't want to be bothered now.'

'Donny Keegan's laughing like a loon in the kitchen! And—'

'He said he didn't want to be bothered now,' Sonny said. 'Didn't you hear him?'

But Casey was too dismayed to stop. '—and it sounds like there's a riot going on in the common room! Yelling! Screaming! And it sounds like—'

Suddenly, Jack's mind filled with a bellow of incredible force and vitality:

Jacky! Where are you? Wolf! Where are you right here and now?

'—there's a dog-pack or something loose up there!'

Gardener was looking at Casey now, eyes narrow, lips pressed tightly together.

Gardener's office! Downstairs! Where we were before!

DOWN-side, Jacky?

Stairs! Down-STAIRS, Wolf!

Right here and now!

That was it; Wolf was gone from his head. From upstairs, Jack heard a thump and a scream.

'Reverend Gardener?' Casey asked. His normally flushed face was deeply pale. 'Reverend Gardener, what is it? What—'

'Shut up!' Gardener said, and Casey recoiled as if slapped, eyes wide and hurt, considerable jowls trembling.

Gardener brushed past him and went to the safe. From it he took an outsized pistol which he stuck in his belt. For the first time, the Reverend Sunlight Gardener looked scared and baffled.

Upstairs, there was a dim shattering sound, followed by a screech. The eyes of Singer, Warwick, and Casey all turned nervously upward – they looked like nervous bomb-shelter occupants listening to a growing whistle above them.

Gardener looked at Jack. A grin surfaced on his face, the corners of his mouth twitching irregularly, as if strings were attached to them, strings that were being pulled by a puppeteer who wasn't particularly good at his job.

'He'll come here, won't he?' Sunlight Gardener said. He nodded as if Jack had answered. 'He'll come . . . but I don't think he'll leave.'

13

Wolf leaped. Heck Bast was able to get his right hand in its plaster cast up in front of his throat. There was a hot flash of pain, a brittle crunch, and a puff of plaster-dust as Wolf bit the cast – and what was left of the hand inside it – off. Heck looked stupidly down at where it had been. Blood jetted from his wrist. It soaked his white turtleneck with bright, hot warmth.

'Please,' Heck whined. 'Please, please, don't—'

Wolf spat out the hand. His head moved forward with the speed of a striking snake. Heck felt a dim pulling sensation as Wolf tore his throat open, and then he knew no more.

14

As he bolted out of the common room, Peabody skidded in Pedersen's blood, went down to one knee, got up, and then ran down the first-floor hall as fast as he could go, vomiting all over himself as he went. Kids were running everywhere, shrieking in panic. Peabody's own panic was not quite that complete. He remembered what he was supposed to do in extreme situations – although he didn't think anyone had ever envisioned a situation as extreme as *this*; he had an idea that Reverend Gardener had been thinking more in terms of a kid going bugfuck and cutting another kid up, something like that.

Beyond the parlor where new boys were brought when they first came to the Sunlight Home was a small upstairs office used only by the thugs Gardener referred to as his 'student aides'.

Peabody locked himself in this room, picked up the phone, and dialled an emergency number. A moment later he was talking to Franky Williams.

'Peabody, at the Sunlight Home,' he said. 'You ought to get up here with as many police as you can get, Officer Williams. All hell has—'

Outside he heard a wailing shriek followed by a crash of breaking wood. There was a snarling, barking roar, and the shriek was cut off.

'—has busted loose up here,' he finished.

'What kind of hell?' Williams asked impatiently. 'Lemme talk to Gardener.'

'I don't know where the Reverend is, but he'd want you up here. There's people dead. *Kids* dead.'

'What?'

'Just get up here with a lot of men,' Peabody said. 'And a lot of guns.'

Another scream. The crash-thud of something heavy – the old highboy in the front hall, probably – being overturned.

'Machine-guns, if you can find them.'

A crystalline jangle as the big chandelier in the hall came down. Peabody cringed. It sounded like that monster was tearing the whole place apart with its bare hands.

'Hell, bring a nuke if you can,' Peabody said, beginning to blubber.

'What—'

Peabody hung up before Williams could finish. He crawled into the kneehole under the desk. Wrapped his arms around his head. And began to pray assiduously that all of this should prove to be only a dream – the worst fucking nightmare he had ever had.

15

Wolf raged along the first-floor hall between the common room and the front door, pausing only to overturn the highboy, then to leap easily up and grab the chandelier. He swung on it like Tarzan until it tore out of the ceiling and spilled diamonds of crystal all over the hallway runner.

DOWN-side. Jacky was on the DOWN-side. Now . . . which side was that?

A boy who was no longer able to stand the agonizing tension of waiting for the thing to be gone jerked open the door of the closet where he had been hiding and bolted for the stairs. Wolf grabbed him and threw him the length of the hall. The boy struck the closed kitchen door with a bone-breaking thud and fell in a heap.

Wolf's head swam with the intoxicating odor of fresh-spilled blood. His hair hung in bloody dreadlocks around his jaw and muzzle. He tried to hold on to thought, but it was hard – hard. He had to find Jacky very quickly now, before he lost the ability to think completely.

He raced back toward the kitchen, where he had come in, dropping to all fours again because movement was faster and easier that way . . . and suddenly, passing a closed door, he remembered. The narrow place. It had been like going down into a grave. The smell, wet and heavy in his throat –

DOWN-side. Behind that door. Right here and now!

'*Wolf!*' he cried, although the boys cringing in their hiding places on the first and second floors heard only a rising, triumphant howl. He raised both of the heavily muscled battering rams that had been his arms and drove them into the door. It burst open in the middle, vomiting splinters down the stairwell. Wolf drove his way through, and yes, here was the narrow place, like a throat; here was the way to the place where the White Man had told his lies while Jack and the Weaker Wolf had to sit and listen.

Jack was down there now. Wolf could smell him.

But he also smelled the White Man . . . and gunpowder.

Careful . . .

Oh yes. Wolfs knew careful. Wolfs could run and tear and kill, but when they had to be . . . Wolfs knew careful.

He went down the stairs on all fours, silent as oiled smoke, eyes as red as brake lights.

16

Gardener was becoming steadily more nervous; to Jack he looked like a man who was entering the freakout zone. His eyes moved jerkily in a triple play, from the studio where Casey was frantically listening, to Jack, and then to the closed door which gave on the hall.

Most of the noises from upstairs had stopped some time ago.

Now Sonny Singer started for the door. 'I'll go up and see what's—'

'You're not going anywhere! Come back here!'

Sonny winced as if Gardener had struck him.

'What's the matter, Reverend Gardener?' Jack asked. 'You look a little nervous.'

Sonny rocked him with a slap. 'You want to watch the way you talk, snotface! You just want to watch it!'

'You look nervous, too, Sonny. And you, Warwick. And Casey in there—'

'*Shut him up!*' Gardener suddenly screamed. '*Can't you do anything? Do I have to do everything around here myself?*'

Sonny slapped Jack again, much harder. Jack's nose began to bleed, but he smiled. Wolf was very close now . . . and Wolf was being careful. Jack had begun to have a crazy hope that they might get out of this alive.

Casey suddenly straightened up and then tore the cans off his head and flicked the intercom switch.

'Reverend Gardener! I hear sirens on the outside mikes!'

Gardener's eyes, now too wide, skidded back to Casey.

'What? How many? How far away?'

'Sounds like a lot,' Casey said. 'Not close yet. But they're coming here. No doubt about that.'

Gardener's nerve broke then; Jack saw it happen. The man sat, indecisive, for a moment, and then he wiped his mouth delicately with the side of his hand.

It isn't whatever happened upstairs, not just the sirens, either. He knows that Wolf is close, too. In his own way he smells him . . . and he doesn't like it. Wolf, we might have a chance! We just might!

Gardener handed the pistol to Sonny Singer. 'I haven't time to deal with the police, or whatever mess there might be upstairs, right now,' he said. 'The important thing is Morgan Sloat. I'm going to Muncie. You and Andy are coming with me, Sonny. You keep this gun on our friend Jack here while I get the car out of the garage. When you hear the horn, come on out.'

'What about Casey?' Andy Warwick rumbled.

'Yes, yes, all right, Casey, too,' Gardener agreed at once, and Jack thought, *He's running out on you, you stupid assholes. He's running out on you, it's so obvious that he might as well take out a billboard on the Sunset Strip and advertise the fact, and your brains are too blown to even know it. You'd go on sitting down here for ten years waiting to hear that horn blow, if the food and toilet paper held out that long.*

Gardener got up. Sonny Singer, his face flushed with new importance, sat down behind his desk and pointed the gun at Jack. 'If his retarded friend shows up,' Gardener said, 'shoot him.'

'How could *he* show up?' Sonny asked. 'He's in the Box.'

'Never mind,' Gardener said. 'He's evil, they're both evil, it's indubitable, it's axiomatic, if the retard shows up, shoot him, shoot them both.'

He fumbled through the keys on his ring and selected one. 'When you hear the horn,' he said. He opened the door and went out. Jack strained his ears for the sound of sirens but heard nothing.

The door closed behind Sunlight Gardener.

17

Time, stretching out.

A minute that felt like two; two that felt like ten; four that felt like an hour. The three of Gardener's 'student aides' who had been left with Jack looked like boys who had been caught in a game of Statue Tag. Sonny sat bolt-upright behind Sunlight Gardener's desk – a place he both relished and coveted. The gun pointed steadily at Jack's face. Warwick stood by the door to the hall. Casey sat in the brightly lighted booth with the cans on his ears again, staring blankly out through the other glass square, into the darkness of the chapel, seeing nothing, only listening.

'He's not going to take you with him, you know,' Jack said suddenly. The sound of his voice surprised him a little. It was even and unafraid.

'Shut up, snotface,' Sonny snapped.

'Don't hold your breath until you hear him honk that horn,' Jack said. 'You'll turn pretty blue.'

'Next thing he says, Andy, break his nose,' Sonny said.

'That's right,' Jack said. 'Break my nose, Andy. Shoot me, Sonny. The cops are coming, Gardener's gone, and they're going to find the three of you standing over a corpse in a strait-jacket.' He paused, and amended: 'A corpse in a strait-jacket with a broken nose.'

'Hit him, Andy,' Sonny said.

Andy Warwick moved from the door to where Jack sat, strait-jacketed, his pants and underpants puddled around his ankles.

Jack turned his face openly up to Warwick's.

'That's right, Andy,' he said. 'Hit me. I'll hold still. Hell of a target.'

Andy Warwick balled up his fist, drew it back . . . and then hesitated. Uncertainty flickered in his eyes.

There was a digital clock on Gardener's desk. Jack's eyes shifted to it for a moment, and then back to Warwick's face. 'It's been four minutes, Andy. How long does it take a guy to back a car out of the garage? Especially when he's in a hurry?'

Sonny Singer bolted out of Sunlight Gardener's chair, came around the desk, and charged at Jack. His narrow, secretive face was furious. His fists were balled up. He made as if to hit Jack. Warwick, who was bigger, restrained him. There was trouble on Warwick's face now – deep trouble.

'Wait,' he said.

'I don't have to listen to this! I don't—'

'Why don't you ask Casey how close those sirens are getting?' Jack asked, and Warwick's frown deepened. 'You've been left in the lurch, don't you know that? Do I have to draw you a picture? It's going bad here. He knew it – he *smelled* it! He's leaving you with a bag. From the sounds upstairs—'

Singer broke free of Warwick's half-hearted hold and clouted Jack on the side of the face. His head rocked to one side, then came slowly back.

'—it's a big, messy bag,' Jack finished.

'You shut up or I'll kill you,' Sonny hissed.

The digits on the clock had changed.

'Five minutes now,' Jack said.

'Sonny,' Warwick said with a catch in his voice. 'Let's get him out of that thing.'

'No!' Sonny's cry was wounded, furious . . . ultimately, frightened.

'You know what the Rev'rend said,' Warwick said

rapidly. 'Before. When the TV people came. Nobody can see the straitjackets. They wouldn't understand. They—'

Click! The intercom.

'Sonny! Andy!' Casey sounded panicky. 'They're closer! The sirens! Christ! What are we supposed to do?'

'Let him out *now*!' Warwick's face was pallid, except for two red spots high on his cheekbones.

'Reverend Gardener *also* said—'

'I don't give a fuck *what* he also said!' Warwick's voice dropped, and now he voiced the child's deepest fear: 'We're gonna get *caught*, Sonny! We're gonna get *caught*!'

And Jack thought that now he could hear sirens, or perhaps it was only his imagination.

Sonny's eyes rolled toward Jack with horrible, trapped indecision. He half-raised the gun and for one moment Jack believed Sonny was really going to shoot him.

But it was six minutes now, and still no honk from the Godhead, announcing that the *deus ex machina* was now boarding for Muncie.

'*You* let him loose,' Sonny said sulkily to Andy Warwick. 'I don't even want to touch him. He's a sinner. And he's a queer.'

Sonny retreated to the desk as Andy Warwick's fingers fumbled with the strait-jacket's lacings.

'You better not say anything,' he panted. 'You better not say anything or I'll kill you myself.'

Right arm free.

Left arm free.

They collapsed bonelessly into his lap. Pins and needles coming back.

Warwick hauled the hateful restraint off him, a horror of dun-colored canvas and rawhide lacings. Warwick looked at it in his hands and grimaced. He darted across the room and began to stuff it into Sunlight Gardener's safe.

'Pull up your pants,' Sonny said. 'You think I want to look at your works?'

Jack fumbled up his shorts, got the waistband of his pants, dropped them, and managed to pull them up.

Click! The intercom.

'Sonny! Andy!' Casey's voice, panicked. 'I *hear* something!'

'Are they turning in?' Sonny almost screamed. Warwick redoubled his efforts to stuff the strait-jacket into the safe. 'Are they turning in the front—'

'No! In the chapel! I can't see nothing but I can hear something in the—'

There was an explosion of shattering glass as Wolf leaped from the darkness of the chapel and into the studio.

18

Casey's screams as he pushed back from the control board in his wheel-footed chair were hideously amplified.

Inside the studio there was a brief storm of glass. Wolf landed four-footed on the slanted control board and half-climbed, half-slid down it, his eyes throwing a red glare. His long claws turned dials and flicked switches at random. The big reel-to-reel Sony tape recorder started to turn.

'– *COMMUNISTS!*' the voice of Sunlight Gardener bellowed. He was cranked to maximum volume, drowning out Casey's shrieks and Warwick's screams to shoot it, Sonny, shoot it, *shoot* it! But the voice of Gardener was not alone. In the background, like music from hell, came the mingled warble of many sirens as Casey's mikes picked up a caravan of police cruisers turning into the Sunlight Home's drive.

'OH, THEY'RE GONNA TELL YOU IT'S ALL RIGHT TO LOOK AT THOSE DIRTY BOOKS! THEY'RE GONNA TELL YOU IT DON'T MATTER THAT IT'S AGAINST THE LAW TO PRAY IN THE PUBLIC SCHOOLS! THEY'RE GONNA TELL YOU IT DON'T EVEN MATTER THAT THERE ARE SIXTEEN U.S. REPRESENTATIVES AND TWO U.S. GOVERNORS WHO ARE AVOWED HOMOSEXUALS! THEY'RE GONNA TELL YOU –'

Casey's chair rolled back against the glass wall between the studio and Sunlight Gardener's office. His head turned, and for one moment they could all see his agonized, bulging eyes. Then Wolf leaped from the edge of the control panel. His head struck Casey's gut . . . and plowed into it. His jaws began to open and close with the speed of a cane-cutting machine. Blood flew up and splattered the window as Casey began to convulse.

'*Shoot it, Sonny, shoot the fucking thing!*' Warwick whooped.

'Think I'm gonna shoot him instead,' Sonny said, looking around at Jack. He spoke with the air of a man who has finally arrived at a great conclusion. He nodded, began to grin.

'– DAY IS COMING, BOYS! OH YES, A MIGHTY DAY, AND ON THAT DAY THOSE COMMUNIST HUMANIST HELLBOUND ATHEISTS ARE GONNA FIND OUT THAT THE ROCK WILL NOT SHIELD THEM, THE DEAD TREE WILL NOT GIVE THEM SHELTER! THEY'RE GONNA, OH SAY HALLELUJAH, THEY'RE GONNA –'

Wolf, snarling and ripping.

Sunlight Gardener, ranting about communism and humanism, the hellbound dope-pushers who wanted to see that prayer never made it back into the public schools.

Sirens from outside; slamming car doors; someone telling someone else to take it slow, the kid had sounded scared.

'Yes, you're the one, you made all this trouble.'

He raised the .45. The muzzle of the .45 looked as big as the mouth of the Oatley tunnel.

The glass wall between the studio and the office blew inward with a loud, coughing roar. A gray-black shaggy shape exploded into the room, its muzzle torn nearly in two by a jag of glass, its feet bleeding. It bellowed an almost human sound, and the thought came to Jack so powerfully that it sent him reeling backward:

YOU WILL NOT HARM THE HERD!

'*Wolf!*' he wailed. 'Look out! Look out, he's got a g—'

Sonny pulled the trigger of the .45 twice. The reports were deafening in the closed space. The bullets were not aimed at Wolf; they were aimed at Jack. But they tore into Wolf instead, because at that instant he was between the two boys, in mid-leap. Jack saw huge, ragged, bloody holes open in Wolf's side as the bullets exited. The paths of both slugs were deflected as they pulverized Wolf's ribs, and neither touched Jack, although he felt one whiff past his left cheek.

'Wolf!'

Wolf's dextrous, limber leap had turned awkward. His right shoulder rolled forward and he crashed into the wall, splattering blood and knocking down a framed photograph of Sunlight Gardener in a Shriner's fez.

Laughing, Sonny Singer turned toward Wolf, and shot

him again. He held the gun in both hands and his shoulders jerked with the recoil. Gunsmoke hung in a thick, noxious, unmoving rafter. Wolf struggled up on all fours and then rose somehow to his feet. A shattering, wounded bellow of pain and rage over-topped Sunlight Gardener's thundering recorded voice.

Sonny shot Wolf a fourth time. The slug tore a gaping hole in his left arm. Blood and gristle flew.

JACKY! JACKY OH JACKY, HURTS, THAT HURTS ME –

Jack shambled forward and grabbed Gardener's digital clock; it was simply the first thing that came to hand.

'*Sonny, look out!*' Warwick shouted. 'Look—' Then Wolf, his entire midsection now a gory tangle of blood-matted hair, pounced on him. Warwick grappled with Wolf and for a moment they appeared almost to be dancing.

'*– IN A LAKE OF FIRE FOREVER! FOR THE BIBLE SAYS –*'

Jack brought the digital radio down on Sonny's head with all the force he could muster as Sonny began to turn around. Plastic crunched. The numbers on the front of the clock began to blink randomly.

Sonny reeled around, trying to bring the gun up. Jack swung the radio in a flat, rising arc that ended at Sonny's mouth. Sonny's lips flew back in a great funhouse grin. There was a brittle crunch as his teeth broke. His finger jerked the trigger of the gun again. The bullet went between his feet.

He hit the wall, rebounded, and grinned at Jack from his bloody mouth. Swaying on his feet, he raised the gun.

'Hellbound—'

Wolf threw Warwick. Warwick flew through the air with the greatest of ease and struck Sonny in the back as

Sonny fired. The bullet went wild, hitting one of the turning tape-reels in the sound-studio and pulverizing it. The ranting, screaming voice of Sunlight Gardener ceased. A great bass hum of feedback began to rise from the speakers.

Roaring, staggering, Wolf advanced on Sonny Singer. Sonny pointed the .45 at him and pulled the trigger. There was a dry, impotent click. Sonny's wet grin faltered.

'No,' he said mildly, and pulled the trigger again . . . and again . . . and again. As Wolf reached for him, he threw the gun and tried to run around Gardener's big desk. The pistol bounced off Wolf's skull, and with a final, failing burst of strength, Wolf leaped across Sunlight Gardener's desk after Sonny, scattering everything that had been there. Sonny backed away, but Wolf was able to grab his arm.

'No!' Sonny screamed. *'No, you better not, you'll go back in the Box, I'm a big man around here, I . . . I . . . IYYYYYYYYYYYY—!'*

Wolf twisted Sonny's arm. There was a ripping sound, the sound of a turkey drumstick being torn from the cooked bird by an overenthusiastic child. Suddenly Sonny's arm was in Wolf's big front paw. Sonny staggered away, blood jetting from his shoulder. Jack saw a wet white knob of bone. He turned away and was violently sick.

For a moment the whole world swam into grayness.

19

When he looked around again, Wolf was swaying in the middle of the carnage that had been Gardener's office. His eyes guttered pale yellow, like dying candles. Something was happening to his face, to his arms and legs – he was becoming Wolf again, Jack saw . . . and then understood fully what that meant. The old legends had lied about how only silver bullets could destroy a werewolf, but apparently about some things they did not lie. Wolf was changing back because he was dying.

'Wolf, no!' he wailed, and managed to get to his feet. He got halfway to Wolf, slipped in a puddle of blood, went to one knee, got up again. *'No!'*

'Jacky—' The voice was low, guttural, little more than a growl . . . but understandable.

And, incredibly, Wolf was trying to smile.

Warwick had gotten Gardener's door open. He was backing slowly up the steps, his eyes wide and shocked.

'Go on!' Jack screamed. *'Go on, get outta here!'*

Andy Warwick fled like a scared rabbit.

A voice from the intercom – Franky Williams's voice – cut through the droning buzz of feedback. It was horrified, but filled with a terrible, sickly excitement. 'Christ, lookit this! Looks like somebody went bullshit with a meat-cleaver! Some of you guys check the kitchen!'

'Jacky—'

Wolf collapsed like a falling tree.

Jack knelt, turned him over. The hair was melting away from Wolf's cheeks with the eerie speed of time-lapse photography. His eyes had gone hazel again. And to Jack he looked horribly tired.

'Jacky—' Wolf raised a bloody hand and touched Jack's cheek. 'Shoot . . . you? Did he . . .'

'No,' Jack said, cradling his friend's head. 'No, Wolf, never got me. Never did.'

'I . . .' Wolf's eyes closed and then opened slowly again. He smiled with incredible sweetness and spoke carefully, enunciating each word, obviously needing to convey this if nothing else. 'I . . . kept . . . my herd . . . safe.'

'Yes, you did,' Jack said, and his tears began to flow. They hurt. He cradled Wolf's shaggy, tired head and wept. 'You sure did, good old Wolf—'

'Good . . . good old Jacky.'

'Wolf, I'm gonna go upstairs . . . there are cops . . . an ambulance . . .'

'No!' Wolf once again seemed to rouse himself to a great effort. 'Go on . . . you go on . . .'

'*Not without you, Wolf!*' All the lights had blurred double, treble. He held Wolf's head in his burned hands. 'Not without you, huh-uh, no way—'

'Wolf . . . doesn't want to live in this world.' He pulled a great, shuddering breath into his broad, shattered chest and tried another smile. 'Smells . . . smells too bad.'

'Wolf . . . listen, Wolf—'

Wolf took his hands gently; as he held them, Jack could feel the hair melting from Wolf's palms. It was a ghostly, terrible sensation.

'I love you, Jacky.'

'I love you, too, Wolf,' Jack said. 'Right here and now.'

Wolf smiled.

'Going back, Jacky . . . I can feel it. Going back . . .'

Suddenly Wolf's very hands felt insubstantial in Jack's grip.

'*Wolf!*' he screamed.

'Going back home . . .'

'*Wolf, no!*' He felt his heart stagger and wrench in his chest. It would break, oh yes, hearts could break, he felt that. '*Wolf, come back, I love you!*' There was a sensation of lightness in Wolf now, a feeling that he was turning into something like a milkweed pod . . . or a shimmer of illusion. A Daydream.

'. . . goodbye . . .'

Wolf was fading glass. Fading . . . fading . . .

'Wolf!'

'. . . love you J . . .'

Wolf was gone. There was only a bloody outline on the floor where he had been.

'Oh God,' Jack moaned. 'Oh God, oh God.'

He hugged himself and began to rock back and forth in the demolished office, moaning.

CHAPTER TWENTY-SEVEN
JACK LIGHTS OUT AGAIN

1

Time passed. Jack had no idea how much or how little. He sat with his arms wrapped around himself as if he were in the strait-jacket again, rocking back and forth, moaning, wondering if Wolf could really be gone.

He's gone. Oh yes, he's gone. And guess who killed him, Jack? Guess who?

At some point the feedback hum took on a rasping note. A moment later there was a high-gain crackle of static and everything shorted out – feedback hum, upstairs chatter, idling engines out front. Jack barely noticed.

Go on. Wolf said to go on.

I can't. I can't. I'm tired, and whatever I do is the wrong thing. People get killed –

Quit it, you self-pitying jerk! Think about your mother, Jack.

No! I'm tired. Let me be.

And the Queen.

Please, just leave me alone –

At last he heard the door at the top of the stairs open, and that roused him. He did not want to be found here. Let them take him outside, in the back yard, but not in this stinking, blood-spattered, smokey room where he had been tortured and his friend killed.

Barely thinking about what he was doing, Jack took up the envelope with JACK PARKER written across the front. He looked inside and saw the guitar-pick, the silver dollar, his beat-up wallet, the Rand McNally road atlas. He tilted the envelope and saw the marble. He stuck everything in the pack and slipped it on, feeling like a boy in a state of hypnosis.

Footfalls on the stairs, slow and cautious.

'– where's the damn lights –'

'– funny smell, like a zoo –'

'– watch it, boys –'

Jack's eye happened on the steel file-tray, neatly stacked with envelopes reading I'LL BE A SUNBEAM FOR JESUS. He helped himself to two of them.

Now when they grab you coming out, they can get you for robbery as well as murder.

Didn't matter. He was moving now for the simple sake of movement, no more than that.

The back yard appeared completely deserted. Jack stood at the top of the stairs that exited through a bulkhead and looked around, hardly able to believe it. There were voices from the front, and pulses of light, and occasional smears of static and dispatchers' voices from police radios that had been cranked up all the way to high gain, but the back yard was empty. It made no sense. But he supposed if they were confused enough, rattled enough by what they had found inside . . .

Then a voice, muffled, less than twenty feet away on Jack's left, said, 'Christ! Do you believe this?'

Jack's head snapped around. There, squatting on the

beaten dirt like a crude Iron Age coffin, was the Box. A flashlight was moving around inside. Jack could see shoe-soles sticking out. A dim figure was crouching by the mouth of the Box, examining the door.

'Looks like this thing was ripped right off'n its hinges,' the fellow looking at the door called into the Box. 'I don't know how anyone coulda done it, though. Hinges are steel. But they're just . . . *twisted*.'

'Never mind the damn hinges,' the muffled voice came back. 'This goddam thing . . . they kept *kids* in here, Paulie! I really think they did! *Kids!* There's initials on the walls . . .'

The light moved.

'. . . and Bible verses . . .'

The light moved again.

'. . . and pictures. Little pictures. Little stick-men and-women, like kids draw . . . Christ, do you think Williams knew about this?'

'Must have,' Paulie said, still examining the torn and twisted steel hinges on the Box's door.

Paulie was bending in; his colleague was backing out. Making no special attempt at concealment, Jack walked across the open dooryard behind them. He went along the side of the garage and came out on the shoulder of the road. From here he had an angle on the careless jam of police cars in the Sunlight Home's front yard. As Jack stood watching, an ambulance came tearing up the road, flashers whirling, siren warbling.

'Loved you, Wolf,' Jack muttered, and wiped an arm across his wet eyes. He set off down the road into darkness, thinking he would most likely be picked up before he got a mile west of the Sunlight Home. But three hours later he was still walking; apparently the cops had more than enough to occupy them back there.

2

There was a highway up ahead, over the next rise or the rise after that. Jack could see the orangey glow of high-intensity sodium arcs on the horizon, could hear the whine of the big rigs.

He stopped in a trash-littered ravine and washed his face and hands in the trickle of water coming out of a culvert. The water was almost paralyzingly cold, but at least it silenced the throbbing in his hands for a while. The old cautions were coming back almost unbidden.

Jack stood for a moment where he was, under the dark night sky of Indiana, listening to the whine of the big trucks.

The wind, murmuring in the trees, lifted his hair. His heart was heavy with the loss of Wolf, but even that could not change how good, how very good it was to be free.

An hour later a trucker slowed for the tired, pallid boy standing in the breakdown lane with his thumb cocked. Jack climbed in.

'Where you headed, kiddo?' the trucker asked.

Jack was too tired and too sick at heart to bother with the Story – he barely remembered it, anyway. He supposed it would come back to him.

'West,' he said. 'Far as you're going.'

'That'd be Midstate.'

'Fine,' Jack said, and fell asleep.

The big Diamond Reo rolled through the chilly Indiana night; Charlie Daniels on the tape-player, it rolled west, chasing its own headlights toward Illinois.

CHAPTER TWENTY-EIGHT
JACK'S DREAM

1

Of course he carried Wolf with him. Wolf had gone home, but a big loyal shadow rode beside Jack in all the trucks and Volkswagen vans and dusty cars pounding along the Illinois highways. This smiling ghost pierced Jack's heart. Sometimes he could see – could almost see – Wolf's huge hairy form bounding alongside, romping through the stripped fields. Free, Wolf beamed at him with pumpkin-colored eyes. When he jerked his eyes away, Jack felt the absence of a Wolf-hand folding itself around his. Now that he missed his friend so completely, the memory of his impatience with Wolf shamed him, brought the blood to his face. He had thought about abandoning Wolf more times than he could count. Shameful, shameful. Wolf had been . . . it took Jack a time to take it in, but the word was *noble.* And this noble being, so out of place in this world, had died for him.

I kept my herd safe. Jack Sawyer was the herd no longer. *I kept my herd safe.* There were times when the truckdrivers or insurance salesmen who had picked up this strange, compelling boy on the side of the road – picked him up even though the boy was road-dirty and shaggy, even though they might never have taken on a hitchhiker before in their lives – looked over and saw him blinking back tears.

Jack mourned Wolf as he sped across Illinois. He had somehow known that he would have no trouble getting rides once in that state, and it was true that often all he had to do was stick out his thumb and look an oncoming driver in the eye – instant ride. Most of the drivers did not even demand the Story. All he had to do was give some minimal explanation for travelling alone. 'I'm going to see a friend in Springfield.' 'I have to pick up a car and drive it back home.' 'Great, great,' the drivers said – had they even heard? Jack could not tell. His mind riffled through a mile-high stack of images of Wolf splashing into a stream to rescue his Territories creatures, Wolf nosing into a fragrant box that had held a hamburger, Wolf pushing food into his shed, bursting into the recording studio, taking the bullets, melting away . . . Jack did not want to see these things again and again, but he had to and they made his eyes burn with tears.

Not far out of Danville, a short, fiftyish man with iron-gray hair and the amused but stern expression of one who has taught fifth grade for two decades kept darting sly looks at him from behind the wheel, then finally said, 'Aren't you cold, buster? You ought to have more than that little jacket.'

'Maybe a little,' Jack said. Sunlight Gardener had thought the denim jackets warm enough for field-work right through the winter, but now the weather licked and stabbed right through its pores.

'I have a coat on the back seat,' the man said. 'Take it. No, don't even try to talk your way out of it. That coat's yours now. Believe me, I won't freeze.'

'But—'

'You have no choice at all in the matter. That is now your coat. Try it on.'

Jack reached over the back of the seat and dragged a heavy length of material onto his lap. At first it was shapeless, anonymous. A big patch pocket surfaced, then a toggle button. It was a loden coat, fragrant with pipe tobacco.

'My old one,' the man said. 'I just keep it in the car because I don't know what to do with it – last year, the kids gave me this goosedown thing. So you have it.'

Jack struggled into the big coat, putting it on right over the denim jacket. 'Oh, boy,' he said. It was like being embraced by a bear with a taste for Borkum Riff.

'Good,' the man said. 'Now if you ever find yourself standing out on a cold and windy road again, you can thank Myles P. Kiger of Ogden, Illinois, for saving your skin. Your —' Myles P. Kiger looked as though he were going to say more: the word hung in the air for a second, the man was still smiling; then the smile warped into goofy embarrassment and Kiger snapped his head forward. In the gray morning light, Jack saw a mottled red pattern spread out across the man's cheeks.

Your (something) skin?

Oh, no.

Your beautiful skin. Your touchable, kissable adorable . . . Jack pushed his hands deep into the loden coat's pockets and pulled the coat tightly around him. Myles P. Kiger of Ogden, Illinois, stared straight ahead.

'Ahem,' Kiger said, exactly like a man in a comic book.

'Thanks for the coat,' Jack said. 'Really. I'll be grateful to you whenever I wear it.'

'Sure, okay,' Kiger said, 'forget it.' But for a second his face was oddly like poor Donny Keegan's, back in the

Sunlight Home. 'There's a place up ahead,' Kiger said. His voice was choppy, abrupt, full of phony calm. 'We can get some lunch, if you like.'

'I don't have any money left,' Jack said, a statement exactly two dollars and thirty-eight cents shy of the truth.

'Don't worry about it.' Kiger had already snapped on his turn indicator.

They drove into a windswept, nearly empty parking lot before a low gray structure that looked like a railway car. A neon sign above the central door flashed EMPIRE DINER. Kiger pulled up before one of the diner's long windows and they left the car. This coat would keep him warm, Jack realized. His chest and arms seemed protected by woolen armor. Jack began to move toward the door under the flashing sign, but turned around when he realized that Kiger was still standing beside the car. The gray-haired man, only an inch or two taller than Jack, was looking at him over the car's top.

'Say,' Kiger said.

'Look, I'd be happy to give you your coat back,' Jack said.

'No, that's yours now. I was just thinking I'm not really hungry after all, and if I keep on going I can make pretty good time, get home a little earlier.'

'Sure,' Jack said.

'You'll get another ride here. Easy. I promise. I wouldn't drop you here if you were going to be stranded.'

'Fine.'

'Hold on. I said I'd get you lunch, and I will.' He put his hand in his trouser pocket, then held a bill out across the top of the car to Jack. The chill wind ruffled his hair and flattened it against his forehead. 'Take it.'

'No, honest,' Jack said. 'It's okay. I have a couple dollars.'

'Get yourself a good steak,' Kiger said, and was leaning across the top of the car, holding out the bill as if offering a life preserver, or reaching for one.

Jack reluctantly came forward and took the bill from Kiger's extended fingers. It was a ten. 'Thanks a lot. I mean it.'

'Here, why don't you take the paper, too, have something to read? You know, if you have to wait a little or something.' Kiger had already opened his door, and leaned inside to pluck a folded tabloid newspaper off the back seat. 'I've already read it.' He tossed it over to Jack.

The pockets of the loden coat were so roomy that Jack could slip the folded paper into one of them.

Myles P. Kiger stood for a moment beside his open car door, squinting at Jack. 'If you don't mind my saying so, you're going to have an interesting life,' he said.

'It's pretty interesting already,' Jack said truthfully.

Salisbury steak was five dollars and forty cents, and it came with french fries. Jack sat at the end of the counter and opened the newspaper. The story was on the second page – the day before, he had seen it on the first page of an Indiana newspaper. ARRESTS MADE, RELATED TO SHOCK HORROR DEATHS. Local Magistrate Ernest Fairchild and Police Officer Frank B. Williams of Cayuga, Indiana, had been charged with misuse of public monies and acceptance of bribes in the course of the investigation of the deaths of six boys at the Sunlight Gardener Scripture Home for Wayward Boys. The popular evangelist Robert 'Sunlight' Gardener had apparently escaped from the grounds of the Home shortly before the arrival of the police, and while no warrants had as yet been issued for his arrest he was urgently being sought for questioning. WAS HE ANOTHER JIM JONES? asked a caption beneath a picture of Gardener at his most gorgeous, arms outspread, hair falling in perfect waves. Dogs had led the State Police to an area near the electrified fences where boys' bodies had been buried without ceremony – five bodies, it appeared, most of them so decomposed that identification was not possible. They would probably be able to identify Ferd Janklow. His parents would be able to give him a real burial, all the while wondering what they had done wrong, exactly; all the while wondering just *how* their love for Jesus had condemned their brilliant, rebellious son.

When the Salisbury steak came, it tasted both salty and woolly, but Jack ate every scrap. And soaked up all the thick gravy with the Empire Diner's underdone fries. He had just about finished his meal when a bearded trucker with a Detroit Tigers cap shoved down over long black hair, a parka that seemed to be made from wolfskins, and a thick cigar in his mouth paused beside him and asked, 'You need a ride west, kid? I'm going to Decatur.' Halfway to Springfield, just like that.

2

That night, in a three-dollar-a-night hotel the trucker had told him about, Jack had two distinct dreams: or he later remembered these two out of many that deluged his bed, or the two were actually one long joined dream. He had locked his door, peed into the stained and cracked sink in the corner, put his knapsack under his pillow, and fallen asleep holding the big marble that in the other world was a Territories mirror. There had been a suggestion of music, an almost cinematic touch – fiery alert bebop, at a volume so low Jack could just pick out that the lead instruments were a trumpet and an alto saxophone. *Richard*, Jack drowsily thought, *tomorrow I should be seeing Richard Sloat*, and fell down the slope of the rhythm into brimming unconsciousness.

Wolf was trotting toward him across a blasted, smoking landscape. Strings of barbed wire, now and then coiling up into fantastic and careless barbed-wire intricacies, separated them. Deep trenches too divided the spoiled land, one of which Wolf vaulted easily before nearly tumbling into one of the ranks of wire.

– Watch out, Jack called.

Wolf caught himself before falling into the triple strands of wire. He waved one big paw to show Jack that he was unhurt, and then cautiously stepped over the wires.

Jack felt an amazing surge of happiness and relief pass through him. Wolf had not died; Wolf would join him again.

Wolf made it over the barbed wire and began trotting forward again. The land between Jack and Wolf seemed mysteriously to double in length – gray smoke hanging over the many trenches almost obscured the big shaggy figure coming forward.

– Jason! Wolf shouted. Jason! Jason!

– I'm still here, Jack shouted back.

– Can't make it, Jason! Wolf can't make it!

– Keep trying, Jack bawled. Damn it, don't give up!

Wolf paused before an impenetrable tangle of wire, and through the smoke Jack saw him slip down to all fours and trot back and forth, nosing for an open place. From side to side Wolf trotted, each time going out a greater distance, with every second becoming more evidently disturbed.

Finally Wolf stood up again and placed his hands on the thick tangle of wire and forced a space he could shout through. – Wolf can't! Jason, Wolf can't!

– I love you, Wolf, Jack shouted across the smouldering plain.

– JASON! Wolf bawled back. BE CAREFUL! They are COMING for you! There are MORE of them!

– More what, Jack wanted to shout, but could not. He knew.

Then either the whole character of the dream changed or another dream began. He was back in the ruined recording studio and office at the Sunlight Home, and the smells of gunpowder and burned flesh crowded the air. Singer's mutilated body lay slumped on the floor, and Casey's dead form drooped through the shattered glass panel. Jack sat on the floor cradling Wolf in his arms, and knew again that Wolf was dying. Only Wolf was not Wolf.

Jack was holding Richard Sloat's trembling body, and it was Richard who was dying. Behind the lenses of his sensible black plastic eyeglasses, Richard's eyes skittered aimlessly, painfully. – Oh no, oh no, Jack breathed out in horror. Richard's arm had been shattered, and his chest was a pulp of ruined flesh and blood-stained white shirt. Fractured bones glinted whitely here and there like teeth.

– I don't want to die, Richard said, every word a superhuman effort. Jason, you should not . . . you should not have . . .

– You can't die, too, Jack pleaded, not you, too.

Richard's upper body lurched against Jack's arms, and a long, liquid sound escaped Richard's throat, and then Richard found Jack's eyes with his own suddenly clear and quiet eyes. – Jason. The sound of the name, which was almost appropriate, hung softly in the stinking air. – You killed me, Richard breathed out, or *you killed 'e*, since his lips could not meet to form one of the letters. Richard's eyes swam out of focus again, and his body seemed to grow instantly heavier in Jack's arms. There was no longer life in that body. Jason DeLoessian stared up in shock –

3

– and Jack Sawyer snapped upright in the cold, unfamiliar bed of a flophouse in Decatur, Illinois, and in the yellowish murk shed by a streetlamp outside saw his breath plume out as luxuriantly as if exhaled from two mouths at once. He kept himself from screaming only by clasping his hands, his own two hands, and squeezing them together hard enough to crack a walnut. Another enormous white feather of air steamed out of his lungs.

Richard.

Wolf running across that dead world, calling out . . . what? *Jason.*

The boy's heart executed a quick, decided leap, with the kick of a horse clearing a fence.

CHAPTER TWENTY-NINE
RICHARD AT THAYER

1

At eleven o'clock the next morning an exhausted Jack Sawyer unshouldered his pack at the end of a long playing field covered with crisp brown dead grass. Far away, two men in plaid jackets and baseball caps labored with leaf-blower and rake down on the stretch of lawn surrounding the most distant group of buildings. To Jack's left, directly behind the red-brick backside of the Thayer library, was the faculty parking lot. In the front of Thayer School a great gate opened onto a tree-lined drive which circled around a large quad crisscrossed with narrow paths. If anything stood out on the campus, it was the library – a Bauhaus steamship of glass and steel and brick.

Jack had already seen that a secondary gate opened onto another access road before the library. This ran two-thirds the length of the school and ended at the garbage dumpsters nested in the round cul-de-sac just before the land climbed up to form the plateau of the football field.

Jack began to move across the top of the field toward the rear of the classroom buildings. When the Thayerites began to go to dining hall, he could find Richard's room – Entry 5, Nelson House.

The dry winter grass crunched beneath his feet. Jack pulled Myles P. Kiger's excellent coat tightly about him – the coat at least looked preppy, if Jack did not. He walked between Thayer Hall and an Upper School dormitory named Spence House, in the direction of the quad. Lazy pre-luncheon voices came through the Spence House windows.

2

Jack glanced toward the quad and saw an elderly man, slightly stooped and of a greenish-bronze, standing on a plinth the height of a carpenter's bench and examining the cover of a heavy book. Elder Thayer, Jack surmised. He was dressed in the stiff collar, flowing tie, and frock coat of a New England Transcendentalist. Elder Thayer's brass head inclined over the volume, pointed generally in the direction of the classroom buildings.

Jack took the right-angle at the end of the path. Sudden noise erupted from an upstairs window ahead – boys shouting out the syllables of a name that sounded like 'Etheridge! Etheridge!' Then an irruption of wordless screams and shouts, accompanied by the sounds of heavy furniture moving across a wooden floor. '*Etheridge!*'

Jack heard a door closing behind his back, and looked over his shoulder to see a tall boy with dirty-blond hair rushing down the steps of Spence House. He wore a tweed sport jacket and a tie and a pair of L. L. Bean Maine hunting shoes. Only a long yellow-and-blue scarf wound several times around his neck protected him from the cold. His long face looked both haggard and arrogant, and just now was the face of a senior in a self-righteous rage. Jack pushed the hood of the loden coat over his head and moved down the path.

'I don't want anybody to move!' the tall boy shouted up at the closed window. 'You freshmen just stay put!'

Jack drifted on toward the next building.

'You're moving the chairs!' the tall boy screamed behind him. 'I can hear you doing it! STOP!' Then Jack heard the furious senior call out to him.

Jack turned around, his heart beating loudly.

'Get over to Nelson House right now, whoever you are, on the double, post-haste, immediately. Or I'll go to your house master.'

'Yes sir,' Jack said, and quickly turned away to move in the direction the prefect had pointed.

'*You're at least seven minutes late!*' Etheridge screeched at him, and Jack was startled into jogging. '*On the double, I said!*' Jack turned the jog into a run.

When he started downhill (he hoped it was the right way; it was, anyway, the direction in which Etheridge had seemed to be looking), he saw a long black car – a limousine – just beginning to swing through the main front gates and whisper up the long drive to the quad. He thought that maybe whatever sat behind the tinted windows of the limousine was nothing so ordinary as the parent of a Thayer School sophomore.

The long black car eased forward, insolently slow.

No, Jack thought. I'm spooking myself.

Still he could not move. Jack watched the limousine pull up to the bottom of the quad and stop, its motor running. A black chauffeur with the shoulders of a running back got out of the front seat and opened the rear passenger door. An old white-haired man, a stranger, effortfully got out of the limousine's back seat. He wore a black topcoat which revealed an immaculate white shirtfront and a solid dark tie. The man nodded to his chauffeur and began to toil across the quad in the direction of the main building. He never even looked in Jack's direction. The chauffeur elaborately craned his neck and looked upward, as if speculating about the possibility of snow. Jack stepped backward and watched while the old man made it to the steps of Thayer Hall. The chauffeur continued his specious examination of the sky. Jack melted backward down the path until the side of the building shielded him, and then he turned around and began to trot.

Nelson House was a three-story brick building on the other side of the quadrangle. Two windows on the ground floor showed him a dozen seniors exercising their privileges: reading while sprawled on couches, playing a desultory game of cards on a coffee table; others stared lazily at what must have been a television set parked beneath the windows.

An unseen door slammed shut a little farther up the hill, and Jack caught a glimpse of the tall blond senior, Etheridge, stalking back to his own building after dealing with the freshmen's crimes.

Jack cut across the front of the building and a gust of cold wind smacked up against him as soon as he reached its side. And around the corner was a narrow door and a plaque (wooden this time, white with Gothic black lettering) saying ENTRY 5. A series of windows stretched down to the next corner.

And here, at the third window – relief. For here was Richard Sloat, his eyeglasses firmly hooked around his ears, his necktie knotted, his hands only slightly stained with ink, sitting erect at his desk and reading some fat book as if for dear life. He was positioned sideways to Jack, who had time to take in Richard's dear, well-known profile before he rapped on the glass.

Richard's head jerked up from the book. He stared wildly about him, frightened and surprised by the sudden noise.

'Richard,' Jack said softly, and was rewarded by the sight of his friend's astonished face turning toward him. Richard looked almost moronic with surprise.

'Open the window,' Jack said, mouthing the words with exaggerated care so that his friend could read his lips.

Richard stood up from his desk, still moving with the slowness of shock. Jack mimed pushing the window up. When Richard reached the window he put his hands on the frame and looked down severely at Jack for a moment – in that short and critical glance was a judgement about Jack's dirty face and unwashed, lank hair, his unorthodox arrival, much else. *What on earth are you up to now?* Finally he pushed up the window.

'Well,' Richard said. 'Most people use the door.'

'Great,' Jack said, almost laughing. 'When I'm like most people, I probably will too. Stand back, okay?'

Looking very much as though he had been caught off-guard, Richard stepped a few paces back.

Jack hoisted himself up onto the sill and slid through the window head-first. 'Oof.'

'Okay, hi,' Richard said. 'I suppose it's even sort of nice to see you. But I have to go to lunch pretty soon. You could take a shower, I guess. Everybody else'll be down in the dining room.' He stopped talking, as if startled that he had said so much.

Richard, Jack saw, would require delicate handling. 'Could you bring some food back for me? I'm really starving.'

'Great,' Richard said. 'First you get everybody crazy, including my dad, by running away, then you break in here like a burglar, and now you want me to steal food for you. Fine, sure. Okay. Great.'

'We have a lot to talk about,' Jack said.

'*If*,' Richard said, leaning slightly forward with his hands in his pockets, '*if* you'll start going back to New Hampshire today, or *if* you'll let me call my dad and get him here to take you back, I'll try to grab some extra food for you.'

'I'm willing to talk about anything with you, Richie-boy. Anything. I'll talk about going back, sure.'

Richard nodded. 'Where in the world have you been, anyhow?' His eyes burned beneath their thick lenses. Then a big, surprising blink. 'And *how* in the world can you justify the way you and your mother are treating my father? Shit, Jack. I really think you ought to go back to that place in New Hampshire.'

'I will go back,' Jack said. 'That's a promise. But I have to get something first. Is there anyplace I can sit down? I'm sort of dead tired.'

Richard nodded at his bed, then – typically – flapped one hand at his desk chair, which was nearer Jack.

Doors slammed in the hallway. Loud voices passed by Richard's door, a crowd's shuffling feet.

'You ever read about the Sunlight Home?' Jack asked. 'I was there. Two of my friends died at the Sunlight Home, and get this, Richard, the second one was a werewolf.'

Richard's face tightened. 'Well, that's an amazing coincidence, because—'

'I really was at the Sunlight Home, Richard.'

'So I gather,' said Richard. 'Okay. I'll be back with some food in about half an hour. Then I'll have to tell you who lives next door. But this is Seabrook Island stuff, isn't it? Tell me the truth.'

'Yeah, I guess it is.' Jack let Myles P. Kiger's coat slip off his shoulders and fold itself over the back of the chair.

'I'll be back,' Richard said. He waved uncertainly to Jack on his way out the door.

Jack kicked off his shoes and closed his eyes.

3

The conversation to which Richard had alluded as 'Seabrook Island stuff,' and which Jack remembered as well as his friend, took place in the last week of their final visit to the resort of that name.

The two families had taken joint vacations nearly every year while Phil Sawyer was alive. The summer after his death, Morgan Sloat and Lily Sawyer had tried to keep the tradition going, and booked the four of them into the vast old hotel on Seabrook Island, South Carolina, which had been the site of some of their happiest summers. The experiment had not worked.

The boys were accustomed to being in each other's company. They were also accustomed to places like Seabrook Island. Richard Sloat and Jack Sawyer had scampered through resort hotels and down vast tanned beaches all through their childhood – but now the climate had mysteriously altered. An unexpected seriousness had entered their lives, an awkwardness.

The death of Phil Sawyer had changed the very color of the future. Jack began to feel that final summer at Seabrook that he might not want to sit in the chair behind his father's desk – that he wanted more in his life. More what? He knew – this was one of the few things he did truly know – that this powerful 'moreness' was connected to the Daydreams. When he had begun to see this in himself, he became aware of something else: that his friend Richard was not only incapable of sensing this quality of 'moreness', but that in fact he quite clearly wanted its opposite. Richard wanted less. Richard did not want anything he could not respect.

Jack and Richard had sloped off by themselves in that slow-breathing time composed at good resorts by the hours between lunch and cocktails. In fact they had not gone far – only up to the side of a pine-tree-covered hill overlooking the rear of the inn. Beneath them sparkled the water of the inn's huge rectangular pool, through which Lily Cavanaugh Sawyer smoothly and efficiently swam length after length. At one of the tables set back from the pool sat Richard's father, wrapped in a bulging, fuzzy terry-cloth robe, flip-flops on his white feet, simultaneously eating a club sandwich and wheeling and dealing on the plug-in telephone in his other hand.

'Is this sort of stuff what you want?' he asked Richard, who was seated neatly beside his own sprawl and held – no surprise – a book. *The Life of Thomas Edison.*

'What I want? When I grow up, you mean?' Richard seemed a little nonplussed by the question. 'It's pretty nice, I guess. I don't know if I want it or not.'

'Do you know what you want, Richard? You always say you want to be a research chemist,' Jack said. 'Why do you say that? What does it mean?'

'It means that I want to be a research chemist.' Richard smiled.

'You know what I mean, don't you? What's the *point*

of being a research chemist? Do you think that would be fun? Do you think you'll cure cancer and save millions of people's lives?'

Richard looked at him very openly, his eyes slightly magnified by the glasses he had begun to wear four months earlier. 'I don't think I'll ever cure cancer, no. But that's not even the point. The point is finding out how things work. The point is that things actually really do work in an orderly way, in spite of how it looks, and you can find out about it.'

'Order.'

'Yeah, so why are you smiling?'

Jack grinned. 'You're going to think I'm crazy. I'd like to find something that makes all this – all these rich guys chasing golfballs and yelling into telephones – that makes all this look sick.'

'It already looks sick,' Richard said, with no intention of being funny.

'Don't you sometimes think there's more to life than order?' He looked over at Richard's innocent, skeptical face. 'Don't you want just a little magic, Richard?'

'You know, sometimes I think you just want chaos,' Richard said, flushing a bit. 'I think you're making fun of me. If you want magic, you completely wreck everything I believe in. In fact you wreck reality.'

'Maybe there isn't just one reality.'

'In *Alice in Wonderland*, sure!' Richard was losing his temper.

He stomped off through the pines, and Jack realized for the first time that the talk released by his feelings about the Daydreams had infuriated his friend. Jack's longer legs brought him alongside Richard in seconds. 'I wasn't making fun of you,' he said. 'It's just, I was sort of curious about why you always say you want to be a chemist.'

Richard stopped short and looked soberly up at Jack. 'Just stop driving me crazy with that kind of stuff,' Richard said. 'That's just Seabrook Island talk. It's hard enough being one of the six or seven sane people in America without having my best friend flip out totally.'

From then on, Richard Sloat bristled at any signs of fancifulness in Jack, and immediately dismissed it as 'Seabrook Island stuff'.

4

By the time Richard returned from the dining room, Jack, freshly showered and with his wet hair adhering to his scalp, was idly turning over books at Richard's desk. Jack was wondering, as Richard swung through the door carrying a grease-stained paper napkin clearly wrapped around a substantial quantity of food, whether the conversation to come might be easier if the books on the desk were *The Lord of the Rings* and *Watership Down* instead of *Organic Chemistry* and *Mathematical Puzzles*.

'What was lunch?' Jack asked.

'You got lucky. Southern fried chicken – one of the few things they serve here that don't make you sorry for the animal who died to become part of the food chain.' He handed the greasy napkin over to Jack. Four thick, richly battered sections of chicken sent up an aroma of almost unbelievable goodness and density. Jack waded in.

'How long have you been eating as though you oinked?' Richard pushed his glasses up on his nose and sat down on his narrow bed. Beneath his tweed jacket he wore a patterned brown V-neck sweater, the bottom of which had been tucked into the waistband of his trousers.

Jack had an uneasy moment, wondering if it were really possible to talk about the Territories with someone so tightly buttoned that he tucked his sweaters beneath his belts.

'The last time I ate,' he said mildly, 'was yesterday, around noon. I'm a little hungry, Richard. Thanks for bringing me the chicken. It's great. It's the best chicken I ever ate. You're a great guy, risking expulsion like this.'

'You think that's a joke, do you?' Richard yanked at the sweater, frowning. 'If anybody finds you in here, I probably *will* get expelled. So don't get too funny. We have to figure out how we're going to get you back to New Hampshire.'

Silence then, for a moment: an appraising look from Jack, a stern look from Richard.

'I know you want me to explain what I'm doing, Richard,' Jack said around a mouthful of chicken, 'and believe me, it's not going to be easy.'

'You don't look the same, you know,' Richard said. 'You look . . . older. But that's not all. You're changed.'

'I know I've changed. You'd be a little different too, if you'd been with me since September.' Jack smiled, looked at scowling Richard in his good-boy clothes, and knew that he would never be able to tell Richard about his father. He simply was not capable of that. If events did it for him, so be it; but he himself did not possess the assassin's heart required for that particular disclosure.

His friend continued to frown at Jack, clearly waiting for the story to begin.

Perhaps to stall the moment when he would have to try to convince Rational Richard of the unbelievable, Jack asked, 'Is the kid in the next room quitting school? I saw his suitcases on his bed from outside.'

'Well, yes, that's interesting,' Richard said. 'I mean, interesting in the light of what you said. He *is* leaving – in fact, he's already gone. Someone is supposed to come for his things, I guess. God knows what kind of a fairy tale you'll make of this, but the kid next door was Reuel Gardener. The son of that preacher who ran that home you claim you escaped from.' Richard ignored Jack's sudden fit of coughing. 'In most senses, I should say, Reuel was anything but the normal kid next door, and probably nobody here was too sorry to see him go. Just when the story came out about kids dying at that place his father ran, he got a telegram ordering him to leave Thayer.'

Jack had gotten down the wad of chicken that had tried to choke him. 'Sunlight Gardener's son? That guy had a son? And he was *here?*'

'He came at the start of the term,' Richard said simply. 'That's what I was trying to tell you before.'

Suddenly Thayer School was menacing to Jack in a way that Richard could not begin to comprehend. 'What was he *like?*'

'A sadist,' Richard said. 'Sometimes I heard really peculiar noises coming out of Reuel's room. And once I saw a dead cat on the garbage thing out in back that didn't have any eyes or ears. When you saw him, you'd think he was the kind of person who might torture a cat. And he sort of smelled like rancid English Leather, I thought.' Richard was silent for a carefully timed moment, and then asked, 'Were you really in the Sunlight Home?'

'For thirty days. It was hell, or hell's next-door neighbor.' He inhaled, looking at Richard's scowling but now at least half-convinced face. 'This is hard for you to swallow, Richard, and I know that, but the guy with me was a werewolf. And if he hadn't been killed while he was saving my life he'd be here right now.'

'A werewolf. Hair on the palms of his hands. Changes into a blood-thirsty monster every full moon.' Richard looked musingly around the little room.

Jack waited until Richard's gaze returned to him. 'Do you want to know what I'm doing? Do you want me to tell you why I'm hitchhiking all the way across the country?'

'I'm going to start screaming if you don't,' Richard said.

'Well,' Jack said, 'I'm trying to save my mother's life.' As he uttered it, this sentence seemed to him filled with a wondrous clarity.

'How the hell are you going to do that?' Richard exploded. 'Your mother probably has cancer. As my father has been pointing out to you, she needs doctors and science . . . and you hit the road? What are you going to use to save your mother, Jack? Magic?'

Jack's eyes began to burn. 'You got it, Richard old chum.' He raised his arm and pressed his already damp eyes into the fabric at the crook of his elbow.

'Oh hey, calm down, hey really . . .' Richard said, tugging frantically at his sweater. 'Don't cry, Jack, come on, please, I know it's a terrible thing, I didn't mean to . . . it was just that—' Richard had crossed the room instantly and without noise, and was now awkwardly patting Jack's arm and shoulder.

'I'm okay,' Jack said. He lowered his arm. 'It's not some crazy fantasy, Richard, no matter how it looks to you.' He sat up straight. 'My father called me Travelling Jack, and so did an old man in Arcadia Beach.' Jack hoped he was right about Richard's sympathy opening internal doors; when he looked at Richard's face, he saw that it was true. His friend looked worried, tender, four-square.

Jack began his story.

5

Around the two boys the life of Nelson House went on, both calm and boisterous in the manner of boarding schools, punctuated with shouts and roars and laughter. Footsteps padded past the door but did not stop. From the room above came regular thumps and an occasional drift of music Jack finally recognized as a record by Blue Oyster Cult. He began by telling Richard about the Daydreams. From the Daydreams he went to Speedy Parker. He described the voice speaking to him from the whirling funnel in the sand. And then he told Richard of how he had taken Speedy's 'magic juice' and first flipped into the Territories.

'But I think it was just cheap wine, wino wine,' Jack said. 'Later, after it was all gone, I found out that I didn't need it to flip. I could just do it by myself.'

'Okay,' Richard said noncommittally.

He tried to truly represent the Territories to Richard: the cart-track, the sight of the summer palace, the timelessness and specificity of it. Captain Farren; the dying Queen, which brought him to Twinners; Osmond. The scene at All-Hands' Village; the Outpost Road which was the Western Road. He showed Richard his little collection of sacred objects, the guitar-pick and marble and coin. Richard merely turned these over in his fingers and gave them back without comment. Then Jack relived his wretched time in Oatley.

Richard listened to Jack's tales of Oatley silent but wide-eyed.

Jack carefully omitted Morgan Sloat and Morgan of Orris from his account of the scene at the Lewisburg rest area on I-70 in western Ohio.

Then Jack had to describe Wolf as he had first seen him, that beaming giant in Oshkosh B'Gosh bib overalls, and he felt his tears building again behind his eyes. He did actually startle Richard by weeping while he told about trying to get Wolf into cars, and confessed his impatience with his companion, fighting not to weep again, and was fine for a long time – he managed to get through the story of Wolf's first Change without tears or a constricted throat. Then he struck trouble again. His rage kept him talking freely until he got to Ferd Janklow, and then his eyes grew hot again.

Richard said nothing for a long time. Then he stood up and fetched a clean handkerchief from a bureau drawer. Jack noisily, wetly blew his nose.

'That's what happened,' Jack said. 'Most of it, anyhow.'

'What have you been reading? What movies have you been seeing?'

'Fuck you,' Jack said. He stood up and walked across the room to get his pack, but Richard reached out and put his hand around Jack's wrist. 'I don't think you made it all up. I don't think you made any of it up.'

'Don't you?'

'No. I don't know what I do think, actually, but I'm sure you're not telling me deliberate lies.' He dropped his hand. 'I believe you were in the Sunlight Home, I believe that, all right. And I believe that you had a friend named Wolf, who died there. I'm sorry, but I cannot take the

Territories seriously, and I cannot accept that your friend was a werewolf.'

'So you think I'm nuts,' Jack said.

'I think you're in trouble. But I'm not going to call my father, and I'm not going to make you leave now. You'll have to sleep in the bed here tonight. If we hear Mr Haywood coming around to do bed checks, you'll be able to hide under the bed.'

Richard had taken on a faintly executive air, and he put his hands on his hips and glanced critically around his room. 'You have to get some rest. I'm sure that's part of the problem. They worked you half to death in that horrible place, and your mind got twisted, and now you need to rest.'

'I do,' Jack admitted.

Richard rolled his eyes upward. 'I have to go to intramural basketball pretty soon, but you can hide in here, and I'll bring some more food back from the dining room later on. The important thing is, you need rest and you need to get back home.'

Jack said, 'New Hampshire isn't home.'

CHAPTER THIRTY

THAYER GETS WEIRD

1

Through the window Jack could see boys in coats, hunched against the cold, crossing to and fro between the library and the rest of the school. Etheridge, the senior who had spoken to Jack that morning, bustled by, his scarf flying out behind him.

Richard took a tweed sport jacket from the narrow closet beside the bed. 'Nothing is going to make me think that you should do anything but go back to New Hampshire. I have to go to basketball now, because if I don't Coach Frazer'll make me do ten punishment laps as soon as he comes back. Some other coach is taking our practice today, and Frazer said he'd run us into the ground if we cut out. Do you want to borrow some clean clothes? I at least have a shirt that'll fit you – my father sent it to me from New York, and Brooks Brothers got the size wrong.'

'Let's see it,' Jack said. His clothes had become definitely disreputable, so stiff with filth that whenever he noticed it Jack felt like Pigpen, the 'Peanuts' character who lived in a mist of dirt and disapproval. Richard gave him a white button-down still in its plastic bag. 'Great, thanks,' Jack said. He took it out of the bag and began removing the pins. It would almost fit.

'There's a jacket you might try on, too,' Richard said. 'The blazer hanging at the end of the closet. Try it on, okay? And you might as well use one of my ties, too. Just in case anyone comes in. Say you're from Saint Louis Country Day, and you're on a Newspaper Exchange. We do two or three of those a year – kids from here go there, kids from there come here, to work on the other school's paper.' He went toward the door. 'I'll come back before dinner and see how you are.'

Two ballpoints were clipped to a plastic insert in his jacket pocket, Jack noticed, and all the buttons of the jacket were buttoned.

Nelson House grew perfectly quiet within minutes. From Richard's window Jack saw boys seated at desks in the big library windows. Nobody moved on the paths or over the crisp brown grass. An insistent bell rang, marking the beginning of fourth period. Jack stretched his arms out and yawned. A feeling of security returned to him – a school around him, with all those familiar rituals of bells and classes and basketball practices. Maybe he would be able to stay another day; maybe he would even be able to call his mother from one of the Nelson House phones. He would certainly be able to catch up on his sleep.

Jack went to the closet and found the blazer hanging where Richard had said it would be. A tag still hung from one of the sleeves: Sloat had sent it from New York, but Richard had never worn it. Like the shirt, the blazer was one size too small for Jack and clung too tightly to his shoulders, but the cut was roomy and the sleeves allowed the white shirt cuffs to peek out half an inch.

Jack lifted a necktie from the hook just inside the closet – red, with a pattern of blue anchors. Jack slipped the tie around his neck and laboriously knotted it. Then he examined himself in the mirror and laughed out loud. Jack saw that he had made it at last. He looked at the beautiful new blazer, the club tie, his snowy shirt, his rumpled jeans. He was there. He was a preppy.

2

Richard had become, Jack saw, an admirer of John McPhee and Lewis Thomas and Stephen Jay Gould. He picked *The Panda's Thumb* from the row of books on Richard's shelves because he liked the title and returned to the bed.

Richard did not return from his basketball practice for what seemed an impossibly long time. Jack paced back and forth in the little room. He could not imagine what would keep Richard from returning to his room, but his imagination gave him one calamity after another.

After the fifth or sixth time Jack checked his watch, he noticed that he could see no students on the grounds.

Whatever had happened to Richard had happened to the entire school.

The afternoon died. Richard too, he thought, was dead. Perhaps all Thayer School was dead – and he was a plague-bearer, a carrier of death. He had eaten nothing all day since the chicken Richard had brought him from the dining room, but he wasn't hungry. Jack sat in numb misery. He brought destruction wherever he went.

3

Then there were footfalls in the corridor once more.

From the floor above, Jack now dimly heard the *thud*

thud thud of a bass pattern, and then again recognized it as being from a record by Blue Oyster Cult. The footsteps paused outside the door. Jack hurried to the door.

Richard stood in the doorway. Two boys with corn-silk hair and half-mast ties glanced in and kept moving down the corridor. The rock music was much more audible in the corridor.

'Where were you all afternoon?' Jack demanded.

'Well, it was sort of freaky,' Richard said. 'They cancelled all the afternoon classes. Mr Dufrey wouldn't even let kids go back to their lockers. And then we all had to go to basketball practice, and that was even weirder.'

'Who's Mr Dufrey?'

Richard looked at him as if he'd just tumbled out of a bassinette. 'Who's Mr Dufrey? He's the headmaster. Don't you know anything at all about this school?'

'No, but I'm getting a few ideas,' Jack said. 'What was so weird about practice?'

'Remember I told you that Coach Frazer got some friend of his to handle it today? Well, he said we'd all get punishment laps if we tried to cut out, so I thought his friend would be some Al Maguire type, you know, some real hotshot. Thayer School doesn't have a very good athletic tradition. Anyhow, I thought his replacement must be somebody really special.'

'Let me guess. The new guy didn't look like he had anything to do with sports.'

Richard lifted his chin, startled. 'No,' he said. 'No, he didn't.' He gave Jack a considering look. 'He smoked all the time. And his hair was really long and greasy – he didn't look anything like a coach. He looked like somebody most coaches would like to step on, to tell you the truth. Even his eyes looked funny. I bet you he smokes pot.' Richard tugged at his sweater. 'I don't think he knew anything about basketball. He didn't even make us practice our patterns – that's what we usually do, after the warm-up period. We sort of ran around and threw baskets and he shouted at us. Laughing. Like kids playing basketball was the most ridiculous thing he'd seen in his whole life. You ever see a coach who thought sports was funny? Even the warm-up period was strange. He just said, "Okay, do pushups," and smoked his cigarette. No count, no cadence, everybody just doing them by themselves. After that it was "Okay, run around a little bit." He looked . . . really wild. I think I'm going to complain to Coach Frazer tomorrow.'

'I wouldn't complain to him or the headmaster either,' Jack said.

'Oh, I get it,' Richard said. 'Mr *Dufrey's* one of them. One of the Territories people.'

'Or he works for them,' Jack said.

'Don't you see that you could fit *anything* into that pattern? *Anything* that goes wrong? It's too easy – you could explain everything that way. That's how craziness works. You make connections that aren't real.'

'And see things that aren't there.'

Richard shrugged, and despite the insouciance of the gesture, his face was miserable. 'You said it.'

'Wait a minute,' Jack said. 'You remember me telling you about the building that collapsed in Angola, New York?'

'The Rainbird Towers.'

'What a memory. I think that accident was my fault.'

'Jack, you're—'

Jack said: 'Crazy, I know. Look, would anyone blow the whistle on me if we went out and watched the evening news?'

'I doubt it. Most kids are studying now, anyway. Why?'

Because I want to know what's been happening around here, Jack thought but did not say. *Sweet little fires, nifty little earthquakes – signs that they're coming through. For me. For* us.

'I need a change of scenery, Richard old chum,' Jack said, and followed Richard down the watery green corridor.

CHAPTER THIRTY-ONE

THAYER GOES TO HELL

1

Jack became aware of the change first and recognized what had happened; it had happened before, while Richard was out, and he was sensitized to it.

The screaming heavy metal of Blue Oyster Cult's 'Tattoo Vampire' was gone. The TV in the common room, which had been cackling out an episode of *Hogan's Heroes* instead of the news, had fallen dormant.

Richard turned toward Jack, opening his mouth to speak.

'I don't like it, Gridley,' Jack said first. 'The native tom-toms have stopped. It's too quiet.'

'Ha-ha,' Richard said thinly.

'Richard, can I ask you something?'

'Yes, of course.'

'Are you scared?'

Richard's face said that he wanted more than anything to say *No, of course not – it always gets quiet around Nelson House this time of the evening.* Unfortunately, Richard was utterly incapable of telling a lie. Dear old Richard. Jack felt a wave of affection.

'Yes,' Richard said. 'I'm a little scared.'

'Can I ask you something else?'

'I guess so.'

'Why are we both whispering?'

Richard looked at him for a long time without saying anything. Then he started down the green corridor again.

The doors of the other rooms on the corridor were either open or ajar. Jack smelled a very familiar odor wafting through the half-open door of Suite 4, and pushed the door all the way open with tented fingers.

'Which one of them is the pothead?' Jack asked.

'What?' Richard replied uncertainly.

Jack sniffed loudly. 'Smell it?'

Richard came back and looked into the room. Both study lamps were on. There was an open history text on one desk, an issue of *Heavy Metal* on the other. Posters decorated the walls: the Costa del Sol, Frodo and Sam trudging across the cracked and smoking plains of Mordor toward Sauron's castle, Eddie Van Halen. Earphones lay on the open issue of *Heavy Metal*, giving out little tinny squeaks of music.

'If you can get expelled for letting a friend sleep under your bed, I doubt if they just slap your wrist for smoking pot, do they?' Jack said.

'They expel you for it, of course.' Richard was looking at the joint as if mesmerized, and Jack thought he looked more shocked and bewildered than he had at any other time, even when Jack had shown him the healing burns between his fingers.

'Nelson House is empty,' Jack said.

'Don't be ridiculous!' Richard's voice was sharp.

'It is, though.' Jack gestured down the hall. 'We're the only ones left. And you don't get thirty-some boys out of a dorm without a sound. They didn't just leave; they disappeared.'

'Over into the Territories, I suppose.'

'I don't know,' Jack said. 'Maybe they're still here, but on a slightly different level. Maybe they're there. Maybe they're in Cleveland. But they're not where we are.'

'Close that door,' Richard said abruptly, and when Jack didn't move quickly enough to suit him, Richard closed it himself.

'Do you want to put out the—'

'I don't even want to touch it,' Richard said. 'I ought to report them, you know. I ought to report them both to Mr Haywood.'

'Would you do that?' Jack asked, fascinated.

Richard looked chagrined. 'No . . . probably not,' he said. 'But I don't like it.'

'Not orderly,' Jack said.

'Yeah.' Richard's eyes flashed at him from behind his spectacles, telling him that was exactly right, he had hit the nail on the head, and if Jack didn't like it, he could lump it. He started down the hall again. 'I want to know what's going *on* around here,' he said, 'and believe me, I'm going to find out.'

That might be a lot more hazardous to your health than marijuana, Richie-boy, Jack thought, and followed his friend.

2

They stood in the lounge, looking out. Richard pointed toward the quad. In the last of the dying light, Jack saw a bunch of boys grouped loosely around the greenish-bronze statue of Elder Thayer.

'They're smoking!' Richard cried angrily. 'Right on the quad, they're *smoking*!'

Jack thought immediately of the pot-smell in Richard's hall.

'They're smoking, all right,' he said to Richard, 'and not the kind of cigarettes you get out of a cigarette machine, either.'

Richard rapped his knuckles angrily on the glass. For him, Jack saw, the weirdly deserted dorm was forgotten; the leather-jacketed, chain-smoking substitute coach was forgotten; Jack's apparent mental aberration was forgotten. That look of outraged propriety on Richard's face said *When a bunch of boys stand around like that, smoking joints within touching distance of the statue of the founder of this school, it's as if someone were trying to tell me that the earth is flat, or that prime numbers may sometimes be divisible by two, or something equally ridiculous.*

Jack's heart was full of pity for his friend, but it was also full of admiration for an attitude which must seem so reactionary and even eccentric to his school-mates. He wondered again if Richard could stand the shocks which might be on the way.

'Richard,' he said, 'those boys aren't from Thayer, are they?'

'God, you really *have* gone crazy, Jack. They're Uppers. I recognize every last one of them. The guy wearing that stupid leather flying hat is Norrington. The one in the green sweat-pants is Buckley. I see Garson . . . Littlefield . . . the one with the scarf is Etheridge,' he finished.

'Are you *sure* it's Etheridge?'

'*Of course it's him!*' Richard shouted. He suddenly turned the catch on the window, rammed it up, and leaned out into the cold air.

Jack pulled Richard back. 'Richard, please, just listen—'

Richard didn't want to. He turned and leaned out into the cold twilight.

'Hey!'

No, don't attract their attention, Richard, for Christ's sake –

'Hey, you guys! Etheridge! Norrington! Littlefield! What in the hell is going on out there?'

The talk and rough laughter broke off. The fellow who was wearing Etheridge's scarf turned toward the sound of Richard's voice. He tilted his head slightly to look up at them. The lights from the library and the sullen furnace afterglow of the winter sunset fell on his face. Richard's hands flew to his mouth.

The right half of the face disclosed was actually a bit like Etheridge's – an older Etheridge, an Etheridge who had been in a lot of places nice prep-school boys didn't go and who had done a lot of things nice prep-school boys didn't do. The other half was a twisted mass of scars. A glittery crescent that might have been an eye peered from a crater in the lumpy mess of flesh below the forehead. It looked like a marble that had been shoved deeply into a puddle of half-melted tallow. A single long fang hooked out of the left corner of the mouth.

It's his Twinner, Jack thought with utter calm certainty. *That's Etheridge's Twinner down there. Are they all Twinners? A Littlefield Twinner and a Norrington Twinner and a Buckley Twinner and so on and so on? That can't be, can it?*

'Sloat!' the Etheridge-thing cried. It shambled two steps toward Nelson House. The glow from the streetlights on the drive now fell directly onto its ruined face.

'Shut the window,' Richard whispered. 'Shut the window. I was wrong. It sort of looks like Etheridge but it's not, maybe it's his older brother, maybe someone threw battery acid or something in Etheridge's brother's face and now he's crazy, but it's not Etheridge so *close the window Jack close it right n—*'

Below, the Etheridge-thing shambled yet another step toward them. It grinned. Its tongue, hideously long, fell out of its mouth like an unrolling party favor.

'Sloat!' it cried. 'Give us your passenger!'

Jack and Richard both jerked around, looking at each other with strained faces.

A howl shivered in the night . . . for it *was* night now; twilight was done.

Richard looked at Jack, and for a moment Jack saw something like real hate in the other boy's eyes – a flash of his father. *Why did you have to come here, Jack? Huh? Why did you have to bring me this mess? Why did you have to bring me all this goddam Seabrook Island Stuff?*

'Do you want me to go?' Jack asked softly.

For a moment that look of harried anger remained in Richard's eyes, and then it was replaced by Richard's old kindness.

'No,' he said, running distracted hands through his hair. 'No, you're not going anywhere. There are . . . there are wild dogs out there. Wild dogs, Jack, on the Thayer campus! I mean . . . did you see them?'

'Yeah, I saw em, Richie-boy,' Jack said softly, as Richard ran his hands through his formerly neat hair again, mussing it into ever wilder tangles. Jack's neat and orderly friend was starting to look a little bit like Donald Duck's amiably mad inventor cousin, Gyro Gearloose.

'Call Boynton, he's Security, that's what I have to do,' Richard said. 'Call Boynton, or the town police, or—'

A howl rose from the trees on the far side of the quad,

from the gathered shadows there – a rising, wavering howl that was really almost human. Richard looked toward it, mouth trembling in an infirm old person's way, and then he looked pleadingly at Jack.

'Close the window, Jack, okay? I feel feverish. I think maybe I've gotten a chill.'

'You bet, Richard,' Jack said, and closed it, shutting the howl out as best he could.

CHAPTER THIRTY-TWO
'SEND OUT YOUR PASSENGER!'

1

'Help me with this, Richard,' Jack grunted.

'I don't want to move the bureau, Jack,' Richard said in a childish, lecturing voice. Those dark circles under his eyes were even more pronounced now than they had been in the lounge. 'That's not where it belongs.'

Out on the quad, that howl rose in the air again.

The bed was in front of the door. Richard's room was now pulled entirely out of shape. Richard stood looking around at this, blinking. Then he went to his bed and pulled off the blankets. He handed one to Jack without speaking, then took his and spread it on the floor. He took his change and his billfold out of his pockets, and put them neatly on the bureau. Then he lay down in the middle of his blanket, folded the sides over himself and then just lay there on the floor, his glasses still on, his face a picture of silent misery.

The silence outside was thick and dreamlike, broken only by the distant growls of the big rigs on the turnpike. Nelson House itself was eerily silent.

'I don't want to talk about what's outside,' Richard said. 'I just want that up front.'

'Okay, Richard,' Jack said soothingly. 'We won't talk about it.'

'Good night, Jack.'

'Good night, Richard.'

Richard gave him a smile that was wan, and terribly tired; yet there was enough sweet friendliness in it to both warm Jack's heart and wrench it. 'I'm still glad you came,' Richard said, 'and we'll talk about all of this in the morning. I'm sure it will make more sense then. This little fever I have will be gone then.'

Richard rolled over on his right side and closed his eyes. Five minutes later, in spite of the hard floor, he was deeply asleep.

Jack sat up for a long time, looking out into the darkness. Sometimes he could see the lights of passing cars on Springfield Avenue; at other times both the headlights and the streetlamps themselves seemed to be gone, as if the entire Thayer School kept sideslipping out of reality and hanging in limbo for a while before slipping back in again.

A wind was rising. Jack could hear it rattling the last frozen leaves from the trees on the quad; could hear it knocking the branches together like bones, could hear it shrieking coldly in the spaces between the buildings.

2

'That guy's coming,' Jack said tensely. It was an hour or so later. 'Etheridge's Twinner.'

'Huzzzat?'

'Never mind,' Jack said. 'Go back to sleep. You don't want to see.'

But Richard was sitting up. Before his eye could fix

on the slumped, somehow twisted form walking toward Nelson House, it was abducted by the campus itself. He was profoundly shocked, deeply frightened.

The ivy on the Monkson Fieldhouse, which had that morning been skeletal but still faintly green, had now gone an ugly, blighted yellow. '*Sloat! Give us your passenger!*'

Suddenly all Richard wanted to do was to go back to sleep – go to sleep until his flu was all gone (he had awakened deciding it *must* be the flu; not just a chill or fever but a real case of the flu); the flu and the fever that was giving him such horrid, twisted hallucinations. He should never have stood by that open window . . . or, earlier, allowed Jack through the window of his room. Richard thought this, and was then deeply and immediately ashamed.

3

Jack shot a quick sideways glance at Richard – but his pallid face and bulging eyes suggested to Jack that Richard was edging farther and farther into The Magical Land of Overload.

The thing out there was short. It stood on the frost-whitened grass like a troll that had crawled out from under some bridge, its long-clawed hands hanging almost to its knees. It wore an Army duffel coat with ETHERIDGE stencilled above the left pocket. The jacket hung unzipped and open. Beneath it, Jack could see a torn and rumpled Pendleton shirt. A dark stain which might have been either blood or vomit was splashed over one side. It was wearing a rumpled blue tie with tiny gold upper-case *E*'s woven into the rep fabric; a couple of burrs were stuck on it like grotesque tie-tacks.

Only half of this new Etheridge's face worked right. There was dirt in its hair and leaves on its clothes.

'Sloat! Give us your passenger!'

Jack looked down at Etheridge's freakish Twinner again. He was caught and held by its eyes, which were somehow vibrating in their sockets, like tuning forks moving rapidly in their lab-mounts. He had to work to drag his eyes away.

'Richard!' he grunted. 'Don't look in its eyes.'

Richard didn't reply; he was staring down at the grinning troll-version of Etheridge with drugged and pallid interest.

Scared, Jack butted his friend with his shoulder.

'Oh,' Richard said. Abruptly he snatched up Jack's hand and pressed it against his forehead. 'How hot do I feel?' he demanded.

Jack pulled his hand away from Richard's forehead, which was a bit warm but no more.

'Pretty hot,' he lied.

'I knew it,' Richard said with real relief. 'I'm going to the infirmary pretty soon, Jack. I think I need an antibiotic.'

'Give him to us, Sloat!'

'Let's get the bureau in front of the window,' Jack said.

'You're in no danger, Sloat!' Etheridge called. It grinned reassuringly – the right half of its face grinned reassuringly, anyway; the left half only continued its corpselike gape.

'How can it look so much like Etheridge?' Richard asked with unsettling, eerie calmness. 'How can its voice come through the glass so clearly? What's wrong with its face?' His voice sharpened a little and recovered some of its earlier dismay as he asked a final question, one which seemed to be at that moment the most vital question of all, at least to Richard Sloat: '*Where did it get Etheridge's tie, Jack?*'

'I don't know,' Jack said. *We're back on Seabrook Island for sure, Richie-boy, and I think we're gonna boogy till you puke.*

'Give him to us, Sloat, or we'll come in and get him!'

The Etheridge-thing showed its single fang in a ferocious cannibal's grin.

'Send your passenger out, Sloat, he's dead! He's dead and if you don't send him out soon, you'll smell him when he starts to stink!'

'Help me move the frigging bureau!' Jack hissed.

'Yes,' Richard said. 'Yes, okay. We'll move the bureau and then I'll lie down, and maybe later I'll go over to the infirmary. What do you think, Jack? What do you say? Is that a good plan?' His face begged Jack to say it was a good plan.

'We'll see,' Jack said. 'First things first. The bureau. They might throw stones.'

4

Soon after, Richard began to mutter and moan in the sleep which had overtaken him again. That was bad enough; then tears began to squeeze from the corners of his eyes and that was worse.

'I can't give him up,' Richard moaned in the weepy, bewildered voice of a five-year-old. Jack stared at him, his skin cold. 'I can't give him up, I want my daddy, please someone tell me where my daddy is, he went into the closet but he's not in the closet now, I want my daddy, he'll tell me what to do, please—'

A rock came crashing through the window. Jack screamed.

It boomed against the back of the bureau in front of

the window. A few splinters of glass flew through the gaps to the left and right of the bureau and shattered into smaller pieces on the floor.

'Give us your passenger, Sloat!'

'Can't,' Richard moaned, writhing inside the blanket.

'*Give him to us!*' another laughing, howling voice from outside screamed. '*We'll take him back to Seabrook Island, Richard! Back to Seabrook Island, where he belongs!*'

Another rock. Jack ducked instinctively, although this rock also bounced off the back of the bureau. Dogs howled and yapped and snarled.

'No Seabrook Island,' Richard was muttering in his sleep. 'Where's my daddy? I want him to come out of that closet! Please, *please, no Seabrook Island stuff, PLEASE*—'

Then Jack was on his knees, shaking Richard as hard as he dared, telling him to wake up, it was just a dream, wake up, for Christ's sake, *wake up*!

'Pleeze-pleeze-pleeze.' A hoarse, inhuman chorus of voices rose outside. The voices sounded like a chorus of manimals from Wells's *Island of Dr Moreau*.

'*Way-gup, way-gup, way-gup!*' a second chorus responded.

Dogs howled.

A flurry of stones flew, knocking more glass from the window, bonking against the back of the bureau, making it rock.

'DADDY'S IN THE CLOSET!' Richard screamed. '*DADDY, COME OUT, PLEASE COME OUT, I'M AFRAID!*'

'Pleeze-pleeze-pleeze!'

'Way-gup, way-gup, way-gup!'

Richard's hands waving in the air.

Stones flying, striking the bureau; soon a rock big

enough to either punch straight through the cheap piece of furniture or to simply knock it over on top of them would come through the window, Jack thought.

Outside, they laughed and bellowed and chanted in their hideous troll-voices. Dogs – packs of them now, it seemed – howled and growled.

'DADEEEEEEEEE—!!' Richard screamed in a chilling, rising voice.

Jack slapped him.

Richard's eyes jerked open. He stared up at Jack for a moment with a dreadful lack of recognition, as if the dream he'd been having had burned away his sanity. Then he pulled in a long, shaking breath and let it out in a sigh.

'Nightmare,' he said. 'Part of the fever, I guess. Horrible. But I don't remember exactly what it was!' he added sharply, as if Jack might ask him this at any moment.

'Richard, I want us to get out of this room,' Jack said.

'Out of this—?' Richard looked at Jack as though he must be crazy. 'I can't do that, Jack. I'm running a fever of . . . it must be a hundred and three at least, might be a hundred and four or five. I can't—'

'You've got a degree of fever at most, Richard,' Jack said calmly. 'Probably not even that—'

'I'm burning up!' Richard protested.

'They're throwing stones, Richard.'

'Hallucinations can't throw stones, Jack,' Richard said, as if explaining some simple but vital fact to a mental defective. 'That's Seabrook Island stuff. It's—'

Another volley of rocks flew through the window.

'*Send out your passenger, Sloat!*'

'Come on, Richard,' Jack said, getting the other boy to his feet. He led him to the door and outside. He felt enormously sorry for Richard now – perhaps not as sorry as he had felt for Wolf . . . but he was getting there.

'No . . . sick . . . fever . . . I can't . . .'

More rocks thudded against the bureau behind them.

Richard shrieked and clutched at Jack like a boy who is drowning.

Wild, cackling laughter from outside. Dogs howled and fought with each other.

Jack saw Richard's white face grow whiter still, saw him sway, and got up in a hurry. But he was not quite in time to catch Richard before he collapsed in Reuel Gardener's doorway.

5

It was a simple fainting spell, and Richard came around quickly enough when Jack pinched the delicate webbings between his thumbs and forefingers. He would not talk about what was outside – affected, in fact, not to know what Jack was talking about.

They moved cautiously down the hallway toward the stairs. At the common room Jack poked his head in and whistled. 'Richard, look at this!'

Richard looked reluctantly in. The common room was a shambles. Chairs were overturned. The cushions on the couch had been slashed open. The oil portrait of Elder Thayer on the far wall had been defaced – someone had crayoned a pair of devil's horns poking out of his neat white hair, someone else had added a moustache under his nose, and a third had used a nail-file or similar implement to scratch a crude phallus on his crotch. The glass of the trophy case was shattered.

Jack didn't much care for the look of drugged, unbelieving horror on Richard's face. In some ways, elves trooping up and down the halls in glowing, unearthly platoons or dragons over the quad would have been easier for Richard to take than this constant erosion of the Thayer School he had come to know and love . . . The Thayer School Richard undoubtedly believed to be noble and good, an undisputed bulwark against a world where nothing could be counted on for long . . . not even, Jack thought, that fathers would come back out of the closets they had gone into.

'Who did this?' Richard asked angrily. 'Those freaks did it,' he answered himself. 'That's who.' He looked at Jack, a great, cloudy suspicion beginning to dawn on his face. 'They might be Colombians,' he said suddenly. 'They might be Colombians, and this might be some sort of drug-war, Jack. Has that occurred to you?'

Jack had to throttle an urge to bellow out mad gusts of laughter. Here was an explanation which perhaps only Richard Sloat could have conceived. It was the Colombians. The cocaine range-wars had come to Thayer School in Springfield, Illinois. Elementary, my dear Watson; this problem has a seven and a half per cent solution.

'I guess anything's possible,' Jack said. 'Let's take a look upstairs.'

'What in God's name for?'

'Well . . . maybe we'll find someone else,' Jack said. He didn't really believe this, but it was something to say. 'Maybe someone's hiding out up there. Someone normal like us.'

Richard looked at Jack, then back at the shambles of the common room. That look of haunted pain came back into his face again, the look that said *I don't really want to look at this, but for some reason it seems to be all I DO want to look at right now; it's bitterly compulsive, like biting a lemon, or scratching your fingernails across a blackboard, or scraping the tines of a fork on the porcelain of a sink.*

'Dope is rampant in the country,' Richard said in eerie lecturehall tones. 'I read an article on drug proliferation in *The New Republic* just last week. Jack, all those people out there could be doped up! They could be freebasing! They could be—'

'Come on, Richard,' Jack said quietly.

'I'm not sure I can climb the stairs,' Richard said, weakly querulous. 'My fever may be too bad for me to climb stairs.'

'Well, give it the good old Thayer try,' Jack said, and continued to lead him in that direction.

6

As they reached the second-floor landing, sound bled back into the smooth, almost breathless silence that had held inside Nelson House.

Dogs snarled and barked outside – it sounded as if there were not just dozens or scores of them now, but hundreds. The bells in the chapel burst into a wild jangle of sound.

The bells were driving the mongrel dogs racing back and forth across the quad absolutely nuts. They turned on each other, rolled over and over on the grass – which was beginning to look ragged, weedy, and unkempt – and savaged anything within mouthshot. As Jack watched, one of them attacked an elm tree. Another launched itself at the statue of Elder Thayer. As its biting, snapping muzzle collided with the solid bronze, blood splashed and sprayed.

Jack turned away, sickened. 'Come on, Richard,' Jack said.

Richard came willingly enough.

7

The second floor was a jumbled confusion of overturned furniture, shattered windows, fistfuls of stuffing, records that had apparently been thrown like Frisbees, clothes that had been tossed everywhere.

The third floor was cloudy with steam and as warmly moist as a tropical rain-forest. As they got closer to the door marked SHOWERS, the heat went up to sauna levels. The mist they had first encountered creeping down the stairs in thin tendrils grew foglike and opaque.

'Stay here,' Jack said. 'Wait for me.'

'Sure, Jack,' Richard said serenely, raising his voice enough to be heard over the drumming showers. His glasses had fogged up, but he made no effort to wipe them off.

Jack pushed the door open and went in. The heat was soggy and thick. His clothes were soaked at once from sweat and the hot, foggy moisture. The tile-lined room roared and drummed with water. All twenty of the showers had been turned on, and the driving needle-spray from all twenty had been focussed on a pile of sports equipment in the middle of the tiled room. The water was able to drain through this crazy pile, but only slowly, and the room was awash. Jack took off his shoes and circled the room, sliding under the showers to keep himself as dry as possible, and also to keep himself from being scalded – whoever had turned on the showers hadn't bothered with the cold faucets, apparently. He turned all of them off, one by one. There was no reason for him to do this, no reason at all, and he scolded himself for wasting time in such a way, when he should be trying to think of a way for them to get out of here – out of Nelson House and off the Thayer School grounds – before the axe fell.

No reason for it, except that maybe Richard wasn't the only one with a need to create order out of chaos . . . to create order and to maintain it.

He went back into the hall and Richard was gone.

'Richard?' He could feel his heartbeat picking up in his chest.

There was no answer. 'Richard!'

Spilled cologne hung on the air, noxiously heavy.

'Richard, where the hell are you!'

Richard's hand fell on Jack's shoulder, and Jack shrieked.

8

'I don't know why you had to yell like that,' Richard said later. 'It was only me.'

'I'm just nervous,' Jack said wanly.

They were sitting in the third-floor room of a boy with the strangely harmonious name of Albert Humbert. Richard told him that Albert Humbert, whose nickname was Albert the Blob, was the fattest boy in school, and Jack could believe it; his room contained an amazing variety of junk food – it was the stash of a kid whose worst nightmare isn't getting cut from the basketball team or flunking a trig test but rather waking up in the night and not being able to find a Ring-Ding or a Reese's Peanut Butter Cup. A lot of the stuff had been thrown around. The glass jar containing the Marshmallow Fluff had been broken, but Jack had never been very wild about Marshmallow Fluff, anyway. He also passed on the licorice whips – Albert the Blob had a whole carton of them stashed on the upper shelf of his closet. Written across one of the carton-flaps was *Happy birthday, dear, from Your Loving Mom.*

Some Loving Moms send cartons of licorice whips, and some Loving Dads send blazers from Brooks Brothers, Jack thought wearily, *and if there's any difference, Jason alone knows what it is.*

They found enough food in the room of Albert the Blob to make a crazy sort of meal – Slim Jims, pepperoni slices, Salt 'n Vinegar potato chips. Now they were finishing up with a package of cookies. Jack had retrieved Albert's chair from the hall and was sitting by the window. Richard was sitting on Albert's bed.

'Well, you sure *are* nervous,' Richard agreed, shaking his head in refusal when Jack offered him the last cookie. 'Paranoid, actually. It comes from spending the last couple of months on the road. You'll be okay once you get home to your mother, Jack.'

'Richard,' Jack said, tossing away the empty Famous Amos bag, 'let's cut the shit. Do you *see* what's going on outside on your campus?'

Richard wet his lips. 'I *explained* that,' he said. 'I have a fever. Probably none of this is happening at all, and if it is, then perfectly ordinary things are going on and my mind is twisting them, heightening them. That's one possibility. The other is . . . well . . . drug-pushers.'

Richard sat forward on Albert the Blob's bed.

'*You* haven't been experimenting with drugs, have you, Jack? While you were on the road?' The old intelligent, incisive light had suddenly rekindled in Richard's eyes. *Here's a possible explanation, a possible way out of this madness*, his eyes said. *Jack has gotten involved in some crazy drug-scam, and all these people have followed him here.*

'No,' Jack said wearily. 'I always used to think of you as the master of reality, Richard,' Jack said. 'I never thought I'd live to see you – *you*! – using your brains to twist the facts.'

'Jack, that's just a . . . a crock, and you know it!'

'Drug-wars in Springfield, Illinois?' Jack asked. 'Who's talking Seabrook Island stuff now?'

And that was when a rock suddenly crashed in through Albert Humbert's window, spraying glass across the floor.

CHAPTER THIRTY-THREE
RICHARD IN THE DARK

1

Richard screamed and threw an arm up to shield his face. Glass flew.

'Send him out, Sloat!'

Jack got up. Dull fury filled him.

Richard grabbed his arm. 'Jack, no! Stay away from the window!'

'Fuck that,' Jack almost snarled. 'I'm tired of being talked about like I was a pizza.'

The Etheridge-thing stood across the road. It was on the sidewalk at the edge of the quad, looking up at them.

'Get out of here!' Jack shouted at it. A sudden inspiration burst in his head like a sunflare. He hesitated, then bellowed: '*I order you out of here! All of you! I order you to leave in the name of my mother, the Queen!*'

The Etheridge-thing flinched as if someone had used a whip to lay a stripe across its face.

Then the look of pained surprise passed and the Etheridge-thing began to grin. 'She's dead, Sawyer!' it shouted up – but Jack's eyes had grown sharper, somehow, in his time on the road, and he saw the expression of twitchy unease under the manufactured triumph. 'Queen

Laura's dead and your mother's dead, too . . . dead back in New Hampshire . . . dead and *stinking*.'

'*Begone!*' Jack bellowed, and he thought that the Etheridge-thing flinched back in baffled fury again.

Richard had joined him at the window, pallid and distracted. 'What are you two yelling about?' he asked. He looked fixedly at the grinning travesty below them and across the way. 'How does Etheridge know your mother's in New Hampshire?'

'*Sloat!*' the Etheridge-thing yelled up. '*Where's your tie?*'

A spasm of guilt contracted Richard's face; his hands jerked toward the open neck of his shirt.

'*We'll let it go this time, if you send out your passenger, Sloat!*' the Etheridge-thing yelled up. '*If you send him out, everything can go back to the way it was! You want that, don't you?*'

Richard was staring down at the Etheridge-thing, nodding – Jack was sure of it – quite unconsciously. His face was a knotted rag of misery, his eyes bright with unshed tears. He wanted everything to go back to the way it had been, oh yes.

'*Don't you love this school, Sloat?*' the Etheridge-thing bellowed up at Albert's window.

'Yes,' Richard muttered, and gulped down a sob. 'Yes, of *course* I love it.'

'You know what we do to little punks who don't love this school? Give him to us! It'll be like he was never here!'

Richard turned slowly and looked at Jack with dreadfully blank eyes.

'You decide, Richie-boy,' Jack said softly.

'He's carrying drugs, Richard!' the Etheridge-thing called up. 'Four or five different kinds! Coke, hash, angel-dust! He's been selling all of that stuff to finance his trip west! Where do you think he got that nice coat he was wearing when he showed up on your doorstep?'

'Drugs,' Richard said with great, shuddery relief. 'I knew it.'

'But you don't believe it,' Jack said. 'Drugs didn't change your school, Richard. And the dogs—'

'Send him out, Sl . . .' the Etheridge-thing's voice was fading, fading.

When the two boys looked down again, it was gone.

'Where did your father go, do you think?' Jack asked softly. 'Where do you think he went when he didn't come out of the closet, Richard?'

Richard turned slowly to look at him, and Richard's face, usually so calm and intelligent and serene, now began to shiver into pieces. His chest began to hitch irregularly. Richard suddenly fell into Jack's arms, clutching at him with a blind, panicky urgency. '*It t-t-touched muh-me-eeee!*' he screamed at Jack. His body trembled under Jack's hands like a winchwire under a near-breaking strain. *'It touched me, it t-touched m-me, something in there t-t-touched me AND I DON'T NUH-NUH-KNOW WHAT IT WAS!'*

2

With his burning forehead pressed against Jack's shoulder, Richard coughed out the story he had held inside him all these years. It came in hard little chunks, like deformed bullets. As he listened, Jack found himself remembering the time his own father had gone into the garage . . . and had come back two hours later, from around the block. That had been bad, but what had happened to Richard had been a lot worse. It explained Richard's iron, no-compromise insistence on reality, the whole reality, and nothing *but* the reality. It explained his rejection of any sort of fantasy, even science fiction . . . and, Jack knew from his own school experience, technies like Richard usually ate and drank sf . . . as long as it was the hard stuff, that was, your basic Heinlein, Asimov, Arthur C. Clarke, Larry Niven – spare us the metaphysical bullshit of the Robert Silverbergs and Barry Malzbergs, please, but we'll read the stuff where they get all the stellar quadrants and logarithms right until it's running out of our ears. Not Richard, though. Richard's dislike of fantasy ran so deep that he would not pick up *any* novel unless it was an assignment – as a kid, he had let Jack pick out the books he read for free-choice book reports, not caring what they were, chewing them up as if they were cereal. It became a challenge to Jack to find a story – *any* story – which would please Richard, divert Richard, carry Richard away as good novels and stories sometimes carried Jack away . . . the good ones, he thought, were almost as good as the Daydreams, and each mapped out its own version of the Territories. But he was never able to produce any *frisson*, any spark, any reaction at all. Whether it was *The Red Pony*, *Dragstrip Demon*, *The Catcher in the Rye*, or *I Am Legend*, the reaction was always the same – frowning, dull-eyed concentration, followed by a frowning, dull-eyed book report that would earn either a hook or, if his English teacher was feeling particularly generous that day, a B–. Richard's Cs in English were what kept him off the honor roll during the few marking periods when he missed it.

Jack had finished William Golding's *Lord of the Flies*, feeling hot and cold and trembly all over – both exalted and frightened, most of all wishing what he always wished when the story was most particularly good – that it didn't have to stop, that it could just roll on and on, the way that life did (only life was always so much more boring and so much more pointless than stories). He knew Richard had a book report due and so he had given him the lap-eared paperback, thinking that this must surely do it, this would turn the trick, Richard must react to the story of these lost boys and their descent into savagery. But Richard had plodded through *Lord of the Flies* as he had plodded through all the other novels before it, and wrote another book report which contained all the zeal and fire of a hung-over pathologist's post-mortem on a traffic accident victim. *What is it with you?* Jack had burst out, exasperated. *What in God's name have you got against a good story, Richard?* And Richard had looked at him, flabbergasted, apparently really not understanding Jack's anger. *Well, there's really no such thing as a good made-up story, is there?* Richard had responded.

Jack had gone away that day sorely puzzled by Richard's total rejection of make-believe, but he thought he understood better now – better than he really wanted to, perhaps. Perhaps to Richard each opening storybook cover had looked a little like an opening closet door; perhaps each bright paperback cover, illustrating people who never were as if they were perfectly real, reminded Richard of the morning when he had Had Enough, Forever.

3

Richard sees his father go into the closet in the big front bedroom, pulling the folding door shut behind him. He is five, maybe . . . or six . . . surely not as old as seven. He waits five minutes, then ten, and when his father still hasn't come out of the closet he begins to be a little frightened. He calls. He calls

(for his pipe he calls for his bowl he calls for his)

father and when his father doesn't answer he calls in a louder and louder voice and he goes closer and closer to the closet as he calls and finally, when fifteen minutes have gone by and his father still hasn't come out, Richard pulls the folding door open and goes in. He goes into darkness like a cave.

And something happens.

After pushing through the rough tweeds and the smooth cottons and the occasional slick silks of his father's coats and suits and sport jackets, the smell of cloth and mothballs and closed-up dark closet air begins to give way to another smell – a hot, fiery smell. Richard begins to blunder forward, screaming his father's name, he thinking there must be a fire back here and his father may be burning in it, because it smells like a fire . . . and suddenly he realizes that the boards are gone under his feet, and he is standing in black dirt. Weird black insects with clustered eyes on the ends of long stalks are hopping all around his fuzzy slippers. Daddy! he screams. The coats and suits are gone, the floor is gone, but it isn't crisp white snow underfoot; it's stinking black dirt which is apparently the birthing ground for these unpleasant black jumping insects; this place is by no stretch of the imagination Narnia. Other screams answer Richard's scream – screams and mad, demented laughter. Smoke drifts around him on a dark idiot wind and Richard turns, stumbling back the way he came, hands outstretched like the hands of a blind man, feeling frantically for the coats, smelling for the faint, acrid reek of mothballs –

And suddenly a hand slithers around his wrist.

Daddy? *he asks, but when he looks down he sees not a human hand but a scaly green thing covered with writhing suckers, a green thing attached to a long, rubbery arm which stretches off into the darkness and toward a pair of yellow, up-slanted eyes that stare at him with flat hunger.*

Screeching, he tears free and flings himself blindly into the black . . . and just as his groping fingers find his father's sport coats and suits again, as he hears the blessed, rational sound of jangling coathangers, that green, sucker-lined hand waltzes dryly across the back of his neck again . . . and is gone.

He waits, trembling, as pallid as day-old ashes in a cold stove, for three hours outside that damned closet, afraid to go back in, afraid of the green hand and the yellow eyes, more and more sure that his father must be dead. And when his father comes back into the room near the end of the fourth hour, not from the closet but from the door which communicates between the bedroom and the upstairs hall – the door BEHIND *Richard – when that happens, Richard rejects fantasy for good and all; Richard negates fantasy; Richard refuses to deal with fantasy, or treat with it, or compromise with it. He has, quite simply, Had Enough, Forever. He jumps up, runs to his father, to the beloved Morgan Sloat, and hugs him so tightly that his arms will be sore all that week. Morgan lifts him up, laughs, and asks him why he looks so pale. Richard smiles, and tells him that it was probably something he ate for breakfast, but he feels better now, and he kisses his father's cheek, and smells the beloved smell of mingled sweat and Raj cologne. And later that day, he takes all of his storybooks – the Little Golden Books, the pop-up books, the I-Can-Read books, the Dr Seuss books, the Green Fairy*

Book for Young Folks, and he puts them in a carton, and he puts the carton down in the basement, and he thinks: 'I would not care if an earthquake came now and opened a crack in the floor and swallowed up every one of those books. In fact, it would be a relief. In fact, it would be such a relief that I would probably laugh all day and most of the weekend.' This does not happen, but Richard feels a great relief when the books are shut in double darkness – the darkness of the carton and the darkness of the cellar. He never looks at them again, just as he never goes in his father's closet with the folding door again, and although he sometimes dreams that there is something under his bed or in his closet, something with flat yellow eyes, he never thinks about that green, sucker-covered hand again until the strange time comes to Thayer School and he bursts into unaccustomed tears in his friend Jack Sawyer's arms.

He has Had Enough, Forever.

4

Jack had hoped that with the telling of his story and the passing of his tears, Richard would return – more or less – to his normal, sharply rational self. Jack didn't really care if Richard bought the whole nine yards or not; if Richard could just reconcile himself to accepting the leading edge of this craziness, he could turn his formidable mind to helping Jack find a way out . . . a way off the Thayer campus, anyway, and out of Richard's life before Richard went totally bananas.

But it didn't work that way. When Jack tried to talk to him – to tell Richard about the time his own father, Phil, had gone into the garage and hadn't come out – Richard refused to listen. The old secret of what had happened that day in the closet was out (sort of; Richard still clung stubbornly to the idea that it had been a hallucination), but Richard had still Had Enough, Forever.

The next morning, Jack went downstairs. He got all of his own things and those things he thought Richard might want – toothbrush, textbooks, notebooks, a fresh change of clothes. They would spend that day in Albert the Blob's room, he decided. They could keep an eye on the quad and the gate from up there. When night fell again, maybe they could get away.

5

Jack hunted through Albert's desk and found a bottle of baby aspirin. He looked at this for a moment, thinking that these little orange pills said almost as much about the departed Albert's Loving Mom as the carton of licorice whips on the closet shelf. Jack shook out half a dozen pills. He gave them to Richard and Richard took them absently. 'Come on over here and lie down,' Jack said.

'No,' Richard answered – his tone was cross and restless and terribly unhappy. He returned to the window. 'I ought to keep a watch, Jack. If this sort of thing is going to happen, someone ought to keep a watch. So a full report can be made to . . . to . . . to the trustees. Later.'

Jack touched Richard's brow lightly. And although it was cool – almost chilly – he said: 'Your fever's worse, Richard. Better lie down until that aspirin goes to work.'

'Worse?' Richard looked at him with pathetic gratitude. 'Is it?'

'It is,' Jack said gravely. 'Come on and lie down.'

Richard was asleep five minutes after he lay down.

Jack sat in Albert the Blob's easy chair, its seat nearly as sprung as the middle of Albert's mattress. Richard's pale face glowed waxily in the growing daylight.

6

Somehow the day passed, and around four o'clock, Jack fell asleep. He awoke to darkness, not knowing how long he had been out. He only knew there had been no dreams, and for that he was grateful. Richard was stirring uneasily and Jack guessed he would be up soon. He stood and stretched, wincing at the stiffness in his back. He went to the window, looked out, and stood motionless, eyes wide. His first thought was *I don't want Richard to see this. Not if I can help it.*

O God, we've got to get out of here, and just as soon as we can, Jack thought, frightened. *Even if, for whatever reasons, they're afraid to come straight at us.*

But was he really going to take Richard out of here? They didn't think he would do it, he knew that – they were counting on his refusing to expose his friend to any more of this craziness.

Flip, Jack-O. You've got to flip over, and you know it. And you've got to take Richard with you because this place is going to hell.

I can't. Flipping into the Territories would blow Richard's wheels completely.

Doesn't matter. You have to do it. It's the best thing, anyway – maybe the only thing – because they won't be expecting it.

'Jack?' Richard was sitting up. His face had a strange, naked look without his glasses. 'Jack, is it over? Was it a dream?'

Jack sat down on the bed and put an arm around Richard's shoulders. 'No,' he said, his voice low and soothing. 'It's not over yet, Richard.'

'I think my fever's worse,' Richard announced, pulling away from Jack. He drifted over to the window, one of the bows of his glasses pinched delicately between the thumb and forefinger of his right hand. He put his spectacles on and looked out. Shapes with glowing eyes roamed back and forth. He stood there for a long time, and then he did something so un-Richardlike that Jack could barely credit it. He took his glasses off again and deliberately dropped them. There was a frigid little crunch as one lens cracked. Then he stepped deliberately back on them, shattering both lenses to powder.

He picked them up, looked at them, and then tossed them unconcernedly toward Albert the Blob's wastebasket. He missed by a wide margin. There was now something softly stubborn in Richard's face, too – something that said *I don't want to see any more, so I won't see any more, and I have taken care of the problem. I have Had Enough, Forever.*

'Look at that,' he said in a flat, unsurprised voice. 'I broke my glasses. I had another pair, but I broke them in gym two weeks ago. I'm almost blind without them.'

Jack knew this wasn't true, but he was too flabbergasted to say anything. He could think of absolutely no appropriate response to the radical action Richard had just taken – it had been too much like a calculated last-ditch stand against madness.

'I think my fever's worse too,' Richard said. 'Have you got any more of those aspirin, Jack?'

Jack opened the desk drawer and wordlessly handed

Richard the bottle. Richard swallowed six or eight of them, then lay down again.

7

As the night deepened, Richard, who repeatedly promised to discuss their situation, repeatedly went back on his word. He couldn't discuss leaving, he said, couldn't discuss *any* of this, not now, his fever had come back and it felt much, much worse, he thought it might be as high as a hundred and five, possibly a hundred and six. He said he needed to go back to sleep.

'Richard, for Christ's sake!' Jack roared. 'You're punking out on me! Of all the things I never expected from you—'

'Don't be silly,' Richard said, falling back onto Albert's bed. 'I'm just sick, Jack. You can't expect me to talk about all these crazy things when I'm sick.'

'Richard, do you want me to go away and leave you?'

Richard looked back over his shoulder at Jack for a moment, blinking slowly. 'You won't,' he said, and then went back to sleep.

8

Around nine o'clock, the campus entered another of those mysterious quiet periods, and Richard, perhaps sensing that there would be less strain put on his tottering sanity now, woke up and swung his legs over the bed. Brown spots had appeared on the walls, and he stared at them until he saw Jack coming toward him.

'I feel a lot better, Jack,' he said hastily, 'but it really won't do us any good to talk about leaving, it's dark, and—'

'We have to leave tonight,' Jack said grimly. 'All they have to do is wait us out. There's fungus growing on the walls, and don't tell me you don't see *that*.'

Richard smiled with a blind tolerance that nearly drove Jack mad. He loved Richard, but he could cheerfully have pounded him through the nearest fungus-rotted wall.

At that precise moment, long, fat white bugs began to squirm into Albert the Blob's room. They came pushing out of the brown fungoid spots on the wall as if the fungus were in some unknown way giving birth to them. They twisted and writhed, half in and half out of the soft brown spots, then plopped to the floor and began squirming blindly toward the bed.

Jack had begun to wonder if Richard's sight weren't really a lot worse than he remembered, or if it had degenerated badly since he had last seen Richard. Now he saw that he had been right the first time. Richard could see quite well. He certainly wasn't having any trouble picking up the gelatinous things that were coming out of the walls, anyway. He screamed and pressed against Jack, his face frantic with revulsion.

'Bugs, Jack! Oh, Jesus! Bugs! Bugs!'

'We'll be all right – right, Richard?' Jack said. He held Richard in place with a strength he didn't know he had. 'We'll just wait for the morning, right? No problem, right?'

They were squirming out in dozens, in hundreds, plump, waxy-white things like overgrown maggots. Some burst open when they struck the floor. The rest humped sluggishly across the floor toward them.

'Bugs, Jesus, we have to get out, we have to—'

'Thank God, this kid finally sees the light,' Jack said.

He slung his knapsack over his left arm and grabbed Richard's elbow in his right hand. He hustled Richard to the door. White bugs squashed and splattered under their shoes. Now they were pouring out of the brown patches in a flood; an obscene, ongoing multiple birth that was happening all over Albert's room. A stream of the white bugs fell from a patch on the ceiling and landed, squirming, on Jack's hair and shoulders; he brushed them away as best he could and hauled the screaming, flailing Richard out the door.

I think we're on our way, Jack thought. *God help us, I really think we are.*

9

They were in the common room again. Richard, it turned out, had even less idea of how to sneak off the Thayer campus than Jack did himself. Jack knew one thing very well: he was not going to trust that deceptive quiet and go out any of Nelson House's Entry doors.

Looking hard to the left out of the wide common-room window, Jack could see a squat octagonal brick building.

'What's that, Richard?'

'Huh?' Richard was looking at the gluey, sluggish torrents of mud flowing over the darkening quad.

'Little squatty brick building. You can just barely see it from here.'

'Oh. The Depot.'

'What's a Depot?'

'The name itself doesn't mean anything anymore,'

Richard said, still looking uneasily out at the mud-drenched quad. 'Like our infirmary. It's called The Creamery because there used to be a real dairy barn and milk-bottling plant over there. Until 1910 or so there was, anyway. Tradition, Jack. It's very important. It's one of the reasons I like Thayer.'

Richard looked forlornly out at the muddy campus again.

'One of the reasons I always did, anyway.'

'The Creamery, okay. How come The Depot?'

Richard was slowly warming to the twin ideas of Thayer and Tradition.

'This whole area of Springfield used to be a railhead,' he said. 'In fact, in the old days—'

'Which old days are we talking about, Richard?'

'Oh. The eighteen-eighties. Eighteen-nineties. You see . . .'

Richard trailed off. His nearsighted eyes began moving around the common room – looking for more bugs, Jack supposed. There weren't any . . . at least not yet. But he could already see a few brown patches beginning to form on the walls. The bugs weren't here yet, but they would be along.

'Come on, Richard,' Jack prompted. 'No one used to have to prime you to get you to run your mouth.'

Richard smiled a little. His eyes returned to Jack. 'Springfield was one of the three or four biggest American railheads during the last two decades of the nineteenth century. It was geographically handy to all the points of the compass.' He raised his right hand toward his face, fore-finger extended to push his glasses up on his nose in a scholarly gesture, realized they were no longer there, and lowered the hand again, looking a bit embarrassed. 'There were main rail routes leaving Springfield for everywhere. This school exists because Andrew Thayer saw the possibilities. He made a fortune in rail shippage. Mostly to the west coast. He was the first one to see the potential in shipping west as well as east.'

A bright light suddenly went on in Jack's head, bathing all of his thoughts in its harsh glare.

'West coast?' His stomach lurched. He could not yet identify the new shape that bright light had shown him, but the word that leaped into his mind was fiery and utterly clear:

Talisman!

'*West* coast, did you say?'

'Of course I did.' Richard looked at Jack strangely. 'Jack, are you going deaf?'

'No,' Jack said. *Springfield was one of the three or four biggest American railheads* . . . 'No, I'm fine.' *He was the first one to see the potential in shipping west* . . .

'Well, you looked damn funny for a minute.'

He was, you might say, the first one to see the potential of shipping stuff by rail to the Outposts.

Jack knew, utterly *knew*, that Springfield was still a pressure point of some kind, perhaps still a shipping point. That was, perhaps, why Morgan's magic worked so well here.

'There were coal-piles and switching yards and roundhouses and box-car sheds and about a billion miles of tracks and sidings,' Richard was saying. 'It covered this whole area where Thayer School is now. If you dig down a few feet under this turf anywhere, you find cinders and pieces of rail and all sorts of stuff. But all that's left now is that little building. The Depot. Of course it never was a real depot;

it's too small, anyone could see that. It was the main rail-yard office, where the stationmaster and the rail-boss did their respective things.'

'You know a hell of a lot about it,' Jack said, speaking almost automatically – his head was still filled with that savage new light.

'It's part of the Thayer tradition,' Richard said simply.

'What's it used for now?'

'There's a little theater in there. It's for Dramatics Club productions, but the Dramatics Club hasn't been very active over the last couple of years.'

'Do you think it's locked?'

'Why would anyone lock The Depot?' Richard asked. 'Unless you think someone would be interested in stealing a few flats from the 1979 production of *The Fantasticks*.'

'So we could get in there?'

'I think so, yes. But why—'

Jack pointed to a door just beyond the Ping-Pong tables. 'What's in there?'

'Vending machines. And a coin-op microwave to heat up snacks and frozen dinners. Jack—'

'Come on.'

'Jack, I think my fever's coming back again.' Richard smiled weakly. 'Maybe we should just stay here for a while. We could rack out on the sofas for the night—'

'See those brown patches on the walls?' Jack said grimly, pointing.

'No, not without my glasses, of course not!'

'Well, they're there. And in about an hour, those white bugs are going to hatch out of—'

'All right,' Richard said hastily.

10

The vending machines stank.

It looked to Jack as if all the stuff inside them had spoiled. Blue mould coated the cheese crackers and Doritos and Jax and fried pork-rinds. Sluggish creeks of melted ice cream were oozing out of the panels in the front of the Hav-a-Kone machine.

Jack pulled Richard toward the window. He looked out. From here Jack could make out The Depot quite well. Beyond it he could see the chain-link fence and the service road leading off-campus.

'We'll be out in a few seconds,' Jack whispered back. He unlocked the window and ran it up.

This school exists because Andrew Thayer saw the possibilities . . . do you *see the possibilities, Jack-O?*

He thought maybe he did.

'Are there any of those people out there?' Richard asked nervously.

'No,' Jack said, taking only the most cursory of glances. It didn't really matter if there were or not, anymore.

One of the three or four biggest American railheads . . . *a fortune in rail shippage . . . mostly to the west coast . . . he was the first one to see the potential in shipping west . . . west . . . west . . .*

A thick, mucky mixture of tidal-flat aroma and garbage stench drifted in the window. Jack threw one leg over the sill and grabbed for Richard's hand. 'Come on,' he said.

Richard drew back, his face long and miserable with fright.

'Jack . . . I don't know . . .'

'The place is falling apart,' Jack said, 'and pretty soon

it's going to be crawling with bugs as well. Now come on. Someone's going to see me sitting here in this window and we'll lose our chance to scurry out of here like a couple of mice.'

'I don't understand any of this!' Richard wailed. 'I don't understand what in the goddam hell is going on here!'

'Shut up and come on,' Jack said. 'Or I will leave you, Richard. Swear to God I will. I love you, but my mother is dying. I'll leave you to fend for yourself.'

Richard looked at Jack's face and saw – even without his glasses – that Jack was telling the truth. He took Jack's hand. 'God, I'm scared,' he whispered.

'Join the club,' Jack said, and pushed off. His feet hit the mucky lawn a second later. Richard jumped down beside him.

'We're going to cross to The Depot,' Jack whispered. 'I make it about fifty yards. We'll go in if it's unlocked, try to hide as well as we can on the Nelson House side of it if it isn't. Once we're sure no one's seen us and the place is still quiet—'

'We go for the fence.'

'Right.' Or maybe we'll have to flip, but never mind that just now. 'The service road. I've got an idea that if we can get off the Thayer grounds, everything will be okay again. Once we get a quarter of a mile down the road, you may look back over your shoulder and see the lights in the dorms and the library just as usual, Richard.'

'That'd be *so* great,' Richard said with a wistfulness that was heart-breaking.

'Okay, you ready?'

'I guess so,' Richard said.

'Run to The Depot. Freeze against the wall on this side. Low, so those bushes screen you. See them?'

'Yes.'

'Okay . . . go for it!'

They broke away from Nelson House and ran for The Depot side by side.

11

They were less than halfway there, breath puffing out of their mouths in clear white vapor, feet pounding the mucky ground, when the bells in the chapel broke into a hideous, grinding jangle of sound. A howling chorus of dogs answered the bells.

They were back, all these were-prefects. Jack groped for Richard and found Richard groping for him. Their hands linked together.

Richard screamed and tried to pull him off to the left. His hand tightened down on Jack's until the finger-bones grated together paralyzingly. A lean white wolf, a Board Chairman of Wolves, came around The Depot and was now racing toward them. That was the old man from the limousine, Jack thought. Other wolves and dogs followed . . . and then Jack realized with sick surety that some of them were not dogs; some of them were half-transformed boys, some grown men – teachers, he supposed.

'*Mr Dufrey!*' Richard shrieked, pointing with his free hand (*Gee, you see pretty well for someone who's lost his glasses, Richie-boy*, Jack thought crazily). '*Mr Dufrey! Oh God, it's Mr Dufrey! Mr Dufrey! Mr Dufrey!*'

So Jack got his first and only look at Thayer School's headmaster – a tiny old man with gray hair, a big, bent nose, and the wizened, hairy body of an organ grinder's monkey. He ran swiftly along on all fours with the dogs and the boys, a mortarboard bobbing crazily up and down on his head and somehow refusing to fall off. He grinned at Jack and Richard, and his tongue, long and lolling and stained yellow with nicotine, fell out through the middle of his grin.

'Mr Dufrey! Oh God! Oh dear God! Mr Dufrey! Mr Du—'

He was yanking Jack harder and harder toward the left. Jack was bigger, but Richard was in the grip of panic. Explosions rocked the air. That foul, garbagey smell grew thicker and thicker. Jack could hear the soft *flupping* and *plupping* of mud squeezing out of the earth. The white wolf which led the pack was closing the distance and Richard was trying to pull them away from it, trying to pull them toward the fence, and that was right, but it was wrong, too, it was wrong because it was The Depot they had to get to, not the fence. That was the spot, that was the spot because this had been one of the three or four biggest American railheads, because Andrew Thayer had been the first one to see the potential in shipping west, because Andrew Thayer had seen the potential and now he, Jack Sawyer, saw the potential, as well. All of this was of course only intuition, but Jack had come to believe that, in these universal matters, his intuition was the only thing he could trust.

'*Let go of your passenger, Sloat!*' Dufrey was gobbling. '*Let go of your passenger, he's too pretty for you!*'

But what's a passenger? Jack thought in those last few seconds, as Richard tried blindly to pull them off-course and Jack yanked him back on, toward the mixed bunch of mongrels and boys and teachers that ran behind the big white wolf, toward The Depot. *I'll tell you what a passenger is; a passenger is one who rides. And where does a passenger begin to ride? Why, at a depot . . .*

'Jack, it'll bite!' Richard screamed.

The wolf outran Dufrey and leaped at them, its jaws dropping open like a loaded trap. From behind them there was a thick, crunching thud as Nelson House split open like a rotten cantaloupe.

Now it was Jack who was bearing down on Richard's fingerbones, clamping tight and tighter and tightest as the night rang with crazy bells and flared with gasoline bombs and rattled with firecrackers.

'Hold on!' he screamed. '*Hold on, Richard, here we go!*'

He had time to think: *Now the shoe is on the other foot; now it's Richard who is the herd, who is my passenger. God help us both.*

'Jack, what's happening?' Richard shrieked. '*What are you doing? Stop it! STOP IT! STOP—*'

Richard was still shrieking, but Jack no longer heard him – suddenly, triumphantly, that feeling of creeping doom cracked open like a black egg and his brain filled up with light – light and a sweet purity of air; air so pure that you could smell the radish a man pulled out of his garden half a mile away. Suddenly Jack felt as if he could simply push off and jump all the way across the quad . . . or fly, like those men with the wings strapped to their backs.

Oh, there was light and clear air replacing that foul, garbagey stench and a sensation of crossing voids of darkness, and for a moment everything in him seemed clear and full of radiance; for a moment everything was rainbow, rainbow, rainbow.

So Jack Sawyer flipped into the Territories again, this time while running headlong across the degenerating Thayer campus, with the sound of cracked bells and snarling dogs filling the air.

And this time he dragged Morgan Sloat's son Richard with him.

INTERLUDE

SLOAT IN THIS WORLD/ORRIS IN THE TERRITORIES (III)

Shortly after seven a.m. on the morning following Jack and Richard's flip out from Thayer, Morgan Sloat drew up to the curb just outside the main gates of Thayer School. He parked. The space was marked with a HANDICAPPED ONLY sign. Sloat glanced at it indifferently, then reached into his pocket, drew out a vial of cocaine, and used some of it. In a few moments the world seemed to gain color and vitality. It was wonderful stuff. He wondered if it would grow in the Territories, and if it would be more potent over there.

Gardener himself had awakened Sloat in his Beverly Hills home at two in the morning to tell him what had happened – it had been midnight in Springfield. Gardener's voice had been trembling. He was obviously terrified that Morgan would fly into a rage, and furious that he had missed Jack Sawyer by less than an hour.

'That boy . . . that bad, bad boy . . .'

Sloat had not flown into a rage. Indeed, he had felt extraordinary calm. He felt a sense of predestination which he suspected came from that other part of him – what he thought of as 'his Orris-ness' in a half-understood pun on royalty.

'Be calm,' Sloat had soothed. 'I'll be there as soon as I can. Hang in there, baby.'

He had broken the connection before Gardener could say any more, and lain back on the bed. He had crossed his hands on his stomach and closed his eyes. There was a moment of weightlessness . . . just a moment . . . and then he felt a sensation of movement beneath him. He heard the creak of leather traces, the groan and thump of rough iron springs, the curses of his driver.

He had opened his eyes as Morgan of Orris.

As always, his first reaction was pure delight: this made coke seem like baby aspirin. His chest was narrower, his weight less. Morgan Sloat's heartbeat ran anywhere from eighty-five beats a minute to a hundred and twenty when he was pissed off; Orris's rarely went higher than sixty-five or so. Morgan Sloat's eyesight was tested at 20/20, but Morgan of Orris nonetheless saw better. He could see and trace the course of every minute crack in the sidewall of the diligence, could marvel over the fineness of the mesh curtains which blew through the windows. Cocaine had clogged Sloat's nose, dulling his sense of smell; Orris's nose was totally clear and he could smell dust and earth and air with perfect fidelity – it was as if he could sense and appreciate every molecule.

Behind him he had left an empty double bed still marked with the shape of his large body. Here he was sitting on a bench seat plusher than the seat in any Rolls-Royce ever made, riding west toward the end of the Outposts, toward a place which was called Outpost Depot. Toward a man named Anders. He knew these things, knew exactly where he was, because Orris was still here, inside his head – speaking to him the way the right side of the brain may speak to the rational left during daydreams, in a low but perfectly clear voice. Sloat had spoken to Orris in this same low undervoice on the few occasions when Orris had Migrated to what Jack had come to think of as the American Territories. When one Migrated and entered the body of one's Twinner, the result was a kind of benign possession. Sloat had read of more violent cases of possession, and although the subject did not greatly interest him, he guessed that the poor, unlucky slobs so afflicted had been taken over by mad hitchhikers from other worlds – or perhaps it was the American world itself which had driven them mad. That seemed more than possible; it had certainly done a number on poor old Orris's head the first two or three times he had popped over, although he had been wildly excited as well as terrified.

The diligence took a mighty bounce – in the Outposts, you took the roads as you found them and thanked God they were there at all. Orris shifted in his seat and his club-foot muttered dull pain.

'Hold on steady, God pound you,' the driver muttered up above. His whip whistled and popped. 'Roll, you sons of dead whores! Roll on!'

Sloat grinned with the pleasure of being here, even though it would only be for moments. He already knew what he needed to know; Orris's voice had muttered it to him. The diligence would arrive at Outpost Depot – Thayer School in the other world – well before morning. It might be possible to take them there if they had lingered; if not, the Blasted Lands awaited them. It hurt and enraged him to think that Richard was now with the Sawyer brat, but if a sacrifice was demanded . . . well, Orris had lost *his* son and survived.

The only thing that had kept Jack alive this long was the maddening fact of his single nature – when the whelp flipped to a place, he was always in the analogue of the place he had left. Sloat, however, always ended up where Orris was, which might be miles away from where he needed to be . . . as was the case now. He had been lucky at the rest area, but Sawyer had been luckier.

'Your luck will run out soon enough, my little friend,' Orris said. The diligence took another terrific bounce. He grimaced, then grinned. If nothing else, the situation was simplifying itself even as the final confrontation took on wider and deeper implications.

Enough.

He closed his eyes and crossed his arms. For just a moment he felt another dull thud of pain in the deformed foot . . . and when he opened his eyes, Sloat was looking up at the ceiling of his apartment. As always, there was a moment when the extra pounds fell into him with sickening weight, when his heart reacted with a surprised double-beat and then sped up.

He had gotten to his feet then and had called West Coast Business Jet. Seventy minutes later he had been leaving LAX. The Lear's steep and abrupt takeoff stance made him feel as it always did – it was as if a blowtorch had been strapped to his ass. They had touched down in Springfield at five-fifty central time, just as Orris would be approaching Outpost Depot in the Territories. Sloat had rented a Hertz sedan and here he was. American travel *did* have its advantages.

He got out of the car and, just as the morning bells began to ring, he walked onto the Thayer campus his own son had so lately quitted.

Everything was the essence of an early Thayer weekday morning. The chapel bells were playing a normal morning tune, something classical but not quite recognizable which sounded a bit like 'Te Deum' but wasn't. Students passed Sloat on their way to the dining hall or to morning work-outs. They were perhaps a little more silent than usual, and they shared a look – pale and slightly dazed, as if they had all shared a disquieting dream.

Which, of course, they had, Sloat thought. He stopped for a moment in front of Nelson House, looking at it thoughtfully. They simply didn't know how fundamentally unreal they all were, as all creatures who live near the thin places between worlds must be. He walked around to the side and watched a maintenance man picking up broken glass that lay on the ground like trumpery diamonds. Beyond his bent back Sloat could see into the Nelson House lounge, where an unusually quiet Albert the Blob was sitting and looking blankly at a Bugs Bunny cartoon.

Sloat started across toward The Depot, his thoughts turning to the first time that Orris had flipped over into this world. He found himself thinking of that time with a nostalgia that was, when one really stopped to think about it, damned near grotesque – after all, he had nearly died. *Both* of them had nearly died. But it had been in the middle fifties, and now he was in *his* middle fifties – it made all the difference in the world.

He had been coming back from the office and the sun had been going down in a Los Angeles haze of smudged purples and smokey yellows – this had been in the days before the L.A. smog had really begun to thicken up. He had been on Sunset Boulevard and looking at a billboard advertising a new Peggy Lee record when he had felt a coldness in his mind. It had been as if a wellspring had suddenly opened somewhere in his subconscious, spilling out some alien weirdness that was like . . . like . . .

(like semen)

. . . well, he didn't know exactly *what* it had been like. Except that it had quickly become warm, gained cognizance, and he had just had time to realize it was *he*, Orris, and then everything had turned topsy-turvy like a secret door on its gimbal – a bookcase on one side, a Chippendale dresser on the other, both fitting the ambience of the room perfectly – and it had been Orris sitting behind the wheel of a 1952 bullet-nosed Ford, Orris wearing the brown double-breasted suit and the John Penske tie, Orris who was reaching down toward his crotch, not in pain but in slightly disgusted curiosity – Orris who had, of course, never worn undershorts.

There had been a moment, he remembered, when the Ford had nearly driven up onto the sidewalk, and then Morgan Sloat – now very much the undermind – had taken over that part of the operation and Orris had been free to go along his way, goggling at everything, nearly half-mad with delight. And what remained of Morgan Sloat had also been delighted; he had been delighted the way a man is delighted when he shows a friend around his new home for the first time and finds that his friend likes it as much as he likes it himself.

Orris had cruised into a Fat Boy Drive-in, and after some fumbling with Morgan's unfamiliar paper money, he had ordered a hamburger and french fries and a chocolate thickshake, the words coming easily out of his mouth – welling up from that undermind as water wells up from a spring. Orris's first bite of the hamburger had been tentative . . . and then he had gobbled the rest with the speed of Wolf gobbling his first Whopper. He had crammed the fries into his mouth with one hand while dialling the radio with the other, picking up an enticing babble of bop and Perry Como and some big band and early rhythm and blues. He had sucked down the shake and then had ordered more of everything.

Halfway through the second burger he – Sloat as well as Orris – began to feel sick. Suddenly the fried onions had seemed too strong, too cloying; suddenly the smell of car exhaust was everywhere. His arms had suddenly begun to itch madly. He pulled off the coat of the double-breasted suit (the second thickshake, this one mocha, fell unheeded to one side, dribbling ice cream across the Ford's seat) and looked at his arms. Ugly red blotches with red centers were growing there, and spreading. His stomach lurched, he leaned out the window, and even as he puked into the tray that was fixed there, he had felt Orris fleeing from him, going back into his own world . . .

'Can I help you, sir?'

'Hmmmm?' Startled out of his reverie, Sloat looked around. A tall blond boy, obviously an upperclassman, was standing there. He was dressed prep – an impeccable blue flannel blazer worn over an open-collared shirt and a pair of faded Levi's.

He brushed hair out of his eyes which had that same dazed, dreaming look. 'I'm Etheridge, sir. I just wondered if I could help you. You looked . . . lost.'

Sloat smiled. He thought of saying – but did not – *No,*

that's how you look, my friend. Everything was all right. The Sawyer brat was still on the loose, but Sloat knew where he was going and that meant that Jacky was on a chain. It was invisible, but it was still a chain.

'Lost in the past, that's all,' he said. 'Old times. I'm not a stranger here, Mr Etheridge, if that's what you're worried about. My son's a student. Richard Sloat.'

Etheridge's eyes grew even dreamier for a moment – puzzled, lost. Then they cleared. 'Sure. Richard!' he exclaimed.

'I'll be going up to see the headmaster in a bit. I just wanted to have a poke around first.'

'Well, I guess that's fine.' Etheridge looked at his watch. 'I have table-duty this morning, so if you're sure you're okay . . .'

'I'm sure.'

Etheridge gave him a nod, a rather vague smile, and started off.

Sloat watched him go, and then he surveyed the ground between Nelson House and here. Noted the broken window again. A straight shot. It was fair – more than fair – to assume that, somewhere between Nelson House and this octagonal brick building, the two boys had Migrated into the Territories. If he liked, he could follow them. Just step inside – there was no lock on the door – and disappear. Reappear wherever Orris's body happened to be at this moment. It would be somewhere close; perhaps even, in fact, in front of the depot-keeper himself. No nonsense about Migrating to a spot which might be a hundred miles away from the point of interest in Territories geography and no way to cover the intervening distance but by wagon or, worse, what his father had called shanks' mare.

The boys would already have gone on, in all likelihood.

Into the Blasted Lands. If so, the Blasted Lands would finish them. And Sunlight Gardener's Twinner, Osmond, would be more than capable of squeezing out all the information that Anders knew. Osmond and his horrid son. No need to Migrate at all.

Except maybe for a look-see. For the pleasure and refreshment of becoming Orris again, if only for a few seconds.

And to Make Sure, of course. His entire life, from childhood onward, had been an exercise in Making Sure.

He looked around once to assure himself that Etheridge had not lingered; then he opened the door of The Depot and went inside.

The smell was stale, dark, and incredibly nostalgic – the smell of old makeup and canvas flats. For a moment he had the crazy idea that he had done something even more incredible than Migrating; he felt that he might have travelled back through time to those undergraduate days when he and Phil Sawyer had been theater-mad college students.

Then his eyes adjusted to the dimness and he saw the unfamiliar, almost mawkish props – a plaster bust of Pallas for a production of *The Raven*, an extravagantly gilt bird-cage, a bookcase full of false bindings – and remembered that he was in the Thayer School excuse for a 'little theater'.

He paused for a moment, breathing deeply of the dust; he turned his eyes up to one dusty sunray falling through a small window. The light wavered and was suddenly a deeper gold, the color of lamplight. He was in the Territories. Just like that, he was in the Territories. There was a moment of almost staggering exhilaration at the speed of the change. Usually there was a pause, a sense of sideslipping from one place to another. This caesura seemed to be in direct proportion to the distance between the physical bodies of his two selves, Sloat and Orris. Once, when he had Migrated from Japan, where he was negotiating a deal with the Shaw brothers for a terrible novel about Hollywood stars menaced by a crazed *ninja*, the pause had gone on so long that he had feared he might be lost forever somewhere in the empty, senseless purgatory that exists between the worlds. But this time they had been close . . . so close! It was like those few times, he thought

(Orris thought)

when a man and woman achieve orgasm at the exact same instant and die in sex together.

The smell of dried paint and canvas was replaced with the light, pleasant smell of Territories burning-oil. The lamp on the table was guttering low, sending out dark membranes of smoke. To his left a table was set, the remains of a meal congealing on the rough plates. Three plates.

Orris stepped forward, dragging his clubfoot a little as always. He tipped one of the plates up, let the guttering lamplight skate queasily across the grease. *Who ate from this one? Was it Anders, or Jason, or Richard . . . the boy would also have been Rushton if my son had lived?*

Rushton had drowned while swimming in a pond not far from the Great House. There had been a picnic. Orris and his wife had drunk a quantity of wine. The sun had been hot. The boy, little more than an infant, had been napping. Orris and his wife had made love and then they had also fallen asleep in the sweet afternoon sunshine. He had been awakened by the child's cries. Rushton had awakened and gone down to the water. He had been able to dog-paddle a little, just enough to get well out beyond his depth before panicking. Orris had limped to the water, dived in, and swum as fast as he could out to where the boy floundered. It was his foot, his damned foot, that had hampered him and perhaps cost his son his life. When he reached the boy, he had been sinking. Orris had managed to catch him by the hair and pull him to shore . . . but by then Rushton had been blue and dead.

Margaret had died by her own hand less than six weeks later.

Seven months after that, Morgan Sloat's own young son had nearly drowned in a Westwood YMCA pool during a Young Paddlers class. He had been pulled from the pool as blue and dead as Rushton . . . but the lifeguard had applied mouth-to-mouth resuscitation, and Richard Sloat had responded.

God pounds His nails, Orris thought, and then a deep, blurry snore snapped his head around.

Anders, the depot-keeper, lay on a pallet in the corner with his kilt rudely pulled up to his breeks. An earthen jug of wine lay overturned nearby. Much of the wine had flowed into his hair.

He snored again, then moaned, as if with bad dreams.

No dream you might have could be as bad as your future now is, Orris thought grimly. He took a step closer, his cloak flapping around him. He looked down on Anders with no pity.

Sloat was able to plan murder, but it had been Orris, time and time again, who had Migrated to carry out the act itself. It had been Orris in Sloat's body who had attempted to smother the infant Jack Sawyer with a pillow while a wrestling announcer droned on and on in the background. Orris who had overseen the assassination of Phil Sawyer in Utah (just as he had overseen the assassination of Phil Sawyer's counterpart, the commoner Prince Philip Sawtelle, in the Territories).

Sloat had a taste for blood, but ultimately he was as allergic to it as Orris was to American food and American air. It was Morgan of Orris, once derided as Morgan Thudfoot, who had always done the deeds Sloat had planned.

My son died; his still lives. Sawtelle's son died. Sawyer's still lives. But these things can be remedied. Will *be remedied. No Talisman for you, my sweet little friends. You are bound for a radioactive version of Oatley, and you each owe the balance-scales a death. God pounds His nails.*

'And if God doesn't, you may be sure I will,' he said aloud.

The man on the floor moaned again, as if he had heard. Orris took another step toward him, perhaps meaning to kick him awake, and then cocked his head. In the distance he heard hoof-beats, the faint creak and jingle of harness, the hoarse cries of drovers.

That would be Osmond, then. Good. Let Osmond take care of business here – he himself had little interest in questioning a man with a hangover when he knew well enough what the man would have to say.

Orris clumped across to the door, opened it, and looked out on a gorgeous peach-colored Territories sunrise. It was from this direction – the direction of the sunrise – that the sounds of approaching riders came. He allowed himself to drink in that lovely glow for a moment and then turned toward the west again, where the sky was still the color of a fresh bruise. The land was dark . . . except for where the first sunlight bounced off a pair of bright parallel lines.

Boys, you have gone to your deaths, Orris thought with satisfaction . . . and then a thought occurred which brought even more satisfaction: their deaths might already have happened.

'Good,' Orris said, and closed his eyes.

A moment later Morgan Sloat was gripping the handle of the door of Thayer School's little theater, opening his own eyes, and planning his trip back to the west coast.

It might be time to take a little trip down memory lane, he thought. To a town in California called Point Venuti. A trip back east first, perhaps – a visit to the Queen – and then . . .

'The sea air,' he said to the bust of Pallas, 'will do me good.'

He ducked back inside, had another jolt from the small vial in his pocket (hardly noticing the smells of canvas and makeup now), and, thus refreshed, he started back downhill toward his car.

·IV·

The Talisman

CHAPTER THIRTY-FOUR
ANDERS

1

Jack suddenly realized that, although he was still running, he was running on thin air, like a cartoon character who has time for one surprised double-take before plunging two thousand feet straight down. But it wasn't two thousand feet. He had time – just – to realize that the ground wasn't there anymore, and then he dropped four or five feet, still running. He wobbled and might have remained upright, but then Richard came piling into him and they both went tumbling.

'*Look out, Jack!*' Richard was screaming – he was apparently not interested in taking his own advice, because his eyes were squeezed tightly shut. '*Look out for the wolf! Look out for Mr Dufrey! Look out—*'

'Stop it, Richard!' These breathless screams frightened him more than anything else had done. Richard sounded mad, absolutely mad. 'Stop it, we're all right! They're gone!'

'*Look out for Etheridge! Look out for the bugs! Look out, Jack!*'

'Richard, they're *gone*! Look around you, for Jason's sake!' Jack hadn't had a chance to do this himself, but he knew they had made it – the air was still and sweet, the night perfectly silent except for a slim breeze that was blessedly warm.

'Look out, Jack! Look out, Jack! Look out, look out—'

Like a bad echo inside his head, he heard a memory of the dog-boys outside Nelson House chorusing *Way-gup, way-gup, way-gup! Pleeze, pleeze, pleeze!*

'Look out, Jack!' Richard wailed. His face was slammed into the earth and he looked like an overenthusiastic Moslem determined to get in good with Allah. *'LOOK OUT! THE WOLF! PREFECTS! THE HEADMASTER! LOOK O—'*

Panicked by the idea that Richard actually *had* gone crazy, Jack yanked his friend's head up by the back of his collar and slapped his face.

Richard's words were cut cleanly off. He gaped at Jack, and Jack saw the shape of his own hand rising on Richard's pale cheek, a dim red tattoo. His shame was replaced by an urgent curiosity to know just where they were. There was light; otherwise he wouldn't have been able to see that mark.

A partial answer to the question came from inside him – it was certain and unquestionable . . . at least, as far as it went.

The Outposts, Jack-O. You're in the Outposts now.

But before he could spend any time mulling that over, he had to try to get Richard shipshape.

'Are you all right, Richie?'

He was looking at Jack with numb, hurt surprise. 'You hit me, Jack.'

'I slapped you. That's what you're supposed to do with hysterical people.'

'I wasn't hysterical! I've never been hysterical in my l—' Richard broke off and jumped to his feet, looking around wildly. 'The wolf! We have to look out for the wolf, Jack! If we can get over the fence he won't be able to get us!'

He would have gone sprinting off into the darkness right then, making for a cyclone fence which was now in another world, if Jack hadn't grabbed him and held him back.

'The wolf is gone, Richard.'

'Huh?'

'We made it.'

'What are you talking abou—'

'The Territories, Richard! We're in the Territories! We flipped over!' *And you almost pulled my damn arm out of its socket, you unbeliever,* Jack thought, rubbing his throbbing shoulder. *The next time I try to haul someone across, I'm going to find myself a real little kid, one who still believes in Santa Claus and the Easter Bunny.*

'That's ridiculous,' Richard said slowly. 'There's no such thing as the Territories, Jack.'

'If there isn't,' Jack said grimly, 'then how come that great big white wolf isn't biting your ass? Or your own damn headmaster?'

Richard looked at Jack, opened his mouth to say something, then closed it again. He looked around, this time with a bit more attention (at least Jack hoped so). Jack did the same, enjoying the warmth and the clarity of the air as he did so. Morgan and his crowd of snake-pit crazies might come bursting through at any second, but for now it was impossible not to luxuriate in the pure animal joy of being back here again.

They were in a field. High, yellowish grass with bearded heads – not wheat, but something like wheat; some edible grain, anyway – stretched off into the night in every direction. The warm breeze rippled it in mysterious but rather lovely waves. To the right was a wooden building standing on a slight knoll, a lamp mounted on a pole in front of it. A yellow flame almost too bright to look at burned clearly inside the lamp's glass globe. Jack saw that the building was octagonal. The two boys had come into the Territories on the outermost edge of the circle of light that lamp threw – and there was something on the far side of the circle, something metallic that threw back the lamplight in broken glimmers. Jack squinted at that faint, silvery glow . . . and then understood. What he felt was not so much wonder as a sense of fulfilled expectation. It was as if two very large jigsaw-puzzle pieces, one in the American Territories and one over here, had just come neatly together.

Those were railroad tracks. And although it was impossible to tell direction in the darkness, Jack thought he knew in which direction those tracks would travel:

West.

2

'Come on,' Jack said.

'I don't want to go up there,' Richard said.

'Why not?'

'Too much crazy stuff going on.' Richard wet his lips. 'Could be anything up there in that building. Dogs. Crazy people.' He wet his lips again. 'Bugs.'

'I told you, we're in the Territories now. The craziness has all blown away – it's clean here. Hell, Richard, can't you *smell* it?'

'There are no such things as *Territories*,' Richard said thinly.

'Look around you.'

'No,' Richard said. His voice was thinner than ever, the voice of an infuriatingly stubborn child.

Jack snatched up a handful of the heavily bearded grass. 'Look at this!'

Richard turned his head.

Jack had to actively restrain an urge to shake him.

Instead of doing that, he tossed the grass away, counted mentally to ten, and then started up the hill. He looked down and saw that he was now wearing something like leather chaps. Richard was dressed in much the same way, and he had a red bandanna around his neck that looked like something out of a Frederic Remington painting. Jack reached up to his own neck and felt a similar bandanna. He ran his hands down along his body and discovered that Myles P. Kiger's wonderfully warm coat was now something very like a Mexican serape. *I bet I look like an advertisement for Taco Bell*, he thought, and grinned.

An expression of utter panic came over Richard's face when Jack started up the hill, leaving him alone at the bottom.

'Where are you going?'

Jack looked at Richard and came back. He put his hands on Richard's shoulders and looked soberly into Richard's eyes.

'We can't stay here,' he said. 'Some of them must have seen us flip. It may be that they can't come right after us, or it may be that they can. I don't know. I know as much about the laws governing all of this as a kid of five knows about magnetism – and all a kid of five knows on the subject is that sometimes magnets attract and sometimes they repel.

But for the time being, that's all I have to know. We have to get out of here. End of story.'

'I'm dreaming all this, I know I am.'

Jack nodded toward the ramshackle wooden building. 'You can come or you can stay here. If you want to stay here, I'll come back for you after I check the place out.'

'None of this is happening,' Richard said. His naked, glasses-less eyes were wide and flat and somehow dusty. He looked for a moment up at the black Territories sky with its strange and unfamiliar sprawl of stars, shuddered, and looked away. 'I have a fever. It's the flu. There's been a lot of flu around. This is a delirium. You're guest-starring in my delirium, Jack.'

'Well, I'll send somebody around to the Delirium Actors' Guild with my AFTRA card when I get a chance,' Jack said. 'In the meantime, why don't you just stay here, Richard? If none of this is happening, then you have nothing to worry about.'

He started away again, thinking that it would take only a few more of these Alice-at-the-teaparty conversations with Richard to convince him that *he* was crazy, as well.

He was halfway up the hill when Richard joined him.

'I would have come back for you,' Jack said.

'I know,' Richard said. 'I just thought that I might as well come along. As long as all of this is a dream, anyway.'

'Well, keep your mouth shut if there's anyone up there,' Jack said. 'I think there is – I think I saw someone looking out that front window at me.'

'What are you going to do?' Richard asked.

Jack smiled. 'Play it by ear, Richie-boy,' he said. 'That's what I've been doing ever since I left New Hampshire. Playing it by ear.'

3

They reached the porch. Richard clutched Jack's shoulder with panicky strength. Jack turned toward him wearily; Richard's patented Kansas City Clutch was something else that was getting old in a big hurry.

'What?' Jack asked.

'This is a dream, all right,' Richard said, 'and I can prove it.'

'How?'

'We're not talking English anymore, Jack! We're talking some language, and we're speaking it perfectly, but it's not English!'

'Yeah,' Jack said. 'Weird, isn't it?'

He started up the steps again, leaving Richard standing below him, gape-mouthed.

4

After a moment or two, Richard recovered himself and scrambled up the steps after Jack. The boards were warped and loose and splintery. Stalks of that richly bearded grain-grass grew up through some of them. Off in the deep darkness, both boys could hear the sleepy hum of insects – it was not the reedy scratch of crickets but a sweeter sound – so much was sweeter over here, Jack thought.

The outside lamp was now behind them; their shadows ran ahead of them across the porch and then made right-angles to climb the door. There was an old, faded sign on that door. For a moment it seemed to Jack to be written in strange Cyrillic letters, as indecipherable as Russian. Then they came clear, and the word was no surprise. DEPOT.

Jack raised his hand to knock, then shook his head a

little. No. He would not knock. This was not a private dwelling; the sign said DEPOT, and that was a word he associated with public buildings – places to wait for Greyhound buses and Amtrak trains, loading zones for the Friendly Skies.

He pushed the door open. Friendly lamplight and a decidedly unfriendly voice came out onto the porch together.

'Get away, ye devil!' the cracked voice screeched. *'Get away, I'm going in the morning! I swear! The train's in the shed! Go away! I swore I'd go and I will go, s'now YE go . . . go and leave me some peace!'*

Jack frowned. Richard gaped. The room was clean but very old. The boards were so warped that the walls seemed almost to ripple. A picture of a stagecoach which looked almost as big as a whaling ship hung on one wall. An ancient counter, its flat surface almost as ripply as the walls, ran across the middle of the room, splitting it in two. Behind it, on the far wall, was a slate board with STAGE ARRIVES written above one column and STAGE LEAVES written above the other. Looking at the ancient board, Jack guessed it had been a good long time since any information had been written there; he thought that if someone tried to write on it with even a piece of soft chalk, the slate would crack in pieces and fall to the weathered floor.

Standing on one side of the counter was the biggest hourglass Jack had ever seen – it was as big as a magnum of champagne and filled with green sand.

'Leave me alone, can't you? I've promised ye I'd go, and I will! Please, Morgan! For yer mercy! I've promised, and if ye don't believe me, look in the shed! The train is ready, I swear the train is ready!'

There was a good deal more gabble and gobble in this same vein. The large, elderly man spouting it was cringing in the far right-hand corner of the room. Jack guessed the oldster's height at six-three at least – even in his present servile posture, The Depot's low ceiling was only four inches or so above his head. He might have been seventy; he might have been a fairly well preserved eighty. A snowy white beard began under his eyes and cascaded down over his breast in a spray of baby-fine hair. His shoulders were broad, although now so slumped that they looked as if someone had broken them by forcing him to carry heavy weights over the course of many long years. Deep crow's-feet radiated out from the corners of his eyes; deep fissures undulated on his forehead. His complexion was waxy-yellow. He was wearing a white kilt shot through with bright scarlet threads, and he was obviously scared almost to death. He was brandishing a stout staff, but with no authority at all.

Jack glanced sharply around at Richard when the old man mentioned the name of Richard's father, but Richard was currently beyond noticing such fine points.

'I am not who you think I am,' Jack said, advancing toward the old man.

'Get away!' he shrieked. *'None of yer guff! I guess the devil can put on a pleasing face! Get away! I'll do it! She's ready to go, first thing in the morning! I said I'd do it and I mean to, now get away, can't ye?'*

The knapsack was now a haversack hanging from Jack's arm. As Jack reached the counter, he rummaged in it, pushing aside the mirror and a number of the jointed money-sticks. His fingers closed around what he wanted and brought it out. It was the coin Captain Farren had given him so long ago, the coin with the Queen on one side and the gryphon on the other. He slammed it down on the counter, and the room's mellow light caught the lovely profile of Laura

DeLoessian – again he was struck with wonder by the similarity of that profile to the profile of his mother. *Did they look that much alike at the beginning? Is it just that I see the similarities more as I think about them more? Or am I actually bringing them together somehow, making them one?*

The old man cringed back even farther as Jack came forward to the counter; it began to seem as though he might push himself right through the back of the building. His words began to pour out in a hysterical flood. When Jack slammed the coin down on the counter like a badman in a Western movie demanding a drink, he suddenly stopped talking. He stared at the coin, his eyes widening, the spit-shiny corners of his mouth twitching. His widening eyes rose to Jack's face and really saw him for the first time.

'Jason,' he whispered in a trembling voice. Its former weak bluster was gone. It trembled now not with fear but with awe. 'Jason!'

'No,' he said. 'My name is—' Then he stopped, realizing that the word which would come out in this strange language was not *Jack* but –

'Jason!' the old man cried, and fell on his knees. 'Jason, ye've come! Ye've come and a' wi' be well, aye, a' wi' be well, a' wi' be well, and a' manner a' things wi' be well!'

'Hey,' Jack said. 'Hey, really—'

'Jason! Jason's come and the Queen'll be well, aye, a' manner a' things wi' be well!'

Jack, less prepared to cope with this weepy adoration than he had been to deal with the old depot-keeper's terrified truculence, turned toward Richard . . . but there was no help there. Richard had stretched out on the floor to the left of the door and had either gone to sleep or was giving a damned good facsimile thereof.

'Oh *shit,*' Jack groaned.

The old man was on his knees, babbling and weeping. The situation was rapidly passing from the realms of the merely ridiculous into those of the cosmically comic. Jack found a flip-up partition and went behind the counter.

'Ah, rise, you good and faithful servant,' Jack said. He wondered blackly if Christ or Buddha had ever had problems like this. 'On your feet, fella.'

'Jason! Jason!' the old man sobbed. His white hair obscured Jack's sandaled feet as he bent over them and began to kiss them – they weren't little kisses, either, but good old spooning-in-the-hayloft smackers. Jack began to giggle helplessly. He had managed to get them out of Illinois, and here they were in a ramshackle depot at the center of a great field of grain which wasn't quite wheat, somewhere in the Outposts, and Richard was sleeping by the door, and this strange old man was kissing his feet and his beard tickled.

'Rise!' Jack yelled, giggling. He tried to step back but hit the counter. *'Rise up, O good servant! Get on your frigging feet, get up, that's enough!'*

'Jason!' Smack! 'A' wi' be well!' Smack-smack!

And a' manner a' things wi' be well, Jack thought crazily, giggling as the old man kissed his toes through the sandals. *I didn't know they read Robert Burns over here in the Territories, but I guess they must –*

Smack-smack-smack.

Oh, no more of this, I really can't stand it.

'RISE!' he bellowed at the top of his voice, and the old man finally stood before him, trembling and weeping, unable to meet Jack's eye. But his amazingly broad shoulders had come up a bit, had lost that broken look, and Jack was obscurely glad of that.

5

It was an hour or better before Jack could manage a coherent run of conversation with the old man. They would *begin* talking, and then Anders, who was a liveryman by trade, would go off on another of his O-Jason-my-Jason-how-great-thou-art jags and Jack would have to quiet him down as quickly as he could . . . certainly before the feet-kissing started again. Jack liked the old man, however, and sympathized. In order to sympathize, all he had to do was imagine how he would feel if Jesus or Buddha turned up at the local car-wash or in the school lunch line. And he had to acknowledge one other clear and present fact: there was a part of him which was not entirely surprised by Anders's attitude. Although he felt like Jack, he was coming more and more to also feel like . . . The other one.

But he'd died.

That was true; undeniably true. Jason had died, and Morgan of Orris had probably had something to do with his death. But guys like Jason had a way of coming back, didn't they?

Jack considered the time it took to get Anders talking well spent if only because it allowed him to be sure that Richard wasn't shamming; that he really had gone back to sleep again. This was good, because Anders had a lot to say about Morgan.

Once, he said, this had been the last stage depot in the known world – it went by the euphonious name of Outpost Depot. Beyond here, he said, the world became a monstrous place.

'Monstrous how?' Jack asked.

'I don't know,' Anders said, lighting his pipe. He looked

out into the darkness, and his face was bleak. 'There are stories about the Blasted Lands, but each is apt to be different from each, and they always begin something like "I know a man who met a man who was lost on the edge of the Blasted Lands for three days and he said . . ." But I never heard a story that begun "*I* was lost on the edge of the Blasted Lands for three days and *I* say . . ."Ye ken the difference, Jason my Lord?'

'I ken it,' Jack said slowly. *The Blasted Lands*. Just the sound of that had raised the hairs on his arms and the nape of his neck. 'No one knows what they are, then?'

'Not for sure,' Anders said. 'But if even a quarter of what I've heard is true—'

'What have you heard?'

'That there are monstrosities out there that makes the things in Orris's ore-pits look almost normal. That there are balls of fire that go rolling across the hills and empty places, leaving long black trails behind them – the trails are black in the daytime, anyway, but I've heard they glow at night. And if a man gets too close to one of those fireballs, he gets turrible sick. He loses his hair, and sores're apt to raise all over his body, and then he begins to vomit; and mayhap he gets better, but more often he only vomits and vomits until his stomach ruptures and his throat bursts and then . . .'

Anders rose.

'My Lord! Why d'ye look so? Have y'seen something out the window? Have y'seen a spook along those double-damned tracks?'

Anders looked wildly toward the window.

Radiation poisoning, Jack thought. *He doesn't know it, but he's described the symptoms of radiation poisoning almost to a* T.

They had studied both nuclear weapons and the

consequences of exposure to radiation in a physical science mod the year before – because his mother was at least casually involved in both the nuclear-freeze movement and the movement to prevent the proliferation of nuclear power plants, Jack had paid very close attention.

How well, he thought, how well radiation poisoning fitted with the whole idea of the Blasted Lands! And then he realized something else, as well: the west was where the first tests had been carried out – where the prototype of the Hiroshima bomb had been hung from a tower and then exploded, where any number of suburbs inhabited only by department-store mannequins had been destroyed so the Army could get a more or less accurate idea of what a nuclear explosion and the resulting firestorm would really do. And in the end they had returned to Utah and Nevada, among the last of the *real* American Territories, and had simply resumed testing underground. There was, he knew, a lot of government land out there in those great wastes, those tangles of buttes and mesas and crenellated badlands, and bombs were not all they were testing out there.

How much of that shit would Sloat bring over here if the Queen died? How much of that shit had he *already* brought? Was this stageline-*cum*-railhead part of the shipping system for it?

'Ye don't look good, my Lord, not at all. Ye look as white as a sheet; I'll take an oath that ye do!'

'I'm fine,' Jack said slowly. 'Sit down. Go on with your story. And light your pipe, it's gone out.'

Anders took his pipe from his mouth, relit it, and looked from Jack to the window again . . . and now his face was not just bleak; it was haggard with fright. 'But I'll know soon enough if the stories are true, I suppose.'

'Why is that?'

'Because I start through the Blasted Lands tomorrow morning, at first light,' Anders said. 'I start through the Blasted Lands, driving Morgan of Orris's devil-machine in yon shed, and carrying God alone knows what sort of hideous devil's work.'

Jack stared at him, his heart pumping hard, the blood humming in his head.

'Where? How far? To the ocean? The big water?'

Anders nodded slowly. 'Aye,' he said. 'To the water. And—' His voice dropped, became a strengthless whisper. His eyes rolled toward the dark windows, as if he feared some nameless thing might be peering in, watching, eavesdropping

'And there Morgan will meet me, and we're to take his goods on.'

'On to where?' Jack asked.

'To the black hotel,' Anders finished in a low, trembling voice.

6

Jack felt that urge to break into wild cackles of laughter again. *The Black Hotel* – it sounded like the title of a lurid mystery novel. And yet . . . and yet . . . all of this had begun at a hotel, hadn't it? The Alhambra in New Hampshire, on the Atlantic coast. Was there some other hotel, perhaps even another rambling old Victorian monstrosity of a hotel, on the Pacific coast? Was that where his long, strange adventure was supposed to end? In some analogue of the Alhambra and with a seedy amusement park close at hand? This idea was terribly persuasive; in an odd, yet precise way, it even seemed to pick up the idea of Twinners and Twinning . . .

'Why do ye look at me so, my Lord?'

Anders sounded agitated and upset. Jack shifted his gaze away quickly. 'I'm sorry,' he said. 'I was just thinking.'

He smiled reassuringly, and the liveryman smiled tentatively back at him.

'And I wish you'd stop calling me that.'

'Calling ye what, my Lord?'

'My Lord.'

'My Lord?' Anders looked puzzled. He was not echoing what Jack had said but asking for clarification. Jack had a feeling that if he tried to push on with this, he would end up in the middle of a 'Who's on first, What's on second' sort of sketch.

'Never mind,' Jack said. He leaned forward. 'I want you to tell me everything. Can you do that?'

'I'll try, my Lord,' Anders said.

7

His words came slowly at first. He was a single man who had spent his entire life in the Outposts and he was not used to talking much at the best of times. Now he had been commanded to speak by a boy whom he considered to be at least royalty, and perhaps even something like a god. But, little by little, his words began to come faster, and by the end of his inconclusive but terribly provocative tale, the words were nearly pouring out. Jack had no trouble following the tale he told in spite of the man's accent, which his mind kept translating into a sort of ersatz Robert Burns burr.

Anders knew Morgan because Morgan was, quite simply, Lord of the Outpost. His real title, Morgan of Orris, was not so grand, but as a practical matter, the two came to nearly the same. Orris was the easternmost cantonment of the Outposts, and the only really organized part of that large, grassy area. Because he ruled Orris utterly and completely, Morgan ruled the rest of the Outposts by default. Also, the bad Wolfs had begun to gravitate to Morgan in the last fifteen years or so. At first that meant little, because there were only a few bad (except the word Anders used also sounded a bit like *rabid* to Jack's ears) Wolfs. But in later years there had been more and more of them, and Anders said he had heard tales that, since the Queen had fallen ill, more than half the tribe of skin-turning shepherds were rotten with the sickness. Nor were these the only creatures at Morgan of Orris's command, Anders said; there were others, even worse – some, it was told, could drive a man mad at a single look.

Jack thought of Elroy, the bogeyman of the Oatley tap, and shuddered.

'Does this part of the Outposts we're in have a name?' Jack asked.

'My Lord?'

'This part we're in now.'

'No real name, my Lord, but I've heard people call it Ellis-Breaks.'

'Ellis-Breaks,' Jack said. A picture of Territories geography, vague and probably in many ways incorrect, was finally beginning to take shape in Jack's mind. There were the Territories, which corresponded to the American east; the Outposts, which corresponded to the American midwest and great plains (Ellis-Breaks? Illinois? Nebraska?); and the Blasted Lands, which corresponded to the American west.

He looked at Anders so long and so fixedly that at last the liveryman began to stir uneasily again. 'I'm sorry,' Jack said. 'Go on.'

His father, Anders said, had been the last stage driver who 'drove out east' from Outpost Depot. Anders had been his 'prentice. But even in those days, he said, there were great confusions and upheavals in the east; the murder of the old King and the short war which had followed it had seen the beginning of those upheavals, and although the war had ended with the installation of Good Queen Laura, the upheavals had gone on ever since, seeming to work their way steadily eastward, out of the spoiled and twisted Blasted Lands. There were some, Anders said, who believed the evil had begun all the way west.

'I'm not sure I understand you,' Jack said, although in his heart he thought he did.

'At land's end,' Anders said. 'At the edge of the big water, where I am bound to go.'

In other words, it began in the same place my father came from . . . my father, and me, and Richard . . . and Morgan. Old Bloat.

The troubles, Anders said, had come to the Outposts, and now the Wolf tribe was partly rotten – just how rotten none could say, but the liveryman told Jack he was afraid that the rot would be the end of them if it didn't stop soon. The upheavals had come here, and now they had even reached the east, where, he had heard, the Queen lay ill and near death.

'That's not true, is it, my Lord?' Anders asked . . . almost begged.

Jack looked at him. 'Should I know how to answer that?' he asked.

'Of course,' Anders said. 'Are ye not her son?'

For a moment, the entire world seemed to Jack to become very quiet. The sweet hum of the bugs outside stilled. Richard seemed to pause between heavy, sluggish breaths.

Even his own heart seemed to pause . . . perhaps that most of all.

Then, his voice perfectly even, he said, 'Yes . . . I am her son. And it's true . . . she's very ill.'

'But dying?' Anders persisted, his eyes nakedly pleading now. 'Is she dying, my Lord?'

Jack smiled a little and said: 'That remains to be seen.'

8

Anders said that until the troubles began, Morgan of Orris had been a little-known frontier lord and no more; he had inherited his comic-opera title from a father who had been a greasy, evil-smelling buffoon. Morgan's father had been something of a laughing-stock while alive, Anders went on, and had even been a laughing-stock in his manner of dying.

'He was taken with the squitters after a day of drinking peach-fruit wine and died while on the trots.'

People had been prepared to make the old man's son a laughing-stock as well, but the laughing had stopped soon after the hangings in Orris began. And when the troubles began in the years after the death of the old King, Morgan had risen in importance as a star of evil omen rises in the sky.

All of this meant little this far out in the Outposts – these great empty spaces, Anders said, made politics seem unimportant. Only the deadly change in the Wolf tribe made a practical difference to them, and since most of the bad Wolfs went to the Other Place, even that didn't make much difference to them ('It fashes us little, my Lord' was what Jack's ears insisted they had heard).

Then, not long after the news of the Queen's illness had reached this far west, Morgan had sent out a crew of grotesque, twisted slaves from the ore-pits back east; these slaves were tended by stolen Wolfs and other, stranger creatures. Their foreman was a terrible man who carried a whip; he had been here almost constantly when the work began, but then he had disappeared. Anders, who had spent most of those terrible weeks and months cowering in his house, which was some five miles south of here, had been delighted to see him go. He had heard rumors that Morgan had called the man with the whip back east, where affairs were reaching some great point of climax; Anders didn't know if this was true or not, and didn't care. He was simply glad that the man, who was sometimes accompanied by a scrawny, somehow gruesome-looking little boy, was gone.

'His name,' Jack demanded. 'What was his name?'

'My Lord, I don't know. The Wolfs called him He of the Lashes. The slaves just called him the devil. I'd say they were both right.'

'Did he dress like a dandy? Velvet coats? Shoes with buckles on the tops, maybe?'

Anders was nodding.

'Did he wear a lot of strong perfume?'

'Aye! Aye, he did!'

'And the whip had little rawhide strings with metal caps on them.'

'Aye, my Lord. An evil whip. And he was fearsome good with it, aye, he was.'

It was Osmond. It was Sunlight Gardener. He was here, overseeing some project for Morgan . . . then the Queen got sick and Osmond was called back to the summer palace, where I first made his cheerful acquaintance.

'His son,' Jack said. 'What did his son look like?'

'Skinny,' Anders said slowly. 'One eye was afloat. That's all I can remember. He . . . my Lord, the Whipman's son was hard to see. The Wolfs seemed more afraid of him than of his father, although the son carried no whip. They said he was *dim*.'

'Dim,' Jack mused.

'Yes. It is their word for one who is hard to see, no matter how hard ye look for that one. Invisibility is impossible – so the Wolfs say – but one can make himself *dim* if only he knows the trick of it. Most Wolfs do, and this little whoreson knew it, too. So all I remember is how thin he was, and that floating eye, and that he was as ugly as black, syphilitic sin.'

Anders paused.

'He liked to hurt things. Little things. He used to take them under the porch and I'd hear the most awful screams . . .' Anders shuddered. 'That was one of the reasons I kept to my house, you know. I don't like to hear wee animals in pain. Makes me feel turrible bad, it does.'

Everything Anders said raised a hundred fresh questions in Jack's mind. He would particularly have liked to know all that Anders knew about the Wolfs – just hearing of them woke simultaneous pleasure and a deep, dully painful longing for *his* Wolf in his heart.

But time was short; this man was scheduled to drive west into the Blasted Lands in the morning, a horde of crazy scholars led by Morgan himself might burst through from what the liveryman called the Other Place at any moment, Richard might wake up and want to know who this Morgan was they were discussing, and who this *dim* fellow was – this *dim* fellow who sounded suspiciously like the fellow who had lived next door to him in Nelson House.

'They came,' he prompted, 'this crew came, and Osmond was their foreman – at least until he was called away or whenever he had to lead the devotions at night-chapel back in Indiana—'

'My Lord?' Anders's face was again ponderous with puzzlement.

'They came, and they built . . . what?' He was sure he already knew the answer to this, but he wanted to hear Anders himself say it.

'Why, the tracks,' Anders said. 'The tracks going west into the Blasted Lands. The tracks I must travel myself tomorrow.' He shuddered.

'No,' Jack said. A hot, terrible excitement exploded in his chest like a sun, and he rose to his feet. Again there was that click in his head, that terrible, persuasive feeling of great things coming together.

Anders fell on his knees with a crash as a terrible, beautiful light filled Jack's face. Richard stirred at the sound and sat sleepily up.

'Not you,' Jack said. 'Me. And him.' He pointed at Richard.

'Jack?' Richard looked at him with sleepy, nearsighted confusion. 'What are you talking about? And why is that man sniffing the floor?'

'My Lord . . . yer will, of course . . . but I don't understand . . .'

'Not you,' Jack said, 'us. We'll take the train for you.'

'But my Lord, why?' Anders managed, not yet daring to look up.

Jack Sawyer looked out into the darkness.

'Because,' he said, 'I think there's something at the end of the tracks – at the end of the tracks or near the end – that I have to get.'

INTERLUDE

SLOAT IN THIS WORLD (IV)

On the tenth of December, a bundled-up Morgan Sloat was sitting on the uncomfortable little wooden chair beside Lily Sawyer's bed – he was cold, so he had his heavy cashmere coat wrapped around him and his hands thrust deep into its pockets, but he was having a much better time than his appearance suggested. Lily was dying. She was going out, away, to that place from which you never came back, not even if you were a Queen in a football-field-sized bed.

Lily's bed was not so grand, and she did not in the least resemble a Queen. Illness had subtracted her good looks, had skinned down her face and aged her a quick twenty years. Sloat let his eyes roam appreciatively over the prominent ridges of bone about her eyes, the tortoiselike shell of her forehead. Her ravaged body barely made a lump beneath the sheets and blankets. Sloat knew that the Alhambra had been well paid to leave Lily Cavanaugh Sawyer alone, for it was he who had paid them. They no longer bothered to send heat up to her room. She was the hotel's only guest. Besides the desk clerk and cook, the only employees still in the Alhambra were three Portuguese maids who spent all their time cleaning the lobby – it must have been the maids who kept Lily piled high with blankets. Sloat himself had commandeered the suite across the hall, and ordered the desk clerk and the maids to keep a close eye on Lily.

To see if she would open her eyes, he said, 'You're looking better, Lily. I really think I see signs of improvement.'

Without moving anything but her mouth, Lily said, 'I don't know why you pretend to be human, Sloat.'

'I'm the best friend you have,' Sloat responded.

Now she did open her eyes, and they were not dull enough to suit him. 'Get out of here,' she whispered. 'You're obscene.'

'I'm trying to help you, and I wish you'd remember that. I have all the papers, Lily. All you have to do is sign them. Once you do, you and your son are taken care of for life.' Sloat regarded Lily with an expression of satisfied gloom. 'I haven't had much luck in locating Jack, by the way. Spoken to him lately?'

'You know I haven't,' she said. And did not weep, as he had hoped.

'I really do think the boy ought to be here, don't you?'

'Piss up a stick,' Lily said.

'I think I *will* use your bathroom, if you don't mind,' he said, and stood up. Lily closed her eyes again, ignoring him. 'I hope he's staying out of trouble, anyhow,' Sloat said, slowly walking down the side of the bed. 'Terrible things happen to boys on the road.' Lily still did not respond. 'Things I hate to think about.' He reached the end of the bed and continued on to the bathroom door. Lily lay under her sheets and blankets like a crumpled piece of tissue paper. Sloat went into the bathroom.

He rubbed his hands together, gently closed the door, and turned on both taps over the sink. From the pocket of his suitcoat he extracted a small brown two-gram vial, from his inner jacket pocket a small case containing a mirror, a razor blade, and a short brass straw. Onto the mirror he tapped about an eighth of a gram of the purest Peruvian Flake cocaine he'd been able to find. Then he chopped it ritualistically with his blade, forming it into two stubby lines. He snorted the lines through the brass straw, gasped, inhaled sharply, and held his breath for a second or two. 'Aah.' His nasal passages opened up as wide as tunnels. Way back there, a drip began to deliver the goodies. Sloat ran his hands under the water, then for the sake of his nose drew a little of the moisture on his thumb and index finger up into his nostrils. He dried his hands and his face.

That lovely train, he allowed himself to think, *that lovely lovely train, I bet I'm prouder of it than I am of my own son.*

Morgan Sloat revelled in the vision of his precious train, which was the same in both worlds and the first concrete manifestation of his long-held plan to import modern technology into the Territories, arriving in Point Venuti loaded with its useful cargo. Point Venuti! Sloat smiled as the coke blasted through his brain, bringing its usual message that all would be well, all would be well. Little Jacky Sawyer would be a very lucky boy *ever* to leave the odd little town of Point Venuti. In fact, he'd be lucky ever to get there in the first place, considering that he'd have to make his way across the Blasted Lands. But the drug reminded Sloat that in some ways he'd prefer Jack to make it to dangerous, warped little Point Venuti, he'd even prefer Jack to survive his exposure to the black hotel, which was not merely boards and nails, bricks and stone, but was also somehow alive . . . because it was possible that he might walk out with the Talisman in his thieving little hands. And if that were to happen . . .

Yes, if that absolutely wonderful event were to take place, all would indeed be well.

And both Jack Sawyer and the Talisman would be broken in half.

And he, Morgan Sloat, would finally have the canvas his talents deserved. For a second he saw himself spreading his arms over starry vastnesses, over worlds folded together like lovers on a bed, over all that the Talisman protected, and all that he had coveted so when he'd bought the Agincourt, years back. Jack could get all that for him. Sweetness. Glory.

To celebrate this thought, Sloat brought the vial out of his pocket again and did not bother with the ritual of razor and mirror, but simply used the attached little spoon to raise the medicinal white powder to first one nostril, then the other. Sweetness, yes.

Sniffing, he came back into the bedroom. Lily appeared slightly more animated, but his mood now was so good that even this evidence of her continuing life did not darken it. Bright and oddly hollow within their circles of bone, her eyes followed him. 'Uncle Bloat has a new loathsome habit,' she said.

'And you're dying,' he said. 'Which one would you choose?'

'Do enough of that stuff, and you'll be dying, too.'

Undeterred by her hostility, Sloat returned to the rickety wooden chair. 'For God's sake, Lily, grow up,' he said.

'Everybody does coke now. You're out of touch – you've been out of touch for years. You wanna try some?' He lifted the vial from his pocket and swung it by the chain attached to the little spoon.

'Get out of here.'

Sloat waggled the vial closer to her face.

Lily sat up in bed as smartly as a striking snake and spat in his face.

'Bitch!' He recoiled, grabbing for his handkerchief as the wad of spittle slid down his cheek.

'If that crap is so wonderful, why do you have to sneak into the toilet to take it? Don't answer, just leave me alone. I don't want to see you again, Bloat. Take your fat ass out of here.'

'You're going to die alone, Lily,' he said, now perversely filled with a cold, hard joy. 'You're going to die alone, and this comic little town is going to give you a pauper's burial, and your son is going to be killed because he can't possibly handle what's lying in wait for him, and no one will ever hear of either one of you again.' He grinned at her. His plump hands were balled into white hairy fists. 'Remember Asher Dondorf, Lily? Our client? The sidekick on that series *Flanagan and Flanagan?* I was reading about him in *The Hollywood Reporter* – some issue a few weeks ago. Shot himself in his living room, but his aim wasn't too cool, because instead of killing himself he just blew away the roof of his mouth and put himself in a coma. Might hang on for years, I hear, just rotting away.' He leaned toward her, his forehead corrugating. 'You and good old Asher have a lot in common, it seems to me.'

She stonily looked back. Her eyes seemed to have crawled back inside her head, and at that moment she resembled some hard-bitten old frontier woman with a squirrel rifle in one hand and Scripture in the other. 'My son is going to save my life,' she said. 'Jack is going to save my life, and you won't be able to stop him.'

'Well, we'll see, won't we?' Sloat answered. 'We'll just see about that.'

CHAPTER THIRTY-FIVE
THE BLASTED LANDS

1

'But will ye be safe, my Lord?' Anders asked, kneeling down before Jack with his white-and-red kilt out around him like a skirt.

'Jack?' Richard asked, his voice a whiny, irrelevant skirl of sound.

'Would you be safe yourself?' Jack asked.

Anders twisted his big white head sideways and squinted up at Jack as if he had just asked a riddle. He looked like a huge puzzled dog.

'I mean, I'll be about as safe as you would be yourself. That's all I mean.'

'But my Lord . . .'

'Jack?' came Richard's querulous voice again. 'I fell asleep, and now I should be awake, but we're still in this weird place, so I'm still dreaming . . . but I want to be awake, Jack, I don't want to have this dream anymore. No. I don't want to.'

And that's why you busted your damn glasses, Jack said to himself. Aloud, he said, 'This isn't a dream, Richie-boy. We're about to hit the road. We're gonna take a train ride.'

'Huh?' Richard said, rubbing his face and sitting up.

If Anders resembled a big white dog in skirts, Richard looked like nothing so much as a newly awakened baby.

'My Lord Jason,' Anders said. Now he seemed as if he might weep – with relief, Jack thought. 'It is yer will? It is yer will to drive that devil-machine through the Blasted Lands?'

'It sure is,' Jack said.

'Where are we?' Richard said. 'Are you sure they're not following us?'

Jack turned toward him. Richard was sitting up on the undulating yellow floor, blinking stupidly, terror still drifting about him like a fog. 'Okay,' he said. 'I'll answer your questions. We're in a section of the Territories called Ellis-Breaks—'

'My head hurts,' Richard said. He had closed his eyes.

'And,' Jack went on, 'we're going to take this man's train all the way through the Blasted Lands to the black hotel, or as close to it as we can get. That's it, Richard. Believe it or not. And the sooner we do it, the sooner we'll get away from whatever just might be trying to find us.'

'Etheridge,' Richard whispered. 'Mr Dufrey.' He looked around the mellow interior of The Depot as if he expected all their pursuers to suddenly pour through the walls. 'It's a brain tumor, you know,' he said to Jack in a tone of perfect reasonableness. 'That's what it is – my headache.'

'My Lord Jason,' old Anders was saying, bowing so low that his hair settled down on the rippling floorboards. 'How good ye are, O High One, how good to yer lowliest servant, how good to those who do not deserve yer blessed presence . . .' He crawled forward, and Jack saw with horror that he was about to begin that moony foot-kissing all over again.

'Pretty far advanced, too, I'd say,' Richard offered.

'Get up, please, Anders,' Jack said, stepping back. 'Get up, come on, that's enough.' The old man continued to crawl forward, babbling with his relief at not having to endure the Blasted Lands. 'ARISE!' Jack bellowed.

Anders looked up, his forehead wrinkled. 'Yes, my Lord.' He slowly got up.

'Bring your brain tumor over here, Richard,' Jack said. 'We're going to see if we can figure out how to drive this damn train.'

2

Anders had moved over behind the long, rippling counter, and was rooting in a drawer. 'I believe it works on devils, my Lord,' he said. 'Strange devils, all hurtled down together. They do not appear to live, yet they do. Aye.' He fetched out of the drawer the longest, fattest candle that Jack had ever seen. From a box atop the counter Anders selected a foot-long, narrow softwood strip, then lowered one of its ends into a glowing lamp. The strip of wood ignited, and Anders used it to light his enormous candle. Then he waved the 'match' back and forth until the flame expired in a curl of smoke.

'Devils?' Jack asked.

'Strange square things – I believe the devils are contained therein. Sometimes how they spit and spark! I shall show this to ye, Lord Jason.'

Without another word he swept toward the door, the warm glow of the candle momentarily erasing the wrinkles from his face. Jack followed him outside into the sweetness and amplitude of the deep Territories. He remembered a photograph on the wall of Speedy Parker's office, a photograph even then filled with an inexplicable power, and realized that he was actually near the site of that photograph. Far off rose a familiar-looking mountain. Down the little knoll the fields of grain rolled away in all directions, waving in smooth, wide patterns. Richard Sloat moved hesitantly beside Jack, rubbing his forehead. The silvery bands of metal, out of key with the rest of the landscape, stretched inexorably west.

'The shed is in back, my Lord,' Anders said softly, and almost shyly turned away toward the side of The Depot. Jack took another glance at the far-off mountain. Now it looked less like the mountain in Speedy's photograph – newer – a western, not an eastern, mountain.

'What's with that Lord Jason business?' Richard whispered right into his ear. 'He thinks he knows you.'

'It's hard to explain,' Jack said.

Richard tugged at his bandanna, then clamped a hand on Jack's biceps. The old Kansas City Clutch. 'What happened to the school, Jack? What happened to the dogs? Where are we?'

'Just come along,' Jack said. 'You're probably still dreaming.'

'Yes,' Richard said in the tone of purest relief. 'Yes, that's it, isn't it? I'm still asleep. You told me all that crazy stuff about the Territories, and now I'm dreaming about it.'

'Yeah,' Jack said, and set off after Anders. The old man was holding up the enormous candle like a torch and drifting down the rear side of the knoll toward another, slightly larger, octagonal wooden building. The two boys followed him through the tall yellow grass. Light spilled from another of the transparent globes, revealing that this second building was open at opposite ends, as if two matching faces of the octagon had been neatly sliced away. The silvery train tracks ran through these open ends. Anders reached the large shed and turned around to wait for the boys. With the flaring, sputtering, upheld candle, his long beard and odd clothes, Anders resembled a creature from legend or faery, a sorcerer or wizard.

'It sits here, as it has since it came, and may the demons drive it hence.' Anders scowled at the boys, and all his wrinkles deepened. 'Invention of hell. A foul thing, d'ye ken.' He looked over his shoulder when the boys were before him. Jack saw that Anders did not even like being in the shed with the train. 'Half its cargo is aboard, and it too stinks of hell.'

Jack stepped into the open end of the shed, forcing Anders to follow him. Richard stumbled after, rubbing his eyes. The little train sat pointing west on the tracks – an odd-looking engine, a boxcar, a flatcar covered with a straining tarp. From this last car came the smell Anders so disliked. It was a wrong smell, not of the Territories, both metallic and greasy.

Richard immediately went to one of the interior angles of the shed, sat down on the floor with his back to the wall, and closed his eyes.

'D'ye ken its workings, my Lord?' Anders asked in a low voice.

Jack shook his head and walked up along the tracks to the head of the train. Yes, there were Anders's 'demons'. They were box batteries, just as Jack had supposed. Sixteen of them, in two rows strung together in a metal container supported by the cab's first four wheels. The entire front part of the train looked like a more sophisticated version of a deliveryboy's bicycle-cart – but where the bicycle itself should have been was a little cab which reminded Jack of something else . . . something he could not immediately identify.

'The demons talk to the upright stick,' Anders said from behind him.

Jack hoisted himself up into the little cab. The 'stick' Anders had mentioned was a gearshift set in a slot with three notches. Then Jack knew what the little cab resembled. The whole train ran on the same principle as a golf cart. Battery-powered, it had only three gears: forward, neutral, and reverse. It was the only sort of train that might possibly work in the Territories, and Morgan Sloat must have had it specially constructed for him.

'The demons in the boxes spit and spark, and talk to the stick, and the stick moves the train, my Lord.' Anders hovered anxiously beside the cab, his face contorting into an astonishing display of wrinkles.

'You were going to leave in the morning?' Jack asked the old man.

'Aye.'

'But the train is ready now?'

'Yes, my Lord.'

Jack nodded, and jumped down. 'What's the cargo?'

'Devil-things,' Anders said grimly. 'For the bad Wolfs. To take to the black hotel.'

I'd be a jump ahead of Morgan Sloat if I left now, Jack thought. And looked uneasily over at Richard, who had managed to put himself asleep again. If it weren't for pig-headed, hypochondriacal Rational Richard, he would never have stumbled onto Sloat's choo-choo; and Sloat would have been able to use the 'devil-things' – weapons of some kind, surely – against him as soon as he got near the black hotel.

For the hotel was the end of his quest, he was sure of that now. And all of that seemed to argue that Richard, as helpless and annoying as he now was, was going to be more important to his quest than Jack had ever imagined. The son of Sawyer and the son of Sloat: the son of Prince Philip Sawtelle and the son of Morgan of Orris. For an instant the world wheeled above Jack and he snagged a second's insight that Richard might just be essential to whatever he was going to have to do in the black hotel. Then Richard snuffled and let his mouth drop open, and the feeling of momentary comprehension slipped away from Jack.

'Let's have a look at those devil-things,' he said. He whirled around and marched back down the length of the train, along the way noticing for the first time that the floor of the octagonal shed was in two sections – most of it was one round circular mass, like an enormous dinner plate. Then there was a break in the wood, and what was beyond the perimeter of the circle extended to the walls. Jack had never heard of a roundhouse, but he understood the concept: the circular part of the floor could turn a hundred and eighty degrees. Normally, trains or coaches came in from the east, and returned in the same direction.

The tarpaulin had been tied down over the cargo with thick brown cord so hairy it looked like steel wool. Jack strained to lift an edge, peered under, saw only blackness. 'Help me,' he said, turning to Anders.

The old man stepped forward, frowning, and with one strong, deft motion released a knot. The tarpaulin loosened and sagged. Now when Jack lifted its edge, he saw that half of the flatcar held a row of wooden boxes stencilled MACHINE PARTS. *Guns*, he thought: Morgan is arming his rebel Wolfs. The other half of the space beneath the tarp was occupied by bulky rectangular packages of a squashy-looking substance wrapped in layers of clear plastic sheeting. Jack had no idea what this substance might be, but he was pretty sure it wasn't Wonder Bread. He dropped the tarpaulin and stepped back, and Anders pulled at the thick rope and knotted it again.

'We're going tonight,' Jack said, having just decided this.

'But my Lord Jason . . . the Blasted Lands . . . at night . . . d'ye ken—'

'I ken, all right,' Jack said, 'I ken that I'll need all the surprise I can whip up. Morgan and that man the Wolfs call He of the Lashes are going to be looking for me, and if I show up twelve hours before anybody is expecting this train, Richard and I might get away alive.'

Anders nodded gloomily, and again looked like an oversize dog accommodating itself to unhappy knowledge.

Jack looked at Richard again – asleep, sitting up with his mouth open. As if he knew what was in Jack's mind, Anders too looked toward sleeping Richard. 'Did Morgan of Orris have a son?' Jack asked.

'He did, my Lord. Morgan's brief marriage had issue – a boy-child named Rushton.'

'And what became of Rushton? As if I couldn't guess.'

'He died,' Anders said simply. 'Morgan of Orris was not meant to be a father.'

Jack shuddered, remembering how his enemy had torn his way through the air and nearly killed Wolf's entire herd.

'We're going,' he said. 'Will you please help me get Richard into the cab, Anders?'

'My Lord . . .' Anders hung his head, then lifted it and gave Jack a look of almost parental concern. 'The journey will require at least two days, perhaps three, before ye reach the western shore. Have ye any food? Would ye share my evening meal?'

Jack shook his head, impatient to begin this last leg of his journey to the Talisman, but then his stomach abruptly growled, reminding him of how long it had been since he had eaten anything but the Ring-Dings and stale Famous Amos cookies in Albert the Blob's room. 'Well,' he said, 'I suppose another half hour won't make any difference. Thank you, Anders. Help me get Richard up on his feet, will you?' And maybe, he thought, he wasn't so eager to cross the Blasted Lands after all.

The two of them jerked Richard to his feet. Like the Dormouse, he opened his eyes, smiled, and sagged back to sleep again. 'Food,' Jack said. 'Real food. You up for that, chum?'

'I never eat in my dreams,' Richard answered with surreal rationality. He yawned, then wiped his eyes. He gradually had found his feet, and no longer leaned against Anders and Jack. 'I am pretty hungry, though, to tell you the truth. I'm having a long dream, aren't I, Jack?' He seemed almost proud of it.

'Yep,' said Jack.

'Say, is that the train we're going to take? It looks like a cartoon.'

'Yep.'

'Can you drive that thing, Jack? It's my dream, I know, but—'

'It's about as hard to operate as my old electric train set,' Jack said. 'I can drive it, and so can you.'

'I don't want to,' Richard said, and that cringing, whining tone came back into his voice again. 'I don't want to get on that train at all. I want to go back to my room.'

'Come and have some food instead,' Jack said, and

found himself leading Richard out of the shed. 'Then we're on our way to California.'

And so the Territories showed one of its best faces to the boys immediately before they entered the Blasted Lands. Anders gave them thick sweet slices of bread clearly made from the grain growing around The Depot, kebabs of tender sections of meat and plump juicy unfamiliar vegetables, a spicy pink juice that Jack for some reason thought of as papaya though he knew it was not. Richard chewed in a happy trance, the juice running down his chin until Jack wiped it off for him. 'California,' he said once. 'I should have known.' Assuming that he was alluding to that state's reputation for craziness, Jack did not question him. He was more concerned about what the two of them were doing to Anders's presumably limited stock of food, but the old man kept nipping behind the corner, where he or his father before him had installed a small wood-burning stove, and returning with yet more food. Corn muffins, calf's-foot jelly, things that looked like chicken legs but tasted of . . . what? Frankincense and myrrh? Flowers? The taste fairly exploded over his tongue, and he thought that he too might begin to drool.

The three of them sat around a little table in the warm and mellow room. At the end of the meal Anders almost shyly brought forth a heavy beaker half-filled with red wine. Feeling as if he were following someone else's script, Jack drank a small glassful.

3

Two hours later, beginning to feel drowsy, Jack wondered if that enormous meal had been an equally enormous error.

First of all, there had been the departure from Ellis-Breaks and The Depot, which had not gone easily; secondly, there was Richard, who threatened to go seriously crazy; and thirdly, and above all else, there were the Blasted Lands. Which were far crazier than Richard would ever be, and which absolutely demanded concentrated attention.

After the meal the three of them had returned to the shed, and the trouble had started. Jack knew that he was fearful of whatever might be ahead – and, he now knew, that fear was perfectly justified – and perhaps his trepidation had made him behave less well than he should have. The first difficulty had come when he tried to pay old Anders with the coin Captain Farren had given him. Anders responded as if his beloved Jason had just stabbed him in the back. Sacrilege! Outrage! By offering the coin, Jack had done more than merely insult the old liveryman, he had metaphorically smeared mud on his religion. Supernaturally restored divine beings apparently were not supposed to offer coins to their followers. Anders had been upset enough to smash his hand into the 'devil-box', as he called the metal container for the rank of batteries, and Jack knew that Anders had been mightily tempted to strike another target besides the train. Jack had managed only a semi-truce: Anders did not want his apologies any more than he wanted his money. The old man had finally calmed down once he realized the extent of the boy's dismay, but he did not really return to his normal behavior until Jack speculated out loud that the Captain Farren coin might have other functions, other roles for him. 'Ye're not Jason entire,' the old man gloomed, 'yet the Queen's coin may aid ye toward yer destiny.' He shook his head heavily. His farewell wave had been distinctly half-hearted.

But a good portion of that had been due to Richard. What had begun as a sort of childish panic had quickly blossomed into full-blown terror. Richard had refused to get in the cab. Up until that moment he had mooned around the shed, not looking at the train, seemingly in an uncaring daze. Then he had realized that Jack was serious about getting him on that thing, and he had freaked – and, strangely, it had been the idea of ending up in California which had disturbed him most. 'NO! NO! CAN'T!' Richard had yelled when Jack urged him toward the train. 'I WANT TO GO BACK TO MY ROOM!'

'They might be following us, Richard,' Jack said wearily. 'We have to get going.' He reached out and took Richard's arm. 'This is all a dream, remember?'

'Oh my Lord, oh my Lord,' Anders had said, moving aimlessly around in the big shed, and Jack understood that for once the liveryman was not addressing him.

'I HAVE TO GO BACK TO MY ROOM!' Richard squalled. His eyes were clamped shut so tightly that a single painful crease ran from temple to temple.

Echoes of Wolf again. Jack had tried to pull Richard toward the train, but Richard had stuck fast, like a mule. 'I CAN'T GO THERE!' he yelled.

'Well, you can't stay here, either,' Jack said. He made another futile effort at yanking Richard toward the train, and this time actually budged him a foot or two. 'Richard,' he said, 'this is ridiculous. Do you want to be here alone? Do you want to be left alone in the Territories?' Richard shook his head. 'Then come with me. It's time. In two days we'll be in California.'

'Bad business,' Anders muttered to himself, watching the boys. Richard simply continued to shake his head, offering a single comprehensive negative. 'I can't go there,' he repeated. 'I can't get on that train and I can't go there.'

'California?'

Richard bit his mouth into a lipless seam and closed his eyes again. 'Oh hell,' Jack said. 'Can you help me, Anders?' The huge old man gave him a dismayed, almost disgusted look, then marched across the room and scooped up Richard into his arms – as if Richard were the size of a puppy. The boy let out a distinctly puppyish squeal. Anders dropped him onto the padded bench in the cab. 'Jack!' Richard called, afraid that he somehow was going to wind up in the Blasted Lands all by himself. 'I'm here,' Jack said, and was in fact already climbing into the other side of the cab. 'Thank you, Anders,' he said to the old liveryman, who nodded gloomily and retreated back into a corner of the shed. 'Take care.' Richard had begun to weep, and Anders looked at him without pity.

Jack pushed the ignition button, and two enormous blue sparks shot out from the 'devil-box' just as the engine whirred into life. 'Here goes,' Jack said, and eased the lever forward. The train began to glide out of the shed. Richard whimpered and drew up his knees. Saying something like 'Nonsense' or 'Impossible' – Jack chiefly heard the hiss of the sibilants – he buried his face between his knees. He looked as though he were trying to become a circle. Jack waved to Anders, who waved back, and then they were out of the lighted shed and were covered only by the vast dark sky. Anders's silhouette appeared in the opening through which they had gone, as if he had decided to run after them. The train was not capable of going more than thirty miles an hour, Jack thought, and at present was doing no better than eight or nine. This seemed excruciatingly slow. West,

Jack said to himself, west, west, west. Anders stepped back inside the shed, and his beard lay against his massive chest like a covering of frost. The train lurched forward – another sizzling blue spark snapped upward – and Jack turned around on the padded seat to see what was coming.

'NO!' Richard screamed, almost making Jack fall out of the cab. 'I CAN'T! CAN'T GO THERE!' He had drawn his head up from his knees, but he wasn't seeing anything – his eyes were still clamped shut, and his whole face looked like a knuckle.

'Be quiet,' Jack said. Ahead the tracks arrowed through the endless fields of waving grain; dim mountains, old teeth, floated in the western clouds. Jack glanced one last time over his shoulder and saw the little oasis of warmth and light which was The Depot and the octagonal shed, slipping slowly backward behind him. Anders was a tall shadow in a lighted doorway. Jack gave a final wave, and the tall shadow waved, too. Jack turned around again and looked over the immensity of grain, all that lyric distance. If this was what the Blasted Lands were like, the next two days were going to be positively restful.

Of course they were not, not like that at all. Even in the moonlit dark he could tell that the grain was thinning out, becoming scrubby – about half an hour out of The Depot the change had begun. Even the color seemed wrong now, almost artificial, no longer the beautiful organic yellow he had seen before, but the yellow of something left too near a powerful heat source – the yellow of something with most of the life bleached out of it. Richard now had a similar quality. For a time he had hyperventilated, then he had wept as silently and shamelessly as a jilted girl, then he had fallen into a twitchy sleep. 'Can't go back,' he had muttered in his sleep, or such were the words Jack thought he had heard. In sleep he seemed to dwindle.

The whole character of the landscape had begun to alter. From the broad sweep of the plains in Ellis-Breaks, the land had mutated to secretive little hollows and dark little valleys crowded with black trees. Huge boulders lay everywhere, skulls, eggs, giant teeth. 'The ground itself had changed, become much sandier. Twice the walls of the valleys grew up right alongside the tracks, and all Jack could see on either side were scrubby reddish cliffs covered with low creeping plants. Now and then he thought he saw an animal scurrying for cover, but the light was too weak, and the animal too quick, for him to identify it. But Jack had the eerie feeling that if the animal had frozen absolutely still in the middle of Rodeo Drive at high noon, he would still have been unable to identify it – a suggestion that the head was twice the size it should be, that this animal was better off hiding from human sight.

By the time ninety minutes had elapsed, Richard was moaning in his sleep and the landscape had passed into utter strangeness. The second time they had emerged from one of the claustrophobic valleys, Jack had been surprised by a sense of sudden openness – at first it was like being back in the Territories again, the Daydreams-land. Then he had noticed, even in the dark, how the trees were stunted and bent; then he had noticed the smell. Probably this had been slowly growing in his consciousness, but it was only after he had seen how the few trees scattered on the black plain had coiled themselves up like tortured beasts that he finally noticed the faint but unmistakable odor of corruption in the air. Corruption, hellfire. Here the Territories stank, or nearly.

The odor of long-dead flowers overlaid the land; but beneath it, as with Osmond, was a coarser, more potent odor. If Morgan, in either of his roles, had caused this, then he had in some sense brought death to the Territories, or so Jack thought.

Now there were no more intricate valleys and hollows; now the land seemed a vast red desert. The queerly stunted trees dotted the sloping sides of this great desert. Before Jack, the twin silver rails of the tracks rolled on through darkened reddish emptiness; to his side, empty desert also rolled away through the dark.

The red land seemed empty, anyhow. For several hours Jack never actually caught sight of anything larger than the deformed little animals concealing themselves on the slopes of the railway cuttings – but there were times when he thought he caught a sudden sliding movement in the corner of one eye, turned to see it, and it was gone. At first he thought he was being followed. Then, for a hectic time, no longer than twenty or thirty minutes, he imagined that he was being tracked by the dog-things from Thayer School. Whenever he looked, something had just ceased to move – had nipped behind one of the coiled-up trees or slipped into the sand. During this time the wide desert of the Blasted Lands did not seem empty or dead, but full of slithery, hidden life. Jack pushed forward on the train's gearshift (as if that could help) and urged the little train to go faster, faster. Richard slumped in the ell of his seat, whimpering. Jack imagined all those beings, those things neither canine nor human, rushing toward them, and prayed that Richard's eyes would stay closed.

'NO!' Richard yelled, still sleeping.

Jack nearly fell out of the cab. He could *see* Etheridge

and Mr Dufrey loping after them. They gained ground, their tongues lolling, their shoulders working. In the next second, he realized that he had seen only shadows travelling beside the train. The loping schoolboys and their headmaster had winked out like birthday candles.

'NOT THERE!' Richard bawled. Jack inhaled carefully. He, they, were safe. The dangers of the Blasted Lands were overrated, mainly literary. In not very many hours the sun would lift itself up again. Jack raised his watch to the level of his eyes and saw that they had been on the train just under two hours. His mouth opened in a huge yawn, and he found himself regretting that he had eaten so much back in The Depot.

A piece of cake, he thought, this is going to be –

And just as he was about to complete his paraphrase of the Burns lines old Anders had rather startlingly quoted, he saw the first of the fireballs, which destroyed his complacency forever.

4

A ball of light, at least ten feet in diameter tumbled over the edge of the horizon, sizzling hot, and at first arrowed straight toward the train. 'Holy shit,' Jack muttered to himself, remembering what Anders had said about the balls of fire. *If a man gets too close to one of those fireballs, he gets turrible sick . . . loses his hair . . . sores're apt to raise all over his body . . . he begins to vomit . . . vomits and vomits until his stomach ruptures and his throat bursts . . .* He swallowed, hard – it was like swallowing a pound of nails. 'Please, God,' he said aloud. The giant ball of light sped straight toward him, as though it owned a mind and had decided to erase Jack Sawyer and

Richard Sloat from the earth. Radiation poisoning. Jack's stomach contracted, and his testicles froze up under his body. *Radiation poisoning. Vomits and vomits until his stomach ruptures . . .*

The excellent dinner Anders had given him nearly leaped out of his stomach. The fireball continued to roll straight toward the train, shooting out sparks and sizzling with its own fiery energy. Behind it lengthened a glowing golden trail which seemed magically to instigate other snapping, burning lines in the red earth. Just when the fireball bounced up off the earth and took a zagging bounce like a giant tennis ball, wandering harmlessly off to the left, Jack had his first clear glimpse of the creatures he had all along thought were following them. The reddish-golden light of the wandering fireball, and the residual glow of the old trails in the earth, illuminated a group of deformed-looking beasts which had evidently been following the train. They were dogs, or once had been dogs, or their ancestors had been dogs, and Jack glanced uneasily at Richard to make sure that he was still sleeping.

The creatures falling behind the train flattened out on the ground like snakes. Their heads were doglike, Jack saw, but their bodies had only vestigial hind legs and were, as far as he could see, hairless and tailless. They looked wet – the pink hairless skin glistened like that of newborn mice. They snarled, hating to be seen. It had been these awful mutant dogs that Jack had seen on the banks of the railway cutting. Exposed, flattened out like reptiles, they hissed and snarled and began creeping away – they too feared the fireballs and the trails the fireballs left on the earth. Then Jack caught the odor of the fireball, now moving swiftly, somehow almost angrily, toward the horizon again, igniting an entire row of the stunted trees. Hellfire, corruption.

Another of the fireballs came cruising over the horizon and blazed away off to the boys' left. The stink of missed connections, of blasted hopes and evil desires – Jack, with his heart lodged just under his tongue, imagined he found all this in the foul smell broadcast by the fireball. Mewing, the crowd of mutant dogs had dispersed into the threat of glinting teeth, a whisper of surreptitious movement, the *hushushush* of heavy legless bodies dragged through red dust. How many of them were there? From the base of a burning tree which tried to hide its head in its trunk two of the deformed dogs bared long teeth at him.

Then another fireball lurched over the wide horizon, spinning off a wide glowing track a distance from the train, and Jack momentarily glimpsed what looked like a ramshackle little shed set just below the curve of the desert wall. Before it stood a large humanoid figure, male, looking toward him. An impression of size, hairiness, force, malice . . .

Jack was indelibly conscious of the slowness of Anders's little train, of his and Richard's exposure to anything that might want to investigate them a little more closely. The first fireball had dispatched the horrible dog-things, but human residents of the Blasted Lands might prove more difficult to overcome. Before the light diminished into the glowing trail, Jack saw that the figure before the shed was following his progress, turning a great shaggy head as the train passed by. If what he had seen were dogs, then what would the people be like? In the last of the flaring light from the ball of fire, the manlike being scuttled around the side of its dwelling. A thick reptilian tail swung from its hindquarters, and then the thing had slipped around the side of the building, and then it was dark again and nothing – dogs, man-beast, shed

– was visible. Jack could not even be sure that he had really seen it.

Richard jerked in his sleep, and Jack pushed his hand against the simple gearshift, vainly trying for more speed. The dog-noises gradually faded behind them. Sweating, Jack raised his left wrist again to the level of his eyes and saw that only fifteen minutes had passed since the last time he'd checked his watch. He astonished himself by yawning again, and again regretted eating so much at The Depot.

'NO!' Richard screamed. 'NO! I CAN'T GO THERE!'

There? Jack wondered. Where was 'there'? California? Or was it anywhere threatening, anywhere Richard's precious control, as insecure as an unbroken horse, might slip away from him?

5

All night Jack stood at the gearshift while Richard slept, watching the trails of the departed fireballs flicker along the reddish surface of the earth. Their odor, of dead flowers and hidden corruption, filled the air. From time to time he heard the chatter of the mutant dogs, or of other poor creatures, rising from the roots of the stunted, ingrown trees which still dotted the landscape. The ranks of batteries occasionally sent up snapping arcs of blue. Richard was in a state beyond mere sleep, wrapped in an unconsciousness he both required and had willed. He made no more tortured outcries – in fact he did nothing but slump into his corner of the cab and breathe shallowly, as if even respiration took more energy than he had. Jack half-prayed for, half-feared the coming of the light. When morning came, he would be able to see the animals; but what else might he have to see?

From time to time he glanced over at Richard. His friend's skin seemed oddly pale, an almost ghostly shade of gray.

6

Morning came with a relaxation of the darkness. A band of pink appeared along the bowllike edge of the eastern horizon, and soon a rosy stripe grew up beneath it, pushing the optimistic pinkness higher in the sky. Jack's eyes felt almost as red as that stripe, and his legs ached. Richard lay across the whole of the cab's little seat, still breathing in a restricted, almost reluctant way. It was true, Jack saw – Richard's face did seem peculiarly gray. His eyelids fluttered in a dream, and Jack hoped that his friend was not about to erupt in another of his screams. Richard's mouth dropped open, but what emerged was the tip of his tongue, not a loud outcry. Richard passed his tongue along his upper lip, snorted, then fell back into his stupefied coma.

Although Jack wished desperately to sit down and close his own eyes, he did not disturb Richard. For the more Jack saw as the new light filled in the details of the Blasted Lands, the more he hoped Richard's unconsciousness would endure as long as he himself could endure the conditions on Anders's cranky little train. He was anything but eager to witness the response of Richard Sloat to the idiosyncrasies of the Blasted Lands. A small amount of pain, a quantity of exhaustion – these were a minimal price to pay for what he knew must be a temporary peace.

What he saw through his squinting eyes was a landscape in which nothing seemed to have escaped withering, crippling damage. By moonlight, it had seemed a vast desert, though a desert furnished with trees. Now Jack took in that his 'desert' was actually nothing of the sort. What he had taken for a reddish variety of sand was a loose, powdery soil – it looked as though a man would sink in it up to his ankles, if not his knees. From this starved dry soil grew the wretched trees. Looked at directly, these were much as they appeared by night, so stunted they seemed to be straining over in an attempt to flee back under their own coiling roots. This was bad enough – bad enough for Rational Richard, anyhow. But when you saw one of these trees obliquely, out of the side of your eye, then you saw a living creature in torment – the straining branches were arms thrown up over an agonized face caught in a frozen scream. As long as Jack was not looking directly at the trees, he saw their tortured faces in perfect detail, the open O of the mouth, the staring eyes and drooping nose, the long, agonized wrinkles running down the cheeks. They were cursing, pleading, howling at him – their unheard voices hung in the air like smoke. Jack groaned. Like all the Blasted Lands, these trees had been poisoned.

The reddish land stretched out for miles on either side, dotted here and there with patches of acrid-looking yellow grass bright as urine or new paint. If it had not been for the hideous coloration of the long grass, these areas would have resembled oases, for each lay beside a small round body of water. The water was black, and oily patches floated on its skin. Thicker than water, somehow, itself oily, poisonous. The second of these false oases that Jack saw began to ripple sluggishly as the train went past, and at first Jack thought with horror that the black water itself was alive, a being as tormented as the trees he no longer wished to see. Then he momentarily saw something break the surface of the thick fluid, a broad black back or side which rolled over before a wide, ravenous mouth appeared, biting down on nothing. A suggestion of scales that would have been iridescent if the creature had not been discolored by the pool. *Holy cow,* Jack thought, *was that a fish?* It seemed to him to have been nearly twenty feet long, too big to inhabit the little pool. A long tail roiled the water before the entire enormous creature slipped back down into what must have been the pool's considerable depth.

Jack looked up sharply at the horizon, imagining that he had momentarily seen the round shape of a head peering over it. And then he had another of those shocks of a sudden displacement, similar to that the Loch Ness monster, or whatever it was, had given him. How could a head peer over the *horizon*, for God's sake?

Because the horizon wasn't the real horizon, he finally understood – all night, and for as long as it took him to really see what lay at the end of his vision, he had drastically underestimated the size of the Blasted Lands. Jack finally understood, as the sun began to force its way up into the world again, that he was in a broad valley, and the rim far off to either side was not the edge of the world but the craggy top of a range of hills. Anybody or anything could be tracking him, keeping just out of sight past the rim of the surrounding hills. He remembered the humanoid being with the crocodile's tail that had slipped around the side of the little shed. Could he have been following Jack all night, waiting for him to fall asleep?

The train *poop-pooped* through the lurid valley, moving with a suddenly maddening lack of speed.

He scanned the entire rim of hills about him, seeing nothing but new morning sunlight gild the upright rocks far above him. Jack turned around completely in the cab, fear and tension for the moment completely negating his tiredness. Richard threw one arm over his eyes, and slept on. Anything, anybody might have been keeping pace with them, waiting them out.

A slow, almost hidden movement off to his left made him catch his breath. A movement huge, slithery . . . Jack had a vision of a half-dozen of the crocodile-men crawling over the rim of the hills toward him, and he shielded his eyes with his hands and stared at the place where he thought he had seen them. The rocks were stained the same red as the powdery soil, and between them a deep trail wound its way over the crest of the hills through a cleft in the high-standing rocks. What was moving between two of the standing rocks was a shape not even vaguely human. It was a snake – at least, Jack thought it was . . . It had slipped into a concealed section of the trail, and Jack saw only a huge sleek round reptilian body disappearing behind the rocks. The skin of the creature seemed oddly ridged; burned, too – a suggestion, just before it disappeared, of ragged black holes in its side . . . Jack craned to see the place where it would emerge, and in seconds witnessed the wholly unnerving spectacle of the head of a giant worm, one-quarter buried in the thick red dust, swivelling toward him. It had hooded, filmy eyes, but it was the head of a worm.

Some other animal bolted from under a rock, heavy head and dragging body, and as the worm's big head darted toward it, Jack saw that the fleeing creature was one of the mutant dogs. The worm opened a mouth like the slot of a corner mailbox and neatly scooped up the frantic dog-thing. Jack clearly heard the snapping of bones. The dog's wailing ceased. The huge worm swallowed the dog as neatly as if it were a pill. Now, immediately before the worm's monstrous form, lay one of the black trails left by the fireballs, and as Jack watched, the long creature burrowed into the dust like a cruise ship sinking beneath the surface of the ocean. It apparently understood that the traces of the fireballs could do it damage and, wormlike, it would dig beneath them. Jack watched as the ugly thing completely disappeared into the red powder. And then cast his eyes uneasily over the whole of the long red slope dotted with pubic outpatches of the shiny yellow grass, wondering where it would surface again.

When he could be at least reasonably certain that the worm was not going to try to ingest the train, Jack went back to inspecting the ridge of rocky hills about him.

7

Before Richard woke up late that afternoon, Jack saw:

at least one unmistakable head peering over the rim of the hills; two more jouncing and deadly fireballs careering down at him; the headless skeleton of what he at first took to be a large rabbit, then sickeningly knew was a human baby, picked shining clean, lying beside the tracks and closely followed by:

the round babyish gleaming skull of the same baby, half-sunk in the loose soil. And he saw:

a pack of the big-headed dogs, more damaged than the others he had seen, pathetically come crawling after the train, drooling with hunger;

three board shacks, human habitations, propped up over the thick dust on stilts, promising that somewhere out in that stinking poisoned wilderness which was the Blasted Lands other people schemed and hunted for food;

a small leathery bird, featherless, with – this a real Territories touch – a bearded monkeylike face, and clearly delineated fingers protruding from the tips of its wings;

and worst of all (apart from what he *thought* he saw), two completely unrecognizable animals drinking from one of the black pools – animals with long teeth and human eyes and forequarters like those of pigs, hindquarters like those of big cats. Their faces were matted with hair. As the train pulled past the animals, Jack saw that the testicles of the male had swollen to the size of pillows and sagged onto the ground. What had made such monstrosities? Nuclear damage, Jack supposed, since scarcely anything else had such power to deform nature. The creatures, themselves poisoned from birth, snuffled up the equally poisoned water and snarled at the little train as it passed.

Our world could look like this someday, Jack thought. What a treat.

8

Then there were the things he *thought* he saw. His skin began to feel hot and itchy – he had already dumped the serape-like overgarment which had replaced Myles P. Kiger's coat onto the floor of the cab. Before noon he stripped off his homespun shirt, too. There was a terrible taste in his mouth, an acidic combination of rusty metal and rotten fruit. Sweat ran from his hairline into his eyes. He was so tired he began to dream standing up, eyes open and stinging with sweat. He saw great packs of the obscene dogs scuttling over the hills; he saw the reddish clouds overhead open up and reach down for Richard and himself with long flaming arms, devil's arms. When at last his eyes finally did close, he saw Morgan of Orris, twelve feet tall and dressed in black, shooting thunderbolts all around him, tearing the earth into great dusty spouts and craters.

Richard groaned and muttered, 'No, no, no.'

Morgan of Orris blew apart like a wisp of fog, and Jack's painful eyes flew open.

'Jack?' Richard said.

The red land ahead of the train was empty but for the blackened trails of the fireballs. Jack wiped his eyes and looked at Richard, feebly stretching. 'Yeah,' he said. 'How are you?'

Richard lay back against the stiff seat, blinking out of his drawn gray face.

'Sorry I asked,' Jack said.

'No,' Richard said, 'I'm better, really,' and Jack felt at least a portion of his tension leave him. 'I still have a headache, but I'm better.'

'You were making a lot of noise in your . . . um . . .' Jack said, unsure of how much reality his friend could stand.

'In my sleep. Yeah, I guess I probably did.' Richard's face worked, but for once Jack did not brace himself against a scream. 'I know I'm not dreaming now, Jack. And I know I don't have a brain tumor.'

'Do you know where you are?'

'On that train. That old man's train. In what he called the Blasted Lands.'

'Well, I'll be double-damned,' Jack said, smiling.

Richard blushed beneath his gray pallor.

'What brought this on?' Jack asked, still not quite sure that he could trust Richard's transformation.

'Well, I knew I wasn't dreaming,' Richard said, and his

cheeks grew even redder. 'I guess I . . . I guess it was just time to stop fighting it. If we're in the Territories, then we're in the Territories, no matter how impossible it is.' His eyes found Jack's, and the trace of humor in them startled his friend. 'You remember that gigantic hourglass back in The Depot?' When Jack nodded, Richard said, 'Well, that was it, really . . . when I saw that thing, I knew I wasn't just making everything up. Because I knew I *couldn't* have made up that thing. Couldn't. Just . . . couldn't. If I were going to invent a primitive clock, it'd have all sorts of wheels, and big pulleys . . . it wouldn't be so simple. So I didn't make it up. Therefore it was real. Therefore everything else was real, too.'

'Well, how do you feel now?' Jack asked. 'You've been asleep for a long time.'

'I'm still so tired I can hardly hold my head up. I don't feel very good in general, I'm afraid.'

'Richard, I have to ask you this. Is there some reason why you'd be afraid to go to California?'

Richard looked down and shook his head.

'Have you ever heard of a place called the black hotel?'

Richard continued to shake his head. He was not telling the truth, but as Jack recognized, he was facing as much of it as he could. Anything more – for Jack was suddenly sure that there was more, quite a lot of it – would have to wait. Until they actually reached the black hotel, maybe. Rushton's Twinner, Jason's Twinner: yes, together they would reach the Talisman's home and prison.

'Well, all right,' he said. 'Can you walk okay?'

'I guess so.'

'Good, because there's something I want to do now – since you're not dying of a brain tumor anymore, I mean. And I need your help.'

'What's that?' Richard asked. He wiped his face with a trembling hand.

'I want to open up one or two of those cases on the flatcar and see if we can get ourselves some weapons.'

'I hate and detest guns,' Richard said. 'You should, too. If nobody had any guns, your father—'

'Yeah, and if pigs had wings they'd fly,' Jack said. 'I'm pretty sure somebody's following us.'

'Well, maybe it's my dad,' Richard said in a hopeful voice.

Jack grunted, and eased the little gearshift out of the first slot. The train appreciably began to lose power. When it had coasted to a halt, Jack put the shift in neutral. 'Can you climb down okay, do you think?'

'Oh sure,' Richard said, and stood up quickly. His legs bowed out at the knees, and he sat down hard on the bench. His face now seemed even grayer than it had been, and moisture shone on his forehead and upper lip. 'Ah, maybe not,' he whispered.

'Just take it easy,' Jack said, and moved beside him and placed one hand on the crook of his elbow, the other on Richard's damp, warm forehead. 'Relax.' Richard closed his eyes briefly, then looked into Jack's own eyes with an expression of perfect trust.

'I tried to do it too fast,' he said. 'I'm all pins and needles from staying in the same position for so long.'

'Nice and easy, then,' Jack said, and helped a hissing Richard get to his feet.

'Hurts.'

'Only for a little while. I need your help, Richard.'

Richard experimentally stepped forward, and hissed in air again. 'Ooch.' He moved the other leg forward. Then he leaned forward slightly and slapped his palms against his thighs and calves. As Jack watched, Richard's face altered, but this time not with pain – a look of almost rubbery astonishment had printed itself there.

Jack followed the direction of his friend's eyes and saw one of the featherless, monkey-faced birds gliding past the front of the train.

'Yeah, there're a lot of funny things out here,' Jack said. 'I'm going to feel a lot better if we can find some guns under that tarp.'

'What do you suppose is on the other side of those hills?' Richard asked. 'More of the same?'

'No, I think there are more people over there,' Jack said. 'If you can call them people. I've caught somebody watching us twice.'

At the expression of quick panic which flooded into Richard's face, Jack said, 'I don't think it was anybody from your school. But it could be something just as bad – I'm not trying to scare you, buddy, but I've seen a little more of the Blasted Lands than you have.'

'The Blasted Lands,' Richard said dubiously. He squinted out at the red dusty valley with its scabrous patches of piss-colored grass. 'Oh – that tree – ah . . .'

'I know,' Jack said. 'You have to just sort of learn to ignore it.'

'Who on *earth* would create this kind of devastation?' Richard asked. 'This isn't natural, you know.'

'Maybe we'll find out someday.' Jack helped Richard leave the cab, so that both stood on a narrow running board that covered the tops of the wheels. 'Don't get down in that dust,' he warned Richard. 'We don't know how deep it is. I don't want to have to pull you out of it.'

Richard shuddered – but it may have been because he had just noticed out of the side of his eye another of the screaming, anguished trees. Together the two boys edged along the side of the stationary train until they could swing onto the coupling of the empty boxcar. From there a narrow metal ladder led to the roof of the car. On the boxcar's far end another ladder let them descend to the flatcar.

Jack pulled at the thick hairy rope, trying to remember how Anders had loosened it so easily. 'I think it's here,' Richard said, holding up a twisted loop like a hangman's noose. 'Jack?'

'Give it a try.'

Richard was not strong enough to loosen the knot by himself, but when Jack helped him tug on the protruding cord, the 'noose' smoothly disappeared, and the tarpaulin collapsed over the nest of boxes. Jack pulled the edge back over those closest – MACHINE PARTS – and over a smaller set of boxes Jack had not seen before, marked LENSES. 'There they are,' he said. 'I just wish we had a crowbar.' He glanced up toward the rim of the valley, and a tortured tree opened its mouth and silently yowled. Was that another head up there, peering over? It might have been one of the enormous worms, sliding toward them. 'Come on, let's try to push the top off one of these boxes,' he said, and Richard meekly came toward him.

After six mighty heaves against the top of one of the crates, Jack finally felt movement and heard the nails creak. Richard continued to strain at his side of the box. 'That's all right,' Jack said to him. Richard seemed even grayer and less healthy than he had before exerting himself. 'I'll get it, next push.' Richard stepped back and almost collapsed over one of the smaller boxes. He straightened himself and began to probe further under the loose tarpaulin.

Jack set himself before the tall box and clamped his jaw shut. He placed his hands on the corner of the lid. After taking in a long breath, he pushed up until his muscles began to shake. Just before he was going to have to ease up, the nails creaked again and began to slide out of the wood. Jack yelled 'AAAGH!' and heaved the top off the box.

Stacked inside the carton, slimy with grease, were half a dozen guns of a sort Jack had never seen before – like grease-guns metamorphosing into butterflies, half-mechanical, half-insectile. He pulled one out and looked at it more closely, trying to see if he could figure out how it worked. It was an automatic weapon, so it would need a clip. He bent down and used the barrel of the weapon to pry off the top of one of the LENSES cartons. As he had expected, in the second, smaller box stood a little pile of heavily greased clips packed in plastic beads.

'It's an Uzi,' Richard said behind him. 'Israeli machinegun. Pretty fashionable weapon, I gather. The terrorists' favorite toy.'

'How do you know that?' Jack asked, reaching in for another of the guns.

'I watch television. How do you think?'

Jack experimented with the clip, at first trying to fit it into the cavity upside-down, then finding the correct position. Next he found the safety and clicked it off, then on again.

'Those things are so damn ugly,' Richard said.

'You get one, too, so don't complain.' Jack took a second clip for Richard, and after a moment's consideration took all the clips out of the box, put them in his pockets, tossed two to Richard, who managed to catch them both, and slid the remaining clips into his haversack.

'Ugh,' Richard said.

'I guess it's insurance,' Jack said.

9

Richard collapsed on the seat as soon as they got back to the cab – the trips up and down the two ladders and inching along the narrow strip of metal above the wheels had taken nearly all of his energy. But he made room for Jack to sit down and watched with heavy-lidded eyes while his friend started the train rolling again. Jack picked up his serape and began massaging his gun with it.

'What are you doing?'

'Rubbing the grease off. You'd better do it, too, when I'm done.'

For the rest of the day the two boys sat in the open cab of the train, sweating, trying not to take into account the wailing trees, the corrupt stink of the passing landscape, their hunger. Jack noticed that a little garden of open sores had bloomed around Richard's mouth. Finally Jack took Richard's Uzi from his hand, wiped it free of grease, and pushed in the clip. Sweat burned saltily in cracks on his lips.

Jack closed his eyes. Maybe he had not seen those heads peering over the rim of the valley, maybe they were not followed after all. He heard the batteries sizzle and send off a big snapping spark, and felt Richard jump at it. An instant later he was asleep, dreaming of food.

10

When Richard shook Jack's shoulder, bringing him up out of a world in which he had been eating a pizza the size of a truck tire, the shadows were just beginning to spread across the valley, softening the agony of the wailing trees. Even they, bending low and spreading their hands across their faces, seemed beautiful in the low, receding light. The deep red dust shimmered and glowed. The shadows printed themselves out along it, almost perceptibly lengthening. The terrible yellow grass was melting toward an almost mellow orange. Fading red sunlight painted itself slantingly along the rocks at the valley's rim. 'I just thought you might want to see this,' Richard said. A few more small sores seemed to have appeared about his mouth. Richard grinned weakly. 'It seemed sort of special – the spectrum, I mean.'

Jack feared that Richard was going to launch into a scientific explanation of the color shift at sunset, but his friend was too tired or sick for physics. In silence the two boys watched the twilight deepen all the colors about them, turning the western sky into purple glory.

'You know what else you're carrying on this thing?' Richard asked.

'What else?' Jack asked. In truth, he hardly cared. It could be nothing good. He hoped he might live to see another sunset as rich as this one, as large with feeling.

'Plastic explosive. All wrapped up in two-pound packages – I think, two pounds, anyhow. You've got enough to blow up a whole city. If one of these guns goes off accidentally, or if someone else puts a bullet into those bags, this train is going to be nothing but a hole in the ground.'

'I won't if you won't,' Jack said. And let himself be

taken by the sunset – it seemed oddly premonitory, a dream of accomplishment, and led him into memories of all he had undergone since leaving the Alhambra Inn and Gardens. He saw his mother drinking tea in the little shop, suddenly a tired old woman; Speedy Parker sitting at the base of a tree; Wolf tending his herd; Smokey and Lori from Oatley's horrible Tap; all the hated faces from the Sunlight Home: Heck Bast, Sonny Singer, and the others. He missed Wolf with a particular and sharp poignancy, for the unfolding and deepening sunset summoned him up wholly, though Jack could not have explained why. He wished he could take Richard's hand. Then he thought, *Well, why not?* and moved his hand along the bench until he encountered his friend's rather grubby, clammy paw. He closed his fingers around it.

'I feel so sick,' Richard said. 'This isn't like – before. My stomach feels terrible, and my whole face is tingling.'

'I think you'll get better once we finally get out of this place,' Jack said. *But what proof do you have of that, doctor?* he wondered. *What proof do you have that you're not just poisoning him?* He had none. He consoled himself with his newly invented (newly discovered?) idea that Richard was an essential part of whatever was going to happen at the black hotel. He was going to need Richard Sloat, and not just because Richard Sloat could tell plastic explosive from bags of fertilizer.

Had Richard ever been to the black hotel before? Had he actually been in the Talisman's vicinity? He glanced over at his friend, who was breathing shallowly and laboriously. Richard's hand lay in his own like a cold waxen sculpture.

'I don't want this gun anymore,' Richard said, pushing if off his lap. 'The smell is making me sick.'

'Okay,' Jack said, taking it onto his own lap with his

free hand. One of the trees crept into his peripheral vision and howled soundlessly in torment. Soon the mutant dogs would begin foraging. Jack glanced up toward the hills to his left – Richard's side – and saw a manlike figure slipping through the rocks.

11

'Hey,' he said, almost not believing. Indifferent to his shock, the lurid sunset continued to beautify the unbeautifiable. 'Hey, Richard.'

'What? You sick, too?'

'I think I saw somebody up there. On your side.' He peered up at the tall rocks again, but saw no movement.

'I don't care,' Richard said.

'You'd better care. See how they're timing it? They want to get to us just when it's too dark for us to see them.'

Richard cracked his left eye open and made a half-hearted inspection. 'Don't see anybody.'

'Neither do I, now, but I'm glad we went back and got these guns. Sit up straight and pay attention, Richard, if you want to get out of here alive.'

'You're such a cornball. Jeez.' But Richard did pull himself up straight and open both his eyes. 'I really don't see anything up there, Jack. It's getting too dark. You probably imagined—'

'Hush,' Jack said. He thought he had seen another body easing itself between the rocks at the valley's top. 'There's two. I wonder if there'll be another one?'

'I wonder if there'll be anything at all,' Richard said. 'Why would anyone want to hurt us, anyhow? I mean, it's not—'

Jack turned his head and looked down the tracks ahead of the train. Something moved behind the trunk of one of the screaming trees. Something larger than a dog, Jack recorded.

'Uh-oh,' Jack said. 'I think another guy is up there waiting for us.' For a moment, fear castrated him – he could not think of what to do to protect himself from the three assailants. His stomach froze. He picked up the Uzi from his lap and looked at it dumbly, wondering if he really would be able to use this weapon. Could Blasted Lands hijackers have guns, too?

'Richard, I'm sorry,' he said, 'but this time I think the shit is really going to hit the fan, and I'm going to need your help.'

'What can I do?' Richard asked, his voice squeaky.

'Take your gun,' Jack said, handing it to him. 'And I think we ought to kneel down so we don't give them so much of a target.'

He got on his knees and Richard imitated him in a slow-moving, underwater fashion. From behind them came a long cry, from above them another. 'They know we saw them,' Richard said. 'But where are they?'

The question was almost immediately answered. Still visible in the dark purplish twilight, a man – or what looked like a man – burst out of cover and began running down the slope toward the train. Rags fluttered out behind him. He was screaming like an Indian and raising something in his hands. It appeared to be a flexible pole, and Jack was still trying to work out its function when he heard – more than saw – a narrow shape slice through the air beside his head. 'Holy mackerel! They've got bows and arrows!' he said.

Richard groaned, and Jack feared that he would vomit all over both of them.

'I have to shoot him,' he said.

Richard gulped and made some noise that wasn't quite a word.

'Oh, hell,' Jack said, and flicked off the safety on his Uzi. He raised his head and saw the ragged being behind him just loosing off another arrow. If the shot had been accurate, he would never have seen another thing, but the arrow whanged harmlessly into the side of the cab. Jack jerked up the Uzi and depressed the trigger.

He expected none of what happened. He had thought that the gun would remain still in his hands and obediently expel a few shells. Instead, the Uzi jumped in his hands like an animal, making a series of noises loud enough to damage his eardrums. The stink of powder burned in his nose. The ragged man behind the train threw out his arms, but in amazement, not because he had been wounded. Jack finally thought to take his finger off the trigger. He had no idea of how many shots he had just wasted, or how many bullets remained in the clip.

'Didja get him, didja get him?' Richard asked.

The man was now running up the side of the valley, huge flat feet flapping. Then Jack saw that they were not feet – the man was walking on huge platelike constructions, the Blasted Lands equivalent of snowshoes. He was trying to make it to one of the trees for cover.

He raised the Uzi with both hands and sighted down the short barrel. Then he gently squeezed the trigger. The gun bucked in his hands, but less than the first time. Bullets sprayed out in a wide arc, and at least one of them found its intended target, for the man lurched over sideways as though a truck had just smacked into him. His feet flew out of the snowshoes.

'Give me your gun,' Jack said, and took the second Uzi from Richard. Still kneeling, he fired half a clip into the shadowy dark in front of the train and hoped he had killed the creature waiting up there.

Another arrow rattled against the train, and another thunked solidly into the side of the boxcar.

Richard was shaking and crying in the bottom of the cab. 'Load mine,' Jack said, and jammed a clip from his pocket under Richard's nose. He peered up the side of the valley for the second attacker. In less than a minute it would be too dark to see anything beneath the rim of the valley.

'I see him,' Richard shouted. 'I saw him – right there!' He pointed toward a shadow moving silently, urgently, among the rocks, and Jack spent the rest of the second Uzi's clip noisily blasting at it. When he was done, Richard took the machine-gun from him and placed the other in his hands.

'Nize boyz, goot boyz,' came a voice from the right side – how far ahead of them it was impossible to tell. 'You stop now, I stop now, too, geddit? All done now, dis bizness. You nize boys, maybe you zell me dat gun. You kill plenty goot dat way, I zee.'

'Jack,' Richard whispered frantically, warning him.

'Throw away the bow and arrows,' Jack yelled, still crouching beside Richard.

'Jack, you can't!' Richard whispered.

'I t'row dem 'way now,' the voice came, still ahead of them. Something light puffed into the dust. 'You boyz stop going, zell me gun, geddit?'

'Okay,' Jack said. 'Come up here where we can see you.'

'Geddit,' the voice said.

Jack pulled back on the gearshift, letting the train coast to a halt. 'When I holler,' he whispered to Richard, 'jam it forward as fast as you can, okay?'

'Oh, Jesus,' Richard breathed.

Jack checked that the safety was off on the gun Richard had just given him. A trickle of sweat ran from his forehead directly into his right eye.

'All goot now, yaz,' the voice said. 'Boyz can siddup, yaz. Siddup, boys.'

Way-gup, way-gup, pleeze, pleeze.

The train coasted toward the speaker. 'Put your hands on the shift,' Jack whispered. 'It's coming soon.'

Richard's trembling hand, looking too small and child-like to accomplish anything even slightly important, touched the gear lever.

Jack had a sudden, vivid memory of old Anders kneeling before him on a rippling wooden floor, asking, *But will you be safe, my Lord?* He had answered flippantly, hardly taking the question seriously. What were the Blasted Lands to a boy who had humped out kegs for Smokey Updike?

Now he was a lot more afraid that he was going to soil his pants than that Richard was going to lose his lunch all over the Territories version of Myles P. Kiger's loden coat.

A shout of laughter erupted in the darkness beside the cab, and Jack pulled himself upright, bringing up the gun, and yelled just as a heavy body hit the side of the cab and clung there. Richard shoved the gearshift forward, and the train jerked forward.

A naked hairy arm clamped itself on the side of the cab. *So much for the wild west*, Jack thought, and then the man's entire trunk reared up over them. Richard screeched, and Jack very nearly did evacuate his bowels into his underwear.

The face was nearly all teeth – it was a face as instinctively evil as that of a rattler baring its fangs, and a drop of what Jack as instinctively assumed to be venom fell off one of the long, curved teeth. Except for the tiny nose, the creature looming over the boys looked very like a man with the head of a snake. In one webbed hand he raised a knife. Jack squeezed off an aimless, panicky shot.

Then the creature altered and wavered back for a moment, and it took Jack a fraction of a second to see that the webbed hand and the knife were gone. The creature swung forward a bloody stump and left a smear of red on Jack's shirt. Jack's mind conveniently left him, and his fingers were able to point the Uzi straight at the creature's chest and pull the trigger back.

A great hole opened redly in the middle of the mottled chest, and the dripping teeth snapped together. Jack kept the trigger depressed, and the Uzi raised its barrel by itself and destroyed the creature's head in a second or two of total carnage. Then it was gone. Only a large bloodstain on the side of the cab, and the smear of blood on Jack's shirt, showed that the two boys had not dreamed the entire encounter.

'Watch out!' Richard yelled.

'I got him,' Jack breathed.

'Where'd he go?'

'He fell off,' Jack said. 'He's dead.'

'You shot his *hand* off,' Richard whispered. 'How'd you do that?'

Jack held up his hands before him and saw how they shook. The stink of gunpowder encased them. 'I just sort of imitated someone with good aim.' He put his hands down and licked his lips.

Twelve hours later, as the sun came up again over the Blasted Lands, neither boy had slept – they had spent the entire night as rigid as soldiers, holding their guns in their laps and straining to hear the smallest of noises. Remembering how much ammunition the train was carrying, every now and then Jack randomly aimed a few rounds at the lip of the valley. And that second entire day, if there were people or monsters in this far sector of the Blasted Lands, they let the boys pass unmolested. Which could mean, Jack tiredly thought, that they knew about the guns. Or that out here, so near to the western shore, nobody wanted to mess with Morgan's train. He said none of this to Richard, whose eyes were filmy and unfocussed, and who seemed feverish much of the time.

12

By evening of that day, Jack began to smell saltwater in the acrid air.

CHAPTER THIRTY-SIX
JACK AND RICHARD GO TO WAR

1

The sunset that night was wider – the land had begun to open out again as they approached the ocean – but not so spectacular. Jack stopped the train at the top of an eroded hill and climbed back to the flatcar again. He poked about for nearly an hour – until the sullen colors had faded from the sky and a quarter moon had risen in the east – and brought back six boxes, all marked LENSES.

'Open those,' he told Richard. 'Get a count. You're appointed Keeper of the Clips.'

'Marvellous,' Richard said in a wan voice. 'I knew I was getting all that education for something.'

Jack went back to the flatcar again and pried up the lid of one of the crates marked MACHINE PARTS. While he was doing this he heard a harsh, hoarse cry somewhere off in the darkness, followed by a shrill scream of pain.

'Jack? Jack, you back there?'

'Right here!' Jack called. He thought it very unwise for the two of them to be yelling back and forth like a couple of washerwomen over a back fence, but Richard's voice suggested that he was close to panicking.

'You coming back pretty soon?'

'Be right there!' Jack called, levering faster and harder with the Uzi's barrel. They were leaving the Blasted Lands behind, but Jack still didn't want to stand at a stop for too long. It would have been simpler if he could have just carried the box of machine guns back to the engine, but it was too heavy.

They ain't heavy, they're my Uzis, Jack thought, and giggled a little in the dark.

'*Jack?*' Richard's voice was high-pitched, frantic.

'Hold your water, chum,' he said.

'Don't call me chum,' Richard said.

Nails shrieked out of the crate's lid, and it came up enough for Jack to be able to pull it off. He grabbed two of the grease-guns and was starting back when he saw another box – it was about the size of a portable-TV carton. A fold of the tarp had covered it previously.

Jack went skittering across the top of the boxcar under the faint moonlight, feeling the breeze blow into his face. It was clean – no taint of rotted perfume, no feeling of corruption, just clean dampness and the unmistakable scent of salt.

'What were you doing?' Richard scolded. 'Jack, we *have* guns! And we *have* bullets! Why do you want to go back and get more? Something could have climbed up here while you were playing around!'

'More guns because machine-guns have a tendency to overheat,' Jack said. 'More bullets because we may have to shoot a lot. *I* watch TV too, you see.' He started back toward the flatcar again. He wanted to see what was in that square box.

Richard grabbed him. Panic turned his hand into a birdlike talon.

'Richard, it's going to be all right—'

'Something might grab you off!'

'I think we're almost out of the Bl—'

'Something might grab *me* off! Jack, don't leave me *alone*!'

Richard burst into tears. He did not turn away from Jack or put his hands to his face; he only stood there, his face twisted, his eyes spouting tears. He looked cruelly naked to Jack just then. Jack folded him into his arms and held him.

'If something gets you and kills you, what happens to me?' Richard sobbed. 'How would I ever, ever, get out of this place?'

I don't know, Jack thought. *I really don't know*.

2

So Richard came with him on Jack's last trip to the travelling ammo dump on the flatcar. This meant boosting him up the ladder and then supporting him along the top of the boxcar and helping him carefully down, as one might help a crippled old lady across a street. Rational Richard was making a mental comeback – but physically he was growing steadily worse.

Although preservative grease was bleeding out between its boards, the square box was marked FRUIT. Nor was that completely inaccurate, Jack discovered when they got it open. The box was full of pineapples. The exploding kind.

'Holy Hannah,' Richard whispered.

'Whoever *she* is,' Jack agreed. 'Help me. I think we can each get four or five down our shirts.'

'Why do you want all this firepower?' Richard asked. 'Are you expecting to fight an army?'

'Something like that.'

3

Richard looked up into the sky as he and Jack were recrossing the top of the boxcar, and a wave of faintness overtook him. Richard tottered and Jack had to grab him to keep him from toppling over the side. He had realized that he could recognize constellations of neither the Northern Hemisphere nor the Southern. Those were alien stars up there . . . but there *were* patterns, and somewhere in this unknown, unbelievable world, sailors might be navigating by them. It was that thought which brought the reality of all this home to Richard – brought it home with a final, undeniable thud.

Then Jack's voice was calling him back from far away: 'Hey, Richie! Jason! You almost fell over the side!'

Finally they were in the cab again.

Jack pushed the lever into the forward gear, pressed down on the accelerator bar, and Morgan of Orris's over-sized flashlight started to move forward again. Jack glanced down at the floor of the cab: four Uzi machine-guns, almost twenty piles of clips, ten to a pile, and ten hand grenades with pull-pins that looked like the pop-tops of beercans.

'If we haven't got enough stuff now,' Jack said, 'we might as well forget it.'

'What are you expecting, Jack?'

Jack only shook his head.

'Guess you must think I'm a real jerk, huh?' Richard asked.

Jack grinned. 'Always have, chum.'

'Don't call me chum!'

'Chum-chum-*chum*!'

This time the old joke raised a small smile. Not much,

and it rather highlighted the growing line of lip-blisters on Richard's mouth . . . but better than nothing.

'Will you be okay if I go back to sleep?' Richard asked, brushing machine-gun clips aside and settling in a corner of the cab with Jack's serape over him. 'All that climbing and carrying . . . I think I really must be sick because I feel really bushed.'

'I'll be fine,' Jack said. Indeed, he seemed to be getting a second wind. He supposed he would need it before long.

'I can smell the ocean,' Richard said, and in his voice Jack heard an amazing mixture of love, loathing, nostalgia, and fear. Richard's eyes slipped closed.

Jack pushed the accelerator bar all the way down. His feeling that the end – some sort of end – was now close had never been stronger.

4

The last mean and miserable vestiges of the Blasted Lands were gone before the moon set. The grain had reappeared. It was coarser here than it had been in Ellis-Breaks, but it still radiated a feeling of cleanness and health. Jack heard the faint calling of birds which sounded like gulls. It was an inexpressibly lonely sound, in these great open rolling fields which smelled faintly of fruit and more pervasively of ocean salt.

After midnight the train began to hum through stands of trees – most of them were evergreens, and their piney scent, mixed with the salty tang in the air, seemed to cement the connection between this place he was coming to and the place from which he had set out. He and his mother had never spent a great deal of time in northern

California – perhaps because Bloat vacationed there often – but he remembered Lily's telling him that the land around Mendocino and Sausalito looked very much like New England, right down to the salt-boxes and Cape Cods. Film companies in need of New England settings usually just went upstate rather than travelling all the way across the country, and most audiences never knew the difference.

This is how it should be. In a weird way, I'm coming back to the place I left behind.

Richard: *Are you expecting to fight an army?*

He was glad Richard had gone to sleep, so he wouldn't have to answer that question – at least, not yet.

Anders: *Devil-things. For the bad Wolfs. To take to the black hotel.*

The devil-things were Uzi machine-guns, plastic explosive, grenades. The devil-things were here. The bad Wolfs were not. The boxcar, however, was empty, and Jack found that fact terribly persuasive.

Here's a story for you, Richie-boy, and I'm very glad you're asleep so I don't have to tell it to you. Morgan knows I'm coming and he's planning a surprise party. Only it's werewolves instead of naked girls who are going to jump out of the cake, and they're supposed to have Uzi machine-guns and grenades as party-favors. Well, we sort of hijacked his train, and we're running ten or twelve hours ahead of schedule, but if we're heading into an encampment full of Wolfs waiting to catch the Territories choo-choo – and I think that's just what we're doing – we're going to need all the surprise we can get.

Jack ran a hand up the side of his face.

It would be easier to stop the train well away from wherever Morgan's hit-squad was, and make a big circle around the encampment. Easier and safer, too.

But that would leave the bad Wolfs around, Richie, can you dig it?

He looked down at the arsenal on the floor of the cab and wondered if he could really be planning a commando raid on Morgan's Wolf Brigade. Some commandos. Good old Jack Sawyer, King of the Vagabond Dishwashers, and His Comatose Sidekick, Richard. Jack wondered if he had gone crazy. He supposed he had, because that was exactly what he was planning – it would be the last thing any of them would expect . . . and there had been too much, too much, too goddam much. He had been whipped; Wolf had been killed. They had destroyed Richard's school and most of Richard's sanity, and, for all he knew, Morgan Sloat was back in New Hampshire, harrying his mother.

Crazy or not, payback time had come.

Jack bent over, picked up one of the loaded Uzis, and held it over his arm as the tracks unrolled in front of him and the smell of salt grew steadily stronger.

5

During the small hours of the morning Jack slept awhile, leaning against the accelerator bar. It would not have comforted him much to know such a device was called a dead-man's switch. When dawn came, it was Richard who woke him up.

'Something up ahead.'

Before looking at that, Jack took a good look at Richard. He had hoped that Richard would look better in daylight, but not even the cosmetic of dawn could disguise the fact that Richard was sick. The color of the new day had changed the dominant color in his skin-tone from gray to yellow . . . that was all.

'Hey! Train! Hello you big fuckin train!' This shout was guttural, little more than an animal roar. Jack looked forward again.

They were closing in on a narrow little pillbox of a building.

Standing outside the guardhouse was a Wolf – but any resemblance to Jack's Wolf ended with the flaring orange eyes. This Wolf's head looked dreadfully flattened, as if a great hand had scythed off the curve of skull at the top. His face seemed to jut over his underslung jaw like a boulder teetering over a long drop. Even the present surprised joy on that face could not conceal its thick, brutal stupidity. Braided pigtails of hair hung from his cheeks. A scar in the shape of an X rode his forehead.

The Wolf was wearing something like a mercenary's uniform – or what he imagined a mercenary's uniform would look like. Baggy green pants were bloused out over black boots – but the toes of the boots had been cut off, Jack saw, to allow the Wolf's long-nailed, hairy toes to protrude.

'Train!' he bark-growled as the engine closed the last fifty yards. He began to jump up and down, grinning savagely. He was snapping his fingers like Cab Calloway. Foam flew from his jaws in unlovely clots. *'Train! Train! Fuckin train RIGHT HERE AND NOW!'* His mouth yawned open in a great and alarming grin, showing a mouthful of broken yellow spears. '*You guys some kinda fuckin early, okay, okay!*'

'Jack, what is it?' Richard asked. His hand was clutching Jack's shoulder with panicky tightness, but to his credit, his voice was fairly even.

'It's a Wolf. One of Morgan's.'

There, Jack, you said his name. Asshole!

But there was no time to worry about that now. They

were coming abreast of the guardhouse, and the Wolf obviously meant to swing aboard. As Jack watched, he cut a clumsy caper in the dust, cut-off boots thumping. He had a knife in the leather belt he wore across his naked chest like a bandoleer, but no gun.

Jack flicked the control on the Uzi to single-fire.

'Morgan? Who's Morgan? *Which* Morgan?'

'Not now,' Jack said.

His concentration narrowed down to a fine point – the Wolf. He manufactured a big, plastic grin for his benefit, holding the Uzi down and well out of sight.

'Anders-train! All-fuckin-right! Here and now!'

A handle like a big staple stuck off from the right side of the engine, above a wide step like a running board. Grinning wildly, drizzling foam over his chin and obviously insane, the Wolf grabbed the handle and leaped lightly up onto the step.

'Hey, where's the old man? Wolf! Where's—'

Jack raised the Uzi and put a bullet into the Wolf's left eye.

The glaring orange light puffed out like a candle-flame in a strong gust of wind. The Wolf fell backward off the step like a man doing a rather stupid dive. He thudded loosely on the ground.

'Jack!' Richard pulled him around. His face looked almost as wild as the Wolf's face had been – only it was terror, not joy, that distorted it. *'Did you mean my father? Is my father involved in this?'*

'Richard, do you trust me?'

'Yes, but—'

'Then let it go. *Let it go*. This is not the time.'

'But—'

'Get a gun.'

'Jack—'

'Richard, *get a gun!*'

Richard bent over and got one of the Uzis. 'I hate guns,' he said again.

'Yeah, I know. I'm not particularly keen on them myself, Richie-boy. But it's payback time.'

6

The tracks were now approaching a high stockade wall. From behind it came grunts and yells, cheers, rhythmic clapping, the sound of bootheels punching down on bare earth in steady rhythms. There were other, less identifiable sounds as well, but all of them fell into a vague set for Jack – *military training operation*. The area between the guardhouse and the approaching stockade wall was half a mile wide, and with all this other stuff going on, Jack doubted that anyone had heard his single shot. The train, being electric, was almost silent. The advantage of surprise should still be on their side.

The tracks disappeared beneath a closed double gate in the side of the stockade wall. Jack could see chinks of daylight between the rough-peeled logs.

'Jack, you better slow down.' They were now a hundred and fifty yards from the gate. From behind it, bellowing voices chanted, '*Sound-HOFF! Hun-too! Hree-FO! Sound-HOFF!*' Jack thought again of H. G. Wells's manimals and shivered.

'No way, chum. We're through the gate. You got just about time to do the Fish Cheer.'

'Jack, you're crazy!'

'I know.'

A hundred yards. The batteries hummed. A blue spark jumped, sizzling. Bare earth flowed past them on either side. *No grain here,* Jack thought. *If Noël Coward had written a play about Morgan Sloat, I guess he would have called it* Blight Spirit.

'Jack, what if this creepy little train jumps its tracks?'

'Well, it might, I guess,' Jack said.

'Or what if it breaks through the gate and the tracks just *end*?'

'That'd be one on us, wouldn't it?'

Fifty yards.

'Jack, you really have lost your mind, haven't you?'

'I guess so. Take your gun off safety, Richard.'

Richard flicked the safety.

Thuds . . . grunts . . . marching men . . . the creak of leather . . . yells . . . an inhuman, laughing shriek that made Richard cringe. And yet Jack saw a clear resolution in Richard's face that made Jack grin with pride. *He means to stick by me – old Rational Richard or not, he really means to stick by me.*

Twenty-five yards.

Shrieks . . . squeals . . . shouted commands . . . and a thick, reptilian cry – *Groooo-OOOO!* – that made the hair stand up on the back of Jack's neck.

'If we get out of this,' Jack said, 'I'll buy you a chili-dog at Dairy Queen.'

'*Barf me out!*' Richard yelled, and, incredibly, he began to laugh. In that instant the unhealthy yellow seemed to fade a bit from his face.

Five yards – and the peeled posts which made up the gate looked solid, yes, very solid, and Jack just had time to wonder if he hadn't made a great big fat mistake.

'Get down, chum!'

'Don't call m—'

The train hit the stockade gate, throwing them both forward.

7

The gate was really quite strong, and in addition it was double-barred across the inside with two large logs. Morgan's train was not terribly big, and the batteries were nearly flat after its long run across the Blasted Lands. The collision surely would have derailed it, and both boys might well have been killed in the wreck, but the gate had an Achilles' heel. New hinges, forged according to modern American processes, were on order. They had not yet arrived, however, and the old iron hinges snapped when the engine hit the gate.

The train came rolling into the stockade at twenty-five miles an hour, pushing the amputated gate in front of it. An obstacle course had been built around the stockade's perimeter, and the gate, acting like a snowplow, began shoving makeshift wooden hurdles in front of it, turning them, rolling them, snapping them into splinters.

It also struck a Wolf who had been doing punishment laps. His feet disappeared under the bottom of the moving gate and were chewed off, customized boots and all. Shrieking and growling, his Change beginning, the Wolf began to claw-climb his way up the gate with fingernails which were growing rapidly to the length and sharpness of a telephone lineman's spikes. The gate was now forty feet inside the stockade. Amazingly, he got almost to the top before Jack dropped the gear-lever into neutral. The train stopped. The gate fell over, puffing up big dust and crushing the unfortunate Wolf beneath it. Underneath the last car of the train, the Wolf's severed feet continued to grow hair, and would for several more minutes.

The situation inside the camp was better than Jack had dared hope. The place apparently woke up early, as military installations have a way of doing, and most of the troops seemed to be out, going through a bizarre menu of drills and body-building exercises.

'*On the right!*' he shouted at Richard.

'*Do what?*' Richard shouted back.

Jack opened his mouth and cried out: for Uncle Tommy Woodbine, run down in the street; for an unknown carter, whipped to death in a muddy courtyard; for Ferd Janklow; for Wolf, dead in Sunlight Gardener's filthy office; for his mother; but most of all, he discovered, for Queen Laura DeLoessian, who was also his mother, and for the crime that was being carried out on the body of the Territories. He cried out as Jason, and his voice was thunder.

'*TEAR THEM UP!*' Jack Sawyer/Jason DeLoessian bellowed, and opened fire on the left.

8

There was a rough parade ground on Jack's side, a long log building on Richard's. The log building looked like the bunkhouse in a Roy Rogers movie, but Richard guessed that it was a barracks. In fact, this whole place looked more familiar to Richard than anything he had seen so far in this weird world Jack had taken him into. He had seen places like it on the TV news. CIA-supported rebels training for takeovers of South and Central American countries trained in places like this. Only, the training camps were usually in

Florida, and those weren't *cubanos* pouring out of the barracks – Richard didn't know *what* they were.

Some of them looked a bit like medieval paintings of devils and satyrs. Some looked like degenerate human beings – cave-people, almost. And one of the things lurching into the early-morning sunlight had scaly skin and nictitating eyelids . . . it looked to Richard Sloat like an alligator that was somehow walking upright. As he looked, the thing lifted its snout and uttered that cry he and Jack had heard earlier: *Grooo-OOOOO!* He just had time to see that most of these hellish creatures looked totally bewildered, and then Jack's Uzi split the world with thunder.

On Jack's side, roughly two dozen Wolfs had been doing callies on the parade ground. Like the guardhouse Wolf, most wore green fatigue pants, boots with cut-off toes, and bandoleer belts. Like the guard, they looked stupid, flat-headed, and essentially evil.

They had paused in the middle of a spastic set of jumping jacks to watch the train come roaring in, the gate and the unfortunate fellow who had been running laps at the wrong place and time plastered to the front. At Jack's cry they began to move, but by then they were too late.

Most of Morgan's carefully culled Wolf Brigade, hand-picked over a period of five years for their strength and brutality, their fear of and loyalty to Morgan, were wiped out in one spitting, raking burst of the machine-gun in Jack's hands. They went stumbling and reeling backward, chests blown open, heads bleeding. There were growls of bewildered anger and howls of pain . . . but not many. Most of them simply died.

Jack popped the clip, grabbed another one, slammed it in. On the left side of the parade ground, four of the Wolfs had escaped; in the center two more had dropped below the line of fire. Both of these had been wounded but now both were coming at him, long-nailed toes digging divots in the packed dust, faces sprouting hair, eyes flaring. As they ran at the engine, Jack saw fangs grow out of their mouths and push through fresh, wiry hair growing from their chins.

He pulled the trigger on the Uzi, now holding the hot barrel down only with an effort; the heavy recoil was trying to force the muzzle up. Both of the attacking Wolfs were thrown back so violently that they flipped through the air head-for-heels like acrobats. The other four Wolfs did not pause; they headed for the place where the gate had been two minutes before.

The assorted creatures which had spilled out of the bunkhouse-style barracks building seemed to be finally getting the idea that, although the newcomers were driving Morgan's train, they were a good deal less than friendly. There was no concentrated charge, but they began to move forward in a muttering clot. Richard laid the Uzi's barrel on the chest-high side of the engine cab and opened fire. The slugs tore them open, drove them backward. Two of the things which looked like goats dropped to hands and knees – or hooves – and scurried back inside. Richard saw three others spin and drop under the force of the slugs. A joy so savage that it made him feel faint swept through him.

Bullets also tore open the whitish-green belly of the alligatorthing, and a blackish fluid – ichor, not blood – began to pour out of it. It fell backward, but its tail seemed to cushion it. It sprang back up and leaped at Richard's side of the train. It uttered its rough, powerful cry again . . . and this time it seemed to Richard that there was something hideously feminine in that cry.

He pulled the trigger of the Uzi. Nothing happened. The clip was spent.

The alligator-thing ran with slow, clumsy, thudding determination. Its eyes sparkled with murderous fury . . . and intelligence. The vestiges of breasts bounced on its scaly chest.

He bent, groped, without taking his eyes off the were-alligator, and found one of the grenades.

Seabrook Island, Richard thought dreamily. *Jack calls this place the Territories, but it's really Seabrook Island, and there is no need to be afraid, really no need; this is all a dream and if that thing's scaly claws settle around my neck I will surely wake up, and even if it's not all a dream, Jack will save me somehow – I know he will, I know it; because over here Jack is some kind of god.*

He pulled the pin on the grenade, restrained the strong urge he felt to simply chuck it in a panicky frenzy, and lobbed it gently, underhand. *'Jack, get down!'*

Jack dropped below the level of the engine cab's sides at once, without looking. Richard did, too, but not before he had seen an incredible, blackly comic thing: the alligator-creature had caught the grenade . . . and was trying to eat it.

The explosion was not the dull crump Richard had expected but a loud, braying roar that drilled into his ears, hurting them badly. He heard a splash, as if someone had thrown a bucket of water against his side of the train.

He looked up and saw that the engine, boxcar and flatcar were covered with hot guts, black blood, and shreds of the alligator-creature's flesh. The entire front of the barracks building had been blown away. Much of the splintered rubble was bloody. In the midst of it he saw a hairy foot in a boot with a cut-off toe.

The jackstraw blowdown of logs was thrown aside as he watched, and two of the goatlike creatures began to pull themselves out. Richard bent, found a fresh clip, and slammed it into his gun. It was getting hot, just as Jack had said it would.

Whoopee! Richard thought faintly, and opened fire again.

9

When Jack popped up after the grenade explosion, he saw that the four Wolfs who had escaped his first two fusillades were just running through the hole where the gate had been. They were howling with terror. They were running side by side, and Jack had a clear shot of them. He raised the Uzi – then lowered it again, knowing he would see them later, probably at the black hotel, knowing he was a fool . . . but, fool or not, he was unable to just let them have it in the back.

Now a high, womanish shrieking began from behind the barracks. *'Get out there! Get out there, I say! Move! Move!'* There was the whistling crack of a whip.

Jack knew that sound, and he knew that voice. He had been wrapped up in a strait-jacket when he had last heard it. Jack would have known that voice anywhere.

– If his retarded friend shows up, shoot him.

Well, you managed that, but maybe now it's payback time – and maybe, from the way your voice sounds, you know it.

'Get them, what's the matter with you cowards? Get them, do I have to show you how to do everything? Follow us, follow us!'

Three creatures came from behind what remained of

the barracks, and only one of them was clearly human – Osmond. He carried his whip in one hand, a Sten gun in the other. He wore a red cloak and black boots and white silk pants with wide, flowing legs. They were splattered with fresh blood. To his left was a shaggy goat-creature wearing jeans and Western-style boots. This creature and Jack looked at each other and shared a moment of complete recognition. It was the dreadful barroom cowboy from the Oatley Tap. It was Randolph Scott. It was Elroy. It grinned at Jack; its long tongue snaked out and lapped its wide upper lip.

'Get him!' Osmond screamed at Elroy.

Jack tried to lift the Uzi, but it suddenly seemed very heavy in his arms. Osmond was bad, the reappearance of Elroy was worse, but the thing between the two of them was a nightmare. It was the Territories version of Reuel Gardener, of course; the son of Osmond, the son of Sunlight. And it did indeed look a bit like a child – a child as drawn by a bright kindergarten student with a cruel turn of mind.

It was curdy-white and skinny; one of its arms ended in a wormy tentacle that somehow reminded Jack of Osmond's whip. Its eyes, one of them adrift, were on different levels. Fat red sores covered its cheeks.

Some of it's radiation sickness . . . Jason, I think Osmond's boy might have gotten a little too close to one of those fireballs . . . but the rest of it . . . Jason . . . Jesus . . . what was its mother? In the name of all the worlds, WHAT WAS ITS MOTHER?

'Get the Pretender!' Osmond was shrieking. 'Save Morgan's son but get the Pretender! Get the false Jason! Get out here, you cowards! They're out of bullets!'

Roars, bellows. In a moment, Jack knew, a fresh contingent of Wolfs, supported by Assorted Geeks and Freaks, was going to appear from the back end of the long barracks, where they would have been shielded from the explosion, where they had probably been cowering with their heads down, and where they would have remained . . . except for Osmond.

'Should have stayed off the road, little chicken,' Elroy grunted, and ran at the train. His tail was swishing through the air. Reuel Gardener – or whatever Reuel was in this world – made a thick mewling sound and attempted to follow. Osmond reached out and hauled him back; his fingers, Jack saw, appeared to slide right into the monster-boy's slat-like repulsive neck.

Then he raised the Uzi and fired an entire clip, point-blank, into Elroy's face. It tore the goat-thing's entire head off, and yet Elroy, headless, continued to climb for a moment, and one of his hands, the fingers melted together in two clumps to make a parody of a cloven hoof, pawed blindly for Jack's head before it tumbled backward.

Jack stared at it, stunned – he had dreamed that final nightmarish confrontation at the Oatley Tap over and over again, trying to stumble away from the monster through what seemed to be a dark jungle filled with bedsprings and broken glass. Now here was that creature, and he had somehow killed it. It was hard to get his mind around the fact. It was as if he had killed childhood's bogeyman.

Richard was screaming – and his machine-gun roared, nearly deafening Jack.

'It's Reuel! Oh Jack oh my God oh Jason it's Reuel, it's Reuel—'

The Uzi in Richard's hands coughed out another short burst before falling silent, its clip spent. Reuel shook free of his father. He lurched and hopped toward the train, mewling. His upper lip curled back, revealing long teeth that looked false and flimsy, like the wax teeth children don at Halloween.

Richard's final burst took him in the chest and neck, punching holes in the brown kilt-*cum*-jumper he wore, ripping open flesh in long, ragged furrows. Sluggish rills of dark blood flowed from these wounds, but no more. Reuel might once have been human – Jack supposed it was just possible. If so, he was not human now, the bullets did not even slow him down. The thing which leaped clumsily over Elroy's body was a demon. It smelled like a wet toadstool.

Something was growing warm against Jack's leg. Just warm at first . . . then hot. What was it? Felt like he had a teakettle in his pocket. But he didn't have time to think. Things were unfolding in front of him. In Technicolor.

Richard dropped his Uzi and staggered back, clapping his hands to his face. His horrified eyes stared out at the Reuel-thing through the bars of his fingers.

'Don't let him get me, Jack! Don't let him get meeeee . . .'

Reuel bubbled and mewled. His hands slapped against the side of the engine and the sound was like large fins slapping down on thick mud.

Jack saw there were indeed thick, yellowish webs between his fingers.

'*Come back!*' Osmond was yelling at his son, and the fear in his voice was unmistakable. '*Come back, he's bad, he'll hurt you, all boys are bad, it's axiomatic, come back, come back!*'

Reuel burbled and grunted enthusiastically. He pulled himself up and Richard screamed insanely, backing into the far corner of the cab.

'DON'T LET HIM GET MEEEEEEE—'

More Wolfs, more strange freaks charging around the corner. One of them, a creature with curly ram's horns jutting from the sides of its head and wearing only a pair of patched L'il Abner britches, fell down and was trampled by the others.

Heat against Jack's leg in a circle.

Reuel, now throwing one reedy leg over the side of the cab. It was slobbering, reaching for him, and the leg was writhing, it wasn't a leg at all, it was a tentacle. Jack raised the Uzi and fired.

Half of the Reuel-thing's face sheered away like pudding. A flood of worms began to fall out of what was left.

Reuel was still coming.

Reaching for him with those webbed fingers.

Richard's shrieks, Osmond's shrieks merging, melting together into one.

Heat like a branding iron against his leg and suddenly he knew what it was, even as Reuel's hands squashed down on his shoulders he knew – it was the coin Captain Farren had given him, the coin Anders had refused to take.

He drove his hand into his pocket. The coin was like a chunk of ore in his hand – he made a fist around it, and felt power ram through him in big volts. Reuel felt it, too. His triumphant slobberings and grunts became mewlings of fear. He tried to back away, his one remaining eye rolling wildly.

Jack brought the coin out. It glowed red-hot in his hand. He felt the heat clearly – but it was not burning him.

The profile of the Queen glowed like the sun.

'*In her name, you filthy, aborted thing!*' Jack shouted. '*Get you off the skin of this world!*' He opened his fist and slammed his hand into Reuel's forehead.

Reuel and his father shrieked in harmony – Osmond

a tenor-verging-on-soprano, Reuel a buzzing, insectile bass. The coin slid into Reuel's forehead like the tip of a hot poker into a tub of butter. A vile dark fluid, the color of overbrewed tea, ran out of Reuel's head and over Jack's wrist. The fluid was hot. There were tiny worms in it. They twisted and writhed on Jack's skin. He felt them biting. Nevertheless, he pressed the first two fingers of his right hand harder, driving the coin farther into the monster's head.

'Get you off the skin of this world, vileness! In the name of the Queen and in the name of her son, get you off the skin of this world!'

It shrieked and wailed; Osmond shrieked and wailed with it. The reinforcements had stopped and were milling behind Osmond, their faces full of superstitious terror. To them Jack seemed to have grown; he seemed to be giving off a bright light.

Reuel jerked. Uttered one more bubbling screech. The black stuff running out of his head turned yellow. A final worm, long and thickly white, wriggled out of the hole the coin had made. It fell to the floor of the engine compartment. Jack stepped on it. It broke open under his heel and spattered. Reuel fell in a wet heap.

Now such a screaming wail of grief and fury arose in the dusty stockade yard that Jack thought his skull might actually be split open with it. Richard had curled into a fetal ball with his arms wrapped around his head.

Osmond was wailing. He had dropped his whip and the machine-pistol.

'*Oh, filthy!*' he cried, shaking his fists at Jack. '*Look what you've done! Oh, you filthy, bad boy! I hate you, hate you forever and beyond forever! Oh, filthy Pretender! I'll kill you! Morgan will kill you! Oh my darling only son! FILTHY! MORGAN*

WILL KILL YOU FOR WHAT YOU'VE DONE! MORGAN—'

The others took up the cry in a whispering voice, reminding Jack of the boys in the Sunlight Home: *can you gimme hallelujah.* And then they fell silent, because there was the other sound.

Jack was tumbled back instantly to the pleasant afternoon he had spent with Wolf, the two of them sitting by the stream, watching the herd graze and drink as Wolf talked about his family. It had been pleasant enough . . . pleasant enough, that is, until Morgan came.

And now Morgan was coming again – not flipping over but bludgeoning his way through, raping his way in.

'Morgan! It's –'

'– Morgan, Lord –'

'Lord of Orris –'

'Morgan . . . Morgan . . . Morgan . . .'

The ripping sound grew louder and louder. The Wolfs were abasing themselves in the dust. Osmond danced a shuffling jig, his black boots trampling the steel-tipped rawhide thongs woven into his whip.

'Bad boy! Filthy boy! Now you'll pay! Morgan's coming! Morgan's coming!'

The air about twenty feet to Osmond's right began to blur and shimmer, like the air over a burning incinerator.

Jack looked around, saw Richard curled up in the litter of machine-guns and ammunition and grenades like a very small boy who has fallen asleep while playing war. Only Richard wasn't asleep, he knew, and this was no game, and if Richard saw his father stepping through a hole between the worlds, he feared, Richard would go insane.

Jack sprawled beside his friend and wrapped his arms

tightly around him. That ripping-bedsheet sound grew louder, and suddenly he heard Morgan's voice bellow in terrible rage:

'What is the train doing here NOW, you fools?'

He heard Osmond wail, '*The filthy Pretender has killed my son!*'

'Here we go, Richie,' Jack muttered, and tightened his grip around Richard's wasted upper body. 'Time to jump ship.'

He closed his eyes, concentrated . . . and there was that brief moment of spinning vertigo as the two of them flipped.

CHAPTER THIRTY-SEVEN

RICHARD REMEMBERS

1

There was a sensation of rolling sideways and down, as if there were a short ramp between the two worlds. Dimly, fading, at last wavering into nothingness, Jack heard Osmond screaming, '*Bad! All boys! Axiomatic! All boys! Filthy! Filthy!*'

For a moment they were in thin air. Richard cried out. Then Jack thudded to the ground on one shoulder. Richard's head bounced against his chest. Jack did not open his eyes but only lay there on the ground hugging Richard, listening, smelling.

Silence. Not utter and complete, but large – its size counter-pointed by two or three singing birds.

The smell was cool and salty. A good smell . . . but not as good as the world could smell in the Territories. Even here – wherever *here* was – Jack could smell a faint under-odor, like the smell of old oil ground into the concrete floors of gas-station garage bays. It was the smell of too many people running too many motors, and it had polluted the entire atmosphere. His nose had been sensitized to it and he could smell it even here, in a place where he could hear no cars.

'Jack? Are we okay?'

'Sure,' Jack said, and opened his eyes to see whether he was telling the truth.

His first glance brought a terrifying idea: somehow, in his frantic need to get out of there, to get away before Morgan could arrive, he had not flipped them into the American Territories but pushed them somehow forward in time. This seemed to be the same place, but older, now abandoned, as if a century or two had gone by. The train still sat on the tracks, and the train looked just as it had. Nothing else did. The tracks, which crossed the weedy exercise yard they were standing in and went on to God knew where, were old and thick with rust. The crossties looked spongy and rotted. High weeds grew up between them.

He tightened his hold on Richard, who squirmed weakly in his grasp and opened his own eyes.

'Where are we?' he asked Jack, looking around. There was a long Quonset hut with a rust-splotched corrugated-tin roof where the bunkhouse-style barracks had been. The roof was all either of them could see clearly; the rest was buried in rambling woods ivy and wild weeds. There were a couple of poles in front of it which had perhaps once supported a sign. If so, it was long gone now.

'I don't know,' Jack said, and then, looking at where the obstacle course had been – it was now a barely glimpsed dirt rut overgrown with the remains of wild phlox and goldenrod – he brought out his worst fear: 'I may have pushed us forward in time.'

To his amazement, Richard laughed. 'It's good to know nothing much is going to change in the future, then,' he said, and pointed to a sheet of paper nailed to one of the posts standing in front of the Quonset/barracks.

It was somewhat weather-faded but still perfectly readable:

NO TRESPASSING!
By Order of the Mendocino County Sheriff's Department
By Order of the California State Police
VIOLATORS WILL BE PROSECUTED!

2

'Well, if you *knew* where we were,' Jack said, feeling simultaneously foolish and very relieved, 'why did you ask?'

'I just saw it,' Richard replied, and any urge Jack might have had to chaff Richard anymore over it blew away. Richard looked awful; he looked as if he had developed some weird tuberculosis which was working on his mind instead of on his lungs. Nor was it just his sanity-shaking round trip to the Territories and back – he had actually seemed to be adapting to that. But now he knew something else as well. It wasn't just a reality which was radically different from all of his carefully developed notions; *that* he might have been able to adapt to, if given world enough and time. But finding out that your dad is one of the guys in the black hats, Jack reflected, can hardly be one of life's groovier moments.

'Okay,' he said, trying to sound cheerful – he actually *did* feel a little cheerful. Getting away from such a monstrosity as Reuel would have made even a kid dying of terminal cancer feel a little cheerful, he figured. 'Up you go and up you get, Richie-boy. We've got promises we must keep, miles to go before we sleep, and you are still an utter creep.'

Richard winced. 'Whoever gave you the idea you had a sense of humor should be shot, chum.'

'Bitez mon crank, mon ami.'

'Where are we going?'

'I don't know,' Jack said, 'but it's somewhere around here. I can feel it. It's like a fishhook in my mind.'

'Point Venuti?'

Jack turned his head and looked at Richard for a long time. Richard's tired eyes were unreadable.

'Why did you ask that, chum?'

'Is that where we're going?'

Jack shrugged. *Maybe. Maybe not.*

They began walking slowly across the weed-grown parade ground and Richard changed the subject. 'Was all of that real?' They were approaching the rusty double gate. A lane of faded blue sky showed above the green. 'Was *any* of it real?'

'We spent a couple of days on an electric train that ran at about twenty-five miles an hour, thirty tops,' Jack said, 'and somehow we got from Springfield, Illinois, into northern California, near the coast. Now *you* tell *me* if it was real.'

'Yes . . . yes, but . . .'

Jack held out his arms. The wrists were covered with angry red weals that itched and smarted.

'Bites,' Jack said. 'From the worms. The worms that fell out of Reuel Gardener's head.'

Richard turned away and was noisily sick.

Jack held him. Otherwise, he thought, Richard simply would have fallen sprawling. He was appalled at how thin Richard had become, and how hot his flesh felt through his preppy shirt.

'I'm sorry I said that,' Jack said when Richard seemed a little better. 'It was pretty crude.'

'Yeah, it was. But I guess maybe it's the only thing that could have . . . you know . . .'

'Convinced you?'

'Yeah. Maybe.' Richard looked at him with his naked, wounded eyes. There were now pimples all across his forehead. Sores surrounded his mouth. 'Jack, I have to ask you something, and I want you to answer me . . . you know, straight. I want to ask you—'

Oh, I know what you want to ask me, Richie-boy.

'In a few minutes,' Jack said. 'We'll get to all the questions and as many of the answers as I know in a few minutes. But we've got a piece of business to take care of first.'

'What business?'

Instead of answering, Jack went over to the little train. He stood there for a moment, looking at it: stubby engine, empty boxcar, flatcar. Had he somehow managed to flip this whole thing into northern California? He didn't think so. Flipping with Wolf had been a chore, dragging Richard into the Territories from the Thayer campus had nearly torn his arm out of its socket, and doing both had been a conscious effort on his part. So far as he could remember, he hadn't been thinking of the train at all when he flipped – only getting Richard out of the Wolfs' paramilitary training camp before he saw his old man. Everything else had taken a slightly different form when it went from one world into the other – the act of Migrating seemed to demand an act of translation, as well. Shirts might become jerkins; jeans might become woolen trousers; money might become jointed sticks. But this train looked exactly the same here as it had over there. Morgan had succeeded in creating something which lost nothing in the Migration.

Also, they were wearing blue jeans over there, Jack-O.

Yeah. And although Osmond had his trusty whip, he also had a machine-pistol.

Morgan's machine-pistol. Morgan's train.

Chilly gooseflesh rippled up his back. He heard Anders muttering, *A bad business.*

It was that, all right. A very bad business. Anders was right; it was devils all hurtled down together. Jack reached into the engine compartment, got one of the Uzis, slapped a fresh clip into it, and started back toward where Richard stood looking around with pallid, contemplative interest.

'This looks like an old survivalist camp,' he said.

'You mean the kind of place where soldier-of-fortune types get ready for World War Three?'

'Yes, sort of. There are quite a few places like that in northern California . . . they spring up and thrive for a while, and then the people lose interest when World War Three doesn't start right away, or they get busted for illegal guns or dope, or something. My . . . my father told me that.'

Jack said nothing.

'What are you going to do with the gun, Jack?'

'I'm going to try to get rid of that train. Any objections?'

Richard shuddered; his mouth pulled down in a grimace of distaste. 'None whatever.'

'Will the Uzi do it, do you think? If I shoot into that plastic junk?'

'One bullet wouldn't. A whole clip might.'

'Let's see.' Jack pushed off the safety.

Richard grabbed his arm. 'It might be wise to remove ourselves to the fence before making the experiment,' he said.

'Okay.'

At the ivy-covered fence, Jack trained the Uzi on the flat and squashy packages of *plastique*. He pulled the trigger, and the Uzi bellowed the silence into rags. Fire hung mystically from the end of the barrel for a moment. The gunfire was shockingly loud in the chapellike silence of the deserted camp. Birds squawked in surprised fear and headed out for quieter parts of the forest. Richard winced and pressed his palms against his ears. The tarpaulin flirted and danced. Then, although he was still pulling the trigger, the gun stopped firing. The clip was exhausted, and the train just sat there on the track.

'Well,' Jack said, 'that was great. Have you got any other i—'

The flatcar erupted in a sheet of blue fire and a bellowing roar. Jack saw the flatcar actually starting to rise from the tracks, as if it were taking off. He grabbed Richard around the neck, shoved him down.

The explosions went on for a long time. Metal whistled and flew overhead. It made a steady metallic rain-shower on the roof of the Quonset hut. Occasionally a larger piece made a sound like a Chinese gong, or a crunch as something *really* big just punched on through. Then something slammed through the fence just above Jack's head, leaving a hole bigger than both of his fists laced together, and Jack decided it was time to cut out. He grabbed Richard and started pulling him toward the gates.

'*No!*' Richard shouted. '*The tracks!*'

'What?'

'The tr—'

Something whickered over them and both boys ducked. Their heads knocked together.

'*The tracks!*' Richard shouted, rubbing his skull with one pale hand. '*Not the road! Go for the tracks!*'

'*Gotcha!*' Jack was mystified but unquestioning. They had to go *somewhere*.

The two boys began to crawl along the rusting chain-link fence like soldiers crossing no-man's land. Richard was slightly ahead, leading them toward the hole in the fence where the tracks exited the far side of the compound.

Jack looked back over his shoulder as they went – he could see as much as he needed to, or wanted to, through the partially open gates. Most of the train seemed to have been simply vaporized. Twisted chunks of metal, some recognizable, most not, lay in a wide circle around the place where it had come back to America, where it had been built, bought, and paid for. That they had not been killed by flying shrapnel was amazing; that they had not been even so much as scratched seemed well-nigh impossible.

The worst was over now. They were outside the gate, standing up (but ready to duck and run if there were residual explosions).

'My father's not going to like it that you blew up his train, Jack,' Richard said.

His voice was perfectly calm, but when Jack looked at him, he saw that Richard was weeping.

'Richard—'

'No, he won't like it at all,' Richard said, as if answering himself.

3

A thick and luxuriant stripe of weeds, knee-high, grew up the center of the railroad tracks leading away from the camp, leading away in a direction Jack believed to be roughly south.

The tracks themselves were rusty and long unused; in places they had twisted strangely – rippled.

Earthquakes did that, Jack thought with queasy awe.

Behind them, the plastic explosive continued to explode. Jack would think it was finally over, and then there would be another long, hoarse BREEE-APPP! – it was, he thought, the sound of a giant clearing its throat. Or breaking wind. He glanced back once and saw a black pall of smoke hanging in the sky. He listened for the thick, heavy crackle of fire – like anyone who has lived for any length of time on the California coast, he was afraid of fire – but heard none. Even the woods here seemed New Englandy, thick and heavy with moisture. Certainly it was the antithesis of the pale-brown country around Baja, with its clear, bone-dry air. The woods were almost smug with life; the railway itself was a slowly closing lane between the encroaching trees, shrubs, and ubiquitous ivy (*poison* ivy, I bet, Jack thought, scratching unconsciously at the bites on his hands), with the faded blue sky an almost matching lane overhead. Even the cinders on the railroad bed were mossy. This place seemed secret, a place for secrets.

He set a hard pace, and not only to get the two of them off this track before the cops or the firemen showed up. The pace also assured Richard's silence. He was toiling too hard to keep up to talk . . . or ask questions.

They had gone perhaps two miles and Jack was still congratulating himself on this conversation-strangling ploy when Richard called out in a tiny, whistling voice, 'Hey, Jack—'

Jack turned just in time to see Richard, who had fallen a bit behind, toppling forward. The blemishes stood out on his paper-white skin like birthmarks.

Jack caught him – barely. Richard seemed to weigh no more than a paper bag.

'Oh, Christ, Richard!'

'Felt okay until a second or two ago,' Richard said in that same tiny, whistling voice. His respiration was very fast, very dry. His eyes were half-closed. Jack could see only whites and tiny arcs of blue irises. 'Just got . . . faint. Sorry.'

From behind them came another heavy, belching explosion, followed by the rattling sound of train-debris falling on the tin roof on the Quonset hut. Jack glanced that way, then anxiously up the tracks.

'Can you hang on to me? I'll piggyback you a ways.' *Shades of Wolf*, he thought.

'I can hang on.'

'If you can't, say so.'

'Jack,' Richard said with a heartening trace of that old fussy Richard-irritation, 'if I couldn't hang on, I wouldn't say that I could.'

Jack set Richard on his feet. Richard stood there, swaying, looking as if someone could blow once in his face and topple him over backward. Jack turned and squatted, the soles of his sneakers on one of the old rotted ties. He made his arms into thigh-stirrups, and Richard put his own arms around Jack's neck. Jack got to his feet and started to shag along the crossties at a fast walk that was very nearly a jog. Carrying Richard seemed to be no problem at all, and not just because Richard had lost weight. Jack had been running kegs of beer, carrying cartons, picking apples. He had spent time picking rocks in Sunlight Gardener's Far Field, can you gimme hallelujah. It had toughened him, all of that. But the toughening went deeper into the fiber of his essential self than something as simple and mindless as physical exercise could go. Nor was all of it a simple function of flipping back and forth between the two worlds like an acrobat, or of that other world – gorgeous as it could be – rubbing off on him like wet paint. Jack recognized in a dim sort of way that he had been trying to do more than simply save his mother's life; from the very beginning he had been trying to do something greater than that. He had been trying to do a good work, and his dim realization now was that such mad enterprises must always be toughening.

He *did* begin to jog.

'If you make me seasick,' Richard said, his voice jiggling in time with Jack's footfalls, 'I'll just vomit on your head.'

'I knew I could count on you, Richie-boy,' Jack panted, grinning.

'I feel . . . extremely foolish up here. Like a human pogo stick.'

'Probably just how you look, chum.'

'Don't . . . call me chum,' Richard whispered, and Jack's grin widened. He thought, *Oh Richard, you bastard, live forever.*

4

'I knew that man,' Richard whispered from above Jack.

It startled him, as if out of a doze. He had picked Richard up ten minutes ago, they had covered another mile, and there was still no sign of civilization of any kind. Just the tracks, and that smell of salt in the air.

The tracks, Jack wondered. *Do they go where I think they go?*

'What man?'

'The man with the whip and the machine-pistol. I knew him. I used to see him around.'

'When?' Jack panted.

'A long time ago. When I was a little kid.' Richard then added with great reluctance, 'Around the time that I had that . . . funny dream in the closet.' He paused. 'Except I guess it wasn't a dream, was it?'

'No. I guess it wasn't.'

'Yes. Was the man with the whip Reuel's dad?'

'What do you think?'

'It was,' Richard said glumly. 'Sure it was.'

Jack stopped.

'Richard, where do these tracks go?'

'You know where they go,' Richard said with a strange, empty serenity.

'Yeah – I think I do. But I want to hear you say it.' Jack paused. 'I guess I *need* to hear you say it. Where do they go?'

'They go to a town called Point Venuti,' Richard said, and he sounded near tears again. 'There's a big hotel there. I don't know if it's the place you're looking for or not, but I think it probably is.'

'So do I,' Jack said. He set off once more, Richard's legs in his arms, a growing ache in his back, following the tracks that would take him – both of them – to the place where his mother's salvation might be found.

5

As they walked, Richard talked. He did not come on to the subject of his father's involvement in this mad business all at once, but began to circle slowly in toward it.

'I knew that man from before,' Richard said. 'I'm pretty sure I did. He came to the house. Always to the back of the house. He didn't ring the bell, or knock. He kind of . . . scratched on the door. It gave me the creeps. Scared me so bad I felt like peeing my pants. He was a tall man – oh, all grown men seem tall to little kids, but this guy was *very* tall – and he had white hair. He wore dark glasses most of the time. Or sometimes the kind of sunglasses that have the mirror lenses. When I saw that story on him they had on *Sunday Report,* I knew I'd seen him *somewhere* before. My father was upstairs doing some paperwork the night that show was on. I was sitting in front of the tube, and when my father came in and saw what was on, he almost dropped the drink he was holding. Then he changed the station to a *Star Trek* rerun.

'Only the guy wasn't calling himself Sunlight Gardener when he used to come and see my father. His name . . . I can't quite remember. But it was something like Banlon . . . or Orlon . . .'

'Osmond?'

Richard brightened. '*That* was it. I never heard his first name. But he used to come once every month or two. Sometimes more often. Once he came almost every other night, for a week, and then he was gone for almost half a year. I used to lock myself in my room when he came. I didn't like his smell. He wore some kind of scent . . . cologne, I suppose, but it really smelled stronger than that. Like perfume. Cheap dime-store perfume. But underneath it—'

'Underneath it he smelled like he hadn't had a bath for about ten years.'

Richard looked at him, wide-eyed.

'I met him as Osmond, too,' Jack explained. He had explained before – at least some of this – but Richard had not been listening then. He was listening now. 'In the

Territories version of New Hampshire, before I met him as Sunlight Gardener in Indiana.'

'Then you must have seen that . . . that *thing*.'

'Reuel?' Jack shook his head. 'Reuel must have been out in the Blasted Lands then, having a few more radical cobalt treatments.' Jack thought of the running sores on the creature's face, thought of the worms. He looked at his red, puffy wrists where the worms had bitten, and shuddered. 'I never saw Reuel until the end, and I never saw his American Twinner at all. How old were you when Osmond started showing up?'

'I must have been four. The thing about the . . . you know, the closet . . . that hadn't happened yet. I remember I was more afraid of him after that.'

'After the thing touched you in the closet.'

'Yes.'

'And that happened when you were five.'

'Yes.'

'When we were *both* five.'

'Yes. You can put me down. I can walk for a while.'

Jack did. They walked in silence, heads down, not looking at each other. At five, something had reached out of the dark and touched Richard. When they were both six

(six, Jacky was six)

Jack had overheard his father and Morgan Sloat talking about a place they went to, a place Jacky called the Daydream-country. And later that year, something had reached out of the dark and had touched him and his mother. It had been nothing more or less than Morgan Sloat's voice. Morgan Sloat calling from Green River, Utah. Sobbing. He, Phil Sawyer, and Tommy Woodbine had left three days before on their yearly November hunting trip – another college chum,

Randy Glover, owned a luxurious hunting lodge in Blessington, Utah. Glover usually hunted with them, but that year he had been cruising in the Caribbean. Morgan called to say that Phil had been shot, apparently by another hunter. He and Tommy Woodbine had packed him out of the wilderness on a lashed-together stretcher. Phil had regained consciousness in the back of Glover's Jeep Cherokee, Morgan said, and had asked that Morgan send his love to Lily and Jack. He died fifteen minutes later, as Morgan drove wildly toward Green River and the nearest hospital.

Morgan had not killed Phil; there was Tommy to testify that the three of them had been together when the shot rang out, if any testimony had ever been required (and, of course, none ever was).

But that was not to say he couldn't have hired it done, Jack thought now. And it was not to say that Uncle Tommy might not have harbored his own long doubts about what had happened. If so, maybe Uncle Tommy hadn't been killed just so that Jack and his dying mother would be totally unprotected from Morgan's depredations. Maybe he had died because Morgan was tired of wondering if the old faggot might finally hint to the surviving son that there might have been more to Phil Sawyer's death than an accident. Jack felt his skin crawl with dismay and revulsion.

'Was that man around before your father and my father went hunting together that last time?' Jack asked fiercely.

'Jack, I was four years old—'

'No, you weren't, you were *six*. You were four when he started coming, you were six when my father got killed in Utah. And you don't forget much, Richard. Did he come around before my father died?'

'That was the time he came almost every night for a

week,' Richard said, his voice barely audible. 'Just before the last hunting trip.'

Although none of this was precisely Richard's fault, Jack was unable to contain his bitterness. 'My dad dead in a hunting accident in Utah, Uncle Tommy run down in L.A. The deathrate among your father's friends is very fucking high, Richard.'

'Jack—' Richard began in a small, trembling voice.

'I mean, it's all water over the dam, or spilled milk, or pick your cliché,' Jack said. 'But when I showed up at your school, Richard, you called me crazy.'

'Jack, you don't under—'

'No, I guess I don't. I was tired and you gave me a place to sleep. Fine. I was hungry and you got me some food. Great. But what I needed most was for you to *believe* me. I knew it was too much to expect, but jeepers! You *knew* the guy I was talking about! You *knew* he'd been in your father's life before! And you just said something like "Good old Jack's been spending too much time in the hot sun out there on Seabrook Island and blah-blah-blah!" Jesus, Richard, I thought we were better friends than that.'

'You still don't understand.'

'What? That you were too afraid of Seabrook Island stuff to believe in me a little?' Jack's voice wavered with tired indignation.

'No. I was afraid of more than that.'

'Oh yeah?' Jack stopped and looked at Richard's pale, miserable face truculently. 'What could be more than that for Rational Richard?'

'I was afraid,' Richard said in a perfectly calm voice. 'I was afraid that if I knew any more about those secret pockets . . . that man Osmond, or what was in the closet that time, I wouldn't be able to love my father anymore. And I was right.'

Richard covered his face with his thin, dirty fingers and began to cry.

6

Jack stood watching Richard cry and damned himself for twenty kinds of fool. No matter what else Morgan was, he was still Richard Sloat's father; Morgan's ghost lurked in the shape of Richard's hands and in the bones of Richard's face. Had he forgotten those things? No – but for a moment his bitter disappointment in Richard had covered them up. And his increasing nervousness had played a part. The Talisman was very, very close now, and he felt it in his nerve-endings the way a horse smells water in the desert or a distant grass-fire in the plains. That nerviness was coming out in a kind of prancy skittishness.

Yeah, well, this guy's supposed to be your best buddy, Jack-O – get a little funky if you have to, but don't trample Richard. The kid's sick, just in case you hadn't noticed.

He reached for Richard. Richard tried to push him away. Jack was having none of that. He held Richard. The two of them stood that way in the middle of the deserted railroad bed for a while, Richard's head on Jack's shoulder.

'Listen,' Jack said awkwardly, 'try not to worry too much about . . . you know . . . everything . . . just yet, Richard. Just kind of try to roll with the changes, you know?' Boy, that sounded really stupid. Like telling somebody they had cancer but don't worry because pretty soon we're going to put *Star Wars* on the VCR and it'll cheer you right up.

'Sure,' Richard said. He pushed away from Jack. The

tears had cut clean tracks on his dirty face. He wiped an arm across his eyes and tried to smile. 'A' wi' be well an' a' wi' be well—'

'An' a' manner a' things wi' be well,' Jack chimed in – they finished together, then laughed together, and that was all right.

'Come on,' Richard said. 'Let's go.'

'Where?'

'To get your Talisman,' Richard said. 'The way you're talking, it must be in Point Venuti. It's the next town up the line. Come on, Jack. Let's get going. But walk slow – I'm not done talking yet.'

Jack looked at him curiously, and then they started walking again – but slowly.

7

Now that the dam had broken and Richard had allowed himself to begin remembering things, he was an unexpected fountain of information. Jack began to feel as if he had been working a jigsaw puzzle without knowing that several of the most important pieces were missing. It was Richard who had had most of those pieces all along. Richard had been in the survivalist camp before, that was the first piece. His father had owned it.

'Are you sure it was the same place, Richard?' Jack asked doubtfully.

'I'm sure,' Richard said. 'It even looked a little familiar to me on the other side, there. When we got back over . . . over here . . . I was sure.'

Jack nodded, unsure what else to do.

'We used to stay in Point Venuti. That's where we

always stayed before we came here. The train was a big treat. I mean, how many dads have their own private train?'

'Not many,' Jack said. 'I guess Diamond Jim Brady and some of those guys had private trains, but I don't know if they were dads or not.'

'Oh, my dad wasn't in their league,' Richard said, laughing a little, and Jack thought: *Richard, you might be surprised.*

'We'd drive up to Point Venuti from L.A. in a rental car. There was a motel we stayed at. Just the two of us.' Richard stopped. His eyes had gone misty with love and remembering. 'Then – after we hung out there for a while – we'd take my dad's train up to Camp Readiness. It was just a little train.' He looked at Jack, startled. 'Like the one we came on, I guess.'

'Camp Readiness?'

But Richard appeared not to have heard him. He was looking at the rusted tracks. They were whole here, but Jack thought Richard might be remembering the twisted ripples they had passed some way back. In a couple of places the ends of rail-sections actually curved up into the air, like broken guitar-strings. Jack guessed that in the Territories those tracks would be in fine shape, neatly and lovingly maintained.

'See, there used to be a trolley line here,' Richard said. 'This was back in the thirties, my father said. The Mendocino County Red Line. Only it wasn't owned by the county, it was owned by a private company, and they went broke, because in California . . . you know . . .'

Jack nodded. In California, everyone used cars. 'Richard, why didn't you ever tell me about this place?'

'That was the one thing my dad said never to tell you.

You and your parents knew we sometimes took vacations in northern California and he said that was all right, but I wasn't to tell you about the train, or Camp Readiness. He said if I told, Phil would be mad because it was a secret.'

Richard paused.

'He said if I told, he'd never take me again. I thought it was because they were supposed to be partners. I guess it was more than that.

'The trolley line went broke because of the cars and the freeways.' He paused thoughtfully. 'That was one thing about the place you took me to, Jack. Weird as it was, it didn't stink of hydrocarbons. I could get into that.'

Jack nodded again, saying nothing.

'The trolley company finally sold the whole line – grandfather clause and all – to a development company. *They* thought people would start to move inland, too. Except it didn't happen.'

'Then your father bought it.'

'Yes, I guess so. I don't really know. He never talked much about buying the line . . . or how he replaced the trolley tracks with these railroad tracks.'

That would have taken a lot of work, Jack thought, and then he thought of the ore-pits, and Morgan of Orris's apparently unlimited supply of slave labor.

'I know he replaced them, but only because I got a book on railroads and found out there's a difference in gauge. Trolleys run on ten-gauge track. This is sixteen-gauge.'

Jack knelt, and yes, he could see a very faint double indentation inside the existing tracks – that was where the trolley tracks had been.

'He had a little red train,' Richard said dreamily. 'Just an engine and two cars. It ran on diesel fuel. He used to laugh about it and say that the only thing that separated the men from the boys was the price of their toys. There was an old trolley station on the hill above Point Venuti, and we'd go up there in the rental car and park and go on in. I remember how that station smelled – kind of old, but nice . . . full of old sunlight, sort of. And the train would be there. And my dad . . . he'd say, "All aboard for Camp Readiness, Richard! You got your ticket?" And there'd be lemonade . . . or iced tea . . . and we sat up in the cab . . . sometimes he'd have stuff . . . supplies . . . behind . . . but we'd sit up front . . . and . . . and . . .'

Richard swallowed hard and wiped a hand across his eyes.

'And it was a nice time,' he finished. 'Just him and me. It was pretty cool.'

He looked around, his eyes shiny with unshed tears.

'There was a plate to turn the train around at Camp Readiness,' he said. 'Back in those days. The old days.'

Richard uttered a terrible strangled sob.

'Richard—'

Jack tried to touch him.

Richard shook him off and stepped away, brushing tears from his cheeks with the backs of his hands.

'Wasn't so grown-up then,' he said, smiling. Trying to. '*Nothing* was so grown up then, was it, Jack?'

'No,' Jack said, and now he found he was crying himself.

Oh Richard. Oh my dear one.

'No,' Richard said, smiling, looking around at the encroaching woods and brushing the tears away with the dirty backs of his hands, 'nothing was so grown-up back then. In the old days, when we were just kids. Back when we all lived in California and nobody lived anywhere else.'

He looked at Jack, trying to smile.

'Jack, help me,' he said. 'I feel like my leg is caught in some stuh-stupid truh-truh-hap and I . . . I . . .'

Then Richard fell on his knees with his hair in his tired face, and Jack got down there with him, and I can bear to tell you no more – only that they comforted each other as well as they could, and, as you probably know from your own bitter experience, that is never quite good enough.

8

'The fence was new back then,' Richard said when he could continue speaking. They had walked on a ways. A whip-poorwill sang from a tall sturdy oak. The smell of salt in the air was stronger. 'I remember that. And the sign – CAMP READINESS, that's what it said. There was an obstacle course, and ropes to climb, and other ropes that you hung on to and then swung over big puddles of water. It looked sort of like boot-camp in a World War Two movie about the Marines. But the guys using the equipment didn't look much like Marines. They were fat, and they were all dressed the same – gray sweat-suits with CAMP READINESS written on the chest in small letters, and red piping on the sides of the sweat-pants. They all looked like they were going to have heart-attacks or strokes any minute. Maybe both at the same time. Sometimes we stayed overnight. A couple of times we stayed the whole weekend. Not in the Quonset hut; that was like a barracks for the guys who were paying to get in shape.'

'If that's what they were doing.'

'Yeah, right. If that's what they were doing. Anyway, we stayed in a big tent and slept on cots. It was a blast.'

Again, Richard smiled wistfully. 'But you're right, Jack – not all the guys shagging around the place looked like businessmen trying to get in shape. The others—'

'What about the others?' Jack asked quietly.

'Some of them – a lot of them – looked like those big hairy creatures in the other world,' Richard said in a low voice Jack had to strain to hear. 'The Wolfs. I mean, they looked *sort* of like regular people, but not too much. They looked . . . rough. You know?'

Jack nodded. He knew.

'I remember I was a little afraid to look into their eyes very closely. Every now and then there'd be these funny flashes of light in them . . . like their brains were on fire. Some of the others . . .' A light of realization dawned in Richard's eyes. 'Some of the others looked like that substitute basketball coach I told you about. The one who wore the leather jacket and smoked.'

'How far is this Point Venuti, Richard?'

'I don't know, exactly. But we used to do it in a couple of hours, and the train never went very fast. Running speed, maybe, but not much more. It can't be much more than twenty miles from Camp Readiness, all told. Probably a little less.'

'Then we're maybe fifteen miles or less from it. From—'

(from the Talisman)

'Yeah. Right.'

Jack looked up as the day darkened. As if to show that the pathetic fallacy wasn't so pathetic after all, the sun now sailed behind a deck of clouds. The temperature seemed to drop ten degrees and the day seemed to grow dull – the whippoorwill fell silent.

9

Richard saw the sign first – a simple whitewashed square of wood painted with black letters. It stood on the left side of the tracks, and ivy had grown up its post, as if it had been here for a very long time. The sentiment, however, was quite current. It read: GOOD BIRDS MAY FLY; BAD BOYS MUST DIE. THIS IS YOUR LAST CHANCE: GO HOME.

'You can go, Richie,' Jack said quietly. 'It's okay by me. They'll let you go, no sweat. None of this is your business.'

'I think maybe it is,' Richard said.

'I dragged you into it.'

'No,' Richard said. 'My father dragged me into it. Or fate dragged me into it. Or God. Or Jason. Whoever it was, I'm sticking.'

'All right,' Jack said. 'Let's go.'

As they passed the sign, Jack lashed out with one foot in a passably good kung-fu kick and knocked it over.

'Way to go, chum,' Richard said, smiling a little.

'Thanks. But don't call me chum.'

10

Although he had begun to look wan and tired again, Richard talked for the next hour as they walked down the tracks and into the steadily strengthening smell of the Pacific Ocean. He spilled out a flood of reminiscences that had been bottled up inside of him for years. Although his face didn't reveal it, Jack was stunned with amazement . . . and a deep, welling pity for the lonely child, eager for the least scrap of his father's affection, that Richard was revealing to him, inadvertently or otherwise.

He looked at Richard's pallor, the sores on his cheeks and forehead and around his mouth; listened to that tentative, almost whispering voice that nevertheless did not hesitate or falter now that the chance to tell all these things had finally come; and was glad once more that Morgan Sloat had never been *his* father.

He told Jack that he remembered landmarks all along this part of the railroad. They could see the roof of a barn over the trees at one point, with a faded ad for Chesterfield Kings on it.

'"Twenty great tobaccos make twenty wonderful smokes,"' Richard said, smiling. 'Only, in those days you could see the whole barn.'

He pointed out a big pine with a double top, and fifteen minutes later told Jack, 'There used to be a rock on the other side of this hill that looked just like a frog. Let's see if it's still there.'

It was, and Jack supposed it did look like a frog. A little. If you stretched your imagination. *And maybe it helps to be three. Or four. Or seven. Or however old he was.*

Richard had loved the railroad, and had thought Camp Readiness was really neat, with its track to run on and its hurdles to jump over and its ropes to climb. But he hadn't liked Point Venuti itself. After some self-prodding, Richard even remembered the name of the motel at which he and his father had stayed during their time in the little coastal town. The Kingsland Motel, he said . . . and Jack found that name did not surprise him much at all.

The Kingsland Motel, Richard said, was just down the road from the old hotel his father always seemed interested in. Richard could see the hotel from his window, and he didn't like it. It was a huge, rambling place with turrets and gables and gambrels and cupolas and towers; brass weather-vanes in strange shapes twirled from all of the latter. They twirled even when there was no wind, Richard said – he could clearly remember standing at the window of his room and watching them go around and around and around, strange brass creations shaped like crescent moons and scarab beetles and Chinese ideograms, winking in the sun while the ocean foamed and roared below.

Ah yes, doc, it all comes back to me now, Jack thought.

'It was deserted?' Jack asked.

'Yes. For sale.'

'What was its name?'

'The Agincourt.' Richard paused, then added another child's color – the one most small children are apt to leave in the box. 'It was black. It was made of wood, but the wood looked like stone. Old black stone. And that's what my father and his friends called it. The Black Hotel.'

11

It was partly – but not entirely – to divert Richard that Jack asked, 'Did your father buy that hotel? Like he did Camp Readiness?'

Richard thought about it awhile and then nodded. 'Yes,' he said. 'I think he did. After a while. There was a For Sale sign on the gates in front of the place when he first started taking me there, but one time when we went there it was just gone.'

'But you never stayed there?'

'God, no!' Richard shuddered. 'The only way he could have gotten me in there would have been with a towing chain . . . even then I might not have gone.'

'Never even went in?'

'No. Never did, never will.'

Ah, Richie-boy, didn't anyone ever teach you to never say never?

'That goes for your father as well? He never even went in?'

'Not to my knowledge,' Richard said in his best professional voice. His forefinger went to the bridge of his nose, as if to push up the glasses that weren't there. 'I'd be willing to bet he never went in. He was as scared of it as I was. But with me, that's all I felt . . . just scared. For my father, there was something more. He was . . .'

'Was what?'

Reluctantly, Richard said, 'He was obsessed with the place, I think.'

Richard paused, eyes vague, thinking back. 'He'd go and stand in front of it every day we were in Point Venuti. And I don't mean just for a couple of minutes, or something like that – he'd stand in front of it for, like, three hours. Sometimes more. He was alone most of those times. But not always. He had . . . strange friends.'

'Wolfs?'

'I guess so,' Richard said, almost angrily. 'Yeah, I guess some of them could have been Wolfs, or whatever you call them. They looked uncomfortable in their clothes – they were always scratching themselves, usually in those places where nice people aren't supposed to scratch. Others looked like the substitute coach. Kind of hard and mean. Some of those guys I used to see out at Camp Readiness, too. I'll tell you one thing, Jack – those guys were even more scared of that place than my father was. They just about cringed when they got near it.'

'Sunlight Gardener? Was he ever there?'

'Uh-huh,' Richard said. 'But in Point Venuti he looked more like the man we saw over there . . .'

'Like Osmond.'

'Yes. But those people didn't come very often. Mostly it was just my father, by himself. Sometimes he'd get the restaurant at our motel to pack him some sandwiches, and he'd sit on a sidewalk bench and eat his lunch looking at the hotel. I stood at the window in the lobby of the Kingsland and looked at my father looking at the hotel. I never liked his face at those times. He looked afraid, but he also looked like . . . like he was gloating.'

'Gloating,' Jack mused.

'Sometimes he asked me if I wanted to come with him, and I always said no. He'd nod and I remember once he said, "There'll be time. You'll understand everything, Rich . . . in time." I remember thinking that if it was about that black hotel, I didn't want to understand.

'Once,' Richard said, 'when he was drunk, he said there was something inside that place. He said it had been there for a long time. We were lying in our beds, I remember. The wind was high that night. I could hear the waves hitting the beach, and the squeaky sound of those weathervanes turning on top of the Agincourt's towers. It was a scary sound. I thought about that place, all those rooms, all of them empty—'

'Except for the ghosts,' Jack muttered. He thought he heard footsteps and looked quickly behind them. Nothing; no one. The roadbed was deserted for as far as he could see.

'That's right; except for the ghosts,' Richard agreed. 'So I said, "Is it valuable, Daddy?"

'"It's the most valuable thing there is," he said.

'"Then some junkie will probably break in and steal it," I said. It wasn't – how can I say this? – it wasn't a subject I wanted to pursue, but I didn't want him to go to sleep, either. Not with that wind blowing outside, and the sound of those vanes squeaking in the night.

'He laughed, and I heard a clink as he poured himself a little more bourbon from the bottle on the floor.

'"Nobody is going to steal it, Rich," he said. "And any junkie who went into the Agincourt would see things he *never* saw before." He drank his drink, and I could tell he was getting sleepy. "Only one person in the whole world could ever touch that thing, and he'll never even get close to it, Rich. I can guarantee that. One thing that interests me is that it's the same over there as over here. It doesn't change – at least, as far as I can tell, it doesn't change. I'd like to have it, but I'm not even going to try, at least not now, and maybe not ever. I could do things with it – you bet! – but on the whole, I think I like that thing best right where it is."

'I was getting sleepy myself by then, but I asked him what *it* was that he kept talking about.'

'What did he say?' Jack asked, dry-mouthed.

'He called it—' Richard hesitated, frowning in thought. 'He called it "the axle of all possible worlds". Then he laughed. Then he called it something else. Something you wouldn't like.'

'What was that?'

'It'll make you mad.'

'Come on, Richard, spill it.'

'He called it . . . well . . . he called it "Phil Sawyer's folly".'

It was not anger he felt but a burst of hot, dizzying

excitement. That was it, all right; that was the Talisman. The axle of all possible worlds. How many worlds? God alone knew. The American Territories; the Territories themselves; the hypothetical Territories' Territories; and on and on, like the stripes coming ceaselessly up and out of a turning barber pole. A universe of worlds, a dimensional macrocosm of worlds – and in all of them one thing that was always the same; one unifying force that was undeniably good, even if it now happened to be imprisoned in an evil place; the Talisman, axle of all possible worlds. And was it also Phil Sawyer's folly? Probably so. Phil's folly . . . Jack's folly . . . Morgan Sloat's . . . Gardener's . . . and the hope, of course, of two Queens.

'It's more than Twinners,' he said in a low voice.

Richard had been plodding along, watching the rotted ties disappear beneath his feet. Now he looked nervously up at Jack.

'It's more than Twinners, because there are more than two worlds. There are triplets . . . quadruplets . . . who knows? Morgan Sloat here; Morgan of Orris over there; maybe Morgan, Duke of Azreel, somewhere else. *But he never went inside the hotel!*'

'I don't know what you're talking about,' Richard said in a resigned voice. *But I'm sure you'll go right on, anyway,* that resigned tone said, *progressing from nonsense to outright insanity. All aboard for Seabrook Island!*

'He *can't* go inside. That is, Morgan of California can't – and do you know why? Because Morgan of *Orris* can't. And Morgan of Orris can't because Morgan of *California* can't. If one of them can't go into *his* version of the black hotel, then *none* of them can. Do you see?'

'No.'

Jack, feverish with discovery, didn't hear what Richard said at all.

'Two Morgans, or dozens. It doesn't matter. Two Lilys, or dozens – dozens of Queens in dozens of worlds, Richard, think of that! How does that mess your mind? Dozens of black hotels – only in some worlds it might be a black amusement park . . . or a black trailer court . . . or I don't know what. But Richard—'

He stopped, turned Richard by the shoulders, and stared at him, his eyes blazing. Richard tried to draw away from him for a moment, and then stopped, entranced by the fiery beauty on Jack's face. Suddenly, briefly, Richard believed that all things might be possible. Suddenly, briefly, he felt *healed*.

'What?' he whispered.

'*Some* things are not excluded. Some *people* are not excluded. They are . . . well . . . *single-natured*. That's the only way I can think of to say it. They are like *it* – the Talisman. Single-natured. Me. I'm single-natured. I had a Twinner, but he died. Not just in the Territories world, but in *all* worlds but this one. I know that – I feel that. My dad knew it, too. I think that's why he called me Travelling Jack. When I'm here, I'm not there. When I'm there, I'm not here. And Richard, *neither are you*!'

Richard stared at him, speechless.

'You don't remember; you were mostly in Freakout City while I was talking to Anders. But he said Morgan of Orris had a boy-child. Rushton. Do you know what he was?'

'Yes,' Richard whispered. He was still unable to pull his eyes away from Jack's. 'He was my Twinner.'

'That's right. The little boy died, Anders said. The

Talisman is single-natured. *We're* single-natured. Your father isn't. I've seen Morgan of Orris in that other world, and he's *like* your father, but he's *not* your father. He couldn't go into the black hotel, Richard. He can't now. But he knew you were single-natured, just as he knows I am. He'd like me dead. He needs you on his side.

'Because then, if he decided he *did* want the Talisman, he could always send *you* in to get it, couldn't he?'

Richard began to tremble.

'Never mind,' Jack said grimly. 'He won't have to worry about it. We're going to bring it out, but *he's* not going to have it.'

'Jack, I don't think I can go into that place,' Richard said, but he spoke in a low, strengthless whisper, and Jack, who was already walking on, didn't hear him.

Richard trotted to catch up.

12

Conversation lapsed. Noon came and went. The woods had become very silent, and twice Jack had seen trees with strange, gnarly trunks and tangled roots growing quite close to the tracks. He did not much like the looks of these trees. They looked familiar.

Richard, staring at the ties as they disappeared beneath his feet, at last stumbled and fell over, hitting his head. After that, Jack piggybacked him again.

'There, Jack!' Richard called, after what seemed an eternity.

Up ahead, the tracks disappeared into an old car-barn. The doors hung open on a shadowy darkness that looked dull and moth-eaten. Beyond the car-barn (which might once have been as pleasant as Richard had said, but which only looked spooky to Jack now) was a highway – 101, Jack guessed.

Beyond that, the ocean – he could hear the pounding waves.

'I guess we're here,' he said in a dry voice.

'Almost,' Richard said. 'Point Venuti's a mile or so down the road. God, I wish we didn't have to go there, Jack . . . Jack? Where are you going?'

But Jack didn't look around. He stepped off the tracks, detoured around one of those strange-looking trees (this one not even shrub-high), and headed for the road. High grasses and weeds brushed his road-battered jeans. Something inside the trolley-barn – Morgan Sloat's private train-station of yore – moved with a nasty slithering bump, but Jack didn't even look toward it.

He reached the road, crossed it, and walked to the edge.

13

Near the middle of December in the year 1981, a boy named Jack Sawyer stood where the water and the land came together, hands in the pockets of his jeans, looking out at the steady Pacific. He was twelve years old and extraordinarily beautiful for his age. His brown hair was long – probably too long – but the sea-breeze swept it back from a fine, clear brow. He stood thinking of his mother, who was dying, and of friends, both absent and present, and worlds within worlds, turning in their courses.

I've come the distance, he thought, and shivered. *Coast to coast with Travelling Jack Sawyer.* His eyes abruptly filled with tears. He breathed deeply of the salt. Here he was – and the Talisman was close by.

'Jack!'

Jack didn't look at him at first; his gaze was held by the Pacific, by the sunlight gleaming gold on top of the waves. He was here; he had made it. He –

'*Jack!*' Richard struck his shoulder, bringing him out of his daze.

'Huh?'

'Look!' Richard was gaping, pointing at something down the road, in the direction in which Point Venuti presumably lay. 'Look there!'

Jack looked. He understood Richard's surprise, but he felt none himself – or no more than he had felt when Richard had told him the name of the motel where he and his father had stayed in Point Venuti. No, not much surprise, but –

But it was damned good to see his mother again.

Her face was twenty feet high, and it was a younger face than Jack could remember. It was Lily as she had looked at the height of her career. Her hair, a glorious be-bop shade of brassy blond, was pulled back in a Tuesday Weld ponytail. Her insouciant go-to-hell grin was, however, all her own. No one else in films had ever smiled that way – she had invented it, and she still held the patent. She was looking back over one bare shoulder. At Jack . . . at Richard . . . at the blue Pacific.

It was his mother . . . but when he blinked, the face changed the slightest bit. The line of chin and jaw grew rounder, and the cheekbones less pronounced, the hair darker, the eyes an even deeper blue. Now it was the face of Laura DeLoessian, mother of Jason. Jack blinked again, and it was his mother again – his mother at twenty-eight, grinning her cheerful *fuckya*-if-you-can't-take-a-joke defiance at the world.

It was a billboard. Across the top of it ran this legend:

THIRD ANNUAL KILLER B FILM FESTIVAL
POINT VENUTI, CALIFORNIA
BITKER THEATER
DECEMBER 10TH–DECEMBER 20TH
THIS YEAR FEATURING LILY CAVANAUGH
'QUEEN OF THE B'S'

'Jack, it's your *mother*,' Richard said. His voice was hoarse with awe. 'Is it just a coincidence? It *can't* be, can it?'

Jack shook his head. No, not a coincidence.

The word his eyes kept fixing on, of course, was QUEEN.

'Come on,' he said to Richard. 'I think we're almost there.'

The two of them walked side by side down the road toward Point Venuti.

CHAPTER THIRTY-EIGHT
THE END OF THE ROAD

1

Jack inspected Richard's drooping posture and glistening face carefully as they walked along. Richard now looked as though he were dragging himself along on will power alone. A few more wet-looking pimples had blossomed on his face.

'Are you okay, Richie?'

'No. I don't feel too good. But I can still walk, Jack. You don't have to carry me.' He bent his head and plodded glumly on. Jack saw that his friend, who had so many memories of that peculiar little railway and that peculiar little station, was suffering far more than he from the reality that now existed – rusty, broken ties, weeds, poison ivy . . . and at the end, a ramshackle building from which all the bright, remembered paint had faded, a building where something slithered uneasily in the dark.

I feel like my leg is caught in some stupid trap, Richard had said, and Jack thought he could understand that well enough . . . but not with the *depth* of Richard's understanding. That was more understanding than he was sure he could bear. A slice of Richard's childhood had been burned out of him, turned inside-out. The railway and the dead station with its staring glassless windows must have seemed like dreadful parodies of themselves to Richard – yet more bits of the past destroyed in the wake of everything he was learning or admitting about his father. Richard's entire life, as much as Jack's, had begun to fold into the pattern of the Territories, and Richard had been given much less preparation for this transformation.

2

As for what he had told Richard about the Talisman, Jack would have sworn it was the truth – the Talisman knew they were coming. He had begun feeling it just about when he had seen the billboard shining out with his mother's picture; now the feeling was urgent and powerful. It was as if a great animal had awakened some miles away, and its purring made the earth resonate . . . or as if every single bulb inside a hundred-story building just over the horizon had just gone on, making a blaze of light strong enough to conceal the stars . . . or as if someone had switched on the biggest magnet in the world, which was tugging at Jack's belt buckle, at the change in his pockets and the fillings in his teeth, and would not be satisfied until it had pulled him into its heart. That great animal purring, that sudden and drastic illumination, that magnetic yearning – all these echoed in Jack's chest. Something out there, something in the direction of Point Venuti, wanted Jack Sawyer, and what Jack Sawyer chiefly knew of the object calling him so viscerally was that it was big. Big. No small thing could own such power. It was elephant-sized, city-sized.

And Jack wondered about his capacity to handle

something so monumental. The Talisman had been imprisoned in a magical and sinister old hotel; presumably it had been put there not only to keep it from evil hands but at least in part because it was hard for anybody to handle it, whatever his intentions. Maybe, Jack wondered, Jason had been the only being capable of handling it – capable of dealing with it without doing harm either to himself or to the Talisman itself. Feeling the strength and urgency of its call to him, Jack could only hope that he would not weaken before the Talisman.

'"You'll understand, Rich,"' Richard surprised him by saying. His voice was dull and low. 'My father said that. He said I'd understand. "*You'll understand, Rich.*"'

'Yeah,' Jack said, looking worriedly at his friend. 'How are you feeling, Richard?'

In addition to the sores surrounding his mouth, Richard now had a collection of angry-looking raised red dots or bumps across his pimply forehead and his temples. It was as though a swarm of insects had managed to burrow just under the surface of his protesting skin. For a moment Jack had a flash of Richard Sloat on the morning he had climbed in his window at Nelson House, Thayer School; Richard Sloat with his glasses riding firmly on the bridge of his nose and his sweater tucked neatly into his pants. Would that maddeningly correct, unbudgeable boy ever return?

'I can still walk,' Richard said. 'But is this what he meant? Is *this* the understanding I was supposed to get, or have, or whatever the hell . . . ?'

'You've got something new on your face,' Jack said. 'You want to rest for a while?'

'Naw,' Richard said, still speaking from the bottom of

a muddy barrel. 'And I can feel that rash. It itches. I think I got it all over my back, too.'

'Let me see,' Jack said. Richard stopped in the middle of the road, obedient as a dog. He closed his eyes and breathed through his mouth. The red spots blazed on his forehead and temples. Jack stepped behind him, raised his jacket, and lifted the back of his stained and dirty blue button-down shirt. The spots were smaller here, not as raised or as angry-looking; they spread from Richard's thin shoulderblades to the small of his back, no larger than ticks.

Richard let out a big dispirited unconscious sigh.

'You got em there, but it's not so bad,' Jack said.

'Thanks,' Richard said. He inhaled, lifted his head. Overhead the gray sky seemed heavy enough to come crashing to earth. The ocean seethed against the rocks, far down the rough slope. 'It's only a couple of miles, really,' Richard said. 'I'll make it.'

'I'll piggyback you when you need it,' Jack said, unwittingly exposing his conviction that before long Richard would need to be carried again.

Richard shook his head and made an inefficient stab at shoving his shirt back in his trousers. 'Sometimes I think I . . . sometimes I think I can't—'

'We're going to go into that hotel, Richard,' Jack said, putting his arm through Richard's and half-forcing him to step forward. 'You and me. Together. I don't have the faintest idea of what happens once we get in there, but you and I are going in. No matter who tries to stop us. Just remember that.'

Richard gave him a look half-fearful, half-grateful. Now Jack could see the irregular outlines of future bumps crowding beneath the surface of Richard's cheeks. Again he was conscious of a powerful force pulling at him, forcing him along as he had forced Richard.

'You mean my father,' Richard said. He blinked, and Jack thought he was trying not to cry – exhaustion had magnified Richard's emotions.

'I mean everything,' Jack said, not quite truthfully. 'Let's get going, old pal.'

'But what am I supposed to understand? I don't get —' Richard looked around, blinking his unprotected eyes. Most of the world, Jack remembered, was a blur to Richard.

'You understand a lot more already, Richie,' Jack pointed out.

And then for a moment a disconcertingly bitter smile twisted Richard's mouth. He had been made to understand a great deal more than he had ever wished to know, and his friend found himself momentarily wishing that he had run away from Thayer School in the middle of the night by himself. But the moment in which he might have preserved Richard's innocence was far behind him, if it had ever really existed – Richard was a necessary part of Jack's mission. He felt strong hands fold around his heart; Jason's hands, the Talisman's hands.

'We're on our way,' he said, and Richard settled back into the rhythm of his strides.

'We're going to see my dad down there in Point Venuti, aren't we?' he asked.

Jack said, 'I'm going to take care of you, Richard. You're the herd now.'

'What?'

'Nobody's going to hurt you, not unless you scratch yourself to death.'

Richard muttered to himself as they plodded along.

His hands slid over his inflamed temples, rubbing and rubbing. Now and then he dug his fingers in his hair, scratched himself like a dog, and grunted in an only partially fulfilled satisfaction.

3

Shortly after Richard lifted his shirt, revealing the red blotches on his back, they saw the first of the Territories trees. It grew on the inland side of the highway, its tangle of dark branches and column of thick, irregular bark emerging from a reddish, waxy tangle of poison ivy. Knotholes in the bark gaped, mouths or eyes, at the boys. Down in the thick mat of poison ivy a rustling, rustling of unsatisfied roots agitated the waxy leaves above them, as if a breeze blew through them. Jack said, 'Let's cross the road,' and hoped that Richard had not seen the tree. Behind him he could still hear the thick, rubbery roots prowling through the stems of the ivy.

Is that a BOY? Could that be a BOY up there? A SPECIAL boy perhaps?

Richard's hands flew from his sides to his shoulders to his temples to his scalp. On his cheeks, the second wave of raised bumps resembled horror-movie makeup – he could have been a juvenile monster from one of Lily Cavanaugh's old films. Jack saw that on the backs of Richard's hands the red bumps of the rash had begun to grow together into great red welts.

'Can you really keep going, Richard?' he asked.

Richard nodded. 'Sure. For a while.' He squinted back across the road. 'That wasn't a regular tree, was it? I never saw a tree like that before, not even in a book. It was a Territories tree, wasn't it?'

''Fraid so,' Jack said.

'That means the Territories are really close, doesn't it?'

'I guess it does.'

'So there'll be more of those trees up ahead, won't there?'

'If you know the answers, why ask the questions?' Jack asked. 'Oh Jason, what a dumb thing to say. I'm sorry, Richie – I guess I was hoping that you didn't see it. Yeah, I suppose there'll be more of them up there. Let's just not get too close to them.'

In any case, Jack thought, 'up there' was hardly an accurate way to describe where they were going: the highway slid resolutely down a steady grade, and every hundred feet seemed to take it farther from the light. Everything seemed invaded by the Territories.

'Could you take a look at my back?' Richard asked.

'Sure.' Jack again lifted Richard's shirt. He kept himself from saying anything, though his instinct was to groan. Richard's back was now covered with raised red blotches which seemed almost to radiate heat. 'It's a little worse,' he said.

'I thought it had to be. Only a little, huh?'

'Only a little.'

Before long, Jack thought, Richard was going to look one hell of a lot like an alligator suitcase – Alligator Boy, son of Elephant Man.

Two of the trees grew together a short way ahead, their warty trunks twisted around each other in a way that suggested violence more than love. As Jack stared at them while they hurried past, he thought he saw the black holes in the bark mouthing at them, blowing curses or kisses: and he knew that he heard the roots gnashing together at the base of the joined trees. *(BOY! A BOY's out there! OUR boy's out there!)*

Though it was only mid-afternoon, the air was dark, oddly grainy, like an old newspaper photograph. Where grass had grown on the inland side of the highway, where Queen Anne's lace had bloomed delicately and whitely, low unrecognizable weeds blanketed the earth. With no blossoms and few leaves, they resembled snakes coiled together and smelled faintly of diesel oil. Occasionally the sun flared through the granular murk like a dim orange fire. Jack was reminded of a photograph he had once seen of Gary, Indiana, at night – hellish flames feeding on poison in a black, poisoned sky. From down there the Talisman pulled at him as surely as if it were a giant with its hands on his clothes. The nexus of all possible worlds. He would take Richard into that hell – and fight for his life with all his strength – if he had to haul him along by the ankles. And Richard must have seen this determination in Jack, for, scratching at his sides and shoulders, he toiled along beside him.

I'm going to do this, Jack said to himself, and tried to ignore how greatly he was merely trying to bolster his courage. *If I have to go through a dozen different worlds, I'm going to do it.*

4

Three hundred yards farther down the road a stand of the ugly Territories trees hovered by the side of the highway like muggers. As he passed by on the other side of the road, Jack glanced at their coiling roots and saw half-embedded in the earth through which they wove a small bleached skeleton, once a boy of eight or nine, still wearing a mouldering green-and-black plaid shirt. Jack swallowed and hurried on, trailing Richard behind like a pet on a leash.

5

A few minutes later Jack Sawyer beheld Point Venuti for the first time.

CHAPTER THIRTY-NINE
POINT VENUTI

1

Point Venuti hung low in the landscape, clinging to the sides of the cliff leading down to the ocean. Behind it, another range of cliffs rose massively but raggedly into the dark air. They looked like ancient elephants, hugely wrinkled. The road led down past high wooden walls until it turned a corner by a long brown metal building that was a factory or warehouse, where it disappeared into a descending series of terraces, the dull roofs of other warehouses. From Jack's perspective, the road did not reappear again until it began to mount the rise opposite, going uphill and south toward San Francisco. He saw only the stairlike descent of the warehouse roofs, the fenced-in parking lots, and, way off to the right, the wintry gray of the water. No people moved on any portion of the road visible to him; nobody appeared in the row of little windows at the back of the nearest factory. Dust swirled through the empty parking lots. Point Venuti looked deserted, but Jack knew that it was not. Morgan Sloat and his cohorts – those who had survived the surprise arrival of the Territories choo-choo, anyway – would be waiting for the arrival of Travelling Jack and Rational Richard. The Talisman boomed out to Jack, urging him forward, and he said, 'Well, this is it, kiddo,' and stepped forward.

Two new facets of Point Venuti immediately came into view. The first was the appearance of approximately nine inches of the rear of a Cadillac limousine – Jack saw the glossy black paint, the shiny bumper, part of the right taillight. Jack wished fervently that the renegade Wolf behind the wheel had been one of the Camp Readiness casualties. Then he looked out toward the ocean again. Gray water lathered toward the shore. A slow movement up above the factory and warehouse roofs took his attention in the middle of his next step. COME HERE, the Talisman called in that urgent, magnetic manner. Point Venuti seemed somehow to contract like a hand into a fist. Up above the roofs, and only now visible, a dark but colorless weathervane shaped like the head of a wolf spun erratically back and forth, obeying no wind.

When Jack saw the lawless weathervane tracking left-right, then right-left, and continuing around in a complete circle, he knew that he had just had his first sight of the black hotel – at least a portion of it. From the roofs of the warehouses, from the road ahead, from all of the unseen town, rose an unmistakable feeling of enmity as palpable as a slap in the face. The Territories were bleeding through into Point Venuti, Jack realized; here, reality had been sanded thin. The wolf's head whirled meaninglessly in mid-air, and the Talisman continued to pull at Jack. COME HERE COME HERE COME NOW COME NOW NOW . . . Jack realized that along with its incredible and increasing pull, the Talisman was singing to him. Wordlessly, tunelessly, but singing, a curving rise and fall of whale's melody that would be inaudible to anyone else.

The Talisman knew he had just seen the hotel's weathervane.

Point Venuti might be the most depraved and dangerous place in all North and South America, Jack thought, suddenly bolder by half, but it could not keep him from going into the Agincourt Hotel. He turned to Richard, feeling now as if he had been doing nothing but resting and exercising for a month, and tried not to let his dismay at his friend's condition show in his face. Richard could not stop him, either – if he had to, he'd shove Richard right through the walls of the damned hotel. He saw tormented Richard drag his fingernails through his hair and down the hivelike rash on his temples and cheeks.

'We're going to do this, Richard,' he said. 'I know we are. I don't care how much crazy bullshit they throw at us. We are going to do this.'

'Our troubles are going to have troubles with us,' said Richard, quoting – surely unconsciously – from Dr Seuss. He paused. 'I don't know if I can make it. That's the truth. I'm dead on my feet.' He gave Jack a look of utterly naked anguish. 'What's *happening* to me, Jack?'

'I don't know, but I know how to stop it.' And hoped that that was true.

'Is my father doing this to me?' Richard asked miserably. He ran his hands experimentally over his puffy face. Then he lifted his shirt out of his trousers and examined the red coalescing rash on his stomach. The bumps, shaped vaguely like the state of Oklahoma, began at his waistline and extended around both sides and up nearly to his neck. 'It looks like a virus or something. Did my father give it to me?'

'I don't think he did it on purpose, Richie,' Jack said. 'If that means anything.'

'It doesn't,' Richard said.

'It's all going to stop. The Seabrook Island Express is coming to the end of the line.'

Richard right beside him, Jack stepped forward – and

saw the taillights of the Cadillac flash on, then off, before the car slipped forward out of his sight.

There would be no surprise attack this time, no wonderful slam-bang arrival through a fence with a trainful of guns and ammunition, but even if everybody in Point Venuti knew they were coming, Jack was on his way. He felt suddenly as if he had strapped on armor, as if he held a magic sword. Nobody in Point Venuti had the power to harm him, at least not until he got to the Agincourt Hotel. He was on his way, Rational Richard beside him, and all would be well. And before he had taken three more steps, his muscles singing along with the Talisman, he had a better, more accurate image of himself than of a knight going out to do battle.The image came straight from one of his mother's movies, delivered by celestial telegram. It was as if he were on a horse, a broad-brimmed hat on his head and a gun tied to his hip, riding in to clean up Deadwood Gulch.

Last Train to Hangtown, he remembered; Lily Cavanaugh, Clint Walker, and Will Hutchins, 1960. So be it.

2

Four or five of the Territories trees struggled out of the hard brown soil beside the first of the abandoned buildings. Maybe they had been there all along, snaking their branches over the road nearly to the white line, maybe not; Jack could not remember seeing them when he first looked down toward the concealed town. It was scarcely more conceivable, though, that he could overlook the trees than he could a pack of wild dogs. He could hear their roots rustling along the surface of the ground as he and Richard approached the warehouse.

(OUR boy? OUR boy?)

'Let's get on the other side of the road,' he said to Richard, and took his lumpy hand to lead him across.

As soon as they reached the opposite side of the road, one of the Territories trees visibly stretched out, root and branch, for them. If trees had stomachs, they could have heard its stomach growl. The gnarly branch and the smooth snakelike root whipped across the yellow line, then across half the remaining distance to the boys. Jack prodded gasping Richard in the side with his elbow, then grasped his arm and pulled him along.

(MY MY MY MY BOY! YESSS!!)

A tearing, ripping sound suddenly filled the air, and for a moment Jack thought that Morgan of Orris was raping a passage through the worlds again, becoming Morgan Sloat . . . Morgan Sloat with a final, not-to-be-refused offer involving a machinegun, a blowtorch, a pair of red-hot pincers . . . but instead of Richard's furious father, the crown of the Territories tree struck the middle of the road, bounced once in a snapping of branches, then rolled over on its side like a dead animal.

'Oh my God,' Richard said. 'It came right out of the ground after us.'

Which was precisely what Jack had been thinking. 'Kamikaze tree,' he said. 'I think things are going to be a little wild here in Point Venuti.'

'Because of the black hotel?'

'Sure – but also because of the Talisman.' He looked down the road and saw another clump of the carnivorous trees about ten yards down the hill. 'The vibes or the atmosphere or whatever the ding-dong you want to call it are all screwed up – because everything's evil and good, black and white, all mixed up.'

Jack was keeping his eye on the clump of trees they now slowly approached as he talked, and saw the nearest tree twitch its crown toward them, as if it had heard his voice.

Maybe this whole town is a big Oatley, Jack was thinking, and maybe he would come through after all – but if there was a tunnel up ahead, the last thing Jack Sawyer was going to do was enter it. He really did not want to meet the Point Venuti version of Elroy.

'I'm afraid,' Richard said behind him. 'Jack, what if more of those trees can jump out of the ground like that?'

'You know,' Jack said, 'I've noticed that even when trees are mobile, they can't actually get very far. Even a turkey like you ought to be able to outrun a tree.'

He was rounding the last curve in the road, going downhill past the final warehouses. The Talisman called and called, as vocal as the giant's singing harp in 'Jack and the Beanstalk'. At last Jack came around the curve, and the rest of Point Venuti lay beneath him.

His Jason-side kept him going. Point Venuti might once have been a pleasant little resort town, but those days had passed long ago. Now Point Venuti itself was the Oatley tunnel, and he would have to walk through all of it. The cracked, broken surface of the road dipped toward an area of burned-out houses surrounded by Territories trees – the workers in the empty factories and warehouses would have lived in these small frame houses. Enough was left of one or two of them to show what they had been. The twisted hulks of burned cars lay here and there about the houses, entwined with thick weeds. Through the wasted foundations of the little houses, the roots of the Territories trees slowly prowled. Blackened bricks and boards, upended and smashed bathtubs, twisted pipes littered the burned-out lots.

A flash of white caught Jack's eye, but he looked away as soon as he saw that it was the white bone of a disarranged skeleton hooked beneath the tangle of roots. Once children had piloted bikes through these streets, housewives had gathered in kitchens to complain about wages and unemployment, men had waxed their cars in their driveways – all gone, now. A tipped-over swingset, powdery with rust, poked its limbs through rubble and weeds.

Reddish little flares winked on and off in the murky sky.

Below the two-block-square area of burned houses and feeding trees, a dead stoplight hung over an empty intersection. Across the intersection, the side of a charred building still showed letters reading UH OH! BETTER GET MAA over a pocked, blistered picture of the front end of a car protruding through a plate-glass window. The fire had gone no farther, but Jack wished that it had. Point Venuti was a blighted town; and fire was better than rot. The building with the half-destroyed advertisement for Maaco paint stood first in a row of shops. The Dangerous Planet Bookstore, Tea & Sympathy, Ferdy's Wholefood Healthstore, Neon Village: Jack could read only a few of the names of the shops, for above most of them the paint had long ago flaked and curdled off the facades. These shops appeared to be closed, as abandoned as the factories and warehouses up the hill. Even from where he stood, Jack could see that the plate-glass windows had been broken so long ago they were like empty eyeglass frames, blank idiot eyes. Smears of paint decorated the fronts of the shops, red and black and yellow, oddly bright and scarlike in the dull gray air. A naked woman, so starved Jack could have counted her ribs, twisted slowly and ceremoniously as a weathervane in the littered street before the shops.

Above her pale body with its drooping breasts and mop of pubic hair, her face had been painted blazing orange. Orange, too, was her hair. Jack stopped moving and watched the insane woman with the painted face and dyed hair raise her arms, twist her upper body as deliberately as one doing a Tai Chi movement, kick her left foot out over the flyblown corpse of a dog, and freeze into position like a statue. An emblem of all Point Venuti, the madwoman held her posture. Slowly the foot came down, and the skinny body revolved.

Past the woman, past the row of empty shops, Main Street turned residential – at least Jack supposed that it had once been residential. Here, too, bright scars of paint defaced the buildings, tiny two-story houses once bright white, now covered with the slashes of paint and graffiti. One slogan jumped out at him: YOU'RE DEAD NOW, scrawled up the side of an isolated peeling building that had surely once been a boarding house. The words had been there a long time.

JASON, I NEED YOU, the Talisman boomed out at him in a language both above and beneath speech.

'I can't,' Richard whispered beside him. 'Jack, I know I can't.'

After the row of peeling, hopeless-looking houses, the road dipped again, and Jack could see only the backs of a pair of black Cadillac limousines, one on either side of Main Street, parked with their noses pointed downhill, motors running. Like a trick photograph, looking impossibly large, impossibly sinister, the top – half? third? – of the black hotel reared up over the back ends of the Cadillacs and the despairing little houses. It seemed to float, cut off by the curve of the final hill. 'I can't go in there,' Richard repeated.

'I'm not even sure we can get past those trees,' Jack said. 'Hold your water, Richie.'

Richard uttered an odd, snuffling noise which it took Jack a second to recognize as the sound of crying. He put his arm over Richard's shoulder. The hotel owned the landscape – that much was obvious. The black hotel owned Point Venuti, the air above it, the ground beneath. Looking at it, Jack saw the weathervanes spin in contradictory directions, the turrets and gambrels rise like warts into the gray air. The Agincourt did look as if it were made of stone – thousand-year-old stone, black as tar. In one of the upper windows, a light suddenly flashed – to Jack, it was as if the hotel had winked at him, secretly amused to find him at last so near. A dim figure seemed to glide away from the window: a second later the reflection of a cloud swam across the glass.

From somewhere inside, the Talisman trilled out its song only Jack could hear.

3

'I think it grew,' Richard breathed. He had forgotten to scratch since he had seen the hotel floating past the final hill. Tears ran over and through the raised red bumps on his cheeks, and Jack saw that his eyes were now completely encased by the raised rash – Richard didn't have to squint to squint anymore. 'It's impossible, but the hotel used to be smaller, Jack. I'm sure of it.'

'Right now, nothing's impossible,' Jack said, almost unnecessarily – they had long ago passed into the realm of the impossible. And the Agincourt was so large, so dominating, that it was wildly out of scale with the rest of the town.

The architectural extravagance of the black hotel, all the turrets and brass weathervanes attached to fluted towers, the cupolas and gambrels which should have made it a playful fantasy, instead made it menacing, nightmarish. It looked as though it belonged in some kind of anti-Disneyland where Donald Duck had strangled Huey, Dewey, and Louie and Mickey shot Minnie Mouse full of heroin.

'I'm afraid,' Richard said; and JASON COME NOW, sang out the Talisman.

'Just stick close to me, pal, and we'll go through that place like grease through a goose.'

JASON COME NOW!

The clump of Territories trees just ahead rustled as Jack stepped forward.

Richard, frightened, hung back – it might have been, Jack realized, that Richard was nearly blind by now, deprived of his glasses and with his eyes gradually being squeezed shut. He reached behind him and pulled Richard forward, feeling as he did so how thin Richard's hand and wrist had become.

Richard came stumbling along. His skinny wrist burned in Jack's hand. 'Whatever you do, don't slow down,' Jack said. 'All we have to do is get by them.'

'I can't,' Richard sobbed.

'Do you want me to carry you? I'm being serious, Richard. I mean, this could be a lot worse. I bet if we hadn't blown so many of his troops away back there, he'd have guards every fifty feet.'

'You couldn't move fast enough if you carried me. I'd slow you down.'

What in the Sam Hill do you think you're doing now? went through Jack's mind, but he said, 'Stay on my far side and go like hell, Richie. When I say three. Got it? One . . . two . . . three!'

He jerked Richard's arm and began sprinting past the trees. Richard stumbled, gasped, then managed to right himself and keep on moving without falling down. Geysers of dust appeared at the base of the trees, a commotion of shredding earth and scrambling things that looked like enormous beetles, shiny as shoe polish. A small brown bird took off out of the weeds near the clump of conspiring trees, and a limber root like an elephant's trunk whipped out of the dust and snatched it from the air.

Another root snaked toward Jack's left ankle, but fell short. The mouths in the coarse bark howled and screamed.

(LOVERRR? LOVER BOYYY?)

Jack clenched his teeth together and tried to force Richard Sloat to fly. The heads of the complicated trees had begun to sway and bow. Whole nests and families of roots were slithering toward the white line, moving as though they had independent wills. Richard faltered, then unambiguously slowed as he turned his head to look past Jack toward the reaching trees.

'Move!' Jack yelled, and yanked at Richard's arm. The red lumps felt like hot stones buried beneath the skin. He hauled away at Richard, seeing too many of the whickering roots crawl gleefully toward them across the white line.

Jack put his arm around Richard's waist at the same instant that a long root whistled through the air and wrapped itself around Richard's arm.

'Jesus!' Richard yelled. 'Jason! It got me! It got me!'

In horror Jack saw the tip of the root, a blind worm's head, lift up and stare at him. It twitched almost lazily in the air, then wound itself once again around Richard's burning arm. Other roots came sliding toward them across the road.

Jack yanked Richard back as hard as he could, and gained another six inches. The root around Richard's arm grew taut. Jack locked his arms around Richard's waist and hauled him mercilessly backward. Richard let out an unearthly, floating scream. For a second, Jack was afraid that Richard's shoulder had separated, but a voice large within him said *PULL!* and he dug in his heels and pulled back even harder.

Then they both nearly went tumbling into a nest of crawling roots, for the single tendril around Richard's arm had neatly snapped. Jack stayed on his feet only by backpedalling frantically, bending over at the waist to keep Richard, too, off the road. In this way they got past the last of the trees just as they heard the rending, snapping sounds they had heard once before. This time, Jack did not have to tell Richard to run for it.

The nearest tree came roaring up out of the ground and fell with a ground-shaking thud only three or four feet behind Richard. The others crashed to the surface of the road behind it, waving their roots like wild hair.

'You saved my life,' Richard said. He was crying again, more from weakness and exhaustion and shock than from fear.

'From now on, my old pal, you ride piggy-back,' Jack said, panting, and bent down to help Richard get on his back.

4

'I should have told you,' Richard was whispering. His face burned against Jack's neck, his mouth against Jack's ear. 'I don't want you to hate me, but I wouldn't blame you if you did, really I wouldn't. I know I should have told you.' He seemed to weigh no more than the husk of himself, as if nothing were left inside him.

'About what?' Jack settled Richard squarely in the center of his back, and again had the unsettling feeling that he was carrying only an empty sack of flesh.

'The man who came to visit my father . . . and Camp Readiness . . . and the closet.' Richard's hollow-seeming body trembled against his friend's back. 'I should have told you. But I couldn't even tell *myself*.' His breath, hot as his skin, blew agitatedly into Jack's ear.

Jack thought, *The Talisman is doing this to him.* An instant later he corrected himself. *No. The black hotel is doing this to him.*

The two limousines which had been parked nose-down at the brow of the next hill had disappeared sometime during the fight with the Territories trees, but the hotel endured, growing larger with every forward step Jack took. The skinny naked woman, another of the hotel's victims, still performed her mad slow dance before the bleak row of shops. The little red flares danced, winked out, danced in the murky air. It was no time at all, neither morning nor afternoon nor night – it was time's Blasted Lands. The Agincourt Hotel did seem made of stone, though Jack knew it was not – the wood seemed to have calcified and thickened, to have blackened of itself, from the inside out. The brass weather-vanes, wolf and crow and snake and circular cryptic designs Jack did not recognize, swung about to contradictory winds. Several of the windows flashed a warning at Jack; but that might have been merely a reflection of one of the red flares. He still could not see the bottom of the hill and the Agincourt's ground floor, and would not be able to see them until he had gone past the bookstore, tea shop, and other stores that had escaped the fire. Where was Morgan Sloat?

Where, for that matter, was the whole god-forsaken reception committee? Jack tightened his grip on Richard's sticklike legs, hearing the Talisman call him again, and felt a tougher stronger being rear up within him.

'Don't hate me because I couldn't . . .' Richard said, his voice trailing off at the end.

JASON, COME NOW COME NOW!

Jack gripped Richard's thin legs and walked down past the burned-over area where so many houses had once stood. The Territories trees which used these wasted blocks as their own private lunch counter whispered and stirred, but they were too far away to trouble Jack.

The woman in the midst of the empty littered street slowly swivelled around as she became aware of the boys' progress down the hill. She was in the midst of a complex exercise, but all suggestion of Tai Chi Chuan left her when she dropped her arms and one outstretched leg and stood stockstill beside a dead dog, watching burdened Jack come down the hill toward her. For a moment she seemed to be a mirage, too hallucinatory to be real, this starved woman with her stick-out hair and face the same brilliant orange; then she awkwardly bolted across the street and into one of the shops without a name. Jack grinned, without knowing he was going to do it – the sense of triumph and of something he could only describe as armored virtue took him so much by surprise.

'Can you really make it there?' Richard gasped, and Jack said, 'Right now I can do anything.'

He could have carried Richard all the way back to

Illinois if the great singing object imprisoned in the hotel had ordered him to do it. Again Jack felt that sense of coming resolution, and thought, *It's so dark here because all those worlds are crowded together, jammed up like a triple exposure on film.*

5

He sensed the people of Point Venuti before he saw them. They would not attack him – Jack had known that with absolute certainty ever since the madwoman had fled into one of the shops. They were watching him. From beneath porches, through lattices, from the backs of empty rooms, they peered out at him, whether with fear, rage, or frustration he could not tell.

Richard had fallen asleep or passed out on his back, and was breathing in heated harsh little puffs.

Jack skirted the body of the dog and glanced sideways into the hole where the window of the Dangerous Planet Bookstore should have been. At first he saw only the messy macaroni of used hypodermic needles which covered the floor, atop and beside the splayed books spread here and there. On the walls, the tall shelves stood empty as yawns. Then a convulsive movement in the dim back of the store caught his eye, and two pale figures coalesced out of the gloom. Both had beards and long naked bodies in which the tendons stood out like cords. The whites of four mad eyes flashed at him. One of the naked men had only one hand and was grinning. His erection waved before him, a thick pale club. He couldn't have seen that, he told himself. Where was the man's other hand? He glanced back. Now he saw only a tangle of skinny white limbs.

Jack did not look into the windows of any of the other shops, but eyes tracked him as he passed.

Soon he was walking past the tiny two-story houses. YOU'RE DEAD NOW splayed itself on a side wall. He would not look in the windows, he promised himself, he could not.

Orange faces topped with orange hair wagged through a downstairs window.

'Baby,' a woman whispered from the next house. 'Sweet baby Jason.' This time he did look. *You're dead now.* She stood just on the other side of a broken little window, twiddling the chains that had been inserted in her nipples, smiling at him lopsidedly. Jack stared at her vacant eyes, and the woman dropped her hands and hesitantly backed away from the window. The length of chain drooped between her breasts.

Eyes watched Jack from the backs of dark rooms, between lattices, from crawl spaces beneath porches.

The hotel loomed before him, but no longer straight ahead. The road must have delicately angled, for now the Agincourt stood decidedly off to his left. And did it, in fact, actually *loom* as commandingly as it had? His Jason-side, or Jason himself, blazed up within Jack, and saw that the black hotel, though still very large, was nothing like mountainous.

COME I NEED YOU NOW, sang out the Talisman. YOU ARE RIGHT IT IS NOT AS GREAT AS IT WANTS YOU TO BELIEVE.

At the top of the last hill he stopped and looked down. There they were, all right, all of them. And there was the black hotel, all of *it*. Main Street descended to the beach, which was white sand interrupted by big outcroppings of rocks like jagged discolored teeth. The Agincourt reared up a short distance off to his left, flanked on the ocean side by a massive stone breakwater running far out into the water. Before it, stretching out in a line, a dozen long black limousines, some dusty, others as polished as mirrors, sat, their motors running. Streamers of white exhaust, low-flying clouds whiter than the air, drifted out from many of the cars. Men in FBI-agent black suits patrolled along the fence, holding their hands up to their eyes. When Jack saw two red flashes of light stab out before one of the men's faces, he reflexively dodged sideways around the side of one of the little houses, moving before he was actually conscious that the men carried binoculars.

For a second or two, he must have looked like a beacon, standing upright at the brow of a hill. Knowing that a momentary carelessness had nearly led to his capture, Jack breathed hard for a moment and rested his shoulder against the peeling gray shingles of the house. Jack hitched Richard up to a more comfortable position on his back.

Anyhow, now he knew that he would somehow have to approach the black hotel from its sea side, which meant getting across the beach unseen.

When he straightened up again, he peeked around the side of the house and looked downhill. Morgan Sloat's reduced army sat in its limousines or, random as ants, milled before the high black fence. For a crazy moment Jack recalled with total precision his first sight of the Queen's summer palace. Then, too, he had stood above a scene crowded with people moving back and forth with apparent randomness. What was it like there, now? On that day – which seemed to have taken place in pre-history, so far must he look back – the crowds before the pavillion, the entire scene, had in spite of all an undeniable aura of peace, of order. That would be gone now, Jack knew. Now Osmond would rule the scene before the great tentlike structure, and those people brave enough to enter the pavillion would scurry in, heads averted.

And what of the Queen? Jack wondered. He could not help remembering that shockingly familiar face cradled in the whiteness of bed linen.

And then Jack's heart nearly froze, and the vision of the pavillion and the sick Queen dropped into a slot in Jack's memory. Sunlight Gardener strolled into Jack's line of vision, a bullhorn in his hand. Wind from the sea blew a thick strand of white hair across his sunglasses. For a second Jack was sure that he could smell his odor of sweet cologne and jungle rot. Jack forgot to breathe for perhaps five seconds, and just stood beside the cracked and peeling shingle wall, staring down as a madman yelled orders to black-suited men, pirouetted, pointed at something hidden from Jack, and made an expressive moue of disapproval.

He remembered to breathe.

'Well, we've got an interesting situation here, Richard,' Jack said. 'We got a hotel that can double its size whenever it wants to, I guess, and down there we also have the world's craziest man.'

Richard, who Jack had thought was asleep, surprised him by mumbling something audible only as *guffuf*.

'What?'

'Go for it,' Richard whispered weakly. 'Move it, chum.'

Jack actually laughed. A second later, he was carefully moving downhill past the backs of houses, going through tall horsetail grass toward the beach.

CHAPTER FORTY
SPEEDY ON THE BEACH

1

At the bottom of the hill, Jack flattened out in the grass and crawled, carrying Richard as he had once carried his backpack. When he reached the border of high yellow weeds alongside the edge of the road, he inched forward on his belly and looked out. Directly ahead of him, on the other side of the road, the beach began. Tall weatherbeaten rocks jutted out of the grayish sand; grayish water foamed onto the shore. Jack looked leftward down the street. A short distance past the hotel, on the inland side of the beach road, stood a long crumbling structure like a sliced-off wedding cake. Above it a wooden sign with a great hole in it read KINGSLA   TEL. The Kingsland Motel, Jack remembered, where Morgan Sloat had installed himself and his little boy during his obsessive inspections of the black hotel. A flash of white that was Sunlight Gardener roamed farther up the street, clearly berating several of the black-suited men and flapping his hand toward the hill. *He doesn't know I'm down here already*, Jack realized as one of the men began to trudge across the beach road, looking from side to side. Gardener made another abrupt, commanding gesture, and the limousine parked at the foot of Main Street wheeled away from the hotel and began to coast alongside the man in the black suit. He unbuttoned his jacket as soon as he hit the sidewalk of Main Street and took a pistol from a shoulder holster.

In the limousines the drivers turned their heads and stared up the hill. Jack blessed his luck – five minutes later, and a renegade Wolf with an oversized gun would have ended his quest for that great singing thing in the hotel.

He could see only the top two floors of the hotel, and the madly spinning devices attached to the architectural extravagances on the roof. Because of his worm's-eye angle, the breakwater bisecting the beach on the right side of the hotel seemed to rear up twenty feet or more, marching down the sand and on into the water.

COME NOW COME NOW, called the Talisman in words that were not words, but almost-physical expressions of urgency.

The man with the gun was now out of sight, but the drivers still stared after him as he went uphill toward Point Venuti's lunatics. Sunlight Gardener lifted his bullhorn and roared, 'Root him out! I want him rooted out!' He jabbed the bullhorn at another black-suited man, just raising his binoculars to look down the street in Jack's direction. 'You! Pig-brains! Take the other side of the street . . . and *root that bad boy out*, oh yes, that baddest baddest boy, *baddest* . . .' His voice trailed away as the second man trotted across the street to the opposite sidewalk, his pistol already lengthening his fist.

It was the best chance he'd ever get, Jack realized – nobody was facing down the length of the beach road. 'Hang on tight,' he whispered to Richard, who did not move. 'Time to boogie.' He got his feet up under him, and knew that Richard's back was probably visible above the yellow weeds and tall grass. Bending over, he burst out of the weeds and set his feet on the beach road.

In seconds Jack Sawyer was flat on his stomach in the gritty sand. He pushed himself forward with his feet. One of Richard's hands tightened on his shoulder. Jack wiggled forward across the sand until he had made it behind the first tall outcropping of rock; then he simply stopped moving and lay with his head on his hands, Richard light as a leaf on his back, breathing hard. The water, no more than twenty feet away, beat against the edge of the beach. Jack could still hear Sunlight Gardener screeching about imbeciles and incompetents, his crazy voice drifting down from uphill on Main Street. The Talisman urged him forward, urged him on, on, on . . .

Richard fell off his back.

'You okay?'

Richard raised a thin hand and touched his forehead with his fingers, his cheekbone with his thumb. 'I guess. You see my father?'

Jack shook his head. 'Not yet.'

'But he's here.'

'I guess. He has to be.' The Kingsland, Jack remembered, seeing in his mind the dingy facade, the broken wooden sign. Morgan Sloat would have holed up in the motel he had used so often six or seven years ago. Jack immediately felt the furious presence of Morgan Sloat near him, as if knowing where Sloat was had summoned him up.

'Well, don't worry about him.' Richard's voice was paper-thin. 'I mean, don't worry about me worrying about him. I think he's dead, Jack.'

Jack looked at his friend with a fresh anxiety: could Richard actually be losing his mind? Certainly Richard was feverish. Up on the hill, Sunlight Gardener bawled 'SPREAD OUT!' through his bullhorn.

'You think—'

And then Jack heard another voice, one that had first whispered beneath Gardener's angry command. It was a half-familiar voice, and Jack recognized its timbre and cadence before he had truly identified it. And, oddly, he recognized that the sound of this particular voice made him feel relaxed – almost as if he could stop scheming and fretting now, for everything would be taken care of – before he could name its owner.

'Jack Sawyer,' the voice repeated. 'Over here, sonny.'

The voice was Speedy Parker's.

'I do,' Richard said, and closed his puffy eyes again and looked like a corpse washed up by the tide.

I do think my father is dead, Richard meant, but Jack's mind was far from the ravings of his friend. 'Over here, Jacky,' Speedy called again, and the boy saw that the sound came from the largest group of tall rocks, three joined vertical piles only a few feet from the edge of the water. A dark line, the high-tide mark, cut across the rocks a quarter of the way up.

'Speedy,' Jack whispered.

'Yeah-bob,' came the reply. 'Get yourself over here without them zombies seein you, can you? And bring your frien' along, too.'

Richard still lay face-up on the sand, his hand over his face. 'Come on, Richie,' Jack whispered into his ear. 'We have to move a little bit down the beach. Speedy's here.'

'Speedy?' Richard whispered back, so quietly Jack had trouble hearing the word.

'A friend. See the rocks down there?' He lifted Richard's

head on the reedlike neck. 'He's behind them. He'll help us, Richie. Right now, we could use a little help.'

'I can't really see,' Richard complained. 'And I'm so *tired* . . .'

'Get on my back again.' He turned around and nearly flattened out on the sand. Richard's arms came over his shoulders and feebly joined.

Jack peered around the edge of the rock. Down the beach road, Sunlight Gardener stroked his hair into place as he strode toward the front door of the Kingsland Motel. The black hotel reared up awesomely. The Talisman opened its throat and called for Jack Sawyer. Gardener hesitated outside the door of the motel, swept both hands over his hair, shook his head, and turned smartly about and began walking much more rapidly back up the long line of limousines. The bullhorn lifted. 'REPORTS EVERY FIFTEEN MINUTES!' he screeched. 'YOU POINT MEN – TELL ME IF YOU SEE A BUG MOVE! I MEAN IT, YES I DO!'

Gardener was walking away; everybody else watched him. It was time. Jack kicked off away from his shelter of rock and, bending over while he clasped Richard's skimpy forearms, raced down the beach. His feet kicked up scallops of damp sand. The three joined pillars of rocks, which had seemed so close while he talked to Speedy, now appeared to be half a mile away – the open space between himself and them would not close. It was as if the rocks receded while he ran. Jack expected to hear the crack of a shot. Would he feel the bullet first, or would he hear the report before the bullet knocked him down? At last the three rocks grew larger and larger in his vision, and then he was there, falling onto his chest and skidding behind their protection.

'Speedy!' he said, almost laughing in spite of everything. But the sight of Speedy, who was sitting down beside a colorful little blanket and leaning against the middle pillar of rock, killed the laughter in his throat – killed at least half of his hope, too.

2

For Speedy Parker looked worse than Richard. Much worse. His cracked, leaking face gave Jack a weary nod, and the boy thought that Speedy was confirming his hopelessness. Speedy wore only a pair of old brown shorts, and all of his skin seemed horribly diseased, as if with leprosy.

'Settle down now, ole Travellin Jack,' Speedy whispered in a hoarse, crackling voice. 'There's lots you got to hear, so open your ears up good.'

'How are you?' Jack asked. 'I mean . . . Jesus, Speedy . . . is there anything I can do for you?'

He gently placed Richard down on the sand.

'Open your ears, like I said. Don't you go worryin bout Speedy. I ain't too com'fable, the way you see me now, but I can be com'fable again, if you does the right thing. Your little friend's dad put this hurtin on me – on his own boy, too, looks like. Old Bloat don't want his child in that hotel, no sir. But you got to take him there, son. There ain't but one way about it. You got to do it.'

Speedy seemed to be fading in and out as he talked to Jack, who wanted to scream or wail more than he had at any time since the death of Wolf. His eyes smarted, and he knew he wanted to cry. 'I know, Speedy,' he said. 'I figured that out.'

'You a good boy,' the old man said. He cocked his

head back and regarded Jack carefully. 'You the one, all right. The road laid its mark on you, I see. You the one. You gonna do it.'

'How's my mom, Speedy?' Jack asked. 'Please tell me. She's still alive, isn't she?'

'You can call her soon's you can, find out she's okay,' Speedy answered. 'But first you got to get it, Jack. Because if you *don't* get it, she be dead. And so be Laura, the Queen. She be dead, too.' Speedy hitched himself up, wincing, to straighten his back. 'Let me tell you. Most everybody at the court gave up on her – gave her up for dead already.' His face expressed his disgust. 'They all afraid of Morgan. Because they know Morgan'll take they skin off they backs if they don't swear allegiance to him now. While Laura still got a few breaths in her. But out in the far Territories, two-legged snakes like Osmond and his gang been goin around, tellin folks she already dead. And if she dies, Travellin Jack, if she dies . . .' He levelled his ruined face at the boy. 'Then we got black horror in both worlds. Black horror. And you can call your momma. But first you has to get it. You has to. It's all that's left, now.'

Jack did not have to ask him what he meant.

'I'm glad you understand, son.' Speedy closed his eyes and leaned his head back against the stone.

A second later his eyes slowly opened again. 'Destinies. That's what all this is about. More destinies, more lives, than you know. You ever hear the name Rushton? I spect you might have, all this time gone by.'

Jack nodded.

'All those destinies be the reason your momma brought you all the way to the Alhambra Hotel, Travellin Jack. I was just sittin and waitin, knowin you'd show up. The Talisman pulled you here, boy. Jason. That's a name you heard, too, I spect.'

'It's *me*,' Jack said.

'Then get the Talisman. I brought this l'il thing along, he'p you out some.' He wearily picked up the blanket, which, Jack saw, was of rubber and therefore not a blanket after all.

Jack took the bundle of rubber from Speedy's charred-looking hand. 'How can I get into the hotel, though?' he asked. 'I can't get over the fence, and I can't swim in with Richard.'

'Blow it up.' Speedy's eyes had closed again.

Jack unfolded the object. It was an inflatable raft in the shape of a legless horse.

'Recognize her?' Speedy's voice, ruined as it was, bore a nostalgic lightness. 'You and me picked her up, sometime back. I explained about the names.'

Jack suddenly remembered coming to Speedy, that day that seemed filled with slashes of black and white, and finding him sitting inside a round shed, repairing the merry-go-round horses. *You be takin liberties with the Lady, but I guess she ain't gonna mind if you're helpin me get her back where she belongs*. Now that too had a larger meaning. Another piece of the world locked into place for Jack. 'Silver Lady,' he said.

Speedy winked at him, and again Jack had the eerie sense that everything in his life had conspired to get him to precisely this point. 'Your friend here all right?' It was – almost – a deflection.

'I think so.' Jack looked uneasily at Richard, who had rolled on his side and was breathing shallowly, his eyes shut.

'Then long's you think so, blow up ole Silver Lady here. You gotta bring that boy in with you no matter what. He's a part of it, too.'

Speedy's skin seemed to be getting worse as they sat on the beach – it had a sickly ash-gray tinge. Before Jack put the air nozzle to his mouth he asked, 'Can't I do anything for you, Speedy?'

'Sure. Go to the Point Venuti drugstore and fetch me a bottle of Lydia Pinkham's ointment.' Speedy shook his head. 'You know how to he'p Speedy Parker, boy. Get the Talisman. That's all the he'p I need.'

Jack blew into the nozzle.

3

A very short time later he was pushing in the stopper located beside the tail of a raft shaped like a four-foot-long rubber horse with an abnormally broad back.

'I don't know if I'll be able to get Richard on this thing,' he said, not complaining but merely thinking out loud.

'He be able to follow orders, ole Travellin Jack. Just sit behind him, kind of he'p hold him on. That's all he needs.'

And in fact Richard had pulled himself into the lee of the standing rocks and was breathing smoothly and regularly through his open mouth. He might have been either asleep or awake, Jack could not tell which.

'All right,' Jack said. 'Is there a pier or something out behind that place?'

'Better than a pier, Jacky. Once you gets out beyond the breakwater, you'll see big pilins – they built part of the hotel right out over the water. You'll see a ladder down in them pilins. Get Richard there up the ladder and you be on the big deck out back. Big windows right there – the kind of windows that be doors, you know? Open up one of them window-doors and you be in the dinin room.' He managed to smile. 'Once you in the dinin room, I reckon you'll be able to sniff out the Talisman. And don't be afraid of her, sonny. She's been waitin for you – she'll come to your hand like a good hound.'

'What's to stop all these guys from coming in after me?'

'Shoo, *they* can't go in the black hotel.' Disgust with Jack's stupidity was printed in every line on Speedy's face.

'I know, I mean in the water. Why wouldn't they come after me with a boat or something?'

Now Speedy managed a painful but genuine smile. 'I think you gonna see why, Travellin Jack. Ole Bloat and his boys gotta steer clear of the water, hee hee. Don't worry about that now – just remember what I told you and get to gettin, hear?'

'I'm already there,' Jack said, and edged toward the rocks to peer around at the beach road and the hotel. He had managed to get across the road and to Speedy's cover without being seen: surely he could drag Richard the few feet down to the water and get him on the raft. With any luck at all, he should be able to make it unseen all the way to the pilings – Gardener and the men with binoculars were concentrating on the town and the hillside.

Jack peeked around the side of one of the tall columns. The limousines still stood before the hotel. Jack put his head out an inch or two farther to look across the street. A man in a black suit was just stepping through the door of the wreck of the Kingsland Motel – he was trying, Jack saw, to keep from looking at the black hotel.

A whistle began to shrill, as high and insistent as a woman's scream.

'Move!' Speedy whispered hoarsely.

Jack jerked his head up and saw at the top of the grassy rise behind the crumbling houses a black-suited man blasting away at the whistle and pointing straight downhill at him. The man's dark hair swayed around his shoulders – hair, black suit, and sunglasses, he looked like the Angel of Death.

'FOUND HIM! FOUND HIM!' Gardener bawled. 'SHOOT HIM! A THOUSAND DOLLARS TO THE BROTHER WHO BRINGS ME HIS BALLS!'

Jack recoiled back into the safety of the rocks. A half-second later a bullet spanged off the front of the middle pillar just before the sound of the shot reached them. *So now I know*, Jack thought as he grabbed Richard's arm and pulled him toward the raft. *First you get knocked down, then you hear the gun go off.*

'You gotta go now,' Speedy said in a breathless rush of words. 'In thirty seconds, there's gonna be a lot more shootin. Stay behind the breakwater as long's you can and then cut over. Get her, Jack.'

Jack gave Speedy a frantic, driven look as a second bullet smacked into the sand before their little redoubt. Then he pushed Richard down in the front of the raft and saw with some satisfaction that Richard had enough presence of mind to grasp and hang on to the separate rubbery tufts of the mane. Speedy lifted his right hand in a gesture both wave and blessing. On his knees Jack gave the raft a shove which sent it almost to the edge of the water. He heard another trilling blast of the whistle. Then he scrambled to his feet. He was still running when the raft hit the water, and was wet to the waist when he pulled himself into it.

Jack paddled steadily out to the breakwater. When he reached the end, he turned into unprotected open water and began paddling.

4

After that, Jack concentrated on his paddling, firmly putting out of his mind any considerations of what he would do if Morgan's men had killed Speedy. He had to get under the pilings, and that was that. A bullet hit the water, causing a tiny eruption of droplets about six feet to his left. He heard another ricochet off the breakwater with a *ping*. Jack paddled forward with his whole strength.

Some time, he knew not how long, went by. At last he rolled off the side of the raft and swam to the back, so that he could push it even faster by scissoring his legs. An almost imperceptible current swept him nearer his goal. At last the pilings began, high crusty columns of wood as thick around as telephone poles. Jack raised his chin out of the water and saw the immensity of the hotel lifting itself above the wide black deck, leaning out over him. He glanced back and to his right, but Speedy had not moved. Or had he? Speedy's arms looked different. Maybe –

There was a flurry of movement on the long grassy descent behind the row of falling-down houses. Jack looked up and saw four of the men in black suits racing down toward the beach. A wave slapped the raft, almost taking it from his grasp. Richard moaned. Two of the men pointed toward him. Their mouths moved.

Another high wave rocked the raft and threatened to push both raft and Jack Sawyer back toward the beach.

Wave, Jack thought, what wave?

He looked up over the front of the raft as soon as it dipped again into a trough. The broad gray back of something surely too large to be a mere fish was sinking beneath the surface. A shark? Jack was uneasily conscious of his two legs fluttering out behind him in the water. He ducked his head under, afraid he'd see a long cigar-shaped stomach with teeth sweeping toward him.

He did not see that shape, not exactly, but what he saw astounded him.

The water, which appeared now to be very deep, was as full as an aquarium, though one containing no fish of normal size or description. In this aquarium only monsters swam. Beneath Jack's legs moved a zoo of outsize, sometimes horrendously ugly animals. They must have been beneath him and the raft ever since the water had grown deep enough to accommodate them, for the water was crowded everywhere. The thing that had frightened the renegade Wolfs glided by ten feet down, long as a southbound freight train. It moved upward as he watched. A film over its eyes blinked. Long whiskers trailed back from its cavernous mouth – it had a mouth like an elevator door, Jack thought. The creature glided past him, pushing Jack closer to the hotel with the weight of the water it displaced, and raised its dripping snout above the surface. Its furry profile resembled Neanderthal Man's.

Ole Bloat and his boys gotta steer clear of the water, Speedy had told him, and laughed.

Whatever force had sealed the Talisman in the black hotel had set these creatures in the waters off Point Venuti to make sure that the wrong people kept away; and Speedy had known it. The great bodies of the creatures in the water delicately nudged the raft nearer and nearer the pilings, but the waves they made kept Jack from getting all but the most fragmentary view of what was happening on shore.

He rode up a crest and saw Sunlight Gardener, his hair flowing out behind him, standing beside the black fence levelling a long heavy hunting rifle at his head. The raft sank into the trough; the shell sizzled past far overhead with a noise of a hummingbird's passing; the report came. When Gardener shot next, a fishlike thing ten feet long with a great sail of a dorsal fin rose straight up out of the water and stopped the bullet. In one motion, the creature rolled back down and sliced into the water again. Jack saw a great ragged hole in its side. The next time he rode up a crest, Gardener was trotting off across the beach, clearly on his way to the Kingsland Motel. The giant fish continued to wash him diagonally forward toward the pilings.

5

A ladder, Speedy had said, and as soon as Jack was under the wide deck he peered through the gloom to try to find it. The thick pilings, encrusted with algae and barnacles and dripping with seaweed, stood in four rows. If the ladder had been installed at the time the deck was built it might easily be useless now – at the least a wooden ladder would be hard to see, overgrown with weed and barnacles. The big shaggy pilings were now much thicker than they had been originally. Jack got his forearms over the back of the raft and used the thick rubbery tail to lever himself back inside. Then, shivering, he unbuttoned his sodden shirt – the same white button-down, at least one size too small, Richard had given him on the other side of the Blasted Lands – and dropped it squashily in the bottom of the raft. His shoes had fallen off in the water, and he peeled off the wet socks and tossed them on top of the shirt. Richard sat in the bow of the raft, slouching forward over his knees, his eyes shut and his mouth closed.

'We're looking for a ladder,' Jack said.

Richard acknowledged this with a barely perceptible movement of his head.

'Do you think you could get up a ladder, Richie?'

'Maybe,' Richard whispered.

'Well, it's around here somewhere. Probably attached to one of these pilings.'

Jack paddled with both hands, bringing the raft between two of the pilings in the first row. The Talisman's call was continuous now, and seemed nearly strong enough to pick him up out of the raft and deposit him on the deck. They were drifting between the first and second rows of pilings, already under the heavy black line of the deck above; here as well as outside, little red flares ignited in the air, twisted, winked out. Jack counted: four rows of pilings, five pilings in each row. Twenty places where the ladder might be. With the darkness beneath the deck and the endless refinements of corridors suggested by the pilings, being here was like taking a tour of the Catacombs.

'They didn't shoot us,' Richard said without affect. In the same tone of voice he might have said, 'The store is out of bread.'

'We had some help.' He looked at Richard, slumped over his knees. Richard would never be able to get up a ladder unless he were somehow galvanized.

'We're coming up to a piling,' Jack said. 'Lean forward and shove us off, will you?'

'What?'

'Keep us from bumping into the piling,' Jack repeated. 'Come on, Richard. I need your help.'

It seemed to work. Richard cracked open his left eye and put his right hand on the edge of the raft. As they drifted nearer to the thick piling he held out his left hand to deflect them. Then something on the pillar made a smacking sound, as of lips pulled wetly apart.

Richard grunted and retracted his hand.

'What was it?' Jack said, and Richard did not have to answer – now both boys saw the sluglike creatures clinging to the pilings. Their eyes had been closed, too, and their mouths. Agitated, they began to shift positions on their pillars, clattering their teeth. Jack put his hands in the water and swung the bow of the raft around the piling.

'Oh God,' Richard said. Those lipless tiny mouths held a quantity of teeth. 'God, I can't take—'

'You have to take it, Richard,' Jack said. 'Didn't you hear Speedy back there on the beach? He might even be dead now, Richard, and if he is, he died so he could be certain that I knew you had to go in the hotel.'

Richard had closed his eyes again.

'And I don't care how many slugs we have to kill to get up the ladder, you are going up the ladder, Richard. That's all. That's it.'

'Shit on you,' Richard said. 'You don't have to talk to me like that. I'm sick of your being so high and mighty. I know I'm going up the ladder, wherever it is. I probably have a fever of a hundred and five, but I know I'm going up that ladder. I just don't know if I can take it. So to hell with you.' Richard had uttered this entire speech with his eyes shut. He effortfully forced both eyes open again. 'Nuts.'

'I need you,' Jack said.

'Nuts. I'll get up the ladder, you asshole.'

'In that case, I'd better find it,' Jack said, pushed the raft forward toward the next row of pilings, and saw it.

6

The ladder hung straight down between the two inner rows of pilings, ending some four feet above the surface of the water. A dim rectangle at the top of the ladder indicated that a trapdoor opened onto the deck. In the darkness it was only the ghost of a ladder, half-visible.

'We're in business, Richie,' Jack said. He guided the raft carefully past the next piling, making sure not to scrape against it. The hundreds of sluglike creatures clinging to the piling bared their teeth. In seconds the horse's head at the front of the raft was gliding beneath the bottom of the ladder, and then Jack could reach up to grab the bottom rung. 'Okay,' he said. First he tied one sleeve of his sodden shirt around the rung, the other around the stiff rubbery tail next to him. At least the raft would still be there – if they ever got out of the hotel. Jack's mouth abruptly dried. The Talisman sang out, calling to him. He stood up carefully in the raft and hung on to the ladder. 'You first,' he said. 'It's not going to be easy, but I'll help you.'

'Don't need your help,' Richard said. Standing up, he nearly pitched forward and threw both of them out of the raft.

'Easy now.'

'Don't easy me.' Richard extended both arms and steadied himself. His mouth was pinched. He looked afraid to breathe. He stepped forward.

'Good.'

'Asshole.' Richard moved his left foot forward, raised his right arm, brought his right foot forward. Now he could find the bottom of the ladder with his hands, as he fiercely squinted through his right eye. 'See?'

'Okay,' Jack said, holding both hands palm-out before him, fingers extended, indicating that he would not insult Richard with the offer of physical aid.

Richard pulled on the ladder with his hands, and his feet slid irresistibly forward, pushing the raft with them. In a second he was suspended half over the water – only Jack's shirt kept the raft from zooming out from under Richard's feet.

'Help!'

'Pull your feet back.'

Richard did so, and stood upright again, breathing hard.

'Let me give you a hand, okay?'

'Okay.'

Jack crawled along the raft until he was immediately before Richard. He stood up with great care. Richard gripped the bottom rung with both hands, trembling. Jack put his hands on Richard's skinny hips. 'I'm going to help lift you. Try not to kick out with your feet – just pull yourself up high enough to get your knee on the rung. First put your hands up on the next one.' Richard cracked open an eye and did so.

'You ready?'

'Go.'

The raft slid forward, but Jack yanked Richard upright so high that he could easily place his right knee on the bottom rung. Then Jack grabbed the sides of the ladder and used the strength in his arms and legs to stabilize the raft. Richard was grunting, trying to get his other knee on the rung; in a second he had done it. In another two seconds, Richard Sloat stood upright on the ladder.

'I can't go any farther,' he said. 'I think I'm going to fall off. I feel so sick, Jack.'

'Just go up one more, please. Please. Then I can help you.'

Richard wearily moved his hands up a rung. Jack, looking toward the deck, saw that the ladder must be thirty feet long. 'Now move your feet. Please, Richard.'

Richard slowly placed one foot, then the next, on the second rung.

Jack placed his hands on the outsides of Richard's feet and pulled himself up. The raft swung out in a looping half-circle, but he raised his knees and got both legs securely on the lowest rung. Held by Jack's outstretched shirt, the raft swung back around like a dog on a leash.

A third of the way up the ladder, Jack had to put one arm around Richard's waist to keep him from falling in the black water.

At last the rectangular square of the trapdoor floated in the black wood directly above Jack's head. He clamped Richard to himself – his unconscious head fell against Jack's chest – by reaching around both Richard and ladder with his left hand, and tried the trapdoor with his right. Suppose it had been nailed shut? But it swung up immediately and banged flat against the top of the deck. Jack got his left arm firmly under Richard's armpits and hauled him up out of the blackness and through the hole in the deck.

INTERLUDE

SLOAT IN THIS WORLD (V)

The Kingsland Motel had been empty for nearly six years, and it had the mouldy yellow-newspaper smell of buildings that have been deserted for a long time. This smell had disturbed Sloat at first. His maternal grandmother had died at home when Sloat was a boy – it had taken her four years, but she had finally made the grade – and the smell of her dying had been like this. He did not want such a smell, or such memories, at a moment which was supposed to be his greatest triumph.

Now, however, it didn't matter. Not even the infuriating losses inflicted on him by Jack's early arrival at Camp Readiness mattered. His earlier feelings of dismay and fury had turned into a frenzy of nervous excitement. Head down, lips twitching, eyes bright, he strode back and forth through the room where he and Richard had stayed in the old days. Sometimes he locked his hands behind his back, sometimes he slammed one fist into the other palm, sometimes he stroked his bald pate. Mostly, however, he paced as he had in college, with his hands clenched into tight and somehow anal little fists, the hidden nails digging viciously into his palms. His stomach was by turns sour and giddily light.

Things were coming to a head.

No; no. Right idea, wrong phrase.

Things were coming *together.*

Richard is dead by now. My son is dead. Got to be. He survived the Blasted Lands – barely – but he'll never survive the Agincourt. He's dead. Hold out no false hope for yourself on that score. Jack Sawyer killed him, and I'll gouge the eyes out of his living head for it.

'But *I* killed him, too,' Morgan whispered, stopping for a moment.

Suddenly he thought of his father.

Gordon Sloat had been a dour Lutheran minister in Ohio – Morgan had spent his whole boyhood trying to flee that harsh and frightening man. Finally he had escaped to Yale. He had set his entire mind and spirit on Yale in his sophomore year of high school for one reason above all others, unadmitted by his conscious mind but as deep as bedrock: it was a place where his rude, rural father would never dare to come. If his father ever tried to set foot on the Yale campus, *something* would happen to him. Just what that *something* might be, the high-school-age Sloat was not sure . . . but it would be roughly akin, he felt to what had happened to the Wicked Witch when Dorothy threw the bucket of water over her. And this insight seemed to have been true: his father never *had* set foot on the Yale campus. From Morgan's first day there, Gordon Sloat's power over his son had begun to wane – that alone made all the striving and effort seem worthwhile.

But now, as he stood with his fists clenched and his nails digging into his soft palms, his father spoke up: *What does it profit a man to gain the whole world, if he should lose his own son?*

For a moment that wet yellow smell – the empty-motel-smell, the grandmother-smell, the death-smell – filled his nostrils, seeming to choke him, and Morgan Sloat/Morgan of Orris was afraid.

What does it profit a man –

For it says in The Book of Good Farming *that a man shall not bring the get of his seed to any place of sacrifice, for what –*

What does it profit –

That man shall be damned, and damned, and damned.

– a man to gain the whole world, if he should lose his own son?

Stinking plaster. The dry smell of vintage mouseturds turning to powder in the dark spaces behind the walls. Crazies. There were crazies in the streets.

What does it profit a man?

Dead. One son dead in that world, one son dead in this.

What does it profit a man?

Your son is dead, Morgan. Must be. Dead in the water, or dead under the pilings and floating around under there, or dead – for sure! – topside. Couldn't take it. Couldn't –

What does it profit –

And suddenly the answer came to him.

'*It profits a man the world!*' Morgan shouted in the decaying room. He began to laugh and pace again. 'It profits a man the *world*, and by Jason, the world is enough!'

Laughing, he began to pace faster and faster, and before long, blood had begun to drip out of his clenched fists.

A car pulled up out front about ten minutes later. Morgan went to the window and saw Sunlight Gardener come bursting out of the Cadillac.

Seconds later he was hammering on the door with

both fists, like a tantrumy three-year-old hammering on the floor. Morgan saw that the man had gone utterly crazy, and wondered if this was good or bad.

'Morgan!' Gardener bellowed. 'Open for me, my Lord! News! I have news!'

I saw all your news through my binoculars, I think. Hammer on that door awhile longer, Gardener, while I make up my mind on this. Is it good that you should be crazy, or is it bad?

Good, Morgan decided. In Indiana, Gardener had turned Sunlight Yellow at the crucial moment and had fled without taking care of Jack once and for all. But now his wild grief had made him trustworthy again. If Morgan needed a kamikaze pilot, Sunlight Gardener would be the first one to the planes.

'Open for me, my Lord! News! News! N—'

Morgan opened the door. Although he himself was wildly excited, the face he presented to Gardener was almost eerily serene.

'Easy,' he said. 'Easy, Gard. You'll pop a blood vessel.'

'They've gone to the hotel . . . the beach . . . shot at them while they were on the beach . . . stupid assholes missed . . . in the water, I thought . . . we'll get them in the water . . . then the deep-creatures rose up . . . I had him in my sights . . . I had that bad bad boy RIGHT IN MY SIGHTS . . . and then . . . the creatures . . . they . . . they . . .'

'Slow down,' Morgan said soothingly. He closed the door and took a flask out of his inside pocket. He handed it to Gardener, who spun the cap off and took two huge gulps. Morgan waited. His face was benign, serene, but a vein pulsed in the center of his forehead and his hands opened and closed, opened and closed.

Gone to the hotel, yes. Morgan had seen the ridiculous

raft with its painted horse's head and its rubber tail bobbing its way out there.

'My son,' he said to Gardener. 'Do your men say he was alive or dead when Jack put him in the raft?'

Gardener shook his head – but his eyes said what he believed. 'No one knows for sure, my Lord. Some say they saw him move. Some say not.'

Doesn't matter. If he wasn't dead then, he's dead now. One breath of the air in that place and his lungs will explode.

Gardener's cheeks were full of whiskey-color and his eyes were watering. He didn't give the flask back but stood holding it. That was fine with Sloat. He wanted neither whiskey nor cocaine. He was on what those sixties slobs had called a natural high.

'Start over,' Morgan said, 'and this time be coherent.'

The only thing Gardener had to tell that Morgan hadn't gleaned from the man's first broken outburst was the fact of the old nigger's presence down on the beach, and he almost could have guessed that. Still, he let Gardener go on. Gardener's voice was soothing, his rage invigorating.

As Gardener talked, Morgan ran over his options one final time, dismissing his son from the equation with a brief throb of regret.

What does it profit a man? It profits a man the world, and the world is enough . . . or, in this case, worlds. Two to start with, and more when and if they play out. I can rule them all if I like – I can be something like the God of the Universe.

The Talisman. The Talisman is –

The key?

No; oh no.

Not a key but a door; a locked door standing between

him and his destiny. He did not want to open that door but to destroy it, destroy it utterly and completely and eternally, so it could never be shut again, let alone locked.

When the Talisman was smashed, all those worlds would be *his* worlds.

'Gard!' he said, and began to pace jerkily again.

Gardener looked at Morgan questioningly.

'What does it profit a man?' Morgan chirruped brightly.

'My Lord? I don't underst—'

Morgan stopped in front of Gardener, his eyes feverish and sparkling. His face rippled. Became the face of Morgan of Orris. Became the face of Morgan Sloat again.

'It profits a man the *world*,' Morgan said, putting his hands on Osmond's shoulders. When he took them away a second later, Osmond was Gardener again. 'It profits a man the *world*, and the world is enough.'

'My Lord, you don't understand,' Gardener said, looking at Morgan as if he might be crazy. 'I think they've gone *inside*. Inside where *IT* is. We tried to shoot them, but the creatures . . . the deep-creatures . . . rose up and protected them, just as *The Book of Good Farming* said they would . . . and if they're *inside* . . .' Gardener's voice was rising. Osmond's eyes rolled with mingled hate and dismay.

'I understand,' Morgan said comfortingly. His face and voice were calm again, but his fists worked and worked, and blood dribbled down onto the mildewy carpet. 'Yessirree-bob, yes-indeedy-doo, rooty-patootie. They've gone in, and my son is never going to come out. You've lost yours, Gard, and now I've lost mine.'

'*Sawyer!*' Gardener barked. 'Jack *Sawyer! Jason!* That—'

Gardener lapsed into a horrible bout of cursing that went on for nearly five minutes. He cursed Jack in two languages; his voice racketed and perspired with grief and insane rage. Morgan stood there and let him get it all out of his system.

When Gardener paused, panting, and took another swallow from the flask, Morgan said:

'Right! Doubled in brass! Now listen, Gard – are you listening?'

'Yes, my Lord.'

Gardener/Osmond's eyes were bright with bitter attention.

'My son is never going to come out of the black hotel, and I don't think Sawyer ever will, either. There's a very good chance that he isn't *Jason* enough yet to deal with what's in there. *IT* will probably kill him, or drive him mad, or send him a hundred worlds away. But he *may* come out, Gard. Yes, he *may*.'

'He's the baddest baddest bitch's bastard to ever draw breath,' Gardener whispered. His hand tightened on the flask . . . tightened . . . tightened . . . and now his fingers actually began to make dents in the shell-steel.

'You say the old nigger man is down on the beach?'

'Yes.'

'Parker,' Morgan said, and at the same moment Osmond said, 'Parkus.'

'Dead?' Morgan asked this without much interest.

'I don't know. I think so. Shall I send men down to pick him up?'

'*No!*' Morgan said sharply. 'No – but we're going down near where he is, aren't we, Gard?'

'We are?'

Morgan began to grin.

'Yes. You . . . me . . . all of us. Because if Jack comes

out of the hotel, he'll go there first. He won't leave his old night-fighting buddy on the beach, will he?'

Now Gardener also began to grin. 'No,' he said. 'No.'

For the first time Morgan became aware of dull and throbbing pain in his hands. He opened them and looked thoughtfully at the blood which flowed out of the deep semi-circular wounds in his palms. His grin did not falter. Indeed, it widened.

Gardener was staring at him solemnly. A great sense of power filled Morgan. He reached up to his neck and closed one bloody hand over the key that brought the lightning.

'It profits a man the *world*,' he whispered. 'Can you gimme *hallelujah*.'

His lips pulled even further back. He grinned the sick yellow grin of a rogue wolf – a wolf that is old but still sly and tenacious and powerful.

'Come on, Gard,' he said. 'Let's go to the beach.'

CHAPTER FORTY-ONE
THE BLACK HOTEL

1

Richard Sloat wasn't dead, but when Jack picked his old friend up in his arms, he was unconscious.

Who's the herd now? Wolf asked in his head. *Be careful, Jacky! Wolf! Be –*

COME TO ME! COME NOW! the Talisman sang in its powerful, soundless voice. *COME TO ME, BRING THE HERD, AND ALL WILL BE WELL AND ALL WILL BE WELL AND –*

'– a' manner a' things wi' be well,' Jack croaked.

He started forward and came within an inch of stepping right back through the trapdoor, like a kid participating in some bizarre double execution by hanging. *Swing with a Friend*, Jack thought crazily. His heart was hammering in his ears, and for a moment he thought he might vomit straight down into the gray water slapping at the pilings. Then he caught hold of himself and closed the trapdoor with his foot. Now there was only the sound of the weathervanes – cabalistic brass designs spinning restlessly in the sky.

Jack turned toward the Agincourt.

He was on a wide deck like an elevated verandah, he saw. Once, fashionable twenties and thirties folk had sat out here at the cocktail hour under the shade of umbrellas, drinking gin rickeys and sidecars, perhaps reading the latest Edgar Wallace or Ellery Queen novel, perhaps only looking out toward where Los Cavernes Island could be dimly glimpsed – a blue-gray whale's hump dreaming on the horizon. The men in whites, the women in pastels.

Once, maybe.

Now the boards were warped and twisted and splintered. Jack didn't know what color the deck had been painted before, but now it had gone black, like the rest of the hotel – the color of this place was the color he imagined the malignant tumors in his mother's lungs must be.

Twenty feet away were Speedy's 'window-doors', through which guests would have passed back and forth in those dim old days. They had been soaped over in wide white strokes so that they looked like blind eyes.

Written on one was:

YOUR LAST CHANCE TO GO HOME

Sound of the waves. Sound of the twirling ironmongery on the angled roofs. Stink of sea-salt and old spilled drinks – drinks spilled long ago by beautiful people who were now wrinkled and dead. Stink of the hotel itself. He looked at the soaped window again and saw with no real surprise that the message had already changed.

SHE'S ALREADY DEAD JACK SO WHY BOTHER?

(now who's the herd?)

'You are, Richie,' Jack said, 'but you ain't alone.'

Richard made a snoring, protesting sound in Jack's arms. 'Come on,' Jack said, and began to walk. 'One more mile. Give or take.'

2

The soaped-over windows actually seemed to *widen* as Jack walked toward the Agincourt, as if the black hotel were now regarding him with blind but contemptuous surprise.

Do you really think, little boy, that you can come in here and really hope to ever come out? Do you think there's that much Jason in you?

Red sparks, like those he had seen in the air, flashed and twisted across the soaped glass. For a moment they took form. Jack watched, wondering, as they became tiny fire-imps. They skated down to the brass handles of the doors and converged there. The handles began to glow dully, like a smith's iron in the forge.

Go on, little boy. Touch one. Try.

Once, as a kid of six, Jack had put his finger on the cold coil of an electric range and had then turned the control knob onto the HIGH setting. He had simply been curious about how fast the burner would heat up. A second later he had pulled his finger, already blistering, away with a yell of pain. Phil Sawyer had come running, taken a look, and had asked Jack when he had started to feel this weird compulsion to burn himself alive.

Jack stood with Richard in his arms, looking at the dully glowing handles.

Go on, little boy. Remember how the stove burned? You thought you'd have plenty of time to pull your finger off – 'Hell,' you thought, 'the thing doesn't even start to get red for almost a minute' – but it burned right away, didn't it? Now, how do you think this is going to feel, Jack?

More red sparks skated liquidly down the glass to the handles of the French doors. The handles began to take on the delicate red-edged-with-white look of metal which is no more than six degrees from turning molten and starting to drip. If he touched one of those handles it would sink into his flesh, charring tissue and boiling blood. The agony would be like nothing he had ever felt before.

He waited for a moment with Richard in his arms, hoping the Talisman would call him again, or that the 'Jason-side' of him would surface. But it was his mother's voice that rasped in his head.

Has something or someone always got to push you, Jack-O? Come on, big guy – you set this going by yourself; you can keep going if you really want to. Has that other guy got to do everything for you?

'Okay, Mom,' Jack said: He was smiling a little, but his voice was trembling with fright. 'Here's one for you. I just hope someone remembered to pack the Solarcaine.'

He reached out and grasped one of the red-hot handles.

Except it wasn't; the whole thing had been an illusion. The handle was warm, but that was all. As Jack turned it, the red glow died from all the handles. And as he pushed the glass door inward, the Talisman sang out again, bringing gooseflesh out all over his body:

WELL DONE! JASON! TO ME! COME TO ME!

With Richard in his arms, Jack stepped into the dining room of the black hotel.

3

As he crossed the threshold, he felt an inanimate force – something like a dead hand – try to shove him back out. Jack pushed against it, and a second or two later, that feeling of being repelled ceased.

The room was not particularly dark – but the soaped windows gave it a monochrome whiteness Jack did not like. He felt fogged in, blind. Here were yellow smells of decay inside walls where the plaster was slowly turning to a vile soup: the smells of empty age and sour darkness. But there was more here, and Jack knew it and feared it.

Because this place was not empty.

Exactly what manner of things might be here he did not know – but he knew that Sloat had never dared to come in, and he guessed that no one else would, either. The air was heavy and unpleasant in his lungs, as if filled with a slow poison. He felt the strange levels and canted passageways and secret rooms and dead ends above him pressing down like the walls of a great and complex crypt. There was madness here, and walking death, and gibbering irrationality. Jack might not have had the words to express these things, but he felt them, all the same . . . he knew them for what they were. Just as he knew that all the Talismans in the cosmos could not protect him from those things. He had entered a strange, dancing ritual whose conclusion, he felt, was not at all preordained.

He was on his own.

Something tickled against the back of his neck. Jack swept his hand at it and skittered to one side. Richard moaned thickly in his arms.

It was a large black spider hanging on a thread. Jack

looked up and saw its web in one of the stilled overhead fans, tangled in a dirty snarl between the hardwood blades. The spider's body was bloated. Jack could see its eyes. He couldn't remember ever having seen a spider's *eyes* before. Jack began to edge around the hanging spider toward the tables. The spider turned at the end of its thread, following him.

'Fushing *feef*!' it suddenly squealed at him.

Jack screamed and clutched Richard against him with panicky, galvanic force. His scream echoed across the high-ceilinged dining room. Somewhere in the shadows beyond, there was a hollow metallic clank, and something laughed.

'*Fushing feef, fushing FEEF!*' the spider squealed, and then suddenly it scuttled back up into its web below the scrolled tin ceiling.

Heart thumping, Jack crossed the dining room and put Richard on one of the tables. The boy moaned again, very faintly. Jack could feel the twisted bumps under Richard's clothes.

'Got to leave you for a little while, buddy,' Jack said.

From the shadows high above: '*. . . I'll take . . . take good . . . good care of him you fushing . . . fushing feef . . .*' There was a dark, buzzing little giggle.

There was a pile of linen underneath the table where Jack had laid Richard down. The top two or three tablecloths were slimy with mildew, but halfway through the pile he found one that wasn't too bad. He spread it out and covered Richard with it to the neck. He started away.

The voice of the spider whispered thinly down from the angle of the fan-blades, down from a darkness that stank of decaying flies and silk-wrapped wasps. '. . . I'll take care of him, you fushing feef . . .'

Jack looked up, cold, but he couldn't see the spider. He could imagine those cold little eyes, but imagination was all it was. A tormenting, sickening picture came to him: that spider scuttling onto Richard's face, burrowing its way between Richard's slack lips and into Richard's mouth, crooning all the while *fushing feef, fushing feef, fushing feef* . . .

He thought of pulling the tablecloth up over Richard's mouth as well, and discovered he could not bring himself to turn Richard into something that would look so much like a corpse – it was almost like an invitation.

He went back to Richard and stood there, indecisive, knowing that his very indecision must make whatever forces there were here very happy indeed – anything to keep him away from the Talisman.

He reached into his pocket and came out with the large dark green marble. The magic mirror in the other world. Jack had no reason to believe it contained any special power against evil forces, but it came from the Territories . . . and, Blasted Lands aside, the Territories were innately good. And innate goodness, Jack reasoned, must have its own power over evil.

He folded the marble into Richard's hand. Richard's hand closed, then fell slowly open again as soon as Jack removed his own hand.

From somewhere overhead, the spider chuffed dirty laughter.

Jack bent low over Richard, trying to ignore the smell of disease – so like the smell of this place – and murmured, 'Hold it in your hand, Richie. Hold it tight, chum.'

'Don't . . . chum,' Richard muttered, but his hand closed weakly on the marble.

'Thanks, Richie-boy,' Jack said. He kissed Richard's cheek gently and then started across the dining room toward the closed double doors at the far end. *It's like the Alhambra,* he thought. *Dining room giving on the gardens there, dining room giving on a deck over the water here. Double doors in both places, opening on the rest of the hotel.*

As he crossed the room, he felt that dead hand pushing against him again – it was the hotel repelling him, trying to push him back out.

Forget it, Jack thought, and kept going.

The force seemed to fade almost at once.

We have other ways, the double doors whispered as he approached them. Again, Jack heard the dim, hollow clank of metal.

You're worried about Sloat, the double doors whispered; only now it wasn't just them – now the voice Jack was hearing was the voice of the entire hotel. *You're worried about Sloat, and bad Wolfs, and things that look like goats, and basketball coaches who aren't really basketball coaches; you're worried about guns and plastic explosive and magic keys. We in here don't worry about any of those things, little one. They are nothing to us. Morgan Sloat is no more than a scurrying ant. He has only twenty years to live, and that is less than the space between breaths to us. We in the Black Hotel care only for the Talisman – the nexus of all possible worlds. You've come as a burglar to rob us of what is ours, and we tell you once more: we have other ways of dealing with fushing feeves like you. And if you persist, you'll find out what they are – you'll find out for yourself.*

4

Jack pushed open first one of the double doors, then the other. The casters squealed unpleasantly as they rolled along their recessed tracks for the first time in years.

Beyond the doors was a dark hallway. *That'll go to the lobby,* Jack thought. *And then, if this place really is the same as the Alhambra, I'll have to go up the main staircase one flight.*

On the second floor he would find the grand ballroom. And in the grand ballroom, he would find the thing he had come for.

Jack took one look back, saw that Richard hadn't moved, and stepped into the hallway. He closed the doors behind him.

He began to move slowly along the corridor, his frayed and dirty sneakers whispering over the rotting carpet.

A little further down, Jack could see another set of double doors, with birds painted on them.

Closer by were a number of meeting-rooms. Here was the Golden State Room, directly opposite the Forty-Niner Room. Five paces farther up toward the double doors with the painted birds was the Mendocino Room (hacked into a lower panel of the mahogany door: YOUR MOTHER DIED SCREAMING!). Far down the corridor – impossibly far! – was watery light. The lobby.

Clank.

Jack wheeled around fast, and caught a glimmer of movement just beyond one of the peaked doorways in the stone throat of this corridor –

(?stones?) (?peaked doorways?)

Jack blinked uneasily. The corridor was lined with dark mahogany panelling which had now begun to rot in the ocean-side damp. No stone. And the doors giving on the Golden State Room and the Forty-Niner Room and the Mendocino Room were just doors, sensibly rectangular and with no peaks. Yet for one moment he had seemed to see openings like modified cathedral arches. Filling these openings had been iron drop-gates – the sort that could be raised or lowered by turning a windlass. Drop-gates with hungry-looking iron spikes at the bottom. When the gate was lowered to block the entrance, the spikes fitted neatly into holes in the floor.

No stone archways, Jack-O. See for yourself. Just doorways. You saw drop-gates like that in the Tower of London, on that tour you went on with Mom and Uncle Tommy, three years ago. You're just freaking a little, that's all . . .

But the feeling in the pit of his stomach was unmistakable.

They were there, all right. I flipped – for just a second I was in the Territories.

Clank.

Jack whirled back the other way, sweat breaking out on his cheeks and forehead, hair beginning to stiffen on the nape of his neck.

He saw it again – a flash of something metallic in the shadows of one of those rooms. He saw huge stones as black as sin, their rough surfaces splotched with green moss. Nasty, soft-looking albino bugs squirmed in and out of the large pores of the decaying mortar between the stones. Empty sconces stood at fifteen – or twenty-foot intervals. The torches that the sconces had once held were long since gone.

Clank.

This time he didn't even blink. The world sideslipped before his eyes, wavering like an object seen through clear running water. The walls were blackish mahogany again instead of stone blocks. The doors were *doors* and not latticed-iron drop-gates. The two worlds, which had been separated by a membrane as thin as a lady's silk stocking, had now actually begun to overlap.

And, Jack realized dimly, his Jason-side had begun to overlap with his Jack-side – some third being which was an amalgamation of both was emerging.

I don't know what that combination is, exactly, but I hope it's strong – because there are things behind those doors . . . behind all of them.

Jack began to sidle up the hallway again toward the lobby.

Clank.

This time the worlds didn't change; solid doors remained solid doors and he saw no movement.

Right behind there, though. Right behind –

Now he heard something behind the painted double doors – written in the sky above the marsh scene were the words HERON BAR. It was the sound of some large rusty machine that had been set in motion. Jack swung toward

(Jason swung toward)

toward that opening door

(that rising drop-gate)

his hand plunging into

(the poke)

the pocket

(he wore on the belt of his jerkin)

of his jeans and closing around the guitar-pick Speedy had given him so long ago.

(and closing around the shark's tooth)

He waited to see what would come out of the Heron Bar, and the walls of the hotel whispered dimly: *We have ways of dealing with fushing feeves like you. You should have left while there was still time . . .*

. . . because now, little boy, your time is up.

5

Clank . . . THUD!

Clank . . . THUD!

Clank . . . THUD!

The noise was large and clumsy and metallic. There was something relentless and inhuman about it which frightened Jack more badly than a more human sound would have done.

It moved and shuffled its way forward with its own slow idiot rhythm:

Clank . . . THUD!

Clank . . . THUD!

There was a long pause. Jack waited, pressed against the far wall a few feet to the right of the painted doors, his nerves so tightly wound they seemed to hum. Nothing at all happened for a long time. Jack began to hope the clanker had fallen back through some interdimensional trapdoor and into the world it had come from. He became aware that his back ached from his artificially still and tautly erect posture. He slumped.

Then there was a splintering crash, and a huge mailed fist with blunt two-inch spikes sprouting from the knuckles slammed through the peeling blue sky on the door. Jack shrank back against the wall again, gaping.

And, helplessly, flipped into the Territories.

6

Standing on the other side of the drop-gate was a figure in blackish, rusty armor. Its cylindrical helmet was broken only by a black horizontal eye-slit no more than an inch wide.

The helmet was topped by a frowzy red plume – white bugs squirmed in and out of it. They were the same sort, Jason saw, as those which had come out of the walls first in Albert the Blob's room and then all over Thayer School. The helmet ended in a coif of mail which draped the rusty knight's shoulders like a lady's stole. The upper arms and forearms were plated with heavy steel brassards. They were joined at the elbows with cubitieres. These were crusted with layers of ancient filth, and when the knight moved, the cubitieres squealed like the high, demanding voices of unpleasant children.

Its armored fists were crazy with spikes.

Jason stood against the stone wall, looking at it, unable in fact to look away; his mouth was dry as fever and his eyeballs seemed to be swelling rhythmically in their sockets in time to his heartbeat.

In the knight's right hand was *le martel de fer* – a battle-hammer with a rusty thirty-pound forged-steel head, as mute as murder.

The drop-gate; remember that the drop-gate is between you and it –

But then, although no human hand was near it, the windlass began to turn; the iron chain, each link as long as Jack's forearm, began to wind around the drum, and the gate began to rise.

7

The mailed fist was withdrawn from the door, leaving a splintered hole that changed the mural at once from faded pastoral romantic to surrealist bar-sinister: it now looked as if some apocalyptic hunter, disappointed by his day in the marshes, had put a load of birdshot through the sky itself in a fit of pique. Then the head of the battle-hammer exploded through the door in a huge blunt swipe, obliterating one of the two herons struggling to achieve liftoff. Jack raised his hand in front of his face to protect it from splinters. The *martel de fer* was withdrawn. There was another brief pause, almost long enough for Jack to think about running again. Then the spiked fist tore through again. It twisted first one way and then the other, widening the hole, then withdrew. A second later the hammer slammed through the middle of a reedbed and a large chunk of the right-hand door fell to the carpet.

Jack could now see the hulking armored figure in the shadows of the Heron Bar. The armor was not the same as that worn by the figure confronting Jason in the black castle; that one wore a helmet which was nearly cylindrical, with a red plume. This one wore a helmet that looked like the polished head of a steel bird. Horns rose from either side, sprouting from the helmet at roughly ear level. Jack saw a breastplate, a kilt of plate-mail, a hemming of chain-mail below that. The hammer was the same in both worlds, and in both worlds the knight-Twinners dropped it at the same instant, as if in contempt – who would need a battle-hammer to deal with such a puny opponent as this?

Run! Jack, run!

That's right, the hotel whispered. *Run! That's what fushing feeves are supposed to do! Run! RUN!*

But he would not run. He might die, but he would not run – because that sly, whispering voice was right. Running was exactly what fushing feeves did.

But I'm no thief, Jack thought grimly. *That thing may kill me, but I won't run. Because I'm no thief.*

'*I won't run!*' Jack shouted at the blank, polished-steel birdface. '*I'm no thief! Do you hear me? I've come for what's mine and I'M NO THIEF!*'

A groaning scream came from the breathing-holes at the bottom of the bird-helmet. The knight raised its spiked fists and brought them down, one on the sagging left door, one on the sagging right. The pastoral marsh-world painted there was destroyed. The hinges snapped . . . and as the doors fell toward him, Jack actually saw the one painted heron who remained go flying away like a bird in a Walt Disney cartoon, its eyes bright and terrified.

The suit of armor came toward him like a killer robot, its feet rising and then crashing down. It was more than seven feet tall, and when it came through the door the horns rising from its helmet tore a set of ragged slashes into the upper jamb. They looked like quotation marks.

Run! a yammering voice in his mind screamed.

Run, you feef, the hotel whispered.

No, Jack answered. He stared up at the advancing knight, and his hand wrapped itself tightly around the guitar-pick in his pocket. The spike-studded gauntlets came up toward the visor of its bird-helmet. They raised it. Jack gaped.

The inside of the helmet was empty.

Then those studded hands were reaching for Jack.

8

The spike-studded hands came up and grasped either side of the cylindrical helmet. They lifted it slowly off, disclosing the livid, haggard face of a man who looked at least three hundred years old. One side of this ancient's head had been bashed in. Splinters of bone like broken eggshell poked out through the skin, and the wound was caked with some black goop which Jason supposed was decayed brains. It was not breathing, but the red-rimmed eyes which regarded Jason were sparkling and hellishly avid. It grinned, and Jason saw the needle-sharp teeth with which this horror would rip him to pieces.

It clanked unsteadily forward . . . but that wasn't the only sound.

He looked to his left, toward the main hall

(lobby)

of the castle

(hotel)

and saw a second knight, this one wearing the shallow, bowl-shaped head-guard known as the Great Helm. Behind it were a third . . . and a fourth. They came slowly down the corridor, moving suits of ancient armor which now housed vampires of some sort.

Then the hands seized him by the shoulders. The blunt spikes on the gloves slid into his shoulders and arms. Warm blood flowed and the livid, wrinkled face drew into a horrid hungry grin. The cubitieres at the elbows screeched and wailed as the dead knight drew the boy toward itself.

9

Jack howled with the pain – the short blunt-tipped spikes on its hands were *in* him, *in* him, and he understood once and for all that this was real, and in another moment this thing was going to kill him.

He was yanked toward the yawning, empty blackness inside the helmet –

But was it really empty?

Jack caught a blurred, faded impression of a double red glow in the darkness . . . something like eyes. And as the armored hands drew him up and up, he felt freezing cold, as if all the winters that ever were had somehow combined, had somehow become one winter . . . and that river of frigid air was now pouring out of that empty helmet.

It's really going to kill me and my mother will die, Richard will die, Sloat will win, going to kill me, going to

(tear me apart rip me open with its teeth)

freeze me solid –

JACK! Speedy's voice cried.

(JASON! Parkus's voice cried.)

The pick, boy! Use the pick! Before it's too late! FOR JASON'S SAKE USE THE PICK BEFORE IT'S TOO LATE!

Jack's hand closed around it. It was as hot as the coin had been, and the numbing cold was replaced with a sudden sense of brain-busting triumph. He brought it out of his pocket, crying out in pain as his punctured muscles flexed against the spikes driven into him, but not losing that sense of triumph – that lovely sensation of Territories *heat*, that clear feeling of *rainbow*.

The pick, for it was a pick again, was in his fingers, a strong and heavy triangle of ivory, filigreed and inlaid with strange designs – and in that moment Jack

(and Jason)

saw those designs come together in a face – the face of Laura DeLoessian.

(the face of Lily Cavanaugh Sawyer.)

10

'In her name, you filthy, aborted thing!' they shouted together – but it was one shout only: the shout of that single nature, Jack/Jason. *'Get you off the skin of this world! In the name of the Queen and in the name of her son, get you off the skin of this world!'*

Jason brought the guitar-pick down into the white, scrawny face of the old vampire-thing in the suit of armor; at the same instant he sideslipped without blinking into Jack and saw the pick whistle down into a freezing black emptiness. There was another moment as Jason when he saw the vampire-thing's red eyes bulge outward in disbelief as the tip of the pick plunged into the center of its deeply wrinkled forehead. A moment later the eyes themselves, already filming over, exploded, and a black, steaming ichor ran over his hand and wrist. It was full of tiny biting worms.

11

Jack was flung against the wall. He hit his head. In spite of that and of the deep, throbbing pain in his shoulders and upper arms, he held on to the pick.

The suit of armor was rattling like a scarecrow made out of tin cans. Jack had time to see it was *swelling* somehow, and he threw a hand up to shield his eyes.

The suit of armor self-destructed. It did not spray shrapnel everywhere, but simply fell apart – Jack thought if he had seen it in a movie instead of as he saw it now, huddled in a lower hallway of this stinking hotel with blood trickling into his armpits, he would have laughed. The polished-steel helmet, so like the face of a bird, fell onto the floor with a muffled thump. The curved gorget, meant to keep the knight's enemy from running a blade or a spear-point through the knight's throat, fell directly inside it with a jingle of tightly meshed rings of mail. The cuirasses fell like curved steel bookends. The greaves split apart. Metal rained down on the mouldy carpet for two seconds, and then there was only a pile of something that looked like scrap-heap leftovers.

Jack pushed himself up the wall, staring with wide eyes as if he expected the suit of armor to suddenly fly back together. In fact, he really did expect something like that. But when nothing happened he turned left, toward the lobby . . . and saw three more suits of armor moving slowly toward him. One held a cheesy, mould-caked banner, and on it was a symbol Jack recognized: he had seen it fluttering from guidons held by Morgan of Orris's soldiers as they escorted Morgan's black diligence down the Outpost Road and toward Queen Laura's pavillion. Morgan's sign – but these were not Morgan's creatures, he understood dimly; they carried his banner as a kind of morbid joke on this frightened interloper who presumed to steal away their only reason for being.

'No more,' Jack whispered hoarsely. The pick trembled between his fingers. Something had happened to it; it had been damaged somehow when he used it to destroy the suit of armor which had come from the Heron Bar. The ivory, formerly the color of fresh cream, had yellowed noticeably. Fine cracks now crisscrossed it.

The suits of armor clanked steadily toward him. One slowly drew a long sword which ended in a cruel-looking double point.

'No more,' Jack moaned. 'Oh God please, no more, I'm tired, I can't, please, no more, no more—'

Travellin Jack, ole Travellin Jack –

'*Speedy, I can't!*' he screamed. Tears cut through the dirt on his face. The suits of armor approached with all the inevitability of steel autoparts on an assembly line. He heard an Arctic wind whistling inside their cold black spaces.

– you be here in California to bring her back.

'Please, Speedy, no more!'

Reaching for him – black-metal robot-faces, rusty greaves, mail splotched and smeared with moss and mould.

Got to do your best, Travellin Jack, Speedy whispered, exhausted, and then he was gone and Jack was left to stand or fall on his own.

CHAPTER FORTY-TWO
JACK AND THE TALISMAN

1

You made a mistake – a ghostly voice in Jack Sawyer's head spoke up as he stood outside the Heron Bar and watched these other suits of armor bear down on him. In his mind an eye opened wide and he saw an angry man – a man who was really not much more than an overgrown boy – striding up a Western street toward the camera, buckling on first one gunbelt and then another, so that they crisscrossed his belly. *You made a mistake – you shoulda killed* both *of the Ellis brothers!*

2

Of all his mother's movies, the one Jack had always liked the best was *Last Train to Hangtown*, made in 1960 and released in 1961. It had been a Warner Brothers picture, and the major parts – as in many of the lower-budget pictures Warners made during that period – were filled by actors from the half-dozen Warner Brothers TV series which were in constant production. Jack Kelly from the *Maverick* show had been in *Last Train* (the Suave Gambler), and Andrew Duggan from *Bourbon Street Beat* (the Evil Cattle-Baron). Clint Walker, who played a character called Cheyenne Bodie on TV, starred as Rafe Ellis (the Retired Sheriff Who Must Strap on His Guns One Last Time). Inger Stevens had been originally slated to play the part of the Dance Hall Girl with Willing Arms and a Heart of Gold, but Miss Stevens had come down with a bad case of bronchitis and Lily Cavanaugh had stepped into the part. It was of a sort she could have done competently in a coma. Once, when his parents thought he was asleep and were talking in the living room downstairs, Jack overheard his mother say something striking as he padded barefoot to the bathroom to get a glass of water . . . it was striking enough, at any rate, so that Jack never forgot it. 'All the women I played knew how to fuck, but not one of them knew how to fart,' she told Phil.

Will Hutchins, who starred in *another* Warner Brothers program (this one was called *Sugarfoot*), had also been in the film. *Last Train to Hangtown* was Jack's favorite chiefly because of the character Hutchins played. It was this character – Andy Ellis, by name – who came to his tired, tottering, overtaxed mind now as he watched the suits of armor marching down the dark hallway toward him.

Andy Ellis had been the Cowardly Kid Brother Who Gets Mad in the Last Reel. After skulking and cowering through the entire movie, he had gone out to face Duggan's evil minions after the Chief Minion (played by sinister, stubbly, wall-eyed Jack Elam, who played Chief Minions in all sorts of Warner epics, both theatrical and televisional) had shot his brother Rafe in the back.

Hutchins had gone striding down the dusty wide-screen street, strapping on his brother's gunbelts with clumsy fingers, shouting, 'Come on! Come on, I'm ready for ya! You made a mistake! You shoulda killed *both* of the Ellis brothers!'

Will Hutchins had not been one of the greatest actors of all time, but in that moment he had achieved – at least in Jack's eyes – a moment of clear truth and real brilliance. There was a sense that the kid was going to his death, and knew it, *but meant to go on, anyway.* And although he was frightened, he was not striding up that street toward the showdown with the slightest reluctance; he went eagerly, sure of what he meant to do, even though he had to fumble again and again with the buckles of the gunbelts.

The suits of armor came on, closing the distance, rocking from side to side like toy robots. *They should have keys sticking out of their backs,* Jack thought.

He turned to face them, the yellowed pick held between the thumb and forefinger of his right hand, as if to strum a tune.

They seemed to hesitate, as if sensing his fearlessness. The hotel itself seemed to suddenly hesitate, or to open its eyes to a danger that was deeper than it had at first thought; floors groaned their boards, somewhere a series of doors clapped shut one after the other, and on the roofs, the brass ornaments ceased turning for a moment.

Then the suits of armor clanked forward again. They now made a single moving wall of plate- and chain-mail, of greaves and helmets and sparkling gorgets. One held a spiked iron ball on a wooden haft; one a *martel de fer*; the one in the center held the double-pointed sword.

Jack suddenly began to walk toward them. His eyes lit up; he held the guitar-pick out before him. His face filled with that radiant Jason-glow. He

sideslipped

momentarily into

the Territories and *became* Jason; here the shark's tooth which had been a pick seemed to be aflame. As he approached the three knights, one pulled off its helmet, revealing another of those old, pale faces – this one was thick with jowls, and the neck hung with waxy wattles that looked like melting candlewax. It heaved its helmet at him. Jason dodged it easily

and

slipped back

into his Jack-self as a helmet crashed off a panelled wall behind him. Standing in front of him was a headless suit of armor.

You think that scares me? he thought contemptuously. *I've seen that trick before. It doesn't scare me, you don't scare me, and I'm going to get it, that's all.*

This time he did not just feel the hotel *listening*; this time it seemed to recoil all around him, as the tissue of a digestive organ might recoil from a poisoned bit of flesh. Upstairs, in the five rooms where the five Guardian Knights had died, five windows blew out like gunshots. Jack bore down on the suits of armor.

The Talisman sang out from somewhere above in its clear and sweetly triumphant voice:

JASON! TO ME!

'*Come on!*' Jack shouted at the suits of armor, and began to laugh. He couldn't help himself. Never had laughter seemed so strong to him, so potent, so good as this – it was like water from a spring, or from some deep river. '*Come on, I'm ready for ya! I don't know what fucked-up Round Table you guys came from, but you shoulda stayed there! You made a mistake!*'

Laughing harder than ever but as grimly determined

inside as Wotan on the Valkyries' rock, Jack leaped at the headless, swaying figure in the center.

'*You shoulda killed* both *of the Ellis brothers!*' he shouted, and as Speedy's guitar-pick passed into the zone of freezing air where the knight's head should have been, the suit of armor fell apart.

3

In her bedroom at the Alhambra, Lily Cavanaugh Sawyer suddenly looked up from the book she had been reading. She thought she had heard someone – no, not just someone, *Jack!* – call out from far down the deserted corridor, perhaps even from the lobby. She listened, eyes wide, lips pursed, heart hoping . . . but there was nothing. Jack-O was still gone, the cancer was still eating her up a bite at a time, and it was still an hour and a half before she could take another of the big brown horse-pills that damped down the pain a little bit.

She had begun to think more and more often of taking all the big brown horse-pills at once. That would do more than damp the pain for a bit; that would finish it off forever. *They say we can't cure cancer, but don't you believe that bullshit, Mr C – try eating about two dozen of these. What do you say? Want to go for it?*

What kept her from doing it was Jack – she wanted so badly to see him again that now she was imagining his voice . . . not just doing a simple albeit corny sort of thing like calling her name, either, but quoting from one of her old pictures.

'You are one crazy old bitch, Lily,' she croaked, and lit a Herbert Tarrytoon with thin, shaking fingers. She took two puffs and then put it out. Any more than two puffs started the coughing these days, and the coughing tore her apart. 'One crazy old bitch.' She picked up her book again but couldn't read because the tears were coursing down her face and her guts hurt, they hurt, oh they hurt, and she wanted to take all the brown pills but she wanted to see him again first, her dear son with his clear handsome forehead and his shining eyes.

Come home, Jack-O, she thought, *please come home soon or the next time I talk to you it'll be by Ouija board. Please, Jack, please come home.*

She closed her eyes and tried to sleep.

4

The knight which had held the spike-ball swayed a moment longer, displaying its vacant middle, and then it also exploded. The one remaining raised its battle-hammer . . . and then simply fell apart in a heap. Jack stood amid the wreckage for a moment, still laughing, and then stopped as he looked at Speedy's pick.

It was a deep and ancient yellow now; the crack-glaze had become a snarl of fissures.

Never mind, Travellin Jack. You get on. I think there may be one more o' those walkin Maxwell House cans aroun someplace. If so, you'll take it on, won't you?

'If I have to, I will,' Jack muttered aloud.

Jack kicked aside a greave, a helmet, a breastplate. He strode down the middle of the hall, the carpet squelching under his sneakers. He reached the lobby and looked around briefly.

JACK! COME TO ME! JASON! COME TO ME! the Talisman sang.

Jack started up the staircase. Halfway up he looked at the landing and saw the last of the knights, standing and looking down at him. It was a gigantic figure, better than eleven feet tall; its armor and its plume were black, and a baleful red glare fell through the eye-slit in its helmet.

One mailed fist gripped a huge mace.

For a moment, Jack stood frozen on the staircase, and then he began to climb again.

5

They saved the worst for last, Jack thought, and as he advanced steadily upward toward the black knight he

slipped

through

again

into Jason. The knight still wore black armor, but of a different sort; its visor was tilted up to reveal a face that had been almost obliterated by old dried sores. Jason recognized them. This fellow had gotten a little too close to one of those rolling balls of fire in the Blasted Lands for his own good.

Other figures were passing him on the stairs, figures he could not quite see as his fingers trailed over a wide bannister that was not mahogany from the West Indies but ironwood from the Territories. Figures in doublets, figures in blouses of silk-sack, women in great belling gowns with gleaming white cowls thrown back from their gorgeously dressed hair; these people were beautiful but doomed – and so, perhaps, ghosts always seem to the living. Why else would even the idea of ghosts inspire such terror?

JASON! TO ME! the Talisman sang, and for a moment all partitioned reality seemed to break down; he did not flip but seemed to *fall* through worlds like a man crashing through the rotted floors of an ancient wooden tower, one after the other. He felt no fear. The idea that he might never be able to get back – that he might just go on falling through a chain of realities forever, or become lost, as in a great wood – occurred to him, but he dismissed it out of hand. All of this was happening to Jason

(and Jack)

in an eyeblink; less time than it would take for his foot to go from one riser on the broad stairs to the next. He would come back; he was single-natured, and he did not believe it was possible for such a person to become lost, because he had a place in all of these worlds. *But I do not exist simultaneously in all of them,* Jason

(Jack)

thought. *That's the important thing, that's the difference; I'm flickering through each of them, probably too fast to see, and leaving a sound like a handclap or a sonic boom behind me as the air closes on the vacancy where, for a millisecond, I took up space.*

In many of these worlds, the black hotel was a black ruin – these were worlds, he thought dimly, where the great evil that now impended on the tightwire drawn between California and the Territories had already happened. In one of them the sea which roared and snarled at the shore was a dead, sickly green; the sky had a similar gangrenous look. In another he saw a flying creature as big as a Conestoga wagon fold its wings and plummet earthward like a hawk. It grabbed a creature like a sheep and swooped up again, holding the bloody hindquarters in its beak.

Flip . . . flip . . . flip. Worlds passed by his eyes like cards shuffled by a riverboat gambler.

Here was the hotel again, and there were half a dozen

different versions of the black knight above him, but the intent in each was the same, and the differences were as unimportant as the stylings of rival automobiles. Here was a black tent filled with the thick dry smell of rotting canvas – it was torn in many places so that the sun shone through in dusty, conflicting rays. In this world Jack/Jason was on some sort of rope rigging, and the black knight stood inside a wooden basket like a crow's nest, and as he climbed he flipped again . . . and again . . . and again.

Here the entire ocean was on fire; here the hotel was much as it was in Point Venuti, except it had been half-sunk into the ocean. For a moment he seemed to be in an elevator car, the knight standing on top of it and peering down at him through the trapdoor. Then he was on a rampway, the top of which was guarded by a huge snake, its long, muscular body armored with gleaming black scales.

And when do I get to the end of everything? When do I stop crashing through floors and just smash my way into the blackness?

JACK! JASON! the Talisman called, and it called in all the worlds. *TO ME!*

And Jack came to it, and it was like coming home.

6

He was right, he saw; he had come up only a single stair. But reality had solidified again. The black knight – *his* black knight, Jack Sawyer's black knight – stood blocking the stair-landing. It raised its mace.

Jack was afraid, but he kept climbing, Speedy's pick held out in front of him.

'I'm not going to mess with you,' Jack said. 'You better get out of my—'

The black figure swung the mace. It came down with incredible force. Jack dodged aside. The mace crashed into the stair where he had been standing and splintered the entire riser down into hollow blackness.

The figure wrenched the mace free. Jack lunged up two more stairs, Speedy's pick still held between his thumb and forefinger . . . and suddenly it simply disintegrated, falling in a little eggshell rain of yellowed ivory fragments. Most of these sprinkled the tops of Jack's sneakers. He stared stupidly at them.

The sound of dead laughter.

The mace, tiny splinters of wood and chews of old dank stair-runner still clinging to it, was upraised in the knight's two armored gloves. The specter's hot glare fell through the slit in its helmet. It seemed to slice blood from Jack's upturned face in a horizontal line across the bridge of his nose.

That chuffing sound of laughter again – not heard with his ears, because he knew this suit of armor was as empty as the rest, nothing but a steel jacket for an undead spirit, but heard inside his head. *You've lost, boy – did you really think that puny little thing could get you past me?*

The mace whistled down again, this time slicing on a diagonal, and Jack tore his eyes away from that red gaze just in time to duck low – he felt the head of the mace pass through the upper layer of his long hair a second before it ripped away a four-foot section of bannister and sent it sailing out into space.

A scraping clack of metal as the knight leaned toward him, its cocked helmet somehow a hideous and sarcastic parody of solicitude – then the mace drew back and up again for another of those portentous swings.

Jack, you didn't need no magic juice to git ovah, and you don't need no magic pick to pull the chain on this here coffee can, neither!

The mace came blasting through the air again – *wheeeeossshhhh!* Jack lurched backward, sucking in his stomach; the web of muscles in his shoulders screamed as they pulled around the punctures the spiked gloves had left.

The mace missed the skin of his chest by less than an inch before passing beyond him and swiping through a line of thick mahogany balusters as if they had been toothpicks. Jack tottered on emptiness, feeling Buster Keatonish and absurd. He snatched at the ragged ruins of the bannister on his left and got splinters under two of his fingernails instead. The pain was so wire-thin excruciating that he thought for a moment that his eyeballs would explode with it. Then he got a good hold with his right hand and was able to stabilize himself and move away from the drop.

All the magic's in YOU, Jack! Don't you know that by now?

For a moment he only stood there, panting, and then he started up the stairs again, staring at the blank iron face above him.

'Better get thee gone, Sir Gawain.'

The knight cocked its great helmet again in that strangely delicate gesture – *Pardon, my boy . . . can you actually be speaking to me?* Then it swung the mace again.

Perhaps blinded by his fear, Jack hadn't noticed until now how slow its setup for those swings was, how clearly it telegraphed the trajectory of each portentous blow. Maybe its joints were rusted, he thought. At any rate, it was easy enough for him to dive inside the circle of its swing now that his head was clear again.

He stood on his toes, reached up, and seized the black helmet in both hands. The metal was sickeningly warm – like hard skin that carried a fever.

'Get you off the skin of this world,' he said in a voice that was low and calm, almost conversational. 'In *her* name I command you.'

The red light in the helmet puffed out like the candle inside a carved pumpkin, and suddenly the weight of the helmet – fifteen pounds at least – was all in Jack's hands, because there was nothing else supporting it; beneath the helmet, the suit of armor had collapsed.

'You shoulda killed *both* of the Ellis brothers,' Jack said, and threw the empty helmet over the landing. It hit the floor far below with a hard *bang* and rolled away like a toy. The hotel seemed to cringe.

Jack turned toward the broad second-floor corridor, and here, at last, was light: clean, clear light, like that on the day he had seen the flying men in the sky. The hallway ended in another set of double doors and the doors were closed, but enough light came from above and below them, as well as through the vertical crack where they were latched together, to tell him that the light inside must be very bright indeed.

He wanted very badly to see that light, and the source of that light; he had come far to see it, and through much bitter darkness.

The doors were heavy and inlaid with delicate scroll-work. Written above them in gold leaf which had flaked a bit but which was still perfectly readable for a' that an' a' that, were the words TERRITORIES BALLROOM.

'Hey, Mom,' Jack Sawyer said in a soft, wondering voice as he walked into that glow. Happiness lit his heart – that feeling was rainbow, rainbow, rainbow. 'Hey, Mom, I think I'm here, I really think I'm here.'

Gently then, and with awe, Jack grasped a handle with each hand, and pressed them down. He opened the doors, and as he did, a widening bar of clean white light fell on his upturned, wondering face.

7

Sunlight Gardener happened to be looking back up the beach at the exact moment Jack dispatched the last of the five Guardian Knights. He heard a dull boom, as if a low charge of dynamite had gone off somewhere inside the hotel. At the same moment, bright light flashed from all of the Agincourt's second-floor windows, and all of the carved brass symbols – moons and stars and planetoids and weird crooked arrows – came to a simultaneous stop.

Gardener was decked out like some sort of goony Los Angeles SWAT squad cop. He had donned a puffy black flak-vest over his white shirt and carried a radio pack-set on a canvas strap over one shoulder. Its thick, stubby antenna wavered back and forth as he moved. Over his other shoulder was slung a Weatherbee .360. This was a hunting rifle almost as big as an anti-aircraft gun; it would have made Robert Ruark himself drool with envy. Gardener had bought it six years ago, after circumstances had dictated that he must get rid of his old hunting rifle. The Weatherbee's genuine zebra-skin case was in the trunk of a black Cadillac, along with his son's body.

'Morgan!'

Morgan did not turn around. He was standing behind and slightly to the left of a leaning grove of rocks that jutted out of the sand like black fangs. Twenty feet beyond this rock and only five feet above the high-tide line lay Speedy Parker, aka Parkus. As Parkus, he had once ordered Morgan of Orris marked – there were livid scars down the insides of that Morgan's large white thighs, the marks by which a traitor is known in the Territories. It had only been through the intercession of Queen Laura herself that those scars had not been made to run down his cheeks instead of his inner thighs, where they were almost always hidden by his clothes. Morgan – this one as well as that one – had not loved the Queen any better for her intercession . . . but his hatred for Parkus, who had sniffed out that earlier plot, had grown exponentially.

Now Parkus/Parker lay face-down on the beach, his skull covered with festering sores. Blood dribbled listlessly from his ears.

Morgan wanted to believe that Parker was still alive, still suffering, but the last discernible rise and fall of his back had been just after he and Gardener arrived down here at these rocks, some five minutes ago.

When Gardener called, Morgan didn't turn because he was rapt in his study of his old enemy, now fallen. Whoever had claimed revenge wasn't sweet had been so wrong.

'Morgan!' Gardener hissed again.

Morgan turned this time, frowning. 'Well? What?'

'Look! The roof of the hotel!'

Morgan saw that all of the weathercocks and roof ornaments – beaten brass shapes which spun at exactly the same speed whether the wind was perfectly calm or howling up a hurricane – had stopped moving. At the same instant the earth rippled briefly under their feet and then was still again. It was as if a subterranean beast of enormous size had shrugged in its hibernal sleep. Morgan would almost have believed he had imagined it if it had not been for the widening of Gardener's bloodshot eyes. *I'll bet you wish you never left Indiana, Gard,* Morgan thought. *No earthquakes in Indiana, right?*

Silent light flashed in all of the Agincourt's windows again.

'What does it mean, Morgan?' Gardener asked hoarsely. His insane fury over the loss of his son had for the first time moderated into fear for himself, Morgan saw. That was a bore, but he could be whipped back into his previous frenzy again, if necessary. It was just that Morgan hated to have to waste energy on anything at this point that didn't bear directly on the problem of ridding the world – *all the worlds* – of Jack Sawyer, who had begun as a pest and who had developed into the most monstrous problem of Sloat's life.

Gardener's pack-set squawked.

'Red Squad Leader Four to the Sunlight Man! Come in, Sunlight Man!'

'Sunlight Man here, Red Squad Leader Four,' Gardener snapped. 'What's up?'

In quick succession Gardener took four gabbling, excited reports that were all exactly the same. There was no intelligence the two of them hadn't seen and felt for themselves – flashes of light, weathercocks at a standstill, something that might have been a ground-temblor or possibly an earthquake preshock – but Gardener labored with sharp-eyed enthusiasm over each report just the same, asking sharp questions, snapping *'Over!'* at the end of each transmission, sometimes breaking in with 'Say again' or

'Roger.' Sloat thought he was acting like a bit player in a disaster movie.

But if it eased him, that was fine with Sloat. It saved him from having to answer Gardener's question . . . and now that he thought about it, he supposed it was just possible that Gardener didn't *want* his question answered, and that was why he was going through this rigmarole with the radio.

The Guardians were dead, or out of commission. That was why the weathercocks had stopped, and that's what the flashes of light meant. Jack didn't have the Talisman . . . at least, not yet. If he got that, things in Point Venuti would *really* shake, rattle, and roll. And Sloat now thought that Jack *would* get it . . . that he had always been *meant* to get it. This did not frighten him, however.

His hand reached up and touched the key around his neck.

Gardener had run out of *overs* and *rogers* and *ten-fours*. He reshouldered the pack-set and looked at Morgan with wide, frightened eyes. Before he could say a word, Morgan put gentle hands on Gardener's shoulders. If he could feel love for anyone other than his poor dead son, he felt love – of a twisted variety, most certainly – for this man. They went back a long way, both as Morgan of Orris and Osmond and as Morgan Sloat and Robert 'Sunlight' Gardener.

It had been with a rifle much like the one now slung over Gardener's shoulder that Gardener had shot Phil Sawyer in Utah.

'Listen, Gard,' he said calmly. 'We are going to win.'

'Are you sure of that?' Gardener whispered. 'I think he's killed the Guardians, Morgan. I know that sounds crazy, but I really think—' He stopped, mouth trembling infirmly, lips sheened with a thin membrane of spittle.

'We are going to win,' Morgan repeated in that same calm voice, and he meant it. There was a sense of clear predestination in him. He had waited many years for this; his resolve had been true; it remained true now. Jack would come out with the Talisman in his arms. It was a thing of immense power . . . but it was fragile.

He looked at the scoped Weatherbee, which could drop a charging rhino, and then he touched the key that brought the lightning.

'We're well equipped to deal with him when he comes out,' Morgan said, and added, 'In either world. Just as long as you keep your courage, Gard. As long as you stick right by me.'

The trembling lips firmed a bit. 'Morgan, of course I'll—'

'Remember who killed your son,' Morgan said softly.

At the same instant that Jack Sawyer had jammed the burning coin into the forehead of a monstrosity in the Territories, Reuel Gardener, who had been afflicted with relatively harmless petit mal epileptic seizures ever since the age of six (the same age at which Osmond's son had begun to show signs of what was called Blasted Lands Sickness), apparently suffered a grand mal seizure in the back of a Wolf-driven Cadillac on I-70, westbound to California from Illinois.

He had died, purple and strangling, in Sunlight Gardener's arms.

Gardener's eyes now began to bulge.

'Remember,' Morgan repeated softly.

'Bad,' Gardener whispered. 'All boys. Axiomatic. That boy in particular.'

'Right!' Morgan agreed. 'Hold that thought! We can

stop him, but I want to make damn sure that he can only come out of the hotel on dry land.'

He led Gardener down to the rock where he had been watching Parker. Flies – bloated albino flies – had begun to light on the dead nigger, Morgan observed. That was just as fine as paint with him. If there had been a *Variety* magazine for flies, Morgan would gladly have bought space, advertising Parker's location. Come one, come all. They would lay their eggs in the folds of his decaying flesh, and the man who had scarred his Twinner's thighs would give birth to maggots. That was fine indeed.

He pointed out toward the dock.

'The raft's under there,' he said. 'It looks like a horse, Christ knows why. It's in the shadows, I know. But you were always a hell of a shot. If you can pick it up, Gard, put a couple of bullets in it. Sink the fucking thing.'

Gardener unshouldered the rifle and peered into the scope. For a long time the muzzle of the big gun wandered minutely back and forth.

'I see it,' Gardener whispered in a gloating voice, and triggered the gun. The echo pealed off across the water in a long curl that at last Doppplered away into nothing. The barrel of the gun rose, then came back down. Gardener fired again. And again.

'I got it,' Gardener said, lowering the gun. He'd got his courage back; his pecker was up again. He was smiling the way he had been smiling when he had come back from that errand in Utah. 'It's just a dead skin on the water now. You want a look in the scope?' He offered the rifle to Sloat.

'No,' Sloat said. 'If you say you got it, you got it. Now he has to come out by land, and we know what direction he'll be coming in. I think he'll have what's been in our way for so many years.'

Gardener looked at him, shiny-eyed.

'I suggest that we move up there.' He pointed to the old boardwalk. It was just inside the fence where he had spent so many hours watching the hotel and thinking about what was in the ballroom.

'All r—'

That was when the earth began to groan and heave under their feet – that subterranean creature had awakened; it was shaking itself and roaring.

At the same instant, dazzling white light filled every window of the Agincourt – the light of a thousand suns. The windows blew out all at once. Glass flew in diamond showers.

'REMEMBER YOUR SON AND FOLLOW ME!' Sloat roared. That sense of predestination was clear in him now, clear and undeniable. *He was meant to win, after all.*

The two of them began to run up the heaving beach toward the boardwalk.

8

Jack moved slowly, filled with wonder, across the hardwood ballroom floor. He was looking up, his eyes sparkling. His face was bathed in a clear white radiance that was all colors – sunrise colors, sunset colors, *rainbow* colors. The Talisman hung in the air high above him, slowly revolving.

It was a crystal globe perhaps three feet in circumference – the corona of its glow was so brilliant it was impossible to tell exactly how big it was. Gracefully curving lines seemed to groove its surface, like lines of longitude and latitude . . . *and why not?* Jack thought, still in a deep daze of awe and amazement. *It is the world – ALL worlds – in microcosm. More; it is the axis of all possible worlds.*

Singing; turning; *blazing.*

He stood beneath it, bathed in its warmth and clear sense of well-meant force; he stood in a dream, feeling that force flow into him like the clear spring rain which awakens the hidden power in a billion tiny seeds. He felt a terrible joy lift through his conscious mind like a rocket, and Jack Sawyer lifted both hands over his upturned face, laughing, both in response to that joy and in imitation of its rise.

'Come to me, then!' he shouted,

and slipped

(through? across?)

into

Jason.

'Come to me, then!' he shouted again in the sweetly liquid and slightly slippery tongue of the Territories – he cried it laughing, but tears coursed down his cheeks. And he understood that the quest had begun with the other boy and thus must end with him; so he let go and

slipped

back

into

Jack Sawyer.

Above him, the Talisman trembled in the air, slowly turning, throwing off light and heat and a sensation of true goodness, of *whiteness.*

'Come to me!'

It began to descend through the air.

9

So, after many weeks, and hard adventuring, and darkness and despair; after friends found and friends lost again; after days of toil, and nights spent sleeping in damp haystacks; after facing the demons of dark places (not the least of which lived in the cleft of his own soul) – after all these things, it was in this wise that the Talisman came to Jack Sawyer:

He watched it come down, and while there was no desire to flee, he had an overwhelming sense of worlds at risk, worlds in the balance. Was the Jason-part of him real? Queen Laura's son had been killed; he was a ghost whose name the people of the Territories swore by. Yet Jack decided he was. Jack's quest for the Talisman, a quest that had been meant for Jason to fulfill, had made Jason live again for a little while – Jack really *had* had a Twinner, at least of a sort. If Jason was a ghost, just as the knights had been ghosts, he might well disappear when that radiant, twirling globe touched his upstretched fingers. Jack would be killing him again.

Don't worry, Jack, a voice whispered. That voice was warm and clear.

Down it came, a globe, a world, *all* worlds – it was glory and warmth, it was goodness, it was the coming-again of the white. And, as has always been with the white and must always be, it was dreadfully fragile.

As it came down, worlds reeled about his head. He did not seem to be crashing through layers of reality now but seeing an entire cosmos of realities, all overlapping one another, linked like a shirt of

(reality)

chain-mail.

You're reaching up to hold a universe of worlds, a cosmos of good, Jack – this voice was his father's. *Don't drop it, son. For Jason's sake, don't drop it.*

Worlds upon worlds upon worlds, some gorgeous, some hellish, all of them for a moment illumined in the warm white light of this star that was a crystal globe chased with fine engraved lines. It came slowly down through the air toward Jack Sawyer's trembling, outstretched fingers.

'Come to me!' he shouted to it as it had sung to him. '*Come to me now!'*

It was three feet above his hands, branding them with its soft, healing heat; now two; now one. It hesitated for a moment, rotating slowly, its axis slightly canted, and Jack could see the brilliant, shifting outlines of continents and oceans and ice-caps on its surface. It hesitated . . . and then slowly slipped down into the boy's reaching hands.

CHAPTER FORTY-THREE
NEWS FROM EVERYWHERE

1

Lily Cavanaugh, who had fallen into a fitful doze after imagining Jack's voice somewhere below her, now sat bolt-upright in bed. For the first time in weeks bright color suffused her waxy yellow cheeks. Her eyes shone with a wild hope.

'Jason?' she gasped, and then frowned; that was not her son's name. But in the dream from which she had just been startled awake she had had a son by such a name, and in that dream she had been someone else. It was the dope, of course. The dope had queered her dreams to a fare-thee-well.

'Jack?' she tried again. 'Jack, where *are* you?'

No answer . . . but she *sensed* him, knew for sure that he was alive. For the first time in a long time – six months, maybe – she felt really good.

'Jack-O,' she said, and grabbed her cigarettes. She looked at them for a moment and then heaved them all the way across the room, where they landed in the fireplace on top of the rest of the shit she meant to burn later in the day. 'I think I just quit smoking for the second and last time in my life, Jack-O,' she said. 'Hang in there, kid. Your momma loves you.'

And she found herself for no reason grinning a large idiotic grin.

2

Donny Keegan, who had been pulling Sunlight Home kitchen duty when Wolf escaped from the box, had survived that terrible night – George Irwinson, the fellow who had been pulling the duty with him, had not been so lucky. Now Donny was in a more conventional orphans' home in Muncie, Indiana. Unlike some of the other boys at the Sunlight Home, Donny had been a real orphan; Gardener had needed to take a token few to satisfy the state.

Now, mopping a dark upstairs hall in a dim daze, Donny looked up suddenly, his muddy eyes widening. Outside, clouds which had been spitting light snow into the used-up fields of December suddenly pulled open in the west, letting out a single broad ray of sunshine that was terrible and exalting in its isolated beauty.

'*You're right, I DO love him!*' Donny shouted triumphantly. It was Ferd Janklow that Donny was shouting to, although Donny, who had too many toys in his attic to accommodate many brains, had already forgotten his name. '*He's beautiful and I DO love him!*'

Donny honked his idiot laugh, only now even *his laugh* was nearly beautiful. Some of the other boys came to their doors and stared at Donny in wonder. His face was bathed in the sunlight from that one clear, ephemeral ray, and one of the other boys would whisper to a close friend that night that for a moment Donny Keegan had looked like Jesus.

The moment passed; the clouds moved over that weird clear place in the sky, and by evening the snow had intensified into the first big winter storm of the season. Donny had known – for one brief moment he had known – what that feeling of love and triumph actually meant. That passed quickly, the way dreams do upon waking . . . but he never forgot the feeling itself, that almost swooning sensation of grace for once fulfilled and delivered instead of promised and then denied; that feeling of clarity and sweet, marvellous love; that feeling of ecstasy at the coming once more of the white.

3

Judge Fairchild, who had sent Jack and Wolf to the Sunlight Home, was no longer a judge of any kind, and as soon as his final appeals ran out, he would be going to jail. There no longer seemed any question that jail was where he would fetch up, and that he would do hard time there. Might never come out at all. He was an old man, and not very healthy. If they hadn't found the damned *bodies* . . .

He had remained as cheerful as possible under the circumstances, but now, as he sat cleaning his fingernails with the long blade of his pocket-knife in his study at home, a great gray wave of depression crashed over him. Suddenly he pulled the knife away from his thick nails, looked at it thoughtfully for a moment, and then inserted the tip of the blade into his right nostril. He held it there for a moment and then whispered, 'Oh shit. Why not?' He jerked his fist upward, sending the six-inch blade on a short, lethal trip, skewering first his sinuses and then his brain.

4

Smokey Updike sat in a booth at the Oatley Tap, going over invoices and totting up numbers on his Texas Instruments calculator, just as he had been doing on the day Jack had met him. Only now it was early evening and Lori was serving the evening's first customers. The juke-box was playing 'I'd Rather Have a Bottle in Front of Me (Than a Frontal Lobotomy).'

At one moment everything was normal. At the next Smokey sat bolt-upright, his little paper cap tumbling backward off his head. He clutched his white T-shirt over the left side of his chest, where a hammering bolt of pain had just struck like a silver spike. *God pounds his nails,* Wolf would have said.

At the same instant the grill suddenly exploded into the air with a loud bang. It hit a Busch display sign and tore it from the ceiling. It landed with a crash. A rich smell of LP gas filled the area in back of the bar almost at once. Lori screamed.

The juke-box speeded up: 45 rpms, 78, 150, 400! The woman's serio-comic lament became the speedy gabble of deranged chipmunks on a rocket-sled. A moment later the top blew off the juke. Colored glass flew everywhere.

Smokey looked down at his calculator and saw a single word blinking on and off in the red window:

TALISMAN-TALISMAN-TALISMAN-TALISMAN

Then his eyes exploded.

'*Lori, turn off the gas!*' one of the customers screamed. He got down off his stool, and turned toward Smokey.

'Smokey, tell her—' The man wailed with fright as he saw blood gushing from the holes where Smokey Updike's eyes had been.

A moment later the entire Oatley Tap blew sky-high, and before the fire-trucks could arrive from Dogtown and Elmira, most of downtown was in flames.

No great loss, children, can you say amen.

5

At Thayer School, where normality now reigned as it always had (with one brief interlude which those on campus remembered only as a series of vague, related dreams), the last classes of the day had just begun. What was light snow in Indiana was a cold drizzle here in Illinois. Students sat dreaming and thoughtful in their classes.

Suddenly the bells in the chapel began to peal. Heads came up. Eyes widened. All over the Thayer campus, fading dreams suddenly seemed to renew themselves.

6

Etheridge had been sitting in advanced-math class and pressing his hand rhythmically up and down against a raging hard-on while he stared unseeingly at the logarithms old Mr Hunkins was piling up on the blackboard. He was thinking about the cute little townie waitress he would be boffing later on. She wore garter-belts instead of pantyhose, and was more than willing to leave her stockings on while they fucked. Now Etheridge stared around at the windows, forgetting his erection, forgetting the waitress with her long legs and smooth nylons – suddenly, for no reason at all, Sloat was on his mind. Prissy little Richard Sloat, who should have been safely classifiable as a wimp but who somehow wasn't. He thought about Sloat and wondered if he was all right. Somehow he thought that maybe Sloat, who had left school unexcused four days ago and who hadn't been heard from since, wasn't doing so good.

In the headmaster's office, Mr Dufrey had been discussing the expulsion of a boy named George Hatfield for cheating with his furious – and rich – father when the bells began to jingle out their unscheduled little tune. When it ended, Mr Dufrey found himself on his hands and knees with his gray hair hanging in his eyes and his tongue lolling over his lips. Hatfield the Elder was standing by the door – cringing against it, actually – his eyes wide and his jaw agape, his anger forgotten in wonder and fear. Mr Dufrey had been crawling around on his rug, barking like a dog.

Albert the Blob had just been getting himself a snack when the bells began to ring. He looked toward the window for a moment, frowning the way a person frowns when he is trying to remember something that is right on the tip of his tongue. He shrugged and went back to opening a bag of nacho chips – his mother had just sent him a whole case. His eyes widened. He thought – just for a moment, but a moment was long enough – that the bag was full of plump, squirming white bugs.

He fainted dead away.

When he awoke and worked up enough courage to peer into the bag again, he saw it had been nothing but a hallucination. Of course! What else? All the same, it was a hallucination which exercised a strange power over him in the future; whenever he opened a bag of chips, or a candy-bar, or a Slim Jim, or a package of Big Jerk beef jerky, he saw those bugs in his mind's eye. By spring, Albert had lost thirty-five pounds, was playing on the Thayer tennis team, and had gotten laid. Albert was delirious with ecstasy. For the first time in his life he felt that he might survive his mother's love.

7

They all looked around when the bells began to ring. Some laughed, some frowned, a few burst into tears. A pair of dogs howled from somewhere, and that was passing strange because no dogs were allowed on campus.

The tune the bells rang was not in the computerized schedule of tunes – the disgruntled head custodian later verified it. A campus wag suggested in that week's issue of the school paper that some eager beaver had programmed the tune with Christmas vacation in mind.

It had been 'Happy Days Are Here Again'.

8

Although she had believed herself far too old to catch pregnant, no blood had come to the mother of Jack Sawyer's Wolf at the time of the Change some twelve months ago. Three months ago she had given birth to triplets – two litter-sisters and one litter-brother. Her labor had been hard, and the foreknowledge that one of her older children was about to die had been upon her. That child, she knew, had gone into the Other Place to protect the herd, and he would die in that Other Place, and she would never see him anymore. This was very hard, and she had wept in more than the pain of her delivery.

Yet now, as she slept with her new young beneath a full moon, all of them safely away from the herd for the time being, she rolled over with a smile on her face and pulled the newest litter-brother to her and began to lick him. Still sleeping himself, the Wolfling put his arms around his mother's shaggy neck and pressed his cheek against her downy breast, and now they both smiled; in her alien sleep a human thought arose: *God pounds his nails well and true.* And the moonlight of that lovely world where all smells were good shone down on the two of them as they slept in each other's arms with the litter-sisters nearby.

9

In the town of Goslin, Ohio (not far from Amanda, and some thirty miles south of Columbus), a man named Buddy Parkins was shovelling chickenshit in a henhouse at dusk. A cheesecloth mask was tied over his mouth and nose to keep the choking white cloud of powdered guano he was raising from getting up his nose and into his mouth. The air reeked of ammonia. The stink had given him a headache. He also had a backache, because he was tall and the henhouse wasn't. All things considered, he would have to say that this was one bitch-kitty of a job. He had three sons, and every damned one of them seemed to be unavailable when the henhouse needed to be swamped out. Only thing to be said about it was that he was almost done, and –

The kid! Jesus Christ! That kid!

He suddenly remembered the boy who had called himself Lewis Farren with total clarity and a stunned kind of love. The boy who had claimed to be going to his aunt, Helen Vaughan, in the town of Buckeye Lake; the boy who had turned to Buddy when Buddy had asked him if he was running away and had, in that turning, revealed a face filled with honest goodness and an unexpected, amazing beauty – a beauty that had made Buddy think of rainbows glimpsed at the end of storms, and sunsets at the end of days that have groaned and sweated with work that has been well done and not scamped.

He straightened up with a gasp and bonked his head on the henhouse beams hard enough to make his eyes water . . . but he was grinning crazily all the same. *Oh my God, that boy is THERE, he's THERE*, Buddy Parkins thought, and although he had no idea of where 'there' was, was suddenly overtaken by a sweet, violent feeling of absolute adventure; never, since reading *Treasure Island* at the age of twelve and cupping a girl's breast in his hand for the first time at fourteen, had he felt so staggered, so excited, so full of warm joy. He began to laugh. He dropped his shovel, and while the hens stared at him with stupid amazement, Buddy Parkins danced a shuffling jig in the chickenshit, laughing behind his mask and snapping his fingers.

'He's there!' Buddy Parkins yelled to the chickens, laughing. 'By diddly-damn, he's there, he made it after all, he's there *and he's got it*!'

Later, he almost thought – almost, but never quite – that he must have somehow gotten high on the stench of the chicken-dust. That *wasn't* all, dammit, that *wasn't*. He had had some kind of revelation, but he could no longer remember what it had been . . . he supposed it was like that British poet some high-school English teacher had told them about: the guy had taken a big dose of opium and had started to write some poem about a make-believe Chink whorehouse while he was stoned . . . except when he came down to earth again he couldn't finish it.

Like that, he thought, but somehow he knew it wasn't; and although he couldn't remember exactly what had caused the joy, he, like Donny Keegan, never forgot the way the joy had come, all deliciously unbidden – he never forgot that sweet, violent feeling of having touched some great adventure, of having looked for a moment at some beautiful white light that was, in fact, every color of the rainbow.

10

There's an old Bobby Darin song which goes: '*And the ground coughs up some roots/wearing denim shirts and boots,/haul em away . . . haul em away*.' This was a song the children in the area of Cayuga, Indiana, could have related to enthusiastically, if it hadn't been popular quite a bit before their time. The Sunlight Home had been empty for only a little more than a week, and already it had gotten a reputation with the local kids as a haunted house. Considering the grisly remains the payloaders had found near the rock wall at the back of Far Field, this was not surprising. The local realtor's FOR SALE sign looked as if it had been standing on the lawn for a year instead of just nine days, and the realtor had already dropped the price once and was thinking about doing it again.

As it happened, he would not have to. As the first snow began to spit down from the leaden skies over Cayuga (and as Jack Sawyer was touching the Talisman some two thousand miles away), the LP tanks behind the kitchen exploded. A workman from Eastern Indiana Gas and Electric had come the week before and had sucked all the gas back into his truck, and he would have sworn you could have crawled right inside one of those tanks and lit up a cigarette, but they exploded anyway – they exploded at the exact moment the windows of the Oatley Tap were exploding out into the street (along with a number of patrons wearing denim shirts and boots . . . the Elmira rescue units hauled em away).

The Sunlight Home burned to the ground in almost no time at all.

Can you gimme hallelujah?

11

In all worlds, something shifted and settled into a slightly new position like a great beast . . . but in Point Venuti the beast was in the earth; it had been awakened and was roaring. It did not go to sleep for the next seventy-nine seconds, according to the Institute of Seismology at CalTech.

The earthquake had begun.

CHAPTER FORTY-FOUR
THE EARTHQUAKE

1

It was some time before Jack became aware that the Agincourt was shaking itself to pieces around him, and this was not surprising. He was transported with wonder. In one sense he was not in the Agincourt at all, not in Point Venuti, not in Mendocino County, not in California, not in the American Territories, not in those other Territories; but he *was* in them, and in an infinite number of other worlds as well, and all at the same time. Nor was he simply in one place in all those worlds; he was in them everywhere because he *was* those worlds. The Talisman, it seemed, was much more than even his father had believed. It was not just the axle of all possible worlds, but the worlds themselves – the worlds, and the spaces between those worlds.

Here was enough transcendentalism to drive even a cavedwelling Tibetan holy man insane. Jack Sawyer was everywhere; Jack Sawyer was everything. A blade of grass on a world fifty thousand worlds down the chain from earth died of thirst on an inconsequential plain somewhere in the center of a continent which roughly corresponded in position to Africa; Jack died with that blade of grass. In another world, dragons were copulating in the center of a cloud high above the planet, and the fiery breath of their ecstasy mixed with the cold air and precipitated rain and floods on the ground below. Jack was the he-dragon; Jack was the she-dragon; Jack was the sperm; Jack was the egg. Far out in the ether a million universes away, three specks of dust floated near one another in interstellar space. Jack was the dust, and Jack was the space between. Galaxies unreeled around his head like long spools of paper, and fate punched each in random patterns, turning them into macro-cosmic player-piano tapes which would play everything from ragtime to funeral dirges. Jack's happy teeth bit an orange; Jack's unhappy flesh screamed as the teeth tore him open. He was a trillion dust-kitties under a billion beds. He was a joey dreaming of its previous life in its mother's pouch as the mother bounced over a purple plain where rabbits the size of deer ran and gambolled. He was ham on a hock in Peru and eggs in a nest under one of the hens in the Ohio henhouse Buddy Parkins was cleaning. He was the powdered henshit in Buddy Parkins's nose; he was the trembling hairs that would soon cause Buddy Parkins to sneeze; he was the sneeze; he was the germs in the sneeze; he was the atoms in the germs; he was the tachyons in the atoms travelling backward through time toward the big bang at the start of creation.

His heart skipped and a thousand suns flashed up in novas.

He saw a googolplex of sparrows in a googolplex of worlds and marked the fall or the well-being of each.

He died in the Gehenna of Territories ore-pit mines.

He lived as a flu-virus in Etheridge's tie.

He ran in a wind over far places.

He was . . .

Oh he was . . .

He was God. God, or something so close as to make no difference.

No! Jack screamed in terror. *No, I don't want to be God! Please! Please, I don't want to be God, I ONLY WANT TO SAVE MY MOTHER'S LIFE!*

And suddenly infinitude closed up like a losing hand folding in a cardsharp's grasp. It narrowed down to a beam of blinding white light, and this he followed back to the Territories Ballroom, where only seconds had passed. He still held the Talisman in his hands.

2

Outside, the ground had begun to do a carny kooch dancer's bump and grind. The tide, which had been coming in, rethought itself and began to run backward, exposing sand as deeply tanned as a starlet's thighs. Flopping on this uncovered sand were strange fish, some which seemed to be no more than gelatinous clots of eyes.

The cliffs behind the town were nominally of sedimentary rock, but any geologist would have taken one look and told you at once that these rocks were to the sedimentary classification as the nouveau riche were to the Four Hundred. The Point Venuti Highlands were really nothing but mud with a hard-on and now they cracked and split in a thousand crazy directions. For a moment they held, the new cracks opening and closing like gasping mouths, and then they began to collapse in landslides on the town. Showers of dirt came sifting down. Amid the dirt were boulders as big as Toledo tire-factories.

Morgan's Wolf Brigade had been decimated by Jack and Richard's surprise attack on Camp Readiness. Now the number was even further reduced as many of them ran screaming and wailing in superstitious fear. Some catapulted back into their own world. Some of these got away, but most were swallowed by the upheavals that were happening there. A core of similar cataclysms ran from this place through all the worlds, as if punched through by a surveyor's hollow sampling rod. One group of three Wolfs dressed in Fresno Demons motorcycle jackets gained their car – a horny old Lincoln Mark IV – and managed to drive a block and a half with Harry James bellowing brass out of the tape-deck before a chunk of stone fell from the sky and crushed the Connie flat.

Others simply ran shrieking in the streets, their Change beginning. The woman with the chains in her nipples strolled serenely in front of one of these. She was serenely ripping her hair out in great chunks. She held one of these chunks out to the Wolf. The bloody roots wavered like the tips of sea-grass as she waltzed in place on the unsteady earth.

'Here!' she cried, smiling serenely. 'A bouquet! For you!'

The Wolf, not a bit serene, tore her head off with a single snap of his jaws and ran on, on, on.

3

Jack studied what he had captured, as breathless as a child who has a shy woodland creature come out of the grass and eat from his hand.

It glowed between his palms, waxing and waning, waxing and waning.

With my heartbeat, he thought.

It seemed to be glass, but it had a faintly yielding feeling in his hands. He pressed and it gave a little. Color shot inward from the points of his pressure in enchanting billows: inky blue from his left hand, deepest carmine from the right. He smiled . . . and then the smile faded.

You may be killing a billion people doing that – fires, floods, God knows what. Remember the building that collapsed in Angola, New York, after –

No, Jack, the Talisman whispered, and he understood why it had yielded to the gentle pressure of his hands. It was alive; of course it was. *No, Jack: All will be well . . . all will be well . . . and all manner of things will be well. Only believe; be true; stand; do not falter now.*

Peace in him – oh such deep peace.

Rainbow, rainbow, rainbow, Jack thought, and wondered if he could ever bring himself to let this wondrous bauble go.

4

On the beach below the wooden walk, Gardener had fallen flat on his belly in terror. His fingers hooked into the loose sand. He was mewling.

Morgan reeled toward him like a drunk and ripped the pack-set from Gardener's shoulder.

'*Stay outside!*' he roared into it, and then realized he had forgotten to press the SEND button. He did it now. '*STAY OUTSIDE! IF YOU TRY TO GET OUT OF TOWN THE MOTHERFUCKING CLIFFS WILL FALL ON YOU! GET DOWN HERE! COME TO ME! THIS IS NOTHING BUT A BUNCH OF GODDAM SPECIAL EFFECTS! GET DOWN HERE! FORM A RING AROUND THE BEACH! THOSE OF YOU WHO COME WILL BE REWARDED! THOSE OF YOU WHO DON'T*

WILL DIE IN THE PITS AND IN THE BLASTED LANDS! GET DOWN HERE! IT'S OPEN! GET DOWN HERE WHERE NOTHING CAN FALL ON YOU! GET DOWN HERE, DAMMIT!'

He threw the pack-set aside. It split open. Beetles with long feelers began to squirm out by the dozens.

He bent down and yanked the howling, whey-faced Gardener up. 'On your feet, beautiful,' he said.

5

Richard cried out in his unconsciousness as the table he was lying on bucked him off onto the floor. Jack heard the cry, and it dragged him out of his fascinated contemplation of the Talisman.

He became aware that the Agincourt was groaning like a ship in a high gale. As he looked around, boards snapped up, revealing dusty beamwork beneath. The beams were sawing back and forth like shuttles in a loom. Albino bugs scuttered and squirmed away from the Talisman's clear light.

'*I'm coming, Richard!*' he shouted, and began to work his way back across the floor. He was thrown over once and he went down holding the glowing sphere high, knowing it was vulnerable – if it was hit hard enough, it would break. What then, God knew. He got to one knee, was thrown back down on his butt, and lurched to his feet again.

From below, Richard screamed again.

'Richard! Coming!'

From overhead, a sound like sleigh-bells. He looked up and saw the chandelier penduluming back and forth, faster and faster. Its crystal pendants were making that sound. As Jack watched, the chain parted and it hit the unravelling floor like a bomb with diamonds instead of high explosive in its nose. Glass flew.

He turned and exited the room in big, larruping strides – he looked like a burlesque comic doing a turn as a drunken sailor.

Down the hall. He was thrown against first one wall and then the other as the floor seesawed and split open. Each time he crashed into a wall he held the Talisman out from him, his arms like tongs in which it glowed like a white-hot coal.

You'll never make it down the stairs.

Gotta. Gotta.

He reached the landing where he had faced the black knight. The world heaved a new way; Jack staggered and saw the helmet on the floor below roll crazily away.

Jack continued to look down. The stairs were moving in great tortured waves that made him feel like puking. A stair-level snapped upward, leaving a writhing black hole.

'Jack!'

'Coming, Richard!'

No way you can make it down those stairs. No way, baby.

Gotta. Gotta.

Holding the precious, fragile Talisman in his hands, Jack started down a flight of stairs that now looked like an Arabian flying carpet caught in a tornado.

The stairs heaved and he was flung toward the same gap through which the black knight's helmet had fallen. Jack screamed and staggered backward toward the drop, holding the Talisman against his chest with his right hand and flailing behind him with his left. Flailing at nothing. His heels hit the drop and tilted backward over oblivion.

6

Fifty seconds had passed since the earthquake began. Only fifty seconds – but earthquake survivors will tell you that objective time, clock-time, loses all meaning in an earthquake. Three days after the '53 earthquake in Los Angeles, a television news reporter asked a survivor who had been near the epicenter how long the quake had lasted.

'It's still going on,' the survivor said calmly.

Sixty-two seconds after the quake began, almost all of the Point Venuti Highlands decided to give in to destiny and become the Point Venuti Lowlands. They fell on the town with a muddy *kurrummmmp*, leaving only a single jut of slightly harder rock, which pointed at the Agincourt like an accusing finger. From one of the new slumped hills a dirty smokestack pointed like a randy penis.

7

On the beach, Morgan Sloat and Sunlight Gardener stood supporting each other, appearing to hula. Gardener had unslung the Weatherbee. A few Wolfs, their eyes alternately bulging with terror and glaring with hellacious rage, had joined them. More were coming. They were all Changed or Changing. Their clothes hung from them in tatters. Morgan saw one of them dive at the ground and begin to bite at it, as if the uneasy earth were an enemy that could be killed. Morgan glanced at this madness and dismissed it. A van with the words WILD CHILD written on the sides in psychedelic lettering plowed hell-for-leather across Point Venuti Square, where children had once begged their parents for ice creams and pennants emblazoned with the Agincourt's likeness. The van made it to the far side, jumped across the sidewalk, and then roared toward the beach, plowing through boarded-up concessions as it came. One final fissure opened in the earth and the WILD CHILD that had killed Tommy Woodbine disappeared forever, nose first. A jet of flame burst up as its gas-tank exploded. Watching, Sloat thought dimly of his father preaching about the Pentecostal Fire. Then the earth snapped shut.

'Hold steady,' he shouted at Gardener. 'I think the place is going to fall on top of him and crush him flat, but if he gets out, you're going to shoot him, earthquake or no earthquake.'

'Will we know if IT breaks?' Gardener squealed.

Morgan Sloat grinned like a boar in a canebrake.

'We'll know,' he said. 'The sun will turn black.'

Seventy-four seconds.

8

Jack's left hand scrabbled a grip on the ragged remains of the bannister. The Talisman glowed fiercely against his chest, the lines of latitude and longitude which girdled it shining as brightly as the wire filaments in a lightbulb. His heels tilted and his soles began to slide.

Falling! Speedy! I'm going to –

Seventy-nine seconds.

It stopped.

Suddenly, it just stopped.

Only, for Jack, as for that survivor of the '53 quake, it was still going on, at least in part of his brain. In part of his brain the earth would continue to shake like a church-picnic Jell-O forever.

He pulled himself back from the drop and staggered to the middle of the twisted stair. He stood, gasping, his face shiny with sweat, hugging the bright round star of the Talisman against his chest. He stood and listened to the silence.

Somewhere something heavy – a bureau or a wardrobe, perhaps – which had been tottering on the edge of balance now fell over with an echoing crash.

'Jack! Please! I think I'm dying!' Richard's groaning, helpless voice did indeed sound like that of a boy in his last extremity.

'Richard! Coming!'

He began to work his way down the stairs, which were now twisted and bent and tottery. Many of the stair-levels were gone, and he had to step over these spaces. In one place four in a row were gone and he leaped, holding the Talisman to his chest with one hand and sliding his hand along the warped bannister with the other.

Things were still falling. Glass crashed and tinkled. Somewhere a toilet was flushing manically, again and again.

The redwood registration desk in the lobby had split down the middle. The double doors were ajar, however, and a bright wedge of sunlight came through them – the old dank carpet seemed to sizzle and steam in protest at that light.

The clouds have broken, Jack thought. *Sun's shining outside.* And then: *Going out those doors, Richie-boy. You and me. Big as life and twice as proud.*

The corridor which led past the Heron Bar and down to the dining room reminded him of sets in some of the old *Twilight Zone* shows, where everything was askew and out of kilter. Here the floor tilted left; here to the right; here it was like the twin humps of a camel. He negotiated the dimness with the Talisman lighting his way like the world's biggest flashlight.

He shoved into the dining room and saw Richard lying on the floor in a tangle of tablecloth. Blood was running from his nose. When he got closer he saw that some of those hard red bumps had split open and white bugs were working their way out of Richard's flesh and crawling sluggishly over Richard's cheeks. As he watched, one birthed itself from Richard's nose.

Richard screamed, a weak, bubbling, wretched scream, and clawed at it. It was the scream of someone who is dying in agony.

His shirt humped and writhed with the things.

Jack stumbled across the distorted floor toward him . . . and the spider swung down from the dimness, squirting its poison blindly into the air.

'*Fushing feef!*' it gibbered in its whining, droning insect's voice. '*Oh you fushing feef, put it back put it back put it back!*'

Without thinking, Jack raised the Talisman. It flashed clean white fire – rainbow fire – and the spider shrivelled and turned black. In only a second it was a tiny lump of smoking coal penduluming slowly to a dead stop in the air.

No time to gawp at this wonder. Richard was dying.

Jack reached him, fell on his knees beside him, and stripped back the tablecloth as if it were a sheet.

'Finally made it, chum,' he whispered, trying not to see the bugs crawling out of Richard's flesh. He raised the Talisman, considered, and then placed it on Richard's forehead. Richard shrieked miserably and tried to writhe away. Jack placed an arm on Richard's scrawny chest and held him – it wasn't hard to do. There was a stench as the bugs beneath the Talisman fried away.

Now what? There's more, but what?

He looked across the room and his eye happened to fix upon the green croaker marble that he had left with Richard – the marble that was a magic mirror in that other world. As he looked, it rolled six feet of its own volition, and then stopped. It rolled, yes. It rolled because it was a marble, and it was a marble's job to roll. Marbles were round. Marbles were round and so was the Talisman.

Light broke in his reeling mind.

Holding Richard, Jack slowly rolled the Talisman down the length of his body. After he reached Richard's chest, Richard stopped struggling. Jack thought he had probably fainted, but a quick glance showed him this wasn't so. Richard was staring at him with dawning wonder . . .

. . . and the pimples on his face were gone! The hard red bumps were fading!

'Richard!' he yelled, laughing like a crazy loon. 'Hey, Richard, look at this! Bwana make juju!'

He rolled the Talisman slowly down over Richard's belly, using his palm. The Talisman glowed brightly, singing a clear, wordless harmonic of health and healing. Down over Richard's crotch. Jack moved Richard's thin legs together and rolled it down the groove between them to Richard's ankles. The Talisman glowed bright blue . . . deep red . . . yellow . . . the green of June meadow-grass.

Then it was white again.

'Jack,' Richard whispered. 'Is that what we came for?'

'Yes.'

'It's beautiful,' Richard said. He hesitated. 'May I hold it?'

Jack felt a sudden twist of Scrooge-miserliness. He snatched the Talisman close to himself for a moment. *No!*

You might break it! Besides, it's mine! I crossed the country for it! I fought the knights for it! You can't have it! Mine! Mine! Mi—

In his hands the Talisman suddenly radiated a terrible chill, and for a moment – a moment more frightening to Jack than all the earthquakes in all the worlds that ever had been or ever would be – it turned a Gothic black. Its white light was extinguished. In its rich, thundery, thanatropic interior he saw the black hotel. On turrets and gambrels and gables, on the roofs of cupolas which bulged like warts stuffed with thick malignancies, the cabalistic symbols turned – wolf and crow and twisted genital star.

Would you be the new Agincourt, then? the Talisman whispered. *Even a boy can be a hotel . . . if he would be.*

His mother's voice, clear in his head: *If you don't want to share it, Jack-O, if you can't bring yourself to risk it for your friend, then you might as well stay where you are. If you can't bring yourself to share the prize – risk the prize – don't even bother to come home. Kids hear that shit all their lives, but when it comes time to put up or shut up, it's never quite the same, is it? If you can't share it, let me die, chum, because I don't want to live at that price.*

The weight of the Talisman suddenly seemed immense, the weight of dead bodies. Yet somehow Jack lifted it, and put it in Richard's hands. His hands were white and skeletal . . . but Richard held it easily, and Jack realized that sensation of weight had been only his own imagination, his own twisted and sickly wanting. As the Talisman flashed into glorious white light again, Jack felt his own interior darkness pass from him. It occurred to him dimly that you could only express your ownership of a thing in terms of how freely you could give it up . . . and then that thought passed.

Richard smiled, and the smile made his face beautiful.

Jack had seen Richard smile many times, but there was a peace in this smile he had never seen before; it was a peace which passed his understanding. In the Talisman's white, healing light, he saw that Richard's face, although still ravaged and haggard and sickly, was healing. He hugged the Talisman against his chest as if it were a baby, and smiled at Jack with shining eyes.

'If *this* is the Seabrook Island Express,' he said, 'I may just buy a season ticket. *If* we ever get out of this.'

'You feel better?'

Richard's smile shone like the Talisman's light. *'Worlds* better,' he said. 'Now help me up, Jack.'

Jack moved to take his shoulder. Richard held out the Talisman.

'Better take this first,' he said. 'I'm still weak, and it wants to go back with you. I feel that.'

Jack took it and helped Richard up. Richard put an arm around Jack's neck.

'You ready . . . *chum*?'

'Yeah,' Richard said. 'Ready. But I somehow think the seagoing route's out, Jack. I think I heard the deck out there collapse during the Big Rumble.'

'We're going out the front door,' Jack said. 'Even if God put down a gangway over the ocean from the windows back there to the beach, I'd still go out the front door. We ain't ditching this place, Richie. We're going out like paying guests. I feel like I've paid plenty. What do you think?'

Richard held out one thin hand, palm-up. Healing red blemishes still glared on it.

'I think we ought to go for it,' he said. 'Gimme some skin, Jacky.'

Jack slapped his palm down on Richard's, and then the

two of them started back toward the hallway, Richard with one arm around Jack's neck.

Halfway down the hall, Richard stared around at the litter of dead metal. 'What in heck?'

'Coffee cans,' Jack said, and smiled. 'Maxwell House.'

'Jack, what in the world are you t—'

'Never mind, Richard,' Jack said. He was grinning, and he still felt good, but wires of tension were working into his body again just the same. The earthquake was over . . . but it wasn't over. Morgan would be waiting for them now. And Gardener.

Never mind. Let it come down the way it will.

They reached the lobby and Richard looked around wonderingly at the stairs, the broken registration desk, the tumbled trophies and flag-stands. The stuffed head of a black bear had its nose in one of the pigeonholes of the mail depository, as if smelling something good – honey, perhaps.

'Wow,' Richard said. 'Whole place just about fell down.'

Jack got Richard over to the double doors, and observed Richard's almost greedy appreciation of that little spray of sunlight.

'Are you really ready for this, Richard?'

'Yes.'

'Your father's out there.'

'No, he's not. He's dead. All that's out there is his . . . what do you call it? His Twinner.'

'Oh.'

Richard nodded. In spite of the Talisman's proximity, he was beginning to look exhausted again. 'Yes.'

'There's apt to be a hell of a fight.'

'Well, I'll do what I can.'

'I love you, Richard.'

Richard smiled wanly. 'I love you, too, Jack. Now let's go for it before I lose my nerve.'

9

Sloat really believed he had everything under control – the situation, of course, but more important, himself. He went right on believing this until he saw his son, obviously weak, obviously sick, but still very much alive, come out of the black hotel with his arm around Jack Sawyer's neck and his head leaning against Jack's shoulder.

Sloat had also believed he finally had his feelings about Phil Sawyer's brat under control – it was his previous rage that had caused him to miss Jack, first at the Queen's pavillion, then in the midwest. Christ, he had crossed Ohio unscathed – and Ohio was only an eyeblink from Orris, that other Morgan's stronghold. But his fury had led to uncontrolled behavior, and so the boy had slipped through. He had suppressed his rage – but now it flared up with wicked and unbridled freedom. It was as if someone had hosed kerosene on a well-banked fire.

His son, still alive. And his beloved son, to whom he had meant to turn over the kingship of worlds and universes, was leaning on Sawyer for support.

Nor was that all. Glimmering and flashing in Sawyer's hands like a star which had fallen to earth was the Talisman. Even from here Sloat could feel it – it was as if the planet's gravitational field had suddenly gotten stronger, pulling him down, making his heart labor; as if time were speeding up, drying out his flesh, dimming his eyes.

'It hurts!' Gardener wailed beside him.

Most of the Wolfs who had stood up to the quake and

rallied to Morgan were now reeling away, hands before their faces. A couple of them were vomiting helplessly.

Morgan felt a moment of swooning fear . . . and then his rage, his excitement, and the lunacy that had been feeding on his increasingly grandiose dreams of overlordship – these things burst apart the webbing of his self-control.

He raised his thumbs to his ears and slammed them deep inside, so deep it hurt. Then he stuck out his tongue and waggled his fingers at Mr Jack Dirty Motherfuck and Soon-to-be-Dead Sawyer. A moment later his upper teeth descended like a drop-gate and severed the tip of his wagging tongue. Sloat didn't even notice it. He seized Gardener by the flak-vest.

Gardener's face was moony with fear. 'They're out, he's got IT, Morgan . . . my Lord . . . we ought to run, we *must* run—'

'*SHOOT HIM!*' Morgan screamed into Gardener's face. Blood from his severed tongue flew in a fine spray. '*SHOOT HIM, YOU ETHIOPIAN JUG-FUCKER, HE KILLED YOUR BOY! SHOOT HIM AND SHOOT THE FUCKING TALISMAN! SHOOT RIGHT THROUGH HIS ARMS AND BREAK IT!*'

Sloat now began to dance slowly up and down before Gardener, his face working horribly, his thumbs back in his ears, his fingers waggling beside his head, his amputated tongue popping in and out of his mouth like one of those New Year's Eve party favors that unroll with a tooting sound. He looked like a murderous child – hilarious, and at the same time awful.

'HE KILLED YOUR SON! AVENGE YOUR SON! SHOOT HIM! SHOOT IT! YOU SHOT HIS FATHER, NOW SHOOT HIM!'

'Reuel,' Gardener said thoughtfully. 'Yes. He killed Reuel. He's the baddest bitch's bastard to ever draw a breath. *All* boys. Axiomatic. But he . . . *he* . . .'

He turned toward the black hotel and raised the Weatherbee to his shoulder. Jack and Richard had reached the bottom of the twisted front steps and were beginning to move down the broad walkway, which had been flat a few minutes ago and which was now crazy-paved. In the Judkins scope, the two boys were as big as house-trailers.

'*SHOOT HIM!*' Morgan bellowed. He ran out his bleeding tongue again and made a hideously triumphant nursery-school sound: *Yadda-yadda-yadda-yah!* His feet, clad in dirty Gucci loafers, bumped up and down. One of them landed squarely on the severed tip of his tongue and tromped it deeper into the sand.

'*SHOOT HIM! SHOOT IT!*' Morgan howled.

The muzzle of the Weatherbee circled minutely as it had when Gardener was preparing to shoot the rubber horse. Then it settled. Jack was carrying the Talisman against his chest. The crosshairs were over its flashing, circular light. The .360 slug would pass right through it, shattering it, and the sun would turn black . . . *but before it does,* Gardener thought, *I will see that baddest bad boy's chest explode.*

'He's dead meat,' Gardener whispered, and began to settle pressure against the Weatherbee's trigger.

10

Richard raised his head with great effort and his eyes were sizzled by reflected sunlight.

Two men. One with his head slightly cocked, the other seeming to dance. That flash of sunlight again, and Richard understood. He understood . . . and Jack was looking in the wrong place. Jack was looking down toward the rocks where Speedy lay.

'*Jack, look out!*' he screamed.

Jack looked around, surprised. 'What—'

It happened fast. Jack missed it almost entirely. Richard saw it and understood it, but could never quite explain what had happened to Jack. The sunlight flashed off the shooter's riflescope again. The ray of reflected light this time struck the Talisman. And the Talisman reflected it back directly at the shooter. This was what Richard later told Jack, but that was like saying the Empire State Building is a few stories high.

The Talisman did not just reflect the sunflash; it *boosted* it somehow. It sent back a thick ribbon of light like a deathray in a space movie. It was there only for a second, but it imprinted Richard's retinas for almost an hour afterward, first white, then green, then blue, and finally, as it faded, the lemony yellow of sunshine.

11

'He's dead meat,' Gardener whispered, and then the scope was full of living fire. Its thick glass lenses shattered. Smoking, fused glass was driven backward into Gardener's right eye. The shells in the Weatherbee's magazine exploded, tearing its midsection apart. One of the whickers of flying metal amputated most of Gardener's right cheek. Other hooks and twists of steel flew around Sloat in a storm, leaving him incredibly untouched. Three Wolfs had remained through everything. Now two of them took to their heels. The third lay dead on his back, glaring into the sky. The Weatherbee's trigger was planted squarely between his eyes.

'What?' Morgan bellowed. His bloody mouth hung open. 'What? What?'

Gardener looked weirdly like Wile E. Coyote in the Roadrunner cartoons after one of his devices from the Acme Company has misfired.

He cast the gun aside, and Sloat saw that all the fingers had been torn from Gard's left hand.

Gardener's right hand pulled out his shirt with effeminate, tweezing delicacy. There was a knife-case clipped to the inner waistband of his pants – a narrow sleeve of fine-grained kid leather. From it Gardener took a piece of chrome-banded ivory. He pushed a button, and a slim blade seven inches long shot out.

'Bad,' he whispered. 'Bad!' His voice began to rise. 'All boys! *Bad! It's axiomatic! IT'S AXIOMATIC!*' He began to run up the beach toward the Agincourt's walk, where Jack and Richard stood. His voice continued to rise until it was a thin, febrile shriek.

'BAD! EVIL! BAD! EEVIL! BAAAD! EEEEE-EEEEEEEEEEE—'

Morgan stood a moment longer, then grasped the key around his neck. By grasping it, he seemed also to grasp his own panicked, flying thoughts.

He'll go to the old nigger. And that's where I'll take him.

'*EEEEEEEEEEEEEEEE—*' Gardener shrieked, his killer knife held out before him as he ran.

Morgan turned and ran down the beach. He was vaguely aware that the Wolfs, all of them, had fled. That was all right.

He would take care of Jack Sawyer – and the Talisman – all by himself.

CHAPTER FORTY-FIVE

IN WHICH MANY THINGS ARE RESOLVED ON THE BEACH

1

Sunlight Gardener ran dementedly toward Jack, blood streaming down his mutilated face. He was the center of a devastated madness. Under bright blistering sunshine for the first time in what must have been decades, Point Venuti was a ruin of collapsed buildings and broken pipes and sidewalks heaved up like books tilting and leaning on a shelf. Actual books lay here and there, their ripped jackets fluttering in raw seams of earth. Behind Jack the Agincourt Hotel uttered a sound uncannily like a groan; then Jack heard the sound of a thousand boards collapsing in on themselves, of walls tipping over in a shower of snapped lath and plaster-dust. The boy was faintly conscious of the beelike figure of Morgan Sloat slipping down the beach and realized with a stab of unease that his adversary was going toward Speedy Parker – or Speedy's corpse.

'He's got a knife, Jack,' Richard whispered.

Gardener's ruined hand carelessly smeared blood on his once-spotless white silk shirt. 'EEEEEEVIL!' he screeched, his voice still faint over the constant pounding of the water on the beach and the continuing, though intermittent, noises of destruction. 'EEEEEEEEEEE . . .'

'What are you going to do?' Richard asked.

'How should I know?' Jack answered – it was the best, truest answer he could give. He had no idea of how he could defeat this madman. Yet he would defeat him. He was certain of that. 'You shoulda killed *both* of the Ellis brothers,' Jack said to himself.

Gardener, still shrieking, came racing across the sand. He was even now a good distance away, about halfway between the end of the fence and the front of the hotel. A red mask covered half his face. His useless left hand leaked a steady spattering stream of blood onto the sandy ground. The distance between the madman and the boys seemed to halve in a second. Was Morgan Sloat on the beach by now? Jack felt an urgency like the Talisman's, pushing him forward, pushing him on.

'Evil! Axiomatic! Evil!' Gardener screamed.

'Flip!' Richard loudly said –

and Jack

sidestepped

as he had inside the black hotel.

And then found himself standing in front of Osmond in blistering Territories sunlight. Most of his certainty abruptly left him. Everything was the same but everything was different. Without looking, he knew that behind him was something much worse than the Agincourt – he had never seen the exterior of the castle the hotel became in the Territories, but he suddenly *knew* that through the great front doors a tongue was coiling out for him . . . and that Osmond was going to drive him and Richard back toward it.

Osmond wore a patch over his right eye and a stained glove on his left hand. The complicated tendrils of his whip came slithering off his shoulder. 'Oh, yes,' he half-hissed, half-whispered. '*This* boy. Captain Farren's boy.' Jack pulled the Talisman protectively into his belly. The intricacies of the whip slid over the ground, as responsive to Osmond's minute movements of hand and wrist as is a racehorse to the hand of the jockey. 'What does it profit a boy to gain a glass bauble if he lose the world?' The whip seemed almost to lift itself off the ground. 'NOTHING! NAUGHT!' Osmond's true smell, that of rot and filth and hidden corruption, boomed out, and his lean crazy face somehow rippled, as if a lightning-bolt had cracked beneath it. He smiled brightly, emptily, and raised the coiling whip above his shoulder.

'Goat's-penis,' Osmond said, almost lovingly. The thongs of the whip came singing down toward Jack, who stepped backward, though not far enough, in a sudden sparkling panic.

Richard's hand gripped his shoulder as he flipped again, and the horrible, somehow laughing noise of the whip instantly erased itself from the air.

Knife! he heard Speedy say.

Fighting his instincts, Jack stepped inside the space where the whip had been, not backward as almost all of him wished to do. Richard's hand fell away from the ridge of his shoulder, and Speedy's voice went wailing and lost. Jack clutched the glowing Talisman into his belly with his left hand and reached up with his right. His fingers closed magically around a bony wrist.

Sunlight Gardener giggled.

'JACK!' Richard bellowed behind him.

He was standing in this world again, under streaming cleansing light, and Sunlight Gardener's knife hand was straining down toward him. Gardener's ruined face hung only inches from his own. A smell as of garbage and long-dead animals left on the road blanketed them. 'Naught,' Gardener said. 'Can you give me hallelujah?' He pushed down with the elegant lethal knife, and Jack managed to hold it back.

'JACK!' Richard yelled again.

Sunlight Gardener stared at him with a bright bird-like air. He continued to push down with his knife.

Don't you know what Sunlight done? said Speedy's voice. *Don't you know yet?*

Jack looked straight into Gardener's crazily dancing eye. Yes.

Richard rushed in and kicked Gardener in the ankle, then clouted a weak fist into his temple.

'You killed my father,' Jack said.

Gardener's single eye sparkled back. 'You killed my boy, baddest bastard!'

'Morgan Sloat told you to kill my father and you did.'

Gardener pushed the knife down a full two inches. A knot of yellow gristly stuff and a bubble of blood squeezed out of the hole that had been his right eye.

Jack screamed – with horror, rage, and all the long-hidden feelings of abandonment and helplessness which had followed his father's death. He found that he had pushed Gardener's knife hand all the way back up. He screamed again. Gardener's fingerless left hand battered against Jack's own left arm. Jack was just managing to twist Gardener's wrist back when he felt that dripping pad of flesh insinuate itself between his chest and his arm. Richard continued to skirmish about Gardener, but Gardener was managing to get his fingerless hand very near the Talisman.

Gardener tilted his face right up to Jack's.

'*Hallelujah*,' he whispered.

Jack twisted his entire body around, using more strength than he'd known he had. He hauled down on Gardener's knife hand. The other, fingerless hand flew to the side. Jack *squeezed* the wrist of the knife hand. Corded tendons wriggled in his grasp. Then the knife dropped, as harmless now as the fingerless cushion of skin which struck repeatedly at Jack's ribs. Jack rolled his whole body into the off-center Gardener and sent him lurching away.

He shoved the Talisman toward Gardener. Richard squawked, *What are you doing?* This was right, right, right. Jack moved in toward Gardener, who was still gleaming at him, though with less assurance, and thrust the Talisman out toward him. Gardener grinned, another bubble of blood bulging fatly in the empty eyesocket, and swung wildly at the Talisman. Then he ducked for the knife. Jack rushed in and touched the Talisman's grooved warm skin against Gardener's own skin. Like Reuel, like Sunlight. He jumped back.

Gardener howled like a lost, wounded animal. Where the Talisman had brushed against him, the skin had blackened, then turned to a slowly sliding fluid, skimming away from the skull. Jack retreated another step. Gardener fell to his knees. All the skin on his head turned waxy. Within half a second, only a gleaming skull protruded through the collar of the ruined shirt.

That's you taken care of, Jack thought, *and good riddance!*

2

'All right,' Jack said. He felt full of crazy confidence. 'Let's go get him, Richie. Let's—'

He looked at Richard and saw that his friend was on the verge of collapsing again. He stood swaying on the sand, his eyes half-lidded and dopey.

'Maybe you better just sit this one out, on second thought,' Jack said.

Richard shook his head. 'Coming, Jack. Seabrook Island. All the way . . . to the end of the line.'

'I'm going to have to kill him,' Jack said. 'That is, if I can.'

Richard shook his head with dogged, stubborn persistence. 'Not my father. Told you. Father's dead. If you leave me I'll crawl. Crawl right through the muck *that* guy left behind, if I have to.'

Jack looked toward the rocks. He couldn't see Morgan, but he didn't think there was much question that Morgan was there. And if Speedy was still alive, Morgan might at this moment be taking steps to remedy that situation.

Jack tried to smile but couldn't make it. 'Think of the germs you might pick up.' He hesitated a moment longer, then held the Talisman reluctantly out to Richard. 'I'll carry you, but you'll have to carry this. Don't drop the ball, Richard. If you drop it—'

What was it Speedy had said?

'If you drop it, all be lost.'

'I won't drop it.'

Jack put the Talisman into Richard's hands, and again Richard seemed to improve at its touch . . . but not so much. His face was terribly wan. Washed in the Talisman's bright glow, it looked like the face of a dead child caught in the glare of a police photographer's flash.

It's the hotel. It's poisoning him.

But it wasn't the hotel; not entirely. It was Morgan. *Morgan* was poisoning him.

Jack turned around, discovering he was loath to look away from the Talisman even for a moment. He bent his back and curved his hands into stirrups.

Richard climbed on. He held to the Talisman with one hand and curled the other around Jack's neck. Jack grabbed Richard's thighs.

He is as light as a thistle. He has his own cancer. He's had it all his life. Morgan Sloat is radioactive with evil and Richard is dying of the fallout.

He started to jog down toward the rocks behind which Speedy lay, conscious of the light and heat of the Talisman just above him.

3

He ran around the left side of the clump of rocks with Richard on his back, still full of that crazy assurance . . . and that it *was* crazy was brought home to him with rude suddenness. A plumpish leg clad in light brown wool (and just below the pulled-back cuff Jack caught a blurred glimpse of a perfectly proper brown nylon sock) suddenly stuck straight out from behind the last rock like a toll-gate.

Shit! Jack's mind screamed. *He was waiting for you! You total nerd!*

Richard cried out. Jack tried to pull up and couldn't.

Morgan tripped him up as easily as a schoolyard bully trips up a younger boy on the play-yard. After Smokey

Updike, and Osmond, and Gardener, and Elroy, and something that looked like a cross between an alligator and a Sherman tank, all it really took to bring him down was overweight, hypertensive Morgan Sloat crouched behind a rock, watching and waiting for an overconfident boy named Jack Sawyer to come boogying right down on top of him.

'*Yiyyy!*' Richard cried as Jack stumbled forward. He was dimly aware of their combined shadow tracking out to his left – it seemed to have as many arms as a Hindu idol. He felt the psychic weight of the Talisman shift . . . and then overshift.

'*WATCH OUT FOR IT, RICHARD!*' Jack screamed.

Richard fell over the top of Jack's head, his eyes huge and dismayed. The cords on his neck stood out like piano wire. He held the Talisman up as he went down. His mouth was pulled down at the corners in a desperate snarl. He hit the ground face-first like the nosecone of a defective rocket. The sand here around the place where Speedy had gone to earth was not precisely sand at all but a rough-textured scree stubbly with smaller rocks and shells. Richard came down on a rock that had been burped up by the earthquake. There was a compact thudding sound. For a moment Richard looked like an ostrich with its head buried in the sand. His butt, clad in dirty polished-cotton slacks, wagged drunkenly back and forth in the air. In other circumstances – circumstances unattended by that dreadful compact thudding sound, for instance – it would have been a comic pose, worthy of a Kodachrome: 'Rational Richard Acts Wild and Crazy at the Beach.' But it wasn't funny at all. Richard's hands opened slowly . . . and the Talisman rolled three feet down the gentle slope of the beach and stopped there, reflecting sky and clouds, not on its surface but in its gently lighted interior.

'*Richard!*' Jack bellowed again.

Morgan was somewhere behind him, but Jack had momentarily forgotten him. All his reassurance was gone; it had left him at the moment when that leg, clad in light brown wool, had stuck out in front of him like a toll-gate. Fooled like a kid in a nursery-school play-yard, and Richard . . . Richard was . . .

'Rich—'

Richard rolled over and Jack saw that Richard's poor, tired face was covered with running blood. A flap of his scalp hung down almost to one eye in a triangular shape like a ragged sail. Jack could see hair sticking out of the underside and brushing Richard's cheek like sand-colored grass . . . and where that hair-covered skin had come from he could see the naked gleam of Richard Sloat's skull.

'Did it break?' Richard asked. His voice cracked toward a scream. '*Jack, did it break when I fell?*'

'It's okay, Richie – it's—'

Richard's blood-rimmed eyes bulged widely at something behind him. '*Jack! Jack, look o—!*'

Something that felt like a leather brick – one of Morgan Sloat's Gucci loafers – crashed up between Jack's legs and into his testicles. It was a dead-center hit, and Jack crumpled forward, suddenly living with the greatest pain of his life – a physical agony greater than any he had ever imagined. He couldn't even scream.

'It's okay,' Morgan Sloat said, 'but *you* don't look so good, Jacky-boy. Not

at

all.'

And now the man slowly advancing on Jack – advancing slowly because he was savoring this – was a man to whom Jack had never been properly introduced. He had been a white face in the window of a great black coach for a space of moments, a face with dark eyes that somehow sensed his presence; he had been a rippling, changing shape bludgeoning itself into the reality of the field where he and Wolf had been talking of such wonders as litter-brothers and the big rut-moon; he had been a shadow in Anders's eyes.

But I've never really seen Morgan of Orris until now, Jack thought. And he still *was* Jack – Jack in a pair of faded, dirty cotton pants of a sort you might expect to see an Asian coolie wearing, and sandals with rawhide thongs, but not Jason – Jack. His crotch was a great frozen scream of pain.

Ten yards away was the Talisman, throwing its effulgent glow along a beach of black sand. Richard was not there, but this fact did not impress itself on Jack's conscious mind until a bit later.

Morgan was wearing a dark blue cape held at the neck with a catch of beaten silver. His pants were the same light wool as Sloat's pants, only here they were bloused into black boots.

This Morgan walked with a slight limp, his deformed left foot leaving a line of short hyphens in the sand. The silver catch on his cloak swung loose and low as he moved, and Jack saw that the silver thing had nothing at all to do with the cape, which was held by a simple unadorned dark cord. This was some sort of pendant. He thought for a moment that it was a tiny golf-club, the sort of thing a woman might take off her charm-bracelet and wear around her neck, just for the fun of it. But as Sloat got closer, he saw it was too slim – it did not end in a club-head but came to a point.

It looked like a lightning-rod.

* * *

'No, you don't look well at all, boy,' Morgan of Orris said. He stepped over to where Jack lay, moaning, holding his crotch, legs drawn up. He bent forward, hands planted just above his knees, and studied Jack as a man might study an animal which his car has run over. A rather uninteresting animal like a woodchuck or a squirrel. 'Not a *bit* well.'

Morgan leaned even closer.

'You've been quite a problem for me,' Morgan of Orris said, bending lower. 'You've caused a great deal of damage. But in the end—'

'I think I'm dying,' Jack whispered.

'Not yet. Oh, I know it feels like that, but believe me, you're not dying yet. In five minutes or so, you'll know what dying *really* feels like.'

'No . . . really . . . I'm broken . . . inside,' Jack moaned. 'Lean down . . . I want to tell . . . to ask . . . beg . . .'

Morgan's dark eyes gleamed in his pallid face. It was the thought of Jack begging, perhaps. He leaned down until his face was almost touching Jack's. Jack's legs had drawn up in response to the pain. Now he pistoned them out and up. For a moment it felt as if a rusty blade were ripping up from his genitals and into his stomach, but the sound of his sandals striking Morgan's face, splitting his lips and crunching his nose to one side, more than made up for the pain.

Morgan of Orris flailed backward, roaring in pain and surprise, his cape flapping like the wings of a great bat.

Jack got to his feet. For a moment he saw the black castle – it was much larger than the Agincourt had been; seemed, in fact, to cover acres – and then he was lunging spastically past the unconscious (*or dead!*) Parkus. He lunged for the Talisman, which lay peacefully glowing on the sand,

and as he ran he

flipped back

to the American Territories.

'Oh you bastard!' Morgan Sloat bellowed. *'You rotten little bastard, my face, my face, you hurt my face!'*

There was a crackling sizzle and a smell like ozone. A brilliant blue-white branch of lightning passed just to Jack's right, fusing sand like glass.

Then he had the Talisman – *had it again*! The torn, throbbing ache in his crotch began to diminish at once. He turned to Morgan with the glass ball raised in his hands.

Morgan Sloat was bleeding from the lip and holding one hand up to his cheek – Jack hoped that he had cracked a few of Sloat's teeth while he was at it. In Sloat's other hand, outstretched in a curious echo of Jack's own posture, was the keylike thing which had just sent a lightning-bolt snapping into the sand beside Jack.

Jack moved sideways, his arms straight out before him and the Talisman shifting internal colors like a rainbow machine. It seemed to understand that Sloat was near, for the great grooved glass ball had begun a kind of subtonal *humming* that Jack felt – more than heard – as a tingle in his hands. A band of clear bright white opened in the Talisman, like a shaft of light right through its center, and Sloat jerked himself sideways and pointed the key at Jack's head.

He wiped a smear of blood away from his lower lip. 'You hurt me, you stinking little bastard,' he said. 'Don't think that glass ball can help you now. Its future is a little shorter than your own.'

'Then why are you afraid of it?' the boy asked, thrusting it forward again.

Sloat dodged sideways, as if the Talisman, too, could

shoot out bolts of lightning. *He doesn't know what it can do,* Jack realized: *he doesn't really know anything about it, he just knows he wants it.*

'Drop it right now,' Sloat said. 'Let go of it, you little fraud. Or I'll take the top of your head off right now. Drop it.'

'You're afraid,' Jack said. 'Now that the Talisman is right in front of you, you're afraid to come and get it.'

'I don't have to come and get it,' Sloat said. 'You goddam Pretender. Drop it. Let's see you break it by yourself, Jacky.'

'Come for it, Bloat,' Jack said, feeling a blast of wholly bracing anger shoot through him. *Jacky*. He *hated* hearing his mother's nickname for him in Sloat's wet mouth. 'I'm not the black hotel, Bloat. I'm just a kid. Can't you take a glass ball away from a kid?' Because it was clear to him that they were in stalemate as long as Jack held the Talisman in his hands. A deep blue spark, as vibrant as one of the sparks from Ander's 'demons', flared up and died in the Talisman's center. Another immediately followed. Jack could still feel that powerful *humming* emanating from the heart of the grooved glass ball. He had been destined to get the Talisman – he was *supposed to get it.* The Talisman had known of his existence since his birth, Jack now thought, and ever since had awaited him to set it free. It needed Jack Sawyer and no one else. 'Come on and try for it,' Jack taunted.

Sloat pushed the key toward him, snarling. Blood drooled down his chin. For a moment Sloat appeared baffled, as frustrated and enraged as a bull in a pen, and Jack actually smiled at him. Then Jack glanced sideways to where Richard lay on the sand, and the smile disappeared from his face. Richard's face was literally covered with blood, his dark hair was matted with it.

'You bast—' he began, but it had been a mistake to look away. A searing blast of blue and yellow light smacked into the beach directly beside him.

He turned to Sloat, who was just firing off another lightning bolt at his feet. Jack danced back, and the shaft of destructive light melted the sand at his feet into molten yellow liquid, which almost instantly cooled into a long straight slick of glass.

'Your son is going to die,' Jack said.

'Your mother is going to die,' Sloat snarled back at him. 'Drop that damned thing before I cut your head off. Now. Let go of it.'

Jack said, 'Why don't you go hump a weasel?'

Morgan Sloat opened his mouth and screeched, revealing a row of square bloodstained teeth. 'I'll hump your *corpse*!' The pointing key wavered toward Jack's head, wavered away. Sloat's eyes glittered, and he jerked his hand up so that the key pointed at the sky. A long skein of lightning seemed to erupt upward from Sloat's fist, widening out as it ascended. The sky blackened. Both the Talisman and Morgan Sloat's face shone in the sudden dark, Sloat's face because the Talisman shed its light upon it. Jack realized that his face too must be picked out by the Talisman's fierce illumination. And as soon as he brandished the glowing Talisman toward Sloat, trying God knew what – to get him to drop the key, to anger him, to rub his nose in the fact that he was powerless – Jack was made to understand that he had not yet reached the end of Morgan Sloat's capabilities. Fat snowflakes spun down out of the dark sky. Sloat disappeared behind the thickening curtain of snow. Jack heard his wet laughter.

4

She struggled out of her invalid's bed and crossed to the window. She looked out at the dead December beach, which was lit by a single streetlight on the boardwalk. Suddenly a gull alighted on the sill outside the window. A string of gristle hung from one side of its beak, and in that moment she thought of Sloat. The gull looked like Sloat.

Lily first recoiled, and then came back. She felt a wholly ridiculous anger. A gull couldn't look like Sloat, and a gull couldn't invade her territory . . . it wasn't *right.* She tapped the cold glass. The bird fluffed its wings briefly but did not fly. And she heard a thought come from its cold mind, heard it as clearly as a radio wave:

Jack's dying, Lily . . . Jack's dyyyyyinn . . .

It bent its head forward. Tapped on the glass as deliberately as Poe's raven.

Dyyyyyyinnnn . . .

'NO!' she shrieked at it. 'FUCK OFF, SLOAT!' She did not simply tap this time but slammed her fist forward, driving it through the glass. The gull fluttered backward, squawking, almost falling. Frigid air funnelled in through the hole in the window.

Blood was dripping from Lily's hand – no; no, not just dripping. It was *running.* She had cut herself quite badly in two places. She picked shards of glass out of the pad on the side of her palm and then wiped her hand against the bodice of her nightdress.

'DIDN'T EXPECT THAT, DID YOU, FUCK-HEAD?' she screamed at the bird, which was circling restlessly over the gardens. She burst into tears. '*Now leave him alone! Leave him alone!* LEAVE MY SON ALONE!'

She was all over blood. Cold air blew in the pane she had shattered. And outside she saw the first flakes of snow come skirling down from the sky and into the white glow of that streetlight.

5

'Look out, Jacky.'

Soft. On the left.

Jack pivoted that way, holding the Talisman up like a searchlight. It sent out a beam of light filled with falling snow.

Nothing else. Darkness . . . snow . . . the sound of the ocean.

'Wrong side, Jacky.'

He spun to the right, feet slipping in the icing of snow. Closer. He had been closer.

Jack held up the Talisman. 'Come and get it, Bloat.'

'You haven't got a chance, Jack. I can take you anytime I want to.'

Behind him . . . and closer still. But when he raised the blazing Talisman, there was no Sloat to be seen. Snow roared into his face. He inhaled it and began to cough on the cold.

Sloat tittered from directly in front of him.

Jack recoiled and almost tripped over Speedy.

'Hoo-hoo, Jacky!'

A hand came out of the darkness on his left and tore at Jack's ear. He turned in that direction, heart pumping wildly, eyes bulging. He slipped and went to one knee.

Richard uttered a thick, snoring moan somewhere close by.

Overhead, a cannonade of thunder went off in the darkness Sloat had somehow brought down.

'Throw it at me!' Sloat taunted. He danced forward out of that stormy, exposures-all-jammed-up-together dark. He was snapping the fingers of his right hand and wagging the tin key at Jack with the left. The gestures had a jerky, eccentric syncopation. To Jack, Sloat looked crazily like some old-time Latin bandleader – Xavier Cugat, perhaps. 'Throw it at me, why don't you? Shooting gallery, Jack! Clay pigeon! Big old Uncle Morgan! What do you say, Jack? Have a go? Throw the ball and win a Kewpie doll!'

And Jack discovered he had pulled the Talisman back to his right shoulder, apparently intending to do just that. *He's spooking you, trying to panic you, trying to get you to cough it up, to –*

Sloat faded back into the murk. Snow flew in dust-devils.

Jack wheeled nervously around but could see Sloat nowhere. *Maybe he's taken off. Maybe –*

'Wassa matta, Jacky?'

No, he was still here. Somewhere. On the left.

'I laughed when your dear old daddy died, Jacky. I laughed in his face. When his motor finally quit I felt—'

The voice warbled. Faded for a moment. Came back. On the right. Jack whirled that way, not understanding what was going on, his nerves increasingly frayed.

'—my heart flew like a bird on the wing. It flew like *this*, Jacky-boy.'

A rock came out of the dark – aimed not at Jack but at the glass ball. He dodged. Got a murky glimpse of Sloat. Gone again.

A pause . . . then Sloat was back, and playing a new record.

'Fucked your mother, Jacky,' the voice teased from behind him. A fat hot hand snatched at the seat of his pants.

Jack whirled around, this time almost stumbling over Richard. Tears – hot, painful, outraged – began to squeeze out of his eyes. He hated them, but here they were, and nothing in the world would deny them. The wind screamed like a dragon in a wind-tunnel. *The magic's in you*, Speedy had said, but where was the magic now? Where oh where oh where?

'You shut up about my mom!'

'Fucked her a lot,' Sloat added with smug cheeriness.

On the right again. A fat, dancing shape in the dark.

'Fucked her by *invitation*, Jacky!'

Behind him! *Close!*

Jack spun. Held up the Talisman. It lashed a white slice of light. Sloat danced back out of it, but not before Jack had seen a grimace of pain and anger. That light had touched Sloat, had hurt him.

Never mind what he's saying – it's all lies and you know it. But how can he do that? He's like Edgar Bergen. No . . . he's like Indians in the dark, closing in on the wagon train. How can he do it?

'Singed my whiskers a little that time, Jacky,' Sloat said, and chuckled fruitily. He sounded a bit out of breath, but not enough. Not nearly enough. Jack was panting like a dog on a hot summer day, his eyes frantic as he searched the stormy blackness for Sloat. 'But I'll not hold it against you, Jacky. Now, let's see. What were we talking about? Oh yes. Your mother . . .'

A little warble . . . a little fade . . . and then a stone came whistling out of the darkness on the right and struck Jack's temple. He whirled, but Sloat was gone again, skipping nimbly back into the snow.

'She'd wrap those long legs around me until I *howled* for mercy!' Sloat declared from behind Jack and to the right. '*OWWWWOOOOOO*!'

Don't let him get you don't let him psych you out don't –

But he couldn't help it. It was his *mother* this dirty man was talking about; his *mother.*

'You stop it! You shut up!'

Sloat was in front of him now – so close Jack should have been able to see him clearly in spite of the swirling snow, but there was only a glimmer, like a face seen underwater at night. Another stone zoomed out of the dark and struck Jack in the back of the head. He staggered forward and nearly tripped over Richard again – a Richard who was rapidly disappearing under a mantle of snow.

He saw stars . . . and understood what was happening.

Sloat's flipping! Flipping . . . moving . . . flipping back!

Jack turned in an unsteady circle, like a man beset with a hundred enemies instead of just one. Lightning-fire licked out of the dark in a narrow greenish-blue ray. He reached toward it with the Talisman, hoping to deflect it back at Sloat. Too late. It winked out.

Then how come I don't see him over there? Over there in the Territories?

The answer came to him in a dazzling flash . . . and as if in response, the Talisman flashed a gorgeous fan of white light – it cut the snowy light like the headlamp of a locomotive.

I don't see him over there, don't respond to him over there, because I'm NOT over there! Jason's gone . . . and I'm single-natured! Sloat's flipping onto a beach where there's no one but Morgan of Orris and a dead or dying man named Parkus – Richard isn't there either, because Morgan of Orris's son, Rushton, died a long time ago and Richard's single-natured, too! When I flipped before, the Talisman was there . . . but Richard wasn't! Morgan's flipping . . . moving . . . flipping back . . . trying to freak me out . . .

'Hoo-hoo! Jacky-boy!'

The left.

'Over here!'

The right.

But Jack wasn't listening for the place anymore. He was looking into the Talisman, waiting for the downbeat. The most important downbeat of his life.

From behind. This time he would come from behind.

The Talisman flashed out, a strong lamp in the snow.

Jack pivoted . . . and as he pivoted he flipped into the Territories, into bright sunlight. And there was Morgan of Orris, big as life and twice as ugly. For a moment he didn't realize Jack had tumbled to the trick; he was limping rapidly around to a place which would be behind Jack when he flipped back into the American Territories. There was a nasty little-boy grin on his face. His cloak popped and billowed behind him. His left boot dragged, and Jack saw the sand was covered with those dragging hashmarks all around him. Morgan had been running around him in a harrying circle, all the while goading Jack with obscene lies about his mother, throwing stones, and flipping back and forth.

Jack shouted:

'*I SEE YOU*!' at the top of his lungs.

Morgan stared around at him in utter stunned shock, one hand curled around that silver rod.

'SEE YOU!' Jack shouted again. 'Should we go around one more time, Bloat?'

Morgan of Orris flicked the end of the rod at him,

his face altering in a second from that rubbery simple-minded expression of shock to a much more characteristic look of craft – of a clever man quickly seeing all the possibilities in a situation. His eyes narrowed. Jack almost, in that second when Morgan of Orris looked down his lethal silver rod at him and narrowed his eyes into gunsights, flipped back into the American Territories, and that would have killed him. But an instant before prudence or panic caused him in effect to jump in front of a moving truck, the same insight that had told him that Morgan was flipping between worlds saved him again – Jack had learned the ways of his adversary. He held his ground, again waiting for that almost mystical downbeat. For a fraction of a second Jack Sawyer held his breath. If Morgan had been a shade less proud of his deviousness, he might well have murdered Jack Sawyer, which he so dearly wished to do, at that moment.

But instead, just as Jack had thought it would, Morgan's image abruptly departed the Territories. Jack inhaled. Speedy's body (*Parkus's* body, Jack realized) lay motionless a short distance away. The downbeat came. Jack exhaled and *flipped* back.

A new streak of glass divided the sand on the Point Venuti beach, glimmeringly reflecting the sudden beam of white light which emanated from the Talisman.

'Missed one, did you?' Morgan Sloat whispered out of the darkness. Snow pelted Jack, cold wind froze his limbs, his throat, his forehead. A car's length away, Sloat's face hung before him, the forehead drawn up into its familiar corrugations, the bloody mouth open. He was extending the key toward Jack in the storm, and a ridge of powdery snow adhered to the brown sleeve of his suit. Jack saw a black trail of blood oozing from the left nostril of the incongruously small nose. Sloat's eyes, bloodshot with pain, shone through the dark air.

6

Richard Sloat confusedly opened his eyes. Every part of him was cold. At first he thought, quite without emotion of any kind, that he was dead. He had fallen down somewhere, probably down those steep, tricky steps at the back of the Thayer School grandstand. Now he was cold and dead and nothing more could happen to him. He experienced a second of dizzying relief.

His head offered him a fresh surge of pain, and he felt warm blood ooze out over his cold hand – both of these sensations evidence that, whatever he might welcome at the moment, Richard Llewellyn Sloat was not yet dead. He was only a wounded suffering creature. The whole top of his head seemed to have been sliced off. He had no proper idea of where he was. It was cold. His eyes focussed long enough to report to him that he was lying down in the snow. Winter had happened. More snow dumped on him from out of the sky. Then he heard his father's voice, and everything returned to him.

Richard kept his hand on top of his head, but very slowly tilted his chin so that he could look in the direction of his father's voice.

Jack Sawyer was holding the Talisman – that was the next thing Richard took in. The Talisman was unbroken. He felt the return of a portion of that relief he had experienced when he'd thought he was dead. Even without his glasses, Richard could see that Jack had an undefeated, *unbowed* look that moved him very deeply. Jack looked like . . . like a hero.

That was all. He looked like a dirty, dishevelled, outrageously youthful hero, wrong for the role on almost every count, but undeniably still a hero.

Jack was just Jack now, Richard now saw. That extraordinary *extra* quality, as of a movie star deigning to walk around as a shabbily dressed twelve-year-old, had gone. This made his heroism all the more impressive to Richard.

His father smiled rapaciously. But that was not his father. His father had been hollowed out a long time ago – hollowed out by his envy of Phil Sawyer, by the greed of his ambitions.

'We can keep on going around like this forever,' Jack said. 'I'm never going to give you the Talisman, and you're never going to be able to destroy it with that gadget of yours. Give up.'

The point of the key in his father's hand slowly moved across and down, and it, like his father's greedy needful face, pointed straight at him.

'First I'll blow Richard apart,' his father said. 'Do you really want to see your pal Richard turned into bacon? Hmmmm? Do you? And of course I won't hesitate to do the same favor for that pest beside him.'

Jack and Sloat exchanged short glances. His father was not kidding, Richard knew. He would kill him if Jack did not surrender the Talisman. And then he would kill the old black man, Speedy.

'Don't do it,' he managed to whisper. 'Stuff him, Jack. Tell him to screw himself.'

Jack almost deranged Richard by winking at him.

'Just drop the Talisman,' he heard his father say.

Richard watched in horror as Jack tilted the palms of his hands and let the Talisman tumble out.

7

Jack, no!'

Jack didn't look around at Richard. *You don't own a thing unless you can give it up*, his mind hammered at him. *You don't own a thing unless you can give it up, what does it profit a man, it profits him nothing, it profits him zilch, and you don't learn that in school, you learn it on the road, you learn it from Ferd Janklow, and Wolf, and Richard going head-first into the rocks like a Titan II that didn't fire off right.*

You learned these things, or you died somewhere out in the world where there was no clear light.

'No more killing,' he said in the snow-filled darkness of this California beach afternoon. He should have felt utterly exhausted – it had been, all told, a four-day run of horrors, and now, at the end, he had coughed up the ball like a freshman quarterback with a lot to learn. Had thrown it all away. Yet it was the sure voice of Anders he heard, Anders who had knelt before Jack/Jason with his kilt spread out around him and his head bowed; Anders saying *A' wi' be well, a' wi' be well, and a' manner a' things wi' be well.*

The Talisman glowed on the beach, snow melting down one sweetly gravid side in droplets, and in each droplet was a rainbow, and in that moment Jack knew the staggering cleanliness of *giving up the thing which was required*.

'No more *slaughter*. Go on and break it if you can,' he said. 'I'm sorry for you.'

It was that last which surely destroyed Morgan Sloat. If he had retained a shred of rational thought, he would have unearthed a stone from the unearthly snow and smashed the Talisman . . . as it *could* have been smashed, in its simple unjacketed vulnerability.

Instead, he turned the key on it.

As he did so, his mind was filled with loving, hateful memories of Jerry Bledsoe, and Jerry Bledsoe's wife. Jerry Bledsoe, whom he had killed, and Nita Bledsoe, who should have been Lily Cavanaugh . . . Lily, who had slapped him so hard his nose bled the one time when, drunk, he had tried to touch her.

Fire sang out – green-blue fire spanning out from the cheap-jack barrel of the tin key. It arrowed out at the Talisman, struck it, spread over it, turned it into a burning sun. Every color was there for a moment . . . for a moment every *world* was there. Then it was gone.

The Talisman swallowed the fire from Morgan's key.

Ate it whole.

Darkness came back. Jack's feet slid out from under him and he sat down with a thud on Speedy Parker's limply splayed calves. Speedy made a grunting noise and twitched.

There was a two-second lag when everything held static . . . and then fire suddenly blew back out of the Talisman in a flood. Jack's eyes opened wide in spite of his frantic, tortured thought

(it'll blind you! Jack! it'll)

and the altered geography of Point Venuti was lit up as if the God of All Universes had bent forward to snap a picture. Jack saw the Agincourt, slumped and half-destroyed; he saw the collapsed Highlands that were now the Lowlands; he saw Richard on his back; he saw Speedy lying on his belly with his face turned to one side. Speedy was smiling.

Then Morgan Sloat was driven backward and enveloped in a field of fire from his own key – fire that had been absorbed inside the Talisman as the flashes of light from

Sunlight Gardener's telescopic sight had been absorbed – and which was returned to him a thousandfold.

A hole opened between the worlds – a hole the size of the tunnel leading into Oatley – and Jack saw Sloat, his handsome brown suit burning, one skeletal, tallowy hand still clutching the key, driven through that hole. Sloat's eyes were boiling in their sockets, but they were wide . . . they were *aware*.

And as he passed, Jack saw him change – saw the cloak appear like the wings of a bat that has swooped through the flame of a torch, saw his burning boots, his burning hair. Saw the key become a thing like a miniature lightning-rod.

Saw . . . *daylight*!

8

It came back in a flood. Jack rolled away from it on the snowy beach, dazzled. In his ears – ears deep inside his head – he heard Morgan Sloat's dying scream as he was driven back through all the worlds that were, into oblivion.

'Jack?' Richard was sitting up woozily, holding his head. 'Jack, what happened? I think I fell down the stadium steps.'

Speedy was twitching in the snow, and now he did a sort of girl's pushup and looked toward Jack. His eyes were exhausted . . . but his face was clear of blemishes.

'Good job, Jack,' he said, and grinned. 'Good—' He fell partway forward again, panting.

Rainbow, Jack thought woozily. He stood up and then fell down again. Freezing snow coated his face and then began to melt like tears. He pushed himself to his knees, then stood up again. The field of his vision was filled with spots . . . but he saw the enormous burned swatch in the snow where Morgan had stood. It tailed away like a teardrop.

'*Rainbow!*' Jack Sawyer shouted, and raised his hands to the sky, weeping and laughing. '*Rainbow! Rainbow!*'

He went to the Talisman, and picked it up, still weeping.

He took it to Richard Sloat, who had been Rushton; to Speedy Parker, who was what he was.

He healed them.

Rainbow, rainbow, rainbow!

CHAPTER FORTY-SIX
ANOTHER JOURNEY

1

He healed them, but he was never able to recall exactly how that had gone, or any of the specific details – for a while the Talisman had blazed and sung in his hands, and he had the vaguest possible memory of its fire's actually seeming to *flow out over them* until they glowed in a bath of light. That was all he could bring back.

At the end of it, the glorious light in the Talisman faded . . . faded . . . went out.

Jack, thinking of his mother, uttered a hoarse, wailing cry.

Speedy staggered over to him through the melting snow and put an arm around Jack's shoulders.

'It be back, Travellin Jack,' Speedy said. He smiled, but he looked twice as tired as Jack. Speedy had been healed . . . but he was still not well. *This world is killing him*, Jack thought dimly. *At least, it's killing the part of him that's Speedy Parker. The Talisman healed him . . . but he is still dying.*

'You did for it,' Speedy said, 'and you wanna believe that *it's* gonna do for *you*. Don't worry. Come on over here, Jack. Come on over to where your frien' be layin.'

Jack did. Richard was sleeping in the melting snow.

That horrid loose flap of skin was gone, but there was a long white streak of scalp showing in his hair now – a streak of scalp from which no hair would ever grow.

'Take his han'.'

'Why? What for?'

'We're gonna flip.'

Jack looked at Speedy questioningly, but Speedy offered no explanation. He only nodded, as if to say *Yes; you heard me right.*

Well, Jack thought, *I trusted him this far –*

He reached down and took Richard's hand. Speedy held Jack's other hand.

With hardly a tug at all, the three of them went over.

2

It was as Jack had intuited – the figure standing beside him over here, on this black sand that was stitched everywhere by Morgan of Orris's dragging foot, looked hale and hearty and healthy.

Jack stared with awe – and some unease – at this stranger who looked a bit like Speedy Parker's younger brother.

'Speedy – Mr Parkus, I mean – what are you—'

'You boys need rest,' Parkus said. 'You for sure, this other young squire even more. He came closer to dying than anyone will ever know but himself . . . and I don't think he's the type to do much admitting, even *to* himself.'

'Yeah,' Jack said. 'You got *that* right.'

'He'll rest better over here,' Parkus told Jack, and struck off up the beach, away from the castle, carrying Richard. Jack stumbled along as best he could, but gradually found himself falling behind. He was quickly out of breath, his legs rubbery. His head ached with reaction from the final battle – shock hangover, he supposed.

'Why . . . where . . .' That was all he could pant. He held the Talisman against his chest. It was dull now, its exterior sooty and opaque and uninteresting.

'Just up a little way,' Parkus said. 'You and your friend don't want to rest where *he* was, do you?'

And exhausted as he was, Jack shook his head.

Parkus glanced back over his shoulder, then looked sadly at Jack.

'It stinks of his evil back there,' he said, 'and it stinks of your world, Jack.

'To me, they smell too much alike for comfort.'

He set off again, Richard in his arms.

3

Forty yards up the beach he stopped. Here the black sand had moderated to a lighter color – not white, but a medium gray. Parkus set Richard down gently. Jack sprawled beside him. The sand was warm – blessedly warm. No snow here.

Parkus sat beside him, cross-legged.

'You're going to have a sleep now,' he said. 'Might be tomorrow before you wake up. Won't anybody bother you, if so. Take a look.'

Parkus waved his arm toward the place where Point Venuti had been in the American Territories. Jack first saw the black castle, one entire side of it crumbled and burst, as if there had been a tremendous explosion inside. Now the castle looked almost pedestrian. Its menace was burnt out, its illicit treasure borne away. It was only stones piled up in patterns.

Looking farther, Jack saw that the earthquake had not been so violent over here – and there had been less to destroy. He saw a few overturned huts that looked as if they had been built mostly of driftwood; he saw a number of burst coaches that might or might not have been Cadillacs back in the American Territories; here and there he could see a fallen, shaggy body.

'Those who were here and survived have now gone,' Parkus said. 'They know what has happened, they know Orris is dead, and they'll not trouble you more. The evil that was here has gone. Do you know that? Can you *feel* it?'

'Yes,' Jack whispered. 'But . . . Mr Parkus . . . you're not . . . not . . .'

'Going? Yes. Very soon. You and your friend are going to have a good sleep, but you and I must have a bit of a talk first. It won't take long, so I want you to try and get your head up off your chest, at least for the moment.'

With some effort, Jack got his head up and his eyes all – well, *most* – of the way open again. Parkus nodded.

'When you wake up, strike east . . . but don't flip! You stay right here for a while. Stay in the Territories. There's going to be too much going on over there on your side – rescue units, news crews, Jason knows what else. At least the snow will melt before anybody knows it's there, except for a few people who'll be dismissed as crackpots—'

'Why do you have to go?'

'I just got to ramble some now, Jack. There's a lot of work to be done over here. News of Morgan's death will already be travelling east. Travelling fast. I'm behind that news right now, and I've got to get ahead of it if I can. I want to get back to the Outposts . . . and the east . . . before a lot of pretty bad folks start to head out for other places.' He looked out at the ocean, his eyes as cold and gray as flint. 'When the bill comes due, people have to pay. Morgan's gone, but there's still a debt owing.'

'You're something like a policeman over here, aren't you?'

Parkus nodded. 'I am what you'd call the Judge General and Lord High Executioner all rolled into one. Over here, that is.' He put a strong, warm hand on Jack's head. 'Over there, I'm just this fella who goes around from place to place, does a few odd jobs, strums a few tunes. And sometimes, believe me, I like that a lot better.'

He smiled again, and this time he *was* Speedy.

'And you be seein that guy from time to time, Jacky. Yeah, from time to time and place to place. In a shoppin center, maybe, or a park.'

He winked at Jack.

'But Speedy's . . . not well,' Jack said. 'Whatever was wrong with him, it was something the Talisman couldn't touch.'

'Speedy's *old*,' Parkus said. 'He's my age, but your world made him older than me. Just the same, he's still got a few years left in him. Maybe quite a few. Feel no fret, Jack.'

'You promise?' Jack asked.

Parkus grinned. 'Yeah-bob.'

Jack grinned tiredly back.

'You and your friend head out to the east. Go until you reckon you've done five miles. You get over those low hills and then you'll be fine – easy walking. Look for a big tree – biggest damn tree you've ever seen. You get to that big old tree, Jack, and you take Richard's hand, and you flip back. You'll come out next to a giant redwood with a tunnel cut through the bottom of it to let the road through. The road's Route Seventeen, and you'll be on the outskirts of a little town in northern California called Storeyville. Walk into town. There's a Mobil station at the blinker-light.'

'And then?'

Parkus shrugged. 'Don't know, not for sure. Could be, Jack, you'll meet someone you'll recognize.'

'But how will we get h—'

'Shhh,' Parkus said, and put a hand on Jack's forehead exactly as his mother had done when he was

(baby-bunting, daddy's gone a-hunting, and all that good shit, lala, go to sleep, Jacky, all's well and all's well and)

very small. 'Enough questions. All will be well with you and Richard now, I think.'

Jack lay down. He cradled the dark ball in the crook of one arm. Each of his eyelids now seemed to have a cinderblock attached to it.

'You have been brave and true, Jack,' Parkus said with calm gravity. 'I wish you were my own son . . . and I salute you for your courage. And your faith. There are people in many worlds who owe you a great debt of gratitude. And in some way or other, I think most of them sense that.'

Jack managed a smile.

'Stay a little while,' he managed to say.

'All right,' Parkus said. 'Until you sleep. Feel no fret, Jack. Nothing will harm you here.'

'My mom always said—'

But before he finished the thought, sleep had claimed him.

4

And sleep continued to claim him, in some mysterious wise, the next day when he was technically awake – or if not sleep, then a protective numbing faculty of the mind which turned most of that day slow and dreamlike. He and Richard, who was similarly slow-moving and tentative, stood beneath the tallest tree in the world. All about them spangles of light lay across the floor of the forest. Ten grown men holding hands could not have reached around it. The tree soared up, massive and apart: in a forest of tall trees it was a leviathan, a pure example of Territories exuberance.

Feel no fret, Parkus had said, even while he threatened to fade hazily away like the Cheshire Cat. Jack tilted his head to stare up toward the top of the tree. He did not quite know this, but he was emotionally exhausted. The immensity of the tree aroused only a flicker of wonder in him. Jack rested a hand against the surprisingly smooth bark. *I killed the man who killed my father*, he said to himself. He clutched the dark, seemingly dead ball of the Talisman in his other hand. Richard was staring upward at the giant head of the tree, a skyscraper's height above them. Morgan was dead, Gardener too, and the snow must have melted from the beach by now. Yet not all of it was gone. Jack felt as though a whole beachful of snow filled his head. He had thought once – a thousand years ago, it seemed now – that if he could ever actually get his hands around the Talisman, he would be so inundated with triumph and excitement and awe that he'd have to fizz over. Instead he now felt only the tiniest hint of all that. It was snowing in his head, and he could see no farther than Parkus's instructions. He realized that the enormous tree was holding him up.

'Take my hand,' he said to Richard.

'But how are we going to get home?' Richard asked.

'Feel no fret,' he said, and closed his hand around Richard's. Jack Sawyer didn't need a tree to hold him up. Jack Sawyer had been to the Blasted Lands, he had vanquished the black hotel, Jack Sawyer was *brave and true*. Jack Sawyer was a played-out twelve-year-old boy with snow falling in his brain. He flipped effortlessly back into his own world, and Richard slid through whatever barriers there were right beside him.

5

The forest had contracted; now it was an American forest. The roof of gently moving boughs was noticeably lower, the trees about them conspicuously smaller than in the part of the Territories forest to which Parkus had directed them. Jack was dimly conscious of this alteration in the scale of everything about him before he saw the two-lane blacktop road in front of him: but twentieth-century reality kicked him almost immediately in the shins, for as soon as he saw the road he heard the eggbeater sound of a small motor and instinctively drew himself and Richard back just before a white little Renault Le Car zipped by him. The car sped past and went through the tunnel cut into the trunk of the redwood (which was slightly more than half the size of its Territories counterpart). But at least one adult and two children in the Renault were not looking at the redwoods they had come to see all the way from New Hampshire ('Live Free or Die!'). The woman and the two small children in the back seat had swivelled around to gawp at Jack and Richard. Their mouths were small black caves, open wide.

They had just seen two boys appear beside the road like ghosts, miraculously and instantaneously forming out of nothing, like Captain Kirk and Mr Spock after beaming down from the *Enterprise*.

'You okay to walk for a little while?'

'Sure,' Richard said.

Jack stepped onto the surface of Route 17 and walked through the huge hole in the tree.

He might be dreaming all this, he thought. He might be still on the Territories beach, Richard knocked out beside him, both of them under Parkus's kindly gaze. *My mom always said . . . My mom always said . . .*

6

Moving as if through thick fog (though that day in that part of northern California was in fact sunny and dry), Jack Sawyer led Richard Sloat out of the redwood forest and down a sloping road past dry December meadows.

. . . that the most important person in any movie is usually the cameraman . . .

His body needed more sleep. His mind needed a vacation.

. . . that vermouth is the ruination of a good martini . . .

Richard followed silently along, brooding. He was so much slower that Jack had to stop still on the side of the road and wait for Richard to catch up with him. A little town that must have been Storeyville was visible a half-mile or so ahead. A few low white buildings sat on either side of the road. ANTIQUES, read the sign atop one of them. Past the buildings a blinking stoplight hung over an empty intersection. Jack could see the corner of the MOBIL sign outside the gas station. Richard trudged along, his head so far down his chin nearly rested on his chest. When Richard drew nearer, Jack finally saw that his friend was weeping.

Jack put his arm around Richard's shoulders. 'I want you to know something,' he said.

'What?' Richard's small face was tear-streaked but defiant.

'I love you,' Jack said.

Richard's eyes snapped back to the surface of the road. Jack kept his arm over his friend's shoulders. In a moment Richard looked up – looked straight at Jack – and nodded. And that was like something Lily Cavanaugh Sawyer once or twice really had said to her son: *Jack-O, there are times you don't have to spill your guts out of your mouth.*

'We're on our way, Richie,' Jack said. He waited for Richard to wipe his eyes. 'I guess somebody's supposed to meet us up there at the Mobil station.'

'Hitler, maybe?' Richard pressed the heels of his hands to his eyes. In a moment he was ready again, and the two boys walked into Storeyville together.

7

It was a Cadillac, parked on the shady side of the Mobil station – an El Dorado with a boomerang TV antenna on the back. It looked as big as a house-trailer and as dark as death.

'Oh Jack, *baaaad* shit,' Richard moaned, and grabbed at Jack's shoulder. His eyes were wide, his mouth trembling.

Jack felt adrenaline whippet into his system again. It didn't pump him up any longer. It only made him feel tired. There had been too much, too much, too much.

Clasping the dark junk-shop crystal ball that the Talisman had become, Jack started down the hill toward the Mobil station.

'*Jack!*' Richard screamed weakly from behind him. '*What the hell are you doing? It's one of THEM*! Same cars as at Thayer! Same cars as in Point Venuti!'

'Parkus told us to come here,' Jack said.

'You're crazy, chum,' Richard whispered.

'I know it. But this'll be all right. You'll see. And don't call me chum.'

The Caddy's door swung open and a heavily muscled leg clad in faded blue denim swung out. Unease became active terror when he saw that the toe of the driver's black engineer boot had been cut off so long, hairy toes could stick out.

Richard squeaked beside him like a fieldmouse.

It was a Wolf, all right – Jack knew that even before the guy turned around. He stood almost seven feet tall. His hair was long, shaggy, and not very clean. It hung in tangles to his collar. There were a couple of burdocks in it. Then the big figure turned, Jack saw a flash of orange eyes – and suddenly terror became joy.

Jack sprinted toward the big figure down there, heedless of the gas station attendant who had come out to stare at him, and the idlers in front of the general store. His hair flew back from his forehead; his battered sneakers thumped and flapped; his face was split by a dizzy grin; his eyes shone like the Talisman itself.

Bib overalls: Oshkosh, by gosh. Round rimless spectacles: John Lennon glasses. And a wide, welcoming grin.

'Wolf!' Jack Sawyer screamed. *'Wolf, you're alive! Wolf, you're alive!'*

He was still five feet from Wolf when he leaped. And Wolf caught him with neat, casual ease, grinning delightedly.

'Jack Sawyer! Wolf! Look at this! Just like Parkus said! I'm here at this God-pounding place that smells like shit in a swamp, and you're here, too! Jack and his friend! Wolf! Good! Great! Wolf!'

It was the Wolf's *smell* that told Jack this wasn't *his* Wolf, just as it was the smell that told him this Wolf was some sort of relation . . . surely a very close one.

'I knew your litter-brother,' Jack said, still in the Wolf's shaggy, strong arms. Now, looking at this face, he could see it was older and wiser. But still kind.

'My brother Wolf,' Wolf said, and put Jack down. He reached out one hand and touched the Talisman with the tip of one finger. His face was full of awed reverence. When he touched it, one bright spark appeared and shot deep into the globe's dull depths like a tumbling comet.

He drew in a breath, looked at Jack, and grinned. Jack grinned back.

Richard now arrived, staring at both of them with wonder and caution.

'There are good Wolfs as well as bad in the Territories—' Jack began.

'*Lots* of good Wolfs,' Wolf interjected.

He stuck out his hand to Richard. Richard pulled back for a second and then shook it. The set of his mouth as his hand was swallowed made Jack believe Richard expected the sort of treatment Wolf had accorded Heck Bast a long time ago.

'This is *my* Wolf's litter-brother,' Jack said proudly. He cleared his throat, not knowing exactly how to express his feelings for this being's brother. Did Wolfs understand condolence? Was it a part of their ritual?

'I loved your brother,' he said. 'He saved my life. Except for Richard here, he was just about the best friend I ever had, I guess. I'm sorry he died.'

'He's in the moon now,' Wolf's brother said. 'He'll be back. Everything goes away, Jack Sawyer, like the moon. Everything comes back, like the moon. Come on. Want to get away from this stinking place.'

Richard looked puzzled, but Jack understood and more than sympathized – the Mobil station seemed surrounded with a hot, oily aroma of fried hydrocarbons. It was like a brown shroud you could see through.

The Wolf went to the Cadillac and opened the rear door like a chauffeur – which was, Jack supposed, exactly what he was.

'Jack?' Richard looked frightened.

'It's okay,' Jack said.

'But where—'

'To my mother, I think,' Jack said. 'All the way across the country to Arcadia Beach, New Hampshire. Going first class. Come on, Richie.'

They walked to the car. Shoved over to one side of the wide back seat was a scruffy old guitar case. Jack felt his heart leap up again.

'Speedy!' He turned to Wolf's litter-brother. 'Is Speedy coming with us?'

'Don't know anyone speedy,' the Wolf said. 'Had an uncle who was sort of speedy, then he pulled up lame – Wolf! – and couldn't even keep up with the herd anymore.'

Jack pointed at the guitar case.

'Where did that come from?'

Wolf grinned, showing many big teeth. 'Parkus,' he said. 'Left this for you, too. Almost forgot.'

From his back pocket he took a very old postcard. On the front was a carousel filled with a great many familiar horses – Ella Speed and Silver Lady among them – but the ladies in the foreground were wearing bustles, the boys knickers, many of the men derby hats and Rollie Fingers moustaches. The card felt silky with age.

He turned it over, first reading the print up the middle: ARCADIA BEACH CAROUSEL, JULY 4th, 1894.

It was Speedy – not Parkus – who had scratched two sentences in the message space. His hand was sprawling, not very literate; he had written with a soft, blunt pencil.

You done great wonders, Jack. Use what you need of what's in the case – keep the rest or throw it away.

Jack put the postcard in his hip pocket and got into the back of the Cadillac, sliding across the plush seat. One of the catches on the old guitar case was broken. He unsnapped the other three.

Richard had gotten in after Jack. 'Holy crow!' he whispered.

The guitar case was stuffed with twenty-dollar bills.

8

Wolf took them home, and although Jack grew hazy about many of that autumn's events in a very short time, each moment of that trip was emblazoned on his mind for the rest of his life. He and Richard sat in the back of the El Dorado and Wolf drove them east and east and east. Wolf knew the roads and Wolf drove them. He sometimes played Creedence Clearwater Revival tapes – 'Run Through the

Jungle' seemed to be his favorite – at a volume just short of ear-shattering. Then he would spend long periods of time listening to the tonal variations in the wind as he worked the button that controlled his wing window. This seemed to fascinate him completely.

East, east, east – into the sunrise each morning, into the mysterious deepening blue dusk of each coming night, listening first to John Fogerty and then to the wind, John Fogerty again and then the wind again.

They ate at Stuckeys'. They ate at Burger Kings. They stopped at Kentucky Fried Chicken. At the latter, Jack and Richard got dinners; Wolf got a Family-Style Bucket and ate all twenty-one pieces. From the sounds, he ate most of the bones as well. This made Jack think of Wolf and the popcorn. Where had that been? Muncie. The outskirts of Muncie – the Town Line Sixplex. Just before they had gotten their asses slammed into the Sunlight Home. He grinned . . . and then felt something like an arrow slip into his heart. He looked out the window so Richard wouldn't see the gleam of his tears.

They stopped on the second night in Julesburg, Colorado, and Wolf cooked them a huge picnic supper on a portable barbecue he produced from the trunk. They ate in a snowy field by starlight, bundled up in heavy parkas bought out of the guitar-case stash. A meteor-shower flashed overhead, and Wolf danced in the snow like a child.

'I love that guy,' Richard said thoughtfully.

'Yeah, me too. You should have met his brother.'

'I wish I had.' Richard began to gather up the trash. What he said next flummoxed Jack almost completely. 'I'm forgetting a lot of stuff, Jack.'

'What do you mean?'

'Just that. Every mile I remember a little less about what happened. It's all getting misty. And I think . . . I think that's the way I want it. Look, are you really sure your mother's okay?'

Three times Jack had tried to call his mother. There was no answer. He was not too worried about this. Things were okay. He hoped. When he got there, she would be there. Sick . . . but still alive. He hoped.

'Yes.'

'Then how come she doesn't answer the phone?'

'Sloat played some tricks with the phones,' Jack said. 'He played some tricks with the help at the Alhambra, too, I bet. She's still okay. Sick . . . but okay. Still there. I can feel her.'

'And if this healing thing works—' Richard grimaced a little, then plunged. 'You still . . . I mean, you still think she'd let me . . . you know, stay with you guys?'

'No,' Jack said, helping Richard pick up the remains of supper. 'She'll want to see you in an orphanage, probably. Or maybe in jail. Don't be a dork, Richard, of course you can stay with us.'

'Well . . . after all my father did . . .'

'That was your dad, Richie,' Jack said simply. 'Not you.'

'And you won't always be reminding me? You know . . . jogging my memory?'

'Not if you want to forget.'

'I do, Jack. I really do.'

Wolf was coming back.

'You guys ready? Wolf!'

'All ready,' Jack said. 'Listen, Wolf, how about that Scott Hamilton tape I got in Cheyenne?'

'Sure, Jack. Then how about some Creedence?'

'"Run Through the Jungle", right?'

'Good tune, Jack! Heavy! *Wolf!* God-pounding *heavy* tune!'

'You bet, Wolf.' He rolled his eyes at Richard. Richard rolled his back, and grinned.

The next day they rolled across Nebraska and Iowa; a day later they tooled past the gutted ruin of the Sunlight Home. Jack thought Wolf had taken them past it on purpose, that he perhaps wanted to see the place where his brother had died. He turned up the Creedence tape in the cassette player as loud as it would go, but Jack still thought he heard the sound of Wolf sobbing.

Time – suspended swatches of time. Jack seemed almost to be floating, and there was a feeling of suspension, triumph, valediction. Work honorably discharged.

Around sunset of the fifth day, they crossed into New England.

CHAPTER FORTY-SEVEN
JOURNEY'S END

1

The whole long drive from California to New England seemed, once they had got so far, to have taken place in a single long afternoon and evening. An afternoon that lasted days, an evening perhaps life-long, bulging with sunsets and music and emotions. *Great humping balls of fire,* Jack thought, *I'm really out of it,* when he happened for the second time in what he assumed to be about half an hour to look at the discreet little clock set in the dashboard – and discovered that three hours had winked past him. Was it even the same day? 'Run Through the Jungle' pumped through the air; Wolf bobbed his head in time, grinning unstoppably, infallibly finding the best roads; the rear window showing the whole sky opening in great bands of twilight color, purple and blue and that particular deep plangent red of the downgoing sun. Jack could remember every detail of this long long journey, every word, every meal, every nuance of the music, Zoot Sims or John Fogerty or simply Wolf delighting himself with the noises of the air, but the true span of time had warped itself in his mind to a concentration like a diamond's. He slept in the cushiony back seat and opened his eyes on light or darkness, on sunlight or stars. Among the things he remembered with particular sharpness, once they had crossed into New England and the Talisman began to glow again, signalling the return of normal time – or perhaps the return of time itself to Jack Sawyer – were the faces of people peering into the back seat of the El Dorado (people in parking lots, a sailor and an ox-faced girl in a convertible at a stoplight in a sunny little town in Iowa, a skinny Ohio kid wearing *Breaking Away*-style bicycle gear) in order to see if maybe Mick Jagger or Frank Sinatra had decided to pay them a call. Nope, just us, folks. Sleep kept stealing him away. Once he awoke (Colorado? Illinois?) to the thumping of rock music, Wolf snapping his fingers while keeping the big car rolling smoothly, a bursting sky of orange and purple and blue, and saw that Richard had somewhere acquired a book and was reading it with the aid of the El Dorado's recessed passenger light. The book was *Broca's Brain*. Richard always knew what time it was. Jack rolled his eyes upward and let the music, the evening colors, take him. They had *done it*, they had done *everything* . . . everything except what they would have to do in an empty little resort town in New Hampshire.

Five days, or one long, dreaming twilight? 'Run Through the Jungle.' Zoot Sims's tenor saxophone saying *Here's a story for you, do you like this story?* Richard was his brother, his brother.

Time returned to him about when the Talisman came back to life, during the magical sunset of the fifth day. *Oatley*, Jack thought on the sixth day, *I could have shown Richard the Oatley tunnel, and whatever's left of the Tap,* I could have shown Wolf which way to go . . . but he did not want to see Oatley again, there was no satisfaction or pleasure in that. And he was conscious now of how close they had come, of how far they had travelled while he drifted through time like a thistle. Wolf had brought them to the great broad artery of I-95, now that they were in Connecticut, and Arcadia Beach lay only a few states away, up the indented New England coast. From now on Jack counted the miles, and the minutes too.

2

At quarter past five on the evening of December 21st, some three months after Jack Sawyer had set his face – and his hopes – on the west, a black El Dorado Cadillac swung into the crushed-gravel driveway of the Alhambra Inn and Gardens in the town of Arcadia Beach, New Hampshire. In the west, the sunset was a mellow valediction of reds and oranges fading to yellow . . . and blue . . . and royal purple. In the gardens themselves, naked branches clattered together in a bitter winter wind. Amid them, until a day not quite a week ago, had been a tree which caught and ate small animals – chipmunks, birds, the desk clerk's starveling, slat-sided cat. This small tree had died very suddenly. The other growing things in the garden, though skeletal now, still bided with dormant life.

The El Dorado's steel-belted radials popped and cracked over the gravel. From inside, muffled behind the polarized glass, came the sound of Creedence Clearwater Revival. '*The people who know my magic*,' John Fogerty sang, '*have filled the land with smoke*.'

The Cadillac stopped in front of the wide double doors. There was only darkness beyond them. The double headlights went out and the long car stood in shadow, tailpipe idling white exhaust, orange parking lights gleaming.

Here at the end of day; here at sunset with color fanning up from the western sky in glory.

Here:

Right here and now.

3

The back of the Caddy was lit with faint, uncertain light. The Talisman flickered . . . but its glow was weak, little more than the glow of a dying firefly.

Richard turned slowly toward Jack. His face was wan and frightened. He was clutching Carl Sagan with both hands, wringing the paperback the way a washerwoman might wring a sheet.

Richard's Talisman, Jack thought, and smiled.

'Jack, do you want—'

'No,' Jack said. 'Wait until I call.'

He opened the rear right door, started to get out of the car, then looked back at Richard. Richard sat small and shrunken in his seat, wringing his paperback in his hand. He looked miserable.

Not thinking, Jack came back in for a moment and kissed Richard's cheek. Richard put his arms around Jack's neck for a moment, and hugged fiercely. Then he let Jack go. Neither of them said anything.

4

Jack started for the stairs leading up to the lobby-level . . . and then turned right and walked for a moment to the edge of the driveway instead. There was an iron railing here. Below it, cracked and tiered rock fell to the beach. Farther to his right, standing against the darkling sky, was the Arcadia Funworld roller coaster.

Jack lifted his face to the east. The wind that was harrying through the formal gardens lifted his hair away from his forehead and blew it back.

He lifted the globe in his hands, as if as an offering to the ocean.

5

On December 21st, 1981, a boy named Jack Sawyer stood near the place where the water and the land came together, hands cradling an object of some worth, looking out at the night-steady Atlantic. He had turned thirteen years old that day, although he did not know it, and he was extraordinarily beautiful. His brown hair was long – probably too long – but the sea-breeze swept it back from a fine, clear brow. He stood there thinking about his mother, and about the rooms in this place which they had shared. Was she going to turn on a light up there? He rather suspected she was.

Jack turned, eyes flashing wildly in the Talisman's light.

6

Lily felt along the wall with one trembling, skeletal hand, groping for the light-switch. She found it and turned it on. Anyone who had seen her in that moment might well have turned away. In the last week or so, the cancer had begun to sprint inside her, as if sensing that something might be on the way which would spoil all its fun. Lily Cavanaugh now weighed seventy-eight pounds. Her skin was sallow, stretched over her skull like parchment. The brown circles under her eyes had turned a dead and final black, the eyes themselves stared from their sockets with fevered, exhausted intelligence. Her bosom was gone. The flesh on her arms was gone. On her buttocks and the backs of her thighs, bedsores had begun to flower.

Nor was that all. In the course of the last week, she had contracted pneumonia.

In her wasted condition she was, of course, a prime candidate for that or any other respiratory disease. It might have come under the best of circumstances . . . and these were definitely not those. The radiators in the Alhambra had ceased their nightly clankings some time ago. She wasn't sure just how long – time had become as fuzzy and indefinable to her as it had been for Jack in the El Dorado. She only knew the heat had gone out on the same night she had punched her fist through the window, making the gull that had looked like Sloat fly away.

In the time since that night the Alhambra had become a deserted coldbox. A crypt in which she would soon die.

If Sloat was responsible for what had happened at the Alhambra, he had done one hell of a good job. Everyone was gone. *Everyone*. No more maids in the halls trundling their squeaky carts. No more whistling maintenance man. No more mealy-mouthed desk clerk. Sloat had put them all in his pocket and taken them away.

Four days ago – when she could not find enough in the room to satisfy even her birdlike appetite – she had gotten out of bed and had worked her way slowly down the hall to the elevator. She brought a chair with her on this expedition, alternately sitting on it, her head hanging in exhaustion, and using it as a walker. It took her forty minutes to traverse forty feet of corridor to the elevator shaft.

She had pushed the button for the car repeatedly, but the car did not come. The buttons did not even light.

'Fuck a duck,' Lily muttered hoarsely, and then slowly worked herself another twenty feet down the hall to the stairwell.

'Hey!' she shouted downstairs, and then broke into a fit of coughing, bent over the back of the chair.

Maybe they couldn't hear the yell but they sure as shit must have been able to hear me coughing out whatever's left of my lungs, she thought.

But no one came.

She yelled again, twice, had another coughing fit, and then started back down the hallway, which looked as long as a stretch of Nebraska turnpike on a clear day. She didn't dare go down those stairs. She would never get back up them. And there was no one down there; not in the lobby, not in The Saddle of Lamb, not in the coffee shop, not *anywhere.* And the phones were out. At least, the phone in *her* room was out, and she hadn't heard a single ring anywhere else in this old mausoleum. Not worth it. A bad gamble. She didn't want to freeze to death in the lobby.

'Jack-O,' she muttered, 'where the hell are y—'

Then she began to cough again and this one was really bad and in the middle of it she collapsed to one side in a faint, pulling the ugly sitting-room chair over on top of her, and she lay there on the cold floor for nearly an hour, and that was probably when the pneumonia moved into the rapidly declining neighborhood that was Lily Cavanaugh's body. *Hey there, big C! I'm the new kid on the block! You can call me big P! Race you to the finish line!*

Somehow she had made it back to her room, and since then she had existed in a deepening spiral of fever, listening to her respiration grow louder and louder until her fevered mind began to imagine her lungs as two organic aquariums in which a number of submerged chains were rattling. And yet she held on – held on because part of her mind insisted with crazy, failing certainty that Jack was on his way back from wherever he had been.

7

The beginning of her final coma had been like a dimple in the sand – a dimple that begins to spin like a whirlpool. The sound of submerged chains in her chest became a long, dry exhalation – *Hahhhhhhhh* . . .

Then something had brought her out of that deepening spiral and started her feeling along the wall in the cold darkness for the light-switch. She got out of bed. She did not have strength enough left to do this; a doctor would have laughed at the idea. And yet she did. She fell back twice, then finally made it to her feet, mouth turned down in a snarl of effort. She groped for the chair, found it, and began to lurch her way across the room to the window.

Lily Cavanaugh, Queen of the Bs, was gone. This was a walking horror, eaten by cancer, burned by rising fever.

She reached the window and looked out.

Saw a human shape down there – and a glowing globe.

'*Jack!*' she tried to scream. Nothing came out but a gravelly whisper. She raised a hand, tried to wave. Faintness

(Haahhhhhhhhh . . .)

washed over her. She clutched at the windowsill.

'Jack!'

Suddenly the lighted ball in the figure's hands flashed

up brightly, illuminating his face, and it *was* Jack's face, it was Jack, oh thank God, it was Jack. Jack had come home.

The figure broke into a run.

Jack!

Those sunken, dying eyes grew yet more brilliant. Tears spilled down her yellow, stretched cheeks.

8

'Mom!'

Jack ran across the lobby, seeing that the old-fashioned telephone switchboard was fused and blackened, as if from an electrical fire, and instantly dismissing it. He had seen her and she looked *awful* – it had been like looking at the silhouette of a scarecrow propped in the window.

'Mom!'

He pounded up the stairs, first by twos, then by threes, the Talisman stuttering one burst of pink-red light and then falling dark in his hands.

'Mom!'

Down the hallway to their rooms, feet flying, and now, at last, he heard her voice – no brassy bellow or slightly throaty chuckle now; this was the dusty croak of a creature on the outer edge of death.

'Jacky?'

'Mom!'

He burst into the room.

9

Down in the car, a nervous Richard Sloat stared upward through his polarized window. What was he doing here, what was *Jack* doing here? Richard's eyes hurt. He strained to see the upper windows in the murky evening. As he bent sideways and stared upward, a blinding white flash erupted from several of the upstairs windows, sending a momentary, almost palpable sheet of dazzling light over the entire front of the hotel. Richard put his head between his knees and moaned.

10

She was on the floor beneath the window – he saw her there finally. The rumpled, somehow dusty-looking bed was empty, the whole bedroom, as disordered as a child's room, seemed empty . . . Jack's stomach had frozen and words backed up in his throat. Then the Talisman had shot out another of its great illuminating flashes, in and for an instant turning everything in the room a pure colorless white. She croaked, *'Jacky?'* once more, and he bellowed, '*MOM!*' seeing her crumpled like a candy wrapper under the window. Thin and lank, her hair trailed on the room's dirty carpet. Her hands seemed like tiny animal paws, pale and scrabbling. 'Oh Jesus, Mom, oh jeepers, oh holy moe,' he babbled, and somehow moved across the room without taking a step, he *floated*, he *swam* across Lily's crowded frozen bedroom in an instant that seemed as sharp to him as an image on a photographic plate. Her hair puddled on the grimy carpet, her small knotty hands.

He inhaled the thick odor of illness, of close death. Jack was no doctor, and he was ignorant of most of the things so wrong with Lily's body. But he knew one thing – his mother was dying, her life was falling away through invisible cracks, and she had very little time left. She had uttered his name twice, and that was about all the life left in her would permit. Already beginning to weep, he put his hand on her unconscious head, and set the Talisman on the floor beside her.

Her hair felt full of sand and her head was burning. 'Oh Mom, Mom,' he said, and got his hands under her. He still could not see her face. Through her flimsy nightgown her hip felt as hot as the door of a stove. Against his other palm, her left shoulderblade pulsed with an equal warmth. She had no comfortable pads of flesh over her bones – for a mad second of stopped time it was as though she were a small dirty child somehow left ill and alone. Sudden unbidden tears squirted out of his eyes. He lifted her, and it was like picking up a bundle of clothes. Jack moaned. Lily's arms sprawled loosely, gracelessly.

(Richard)

Richard had felt . . . not as bad as this, not even when Richard had felt like a dried husk on his back, coming down the final hill into poisoned Point Venuti. There had been little but pimples and a rash left of Richard at that point, and he, too, had burned with fever. But Jack realized with a sort of unthinking horror that there had been more actual life, more *substance*, to Richard than his mother now possessed. Still, she had called his name.

(and Richard had nearly died)

She had called his name. He clung to that. She had *made it to the window*. She had *called his name*. It was impossible, unthinkable, immoral to imagine that she could die. One of her arms dangled before him like a reed meant to be cut in half by a scythe . . . her wedding ring had fallen off her finger. He was crying steadily, unstoppably, unconsciously. 'Okay, Mom,' he said, 'okay, it's okay now, okay, it's okay.'

From the limp body in his arms came a vibration that might have been assent.

He gently placed her on the bed, and she rolled weightlessly sideways. Jack put a knee on the bed and leaned over her. The tired hair fell away from her face.

11

Once, at the very beginning of his journey, he had for a shameful moment seen his mother as an old woman – a spent, exhausted old woman in a tea shop. As soon as he had recognized her, the illusion had dissipated, and Lily Cavanaugh Sawyer had been restored to her unaging self. For the real, the true Lily Cavanaugh could never have aged – she was eternally a blonde with a quick switchblade of a smile and a go-to-hell amusement in her face. This had been the Lily Cavanaugh whose picture on a billboard had strengthened her son's heart.

The woman on the bed looked very little like the actress on the billboard. Jack's tears momentarily blinded him. 'Oh don't don't don't,' he said, and laid one palm across her yellowed cheek.

She did not look as though she had enough strength to lift her hand. He took her tight dry discolored claw of a hand into his own hand. 'Please please please don't—' He could not even allow himself to say it.

And then he realized how much an effort this shrunken woman had made. She had been looking for him, he understood in a great giddy rush of comprehension. His mother had known he was coming. She had trusted him to return and in a way that must have been connected to the fact of the Talisman itself, she had known the moment of his return.

'I'm here, Mom,' he whispered. A wad of wet stuff bubbled from his nostrils. He unceremoniously wiped his nose with the sleeve of his coat.

He realized for the first time that his entire body was trembling.

'I brought it back,' he said. He experienced a moment of absolute radiant pride, of pure accomplishment. 'I brought back the Talisman,' he said.

Gently he set her nutlike hand down on the counterpane.

Beside the chair, where he had placed it (every bit as gently) on the floor, the Talisman continued to glow. But its light was faint, hesitant, cloudy. He had healed Richard by simply rolling the globe down the length of his friend's body; he had done the same for Speedy. But this was to be something else. He knew that, but not what 'it' was to be – unless it was a question of knowing and not wanting to believe.

He could not possibly break the Talisman, not even to save his mother's life – that much he *did* know.

Now the interior of the Talisman slowly filled with a cloudy whiteness. The pulses faded into one another and became a single steady light. Jack placed his hands on it, and the Talisman shot forth a blinding wall of light, *rainbow!* which seemed nearly to speak. AT LAST!

Jack went back across the room toward the bed, the Talisman bouncing and spraying light from floor to wall to ceiling, illuminating the bed fitfully, garishly.

As soon as he stood beside his mother's bed, the texture of the Talisman seemed to Jack to subtly alter beneath his fingers. Its glassy hardness *shifted* somehow, became less slippery, more porous. The tips of his fingers seemed almost to sink into the Talisman. The cloudiness filling it boiled and darkened.

And at this moment Jack experienced a strong – in fact, passionate – feeling he would have thought was impossible, that day long ago when he had set off for his first day's walk in the Territories. He knew that in some unforeseen way the Talisman, the object of so much blood and trouble, was going to alter. It was going to change forever, and he was going to lose it. The Talisman would *no longer be his.* Its clear skin was clouding over, too, and the entire beautiful grooved gravid surface was softening. The feeling now was not glass but warming plastic.

Jack hurriedly set the altering Talisman down in his mother's hands. It knew its job; it had been made for this moment; in some fabulous smithy it had been created to answer the requirements of this particular moment and of none other.

He did not know what he expected to happen. An explosion of light? A smell of medicine? Creation's big bang?

Nothing happened. His mother continued visibly but motionlessly to die.

'Oh please,' Jack blurted, 'please – Mom – please—'

His breath solidified in the middle of his chest. A seam, once one of the vertical grooves in the Talisman, had soundlessly opened. Light slowly poured out and pooled over his mother's hands. From the cloudy interior of the loose, emptying ball, more light spilled through the open seam.

From outside came a sudden and loud music of birds celebrating their existence.

12

But of that Jack was only distractedly conscious. He leaned breathlessly forward and watched the Talisman pour itself out onto his mother's bed. Cloudy brightness welled up within it. Seams and sparks of light enlivened it. His mother's eyes twitched. 'Oh Mom,' he whispered. 'Oh . . .'

Gray-golden light flooded through the opening in the Talisman and cloudily drifted up his mother's arms. Her sallow, wizened face very slightly frowned.

Jack inhaled unconsciously.

(What?)

(Music?)

The gray-golden cloud from the heart of the Talisman was lengthening over his mother's body, coating her in a translucent but slightly opaque, delicately moving membrane. Jack watched this fluid fabric slide across Lily's pitiful chest, down her wasted legs. From the open seam in the Talisman a wondrous odor spilled out with the gray-golden cloud, an odor sweet and unsweet, of flowers and earth, wholly good, yeasty; a smell of birth, Jack thought, though he had never attended an actual birth. Jack drew it into his lungs and in the midst of his wonder was gifted with the thought that he himself, Jack-O Sawyer, was being born at this minute – and then he imagined, with a barely perceptible shock of recognition, that the opening in the Talisman was like a vagina. (He had of course never seen a vagina and had only the most rudimentary idea of its structure.) Jack looked directly into the opening in the distended, loosened Talisman.

Now he became conscious for the first time of the incredible racket, in some way all mixed up with faint music, of the birds outside the dark windows.

(Music? What . . . ?)

A small colored ball full of light shot past his vision, flashing in the open seam for a moment, then continued beneath the Talisman's cloudy surface as it dove into the shifting moving gaseous interior. Jack blinked. It had resembled— Another followed, and this time he had time to see the demarcations of blue and brown and green on the tiny globe, the coastal shorelines and tiny mountain ranges. On that tiny world, it occurred to him, stood a paralyzed Jack Sawyer looking down at an even tinier colored speck, and on that speck stood a Jack-O the height of a dust mote staring at a little world the size of an atom. Another world followed the first two, spinning in, out, in, out of the widening cloud within the Talisman.

His mother moved her right hand and moaned.

Jack began openly to weep. She would live. He knew it now. All had worked as Speedy had said, and the Talisman was forcing life back into his mother's exhausted, disease-ridden body, killing the evil that was killing her. He bent forward, for a moment almost giving in to the image of himself kissing the Talisman which filled his mind. The odors of jasmine and hibiscus and freshly overturned earth filled his nostrils. A tear rolled off the end of his nose and sparkled like a jewel in the shafts of light from the Talisman. He saw a belt of stars drift past the open seam, a beaming yellow sun swimming in vast black space. Music seemed to fill the Talisman, the room, the whole world outside. A woman's face, the face of a stranger, moved across the open seam. Children's faces, too, then the faces of other women . . . Tears rolled down his own face, for he had seen swimming in the Talisman his mother's own face, the confident wise-cracking tender features of the Queen of half a hundred quick movies. When he saw his own face drifting among all the worlds and lives falling toward birth within the Talisman, he thought he would burst with feeling. He *expanded*. He breathed in light. And became at last aware of the astonishment of noises taking place all about him when he saw his mother's eyes stay open as long, at least, as a blessed two seconds . . .

(for alive as birds, as alive as the world contained within the Talisman, there came to him the sounds of trombones and trumpets, the cries of saxophones; the joined voices of frogs and turtles and gray doves singing, *The people who know my magic have filled the land with smoke*; there came to him the voices of Wolfs making Wolfmusic at the moon. Water spanked against the bow of a ship and a fish spanked the surface of a lake with the side of its body and a rainbow spanked the ground and a travelling boy spanked a drop of spittle to tell him which way to go and a spanked baby squinched its face and opened its throat; and there came the huge voice of an orchestra singing with its whole massive heart; and the room filled with the smokey trail of a single voice rising and rising and rising over all these forays of sound. Trucks jammed gears and factory whistles blew and somewhere a tire exploded and somewhere a firecracker loudly spent itself and a lover whispered *again* and a child squalled and the voice rose and rose and for a short time Jack was unaware that he could not see; but then he could again).

Lily's eyes opened wide. They stared up into Jack's face with a startled where-am-I expression. It was the expression of a newborn infant who has just been spanked into the world. Then she jerked in a startled breath –

– and a river of worlds and tilted galaxies and universes were pulled up and out of the Talisman as she did. They were pulled up in a stream of rainbow colors. They streamed into her mouth and nose . . . they settled, gleaming, on her sallow skin like droplets of dew, and melted inward. For a moment his mother was all clothed in radiance –

– for a moment his mother was the Talisman.

All the disease fled from her face. It did not happen in the manner of a time-lapse sequence in a movie. It happened *all at once*. It happened *instantly*. She was sick . . . and then she was well. Rosy good health bloomed in her cheeks. Wispy, sparse hair was suddenly full and smooth and rich, the color of dark honey.

Jack stared at her as she looked up into his face.

'Oh . . . oh . . . my GOD . . .' Lily whispered.

That rainbow radiance was fading now – but the health remained.

'Mom?' He bent forward. Something crumpled like cellophane under his fingers. It was the brittle husk of the Talisman. He put it aside on the nighttable. He pushed several of her medicine bottles out of the way to do it. Some crashed on the floor, and it didn't matter. She would not be needing the medicines anymore. He put the husk down with gentle reverence, suspecting – no, *knowing* – that even that would be gone very soon.

His mother smiled. It was a lovely, fulfilled, somewhat surprised smile – *Hello, world, here I am again! What do you know about that?*

'Jack, you came home,' she said at last, and rubbed her eyes as if to make sure it was no mirage.

'Sure,' he said. He tried to smile. It was a pretty good smile in spite of the tears that were pouring down his face. 'Sure, you bet.'

'I feel . . . a lot better, Jack-O.'

'Yeah?' He smiled, rubbed his wet eyes with the heels of his palms. 'That's good, Mom.'

Her eyes were radiant.

'Hug me, Jacky.'

In a room on the fourth floor of a deserted resort hotel on the minuscule New Hampshire seacoast, a thirteen-year-old boy named Jack Sawyer leaned forward, closed his eyes, and hugged his mother tightly, smiling. His ordinary life of school and friends and games and music, a life where there were schools to go to and crisp sheets to slide between at night, the ordinary life of a thirteen-year-old boy (if the life of such a creature can ever, in its color and riot, be considered ordinary) had been returned to him, he realized. The Talisman had done that for him, too. When he remembered to turn and look for it, the Talisman was gone.

EPILOGUE

In a billowing white bedroom filled with anxious women, Laura DeLoessian, Queen of the Territories, opened her eyes.

CONCLUSION

So endeth this chronicle. It being strictly the history of a *boy*, it must stop here; the story could not go much further without becoming the history of a *man*. When one writes a novel about grown people, he knows exactly where to stop – that is, with a marriage; but when he writes of juveniles, he must stop where he best can.

Most of the characters who perform in this book still live, and are prosperous and happy. Some day it may seem worthwhile to take up the story again and see what . . . they turned out to be; therefore, it will be wisest not to reveal any of that part of their lives at present.

– Mark Twain, *Tom Sawyer*

DISCOVER THE WORLD OF THE TALISMAN
BY STEPHEN KING AND PETER STRAUB